Mary Shelley's *Frankenstein* has been described by Stephen King as 'the taproot of Science Fiction' and both the book and the 1931 Boris Karloff film have become twentieth-century cults. The story of the obsessed scientist's experiments to create life has been the inspiration for a group of terrifying short stories, movies and television adaptations.

*The Frankenstein Omnibus* is the most complete collection of horror stories on this theme ever published and underlies Stephen King's statement that 'Frankenstein is a mystical morality tale about what happens when man dares to transgress the limits of knowledge.'

D1440352

300

# Frankenstein

## Or
## The Modern
## Prometheus
## By
## Mary
## Wollstonecraft
## Shelley

London
Gibbings and
Company
Limited

Philadelphia
J. B. Lippincott
Company
1897

Peter Haining is an internationally-known anthologist and writer on crime fiction whose books have been published in over a dozen languages. He is a 1992 Edgar nominee by the Mystery Writers of America for his Centenary study of Agatha Christie's work on stage, film, radio and TV, *Murder in Four Acts*. Peter Haining is married with three children and lives in rural Suffolk.

# The Frankenstein Omnibus

EDITED BY
Peter Haining

**ORION**

An Orion paperback

First published in Great Britain by Orion in 1994
This paperback edition published in 1995
by Orion Books Ltd
Orion House, 5 Upper St Martin's Lane, London WC2H 9EA

A CIP catalogue record for this book is
available from the British Library.

ISBN: 85797 804 8

Typeset by Datix International Limited, Bungay, Suffolk

Printed and bound in Great Britain
by Clays Ltd, St Ives plc

## FOR ANTHONY CHEETHAM

———

In memory of the monster
we created at Barnard's Inn!

# Contents

# Introduction

It had been an overcast and rather chilly spring day that caused darkness to fall earlier than usual over the Villa Diodati on the shores of Lake Geneva in Switzerland. For the five people holidaying at the picturesque mansion on June 16, 1816, the evening was only enlivened by the reading aloud around the fire of some supernatural stories in a small, leather bound book embossed with the title *Fantasmagoriana*. The host, an almost demoniacally handsome young man, had heightened the atmosphere of *frisson* in the room by dramatically reciting a German tale about a luckless bridegroom who had kissed his newlywed wife on their honeymoon night only to find her instantly turned into a rotting corpse . . .

When the group had finally decided to retire to bed, the host offered a last thought to his guests. 'We will each write a ghost story,' he said. 'And then read them to each other to see whose is the best.'

It was an innocent enough suggestion – but one that was to have far-reaching implications. Not only for that group of people – but the whole of literature, too.

The man who issued the challenge was the notorious poet, Lord Byron. He had hired the Villa Diodati for the summer, and invited his friends, another leading English poet Percy Shelley, and his 18-year-old mistress, Mary, the daughter of Mary Wollstonecraft, the campaigner for women's rights, and William Godwin, the political writer and novelist. Completing the house party were Byron's Italian physician, John William Polidori, and Mary's stepsister, Claire Clairmont, who was carrying Byron's child.

The idea of the story was eagerly taken up by the party, all of whom had been growing rather bored during the recent period of poor weather which had prevented them taking advantage of the lake or the surrounding countryside. All proceeded to bed with their minds still alive from the tales they had heard.

The results initially, however, were disappointing. Both Byron and Percy Shelley lost interest after scribbling only a few pages. John Polidori did work on an idea for a story about an undead man which would later be called *The Vampyre*, but it would be some time before he completed the task. Mary Shelley, for her part, could think of nothing that night – or for several nights thereafter. It seemed as if the whole idea would be a failure.

Then, unexpectedly, as she lay in bed about a week later in the half-world between waking and sleeping, Mary experienced a vivid flight of imagination in which she saw a scientist create artificial life in a laboratory. Here was her theme, she knew at once, and the next morning quickly took up her pen.

The result of that dream was *Frankenstein*. But not the famous novel that we know today. Mary, true to the instructions of the challenge, merely wrote a short story around her nightmare, which she then showed to Byron and Shelley. Her host dismissed it with hardly a glance; her lover, though, read the few pages rather more carefully, and then declared it was not really a story. She should perhaps try to turn it into a novel.

It was, in fact, to be two more years before the finished draft would finally be published on March 11, 1818 as *Frankenstein; or, The Modern Prometheus*, in three sturdy volumes from the London publishing house of Lackington, Hughes, Harding, Mayor and Jones. But this publication was not to result in the instant fame for the author and for her story that one might expect for such a seminal work. Indeed, the first edition was actually issued without an author's name on the title page at all, and for a while rumour had it that Percy Shelley was the author – probably because he had written the Introduction. It never crossed anyone's mind that a woman might have been the author – for surely no member of the gentle sex could have written such a tale!

'*Frankenstein* is an uncouth story,' the critic of the *Monthly Review* declared as if echoing such a view, 'setting probability at defiance and leading to no conclusion either moral or philosophical. A serious examination is scarcely necessary for so eccentric a vagary of the imagination as this tale presents.'

Had that reviewer still been alive today he would have cause to regret such a hasty decision in the light of the critical importance that was subsequently attached to the book and continues to be given to it today. For *Frankenstein* is now widely regarded as the book which marked the decline of the Gothic novel and heralded the dawn of Science Fiction. It has also attracted admirers from each new generation of readers and writers: Stephen King and Clive Barker, two of today's leading authors of horror fiction, have both admitted their debt to this masterpiece.

'*Frankenstein* is a mystical morality tale,' Stephen King says, stating what both writers feel, 'about what happened when man dares to transgress the limits of knowledge.'

The fame of the book has spread not only by way of the endless new editions and translations into other languages which have kept it in print for 175 years, but also in the novels and stories which have utilised its ideas, and the films and television adaptations which have brought the story to the screen. It is, with good reason, now generally regarded as *the* single greatest horror story novel ever written and the most widely influential in the genre.

A guide to just how wide this influence has spread is the theme of this anthology. Though by no means exhaustive, it certainly represents the largest and most comprehensive collection of stories on the Frankenstein theme ever collected in one volume. It begins, appropriately, with the short episode that was Mary Shelley's first rendering of her idea, and which she was later to enlarge into the enduring classic.

'I have found it!' Mary Shelley declared enthusiastically to her fellow guests at the Villa Diodata on that June morning, and then repeated in an introduction specially written for a new edition of *Frankenstein* published in 1831. 'What terrified me will terrify others; and I need only describe the spectre which haunted my midnight pillow. I began that day with the words, "It was on a dreary night of November", making a transcript of the grim terrors of my waking dream.'

What she also did that night was to give life to the creature who ever since has walked through all our days and nights in words and illustrations and moving pictures . . .

PETER HAINING
August, 1993

# *Preface*

---

## 'THE CREATURE LIVES!'

It was on a dreary night of November, that I beheld the accomplishment of my toils. With an anxiety that almost amounted to agony, I collected the instruments of life around me, that I might infuse a spark of being into the lifeless thing that lay at my feet. It was already one in the morning; the rain pattered dismally against the panes, and my candle was nearly burnt out, when, by the glimmer of the half-extinguished light, I saw the dull yellow eye of the creature open; it breathed hard, and a convulsive motion agitated its limbs.

How can I describe my emotions at this catastrophe, or how delineate the wretch whom with such infinite pains and care I had endeavoured to form? His limbs were in proportion, and I had selected his features as beautiful. Beautiful! – Great God! His yellow skin scarcely covered the work of muscles and arteries beneath; his hair was of a lustrous black, and flowing; his teeth of a pearly whiteness; but these luxuriances only formed a more horrid contrast with his watery eyes, that seemed almost of the same colour as the dun white sockets in which they were set, his shrivelled complexion and straight black lips.

The different accidents of life are not so changeable as the feelings of human nature. I had worked hard for nearly two years, for the sole purpose of infusing life into an inanimate body. For this I had deprived myself of rest and health. I had desired it with an ardour that far exceeded moderation; but now that I had finished, the beauty of the dream vanished, and breathless horror and disgust filled my heart. Unable to endure the aspect of the being I had created, I rushed out of the room, and continued a long time traversing my bed-chamber, unable to compose my mind to sleep. At length lassitude succeeded to the tumult I had before endured; and I threw myself on the bed in my clothes, endeavouring to seek a few moments of forgetfulness. But it was in vain: I slept, indeed, but I was disturbed by the wildest dreams. I thought I saw Elizabeth, in the bloom of health, walking in the streets of Ingolstadt. Delighted and surprised, I embraced her; but as I imprinted the first kiss on her lips, they became livid with the hue of death; her features appeared to change, and I thought that I held the corpse of my dead mother in my arms; a shroud enveloped her form, and I saw the grave-worms crawling in the folds of the flannel. I started from my sleep with horror; a cold dew covered my forehead, my teeth chattered, and every limb became convulsed: when, by the dim and yellow light of the moon, as it forced its way through the window shutters, I beheld the wretch – the miserable monster whom I had created. He held up the curtain of the bed; and his eyes, if eyes they may be called, were fixed on me. His jaws opened, and he muttered some inarticulate sounds, while a grin wrinkled his cheeks. He might have spoken, but I did not hear; one hand was stretched out, seemingly to detain me, but I escaped, and rushed down stairs. I took refuge in the courtyard belonging to the house which I inhabited; where I remained during the rest of the night, walking up and down in the greatest agitation, listening attentively, catching and fearing each sound as if it were to announce the approach of the demoniacal corpse to which I had so miserably given life.

Oh! no mortal could support the horror of that countenance. A mummy again endued with animation could not be so hideous as that wretch. I had gazed on him while unfinished; he was ugly then; but when those muscles and joints were rendered capable of motion, it became a thing such as even Dante could not have conceived.

I passed the night wretchedly. Sometimes my pulse beat so quickly and hardly, that I felt the palpitation of every artery; at others, I nearly sank to the ground through languor and extreme weakness. Mingled with this horror, I felt the bitterness of disappointment; dreams that had been my food and pleasant rest for so long a space were now become a hell to me; and the change was so rapid, the overthrow so complete!

Morning, dismal and wet, at length dawned, and discovered to my sleepless and aching eyes the church of Ingolstadt, its white steeple and clock, which indicated the sixth hour. The porter opened the gates of the court, which had that night been my asylum, and I issued into the streets, pacing them with quick steps, as if I sought to avoid the wretch whom I feared every turning of the street would present to my view. I did not dare return to the apartment which I inhabited, but felt impelled to hurry on, although drenched by the rain which poured from a black and comfortless sky.

I continued walking in this manner for some time, endeavouring, by bodily exercise, to ease the load that weighed upon my mind. I traversed the streets, without any clear conception of where I was, or what I was doing. My heart palpitated in the sickness of fear; and I hurried on with irregular steps, not daring to look about me: –

> Like one who, on a lonely road,
>     Doth walk in fear and dread,
> And, having once turned round, walks on,
>     And turns no more his head;
> Because he knows a frightful fiend
>     Doth close behind him tread.*

Continuing thus, I came at length opposite to the inn at which the various diligences and carriages usually stopped. Here I paused, I knew not why; but I remained some minutes with my eyes fixed on a coach that was coming towards me from the other end of the street. As it drew nearer, I observed that it was the Swiss diligence: it stopped just where I was standing; and, on the door being opened, I perceived Henry Clerval, who, on seeing me, instantly sprung out. 'My dear Frankenstein,' exclaimed he, 'how glad I am to see you! how fortunate that you should be here at the very moment of my alighting!'

Nothing could equal my delight on seeing Clerval; his presence brought back to my thoughts my father, Elizabeth, and all those scenes of home so dear to my recollection. I grasped his hand, and in a moment forgot my horror and misfortune; I felt suddenly, and for the first time during many months, calm and serene joy. I welcomed my friend, therefore,

* Coleridge's 'Ancient Mariner'.

in the most cordial manner, and we walked towards my college. Clerval continued talking for some time about our mutual friends, and his own good fortune in being permitted to come to Ingolstadt. 'You may easily believe,' said he, 'how great was the difficulty to persuade my father that all necessary knowledge was not comprised in the noble art of book-keeping; and, indeed, I believe I left him incredulous to the last, for his constant answer to my unwearied entreaties was the same as that of the Dutch school-master in the Vicar of Wakefield: – "I have ten thousand florins a year without Greek, I eat heartily without Greek." But his affection for me at length overcame his dislike of learning, and he has permitted me to undertake a voyage of discovery to the land of knowledge.'

'It gives me the greatest delight to see you; but tell me how you left my father, brothers, and Elizabeth.'

'Very well, and very happy, only a little uneasy that they hear from you so seldom. By the by, I mean to lecture you a little upon their account myself. – But, my dear Frankenstein,' continued he, stopping short, and gazing full in my face, 'I did not before remark how very ill you appear; so thin and pale; you look as if you had been watching for several nights.'

'You have guessed right; I have lately been so deeply engaged in one occupation, that I have not allowed myself sufficient rest, as you see: but I hope, I sincerely hope, that all these employments are now at an end, and that I am at length free.'

I trembled excessively; I could not endure to think of, and far less to allude to, the occurrences of the preceding night. I walked with a quick pace, and we soon arrived at my college. I then reflected, and the thought made me shiver, that the creature whom I had left in my apartment might still be there, alive, and walking about. I dreaded to behold this monster; but I feared still more that Henry should see him. Entreating him, therefore, to remain a few minutes at the bottom of the stairs, I darted up towards my own room. My hand was already on the lock of the door before I recollected myself. I then paused; and a cold shivering came over me. I threw the door forcibly open, as children are accustomed to do when they expect a spectre to stand in waiting for them on the other side; but nothing appeared. I stepped fearfully in: the

apartment was empty; and my bedroom was also freed from
its hideous guest. I could hardly believe that so great a
good fortune could have befallen me; but when I became
assured that my enemy had indeed fled, I clapped my hands
for joy, and ran down to Clerval ...

Mary Shelley
FRANKENSTEIN (1818)

# I
## *The Prototypes*

# The Reanimated Man

## By MARY SHELLEY

When Mary Shelley glanced at her morning newspaper on July 4, 1826, she could be forgiven if an uncanny shiver of recognition ran up her spine. For there prominently reported on the front page was the story of an Englishman, one Roger Dodsworth, who had apparently been frozen in a glacier for over a century and, following the recovery of his body, been reanimated 'by the usual remedies' to find himself in a world very different from the one he had last seen before being overwhelemed by an avalanche. To Mary, it must have seemed as if her story had somehow come true and Frankenstein's creature had risen from his icy tomb! It is therefore not surprising to learn that she took a special interest in the reports and later wrote her own version of the events.

With the passage of time, the huge success of Frankenstein has tended to overshadow Mary Shelley's other literary works, in particular her short stories which, with a few exceptions, are little known today. In fact, her famous book was not the only thing she wrote that dealt with scientific experiments in general and the Frankenstein theme in particular. In 1819, for instance, she wrote a short tale, Valerius, about a Roman who had died during the collapse of the Roman Empire and was then brought back to life over nineteen hundred years later to revisit his now much-changed former haunts. There was also The Mortal Immortal (1834) featuring a man who has ceased to age thanks to alchemy, but instead finds himself beset by the problems of a wife who grows older and more jealous as the years leave him physically and intellectually untouched. Even more striking than these is The Transformation (1824) in which a young man exchanges his body with a misshapen dwarf – a story to which I shall be returning later.

The Reanimated Man *was written by Mary in October 1826, following the reprinting of the original story in a number of other English newspapers and magazines and its discussion by various leading scholars including Thomas Moore, William Cobbett and Theodore Hook. What neither she nor these men knew at the time was that the story had actually originated in a French periodical, the* Journal du Commerce de Lyon, *of June 28, 1826, and had been lifted from there by the British press and translated literally word for word. Four months later the 'cryogenic hoax', as it has since been called, was exposed as a piece of pure fiction. But in the minds of a population that had not long before been amazed by the possibilities of creating life as described in Mary's novel, it was perhaps not altogether surprising that the 'reawakening' of Roger Dodsworth should have been given such credence. Mary's story, which has only been reprinted once since its first appearance over a century ago in* Yesterday and Today *(1863), adds a fascinating new dimension to the Frankenstein legend and is an ideal tale with which to begin this collection* ...

It may be remembered, that on the fourth of July last, a paragraph appeared in the papers importing that Dr Hotham, of Northumberland, returning from Italy, over Mount St Gothard, a score or two of years ago, had dug out from under an avalanche, in the neighbourhood of the mountain, a human being whose animation had been suspended by the action of the frost. Upon the application of the usual remedies, the patient was resuscitated, and discovered himself to be Mr Dodsworth, the son of the antiquary Dodsworth, who perished in the reign of Charles I. He was thirty-seven years of age at the time of his inhumation, which had taken place as he was returning from Italy, in 1654. It was added that as soon as he was sufficiently recovered he would return to England, under the protection of his preserver. We have since heard no more of him, and various plans for public benefit, which have started in philanthropic minds on reading the statement, have already returned to their pristine nothingness. The antiquarian society had eaten their way to several votes for medals, and had already begun, in idea, to consider what prices it could afford to offer for Mr Dodsworth's old clothes, and to conjecture what treasures in the way of pamphlet, old song, or autographic letter his pockets might contain. Poems from all quarters, of all kinds, elegiac, congratulatory, burlesque and allegoric, were half written. Mr Godwin had suspended for the sake of such authentic information the history of the Commonwealth he had just begun. It is hard not only that the world should be baulked of these destined gifts from the talents of the country, but also that it should be promised and then deprived of a new subject of romantic wonder and scientific interest. A novel idea is worth much in the commonplace routine of life, but a new fact, an astonishment, a miracle, a palpable wandering from the course of things into apparent impossibilities, is a circumstance to which the imagination must cling with delight, and we say again that it is hard, very hard, that Mr Dodsworth refuses to appear, and that the believers in his resuscitation are forced to undergo the sarcasms and triumphant arguments of those sceptics who always keep on the safe side of the hedge.

Now we do not believe that any contradiction or impossibility is attached to the adventures of this youthful antique. Animation (I believe physiologists agree) can as easily be suspended for an hundred or two years, as for as many seconds. A body hermetically sealed up by the frost, is of necessity preserved in its pristine entireness. That which is totally secluded from the action of external agency, can neither have any thing added to nor taken away from it: no decay can take place, for something can never become nothing; under the influence of that state of being which we call death, change but not annihilation removes from our sight the corporeal atoma; the earth receives sustenance from them, the air is fed by them, each element takes its own, thus seizing forcible repayment of what it had lent. But the elements that hovered round Mr Dodsworth's icy shroud had no power to overcome the obstacle it presented. No zephyr could gather a hair from his head, nor could the influence of dewy night or genial morn penetrate his more than adamantine panoply. The story of the Seven Sleepers rests on a miraculous interposition – they slept. Mr Dodsworth did not sleep; his breast never heaved, his pulses were stopped; death had his finger pressed on his lips which no breath might pass. He has removed it now, the grim shadow is vanquished, and stands wondering. His victim has cast from him the frosty spell, and arises as perfect a man as he had lain down an hundred and fifty years before. We have eagerly desired to be furnished with some particulars of his first conversations, and the mode in which he has learnt to adapt himself to his new scene of life. But since facts are denied to us, let us be permitted to indulge in conjecture. What his first words were may be guessed from the expressions used by people exposed to shorter accidents of the like nature. But as his powers return, the plot thickens. His dress had already excited Doctor Hotham's astonishment – the peaked beard – the love locks – the frill, which, until it was thawed, stood stiff under the mingled influence of starch and frost; his dress fashioned like that of one of Vandyke's portraits, or (a more familiar similitude) Mr Sapio's costume in Winter's Opera of the Oracle, his pointed shoes – all spoke of other times. The curiosity of his preserver was keenly awake, that of Mr Dodsworth was about to be roused. But to be enabled to conjecture with any degree of likelihood the tenor of his first inquiries, we must endeavour to make out what part he played in his former life. He lived at the most interesting period of English History – he was lost to the world when Oliver Cromwell had arrived at the summit of his ambition, and in the eyes of all Europe the commonwealth of England appeared so established as to endure for ever. Charles I. was dead; Charles II. was an outcast, a beggar, bankrupt even in hope. Mr Dodsworth's father, the antiquary, received a salary from the republican general, Lord Fairfax, who was himself a great lover of antiquities, and died the very year that his son went to his long, but not unending sleep, a curious coincidence this, for it would seem that our frost-preserved friend was returning to England on his father's death, to claim probably his inheritance – how short lived are human views! Where now is Mr Dodsworth's patrimony? Where his co-heirs, executors, and fellow legatees? His protracted absence has, we should suppose, given the present possessors to his estate – the world's chronology is an hundred and seventy years older since he seceded from the busy scene, hands after hands have tilled his acres, and then become clods beneath them; we may be permitted to doubt whether one single particle of their surface is individually the same as those which were to have been his – the youthful soil would of itself reject the antique clay of its claimant.

Mr Dodsworth, if we may judge from the circumstance of his being abroad, was no zealous commonwealth's man, yet his having chosen Italy as the country in which to make his tour and his projected return to England on his father's death, renders it probable that he was no violent loyalist. One of those men he seems to be (or to have been) who did not follow Cato's advice as recorded in the Pharsalia; a party, if to be of no party admits of such a term, which Dante recommends us utterly to despise, and which not unseldom falls between the two stools, a seat on either of which is so carefully avoided. Still Mr Dodsworth could hardly fail to feel anxious for the latest news from his native country at so critical a period; his absence might have put his own property in jeopardy; we may imagine therefore that after his limbs had felt the cheerful return of circulation, and after he had refreshed himself with such of earth's products as from all analogy he never could have hoped to live to eat, after he had been told from what peril he had been rescued, and said a prayer thereon which even appeared enormously long to Dr Hotham – we may imagine, we say, that his first question would be: 'If any news had arrived lately from England?'

'I had letters yesterday,' Dr Hotham may well be supposed to reply.

'Indeed,' cries Mr Dodsworth, 'and pray, sir, has any change for better or worse occurred in that poor distracted country?'

Dr Hotham suspects a Radical, and coldly replies: 'Why, sir, it would be difficult to say in what its distraction consists. People talk of starving manufacturers, bankruptcies, and the fall of the Joint Stock Companies – excrescences these, excrescences which will attach themselves to a state of full health. England, in fact, was never in a more prosperous condition.'

Mr Dodsworth now more than suspects the Republican, and, with what we have supposed to be his accustomed caution, sinks for awhile his loyalty, and in a moderate tone asks: 'Do our governors look with careless eyes upon the symptoms of over-health?'

'Our governors,' answers his preserver, 'if you mean our ministry, are only too alive to temporary embarrassment.' (We beg Doctor Hotham's pardon if we wrong him in making him a high Tory; such a quality appertains to our pure anticipated cognition of a Doctor, and such is the only cognizance that we have of this gentleman.) 'It were to be wished that they showed themselves more firm – the king, God bless him!'

'Sir!' exclaims Mr Dodsworth.

Doctor Hotham continues, not aware of the excessive astonishment exhibited by his patient: 'The king, God bless him, spares immense sums from his privy purse for the relief of his subjects, and his example has been imitated by all the aristocracy and wealth of England.'

'The King!' ejaculates Mr Dodsworth.

'Yes, sir,' emphatically rejoins his preserver; 'the king, and I am happy to say that the prejudices that so unhappily and unwarrantably possessed the English people with regard to his Majesty are now, with a few' (with added severity) 'and I may say contemptible exceptions, exchanged for dutiful love and such reverence as his talents, virtues, and paternal care deserve.'

'Dear sir, you delight me,' replies Mr Dodsworth, while his loyalty late a tiny bud suddenly expands into full flower; 'yet I hardly understand; the change is so sudden; and the man – Charles Stuart, King Charles, I may now call him, his murder is I trust execrated as it deserves?'

Dr Hotham put his hand on the pulse of his patient – he feared an access of delirium from such a wandering from the subject. The pulse was calm, and Mr Dodsworth continued: 'That unfortunate martyr looking down from heaven is, I trust, appeased by the reverence paid to his name and the prayers dedicated to his memory. No sentiment, I think I may venture to assert, is so general in England as the compassion and love in which the memory of that hapless monarch is held?'

'And his son, who now reigns? –'

'Surely, sir, you forget; no son; that of course is impossible. No descendant of his fills the English throne, now worthily occupied by the house of Hanover. The despicable race of the Stuarts, long outcast and wandering, is now extinct, and the last days of the last Pretender to the crown of that family justified in the eyes of the world the sentence which ejected it from the kingdom for ever.'

Such must have been Mr Dodsworth's first lesson in politics. Soon, to the wonder of the preserver and preserved, the real state of the case must have been revealed; for a time, the strange and tremendous circumstance of his long trance may have threatened the wits of Mr Dodsworth with a total overthrow. He had, as he crossed Mount Saint Gothard, mourned a father – now every human being he had ever seen dust, each voice he had ever heard is mute. The very sound of the English tongue is changed, as his experience in conversation with Dr Hotham assures him. Empires, religions, races of men, have probably sprung up or faded; his own patrimony (the thought is idle, yet, without it, how can he live?) is sunk into the thirsty gulph that gapes ever greedy to swallow the past; his learning, his acquirements, are probably obsolete; with a bitter smile he thinks to himself, I must take to my father's profession, and turn antiquary. The familiar objects, thoughts, and habits of my boyhood, are now antiquities. He wonders where the hundred and sixty folio volumes of MS. that his father had compiled, and which, as a lad, he had regarded with religious reverence, now are – where – ah, where? His favourite play-mate, the friend of his later years, his destined and lovely bride; tears long frozen are uncongealed, and flow down his young old cheeks.

But we do not wish to be pathetic; surely since the days of the patriarchs, no fair lady had her death mourned by her lover so many years after it had taken place. Necessity, tyrant of the world, in some degree reconciles Mr Dodsworth to his fate. At first he is persuaded that the later generation of man is much deteriorated from his contemporaries; they are neither so tall, so handsome, nor so intelligent. Then by degrees he begins to doubt his first impression. The ideas that had taken possession of his brain before his accident, and which had been frozen up for so many years, begin to thaw and dissolve away, making room for others. He dresses himself in the modern style, and does not object much to anything except the neck-cloth and hardboarded hat. He admires the texture of his shoes and stockings, and looks with admiration on a small Genevese watch, which he often consults, as if he were not yet assured that time had made progress in its accustomed manner, and as if he should find on its dial plate ocular demonstration that he had exchanged his thirty-seventh year for his two hundredth and upwards, and had left A.D. 1654 far behind to find himself suddenly a beholder of the ways of men in this enlightened nineteenth century. His curiosity is insatiable; when he reads, his eyes cannot purvey fast enough to his mind, and every now and then he lights upon some inexplicable passage, some discovery and knowledge familiar to us, but undreamed of in his days, that throws him into wonder and interminable reverie. Indeed, he may be supposed to pass much of his time in that state, now and then interrupting himself with a royalist song against old Noll and the Roundheads, breaking off suddenly, and looking round fearfully to see who were his auditors, and on beholding the modern appearance of his friend the Doctor, sighing to think that it is no longer of import to any, whether he sing a cavalier catch or a puritanic psalm.

It were an endless task to develop all the philosophic ideas to which Mr Dodsworth's resuscitation naturally gives birth. We should like much to converse with this gentleman, and still more to observe the progress of his mind, and the change of his ideas in his very novel situation. If he be a sprightly youth, fond of the shows of the world, careless of the higher human pursuits, he may proceed summarily to cast into the shade all trace of his former life, and endeavour to merge himself at once into the stream of humanity now flowing. It would be curious enough to observe the mistakes he would make, and the medley of manners which would thus be produced. He may think to enter into active life, become whig or tory as his inclinations lead, and get a seat in the, even to him, once called chapel of St Stephens. He may content himself with turning contemplative philosopher, and find sufficient food for his mind in tracing the march of the human intellect, the changes which have been wrought in the dispositions, desires, and powers of mankind. Will he be an advocate for perfectibility or deterioration? He must admire our manufactures, the progress of science, the diffusion of knowledge, and the fresh spirit of enterprise characteristic of our countrymen. Will he find any individuals to be compared to the glorious spirits of his day? Moderate in his views as we have supposed him to be, he will probably fall at once into the temporising tone of mind now so much in vogue. He will be pleased to find a calm in politics; he will greatly admire the ministry who have succeeded in conciliating almost all parties – to find peace where he left feud. The same character which he bore a couple of hundred years ago, will influence him now; he will still be the moderate, peaceful, unenthusiastic Mr Dodsworth that he was in 1647.

For notwithstanding education and circumstances may suffice to direct and form the rough material of the mind, it cannot create, nor give intellect, noble aspiration, and energetic constancy where dullness, wavering of purpose, and grovelling desires, are stamped by nature. Entertaining this belief we have (to forget Mr Dodsworth for awhile) often made conjectures how such and such heroes of antiquity would act, if they were reborn in these times: and then awakened fancy has gone on to imagine that some of them are reborn; that according to the theory explained by Virgil in his sixth Æeid, every thousand years the dead return to life, and their souls endued with the same sensibilities and capacities as before, are turned naked of knowledge into this world, again to dress their skeleton powers in such habiliments as situation, education, and experience will furnish. Pythagoras, we are told, remembered many transmigrations of this sort, as having occurred to himself, though for a philosopher he made very little use of his anterior memories. It would prove an instructive school for kings and statesmen, and in fact for all human beings, called on as they are, to play their part on the stage of the world, could they remember what they had been. Thus we might obtain a glimpse of heaven and of hell, as, the secret of our former identity confined to our own bosoms, we winced or exulted in the blame or praise bestowed on our former selves. While the love of glory and posthumous reputation is as natural to man as his attachment to life itself, he must be, under such a state of things, tremblingly alive to the historic records of his honour or shame. The mild spirit of Fox would have been soothed by the recollection that he had played a worthy part as Marcus Antoninus – the former experiences of Alcibiades or even of the emasculated Steeny of

James I. might have caused Sheridan to have refused to tread over again the same path of dazzling but fleeting brilliancy. The soul of our modern Corinna would have been purified and exalted by a consciousness that once it had given life to the form of Sappho. If at the present moment the witch, memory, were in a freak, to cause all the present generation to recollect that some ten centuries back they had been somebody else, would not several of our free thinking martyrs wonder to find that they had suffered as Christians under Domitian, while the judge as he passed sentence would suddenly become aware, that formerly he had condemned the saints of the early church to the torture, for not renouncing the religion he now upheld – nothing but benevolent actions and real goodness would come pure out of the ordeal. While it would be whimsical to perceive how some great men in parish affairs would strut under the consciousness that their hands had once held a sceptre, an honest artizan or pilfering domestic would find that he was little altered by being transformed into an idle noble or director of a joint stock company; in every way we may suppose that the humble would be exalted, and the noble and the proud would feel their stars and honours dwindle into baubles and child's play when they called to mind the lowly stations they had once occupied. If philosophical novels were in fashion, we conceive an excellent one might be written on the development of the same mind in various stations, in different periods of the world's history.

But to return to Mr Dodsworth, and indeed with a few more words to bid him farewell. We entreat him no longer to bury himself in obscurity; or, if he modestly decline publicity, we beg him to make himself known personally to us. We have a thousand inquiries to make, doubts to clear up, facts to ascertain. If any fear that old habits and strangeness of appearance will make him ridiculous to those accustomed to associate with modern exquisites, we beg to assure him that we are not given to ridicule mere outward shows, and that worth and intrinsic excellence will always claim our respect.

This we say, if Mr Dodsworth is alive. Perhaps he is again no more. Perhaps he opened his eyes only to shut them again more obstinately; perhaps his ancient clay could not thrive on the harvests of these latter days. After a little wonder; a little shuddering to find himself the dead alive – finding no affinity between himself and the present state of things – he has bidden once more an eternal farewell to the sun. Followed to his grave by his preserver and the wondering villagers, he may sleep the true death-sleep in the same valley where he so long reposed. Doctor Hotham may have erected a simple tablet over his twice-buried remains, inscribed –

To the Memory of R. Dodsworth,
An Englishman,
Born April 1, 1617; Died July 16, 1826; Aged 209.

An inscription which, if it were preserved during any terrible convulsion that caused the world to begin its life again, would occasion many learned disquisitions and ingenious theories concerning a race which authentic records showed to have secured the privilege of attaining so vast an age.

# The Mummy

### By JANE WEBB

Frankenstein *was still gaining new readers by the thousands when another teenage girl wrote a sensational novel about reanimation,* The Mummy! A Tale of the Twenty-Second Century, *which was published in 1827 in three volumes. The authoress, Jane Webb (1807–1858), had set out to write the novel because she was, quite literally, penniless. Still only nineteen, she had just lost her father and decided the only course open to someone of her genteel upbringing was to create a bestselling novel in the manner of her contemporaries Ann Radcliffe, Elizabeth Inchbald and, of course, Mary Shelley, all of whom had made fortunes from their books. The result was a mélange of thrills, pathos, heroism and not a little scientific prophecy all surrounding the reanimation of the Ancient Egyptian pharaoh Cheops in the year 2126.*

*Apart from its breathless prose, wooden characterisation and stilted dialogue, not to mention frequent implausible twists in the plot,* The Mummy *nonetheless makes fascinating reading because of its ingenious picture of a future feminist England 'when the country enjoyed peace and tranquility under the absolute dominion of a female sovereign.' Readers also soon discover that mechanical inventions – mostly powered by steam or electricity – have made life much easier for everyone. The weather and agriculture are now completely under man's control; robot doctors look after the sick, and mechanical judges and lawyers take care of justice. Television provides the primary means of communication, while air travel in giant balloons is commonplace. Among the central figures in the story are Dr Entwerfen, 'a clownish genius'; the hero, Edric; and their man-servant Gregory. It is this trio's plan to fly to Egypt and there revive the body of the long-*

*dead pharaoh to prove the efficiency of an electrical reanima-
tion machine which Dr Entwerfen has invented. But when this
is achieved – not without problems – Cheops escapes by
balloon and flies to England where he becomes involved in
the power struggle for the throne. Some six hundred pages
later, the pharaoh finally returns to his pyramid in Egypt,
leaving behind an England once more functioning as a benevolent female monarchy. For this creature there is a happy
ending.*

*Everett Bleiler, the historian of early science fiction, has
described* The Mummy *as 'a strange stew' and wrote in* The
Arkham Sampler *(Spring 1949): 'It is the remnants of* Frankenstein *rehashed, where man is again earnestly adjured not to
meddle scientifically with things beyond his power, where the
mummy of Cheops, revived by unholy science, serves as does
the monster in* Frankenstein *as an active albatross, throttling
the dabbler.' Copies of the novel are now extremely rare
despite the popularity it enjoyed among readers who had
discovered embryo 'science fiction' in* Frankenstein. *However,
I am fortunate in possessing an edition and have selected for
reprinting here the crucial episode in which the mummy is
revived. Like her sensational Gothic story, Jane Webb deserves
to be better known today. In the few biographical notes
about her career that can be found,* The Mummy *receives
rather less attention than the fact that she married an admirer
she met as a result of the book – one John Claudius Loudon,
an expert on horticulture – and thereafter devoted her writing
life to producing a series of popular books about ...
gardening!*

No event of any importance occurred to our travellers in the
course of their aërial voyage. They were too well provided
with all kinds of necessaries to have any occasion to rest by
the way, and in an incredibly short space of time they were
hovering over Egypt. Different, however, how different from
the Egypt of the nineteenth century, was the fertile country

which now lay like a map beneath their feet! Improvement had turned her gigantic steps towards its once deserted plains; Commerce had waved her magic wand; and towns and cities, manufactaries and canals, spread in all directions. No more did the Nile overflow its banks: a thousand channels were cut to receive its waters. No longer did the moving sands of the Desert rise in mighty waves, threatening to overwhelm the wayworn traveller: macadamized turnpike roads supplied their place, over which post-chaises, with anti-attritioned wheels, bowled at the rate of fifteen miles an hour. Steam boats glided down the canals, and furnaces raised their smoky heads amidst groves of palm trees; whilst iron railways intersected orange groves, and plantations of dates and pomegranates might be seen bordering excavations intended for coal pits. Colonies of English and Americans peopled the country, and produced a population that swarmed like bees over the land, and surpassed in numbers, even the wondrous throngs of the ancient Mizraim race; whilst industry and science changed desolation into plenty, and had converted barren plains into fertile kingdoms.

Amidst all these revolutions, however, the Pyramids still raised their gigantic forms, towering to the sky; unchanged, unchangeable, grand, simple, and immoveable, fit symbols of that majestic nature they were intended to represent, and seeming to look down with contempt upon the ephemeral structures with which they were surrounded; as though they would have said, had utterance been permitted to them – 'Avaunt, ye nothings of the day! Respect our dignity and sink into your original obscurity; for, know that we alone are monarchs of the plains.' Indestructible, however, as they had proved themselves, even their granite sides had not been able entirely to resist the corroding influence of the smoke with which they were now surrounded, and a slight crumbling announced the first outward symptom of decay. Still, however, though blackened and disfigured, they shone stupendous monuments of former greatness; and Edric and his tutor gazed upon them with an awe that for some moments deprived them of utterance.

The doctor, however, who was too fond of reasoning ever long to remain willingly silent, after surveying them a few minutes, broke forth as follows: 'What noble piles! What

majesty and grandeur they display in their formation, and yet
what dignified simplicity! Can the imagination of man conceive anything more sublime than the thought that they have
stood thus, frowning in awful magnificence, perhaps since the
very creation of the world, without equals, without even
competitors – mocking the feeble efforts of man to divine
their origin, and seeing generation after generation pass away,
whilst they still remain immutable, and involved in the same
deep and unfathomable mystery as at first?'

'It is very strange,' observed Edric, 'that, in this age of
speculation and discovery, nothing certain should be known
concerning them.'

'It is,' returned the doctor: 'but the thick mysterious veil
that has rested upon them for so many ages, seems not
intended to be removed by mortal hands. They remind one of
the sublime inscription upon the temple of the goddess, Isis,
at Sais: "I am whatever was, whatever is, and whatever shall
be; but no mortal has, as yet, presumed to raise the veil that
covers me."'

'Your quotation is apt, doctor,' resumed Edric, 'for both
relate to Nature. Indeed, Nature appears to be the deity which
the ancient Egyptians worshipped, under all the various forms
in which she presents herself; and their strange and animal
deities were but reverenced as her symbols. It was Nature
which they worshipped as Isis; it was Nature that was typified
in the Pyramids; and the good taste of the Egyptians made
them prefer the simple, the majestic, and the sublime, in those
works which they destined to last for ages. Formerly, from
the immensity of their population, and high state of their
civilization, labour was so divided, and consequently so light-
ened, that multitudes were enabled to exist exempt from toil.
These persons, devoting themselves to study, became *initiati*;
and either enrolled themselves amongst the priesthood, or
passed their lives in making themselves masters of the most
abstract sciences. The consequences were natural: they followed up the ramifications of creation to their original source;
they penetrated into the most profound secrets of Nature,
and traced all her wonders in her works: aware, however,
of the taste of the vulgar for anything above their comprehension, and of the natural craving of the human mind for
mystery, they wrapped the discoveries they had made in a deep

impenetrable veil, and concealed awful and sublime significa-
tions under the meanest and most disgusting images.'

'You are right,' said the doctor, 'in your observations upon
the religion of the ancient Egyptians; but it does not appear
to me that the Pyramids were erected by them.'

'What! I suppose you draw your conclusions from the want
of hieroglyphics in their principal chambers; and, from what
Herodotus says of their having been erected by a shepherd,
you think they were the work of the Pallic race.'

'No; though I allow much may be said in favour of that
hypothesis, particularly as Herodotus says the kings under
whom they were erected, ordered all the Egyptian temples to
be closed, which we know the shepherd or Pallic sovereigns
did; but I cannot imagine that an ignorant, Goth-like race of
shepherds, men accustomed to live in tents or in the open air,
and possessing no talents but for war, were capable of constructing such immense piles. No, no, the Pyramids required
gigantic conceptions, highly cultivated minds, and unwearied
perseverance; all qualities quite incompatible with a warlike
wandering race. I do not think the Palli were capable of
imagining such structures, much less of constructing them. I
think they were the work of evil spirits.'

'Evil spirits!' exclaimed Edric.

'Yes,' returned the doctor. 'We are told that the evil spirits,
after their expulsion from Paradise, were under the command
of the Sultan, or Soliman Giam ben Giam, as he is called by
Arabic writers, but who is supposed to have been the same as
Cheops; and I think that he employed them in this vast
work.'

'I do not know by what analysis etymologists can draw the
name of Cheops from that of Giam ben Giam' responded
Edric, 'but supposing the fact to be correct, that they designated the same person, I think it only proves more strongly
my hypothesis; for the Palli came from Mount Caucasus,
where the evil spirits were said to have been enchained, and if
Cheops was a Pallic king, it is possible the Egyptians might
poetically call their conquerors evil spirits.'

'That is a good idea, Edric; though I do not think it by any
means certain that Cheops was a Pallic king. However, we
shall soon be able to see his tomb, and judge for ourselves;
for we have now approached near enough to the Pyramids to

descend. Foh! what a smoke and what a noise! It is enough to rouse the mummies from their slumbers before their appointed time, and without the aid of galvanism. Have you opened the valves, Edric? Oh yes! I perceive we are getting lower; we will not lose a moment before we visit the Pyramid. But what a crowd of brutes are assembled to witness our arrival! They stare as though they had never seen a balloon before. Egypt is certainly a fine country, but the inhabitants are a century behind us in civilization.'

An immense crowd had gathered together to witness the descent of our travellers, and they did indeed stand staring, lost in stupid astonishment at the strange sight that presented itself; for though the Egyptian people had occasionally seen balloons, they had never before beheld one made of Indian rubber. The odd figure of the doctor, too, amused them exceedingly, as he sat wrapt up in the most dignified manner in an asbestos cloak, his bob-wig pushed a little on one side from the heat of the weather and the warmth of his argument; his round, red, oily face attempting to look solemn, and his little fat, punchy figure trying to assume an air of majesty. The Egyptians were amazingly struck with this apparition, and being, like most colonists, somewhat conceited and not very ceremonious in their manners, they looked at him a few minutes in silence, and then burst into immoderate fits of laughter.

The doctor was exceedingly indignant at this rude reception, and rising, shook his fist at them in anger; a manoeuvre that only redoubled the mirth of the unpolished Egyptians, whose peals of laughter now became so tremendous, that they actually shook the skies, and occasioned a most unpleasant vibration in the balloon. Edric, who was almost as much annoyed as the doctor, had yet sufficient self-command to continue calmly making preparations for his descent; and without taking the least notice of the crowd below, he screwed the top upon the propelling vapour-bottle; he let the inflammable air escape from the balloon, which rapidly collapsed as they approached the earth, and throwing out their patent spring grappling-irons, they caught one of the lower stones of the Great Pyramid, and in a few moments the car in which our travellers were sitting, was safely moored at a convenient distance from the earth for them to alight. Edric now unloosed the descending ladder, and reverentially assisted the doctor, who was encumbered with his long cloak, to reach terra firma in safety – amidst the bustle and exclamations of the crowd, who thronged round them, expressing their wonder and astonishment audibly, in broad English.

'Where the deuce did this spring from?' cried one; 'the car would load a waggon!'

'And what is gone with the balloon?' said another; 'it is clean vanished!'

'Well, I never saw such a thing in all my life before!' exclaimed a third; 'I think they must be come from the moon.'

'Hush! hush!' cried an old gentleman bustling amongst them, who seemed as one having authority. 'What's the matter? What's the matter?'

'We are strangers, Sir,' said Edric, advancing and addressing him. 'We come here to see the wonders of your country, and we wish to explore the Pyramids – but the reception we have met with –'

'Say no more – say no more!' interrupted the worthy justice, for such he was. 'Get about your business, you rapscallions, or I'll read the riot act! Here, Gregory, call out the *posse comitatus*, and set a guard of constables to keep watch over these gentlemen's balloon, whilst they go to explore the Pyramids. Eh, but where is the balloon? I don't see it. I hope neither of the gentlemen has put it in his pocket!' laughing at his own wit.

'No, Sir,' returned Edric, smiling, 'though it is a feat which might easily be accomplished, for that is our balloon,' pointing to the caoutchouc bottle, now shrunk to its original dimensions.

'Very strange, that!' said the justice; 'very curious, very curious indeed! Well, gentlemen, if you wish to proceed immediately, you'll want a guide of course. These cottages at the foot of the Pyramids are all inhabited by guides, who get their living by showing the sights. They are sad rogues, most of them, but I can recommend you to one who is a very honest man. Here, Samuel,' continued he, knocking against a small door, 'Samuel, I say!'

Samuel made his appearance, in the guise of a tall, raw-boned, stupid-looking fellow, with a pair of immensely broad stooping shoulders, which looked as though he could have relieved Atlas occasionally of his burthen, without much trouble to himself. Coming forth from his hut in an awkward shambling pace, he scratched his head, and demanded what his honour was pleased to want.

'You must show these gentlemen the Pyramids,' said the justice.

'Ay, that I will with pleasure!' returned Samuel. 'I've got my living by showing them these fifty years, man and boy; and I know every crink and cranny of them, though I'm old now and somewhat lame. So walk this way, gentlemen.'

'We are very much obliged to you, Sir,' said the doctor, bowing to the justice; who was in fact one of those good-natured, busy, bustling men, who are always better pleased to transact any other person's business than their own; and are never so happy as when a new arrival gives them an opportunity of showing off their consequence. Indeed, there is a pleasure in showing wonders to a stranger, that only those who have little else to occupy their minds can properly estimate: a man of this kind feels his self-love gratified by the superiority his local knowledge gives him over a stranger; and as it is, perhaps, the only chance he ever can have of showing superiority, they must be unreasonable who blame him for making the most of it. Justice Freemantle was accordingly exceedingly delighted with travellers who seemed disposed to submit implicitly to his dictation; and he returned a most gracious reply to the doctor's thanks.

'Don't mention it! Don't mention it, my dear Sir!' said he; 'I am never so happy as when I can make myself useful. Is there any thing else I can do for you? You may command me, I assure you; and you may depend upon it, no injury shall be done to your luggage, whilst you are away.'

'What a very civil, obliging, good-natured old gentleman!' said the doctor, as they walked towards the entrance of the Pyramids; 'I declare he almost reconciles me to the country, though, I own, I thought at first the people were the greatest brutes I had ever met with.'

'Which Pyramid does your honour wish to see?' asked the guide.

'That which contains the tomb of Cheops, man!' cried the doctor solemnly; who, encumbered with his long cloak, and loaded with his walking-stick and galvanic battery, had some difficulty in getting on.

'Won't your honour let me carry that pole and that box?' said the man; 'you'd get on a surprising deal better, if you would.'

'Avaunt, wretch!' exclaimed the doctor, 'nor offer to touch with thy profane fingers the immortal instruments of science.'

The man stared, but fell back, and the whole party walked on in perfect silence.

In the mean time, Edric had advanced before his companions, completely lost in meditation. A crowd of conflicting thoughts rushed through his mind; and now, when he found himself at the very goal of his wishes, the daring nature of the purpose he had so long entertained, seemed to strike him for the first time, and he trembled at the consequences that might attend the completion of his desires. With his arms folded on his breast, he stood gazing on the Pyramids, whilst his ideas wandered uncontrolled through the boundless regions of space.

'And what am I,' thought he, 'weak, feeble worm that I am who dare seek to penetrate into the awful secrets of my Creator? Why should I wish to restore animation to a body now resting in the quiet of the tomb? What right have I to renew the struggles, the pains, the cares, and the anxieties of mortal life? How can I tell the fearful effects that may be produced by the gratification of my unearthly longing? May I not revive a creature whose wickedness may involve mankind in misery? And what if my experiment should fail, and if the moment when I expect my rash wishes to be accomplished, the hand of Almighty vengeance should strike me to the earth, and heap molten fire on my brain to punish my presumption!'

The sound of human voices, as the doctor and the guide approached, grated harshly on the nerves of Edric, already overstrained by the awful nature of the thoughts in which he had been indulging, and he turned away involuntarily, to escape the interruption he dreaded, quite forgetting for the moment from whom the sounds most probably proceeded.

'Lord have mercy on us!' said the guide; 'I declare that gentleman looks as if he were beside himself; and see there if he hasn't walked right by the entrance to the Pyramid without seeing it! Sir! Sir!' hallooed he.

Excessively annoyed, but recalled to his recollection by these shouts, Edric returned.

'These Pyramids are wonderful piles,' said the doctor, as he stumbled forward to meet him. 'I really had no adequate conception of the enormity of their size. They did not even look half so large at a distance as they do now.'

'Immense masses seldom do,' replied Edric, compelling himself with difficulty to speak.

'True,' returned the doctor; 'the simplicity and uniformity of their figures deceive the eyes, and it is only when we approach them that we feel their stupendous magnitude and our own insignificance!'

'They give an amazing idea of the grandeur of the ancient kings of Egypt,' said Edric, without exactly knowing what he was saying. 'Their palaces must have been superb, if they had such mausoleums.'

'How absurdly you reason, Edric!' replied the doctor peevishly; for, being annoyed with his burthens and his cloak, he was not in a humour to bear contradiction. 'I thought we had settled that question before. In the first place, I think it very doubtful whether the Egyptians had anything to do with the building of these monuments; and if they had, I believe they were meant for temples, not mausoleums; and in the next place, even if they were intended for tombs, their greatness affords no argument for the splendour of the surrounding palaces; as the Egyptians were celebrated for the superiority of their burying-places, and for the immense sums they expended upon them. Indeed, you know, ancient writers say they went so far as to call the houses of the living only inns, whilst they considered tombs as everlasting habitations – a circumstance, by the way, that strongly corroborates my hypothesis, at least as far as their opinions go; as it seems to imply that both soul and body were designed to remain there.'

They had now entered the Pyramid, and were proceeding with infinite difficulty along a low, dark, narrow passage.

'Observe, Edric,' said the doctor, 'how the difficulty and obscurity of these winding passages confirm my opinion: you know, the religion of the ancient Egyptians, like that of the ancient Hindoos, was one of penances and personal privations; and, granting that to be the case, what can be more simple than that the passages the *initiati* had to traverse before they reached the adytum, should be painful and difficult of access. Besides this, as, you know, the bones of a bull, no doubt those of the god Apis, were found in a sarcophagus in the second Pyramid, it seems probable that it was sacred to his worship: and its vicinity to the Nile, which was indispensable to the temples of Apis, as, when it was time for him to die, he was drowned in its waters, confirms the fact. Indeed, I am only surprised that any human being, possessing a grain of common sense, can entertain a single doubt upon the subject.'

'How do you account for the tomb we are about to visit being placed in the Pyramid, if you think they were only designed for temples?' asked Edric.

'The question is futile,' said the doctor. 'A strange fancy prevailed in former times, that burying the dead in consecrated places, particularly in temples intended for divine worship, would scare away the evil spirits, and the practice actually prevailed in England even as lately as the nineteenth or twentieth century. Indeed, it was not till after the country had been almost depopulated by the dreadfully infectious disease which prevailed about two hundred years ago, that a law was passed to prevent the interment of the dead in London, and that those previously buried in and near the churches there, were exhumed and placed in cemeteries beyond the walls.'

Edric did not reply, for in fact his ideas were so absorbed by the solemn object before him, that it was painful for him to speak, and the doctor's ill-timed reasoning created such an irritation of his nerves, that he found it required the utmost exertion of his self-command to endure it patiently. The passage they were traversing, now became higher and wider, shelving off occasionally into chambers or recesses on each side, till they approached a kind of vestibule, in the centre of which yawned a deep, dark, gloomy-looking cavity, like a well.

'We must descend that shaft,' said the guide, 'and that will lead us to the tomb of King Cheops; but as the road is dark, and rather dangerous, we had better, each of us, take a torch.'

As he spoke, he drew some torches from a niche where they were deposited, and began to illuminate them from his own. The red glare of the torches flashed fearfully on the massive walls of the Pyramid, throwing part of their enormous masses into deep shadow, as they rose in solemn and sublime dignity around, and seemed frowning upon the presumptuous mortals who had dared to invade their recesses, whilst the deep pit beneath their feet seemed to yawn wide to engulf them in its abyss. Edric's heart beat thick: it throbbed till he even fancied its pulsations audible; and a strange, mysterious thrilling of anxiety, mingled with a wild, undefinable delight, ran through his frame. A few short hours, and his wishes would be gratified, or set at rest for ever. The doctor and the guide had already begun to descend, and their figures seemed changed and unearthly as the gleams of the torches fell upon them. Edric gazed for a moment, and then followed with feelings worked up almost to frenzy by the over-excitement of his nerves; whilst the hollow sounds that re-echoed from the walls, as they struck against them in their descent, thrilled through his whole frame.

No one spoke; and after proceeding for some time along the narrow path, or rather ledge, formed on the sides of the cavity, which gradually shelved downwards, the guide suddenly stopped, and touching a secret spring, a solid block of granite slowly detached itself from the wall, and, rising majestically like the portcullis of an ancient fortress, showed the entrance to a dark and dreary cave. The guide advanced, followed by our travellers, into a gloomy vaulted apartment, where long vistas of ponderous arches stretched on every side, till their termination was lost in darkness, and gave a feeling of immensity and obscurity to the scene.

'I will wait here,' said the guide; 'and here, if you please, you had better leave your torches. That avenue will lead you to the tomb.'

The travellers obeyed; and the guide, placing himself in a recess in the wall, extinguished all the torches except one, which he shrouded so as to leave the travellers in total darkness. Nothing could be now more terrific than their situation: immured in the recesses of the tomb, involved in darkness, and their bosoms throbbing with hopes that they scarcely dared avow even to themselves; with faltering steps they proceeded slowly along the path the guide had pointed out, shuddering even at the hollow echo of their own footsteps, which alone broke the solemn silence that reigned throughout these fearful regions of terror and the tomb.

Suddenly, a vivid light flashed upon them, and, as they

advanced, they found it proceeded from torches placed in the hands of two colossal figures, who, placed in a sitting posture, seemed guarding an enormous portal, surmounted by the image of a fox, the constant guardian of an Egyptian tomb. The immense dimensions and air of grandeur and repose about these colossi had something in it very imposing; and our travellers felt a sensation of awe creep over them as they gazed upon their calm unmoved features, so strikingly emblematic of that immutable nature which they were doubtless placed there to typify.

It was with feelings of indescribable solemnity, that the doctor and Edric passed through this majestic portal, and found themselves in an apartment gloomily illumined by the light shed faintly from an inner chamber, through ponderous brazen gates beautifully wrought. The light thus feebly emitted, showed that the room in which they stood was dedicated to Typhon, the evil spirit, as his fierce and savage types covered the walls; and images of his symbols, the crocodile and the dragon, placed beneath the shadow of the brazen gates, and dimly seen by the imperfect light, seemed starting into life, and grimly to forbid the farther advance of the intruders. Our travellers shuddered, and opening with trembling hand the ponderous gates, they entered the tomb of Cheops.

In the centre of the chamber, stood a superb, highly ornamented sarcophagus of alabaster, beautifully wrought: over this hung a lamp of wondrous workmanship, supplied by a potent mixture, so as to burn for ages unconsumed; thus awfully lighting up with perpetual flame the solemn mansions of the dead, and typifying life eternal even in the silent tomb. Around the room, on marble benches, were arranged mummies simply dried, apparently those of slaves; and close to the sarcophagus was placed one contained in a case, which the doctor approached to examine. This was supposed to be that of Sores, the confidant and prime-minister of Cheops. The chest that enclosed the body was splendidly ornamented with embossed gilt leather, whilst the parts not otherwise covered were stained with red and green curiously blended, and of a vivid brightness.

The mighty Phtah, the Jupiter of the Egyptians, spread its widely extended wings over the head, grasping in his monstrous claws a ring, the emblem of eternity; whilst below, the vulture-form of Rhea proclaimed the deceased a votary of that powerful deity; and on the sides were innumerable hieroglyphics. The doctor removed the lid, and shuddered as the crimson tinge of the everlasting lamp fell upon the hideous and distorted features thus suddenly exhibited to view. This sepulchral light, indeed, added unspeakable horror to the scene, and its peculiar glare threw such a wild and demoniac expression on the dark lines and ghastly lineaments of the mummies, that even the doctor felt his spirits depressed, and a supernatural dread creep over his mind as he gazed upon them.

In the mean time, Edric had stood gazing upon the sarcophagus of Cheops, the sides of which were beautifully sculptured with groups of figures, which, from the peculiar light thrown upon them, seemed to possess all the force and reality of life. On one side was represented an armed and youthful warrior bearing off in his arms a beautiful female, on whom he gazed with the most passionate fondness. He was pursued by a crowd of people and soldiers, who seemed to be rending the air with vehement exclamations against his violence, and endeavouring in vain to arrest his progress; whilst in the background appeared an old man, who was tearing his hair and wringing his hands in ineffectual rage against the ravisher.

The other side presented the same old man wrestling with the youthful warrior, who had just overpowered and stabbed him; the helpless victim raising his withered hands and failing eyes to Heaven as he fell, as though to implore vengeance upon his murderer, whilst the crimson current was fast ebbing from his bosom. The dying look and agony of the old man were forcibly depicted, whilst upon the features of the youthful warrior glowed the fury of a demon.

The sarcophagus was supported by the lion, emblem of royalty, the symbol of the solar god Horus; and above it sat the majestic hawk of Osiris, gazing upwards, and unmindful of the subtle crocodile of Typhon, that, crouching under its feet, was just about to seize its breast in its enormous jaws. Neither of the travellers had as yet spoken, for it seemed like sacrilege to disturb the awful stillness that prevailed even by a whisper. Indeed, the solemn aspect of the chamber thrilled through every nerve, and they moved slowly, gliding along with noiseless steps as though they feared prematurely to break the slumbers of the mighty dead it contained. They gazed, however, with deep, but undefinable interest upon the sculptured mysteries of the tomb of Cheops, vainly endeavouring to decipher their meaning; whilst, as they found their efforts useless, a secret voice seemed to whisper in their bosoms – 'And shall finite creatures like these, who cannot even explain the signification of objects presented before their eyes, presume to dive into the mysteries of their Creator's will? Learn wisdom by this omen, nor seek again to explore secrets above your comprehension! Retire, whilst it is yet time; soon it will be too late!'

Edric started at his own thoughts, as the fearful warning, 'soon it will be too late,' rang in his ears; and a fearful presentiment of evil weighed heavily upon his soul. He turned to look upon the doctor, but he had already seized the lid of the sarcophagus, and, with a daring hand, removed it from its place, displaying in the fearful light the royal form that lay beneath. For a moment, both Edric and the doctor paused, not daring to survey it; and when they did, they both uttered an involuntary cry of astonishment, as the striking features of the mummy met their eyes, for both instantly recognized the sculptured warrior in his traits. Yes, it was indeed the same, but the fierce expression of fiery and ungoverned passions depicted upon the countenance of the marble figure, had settled down to a calm, vindictive and concentrated hatred upon that of its mummy prototype in the tomb.

Awful, indeed, was the gloom that sat upon that brow, and bitter the sardonic smile that curled those haughty lips. All was perfect as though life still animated the form before them, and it had only reclined there to seek a short repose. The dark eyebrows, the thick raven hair which hung upon the forehead, and the snow-white teeth seen through the half-open lips, forbade the idea of death; whilst the fiend-like expression of the features made Edric shudder, as he recollected the purpose that brought him to the tomb, and he trembled at the thought of awakening such a fearful being from the torpor of the grave to all the renewed energies of life.

'Let us go,' whispered the doctor to his pupil, in a low, deep, and unearthly tone, fearfully different from his usually cheerful voice. Edric started at the sound, for it seemed the last sad warning of his better genius, before it abandoned him for ever. The die, however, was cast, and it was too late to recede. Edric felt worked up to frenzy by the over-wrought feelings of the moment. He seized the machine, and resolutely advanced towards the sarcophagus, whilst the doctor gazed upon him with a horror that deprived him of either speech or motion.

Innumerable folds of red and white linen, disposed alternately, swathed the gigantic limbs of the royal mummy; and upon his breast lay a piece of metal, shining like silver, and stamped with the figure of a winged globe. Edric attempted to remove this, but recoiled with horror, when he found it bend beneath his fingers with an unnatural softness; whilst, as the flickering light of the lamp fell upon the face of the mummy, he fancied its stern features relaxed into a ghastly laugh of scornful mockery. Worked up to desperation, he applied the wires of the battery and put the apparatus in motion, whilst a demoniac laugh of derision appeared to ring in his ears, and the surrounding mummies seemed starting from their places and dancing in unearthly merriment. Thunder now roared in tremendous peals through the Pyramids, shaking their enormous masses to the foundation, and vivid flashes of light darted round in quick succession.

Edric stood aghast amidst this fearful convulsion of nature. A horrid creeping seemed to run through every vein, every nerve feeling as though drawn from its extremity, and wrapped in icy chillness round his heart. Still, he stood immoveable, and gazing intently on the mummy, whose eyes had opened with the shock, and were now fixed on those of Edric, shining with supernatural lustre. In vain Edric attempted to rouse himself; in vain to turn away from that withering glance. The mummy's eyes still pursued him with their ghastly brightness; they seemed to possess the fabled fascination of those of the rattle-snake, and though he shrank from their gaze, they still glared horribly upon him. Edric's senses swam, yet he could not move from the spot; he remained fixed, chained, and immoveable, his eyes still riveted upon those of the mummy, and every thought absorbed in horror.

Another fearful peal of thunder now rolled in lengthened vibrations above his head, and the mummy rose slowly, his eyes still fixed upon those of Edric, from his marble tomb. The thunder pealed louder and louder. Yells and groans seemed mingled with its roar; the sepulchral lamp, flared with redoubled fierceness, flashing its rays around in quick succession, and with vivid brightness; whilst by its horrid and uncertain glare, Edric saw the mummy stretch out its withered hand, as though to seize him. He saw it rise gradually – he heard the dry, bony fingers rattle as it drew them forth – he felt its tremendous grip – human nature could bear no more – his senses were rapidly deserting him; he felt, however, the fixed, steadfast eyes of Cheops still glowing upon his failing orbs, as the lamp gave a sudden flash, and then all was darkness! The brazen gates now shut with a fearful clang, and Edric, uttering a shriek of horror, fell senseless upon the ground, whilst his shrill cry of anguish rang wildly through the marble vaults, till its re-echoes seemed like the yell of demons joining in fearful mockery.

How long he lay in this state he knew not; but when he re-opened his eyes, for the moment, he fancied all that had passed a dream. As his senses returned he recollected where he was, and shuddered to find himself yet in that place of horrors. All now was dark, except a faint gleam that shone feebly through the half-open gates; these ponderous portals slowly unclosed, and the form of a man, wrapped in a large cloak, and bearing a torch, entered, peering around as it advanced, as though half afraid to proceed. Edric's feelings were too highly wrought to bear any fresh horrors, and he shrieked in agony as the figure approached. The sound of his voice subdued the terrors of the intruder, and the doctor, for it was he, shouted with joy, as he rushed forward to embrace him.

'Edric! Edric! thank God he is alive!' exclaimed he. 'Edric! My beloved Edric! for God's sake, let us leave this den of horrors! Come, come!'

Reassured by his tutor's voice, Edric arose, and taking one hasty, shuddering glance around as the light gleamed on the sarcophagus, he hurried out of the tomb. Neither he nor the doctor spoke as they passed through the vestibule, where the colossal figures still sat in awful majesty; indeed, as their torches were extinguished, their gigantic forms looked still more terrific than before, from the wavering and indistinct light thrown upon them. Edric shuddered as he looked, and hurried on with hasty strides to the place where they had left the guide, whom they found kneeling in a corner, hiding his face in his hands, and roaring out, 'O Lord, defend us! Heaven have mercy upon us! Lord have mercy upon us! Heaven have mercy upon us!'

'He has been in that state for more than an hour,' said the doctor mournfully, 'for, after I came to myself, I tried to rouse him, but all to no purpose.'

'Then you also fainted?' said Edric, with difficulty compelling himself to speak.

'Why,' resumed the doctor with some hesitation, 'I don't know that you can exactly call it fainting; but the fact was, when I saw you touch the plate upon the mummy's breast, and start back, looking so horribly frightened, I – I thought I had better call for assistance; so as I ran for that purpose; somehow or other I fell down, and lay insensible I don't know how long. When I came to myself, I tried to rouse the guide, and when I found I could not, I came to seek you. But now that we are both recovered, I really don't know what is to become of us; for this fellow will never be able to show us the way out, and I'm sure I don't know the road.'

'Let us try to find it, at any rate,' said Edric faintly.

'Oh, for God's sake, take me too!' screamed the guide. 'If you have any mercy, don't leave me in this fearful place.'

'Take the light then, and lead the way,' said Edric. The guide obeyed, shaking in every limb, and every now and then casting a terrified look behind, whilst the quivering flame of the torch betrayed the unsteadiness of the trembling hands that bore it. In this manner they proceeded, starting at every sound, and frightened even at their own shadows, without daring to stop till they reached the plain.

'Thank God!' cried the doctor, the moment they stepped out of the Pyramid; looking round him, gasping for breath, and inhaling the fresh air with rapture.

'Thank God!' reiterated Edric and the guide, as they walked rapidly towards the place where they had left their balloon. When arrived there, however, they looked for it in vain; and fancying themselves under the influence of a delusion, they rubbed their eyes, and again looked, but without success.

'Dear me, it is very strange!' said the doctor; 'this is certainly the place, and yet, where can it be?'

'Where, indeed!' repeated Edric, 'horrors and unaccountable incidents environ us at every step; I am not naturally timid, yet –'

'Ah!' screamed the doctor, as he tumbled over a man lying with his face upon the ground. 'Oh!' groaned he, as Edric and the guide with difficulty raised him; 'would to Heaven I were safe at home again in my own comfortable little study, indulging in pleasing anticipations of that, which I find is any thing in the world but pleasing in reality.'

The mummy thus strangely recalled to life, was indeed Cheops! And horrible were the sensations that throbbed through every nerve as returning consciousness brought with it all the pangs of his former existence, and renewed circulation thrilled through every vein. His first impulse was to quit the tomb in which he had been so long immured, and seek again the regions of light and day. Instinct seemed to guide him to this; for, as yet, a mist hung over his faculties, and ideas thronged in painful confusion through his mind, which he was incapable of either arranging or analysing.

When, however, he reached the plain, light and air seemed to revive him and restore his scattered senses; and, gazing wildly around, he exclaimed, 'Where am I? what place is this? Methinks all seems wondrous, new, and strange! Where is my father? And where! oh, where, is my Arsinöe? Alas, alas!' continued he wildly; 'I had forgotten – I hoped it was a dream, a fearful dream, for methinks I have been long asleep. Was it, indeed, reality? Are all, all gone? And was that hideous scene true? – Those horrors, which still haunt my memory like a ghastly vision? Speak! speak!' continued he, his voice rising in thrilling energy as he spoke, 'Speak! let me hear the sound of another's voice, before my brain is lost in madness. Have I entered Hades, or am I still on earth? – yes, yes, it is still the earth, for there the mighty Pyramid I caused to be erected towers behind me. Yet where is Memphis? Where are my forts and palaces? What a dark, smoky mass of buildings now surrounds me! Can this be the once proud Queen of Cities? I see no palaces, no temples – Memphis is fallen. The mighty barrier that protected her splendour from the waste of waters, must have been swept away by the encroaching inroads of the swelling Nile. But is this the Nile?' continued he, looking wildly upon the river; 'sure I must be deceived. It is the fatal river of the dead. No papyrine boats glide smoothly on its surface; but strange, infernal vessels, vomiting forth volumes of fire and smoke. Holy Osiris, defend me! Where am I? Where have I been? A misty veil seems thrown upon the face of nature. Awake, awake!' cried he, with a scream of agony; 'set me free; I did not mean to slay him!'

Then throwing himself violently upon the ground, he lay for some moments, apparently insensible. Then slowly rising, he looked at himself, and a deep, unnatural shuddering convulsed his whole frame. His sensations of identity became confused, and he recoiled with horror from himself: 'These are the trappings of a mummy!' murmured he in a hollow whisper. 'Am I then dead?' The next instant, however, he broke into a wild laugh of derision – 'Poor, feeble wretch!' cried he; 'what do I fear? – Need *I* tremble, in whose bosom dwells everlasting fire? Let me rather rejoice. I cannot be more wretched; why should I dread a change? I welcome it with transport, and dare my future fate.'

At this moment the car of the balloon caught his eye: 'Ah! what is that?' cried he; 'I am summoned! 'Tis the boat of Hecate, ready to ferry me across the Mærian Lake, to learn my final doom. I come! I come! I fear no judgment! *My hell* is here!' and, striking his bosom, he leaped into the car, and stamped violently against its sides.

At this instant Gregory awoke, and his terror was not surprising. The dried distorted features of the mummy looked yet more hideous than before, when animated by human passions, and his deep hollow voice, speaking in a language he did not understand, fell heavily upon his ear, like the groans of fiends. Gregory tried to scream, but he could not utter a sound. He attempted to fly, but his feet seemed nailed to the spot on which he stood, and he remained with his eyes fixed upon the mummy, gasping for breath, while a cold sweat distilled from every pore. In the mean time, Cheops had stumbled over the box containing the apparatus for making inflammable air, and striking it violently, had unintentionally set the machinery in motion. The pipes, tubes, and bellows, instantly began to work; and the Indian-rubber bottle became gradually inflated, till it swelled to an enormous magnitude, and fluttered in the air like an imprisoned bird, beating itself against the massive walls to which it was still attached.

'Still it goes not,' cried Cheops, again stamping impatiently. The quicksilver vapour bottle had fallen beneath his feet, and it broke as he trod upon it. The vapour burst from it with inconceivable violence, and tearing the balloon from its fastenings, sent it off through the air, like an arrow darting from a bow.

# The New Frankenstein

## By WILLIAM MAGINN

It is perhaps not surprising that the success of Frankenstein
should have eventually attracted the attention of the parodists,
and my researches indicate that the first story to burlesque
Mary Shelley's novel was 'The New Frankenstein' which
appeared in the January 1837 issue of the fashionable monthly
journal, Fraser's Magazine. Though published anonymously,
there is strong evidence that the author was William Maginn
(1794–1842), the co-founder of the magazine, who was also
one of its most prolific contributors and especially noted for
his humorous tales and parodies. As the January issue contained several other items bearing his name, it is understand-
able in an age when a good deal was published anonymously
that Maginn should have withheld his name from a tale that
was, after all, deliberately making fun of a popular literary
work written by an authoress who may well have been known
to him personally. The style of the tale is also undeniably
similar to that of many of Maginn's other parodies.

Maginn, who was born in Cork and educated at Trinity
College, Dublin, was employed as a teacher for ten years
before moving to London and thereafter earned his living as a
magazine contributor to publications such as Blackwoods and
the Standard. In helping to launch Fraser's Magazine with the
Regent Street publisher, James Fraser, he also opened up
another outlet for his versatile pen. He was an admitted
admirer of Percy Shelley's work – and is believed to have met
him on several occasions – and is claimed to have reviewed
Mary's Frankenstein for one of the literary journals, though
this has not as yet been traced. In 'The New Frankenstein' he
describes the attempts of a experimenter not only to create a
man, but also to instil his creature with great knowledge and

*wisdom. There is circumstantial evidence that Maginn may have read Jane Webb's The Mummy, too, for the closing scenes of his story also take place in the pyramids of Egypt in a burst of pyrotechnical and supernatural occurrences . . .*

At the Lazaretto of Genoa, by good fortune, I met with a German who was travelling to the Vatican, in search of Palimpsests. He was scarcely thirty, though he might have passed for ten years older, as is often observed to be the case with those who have devoted much of their time to intense study. His shoulders inclined forward, and his light, flaxen hair hung much below his travelling cap. In his eye there were a wildness, and a glassiness, that bespoke, if not alienation of mind, at least eccentricity.

During our captivity in quarantine, we endeavoured to kill time by relating our several adventures; and, one evening, the German, having been called upon to continue our *soirées*, looked round for a while, as though he were waiting for the dictation of some familiar spirit – some monitor, like a second Socrates; and, with a voice not unresembling a cracked instrument, without preface, in his own idiomatic language, which I will endeavour to translate, thus commenced : –

I came into the world on the same day as Hoffman's celebrated cat Mürr, – ay, not only on the same day, but the same hour of the day, if the obstetrix kept a good reckoning. You may smile, gentlemen; but did not one of your poets boast that he was born on the anniversary of another great poet. *C'est une autre affaire*, perhaps you will say. But a cat's birth, what can that have to do with yours? Don't be impatient – much; for it was to this fortunate coincidence, to the circumstance of my mother's presenting Mürr, when a kitten, to Hoffman – a gift for which he was ever grateful – that I became acquainted with that poet, painter, classic, musician, novelist – that *bel esprit*, the pride of Germany.

'Love me, love my cat,' is an old adage. My affection for

Mürr begat a return of it in his master; and it was for the amusement of my childhood that he wrote *Little Zachary*.

Who does not remember Mürr? – that back which outvied the enamel of the tortoise in the brilliancy and variety of its colours – that coat, finer than ermine – that voice, whose purr was more melodious than the whispered voice of lovers – and then, his eye, there was something in it not feline, nor human, nor divine; but enough has been said to shew that he was no ordinary *maton*, or, as your Shakespeare has it, jibe cat. I will now let you into a secret [said the narrator, in a mysterious whisper]. Mürr was strongly suspected of being more than a familiar – an emanation, an incarnation, of one to whom Hoffman, like Calcott, was so much indebted, – it being to a *certain* dictation that he owed so many of his nocturnal and diabolical tales, and, among the rest, that marvel of his genius, the *Pot of Gold*. I wish to shew you, gentlemen, what gave the bent and impulse to my genius, and how seemingly insignificant causes are the parents of the great events of our lives. But Mürr paid the debt of nature, and Hoffman never recovered his loss.

At twelve years of age I was sent to the university of Leipsic, and at fifteen was thoroughly master of the dead languages; but my favourite author was Apuleius, the most romantic of all the ancient writers; and I had got almost by heart the first book of the *Golden Ass*, fully believing in all the wild traditions, the fantastic fables, and visions that it embodied. I thus early divided the life of man into two sets of sensation, but not of equal value in my eyes – a waking sleep, and a sleeping sleep; for it seemed to me, that no one could dispute the superior advantages of the latter in perceiving the only world that is worth perceiving – the imaginary one. But more on this subject hereafter. I only mention it *en passant*, to shew that natural philosophy was the great object of my pursuit; and it must be confessed that my tutor – for I had a private one, and seldom attended the public lectures – was admirably qualified to direct this branch of my studies. How he had acquired all his learning was a mystery; for he never read, and yet had hardly, to all appearance, passed his twenty-fifth year. Where he had been educated, or from what country he came, was equally unknown – for he spoke all languages with equal fluency. As Goethe says of the mere kats, 'Even with those little people one would not wish to be alone.' Thus he was a man in whose company I never felt quite at ease, and yet was attracted to him by a kind of resistless impetus. Though his features were good, his face was a continual mask; his eyes, dark and lustrous, had in them an extraordinary and supernatural power of inquisition. There was an expression in his countenance the most gloomy, a desolateness the most revolting; the depravity of human nature seemed to him a delight. He was never known to laugh but at what would have moved others to tears. Though he watched over me as if his own life depended on mine, there was hardly a drunken orgy, or a duel, its natural consequence (for you know such take place daily at our universities), that Starnstein − for that was his name − was not the exciting cause. You saw me look round just now. I often fancy him at my elbow; and thought, since I began talking of him, that he whispered in my ear.

Being destined for a physician, I repaired, after taking my degree, to Paris, for the purpose of attending the anatomical school. There, however, the only dissections in which I took an interest were those of the brain, which opened to me a new world of speculations − one of which was, that all our sentiments are nothing more than a subtle kind of mind, and that mind itself is only a modification of matter. I now set no bounds to the power of *Mater Ia*, and soon attributed to her all creation; being much assisted in coming to this conclusion by Buffon and Cuvier. Their researches, particularly those of the latter great naturalist, proved to my satisfaction that there was a period when this planet was inhabited by a nameless progeny of monstrous forms, engendered by a peculiar state of the atmosphere − a dense congregation of putrid vapours that brooded over chaos; that all this Megatherian and Saurian brood, those flying liquids, long as the 'mast of some high admiral,' disappeared at the first ray of light, and gave place to a new and better order of existences; but as inferior to man, or the present race of the inhabitants of our globe, as man is to the ape − himself the original of our species; as La Croix, in his scale of created beings, has proved in demonstration. But I was the first to discern that crystals are to be produced by the galvanic battery, and animal life from acids; to detect in paste, by means of the solar microscope, thousands

of vermicular creatures, which could not have arisen from the
accidental depositions of ova – this genus being, like that of
eels, viviparous. I will describe to you one of my experiments.
I got some volcanic dust from Etna, which I impasted with
muriatic acid, and after a time distinguished, though inaudible
save with an ear trumpet – or thought I could distinguish – a
*hum*, like that of fermentation. What was my delight to find
that there was vitality in the mass – that these atoms daily
grew in size! They were of the *bug* species; not unresembling
what the French call a *punaise*. Their kinds were two; the
larger soon began to devour the smaller, till they were completely destroyed; and in their voracity the survivors preyed
on each other; so that at last only one, the great conqueror,
was left – and he, I speak it to my infinite regret, was crushed
in handling – so crushed, that scarcely anything but slime, not
of the most agreeable odour, was left upon my fingers. I had
promised myself to present him to the Luxembourg, for its
splendid entomological collection. He would have been a
prize, indeed.

I now set no limits to nature; put implicit faith in the story
of Prometheus and Pandora – the Thessalian priestesses – the
resuscitation of Hippolitus – and fancied I could discover by
what sorcery it was that Medea,

> '– with magic spell
> And potent charm evoked the shapes of hell,
> When at her summons Hecate winged her flight,
> And forms of darkness sickening met the sight.
> Here lies a fearful work that loathes the day,
> To wake new being in the extinguished clay.
> They burst the bonds of Nature – by degrees
> Breathe a false spirit through the frame; it sees
> The wan lips quiver, and erect to view
> It speaks, and draws the vital air anew.'

Fully believing in all this, had I known Dupuytren, I should,
without hesitation, have asked him the same question as was
put to Sir H. Davy, whether he could make a man?

This is a long preface, but it is not foreign to my purpose.

I pass over several years of my life, and find myself, in the
summer of 18 –, at Manheim. It is a curious old town; but I

shall not stop to describe it. There it was that I first met with
a German translation of that very ingenious history of Frankenstein. Such was my predisposition to a belief in what might
have seemed to others prodigious, that I read it without a
question or suspicion of its being a fiction. The part, however,
that most interested me was the creation; the scene that
riveted me most, the creation scene. One night I had the
passage open in my hand, when who should walk into the
room, arm-in-arm, but my old tutor and that anatomical man
– that identical phantasmagoric hero. Starnstein, after having
posted him against the oak panelling, turned towards me with
one of his old Sardonic grins, pointed to his *protégé*, and
slipped off before I could have detained him, had I been so
inclined, which, to tell you the truth, I was not. I had never
seen him since I left college; but wished to renew his acquaintance, and sometimes doubt whether it was not his apparition.
But not so the other. He was too palpable to view, and
without any mistake. Thus he was standing in *propriá personá*
– the human monster – the restored ruin – the living phantom
– the creature without a name. I put my hand before my eyes
more than once, to convince myself that it was only a vision
such as a feverish imagination conjured up. No rattle-snake
could have more fascinated its victim. Yes, there he stood in
all his horrible disproportion. His back, as I said, was against
the oak wainscot, and his face turned towards me.

Every one knows the effect produced at Guy's Hospital on
the medical students, when the corpse of a criminal, under the
effect of a powerful galvanic battery, opened its eyes, made
one step from the table against which he was placed, erect,
and stiff, and fell among them. Such was the feeling I experienced, lest he should advance. Horrible sensations for a time
came over me; there was a lurid glare on all the objects in the
room; every thing took, or seemed to take, forms the most
fantastic, and to bear some mysterious relation to the strange
being before me. But by degrees I became familiarised with
his person, and at length thought I should not dislike his
company; I therefore took up the lamp, which was one of
that classical construction common in Italy, with three depending wicks, and with measured and stealthy steps began to
approach my visitor. But this rashness had nearly proved
fatal; for that which had given him life had well nigh caused

my death: so powerful was the galvanism with which he had been charged, that the shock struck me to the ground like a forked flash of lightning. How long I lay I know not; but, on recovering, had learned sufficient prudence to keep a respectful distance from my uninvited guest. There he was in the self-same state. I now examined him steadily; but, instead of his being gifted with the faculties assigned to him by the fair authoress, I found he had only a talismanic existence – was a mere automaton – a machine – a plant without the faculty of motion. His eyes – those yellow eyes so graphically depicted – rolled pendulously in their sunken sockets with a clicking sound not unresembling that of a clock; there was a mechanical trepidation of all his fibres; his nerves quivered, but not with sensibility, and his whole frame had a convulsive motion; whilst his head moved from left to right and right to left, like that of a Chinese mandarin. As I gazed and gazed on the image before me, I insensibly took a greater interest in the *bipes implumis*, the best definition ever given of the *genus homo*. I pitied him, and said to myself, I will be a new Frankenstein, and a greater. Like Prospero, I will have my Ariel. I will have my Paradox, as Rousseau had his Paradox: the Paradox of Jean Jacques was the hate of all mankind; mine shall be its admiration, envy, and despair. Frankenstein has left his work imperfect; he has resuscitated a corpse: I will make him what Thyestes was. Yes, I will give him a mind – a mind; yes, with a frantic joy I shouted, till the room re-echoed in loud vibrations – 'I will create a mind for you, and such a mind as man, till now, never possessed!' But, how to begin? Would Columbus have discovered the New World, had he not overcome all the difficulties he had to encounter from the elements? The *elements*; yes, I had to contend, with elements also. But, how to bring them into subjection was a question might well give me pause. Such an undertaking, till within the last twenty years, would have seemed preposterous and absurd. But, what were all the physicians and metaphysicians of old compared to the philosophers of the new school? There are only two sciences worth cultivating – phrenology and animal magnetism; and it was by their means that I hoped to accomplish the great arcanum.

All who know anything of craniology must be aware that genius, so erroneously defined by Buffon as the product of study and perseverance, depends on organisation, and organisation only – on the elevation and depression of certain bosses in the cerebrum. The cerebellum is another affair. Out upon it! and, were it not for the continuation of the species, perhaps we should be infinitely more perfect without it; but, at all events, in this case, it was not my intention to meddle with the cerebellum. Well, with toil of mind that strengthens with its own fatigue, I made a discovery which, alone, in any other planet, would have immortalised me. I found out what neither Gall nor Spurzheim ever dreamed of; I learned intuitively, or, rather, by that sense through which we see things more real than the dull dross visions to itself in its blind misimaginings – I need not name animal magnetism. I perceived, I say, that every one of those compartments, as laid down in the most approved charts of the head, contains a certain gas, though it has, like the nervous fluid circulating in that curious network of the frame, hitherto escaped analysis or detection. To this gas I have given the appellation of the cerebral afflatus, and now felt satisfied that the protuberances, or subsidations of the cranium, which have been usually attributed to the convolutions of the nerves, called brains, is derived from the action of this mental air pent up in its cells, each in its own Æolian cave. Newton, when the laws of gravitation flashed upon his mind by the apple hitting the boss of mathematics, never experienced the proud gratification this sublime discovery gave me. Εὑοηχμ, I exclaimed, and proceeded forthwith to make my preparations.

Ulysses, as all know, carried about with him the winds in bladders – a contrivance clever enough before the invention of glass; and the Usula of Don Cleophas bottled the lame devil Asmodeus.

These hints were not lost upon me. I set, therefore, my mechanical genius to work, and fabricated a number of tubes, composed of a mixture of divers metals, such as went to the formation of Perkins's Tractors. These tubes had, at one end, tunnels; and to the other I attached phials, in the shape of balls communicating with them, and so contrived as to open and shut by means of screws, or vices, similar to those now used in the air-cushions; so that the fluid of which I was in search, once risen (as it is in the nature of all gases to do) to the top, might be there imprisoned, and, once hermetically closed, could only escape at my option. These tubes were all of one size; but not so the globes, which I blew of a vast thickness, lest it should happen that the expansion of the confined air might endanger the security of my retorts, which, like steam-engines, did not admit of safety-valves.

Thus admirably provided, I locked up my treasure, as carefully as a miser does his gold, and issued, like a new Captain Cook, on a voyage of discovery very much more interesting and important than the great navigator's.

The author of that night-mare – that poem, which, like the kaleidoscope, takes, at every turn of the page, fresh shapes (a puzzle to his commentators), and that makes wise men stare and sets fools blundering – *Faust*, was then at Weimar. Easily accessible to a man of genius like myself, and ignorant of my motives (which, if he had known, his *familiar* would doubtless have befriended me), Goethe was easily persuaded to submit himself to my manipulation. No patient I ever had was easier brought *en rapport*. From him it was that I sought to extract *Imagination*; and I reconciled myself to the theft, knowing that, however much I might appropriate to myself for the use of my *protégé*, Goethe might well spare it. Nor would it be long missed, considering that the working of his fertile brain would soon generate fresh gas to supply the vacuum. So abundant was the stream, or steam, that flowed from my fingers' ends, and thence conducted by my thumb into the tube, that my largest globe was, at the first sitting, almost filled to explosion, and as soon unescapably sealed.

Delighted with the success of my first experiment, I now deliberated which of my compatriots I should next put in requisition. Unhappily, Kant, that mighty mystic! was gone to the land of shadows – himself a shade; but he had bequeathed his spirit to a worthy disciple, who, to the uninitiated, lectures in an unknown tongue. I allude to Sheeling.

Transcendentalism, owing to the habitude of my own organs, has always been to me a wonder and a mystery; but I was determined that it should not be so to my adopted son. The gaseous effluvium which I drew from the professor was of so extra-subtle and super-volatile a nature, that it was long before I could satisfy myself that I had obtained a *quantum sufficit in ullo vehiculo*, as the physicians say; but, by dint of pressure with my finger-pump, in a happy moment I heard a slight crackling, like that of confined air in a bottle of –, I was about to have said champagne, only that its quality most resembles that of Eau de Seltz. Being now *súr de mon affaire*, I would have given worlds for half an hour with Swedenbourg, or Madame Grizon. As I could not resuscitate the dead, I passed in review the living, and bethought me of one who had, as they, a religion of his own. He was [here the narrator turned to me] a compatriot of yours. Socrates, according to the comic dramatist, made his deities the clouds; and, if his busts are to be relied on for accuracy, was not deficient in veneration – of a peculiar kind, certainly, and widely differing from that of the sectarians above mentioned; whose *coronas* – for it is there that veneration is properly placed – possessed no ordinary protuberances.

Imperfect, indeed, would the φοην of my phenomenon have been without this great essential; and, therefore, I crossed the Alps, and found Shelley at the baths of Lucca. I had always conceived his Hermaphrodites in the *Witch of Atlas* as the *beau idéal* of nondescripts, the most perfect of imperfect beings; and, oh! I sighed that mine could be like that enchanting neutral. The great poet's animal magnetic sensibility is well known, and it had been, if possible, increased by a late visit to the Prato Fiorito, where he had fainted with the excess of sweetness of the jonquils that carpet that enamelled mead. He was, at that moment, full of the conception of his *Ode to Intellectual Beauty*; and I extracted enough of that particular sort of devotion to form a recipe for my χοιητης.

Passing through Bologna on my return, I tapped the Bibliotecario Mezzofonti for three hundred and sixty-five languages; which, strange to say, he had acquired without stirring out of his own library.

Travelling night and day, behold me now, as

'I stood tiptoe upon a little hill.'

That little hill was Primrose Hill. I for a moment looked down on the mighty Babylon beneath me, and listened to the hum of the 'million-peopled city vast,' itself hidden in a dense fog. Out of all the multitude, there was only one whom I sought; that one, χατ᾽ ιξυχη, was Coleridge. I found him at no great distance, in his own rural retreat of Highgate, and at that time taking 'his ease in his inn.' No man was more accessible. Talking was not the amusement, but the occupation of his life; and it must be confessed that he was an adept in the art, as should naturally have been a person whose tongue was employed for eighteen hours out of the twenty-four. For the first five of our interview, the clack of a water-mill, the wheels of a steamboat, the waves on a sea-shore, were poor comparisons to express the volubility of his organ. That coma, or trance, with which I endeavoured to inspire him – that sleep of the soul, which is the awakening of reason – that agent unknown – that attribute divine – that double existence – that εζιμα of the nervous system, Somnambulism, into which I had hoped to throw him, was transferred from the operated on to the operator. I called to mind the celebrated epigram:

> 'Safe from the syren's tuneful air
>     The sage Ulysses fled;
> But had that man of prose been there,
>     He would have talked him dead.'

At the same time I must admit, that no one ever talked so well. The mighty stream, 'without o'erflowing, full,' rolled on, and carried all before it – even the floodgates of reason. He was the despair of the animal magnetist, and I almost began to doubt the efficacy, not of the system, but of my own powers, when he filled from a quart bottle a bumper of his favourite beverage, black-drop; and during its opiate influence I felt a vibration of the tube, like the string of a harp in concert-pitch, thrill through every fibre of my frame, to its utmost ramifications. '*Io triumphe!*' the victory was complete.

I will not enumerate any other author whom I laid under contribution in different parts of Europe; for, though I employed the smallest vehicles in my possession, I had great difficulty in filling them with original fluids.

My task being accomplished, there is one thing for which I must give myself credit – disinterestedness. I disdained to appropriate to myself any of the fruits of my labours, trusting to my second self having a sufficiency of the *afflatus* for both; and to his generosity, or gratitude, for supplying me, at any time, with any superfluity he might possess. Besides that, I looked upon his head as a sort of *imperium in imperio* – a head within a head, on whose resources I might always draw, at any time, *ad libitum*.

And now, behold me back to Manheim. No miser, gloating over his stores – no devotee, the possessor of some relic of her patron saint – not Psyche herself, with her precious casket, felt half the raptures I enjoyed as I turned the key of my laboratory.

I found my *homuncio* (which means, I believe, a great ugly fellow, though not such did he seem to me) posted exactly where I had left him, with the same mechanical clicking of the eyes, the same oscillation of the frame. And now for my reward.

One by one did I carefully unvalve my phials, and apply the contents to the portals of the brain – the porticoes of my *innominato*, as the man-fiend is called in the *Promessi Sposi*. Scarcely had I discharged through the olfactory nerves the subtle fluids, when I perceived a strange confusion – a chaos like that of the elements primeval – ensue; and it was easy to perceive that the late arrivals were dissatisfied with their new lodging, finding, doubtless, the apartments not to their taste – too spacious, or too confined for their operations. I was immediately reminded of Casti's *Caso di Coscunza*, in which the spirits of the hero and heroine – a priest and his house-keeper, removed simultaneously from the world – being called back by the prayers of the good peasants of Estramadura to reanimate their clay, by mistake enter the wrong bodies; so that the don finds himself no man, and the donna no woman; a circumstance of extreme awkwardness, that elicited from the witty bard a simile which may serve to exemplify the bizarre position in which our stronger organs found them-selves. The translation is, I beg to say, by a great hand.

> 'As when a fowler, in the leafy season
>     Of June or July – it may be the latter –
> A flight of amorous sparrow, thick as bees on
>     The housetop, clustering views, and by their clatter,
> And twitter, and lascivious ways, has reason
>     To think his distance sure – Bang! At his clatter
> They all fly off at once, and in their terror,
>     One gets into another's nest from error.'

Thus happened it, I should conjecture, with some of the newly imported and imprisoned spirits in my *innominato's* cranium. It was long before quiet was established in that 'dome of thought,' and I waited, in an agony of impatience, to see the effect of my operation.

I observed a picture in one of the exhibitions at Paris, of I forget what year, the subject of which was Pygmalion and his statue. The artist has chosen the moment when the intensity of the sculptor's passion, which is impassable to Love, warmed the marble into life. As the Italians said of one of their school, the French painter had made use of *carne macerato* instead of colour. We might almost see the roseate light of life and youth, as through an alabaster vase, gradually illuminating the perfect form of the nymphalept's creation; and the creator himself contemplating, with delight and wonder, the object of his adoration.

My feelings were different, though not less acute. Motionless as the sculptor, or almost turned to stone as one who had seen Medusa, I stood, all eyes and ears intently fixed on my phenomenon. I saw the glassy and unmeaning glare of *his* eyes give place to the fire of intelligence; the jaundiced, or, rather, livid hue of his cheek, disappear, like the grey of the morning at the uprising of the sun; and, as his lungs became inflated, I could distinctly hear the *a w* – those sounds so expressive of inspiration and expiration – at measured intervals repeated. I now expected that his first impulse would be to fall down and worship me. But, far from this, what was my vexation and disappointment to mark the look of unutterable scorn and hate with which he regarded me. I think I now hear the floor ringing with his heavy tread, as he paced it backwards and forwards to give circulation to his blood, or as though waiting for the chaos of his thoughts to be reduced to form, ere he attempted to give them utterance. At length he found that distinguishing characteristic of man above all other animals – speech. His voice was hollow, hoarse, and unmodulated, resembling most a pair of asthmatic bellows, or a cracked bassoon, rather than aught human. At first, his utterance, like that of a new-born babe, consisted of inarticulate sounds; but, after running up and down the gamut of the vowels, he put together a variety of words, as by way of practice, and with a slow and laboured delivery, and a sort of telegraphic gestures, commenced an harangue. It was composed of all languages, which he called into requisition to express more fully his meaning, or no meaning. I have said, that his delivery was at first slow and difficult, but as he proceeded his facility of pronunciation, his volubility, increased. From a fountain, a rivulet, a river, he poured forth at last a torrent of eloquence, which it was impossible to stop, or almost to make intelligible in words. His merciless imagination flew with the speed of thought from subject to subject, from topic to topic, in a perpetual flux and reflux. It was a labyrinth inextricable — an ill-linked chain of sentences the most involved, parentheses within parentheses — a complication of images and figures the most *outré*. In short, imagine to yourselves the mysticism of Kant, the transcendental philosophy of Coleridge, the metaphysics of Shelley and Goethe, the poetry of Lycophron, mingled and massed together in one jargon, compounded of Greek, Latin, Italian, French, Spanish, German, and English, not to mention tongues known and unknown, and you may form some idea of his style; but of his barbarous pronunciation I can give you none: it was worse than Mezzafonti's. *C'est beaucoup dire*.

I now perceived, to my infinite sorrow, that I had done infinite mischief by this Phrengenesis. Its very creation weighed upon me like remorse upon the guilty. I had now the means of knowing that he had nothing to know, yet knew nothing.

Thus it was that I found out the Theosophs were right in separating entirely the mind from the soul, in considering them diametrically opposite relations — as different principles, as the physic and the phrenic. And I became satisfied that my paradox had no soul. What was to be done now? Should I leave the work imperfect, or endeavour to create one? Was it impious? I scarcely dared put the question. Was not Æsculapius struck dead by the balls of Jove for usurping his power? Were I to evoke the dead — call up the spirit of Adam himself — could he aid me in the undertaking? At which the imagination revolted, and shrank back in terror. Where lay the scent? Was there any tradition on the earth, below the earth, or above the earth, of the Psycogenesis? The more I reflected, the more was I lost and confounded. Abyssus,

Abyssum. In the lowest deep there was yet a lower deep of mystery.

I was about to abandon the task as hopeless, when I remembered the great maxim and axiom of the animal magnetists, that nothing is impossible to faith. But was it an act of volition? Could we command it? Could we inspire ourselves with that waking sleep – master our own senses, so as to produce such a somnambulism.

Imagine yourself to have lost your way, benighted amid some inhospitable desert, some savage range of Alpine solitudes – far from a path, as you suppose, or the abode of man; and when you are about to lay yourself down and die, in your despair, hear all at once the bark of a house-dog, and see the light streaming from the window of a cottage; and, when you enter, find a cheerful fire blazing in the hearth, and a young girl, beautiful as the houris, who welcomes you with a voice tremulous with delight, and presents to your parched lips an exquisite and life-giving cordial.

Thus was it with me, when a scroll of vellum slowly unrolled itself. It was a palimpsest. The writing – the work of some falsely pious monk – that supplied the place of the original MSS., gradually became obliterated, and shewed beneath some characters, dim and indistinct, in a language long lost. It had been one of the hermetic books escaped from the burning of the Alexandrian Library, and once belonged to that of Ragusa, the last temple of the Greek and Roman muses, when Urban Appendini and Sorgo were stars in its brilliant constellation of talent. Oh, the marvellous power of somnambulism! that imparts wisdom to brutes, and furnishes a clue to all sciences and tongues. It was by its mysterious power that my eyes were opened – the film removed from them – that I could decipher in the pictured language, above the rest, these words, *Thebes Adamite King*. Then came a sarcophagus, in which was traced in blood the mystical triangle, enclosed within a circle, the sacred emblem and diagram of the Magi and Brahmans.

Yes, said I, it was in Osiris that the Egyptians supposed to reside all living beings, the genii and the souls of men. To Egypt, then! – there to unravel the mystery.

With my double, my second self, behold me journeying to Alexandria. We ascended the sacred stream of the Nile, and found ourselves among the ruins of ancient Thebes. My first visit was to the cavern in which Belzoni had abode for long twelve months. I instinctively knew that it was only the entrance to the Memphis of that once mighty city.

My revelation was not a false one. At the further extremity of the tomb, I discovered, hollowed out of the rock, a subterranean passage, that seemed to descend into the very bowels of the earth. With a delight unutterable, I led the way down the perpendicular stairs, till we came to a lofty door, the entrance to the Necropolis. On each side of this door crouched two colossal sphynxes, as though they were the guardians of the place.

No human foot had for three thousand years profaned the sanctity of that City of the Dead, into which our venturous steps were treading.

The winding passage widened as we advanced, when, on a sudden, a light burst on my eyes that dimmed the glare of our torches. It proceeded from myriads of Naphtha lamps, held by gigantic figures, part man part beast, in combinations strange as that of the snake-man in the *Inferno*, in whom it was impossible to distinguish where the man began and the reptile ended.

These forms were sculptured out of the solid granite, of an alabaster whiteness; and in long perspective revealed, branching in different directions, vast streets, that seemed interminable. They were like some work of the Cimmerians, and lofty as the cavern of Pausilippo; and on each side were ranged sarcophagi innumerable, some of marble of a dazzling lustre, inlaid with gems, and in workmanship so exquisite, that the hieroglyphical pictures seemed as composed of a single piece. The mosaic on the tomb of the Tajh Mehul at Agra was coarse in comparison. Others were of sandal-wood and ebony, and covered with paintings, as vivid in colour as though they had been only finished a single day. The epicurean, when the mysteries were revealed to him – Vathek, in the caves of Domdamuel, can alone give an idea of the sensations that marvellous spectacle, that silence which made itself to be felt, excited.

With an indefinable terror, that even stilled the eternal 'babel' of my Caliban, we continued to pace those Hades, popular with the dead; and as the azure light flickered and quivered, like serpents' tongues, from the lamps of the colossi, my imagination gifted the vapours with shapes all differing from each other, floating light as the atoms in the sunbeams along the walls, even to the lofty roof.

And now, afar off, murmurs were heard. Was it the many voices of the dead? It became more distinct. 'Tis the Nile rushing above our heads, swollen with the Abyssinian rains. Still we passed on, till its echoes died away in distant music among the catacombs.

Should we sink to rest among these labyrinthian cells, stifled in that dust of centuries, which rose from our feet in volumes – such were some of the reflections that began to suggest themselves, when I was attracted by an illumination, rendered more brilliant than the rest by the impenetrable depth of pitchy darkness of a cavern at its back. This galaxy of light proceeded from lamps held by twelve figures of the natural size, so admirable as a work of art, that they might have been supposed from the chisel of Phydias or Praxiteles; and, on seeing them, I no longer wondered at the perfection of the Egean marbles. They were grouped round a sarcophagus of Egyptian alabaster, which they supported with their hands and arms. So easy and graceful was their attitude, as of persons walking – for the sculptor had almost given them motion – that I fancied them advancing towards me, and stepped aside in order to let them pass. This was my first impulse. Was this the sarcophagus of the mysterious scroll? Did it contain the sacred emblems? My heart beat audibly with hope. I approached, and leaned over the shoulder of one of the bearers. Yes! – it was there! – the sacred diagram! – that most perfect of figures enclosed in its mystic circle! – *there*, as I had seen it in my trance! The rubies of which the triangle were composed threw on the face of the central statue a sanguine hue, that gave him the appearance of life; and as it played lambently on his features, I gazed on them, till I almost spoke to him.

And now for the great arcanum! With hands trembling at the sacrilege I was about to commit, I proceeded to lift off the lid of the sarcophagus. It yielded – slowly yielded – lost its equilibrium, and fell with a heavy crash on the floor. The sound was like that of thunder, and vibrated through the pitchy cavern in long echoes, which, from their repetition, proved it to be of vast extent – perhaps the hades of the Egyptians.

There lay the undecaying corpse of the Adamite king, enwrapt all save the face, in the winding sheet of death. Like to life he was – the hues of life were yet upon his cheek – his eyes were open, and glared on me with more than mortal lustre; and, lit by that reflection, made more wan his lips, that moved and quivered, as though he was only waiting for me to address him, ere he replied in answer to my questions.

At that awful moment, the whole Necropolis rocked and shook, as though rent by an earthquake; and there appeared to rise on all sides, out of the ground, a multitude of hideous fiends, vibrating in their hands torches, from which the ruddy fire flew off in flakes. They came in crowds that seemed to thicken as they approached, and joining in one chorus. The words were these: –

'Papai Satan, Papai Satan, Aleppe!'

At that moment all the tombs opened with one accord, and the dead that had slept for ages rose slowly out of them in their shrouds, pressing forward in throngs from the depths of the streets that branched out on every side. They advanced as to a festival; and the light from their eyes was like that of a distant world, whose ashes are burning after it is extinct.

As they came near, I felt a sort of numbing iciness emanate from their bodies, the poisonous effluvium of the grave, penetrating to my marrow like a thousand points of steel. Yet did my heart beat wildly, panting to respire the atmosphere of life, struggling between life and death, suffocated amid that dust of millennia, the flame of torches, the damp of the catacombs. And imagine to yourself, added to all this, the dæmons of the night howling, roaring in my stunned ears all one chorus – those discordant and mysterious words of invocation:

'Papai Satan, Papai Satan, Aleppe!'

Then, too, the earth seemed to open beneath my feet, and a

red spiral flame issued forth, which by degrees assumed a form, a shape. It was, yet it was not, my old tutor. Then I awoke, and found it was – A DREAM.

# The Bell-Tower

## By HERMAN MELVILLE

*The first writer to attempt a straightforward short tale inspired by* Frankenstein *was the American, Herman Melville (1819–1891), author of the maritime classic,* Moby Dick, *published in 1851. Unlikely though this claim may at first seem, it should be remembered that Melville's great white whale has been described as 'an archetype of the more metaphysical variety of Science Fiction monster' (by Peter Nicholls in his* Encyclopedia of Science Fiction, *1979), while the book itself has proved to be widely influential on modern fantasy fiction, especially writers such as Roger Zelazny and Philip Jose Farmer who wrote a 'sequel',* The Wind Whales of Ishmael *(1971).*

*According to Gerard M. Sweeney, an authority on Herman Melville, the writer had probably read* Frankenstein *as a child, and then consulted the novel again while working on his monumental sea story, for 'Ahab appears as a man-maker in* Moby Dick', *says Mr Sweeney. This authority is, though, in no doubt that Mary Shelley's novel was the inspiration for the short story,* The Bell-Tower, *set in Renaissance Italy, about a machine man constructed to strike the hour on a large bell, but which instead turns on its creator. Once again, experts have seen this story as a warning of the implications of the new era of mechanical invention and science that was taking place in the 1850s when it was written. Curiously, when the tale was first published in* Putnam's Monthly Magazine *in August 1855 it appeared anonymously – just as Mary Shelley's novel had done all those years earlier, and likewise led to a certain amount of confusion about the authorship. In Melville's case, it has been argued that it was a number of omissions and changes demanded by the magazine, nervous*

*about the morality of the tale, which resulted in his decision
to remove his name – but this remains conjecture. The story
hereunder, however, appears precisely as Melville intended,
providing yet another important landmark in the development
of the* Frankenstein *tradition . . .*

In the south of Europe, nigh a once-frescoed capital, now
with dank mould cankering its bloom, central in a plain,
stands what, at distance, seems the black mossed stump of
some immeasurable pine, fallen, in forgotten days, with Anak
and the Titan.

As all along where the pine tree falls, its dissolution leaves
a mossy mound – last-flung shadow of the perished trunk;
never lengthening, never lessening; unsubject to the fleet falsi-
ties of the sun; shade immutable and true gauge which cometh
by prostration – so westward from what seems the stump,
one steadfast spear of lichened ruin veins the plain.

From that tree-top, what birded chimes of silver throats
had rung. A stone pine; a metallic aviary in its crown: the
Bell-Tower, built by the great mechanician, the unblest foundling, Bannadonna.

Like Babel's, its base was laid in a high hour of renovated
earth, following the second deluge, when the waters of the
Dark Ages had dried up, and once more the green appeared.
No wonder that, after so long and deep submersion, the
jubilant expectation of the race should, as with Noah's sons,
soar into Shinar aspiration.

In firm resolve, no man in Europe at that period went
beyond Bannadonna. Enriched through commerce with the
Levant, the state in which he lived voted to have the noblest
Bell-Tower in Italy. His repute assigned him to be architect.

Stone by stone, month by month, the tower rose. Higher,
higher; snail-like in pace, but torch or rocket in its pride.

After the masons would depart, the builder, standing alone
upon its ever-ascending summit, at close of every day saw that
he overtopped still higher walls and trees. He would tarry till

a late hour there, wrapped in schemes of other and still loftier piles. Those who of saints' days thronged the spot – hanging to the rude poles of scaffolding, like sailors on yards, or bees on boughs, unmindful of lime and dust, and falling chips of stone – their homage not the less inspirited him to self-esteem.

At length the holiday of the Tower came. To the sound of viols, the climax-stone slowly rose in air, and, amid the firing of ordnance, was laid by Bannadonna's hands upon the final course. Then mounting it, he stood erect, alone, with folded arms; gazing upon the white summits of blue inland Alps, and whiter crests of bluer Alps off-shore – sights invisible from the plain. Invisible, too, from thence was that eye he turned below, when, like the cannon booms; came up to him the people's combustions of applause.

That which stirred them so was, seeing with what serenity the builder stood three hundred feet in air, upon an unrailed perch. This none but he durst do. But his periodic standing upon the pile, in each stage of its growth – such discipline had its last result.

Little remained now but the bells. These, in all respects, must correspond with their receptacle.

The minor ones were prosperously cast. A highly enriched one followed, of a singular make, intended for suspension in a manner before unknown. The purpose of this bell, its rotary motion, and connection with the clock-work, also executed at the time, will, in the sequel, receive mention.

In the one erection, bell-tower and clock-tower were united, though, before that period, such structures had commonly been built distinct; as the Campanile and Torre dell' Orologio of St Mark to this day attest.

But it was upon the great state-bell that the founder lavished his more daring skill. In vain did some of the less elated magistrates here caution him; saying that though truly the tower was Titanic, yet limit should be set to the dependent weight of its swaying masses. But undeterred, he prepared his mammoth mould, dented with mythological devices; kindled his fires of balsamic firs; melted his tin and copper; and throwing in much plate, contributed by the public spirit of the nobles, let loose the tide.

The unleashed metals bayed like hounds. The workmen shrank. Through their fright, fatal harm to the bell was dreaded. Fearless as Shadrach, Bannadonna, rushing through the glow, smote the chief culprit with his ponderous ladle. From the smitten part, a splinter was dashed into the seething mass, and at once was melted in.

Next day a portion of the work was heedfully uncovered. All seemed right. Upon the third morning, with equal satisfaction, it was bared still lower. At length, like some old Theban king, the whole cooled casting was disinterred. All was fair except in one strange spot. But as he suffered no one to attend him in these inspections, he concealed the blemish by some preparation which none knew better to devise.

The casting of such a mass was deemed no small triumph for the caster; one, too, in which the state might not scorn to share. The homicide was overlooked. By the charitable that deed was but imputed to sudden transports of esthetic passion, not to any flagitious quality. A kick from an Arabian charger: not sign of vice, but blood.

His felony remitted by the judge, absolution given him by the priest, what more could even a sickly conscience have desired!

Honouring the tower and its builder with another holiday, the republic witnessed the hoisting of the bells and clockwork amid shows and pomps superior to the former.

Some months of more than usual solitude on Bannadonna's part ensued. It was not unknown that he was engaged upon something for the belfry, intended to complete it, and surpass all that had gone before. Most people imagined that the design would involve a casting like the bells. But those who thought they had some further insight, would shake their heads, with hints, that not for nothing did the mechanician keep so secret. Meantime, his seclusion failed not to invest his work with more or less of that sort of mystery pertaining to the forbidden.

Ere long he had a heavy object hoisted to the belfry, wrapped in a dark sack or cloak; a procedure sometimes had in the case of an elaborate piece of sculpture, or statue, which, being intended to grace the front of a new edifice, the architect does not desire exposed to critical eyes, till set up, finished, in its appointed place. Such was the impression now. But, as the object rose, a statuary present observed, or thought he did, that it was not entirely rigid, but was, in a manner, pliant. At last, when the hidden thing had attained its final height, and, obscurely seen from below, seemed almost of itself to step into the belfry, as if with little assistance from the crane, a shrewd old blacksmith present ventured the suspicion that it was but a living man. This surmise was thought a foolish one, while the general interest failed not to augment.

Not without demur from Bannadonna, the chief-magistrate of the town, with an associate – both elderly men – followed what seemed the image up the tower. But, arrived at the belfry, they had little recompense. Plausibly entrenching himself behind the conceded mysteries of his art, the mechanician withheld present explanation. The magistrates glanced toward the cloaked object, which, to their surprise, seemed now to have changed its attitude, or else had before been more perplexingly concealed by the violent muffling action of the wind without. It seemed now seated upon some sort of frame, or chair, contained within the domino. They observed that nigh the top, in a sort of square, the web of the cloth, either from accident or design, had its warp partly withdrawn, and the crossthreads plucked out here and there, so as to form a sort of woven grating. Whether it were the low wind or no, stealing through the stone latticework, or only their own perturbed imaginations, is uncertain, but they thought they discerned a slight sort of fitful, spring-like motion, in the domino. Nothing, however incidental or insignificant, escaped their uneasy eyes. Among other things, they prised out, in a corner, an earthen cup, partly corroded and partly encrusted, and one whispered to the other, that this cup was just such a one as might, in mockery, be offered to the lips of some brazen statue, or, perhaps, still worse.

But, being questioned, the mechanician said, that the cup was simply used in his founder's business, and described the purpose; in short, a cup to test the condition of metals in fusion. He added, that it had got into the belfry by the merest chance.

Again, and again, they gazed at the domino, as at some suspicious incognito – at a Venetian mask. All sorts of vague apprehensions stirred them. They even dreaded lest, when they should descend, the mechanician, though without a flesh and blood companion, for all that, would not be left alone.

Affecting some merriment at their disquietude, he begged to relieve them, by extending a coarse sheet of workman's canvas between them and the object.

Meantime he sought to interest them in his other work; nor, now that the domino was out of sight, did they long remain insensible to the artistic wonders lying round them; wonders hitherto beheld but in their unfinished state; because, since hoisting the bells, none but the caster had entered within the belfry. It was one trait of his, that, even in details, he would not let another do what he could, without too great loss of time, accomplish for himself. So, for several preceding weeks, whatever hours were unemployed in his secret design, had been devoted to elaborating the figures on the bells.

The clock-bell, in particular, now drew attention. Under a patient chisel, the latent beauty of its enrichments, before obscured by the cloudings incident to casting that beauty in its shyest grace, was now revealed. Round and round the bell, twelve figures of gay girls, garlanded, hand-in-hand, danced in a choral ring – the embodied hours.

'Bannadonna,' said the chief, 'this bell excels all else. No added touch could here improve. Hark!' hearing a sound, 'was that the wind?'

'The wind, Eccellenza,' was the light response. 'But the figures, they are not yet without their faults. They need some touches yet. When those are given, and the – block yonder,' pointing towards the canvas screen, 'when Haman there, as I merrily call him – him? *it*, I mean – when Haman is fixed on this, his lofty tree, then, gentlemen, will I be most happy to receive you here again.'

The equivocal reference to the object caused some return of restlessness. However, on their part, the visitors forbore further allusion to it, unwilling, perhaps, to let the foundling see how easily it lay within his plebeian art to stir the placid dignity of nobles.

'Well, Bannadonna,' said the chief, 'how long ere you are ready to set the clock going, so that the hour shall be sounded? Our interest in you, not less than in the work itself, makes us anxious to be assured of your success. The people, too – why, they are shouting now. Say the exact hour when you will be ready.'

'To-morrow, Eccellenza, if you listen for it – or should you not, all the same – strange music will be heard. The stroke of one shall be the first from yonder bell,' pointing to the bell adorned with girls and garlands, 'that stroke shall fall there, where the hand of Una clasps Dua's. The stroke of one shall sever that loved clasp. To-morrow, then, at one o'clock, as struck here, precisely here,' advancing and placing his finger upon the clasp, 'the poor mechanic will be most happy once more to give you liege audience, in this his littered shop. Farewell till then, illustrious magnificoes, and hark ye for your vassal's stroke.'

His still, Vulcanic face hiding its burning brightness like a forge, he moved with ostentatious deference towards the scuttle, as if so far to escort their exit. But the junior magistrate, a kind-hearted man, troubled at what seemed to him a certain sardonical disdain, lurking beneath the foundling's humble mien, and in Christian sympathy more distressed at it on his account than on his own, dimly surmising what might be the final fate of such a cynic solitaire, nor perhaps uninfluenced by the general strangeness of surrounding things, this good magistrate had glanced sadly, sideways from the speaker, and thereupon his foreboding eye had started at the expression of the unchanging face of the Hour Una.

'How is this, Bannadonna?' he lowly asked, 'Una looks unlike her sisters.'

'In Christ's name, Bannadonna,' impulsively broke in the chief, his attention, for the first time, attracted to the figure, by his associate's remark, 'Una's face looks just like that of Deborah, the prophetess, as painted by the Florentine, Del Fonca.'

'Surely, Bannadonna,' lowly resumed the milder magistrate, 'you meant the twelve should wear the same jocundly abandoned air. But see, the smile of Una seems but a fatal one. 'Tis different.'

While his mild associate was speaking, the chief glanced, inquiringly, from him to the caster, as if anxious to mark how the discrepancy would be accounted for. As the chief stood, his advanced foot was on the scuttle's curb.

Bannadonna spoke.

'Eccellenza, now that, following your keener eye, I glance upon the face of Una, I do, indeed, perceive some little variance. But look all round the bell, and you will find no two faces entirely correspond. Because there is a law in art – but the cold wind is rising more; these lattices are but a poor defence. Suffer me, magnificoes, to conduct you, at least, partly on your way. Those in whose well-being there is a public stake, should be heedfully attended.'

'Touching the look of Una, you were saying, Bannadonna, that there was a certain law in art,' observed the chief, as the three now descended the stone shaft, 'pray, tell me, then –.'

'Pardon; another time, Eccellenza; – the tower is damp.'

'Nay, I must rest, and hear it now. Here – here is a wide landing, and through this leeward slit, no wind, but ample light. Tell us of your law; and at large.'

'Since, Eccellenza, you insist, know that there is a law in art, which bars the possibility of duplicates. Some years ago, you may remember, I graved a small seal for your republic, bearing, for its chief device, the head of your own ancestor, its illustrious founder. It becoming necessary, for the customs' use, to have innumerable impressions for bales and boxes, I graved an entire plate, containing one hundred of the seals. Now, though, indeed, my object was to have those hundred heads identical, and though, I dare say, people think them so, yet, upon closely scanning an uncut impression from the plate, no two of those five-score faces, side by side, will be found alike. Gravity is the air of all; but, diversified in all. In some, benevolent; in some, ambiguous; in two or three, to a close scrutiny, all but incipiently malign, the variation of less than a hair's breadth in the linear shadings round the mouth sufficing to all this. Now, Eccellenza, transmute that general gravity into joyousness, and subject it to twelve of those variations I have described, and tell me, will you not have my hours here, and Una one of them? But I like –.'

'Hark! is that – a footfall above?'

'Mortar, Eccellenza; sometimes it drops to the belfry-floor from the arch where the stone-work was left undressed. I must have it seen to. As I was about to say: for one, I like this law forbidding duplicates. It evokes fine personalities. Yes, Eccellenza, that strange, and – to you – uncertain smile, and those fore-looking eyes of Una, suit Bannadonna very well.'

'Hark! – sure we left no soul above?'

'No soul, Eccellenza; rest assured, no *soul*. – Again the mortar.'

'It fell not while we were there.'

'Ah, in your presence, it better knew its place, Eccellenza,' blandly bowed Bannadonna.

'But, Una,' said the milder magistrate, 'she seemed intently gazing on you; one would have almost sworn that she picked you out from among us three.'

'If she did, possibly, it might have been her finer apprehension, Eccellenza.'

'How, Bannadonna? I do not understand you.'

'No consequence, no consequence, Eccellenza – but the shifted wind is blowing through the slit. Suffer me to escort you on; and then, pardon, but the toiler must to his tools.'

'It may be foolish, Signore,' said the milder magistrate, as, from the third landing, the two now went down unescorted, 'but, somehow, our great mechanician moves me strangely. Why, just now, when he so superciliously replied, his look seemed Sisera's, God's vain foe, in Del Fonca's painting. – And that young, sculptured Deborah, too. Aye, and that –.'

'Tush, tush, Signore!' returned the chief. 'A passing whim. Deborah? – Where's Jael, pray?'

'Ah,' said the other, as they now stepped upon the sod, 'Ah, Signore, I see you leave your fears behind you with the chill and gloom; but mine, even in this sunny air, remain. Hark!'

It was a sound from just within the tower door, whence they had emerged. Turning, they saw it closed.

'He has slipped down and barred us out,' smiled the chief; 'but it is his custom.'

Proclamation was now made, that the next day, at one hour after meridian, the clock would strike, and – thanks to the mechanician's powerful art – with unusual accompaniments. But what those should be, none as yet could say. The announcement was received with cheers.

By the looser sort, who encamped about the tower all night, lights were seen gleaming through the topmost blindwork, only disappearing with the morning sun. Strange sounds, too, were heard, or were thought to be, by those whom anxious watching might not have left mentally undisturbed, sounds, not only of some ringing implement, but also – so they said – half-suppressed screams and plainings, such as might have issued from some ghostly engine, overplied.

Slowly the day drew on; part of the concourse chasing the

weary time with songs and games, till, at last, the great blurred sun rolled, like a football, against the plain.

At noon, the nobility and principal citizens came from the town in cavalcade; a guard of soldiers, also, with music, the more to honour the occasion.

Only one hour more. Impatience grew. Watches were held in hands of feverish men, who stood, now scrutinizing their small dial-plates, and then, with neck thrown back, gazing toward the belfry, as if the eye might foretell that which could only be made sensible to the ear, for, as yet, there was no dial to the tower-clock.

The hour-hands of a thousand watches now verged within a hair's breadth of the figure I. A silence, as of the expectation of some Shiloh, pervaded the swarming plain. Suddenly a dull, mangled sound – naught ringing in it; scarcely audible, indeed, to the outer circles of the people – that dull sound dropped heavily from the belfry. At the same moment, each man stared at his neighbour blankly. All watches were upheld. All hour-hands were at – had passed – the figure I. No bell-stroke from the tower. The multitude became tumultuous.

Waiting a few moments, the chief magistrate, commanding silence, hailed the belfry, to know what thing unforeseen had happened there.

No response.

He hailed again and yet again.

All continued hushed.

By his order the soldiers burst in the tower-door; when, stationing guards to defend it from the now surging mob, the chief, accompanied by his former associate, climbed the winding stairs. Half-way up, they stopped to listen. No sound. Mounting faster, they reached the belfry; but, at the threshold, startled at the spectacle disclosed. A spaniel which, unbeknown to them, had followed them thus far, stood shivering as before some unknown monster in a brake: or, rather, as if it snuffed footsteps leading to some other world.

Bannadonna lay prostrate and bleeding at the base of the bell which was adorned with girls and garlands. He lay at the feet of the hour Una; his head coinciding, in a vertical line, with her left hand, clasped by the hour Dua. With downcast face impending over him, like Jael over nailed Sisera in the tent, was the domino; now no more becloaked.

It had limbs, and seemed clad in a scaly mail, lustrous as a dragon-beetle's. It was manacled, and its clubbed arms were uplifted, as if, with its manacles, once more to smite its already smitten victim. One advanced foot of it was inserted beneath the dead body, as if in the act of spurning it.

Uncertainty falls on what now followed.

It were but natural to suppose that the magistrates would at first shrink from immediate personal contact with what they saw. At the least, for a time, they would stand in involuntary doubt; it may be, in more or less of horrified alarm. Certain it is, that an arquebuss was called for from below. And some add, that its report, followed by a fierce whiz, as of the sudden snapping of a main-spring, with a steely din, as if a stack of sword blades should be dashed upon a pavement, these blended sounds came ringing to the plain, attracting every eye far upward to the belfry, whence, through the lattice-work, thin wreaths of smoke were curling.

Some averred that it was the spaniel, gone mad by fear, which was shot. This, others denied. True it was, the spaniel never more was seen; and, probably, for some unknown reason, it shared the burial now to be related of the domino. For, whatever the preceding circumstances may have been, the first instinctive panic over, or else all ground of reasonable fear removed, the two magistrates, by themselves, quickly rehooded the figure in the dropped cloak wherein it had been hoisted. The same night, it was secretly lowered to the ground, smuggled to the beach, pulled far out to sea, and sunk. Nor to any after urgency, even in free convivial hours, would the twain ever disclose the full secrets of the belfry.

From the mystery unavoidably investing it, the popular solution of the foundling's fate involved more or less of supernatural agency. But some few less unscientific minds pretended to find little difficulty in otherwise accounting for it. In the chain of circumstantial inferences drawn, there may, or may not, have been some absent or defective links. But, as the explanation in question is the only one which tradition has explicitly preserved, in dearth of better, it will here be given. But, in the first place, it is requisite to present the supposition entertained as to the entire motive and mode, with their origin, of the secret design of Bannadonna; the minds above-mentioned assuming to penetrate as well into his soul as into the event. The disclosure will indirectly involve reference to peculiar matters, none of the clearest, beyond the immediate subject.

At that period, no large bell was made to sound otherwise than as at present, by agitation of a tongue within, by means of ropes, or percussion from without, either from cumbrous machinery, or stalwart watchmen, armed with heavy hammers, stationed in the belfry, or in sentry-boxes on the open roof, according as the bell was sheltered or exposed.

It was from observing these exposed bells, with their watchmen, that the foundling, as was opined, derived the first suggestion of his scheme. Perched on a great mast or spire, the human figure, viewed from below, undergoes such a reduction in its apparent size, as to obliterate its intelligent features. It evinces no personality. Instead of bespeaking volition, its gestures rather resemble the automatic ones of the arms of a telegraph.

Musing, therefore, upon the purely Punchinello aspect of the human figure thus beheld, it had indirectly occurred to Bannadonna to devise some metallic agent, which should strike the hour with its mechanic hand, with even greater precision than the vital one. And, moreover, as the vital watchman on the roof, sallying from his retreat at the given periods, walked to the bell with uplifted mace, to smite it, Bannadonna had resolved that his invention should likewise possess the power of locomotion, and, along with that, the appearance, at least, of intelligence and will.

If the conjectures of those who claimed acquaintance with the intent of Bannadonna be thus far correct, no unenterprising spirit could have been his. But they stopped not here; intimating that though, indeed, his design had, in the first place, been prompted by the sight of the watchman, and confined to the devising of a subtle substitute for him; yet, as is not seldom the case with projectors, by insensible gradations, proceeding from comparatively pigmy aims to Titanic ones, the original scheme had, in its anticipated eventualities, at last, attained to an unheard of degree of daring. He still bent his efforts upon the locomotive figure for the belfry, but only as a partial type of an ulterior creature, a sort of elephantine Helot, adapted to further, in a degree scarcely to be imagined, the universal conveniences and glories of humanity;

supplying nothing less than a supplement to the Six Days' Work; stocking the earth with a new serf, more useful than the ox, swifter than the dolphin, stronger than the lion, more cunning than the ape, for industry an ant, more fiery than serpents, and yet, in patience, another ass. All excellences of all God-made creatures, which served man, were here to receive advancement, and then to be combined in one. Talus was to have been the all-accomplished Helot's name. Talus, iron slave to Bannadonna, and, through him, to man.

Here, it might well be thought that, were these last conjectures as to the foundling's secrets not erroneous, then must he have been hopelessly infected with the craziest chimeras of his age; far outgoing Albert Magnus and Cornelius Agrippa. But the contrary was averred. However marvellous his design, however apparently transcending not alone the bounds of human invention, but those of divine creation, yet the proposed means to be employed were alleged to have been confined within the sober forms of sober reason. It was affirmed that, to a degree of more than sceptic scorn, Bannadonna had been without sympathy for any of the vainglorious irrationalities of his time. For example, he had not concluded, with the visionaries among the metaphysicians, that between the finer mechanic forces and the ruder animal vitality, some germ of correspondence might prove discoverable. As little did his scheme partake of the enthusiasm of some natural philosophers, who hoped, by physiological and chemical inductions, to arrive at a knowledge of the source of life, and so qualify themselves to manufacture and improve upon it. Much less had he aught in common with the tribe of alchemists, who sought, by a species of incantations, to evoke some surprising vitality from the laboratory. Neither had he imagined with certain sanguine theosophists, that, by faithful adoration of the Highest, unheard-of powers would be vouchsafed to man. A practical materialist, what Bannadonna had aimed at was to have been reached, not by logic, not by crucible, not by conjuration, not by altars; but by plain vice-bench and hammer. In short, to solve nature, to steal into her, to intrigue beyond her, to procure some one else to bind her to his hand; – these, one and all, had not been his objects; but, asking no favors from any element or any being, of himself, to rival her, outstrip her, and rule her. He stooped to conquer. With him, common sense was theurgy; machinery, miracle; Prometheus, the heroic name for machinist; man, the true God.

Nevertheless, in his initial step, so far as the experimental automaton for the belfry was concerned, he allowed fancy some little play; or, perhaps, what seemed his fancifulness was but his utilitarian ambition collaterally extended. In figure, the creature for the belfry should not be likened after the human pattern, nor any animal one, nor after the ideals, however wild, of ancient fable, but equally in aspect as in organism be an original production; the more terrible to behold, the better.

Such, then, were the suppositions as to the present scheme, and the reserved intent. How, at the very threshold, so un-looked for a catastrophe overturned all, or, rather, what was the conjecture here, is now to be set forth.

It was thought that on the day preceding the fatality, his visitors having left him, Bannadonna had unpacked the belfry image, adjusted it, and placed it in the retreat provided – a sort of sentry-box in one corner of the belfry; in short, throughout the night, and for some part of the ensuing morning, he had been engaged in arranging every thing connected with the domino: the issuing from the sentry-box each sixty minutes; sliding along a grooved way, like a railway; advancing to the clock-bell, with uplifted manacles; striking it at one of the twelve junctions of the four-and-twenty hands: then wheeling, circling the bell, and retiring to its post, there to bide for another sixty minutes, when the same process was to be repeated; the bell, by a cunning mechanism, meantime turning on its vertical axis, so as to present, to the descending mace, the clasped hands of the next two figures, when it would strike two, three, and so on, to the end. The musical metal in this time-bell being so managed in the fusion, by some art perishing with its originator, that each of the clasps of the four-and-twenty hands should give forth its own peculiar resonance when parted.

But on the magic metal, the magic and metallic stranger never struck but that one stroke, drove but that one nail, severed but that one clasp, by which Bannadonna clung to his ambitious life. For, after winding up the creature in the sentry-box, so that, for the present, skipping the intervening hours, it should not emerge till the hour of one, but should then infallibly emerge, and, after deftly oiling the grooves whereon it was to slide, it was surmised that the mechanician must then have hurried to the bell, to give his final touches to its sculpture. True artist, he here became absorbed; an absorption still further intensified, it may be, by his striving to abate that strange look of Una; which, though, before others, he had treated with such unconcern, might not, in secret, have been without its thorn.

And so, for the interval, he was oblivious of his creature; which, not oblivious of him, and true to its creation, and true to its heedful winding up, left its post precisely at the given moment; along its well-oiled route, slid noiselessly towards its mark; and aiming at the hand of Una, to ring one clangorous note, dully smote the intervening brain of Bannadonna, turned backwards to it; the manacled arms then instantly upspringing to their hovering poise. The falling body clogged the thing's return; so there it stood, still impending over Bannadonna, as if whispering some postmortem terror. The chisel lay dropped from the hand, but beside the hand; the oil-flask spilled across the iron track.

In his unhappy end, not unmindful of the rare genius of the mechanician, the republic decreed him a stately funeral. It was resolved that the great bell – the one whose casting had been jeopardized through the timidity of the ill-starred workman – should be rung upon the entrance of the bier into the cathedral. The most robust man of the country round was assigned the office of bell-ringer.

But as the pall-bearers entered the cathedral porch, nought but a broken and disastrous sound, like that of some lone Alpine land-slide, fell from the tower upon their ears. And then, all was hushed.

Glancing backwards, they saw the groined belfry crashed sideways in. It afterwards appeared that the powerful peasant who had the bell-rope in charge, wishing to test at once the full glory of the bell, had swayed down upon the rope with one concentrated jerk. The mass of quaking metal, too ponderous for its frame, and strangely feeble somewhere at its top, loosed from its fastening, tore sideways down, and tumbling in one sheer fall, three hundred feet to the soft sward below, buried itself inverted and half out of sight.

Upon its disinterment, the main fracture was found to have

started from a small spot in the ear; which, being scraped, revealed a defect, deceptively minute, in the casting; which defect must subsequently have been pasted over with some unknown compound.

The remolten metal soon reässumed its place in the tower's repaired superstructure. For one year the metallic choir of birds sang musically in its belfry-bough-work of sculptured blinds and traceries. But on the first anniversary of the tower's completion – at early dawn, before the concourse had surrounded it – an earthquake came; one loud crash was heard. The stone-pine, with all its bower of songsters, lay overthrown upon the plain.

So the blind slave obeyed its blinder lord; but, in obedience, slew him. So the creator was killed by the creature. So the bell was too heavy for the tower. So that bell's main weakness was where man's blood had flawed it. And so pride went before the fall.*

* It was not deemed necessary to adhere to the peculiar notation of Italian time. Adherence to it would have impaired the familiar comprehension of the story. Kindred remarks might be offered touching an anachronism or two that occur.

# The Vivisector

## By SIR RONALD ROSS

*There is a story told that Sir Ronald Ross (1857–1932), the British physician who won the Nobel Prize for medicine in 1902 for his discovery of the malaria parasite, was introduced to scientific experimentation by reading* Frankenstein *as a young man. True or not, and although he went on to enjoy a distinguished career as a scientist, Sir Ronald admitted when receiving his award that literature had always been his first love. In fact, he wrote a number of novels (including* Child of Ocean *and* The Spirit of the Storm) *as well as a considerable number of fables, poems, satires and his* Memoirs *(1923). Born in Almora, India, he studied medicine at St Bartholomew's in London before returning to his native country to work in the Indian Medical Service from 1881–99. It was his research there that led to his discovery of the malaria parasite in 1895. Sir Ronald finished his career as Professor of Tropical Medicines at Liverpool.*

*Regardless of whether Mary Shelley's story had been his inspiration, Sir Ronald Ross was undoubtedly interested in the concept of creating and extending life, a fact that is evident in* The Vivisector *which he wrote while still living in India in 1881. Almost half a century later, in 1928, he was to go on record with his belief that a man could live for hundreds of years under the right conditions – a statement that had him branded as a 'Frankenstein' in some of the popular journals of the day.*

*'The best and ultimate test of the ability of man to live long beyond his present allotted score of years would be to have a man, from his babyhood up, live in what practically would be a sterilised test-tube,' Sir Ronald wrote. 'He would breathe sterilised air. He would eat sterilised food. He would drink*

*sterilised liquids. He would thus be placed as far as humanly possible beyond the range of the myriad microbes that in many ways are the enemies of man and that bring about many of his ailments. Such a man, growing and living under special conditions, might live to be 200.' (As a matter of interest, this statement inspired the popular American SF writer, Wallace West, to write a short story, 'The Incubator Man' published that same year, in which Sir Ronald's test-tube creature lived for 150 years – only to die as soon as he left his antiseptic environment from catching ... the measles.)*

*The amusing blending of science and humour in the following story of* The Vivisector *has caused several critics to compare the best of the author's work to that of his famous American contemporary, Mark Twain. Certainly Sir Ronald Ross deserves credit as an ingenious fantasy writer as well as a great physician.*

In the Year 1860, I, having completed my medical studies in London, and being a man of some small independence, determined upon visiting the various universities and scientific societies of the world. I travelled through Germany, France, Spain, Italy, Russia, Persia, Turkey, India and China. Having seen much physic poured down many throats, and having listened to the opposing views of five thousand professors, I became in the end assured that for most diseases the best medicine is water, taken internally. I was also convinced of the necessity for a better knowledge of Physiology; for unless we know the working of a watch or machine, how can we hope to mend it? Truly hot oil poured in *may* do good; but it can also possibly clog the wheels. Hygiene is the better part of medicine; physiology, the best part of both: for without it we put on spectacles in the dark. Those great mysteries of Life and Death, birth, maintenance, action and thought were to me Mexicos, their solution El Dorados. Accordingly I set foot in America, the land of experiment, with enthusiasm. I passed eastward, calling on persons long known to me through their works; but I was not satisfied.

At the large city of Snogginsville I met the well-known Dr Silcutt, famous for his excellent work on the encephalon of politicians. He was as ardent a physiologist as myself; and was at the time much excited by his recent excellent discovery that gold produces effects different from those of copper when approached to the different nerves of those engaged in public services. Titillation of the palm with the former metal produces contraction of the flexors, with the latter, contraction of the extensors. He was personally tall, sombre, and not of a humorous disposition. He lived in his private chambers at the Infirmary where I stayed with him so long that we became friends. With him there resided an old gentleman, suffering from dementia, whom at first I took to be his father.

The day before the one on which I intended leaving Snogginsville, Silcutt exhibited to me his private museum of medical curiosities. I remember that when we entered the room, he, being interested in argument, left the door ajar. Passing from specimen to specimen we at last arrived before a most curious contrivance. Roughly described, one would have considered it a double kind of pump with four tubes (two tubes from each pump) leading to a central mechanism. Each pump was a heavy square mass meant to be placed on the ground, with a piston action; the piston being so disposed as to require pushing down and pulling up without a lever. Silcutt seemed inclined to pass it, but I inquired its use; no sooner, however, were the words out of my mouth, than I heard a kind of scream behind me, muffled in laughter. The above-mentioned old gentleman was standing looking at the construction which had interested me. A quick frown passed over Silcutt's face, and he clutched the other by the arm. The old man lifted his right foot and placed it on a low bench close by. His face became tumid with blood until his white hair, eye-brows and scanty whiskers started out, as it were, in contrast. The veins of his neck swelled, and perspiration broke out on his forehead. His teeth were clenched and his eyes bloodshot; and though all this transformation occurred in a few seconds, yet he had every appearance of a man who had undergone severe bodily exercise. He stooped down as if to lift a heavy weight with both hands, and began to pull up and push down with his arms, as if, as I thought, he was working one of the pumps described above. He laughed and screamed alternately; until, after a few seconds more, a foam gathered on his lips, he shrieked, and fell down in an epileptic seizure.

Silcutt said, 'He is not my father. He is accustomed to these fits. He has been located with me for twenty years. To-night, I will give you a manuscript, fully describing this occurrence and that machine; upon the condition that you do not divulge its contents until the death of both of us.'

Upon retiring to rest, I found on my bedroom table a manuscript signed 'William Silcutt, U.Sc. Phil.' Opening it, I read:-

'I attended Snogginsville Infirmary as a medical student from 1838 to 1840. Patrick Maculligan, a man of about forty years of age, was resident medical officer. He was at the time deeply engaged in experimental research on both physiology and therapeutics; and needing an assistant, he fixed on me. I was intensely fond of both these subjects; and we were often engaged together in the laboratory for the whole day. The Infirmary is situated on a hill, and is a long building, turreted at either end. At the time I speak of only one half of the structure was occupied by patients. At the top of the turret belonging to the empty wing, our laboratory was situated. Here we worked, ate, and often slept without seeing anyone but ourselves for twenty-four hours at a stretch. The laboratory consisted of five rooms; an animals' room for keeping live-stock; a chemical room; a miscroscopical room; a workshop for making implements; and the operation room. This last chamber was the top central one of the turret and had a window facing westward. It was painted black so as not to show the blood that was often spurted upon its walls. In a corner were a basin and ewer. Tables with various knives, tweezers, forceps, saws, etc., stood round. At a yard from one wall there was the usual stove with a pipe leading through the roof. In the middle stood the operating-table, which we called the altar of science. It was a complicated contrivance, padded and covered with leather, with a waterproof over all. It could be so drawn out, or pushed in, as to afford room for holding either a donkey or a guinea-pig at will. Numbers of fastening straps were attached. The door and window were padded to prevent the egress of any sound which might disturb the patients below.

'Maculligan was an Irish immigrant. He was of middle stature, pale of complexion, with light sandy hair. He was very grave and had large white front teeth. His hands were long and hairy; and owing to his studies, he was slightly bowed and weakly. A long scar cut from his left eye to the mouth, and the deformity made him the more shy. He was a Protestant, and when not engaged in vivisection, it was his great delight to read over a book of hymns, which he often hummed to himself. He told me that he was the son of an Irish physician and had left home owing to family quarrels, when a lad of seventeen.

'We had often discussed the awful problem of death. Could it be prevented? May not science hope to find its antidote? He said: "Seeing that most tissues are repairable, like bone, re-formable, or like skin to be mended by another structure, I believe that death does not originate in these parts which may be called rather the appurtenances of life than life itself. The older the man, the less able is he to obtain healing of wounds. Why? Because the healing power is older and less vigorous. What is the healing power? Where is it? Either in the nervous system or in the blood, I should say. A man dies, not because his muscles and organs decay; but because either the mecha-nism of his brain, cord, or ganglia is so attrite, and worn out, or his blood is so changed by continual use, as to be of no further service to the body. We cannot give an animal a new brain; but we can provide him with fresh blood. Let us try then whether the blood be not the seat of life. The plan we will adopt is this: I have constructed an artificial heart which may be filled with the fresh blood of an animal recently killed. Now we must obtain a corpse which has died of loss of blood alone: we must quickly after death cut down to his heart, and apply the apparatus to his blood-vessels, pour in a fresh circulation. By this means," he ended, rubbing his hands, "I hope to bring the dead to life."'

To understand the rest of Dr Silcutt's narrative, the reader should know the course of the circulation. This is very simple. The heart is divided into two partitions, a right and a left one. The blood enters the right partition, whence it is squirted into the lungs; from the lungs it returns to the left partition, whence it is squirted all over the body; and from the body it finally returns back to the right partition, and so on *ad infinitum*. The apparatus now shown to Silcutt, described without the use of anatomical words, was an artificial heart, only the two partitions were quite separate, and to be worked by different pressure. The chest was opened and into the large blood-vessels, which convey the blood to and from the heart, long india-rubber tubes were inserted: so that the blood from the body was carried to the right artificial heart or pump, and thence squirted back to the lungs; from the lungs it passed to the left artificial heart or pump, and thence to the body, and so on. These artificial hearts were mere ordinary double-action pumps, with valves, which sucked in the fluid from one direction and expelled it in another; but having to be completely air-tight they were heavily constructed and the pistons were worked only with considerable difficulty. Each pump was placed in a hot-water bath to maintain the blood at the temperature of 100°; and one was to be put on either side of the dead body. To resume the manuscript: –

'It was some time before a fit subject was brought into the hospital. What was required was a person who had simply bled to death without much serious injury except the wound of the blood-vessels. A donkey was kept in readiness to supply the required fluid. We often practised the insertion of the india-rubber tubes into the blood-vessel on dead patients; and had become so skilful as to be able to finish the operation in five minutes.

'At last, on the morning of 5th October 1840, a patient was brought into the Infirmary with a cut wound on the head from which he had bled profusely. He had been cut with a knife in a street row. He was a tall, vigorous man, with an immense amount of red hair and beard and with a vicious leering kind of expression. When I saw him he was fast sinking; for the evident drunken habits of the patient did not predispose him to recovery. I only saw him and attended him (except the nurses); and had him removed to a private ward when he died at 2 p.m. Having previously acquainted Maculligan of the case, I waited below while that gentleman was preparing the apparatus. I sent the nurses out of the ward after the patient's death. I wrapt him in a blanket and drawing his hands over my shoulders carried him out. A violent storm, which had just broken, gave me greater security. I locked the door of the private ward and struggled as I best could with my burden up the narrow stairs of the turret. When I arrived in the laboratory, the apparatus was ready, and the pumps were standing in their baths of hot-water (which was procured from the stove boiler). The donkey had been killed, and his fresh blood was in the cavities of our machine.

'Maculligan was flushed with excitement: "Now," he exclaimed, "we shall get at least some knowledge; either a useful negative result, or a world-reforming fact."

'I placed the body on the bed: on his left side was the pump which I was to work and which sent the blood all over his body; on his right side Maculligan supplied his lungs. In a minute I had fastened the limbs, and made bare the chest of the man. Maculligan seized the knife, and at one swoop cut down to the heart. I held apart the several parts. Almost immediately it seemed he had inserted the tubes into the arteries and veins, and a few seconds sufficed to sew up the chest again, joining the cartilages as well as the skin, and covering all the incision with a quickly congealing gum to exclude the air, and permit breathing. The whole was done by ten minutes after death. The corpse was pale, slightly cold, the eyelids half-open, and the eyes turned upwards beneath them. Blankets were thrown upon it to retain the heat. The storm outside had increased in fury; the rain drenched the window-panes, and the violence of the wind was such that the whole tower seemed to rock. Most unearthly noises, too, were caused by it; and the darkness was so great that we could barely see to do our experiment. I could observe Maculligan trembling with excitement. I myself, though generally stolid, was much moved.

'"Are you ready," said he, taking hold of his pump and speaking hoarsely. "Then away," and down went the pistons simultaneously.

'We told twelve strokes – no blood had oozed from the cut in the chest – all was satisfactory. Another twelve – a slight flushing the cheeks. Maculligan stopped, and we both took off our coats, the wind howling with tenfold fury. We resumed

– suddenly the eyes closed. We went on for fully quarter of an hour.

'"He is breathing," cried my companion.

'Most certainly there was some slight action of the diaphragm. Maculligan suddenly motioned me to stop, and going up to the patient listened to hear the breathing. While he looked into the man's face the eyes suddenly opened, following my friend, who sprang back to his pump, trembling violently. We went on silently; the man, all the while, watching Maculligan whose hair seemed stiff, and whose face was so changed that I should hardly have known him. I myself was so astounded that I could not conceive the occurrence as real. We had never expected that there would be any recovery beyond a comatose condition.

'Suddenly the man, who appeared as if recovering from chloroform, said aloud, "Lave it, will you."

'"Leave what?" asked Maculligan, hoarsely.

'"Lave pulling that out of the ground, for sure it goes bang through the wurrld, and is clamped on the other side. It's o' no use."

'"Bedad," he continued, "but ye're the rummiest egg-flip iver I came across."

'"Egg-flip! Eh, boy?" cried Maculligan, laughing excitedly. "You're another."

'"What!" said the man, smiling with one side of his mouth, "you air a wag, you air – a kind o' wag as tells loodicrus tales to tay-totallers at taymatins, you air."

'"No, I ain't now," exclaimed my friend, lifting his chin, and winking in an excited, ready-boy kind of manner.

'"Wal, friend," continued the patient, "kep your 'air on, an' nobody 'ud tell you warn't a Quaker. But you're too quaky for your occupation – I tak it you're a water-works man, with that 'ere pump, eh? friend." He then spat into the air.

'"What makes you think that, boy," answered my companion, putting his tongue in his cheek, and pumping vigorously.

'"Wal," returned the other, laughing roughly, "I guessed you war by your complexion. I say," he continued, winking, "you don't often git your pipes bunged in these parts by vivisections does yer – no vivisected babbies, now – eh?"

'"Not I, lad, not I," laughed Maculligan boisterously.

'"That's odd now! och! man, sure, an wasn't I a vivisector in ould Ireland, an a phesycian."

'"I hope you got many of 'em," laughed the other.

'"Many o' wot?"

'"Fees – you said you were a feesycian."

'"Wal," laughed the man, winking, "just you write that 'ere goak in yer diary and have a dinner on the annivassery of it, ivery year. Yes, sir, I was a physician, and, sure, an eminent one and got me thousand a year, and lived in Merrion Square, bedad. But I went in for physiology – I went in for physiology, and so got ruined. I say! won't the devil give me hot for my vivisecting – for the cutting – eh? For the fastening up – eh? 'You should have taken the trouble to give chloroform,' he'll say. But I don't care a doight for the devil – eh? – till I am dead – eh? snifflewink?"

'"But what if you are," cried Maculligan, loudly. "Eh, boy, what if you are?"

'"Hey? Wal, stranger, I guess you air goin' it with that 'ere pump. I say," he called out suddenly, "stop it, will you! Every push sends a throb in me chist, you skippin' spalpeen."

'The patient seemed to become alarmed. He had kept his eyes fixed on my associate; he now turned them upon me, and I saw that he recognized me.

'He began to pull at his wrists and ankles, when Maculligan, not knowing what he was saying, kept on repeating, "But, what if you *are* dead?"

'All this while we were both pumping without intermission.

'"Aha!" hissed the man, his face wearing a horrible expression, "what is this? What is this? I am dead! Begorra, I died just now – I died of a cut on the head, and drank a bottle o' whiskey upon it to die drunk! Oh, Lord! I see it – ochone! I am in hell, and I am drunk still!" He wrenched again at his wrists, screaming.

'"So you are, Pat," cried my friend. "So you are."

'"Ah! Lord! What 'ull they say if I come up to court drunk! Maybe I have been in court already, but was so inebriate I did not know it, and have got damned out o' hand, with never a bit of a voice in the matter."

'"So you have, Pat, so you have. You were dead drunk in the dock, you were."

'"Ah! krimy," groaned the man, his eye wandering down to the instrument stuck in his chest, the stitches in his skin and the tubes leading to the pumps. "Och! St Pathrick, I see it! And my punishment is, to be done to as I have been done by. And you are a couple of devils, and I a vivisection; and I shall be vivisected for iver and iver, wurrld without end – Oh! Lord – damn – damn – damn –"

'Here Maculligan inadvertently missed a stroke which caused the patient to gasp violently.

'"Now, don't do it again, honey," he continued. "I'll swear no more, purty deevil that ye are, I did not mane to chaffer ye just now – but ye're the wittiest devil, truly speaking, that I iver saw on earth, or in h – or anywhere. You'll not be studyin' much on me now, will yer, dear?"

'"We shall not do more than tie up your bile duct and establish a fistula in your side to-day, friend," said Maculligan, winking at me.

'"And will you do that? Oh! crikey!"

'"To-morrow we are going to lay out a piece of your mesentery under the microscope to see the blood circulate."

'"Oh, sammy! And what 'ull yer do the day arter?"

'"See how much of your brains we can slice off without stopping your thinking."

'"Why, yer don't imagine I think with the pit of my stomach, do yer? One blessing yer'll have to lave it soon, for there 'ull never be a pickin' place left on me carcase."

'"Not a bit of it, my dear sir," roared Maculligan, who seemed mad from excitement. "You heal up in one place as soon as we go on to another."

'"Well, that knocks all hope out of me. But what are ye doin' now?"

'"Injecting you with donkey's blood to see if you will bray."

'"I'll not do that, anyway, but I tell you what, I feel uncommon sharp and witty like. I 'ud advise you to try a little of the same mixture. Yer not agoin' to have any alcoholic experiments on me, friend, air ye?"

'"No – why?"

'"Wal, yer might find out how much whuskey it 'ull take to make me drunk, anyhow, honey. O Lord!" he ejaculated, looking round, "how well I know them scalpels, directors, retractors, bone-forceps, aneurism needles and the like, and I have often done all the experiments you have mentioned."

'At times the man dropped the coarser Irish brogue, and at other times used a Californian slang.

'"You see," he continued, "I was a man of some eminence in the medical profession."

'"And how did you lose that eminence?"

'"One day I was up to the ears in thought about me theory of diabetes, when a poodle happening to bark about me heels, instead of kicking it away, sure enough I put it in me pocket, thoughtlessly."

'"Well?"

'"Well, that poodle belonged to the vice-queen, or the vice-royess, who offered a hundred pound for it. Now a rapscallion saw me pockit the poodle, tould a policeman, who followed me as I went home one day, entered me house, got up to the laboratory and found the identical poodle with a pay in its fourth ventricle, and a pin in its curvickle ganglion. They had me up for dog-stealing, jist as I had complated me work on the subject in hand, and instid of putting me in the Royal Society, put me in a common prison. When I got out I took to drinking and went to America and the dogs; and I've got there now, begorra! – Yer will not give me chloroform, thin, honey; or a gin-cocktail now? Be Jesus, how the devils are howlin' round about!"

'During this extraordinary conversation the wind had risen still more, and the turret was plainly felt to rock to and fro. The evening, too, began to hasten in, aided by the black, scurrying rack that obscured the sky. We had been toiling for more than an hour, having to keep time like rowers. My arms were getting tired, and I was profusely perspiring. Maculligan was shouting and laughing like a maniac or drunkard, his face bloated with exertion and his long light hair hanging over his eyes. Suddenly I cast my eyes on the thermometer in the bath which maintained the heat of the blood at the necessary 100°. It stood at 97.4°. The fire in the stove was getting low.

'I said: "The fire is getting low; it must be replenished."

'"You pile it up then," said Maculligan; "we must leave off together."

'At a signal from him we both ceased pumping and I, who was nearest, rushed to the stove, knocked the lid off and poured in, in my haste, the whole scuttle full of coals. When I returned the patient had fainted: we immediately resumed.

'I said: "He was nearly out then, Maculligan."

'"Wot's that?" muttered the patient, coming round. "Tarnation take you deevils, how did you gumption that my name was Maculligan?"

'"Is that so?" inquired Maculligan.

'"Is that so! I guess it is – Josephus Maculligan av Maculligan Castle, County Leitrim, son av old Maculligan av the same, and be damned to yer!"

'No sooner were these words uttered than my companion uttered the most horrible yell I ever heard.

'"You are my brother," he shrieked; "Ha! ha! look at this!" showing the long scar on his face. The patient's jaw dropped, and he violently struggled; but when my friend relaxed the speed of pumping he fell back, and began to groan.

'"Oh! oh! Is it me brother they have put to plague me, me twin brother, who I knocked about and gashed down the cheek because he was after bein' five munutes older than myself and had got all the proparty? Ye are not dead, Pathrick dear? Ye are no ghost, avic? Ye will not tormint me though your father and me druv you to Ameriky?"

'"No, no," shouted Maculligan. "I am alive! You are alive! We are all alive! I am surgeon of the Snogginsville Infirmary. I have made an invention for reviving the dead by means of injecting hot, fresh blood into his veins. I required a case for experiment, which had merely bled to death. You were the first that presented. If we leave off pumping for five minutes, or the stove goes out, letting the hot-water cool, the blood will clot in the machine and you will die immediately."

'I cannot describe the face of Josephus Maculligan during this recital. He burst forth into oaths, upbraiding his brother for attempting such an experiment, and shrieking for help. But the wind out-shrieked him. He prayed and cried alternately. My arms were getting intensely tired, and my back was aching, owing to the necessary stoop of the body. Suddenly the setting sun, which was almost touching the horizon, gleamed out from the clouds, and poured a red glow on Patrick Maculligan's face. I shall never forget its expression: he seemed to have become more like an ape than a man. His face was turbid and red; his mouth drawn back at the

corners, showing all his teeth and the very gums. His tongue
hung out, the large veins of the throat and forehead stood
prominent, the long scar on the cheek glistened white, and
seemed to have contracted in length, drawing up the upper
lip, and showing the canine tooth of that side. His necktie and
collar had burst open, and he panted quickly like a dog; while
his eyes, round and lidless, glared on his brother, not with
anger or fear, but without any expression at all. The one
beam of blood-red light, streaming in from the window seemed
to rest upon him on purpose, and, as it were, moved and
twined amongst his hair. He alone was visible: all the rest of
the room was dark; for the ray, after touching him passed
into the workshop beyond. I could see that his hands which
were working the pump were swollen and veined.

'He said: "You have wronged me. We are twin-brothers,
and I being the weaker should have been protected by you,
rather than bullied. We both loved Lucy Hagan; but she
preferred me. One day I said: 'I have brains; I don't want the
property; I will ask Lucy to marry me, and we will go to
Amerika!' I went to ask her passing through a wood. You
were there felling trees. You threw the hatchet at me, saying:
'I'll knock the Polly Beloy dear out of you!' The steel cut my
check. A week afterwards I presented myself to Lucy. She said
she would think about it, and in the evening sent me a refusal
written in French and a hymn-book with her favourite hymns
marked. She informed me that she was going to marry you. I
called upon her to thank her for the hymn-book, and murdered
her on the spot. I then proceeded to America when I heard
that my father was found dead in bed. I said: 'My brother
Joseph has murdered him.' Both of us being murderers, it
was natural enough that we should go a step further and
become vivisectors, and this is our punishment."

'"Wal," returned the other, spitting into the ray of light, "I
guess I'd rayther be you than me in this here investigation
of nature. You are payin' interest and principal together of that
'ere loan across the cheek I gave yer. If yer cannot kep up that
elber-jiggerin work much longer, I will be much obleeged if
you will ax someone to come up and relieve yer, and bring up
a drop or two o' somethin' cooling, cas I am feeling tarnation
warrum."

'"If either of us stop for two minutes you are dead, clear;

and there are no more donkeys in the establishment," answered Patrick. "It won't do for only one to pump, because that will burst up your vessels. And it won't do to call, because no one will hear. It would take at least four minutes to get to the occupied wing of the building and back and by that time clots would be sure to form, any one of which getting in your brain would kill you slick."

'"Wal," asked Josephus, "and cud not both of you go and divide the distance atween yer? I am getting as hot as a taypot."

'Looking at the thermometer in the water-bath of my pump, I observed it stood at 102°. The fire in the stove, drawn by the violent wind, was beginning to roar through the heap of coals.

'"Turn on the cold water," said Patrick.

'It came from the tap with a gush, then stopped – *the water-pipe had been broken by the storm*. The thermometer was rising – if it passed 120° the blood would be heated to the same temperature, and would certainly become coagulated, or would coagulate the nervous matter of the patient. We left off, and I rushed to the stove – *the poker and shovel had both been sent to be mended*. The patient was gasping.

'"If you stop me circulation again, yer spalpeens, I'll skin yer," he said.

'We resumed. The light had left Patrick's face, but the stove glowed out in the darkness, and we heard the roaring of the flames. Patrick was staggering like a drunkard, and breathing stertorously. His tongue was hanging further out; the corners of his mouth were drawn more and more backwards; and at every stroke he pulled, his ears twitched. In my hands there was no feeling left, for as said before, the pumps were very stiff. I pushed and pulled mechanically; there was a dead pain at my heart; I could think of nothing, my eyes were glazed; all I saw was the thermometer slowly rising. Josephus was struggling and howling.

'"Arrah, now," he cried, "ye're running fire into me. Lave it will yer. I guess I'll get up and pummel yer both."

'We stopped for a second, when he yelled out, "Go on yer hell-sparks, or I'll report yer behaviour to the deevil. O Lord," he groaned, "here's faver and no ague."

'The thermometer had reached 106°.

'"Wal," continued Josephus, "this 'ull put me in the very best trainin' for hell cud be imagined. I shall ask for a place as head stoker after this, for I shan't flinch at no fire agin."

'Patrick tried to speak but could not. The flames in the stove shot up through the coaling-hole at top. The thermometer stood at 108°, a temperature seldom reached by the most violent fevers.

'Josephus said, "I poisoned me father with opium and drove me brother to murder his sweetheart, but they ought to let me into heaven arter this, for it's punishment enough sure. It's plaguey hard on a poor boy to make him die twice – to make him pay over agin for his ticket to tarnation. Ah! lads kep it up, lads. Though ye're a runnin' the red-hot blood o' ten thousand jackasses biled in the boilers av the cintre of the wurrld into me Ah-orta, kep it up! Though ye are a sweatin' away yerselves, till there is nothin' left av yer but yer skilitons, and a little ile in yer boots, yet kep it up, lads, kep it up! Brayvo, brayvo! oh! but the warrmth – the warrmth! I'll tak me whusky cold, I thank you. Ice! Thanks, I wull jist tak a limp o' the same."

'He then ceased talking and struggled violently. The last he said was, "Good-bye, Pathrick; I'll vivisect yer, t' other side o' Jourdan;"

'The thermometer had reached 116.5°. The howling of the wind was awful. Patrick was rolling from side to side. The perspiration ran down over my eyes. I could not feel my arms below the shoulders. Patrick suddenly drew in his breath sharply, gave a yell, threw up his arms and fell on his face. Josephus by a last effort wrenched his arms loose, sat up, clutched at his throat and fell back. At the same moment the storm blew in the window with a crash. In came the tempest and rain, a spiral of flame shot up from the stove, and I was hurled to the ground.

'It was morning when I woke. The stove was out and Patrick sleeping soundly. I could not stand, nor move the arms below the elbows. As best I could I crawled downstairs for assistance.

'Josephus Maculligan was stone dead, and was soon buried. Patrick lives, but he is demented and suffers from attacks of epilepsy. I am myself quite well.

'(Signed) WILLIAM SILCUTT.'

Such was the remarkable manuscript I read, and I may well be believed when I state that so great was the horror of vivisection which I derived from the perusal of this account of the impaling and exhaustion to death of living beings, that I took to collecting butterflies in the summer, and hunting in the winter, neglecting the medical profession altogether. After the death of Silcutt and Maculligan, I related the story to the President of the Club for the Total Abolition of Vivisection. He asked me down to the country branch of that club, where I was to read the manuscript.

After our interesting pigeon battue, where more than two hundred birds were killed, we dined. I then read the work; which filled the members with such horror that they passed forty-five resolutions upon the spot, and finished the day with an oyster and white-bait supper. I am sure that the reader who believes this atrocious and fearful tale cannot become anything but a *Total Anti-vivisectionist*.

# The Future Eve

## By VILLIERS DE L'ISLE ADAM

*It was not until 1886 that the first female creature was introduced into the* Frankenstein *canon with* The Future Eve *by the fin-de-siècle French author, Villiers De L'Isle Adam (1840–1889). This extraordinary man, a Count by birth who belonged to a shabby-genteel family of old Breton aristocrats, endured a 'manic and poverty-stricken existence in Paris,' according to his biographer Alan Reitt, writing plays and poetry and a series of beautifully polished weird stories, the best of which were later collected as* Contes Cruels *(Cruel Tales, 1883). Little was, in fact, known for years about the Count beyond the remarks of his immediate circle – one of his devotees, Stephane Mallarmé, the symbolist poet, declaring wryly in 1889, 'His life? I search for anything that corresponds to that expression: truly and in the ordinary sense, did he live?'*

*The Count's life was, in fact, very much that of a Bohemian: living in a succession of squalid lodging houses; writing in cafés and beerhouses where he talked and drank endlessly; and provoking duels with friends while at the same time pursuing a trail of wealthy heiresses, one of whom he hoped to marry and thereby end his poverty. This, like his ambitions for his plays, steadfastly eluded him – but he is still remembered today for* Cruel Tales *and* L'Eve Future, *which is regarded as 'one of the pioneering works of Science Fiction' by Richard Holmes; and 'an important contribution to the Symbolist movement,' according to Peter Nicholls. Villier De L'Isle Adam dedicated the story of his artificial woman to 'aux reveurs, aux railleurs' – to dreamers and scoffers – and probably would not be surprised to learn that no popular edition of the novelette in English appeared for almost half a century.*

The Future Eve *describes how a remarkable scientist, Professor X (believed to be modelled on the American inventor, Thomas Alva Edison) creates an artificial woman for his friend and benefactor, a wealthy and handsome young lord who has despaired of ever finding a suitable wife. The description of the making of this perfect young female is one of the best accounts of its kind in all fiction; while the story itself is fascinating for its philosophical and ironic comments, as well as the accuracy of its scientific prophecies. The following translation of the story was specially made by Florence Crewe-Jones for* Argosy *magazine.*

# I.

Ten miles from the great seething city there stands a large house in the centre of a network of electric wires, surrounded by wide, solitary grounds. A beautiful green park and shady, gravelled paths lead from the massive iron entrance gates to the isolated mansion. This was the home of the world-famed inventor and master electrician, Professor X.

The scientist, a man of about forty years, had more the appearance of a distinguished artist than a plodding scientist. It almost appeared that the face of the artist had been transformed into that of the inventor. The two had the same congenital aptitude with different applications, like mysterious twins who had developed their individual genius.

About five o'clock in the afternoon of a late autumn day the professor retired into the seclusion of his private laboratory, a small grey stone building standing in the rear of his large abode. A few minutes before he had dismissed his five pupils, devoted followers, scholarly and clever, upon whose discretion he could count, and who were his chief help in his scientific work.

Alone, seated in his great leather chair, a cigar in his mouth, his huge frame enveloped in a loose-fitting cloak of

black silk, he seemed lost in thought. With eyes fixed and
absent, he gazed into space, but his mind was working
actively.

On his right was a high window opening toward the
flaming west – the glowing sunset casting on all objects a red-
gold mist. In the room were moulds of various shapes, instruments of precision, piles of blue prints, strange wheelwork,
electrical apparatus, telescopes, reflectors, enormous magnets,
bottles full of peculiar substances, slates covered with
quotations.

Outside, from beyond the horizon, the setting sun threw its
last rays on the curtain of maples and pines which overhung
the steep cliffs near by, and illumined the room at moments
with splashes of brilliance. The golden rays were reflected on
all sides from crystal facets.

The air was keen. There had been a heavy storm during the
day, and the rain had soaked the lawn and drenched the
blown flowers in their green boxes under the windows. Creeping plants and ferns hung somewhat awry from their iron
baskets, due to the violence of the storm. In the subtle urge of
this atmosphere, the strong and keenly vivacious thoughts of
the scientist became attenuated, influenced by the meditative
spirit – and the twilight.

Although the inventor's hair was greying on the temples,
his face was boyish, his smile was frank and winning. Around
his mouth were little lines which told of the struggles and
hardships which he had encountered in the early days of his
career. It had been bitter uphill work, but he now stood on
the pinnacle of fame; he was positive in his opinions, espous-
ing even the most specious of theories only when duly bul-
warked in facts. A humanitarian, he was prouder of his
labours than of his genius.

Like an ordinary mortal, he sometimes abandoned himself
to most fantastic and bizarre reflections. And now he com-
muned with his ego, humbly, sadly.

'How late I come in humanity's history,' he mused. 'I
should have been born centuries ago. Alas, I have come into
this world very late.'

He arose from his chair and began to pace up and down
the laboratory as he thought of the great happenings of olden
days which could have been turned to the world's advantage.

In the midst of his meditations he heard the voice of a young woman speaking softly near him.

'Master!' came the murmur.

And as yet there was not the shadow of a form to be seen.

The professor had started at the ghostly sound.

'You, Sowana?' he asked aloud.

'Yes,' said the voice. 'This evening I needed a good sound sleep, so I took the ring. I have it on my finger now. There is no occasion for you to raise your voice to its natural pitch. I am quite near you, and, for the last few minutes, I have been listening to you speaking your thoughts aloud like a child.'

'Yes, Sowana. But, bodily, where are you?'

'I am stretched out on the fur rugs in the vault behind the bush where the birds are.

'Hadaly seems to be asleep. I have given her some lozenges and some pure water, and – well, they have made her quite *animated*.'

The invisible being whom the inventor had called Sowana laughed as she uttered the last word. Her voice, discreet and low, came from the folds of a velvet curtain, carried from the distance by the electrical current in the sonorous, vibrating plaque in the portières; one of the professor's new condensators through which the pronunciation and the tone of the voice were distinctly transmitted.

'Tell me, Mrs Anderson,' he resumed, 'are you sure that you can hear what another person says to me in this room – now, in the state that you are in?'

'Yes, if you speak distinctly, very low, between your lips, the difference in the intonation between your voice and the replies enables me to understand the dialogue absolutely. You see, I am like one of the jinn of the ring in the "Thousand and One Nights."'

'Then, if that is the case, if I were to ask you to attach the telephone wire by which you speak to me, at this moment, to the person of our beautiful young friend, the miracle in which we are both interested would take place?'

'Without the slightest doubt. I am positive of it,' declared the voice. 'It is a prodigious thing, ingenious and ideal, but, worked out according to these calculations, it will come about naturally.

'Now,' continued the voice, 'for me to be able to hear you

in this marvellous state in which I am at this moment; penetrated as I am with the living fluid in the ring, there is no need for you to have a telephone; but in order that you or any of your visitors should hear me, the mouthpiece of the telephone which I am holding now must be in connection with something which will correspond with the metal sounding plate, no matter how hidden it may be. Is that right?'

'That is exactly right. And now, Mrs Anderson, tell me –'

'Oh!' cried the invisible speaker, with a plaintive catch in her voice. 'Call me by my dream name *here*. I am another being now, not myself. Here I forget my sorrows, and I do not suffer. The other name recalls the horrible things of earth to which I still belong.'

'I will do as you wish, Sowana,' said the professor gravely. 'Now I want you to tell me – you are quite sure of Hadaly, are you not?'

'Ah,' replied Sowana, 'you have given me so much information about your beautiful Hadaly, and I have studied her so thoroughly, that I can reply – well, as I would for my own reflection in a mirror! I would rather exist in that vibrating creature than in my own self.

'What a sublime creation you have, my dear master! She exists in the superior state in which I am at this moment. She is imbued with our two wills; they are united in her; it is a dualism – not conscious – a spirit. When she says to me, "I am a phantom," I feel embarrassed. You know, professor, I have a presentiment – I believe that Hadaly will be incarnated, actually turning to flesh and blood!'

'Ah' said the great electrician, with a little gasp, 'if such a thing could come to pass – but alas, I do not see how that could be!

'Go and sleep now, Sowana,' he continued in a low voice which was almost a whisper; 'but you know that there must be a third living being, in order that Hadaly should become incarnated. The masterpiece could not be produced without a third, and who is there on this earth that we would dare to consider worthy?'

'Yes, that is true,' murmured Sowana, 'but we shall see. I *believe* that it will take place.'

There was a slight pause, and then the voice, in the tone of one who is dropping off to sleep, murmured:

'This evening I shall be ready, master. A flash, and Hadaly will appear. All will be well.'

Then came a mysterious silence after this conversation which was as strange as it was incomprehensible. The engineer stood in the middle of his laboratory with his arms folded across his chest. There was not a sound to be heard now, only, every now and then, a slight inward catch of his breath, as he dwelt on the meaning of the last words Sowana had spoken.

'She thinks Hadaly will be incarnated,' he mused. 'Although I have long familiarized myself with this phenomenon, there are times when I become dizzy, and my brain whirls when I think about it. Sowana believes that Hadaly will be incarnated. How could that be? The speech – aye, that's it – the speech – although I have reproduced the voice in a phonograph, how can I make that voice human? Ah, but science –'

The professor's eyes glowed like fire as he mused thus. He laughed aloud. Why did this great inventor now appear to treat the tremendous problem so lightly, so gaily? He was probing the depths of a great puzzle, but it did not appear now to baffle him completely, for he continued to smile.

Geniuses are so made. It seems almost as if they endeavour to make their brain whirl with their own prodigious thoughts. They wander through the labyrinths of science, and then in a moment, in a flash, they perceive that for which they are seeking. No wonder they appear absent-minded, for their thoughts are far away from matters of the everyday world.

The shadows around him deepened, for night had fallen.

Still meditating, the wizard inventor switched on a soft, pale light which dimly illuminated the great laboratory. Then he lit a second cigar.

He was still in the midst of his reveries when the silence was broken by a clear ring. Going to a phonograph, the resonating plate of which was connected to a telephone, he set in action the metal disk, which relieved him of the necessity of replying in person, for the great man avoided speaking as much as possible to others.

'Well, what is it?' cried the instrument into the mouthpiece of the telephone with the voice of the inventor, slightly impatient. 'Is that you, Martin?'

'Yes, sir. I am in the city, at your office. I am sending you a telegram which came this moment.'

The voice came from the apparatus of a perfect condensator, the secret of which Professor X had not yet divulged to the world, a polyhedral ball suspended from an induction cord which hung from the ceiling.

The professor glanced toward the receiver of a Morse instrument which was standing on a base close to the telephone. It held a telegraph blank.

There was an almost imperceptible fluttering which slightly agitated the double corresponding wires, and the professor stretched out his hand for the paper, which was shot out of its metal socket. Holding the telegram to the light, he read:

Arrived this morning. Hope to see you this evening. Affectionate greetings.

EWALD

Professor X gave a start of pleased surprise when he read the signature.

'Lord Ewald!' he cried. 'So he has come back to this country. Well, I am delighted.'

He continued to smile, and, in his smile, one could not have recognized the sceptic of the few previous moments.

'Ah, my dear, young friend,' he murmured, 'I have not forgotten you. At the time when I most needed a friend, you came – you gave aid to a stranger. It is hardly likely that I could forget my benefactor.'

The professor walked hastily over to a drapery and touched an electric button. The sound of a bell rang out in the park near the great house. Then, almost at once, the gay, happy voice of a little girl was heard.

'What do you want, papa?' she asked.

He seized the mouthpiece of an instrument that was placed between the draperies.

'Lord Ewald will call here this evening,' he said; 'tell the servants that I am expecting him, and that he can enter. He must be made to feel quite at home.'

'Very well, father,' replied the same happy voice, which, owing to a placing of the condensators, appeared to come, this time, from a big reflector of magnesium.

'I will let you know if he will have supper with me,' continued the inventor. 'Do not wait up for me, and mind you be a good little girl. Good night, darling.'

A charming, childish trill of laughter seemed to come from the shadows on all sides; it was as if an invisible elf in the air had replied to the inventor. He smilingly dropped the receiver, and resumed his striding up and down the room.

As he passed near an ebony table upon which various instruments were strewn, he carelessly threw down the telegram he had just received. By chance, the slip of paper happened to fall upon an extraordinary object, a startling object, the presence of which was unexplainable in this room.

The circumstance of this casual encounter of the telegram and this object attracted the scientist's attention. He suddenly stopped his striding, considered the fact, gazed intently at the object and the telegram, and, then, became thoughtful indeed.

## II.

It was a human arm and hand lying on a violet silk cushion. The blood appeared to be congealed around the humeral section. Some crimson splashes on a piece of white linen, which had been thrown down beside it, attested to a recent operation.

It was the arm and hand of a young woman.

A bracelet of chased gold, in the form of a serpent, was clasped around the delicate wrist. On the ring finger of this left hand a sapphire ring flashed brilliantly. And the exquisitely slim fingers still retained their hold on a pearl-grey glove which, evidently, had been worn several times.

The flesh was so lifelike in tint, so soft and satiny, that the sight of it was poignantly cruel.

What could have necessitated this drastic, desperate operation? What unknown, terrible harm could have brought about this frightful amputation? And, above all, what had caused this arm to retain its healthy vitality? The blood still seemed to flow in this sweet and gracious member.

But a chilling, sinister thought would have leaped in the mind of a stranger at the sight of it.

The large country house which stood alone like a gloomy

castle among the trees was an isolated abode, and Professor X, as all the world knows, a daring experimenter. It was only to his closest friends that he showed any signs of affection.

His discoveries as an engineer; his inventions of various kinds, the least strange of which are alone known to the general public; conveyed the impression of an enigmatic positivism.

He had compounded an anaesthetic so powerful in its effect that, in speaking of it, his flatterers said: 'If only one had the time to absorb a few drops of it, one could face the most subtle tortures without being aware of it.' And, now, was he trying a new experiment, before which a doctor might well flinch? Was he striving to fathom the existence of another? Or was he trying to solve his own?

What scientist, worthy of the title, would not, if only for a moment, dwell without remorse, and even without shame, on thoughts of this order, when it was a question of a great discovery?

The press, all over the world, had given much space to describing the nature of some of his experiments. Many of the tests which he had desired to make had been forbidden by the government of his country.

A layman might feel, legitimately, a suspicion that the great scientist had been trying some experiment which had ended fatally, some venture of which this beautiful, radiant arm, rudely severed from its place, was the souvenir.

Meanwhile, as he stood beside the ebony table, Professor X looked meditatively at the telegram which had fallen between two fingers on the hand. He touched the hand, and, then, he started, as though a sudden idea had come to him.

'Ah,' he murmured, 'suppose it should happen, suppose – suppose that Lord Ewald – suppose it is he who will be the one to awaken Hadaly.'

The word 'awaken' was uttered by the scientist in a rather odd, hesitating manner. After a moment he shrugged his shoulders and smiled.

'Bah!' he muttered. 'I must not let my thoughts race ahead in this fashion.'

He resumed his striding up and down the laboratory. He evidently preferred to be in the dark, for he switched off the lights.

Suddenly the moon passed between the clouds, and sinisterly slipped a streak of light onto the black table.

The pale ray caressed the inanimate hand, lingered on the arm, and threw a gleam into the eyes of the gold snake and a flash on the ring.

Then all became dark again.

Professor X pondered, as he paced to and fro in the darkness, upon all the wonderful inventions he had given to the world.

He thought of all the great scientists of the past; those famous engineers who built the temple of Cheops, and all the other wonders which have been left to endure through the ages; of the architects who had left their imprint on colossal, marvellous ruins which were, even now, masterpieces unexcelled. Was it not strange that some of these deep minds had not conceived the things which he had perfected?

As his mind passed down through the cycles of history, he conjured up pictures of the marvellous men and women whose names have been inspiring to us. How beneficial it would be if we could have had preserved for us their actual photographs. What a loss that this art had been so long deferred!

What remarkable progress might have been made possible if we only had actual photographic records of the progressions of natural history. How quickly nature had effaced the traces of her first efforts. What precious visions had been lost!

And he felt a great feeling of thankfulness within him. A thankfulness that, because of his having existed, because of his inventions, mankind would henceforth reap great benefits.

And, more than that, if it were possible – if the great God, the Lord of Life, of whom so many painters and sculptors had tried to give us an image – if this Mighty, Most High would but permit a photograph of Himself to be taken, would but permit the sound of His voice to be recorded, from that day on there would not be left an atheist on the face of the earth.

As it was his habit, the professor had been softly speaking his thoughts aloud as he paced to and fro in the laboratory. He now stopped and looked absently through the openings of the long French windows, staring at the rays of light which the moon cast across the lawn.

'So be it,' he murmured, resuming his soliloquy. 'Let it be

defiance for defiance. Since life will not deign to answer our questions, but treats all our inquiries with a profound and problematic silence, we will defy life-creation. I have already taken the prodigious step, and now have something to show.'

At this moment, the professor caught sight of a human shadow through the glass doors.

'Who is there?' he cried, his fingers closing over the butt of a small revolver in his pocket.

'It is I – Ewald,' replied a voice.

'My dear Lord Ewald. Welcome!' cried the professor, as he came forward to greet his guest.

Three unusually large lamps, with globes of blue glass, simultaneously burst into flame like huge torches of electricity, lighting up the laboratory.

The visitor was about twenty-seven years old, tall, manly, and extremely handsome. He was immaculately groomed, and his magnificent physique suggested his apprenticeship on the crews of Oxford or Cambridge.

His face, calm in repose, was sympathetic in expression, but the look in his eyes was grave and somewhat haughty.

'My dear friend,' said the inventor. 'All that I now have I owe to you, for, without the help you once gave me, I could have accomplished nothing.'

'No, no, professor,' said Lord Ewald, smiling, 'it is I who am indebted to you. Through you I was able to be useful to the rest of humanity. The bit of money meant nothing to me.

'See how fortunate I consider myself in having met you! As soon as I put foot in your country I hasten to call to see you, for I want to renew the friendship that began with a chance meeting.'

Professor X now suddenly detected that there was something subtly wrong with his guest.

'I see you think that I am ill,' continued the younger man, with a slight understanding smile. 'I am not suffering physically, I assure you. But I have an everlasting grief and, I suppose, that would make one look a bit off in the course of time.'

Lord Ewald glanced about the perfectly appointed laboratory, paying particular attention to the lighting.

'I must congratulate you on all that you have accomplished in such a short time,' he continued. 'You are certainly the chosen one — a veritable genius. This marvellous lighting is your own invention, I presume?'

The professor nodded.

'It is like a brilliant afternoon in summer time,' said his lordship.

'Again thanks to you,' his host declared with a smile.

'It is all very wonderful; you are an electrical wizard.'

'Well,' said the professor modestly, 'I have discovered a few little things — and also some important things that I want to tell you about. I was just thinking, before you arrived, that my inventions should have been known centuries ago.'

Lord Ewald listened politely to his host, but it was evident that his secret sorrow obsessed him. The professor's keen eyes scanned the young man's face searchingly. There was a moment's silence.

'My dear Lord Ewald,' said the inventor, gravely, 'permit me to assume the rôle of an old friend and interest myself in you. I can see there is something very wrong. Your trouble?'

The younger man tapped the cold ashes from his cigar, and looked at his host, but said nothing.

'You know that I am a physician also,' continued the professor, 'and I am one of those who believe that there is a remedy for every illness.'

'Oh, the grief in question,' responded Lord Ewald, trying to speak lightly, 'is a very commonplace subject — an unfortunate love affair. It has hit me hard. You see, now, that my secret is very ordinary. I shall always suffer, but, please, do not let us speak about it.'

'*You* unfortunate in a love affair!' cried the doctor, in astonishment. 'You the victim! Why, that almost seems impossible. I —'

'Pardon me,' interrupted his young friend, 'I have only a short time to spend with you and I do not wish to abuse your time. I think the conversation will be far more interesting if we talk of you and what you have accomplished.'

'Why, my time is all yours!' cried the inventor. 'Those who admire and laud me to-day once ignored me and would have allowed me to die like a homeless dog — all but you.

'My affection for you is sincere, and it has rights which are just as sacred as yours, my dear young friend. Perhaps I may be able to cure you, or, at least —'

'No,' interrupted Lord Ewald, with a bitter smile, 'unfortunately, you can do nothing – science cannot go as far as
that.'

'One never knows,' declared the professor. 'Science has
astonished me. I am always working – always probing –
always discovering. Who can tell ?'

'I know that you could not understand the sentiment I have
in this affair,' the young man demurred. 'It would be strange
– inconceivable to you.'

'So much the better,' exclaimed the professor. 'It will be a
challenge to my imagination.'


## III.


Lord Ewald settled back in his chair, crossed his legs, and
after relighting his cigar, spoke as follows :

'For some years past I have been living at Athelwold Castle,
one of the oldest estates in England. It is surrounded by pines,
lakes, and rocky hills.

'Since my return from an expedition into Abyssinia, I have
led an isolated existence there. My parents are dead, and the
only other persons in the castle with me are a few servants
who have grown old in our service.

'One morning I had occasion to run up to London. There
were few vacant compartments in the train. At one of the
stations, a young lady, after looking hastily everywhere else
for a seat, jumped into the carriage where I was seated.

'I need not go into details. In a brief time we became the
best of friends. I fell in love with her.

'Alicia Cleary was only twenty years of age. She was a
Venus, exquisite in form and face. It was the beauty of the
Venus of Milo come to life – or the Venus Victrix.

'Her heavy brown hair, which hung about her like a mantle,
had the radiance of a summer night. Her face was an exquisite
oval. Her hands were not quite as aristocratic as the rest of
her form, but her feet had the same eloquence as the Greek
statues.

'Her eyes were beautiful, her brows perfectly shaped. The
sound of her low voice was so thrilling, the notes of her songs

so stirring, that I was overcome with a strange emotion. My admiration, as you shall see, was of an unknown order.

'In London, at the different Court functions, I had met the most beautiful girls in England, but I scarcely noticed them. I had thoughts of Alicia only.

'From the first days, however, I struggled to combat the peculiar evidences which appeared in her words and actions. I told myself that it was folly to admit their significance, and I sought in every way to put them from my thoughts.

'Yet, I could not forget that in all living beings there is a depth, which gives to their ideas, even the most vague, and to all their impressions, those modifications which are shown externally. This depth gives them their aspect, colour and character; it is in fact the inflection of their true selves. Let us call this substrata the soul, if you wish.

'And, between the body and soul of Alicia Cleary, there was a disproportion which disconcerted me.'

When Lord Ewald made this statement, the professor barely hid a start of surprise. His face paled, but he did not voice his agitation.

'It seemed,' continued Lord Ewald, 'that her inner self was in absolute contradiction to her beautiful form. Her beauty was quite foreign to her words, her conversation appeared out of place in such a voice.

'It seemed that her peculiar personality was not only deprived of what is called by philosophers the "plastic mediator," but actually imprisoned, by a sort of occult punishment, in her body. It is a perpetual contradiction of her ideal beauty.

'Yes, sometimes, I seriously think that this woman has strayed by mistake into the form of the goddess – that this body does not belong to her!'

'An extreme supposition,' murmured the scientist, 'but it is a thought not at all rare. Similar feelings are often evoked in the hearts of those who are in love for the first time. It is, however, probable that Alicia's sublime beauty was not in keeping with the smallness of her soul. You will pardon me, but has this beautiful creature been faithful to you?'

'I would to heaven that she had!' exclaimed Lord Ewald, bitterly. 'No; but I believe that I have the only love of which she is capable.'

'Ah,' said the scientist soberly, 'please go on.'

'I learned that she came from a good family and that her betrothed had forsaken her to marry a girl with a fortune. Alicia left home, intending to lead a Bohemian life as a singer. However, she later gave up this idea.

'Her voice, appearance, and dramatic talent would have provided her with an income sufficient for her needs. But she was glad to have met me just when she was setting forth into the world. She could not be my wife, she said, but she was eager to accept the love and protection which I pressed upon her.'

'Well, at least, that was an honest confession,' said the professor.

Lord Ewald appeared to be approaching a painful part of his story. However, he continued calmly:

'Yes, but that is my version that you have just heard, not hers. She spoke in other words, in another style. I suppose I shall have to speak more clearly so that you may understand her character better.

'What she really told me was that her betrothed was a fickle lover. His status was that of a small manufacturer, and she had been hopeful of marrying him solely because he had a certain amount of money.

'She certainly did not love him, yet she pretended that hers was a *grande passion*. Her plans to ensnare him with her blandishments went astray, however, so she fled from the gossip of the town and hurried to London intending to go on the stage, but, having met me, she changed her mind.

'She told me quite frankly that she was well pleased to have met me. I could see that the fact that I had a title delighted her immensely. Now, after this version, what do you think of her?'

'Well,' said the professor, with a cynical smile, 'your version and hers are different, in truth.'

There was a moment of silence.

'My thoughts are dwelling on the fundamental senses,' resumed Lord Ewald. 'How can this young creature, so wonderfully beautiful, be utterly unappreciative of herself. How can she ignore the divinity – the exquisite perfection – which her body represents?

'How can she fail to have lofty aspirations – high ideals?

To her these wondrous things do not exist; she only forces herself, in a sort of shamefaced manner, to assume them.

'Her golden voice is only an empty instrument to her; she considers it merely as a means of livelihood to make use of when all other means have failed. The happiness that she could give to others with it means nothing to her.

'She so lacks a sense of shame that she delights in relating her unfortunate love affair to me. If she had a remnant of tact it should warn her that she is destroying all the sympathy and admiration that I could have for her.

'This beauty that should be inspiring is so steeped in moral blindness that I am forced to renounce it. I cannot love a woman who has no soul.'

Lord Ewald paused abruptly.

The professor, however, blithely nodded his head as a sign for him to continue. The analysis of Miss Cleary's character apparently gave the listener much pleasure.

'When Alicia is not speaking,' the young nobleman went on, 'and her face is not wearing the expression which her empty, unprincipled remarks call forth, she is divine. Her wondrous beauty then gives the lie to all the base things that she has voiced.

'With a person who is very beautiful, but of ordinary perfection, I should not have this unexplainable sensation which Miss Cleary causes me. I would have known from the beginning – the quality of the lines, the texture of the skin, the coarseness of the hair, a movement, any of these tiny signs would have warned me of the hidden nature – and I should have recognized her identity with *herself*.

'But Alicia's beauty is the Irreproachable, defying the most minute analysis. Exteriorly, from head to feet, she is a veritable Venus Anadyomene; inside, the personality, the *soul*, is entirely foreign to the form.

'Imagine a *commonplace* goddess! I have come to the conclusion that all physiological laws were overthrown in this living, hybrid phenomenon.'

'My dear friend, you are certainly a poet,' declared the professor. 'Disillusionment must have been indeed severe, since it forced you into the heights of poesy to describe the commonplace truth. Your words are as fantastic as the story of a grand opera.'

'Yes, my subtle confessor,' the young man agreed bitterly, 'I know – I am a dreamer, but I have been well punished for my dreams.'

'But,' asked the professor, 'how is it that you are still in love with her, if you are able to analyse her character so correctly?'

'The awakening from a dream does not always bring forgetfulness,' replied Lord Ewald, sadly. 'Man is enchained with his own imagination. That is how it is in my case. I cannot break the tie now that I have awakened. My Delilah has cut my hair during my sleep.

'She does not know what attacks of rage and despair I have to control on her account. There are moments when I feel that I would like to kill her and then destroy myself.

'A mirage has enslaved me to this marvellous, living form with a dead soul. Alicia, to-day, represents for me simply the habit of a presence. I swear that it would be impossible for me to desire her.'

The professor started as if to speak, but hesitated as the disconsolate lover added:

'Yes, we exist together, but we are separated forever.'

Silence fell between the two men.

'Now, just a few questions,' said the professor finally. 'Is Miss Cleary a stupid person?'

'Certainly not,' declared Lord Ewald, smiling slightly. 'There is no trace of that stupidity which is almost saintly. She is not stupid, she is just silly.'

'I understand,' said the scientist. 'A little foolish, insipid. But she has talent, has she not?'

'Great heavens! I should say so!' exclaimed Lord Ewald. 'She is a virtuoso – the direct and mortal enemy of genius and art, in consequence. Art has no bearing, you know, with the virtuoso, neither is genius related to talent.

'Her voice is wonderful, but she will never sing unless I beg her to do so. It bores her to sing, for she considers it only as a part of a profession – one might say, as *work*, for which she does not consider that she was made.'

'Well, the fact is,' said the professor, 'one can't make a horse run fast merely by the fact that it has been entered in a race. Only, it is positively remarkable to me that, in spite of the depth of this analysis of character, you do not perceive that this lady would be the feminine ideal for three-fourths of humanity.'

'But it is killing me,' said Lord Ewald.

Then, giving way to a boyish impulse, which until then he had controlled, he cried:

'Oh, who could put a Soul into that body!'

## IV.

At Lord Ewald's impulsive words a strange gleam, the light of genius, leaped into the professor's grey eyes. He drew in his breath with a slight hissing sound which betrayed the deep emotion he was feeling. But the younger man was too absorbed in his thoughts to heed these signs.

'Yes,' continued Lord Ewald, almost reminiscently, 'I thought I could change her. I tried to give her healthy diversion; I treated her as a sick person.

'I hoped that travelling would educate and improve her mind. But, in Italy, in France, in Spain, it was just the same. She looked jealously at the masterpieces, which she thought deprived her, for the moment, of complete attention, without understanding that she, herself, was a part of the beauty of those masterpieces, without knowing that they were but mirrors, reflecting her own reflection, that I was showing her.

'In Switzerland, we watched the sun rising over the mountains, but, instead of being inspired by the sight, she cried out, with a smile that was as radiant as the sunshine itself: "Oh, I hate these mountains; they just seem to want to crush me."

'In Florence, while we were standing before the wonders of the century of Leon X, she yawned slowly, and said: "Quite interesting, isn't it?"

'Once we were at a concert, listening to Wagner. She wanted to leave before it was half over, exclaiming petulantly: "Oh, I can't get the tune of this music. It is just a lot of bangs, just noise — it's just crazy!" If her sublime face could have portrayed the expression of her soul, she would have worn a distorted grimace.

'In Paris, I had the keenest desire to show this living woman the great statue of Venus — her very image. I wanted to see what she would say in the presence of her counterpart.

I said to her, half jokingly: "Alicia, I am going to take you to the Louvre galleries, and I think that you will see something there that will surprise you."

'We walked through the halls, and, then, quite suddenly, I led her into the presence of the eternal statue.

'This time she raised her veil and gazed at the marble figure with a degree of astonishment, as she cried out naïvely: "Why, that's me!"

'I said nothing. I waited. After a few moments' stupefied pause, she looked at me and said: "Yes, that's me, except that I have not lost my arms, and I am much more aristocratic-looking." Then she shivered a little; she had withdrawn her hand from my arm and was holding the balustrade.

'She now took my arm again, and said, in a low tone: "Oh, these statues, these stones here make me feel so cold. Come on, let's leave!"

'Once outside the historical building, I glanced at her, for she had been silent for some minutes and I had a sort of hope that she had been stirred. She had been stirred, indeed, but – how? After thinking for some time, she came quite close to me and said: "If they make so much fuss over that statue, I ought to be a tremendous success."

'I confess that her words gave me a queer feeling. Her foolishness soared as high as the heavens; it seemed like a damnation. I simply said: "I hope so!"

'I escorted her to her hotel. This duty accomplished, I returned to the museum and again entered the sacred halls. I looked at the goddess, and, then, for the first time in my life, I felt my heart ready to burst with one of those mysterious dry sobs that stifle a human being.

'Picture, then, this woman, an animated duality which repelled and attracted me. My ardent love for her beautiful voice and her exterior charms is now entirely platonic.

'Her moral being has frozen the fires of my senses forever; they have become purely contemplative. I am only attached to her by a sorrowful admiration. I would like to see her dead, if Death would not efface those human features.

'There is nothing that can make Alicia Cleary worthy of a great love. My only wish for her now is to have her go on the stage to the career she desires, and then there will be nothing more in life for me.

'There you have the story. You can see there is no remedy. I must be going. This is good-by. I shall never return.'

'Wait a moment, my dear young friend,' said the professor sharply. 'I can see that you are contemplating a serious step on account of a woman. Bah! It is nonsense.'

'I loved Alicia,' Lord Ewald declared quietly as he arose; 'she represented to me everything that was divine and beautiful.'

The professor saw that the manly youth standing before him had the thought of suicide well defined in his mind.

'Lord Ewald,' he said, sternly, 'you are only the victim of a youthful passion which you have idealized. Time will cure you. Go your way. Forget her.'

'Do you think me so inconsistent?' the young man demanded. 'No, my nature is such that, while I am perfectly aware of the absurdity of this "passion," I do not suffer less.'

'Lord Ewald,' the professor remarked finally, 'you amaze me. You are one of England's richest and most distinguished peers. In your country there are many beautiful, eligible young women.

'You are a brilliant match, and you can certainly find some innocent, ideal girl whose love could only be given once in a lifetime. You could have a wonderful, happy future with such a wife.

'But here you are, shorn of your strength before this coquette. It is absurd!'

'Come, my friend, don't be so hard on me,' Lord Ewald pleaded. 'I have taken myself to task very severely, but it is no use.'

'Yes,' said the elder man, 'but I am now speaking for the young girl who will be your salvation. You have a great deal to accomplish in this world, and she will be at your side to help and comfort you.'

The young nobleman shook his head sadly.

'Yes,' the professor continued as though to himself, 'it is serious, very serious – very grave indeed.'

Then, after a longer pause, he announced:

'Lord Ewald, I am, perhaps, the only physician under heaven who can help you! Now, I want you, for the last time, to give me a reply in a definite fashion:

'Can you not consider this affair merely as a gallant intrigue, as a romantic adventure? Any other man but you would. Can't you consider it as a worldly fancy, intense, if you wish, but of no vital importance?'

'It is impossible,' declared the young man. 'Miss Cleary might to-morrow be the love of but a day to many others – it is quite possible. But I can never change.

'I come of a race that loves only once, and, when we fail, we disappear quietly. The shadings and concessions we leave to others. There is no other form of beauty but hers in this life for me.'

'But, despising her as you do, why do you persist in exalting this point of beauty, if you say that your desires have become forever contemplative and frozen?'

'That is very true. I have no desire for her. But she has become the radiant obsession of my mind.'

'Do you absolutely refuse to take up your social life again?' inquired the professor.

'Absolutely,' replied Lord Ewald, as correct and calm as always, he took up his hat.

His host arose also.

'My dear boy,' he said, 'do you suppose for an instant that I am going to sit calmly by and let you walk out of here to blow out your brains, without making an effort to save you? You saved my life. I owe mine and all that has come into it to what you have done for me. Do you think that I have been questioning you without a motive?

'My dear fellow, you are one of those sick persons who can only be treated with poison, so I have determined, since all other remonstrances are useless, to doctor you thus, if you will permit me. It will be in a terrible way, as your case is an exceptional one. The remedy consists of enabling you to realize your dreams.

'Great heavens! It seems to me now that, unconsciously, I have expected you this evening. Now, I see it. Yes, your dreams shall be realized!

'There are wounds that cannot be cured except by probing deeper into them. I am going to accomplish your dreams in their entirety. When you spoke of Alicia Cleary, did you not utter these words:

'"*Who could put a soul into that body!*"'

'Yes,' murmured the young nobleman.

'I can!' exclaimed the professor. 'I shall put a wonderful soul into that beautiful body!'

## V.

'My lord,' said Professor X, speaking with the solemnity of a great physician, 'do not forget that in carrying out your singular wish I agree to do so only out of necessity.'

The strange tone and the look which accompanied it made Lord Ewald start. A slight tremor of premonition passed over him. He glanced keenly at his host, wondering if he was in possession of his faculties, for the words that he had just uttered passed all intelligence.

But, in spite of this feeling, an irresistible magnetism had come from the professor's last words. The young Englishman had a presentiment of an imminent miracle.

Taking his gaze from the inventor's face, his glance travelled over the various objects strewn about. Under the brilliant light given off by the lamps these marvels of scientific discovery assumed disturbing configurations. The laboratory took on the appearance of a magic grotto.

Lord Ewald was aware that most of his host's discoveries were still unknown to the world. The professor's real character, constantly paradoxical to his reputation, surrounded him, in Lord Ewald's eyes, with an intellectual halo, as he stood in the centre of the wonders to which he belonged. To the young guest his host was like the inhabitant of a superelectrical, a supernatural, realm.

After a few moments he felt himself won over by a blending of sentiments, curiosity and amazement, and with these there was a new feeling, a new *hope*. The vitality of his being was augmented.

'You seem amazed,' the professor remarked. 'It is merely a matter of transsubstantiation. I have already made some tests, and I am well satisfied with my experiments so far.'

He paused a moment, and then demanded brusquely:

'Do you accept the proposition?'

'Are you speaking seriously?' Lord Ewald countered.

'Certainly!'

'Then I'll give you *carte blanche*,' said Lord Ewald, with a sad little smile, which was, however, already a trifle worldly.

'Very well,' said the professor, glancing at the electric clock which hung over the door, 'I will commence, then, for time is precious, and I need three weeks.

'It is now eight thirty-five. Twenty-one days from now, at this same hour, Alicia Cleary will stand before you, not only transformed, not merely a delightful companion, with a mind of the highest intellectual type, but reclothed in a phase of immortality.

'In fact, this dazzling creature will no longer be a woman, but an angel – not only a woman, but the beloved – not the cold Reality, but the Ideal.'

'What an extraordinary statement!' his lordship exclaimed.

'Oh, I will show you how it will be brought about,' said the professor. 'The result will be so marvellous in itself that the apparent disillusions of its scientific analysis will fade away before the sudden and profound splendour of the achievement.

'So, if only to reassure you that I am absolutely sane, and that I am in full possession of my faculties, for I can see from your look that you have your doubts upon this matter, I will take you into my secret this very evening.

'But we must get back to work right now. Where is Miss Cleary now?'

'At the opera.'

'What is the number of her box?'

'Number seven.'

'Did you tell her that you were coming down here to see me alone this evening?'

'No. It would have been of such small interest to her that I did not think it necessary.'

'Has she ever heard of my name?'

'Perhaps, but she would have forgotten it.'

'So much the better – that is important.'

While he was speaking the professor walked over to the phonograph, which was connected to the telephone. Glancing for a moment at the record, he adjusted the needle to a certain spot and started the instrument.

'Are you there, Martin?' the instrument cried out with the professor's voice.

There was no reply.

'I bet the rogue has thrown himself down on my lounge and gone to sleep,' remarked the scientist, smilingly.

Shutting off the machine, he took up the receiver of a perfected microphone, adjusted it to the ear, and observed:

'Ah, it is just as I thought. He has had his nightcap and has gone to sleep. He is snoring loudly enough.'

'Where is this person to whom you wish to speak?' inquired Lord Ewald.

'He is in my office in the city – about twenty-five miles from here.'

'And you can hear a person snoring at that distance?'

'If he snored like this fellow,' said the professor, laughing, 'I could hear him at the North Pole. Strange, isn't it? If you were to tell a fairy story like that to a child, it would say: "That is impossible," and yet it is possible.

'In the near future, no one will be astonished to hear voices and sound from a great distance. I predict this. Now, I am going to give this fellow something that will tickle him.'

As he spoke, he applied the hooded mouthpiece of another piece of apparatus to the transmitter of the telephone.

'Let us hope that this won't scare the horses on the street,' he muttered as he set it in motion.

'Are you there, Martin?' the instrument shouted.

A few seconds later there was heard the deep voice which had spoken to the professor some time before, but which now was startled and evidently coming from a man who had been suddenly awakened from a sound sleep. The tones seemed to come from out of the hat which Lord Ewald held in his hand, which had by chance come in contact with a condensator that was suspended near by.

'What is wrong?' cried the voice. 'Is there a fire?'

'There!' exclaimed the professor. 'I got him to his feet quick enough.'

Then, going over to the telephone into which he had spoken before, he said:

'Don't be alarmed, Martin: just a false alarm to awaken you. The warning is only set at eighteen degrees. I am sending you a message which I want you to get off at once by hand.'

'Very well, sir. I am ready.'

The professor tapped off a message in code on the dial plate of a Morse instrument.

'Have you read it?' he asked.

'Yes, sir,' the voice answered. 'I'll take it myself.'

Whether by accident or by a jocular design on the part of the inventor, who had placed his hand on the central control of the laboratory, the voice appeared to rebound from corner to corner on all sides of the immense room. It appeared as if a dozen individuals, faithful echoes of one another, were all speaking at the same time.

'And, Martin,' added the professor, 'let me have the reply quickly.

'That is settled,' he said, turning round to face Lord Ewald. 'All goes well.'

Then his whole manner changed. He looked at the young man fixedly, and in a tone that was impressive, he declared:

'My lord, I now have to inform you that we are going to leave the domains of normal life. Together we are to enter a world of phenomena which are as unusual as they are impressive.

'I will endeavour to present you with a key to the riddle. At first we are going to verify – nothing more. You are going to be shown a being, a vision of indefinite mentality. Although her aspect will be familiar, the sight of this being will be enough to give you a great shock.

'You will run no physical risks. However, I feel that it is my duty to warn you that you will need all your coolness, and perhaps much courage, to support you at the first sight of the marvel.'

Lord Ewald regarded the scientist closely, hesitatingly. Then, after a brief pause, he replied:

'Thanks for your warning. I hope that I shall be able to control myself. Let us proceed.'

The professor now became very energetic. Going over to the big French windows, he closed them, drawing together the inside shutters and fastening them securely. He then crossed hurriedly to the door leading from the laboratory and pushed the bolt.

This done, he closed the switch of a danger signal which flashed an intense red light above the laboratory, giving warning to those at a distance that a dangerous experiment was being conducted, and that any one who came near the laboratory was doing so at the risk of his life.

Raising a lever, he disconnected all of the micro-telephonic inductors, with the exception of the call bell, which connected the laboratory with the city office.

'Now,' said the scientist, 'we are almost cut off from the world of the living.'

Seating himself at his table full of telegraphic apparatus, he began to arrange several wires with his left hand while with his right he seemed to be tracing some strange characters, his lips moving constantly, as if he were murmuring some weird incantation.

'Haven't you a picture of Miss Cleary on you?' he asked, continuing to write.

'Oh, yes,' replied Lord Ewald. 'I forgot. I might have shown it to you.'

Taking a small picture from his pocket, he handed it to the professor, saying:

'Here she is – in all her statuesque beauty. Look and see for yourself that I have not exaggerated.'

The professor took the photograph and looked at it.

'She is marvellous!' he exclaimed. 'Here certainly is the famous Venus of the sculptor. The resemblance is amazing. You are quite right, she is the Venus de Milo come to life.'

He turned and touched the regulator of a battery near at hand. Immediately there was a flash, as a flaming electrical arc jumped across the huge points of a double wire of platinum. With a sizzling crackle it flickered for several seconds, as though it were searching on all sides for a means of escape.

A blue wire, one end of which was grounded, was near by. The questing arc seized upon it and disappeared.

An instant later a sombre, rumbling noise was heard underneath the feet of the two men. It rolled onward, as though it were coming from the bowels of the earth, or indeed from the profound depths of an abyss. One might have thought that ghostly phantoms were shattering a glacial sepulchre and dragging its long-lost occupant back to the surface of the earth.

The scientist, still holding in his hand the photograph, had his eyes fixed on a point in the wall at the other end of the laboratory. His attitude was tense.

The noise, which had continued to ascend in a crescendo, suddenly ceased.

The hand of the master engineer pressed an ebony lever on the table.

'*Hadaly*!' he called, as if he were summoning some one to appear from the spirit world.

## VI.

As the professor called out this mysterious name, a section of the wall at the extreme south of the laboratory turned on its hinges, silently bringing to view a narrow retreat fashioned between the slabs of stone. All the light from the electrical globes was suddenly focused on this spot.

The concave and semicircular walls were covered with rich draperies of black velvet, which fell luxuriously from an arch of jade to the white marble floor. The heavy folds were hooked back and fastened by retainers of gold, caught here and there through the rich material.

On a dais in the centre of this niche was standing a being whose aspect bore the impression of the Unknown.

The vision appeared to have a face of shadows, phantom-like. In the centre of the forehead a network of pearls caught together and held in place folds of black gauze which completely hid the rest of the head. A suit of armour, fashioned of leaves of burned silver, which were moulded with a myriad of perfect shadings, covered her girlish form.

The front of the black veil crossed over under the round metal collar, and was then thrown over the shoulders and knotted at the back of the head. The flimsy lengths of this veil fell to the waist of the apparition like a cloud of hair and then blended to the floor with the dark shadows of her presence.

A draping of black batiste was drawn around the hips and tied before her. The long black fringes of the drapery which fell behind her appeared to be sewn with sparkling brilliants. Between the folds of her belt could be seen the gleam of a naked weapon of oblique form.

The phantom leaned her right hand on the hilt of this blade while in her left hand, which hung down beside her, she held an everlasting flower of gold. On every finger of her hands sparkled rings set with precious stones, and these circlets in turn were fastened on the delicate gauntlet on her hand.

The mysterious being, after standing motionless for a few moments, descended the one step from the dais, and came forward, towards the two men.

Although her footsteps appeared soft, they resounded throughout the laboratory as she advanced, the powerful lights playing on her gleaming armour.

The vision advanced until it was within three steps of the professor and his guest. Then, in a voice that was exquisitely grave, the apparition said:

'My dear master, I am here.'

Lord Ewald gazed in nervous wonderment at this extraordinary sight.

'The hour has come for you to live, Hadaly,' said the great electrician.

'Ah, master, I do not wish to live,' murmured the soft voice through the hanging veil.

'But this young man has come here to accept life for you,' the inventor explained as he threw into a jade vase the photograph of Alicia Cleary which he had been holding in his hand.

'Then,' said the vision resignedly, after a moment's pause, and with a slight inclination of her head towards Lord Ewald, 'let it be according to his wish.'

When the vision uttered these words the inventor, by regulating the claws of a circuit breaker, caused a sponge of magnesium at the other end of the laboratory to burst into a brilliant flame.

A powerful, pencil-like ray of dazzling light shot forth, directed by a reflector, and this ray was in turn reflected onto an object glass adjusted opposite the photograph of Alicia Cleary. Another reflector, placed above the photograph, multiplied the refraction of the penetrating rays upon it.

Almost instantaneously a square of glass, placed in the centre of the object glass, became tinted. Then the square of glass appeared to lift itself from out of its groove in the object glass and to enter into a metallic cell which had two circular openings.

The incandescent rays entered through one of these openings, passing through the tinted glass in the centre, and came forth on the opposite side, which surrounded the wide cone of a projector.

Immediately, in a large frame on a sheet of white silk stretched on the wall, there appeared, life-size, the luminous and transparent image of a young woman – the blood and flesh and bone statue of the Venus de Milo in truth, if such one ever breathed in this world of illusions.

'I am dreaming!' exclaimed Lord Ewald in bewilderment.

'Hadaly,' said the scientist, 'that is the form in which you will be incarnated!'

The vision took a step toward the radiant image, which she appeared to contemplate for a moment from behind the darkness of her veil. Then she murmured in a soft voice, as if to herself:

'Oh, so beautiful – and to force me to live!'

And bowing her head on her chest with a deep sigh, she whispered:

'So be it!'

The magnesium went out. The vision in the frame disappeared.

Before the spell of emotion which this picture caused had been dispelled, the professor raised his hands to the height of the vision's forehead. She trembled a little, then, without a word, she offered the symbolic golden flower to Lord Ewald, who could not repress a faint chill when he accepted it.

Turning to one side, the phantom began the same somnam-bulistic walk back to the mysterious regions whence she had come. When she reached the threshold she turned, and, raising her two hands towards the black veil over her face, she threw, with a charming gesture, a kiss to the professor and his guest.

Then she entered the opening, lifted a fold of one of the black draperies, and disappeared from view.

The wall closed again. There was the same sombre, rum-bling noise that was heard before, but this time it seemed to be descending and dying away into the bowels of the earth. It stopped as suddenly as it had begun. The two men were again alone under the bright lights of the laboratory.

'Who is this strange being?' Lord Ewald demanded, half fearfully, placing in his lapel the emblematic flower that Hadaly had given to him.

The professor fixed his gaze on Lord Ewald's face as he replied calmly:

'It is not a living being!'

At these words the younger man also stared in turn at the scientist, as if demanding whether he had heard rightly.

'Yes,' the professor continued, replying to the unspoken question in the young man's eyes, 'I affirm that this form which walks, speaks, and obeys, is not a person or a being in the ordinary sense of the word.'

Then, as Lord Ewald still looked at him in silence, he went on:

'At present it is not an entity; it is no one at all! Hadaly, externally, is nothing but an electro-magnetic thing – a being of limbo – a possibility.

'Presently, if you wish, I will unveil to you the secret of her magic nature. But here is something that will give you enlightenment.'


## VII.

He guided the young man through the maze of miscellaneous instruments installed about the room before they stood before the ebony table.

'What impression do you get at sight of that?' he asked, pointing to the white-skinned feminine hand and arm lying on the violet silk cushion.

Lord Ewald gazed with a still greater thrill of astonishment at the unexpected human relic on which the light from the marvellous lamps now focused.

'What is it?' he asked.

'Look at it well,' the professor urged, evasively. 'Examine it.'

The young man leaned over. He lifted up the hand, then he drew back abruptly and demanded:

'What can it mean – a human hand – and it is still warm?'

'Don't you find anything extraordinary in the arm?' the professor inquired.

Lord Ewald resumed his examination for a moment, and exclaimed:

'Good heavens, this is as great a marvel as the phantom. If

it had not been for the excision here, I could not have seen that it was a masterpiece of scientific skill.'

The young Englishman appeared to be fascinated by the object. He took up the arm and began comparing his own hand with the feminine fingers.

'The weight – the form – the colour, even,' he murmured, as if in a stupor. 'Do you mean to tell me that this is not human flesh that I am touching at this moment? Upon my word, my own hand trembles at the very touch of it.'

'That is better than human flesh,' said the scientist simply. 'Human flesh fades and grows old. Here is a composition of delicate substances compounded by chemistry in such a way as might well confuse nature herself.

'But let us say this is a copy of nature – to use this word empirically – which will always appear living and young. A thunderbolt could destroy it, but it will never age. It is artificial flesh, and I can explain how it is produced. You have only to read Berthelot.'

The younger man could only murmur in stupefaction:

'Eh? What did you say?'

'I say that it is artificial flesh,' declared the professor. 'I believe that I am the only one who can fabricate it to such perfection.'

Lord Ewald, who was now in such a state of confusion that he could not readily express his thoughts, again turned to examine the artificial arm.

'But, professor,' he said, 'this pearly fluid – this carnal splendour and the intense life in it – how was it possible to produce such an amazing illusion?'

'Oh, that part of the experiment is a mere nothing. It is done simply by the aid of the sun,' was the smiling response.

'In a certain sense, we can catch the secret of the sun's vibrations, and once the shade of the dermal whiteness is determined I reproduce it by a setting of the object plates.

'Here is how I do that,' he continued. 'Albumin is supple, but it solidifies; the elasticity in this example is due to hydraulic pressure. This material is then made sensitive by a very subtle photochromatic action. Of course, I had a splendid model.

'As for the rest, it is simple; the humerus constructed of ivory contains a galvanic marrow in constant communication with a network of induction wires which are entwined in the same way as nerves and veins, and which are held between the releases of a perpetual calorific unit that gives to it this impression of warmth and malleability.

'If you wish to know where the elements of this network are disposed, how they feed themselves, so to speak, and in what manner the static fluid transforms its action into almost animal heat, I can give you the entire anatomy of it. It is nothing more than a matter of handwork.

'What you see here is an Andraiad of my making, moulded for the first time by the amazing vital agent we call electricity. This gives to my creation the blending, the softness, and the illusion of life.'

'An Andraiad?'

'Yes,' said the professor, 'a human-imitation, if you prefer that phrase. In the future we will have to be careful that the facsimile does not, in the manufacture, surpass the model physically. That is a danger to be avoided.

'I suppose, my dear fellow, that you know the kind of mechanism that has heretofore been employed in the attempt to forge a human image.'

Lord Ewald nodded.

'But,' the professor remarked, with a scornful laugh, 'they tried to work without the proper means of execution – and what was the result? They simply produced monsters – scarecrows for birds.

'These anatomies were only fit for a place in the most hideous waxwork shows, wretched objects that exude a strong odour of wood, rancid oil, and gutta percha. Such false sycophants, instead of giving man a knowledge of his power, could only make him bow his head before the god Chaos.

'You know their jerky and irregular movements, their absurdity of line and colour, the frightful wigs they wore, the noise of their mechanism, their stiffness, and the sensation of emptiness which they created. They were all just horrible masks, all caricatures of our race. Such were the first models of Andraiads.'

The face of the inventor grew severe, his voice became didactic and hard.

'But, to-day,' he went on, 'that time has passed. Scientific discoveries have multiplied. Metaphysical conceptions are refined. Instruments of counterdraw are so accurate, so precise, and so dependable that man is now able to attempt far greater things than formerly.

'We now are able to realize the powerful phantoms of mixed-presences of which our predecessors could never have even conceived an idea. They would have ridiculed the idea and declared it impossible.

'Just now, for instance, when you saw Hadaly, it would have been almost impossible for you to have smiled at her aspect. But, I assure you, that so far she is only a rough diamond. She is only the skeleton of a shadow waiting for the shadow to appear.

'Is it not true that you received the same sensation in touching the limb of that Andraiad that you would have received in touching the limb of a human being?'

Lord Ewald nodded.

'Well, now,' said the professor, 'just make another test. Will you clasp that hand? Perhaps it will return the pressure!'

Lord Ewald took the slim fingers in his and pressed them slightly.

He gasped in amazement. The hand responded to his pressure in an affable manner, so soft and sweet, yet seemingly so far off that he thought it must be a part of an invisible body. With an uncanny feeling he let the shadowy object drop hastily.

'Ghostly!' he exclaimed.

The inventor smiled at the young man's amazement.

'That is nothing,' he said, 'in comparison to what can be done. Oh, this great work – this creation – if you only knew – if you –'

The professor stopped short, as if a sudden, new idea had come to him – an idea so terrible that it cut short his speech.

'Truly,' cried Lord Ewald, with a forced laugh, 'I feel as though I were in the presence of some mighty wizard of the middle ages. What are you thinking of now, professor?'

The great inventor remained silent for a few moments, immersed in deep thought. Then he sat down and looked with a new anxiety at the young man who stood before him.

'My lord,' he said finally, 'I have just perceived that, with a young man of your imagination, an experiment might lead to fatal results! I am dubious.

'Hearken! When one stands on the threshold of a black-smith's shop he sees a man working in the smoke, a fire, and implements. The anvil rings out as the smith fashions bars, blades, tools.

'But the man who is making these things is entirely ignorant of the unexpected usage to which his products will be put. He can only call them by their common names. And that is true with all of us.

'No blacksmith can estimate correctly the true nature of the object he is forging, for the simple reason that all knives may become daggers and do murder. It is the usage that one makes of a thing which re-baptizes and transforms it.

'Our uncertainty of the ultimate use of an object alone makes us irresponsible. Therefore, if one would dare to accomplish anything, he must know how to properly safeguard it.

'The mechanic who melts lead into the form of a bullet says unconsciously, "This is thrown to chance, perhaps it is lost," and he finishes this messenger of death, the soul of which is veiled from his eyes.

'But if the gaping, mortal wound that his bullet is destined to make could, by chance, be made to pass before his eyes, the mould for the bullet would drop from his hands, if he were an honest man. No doubt he would refuse bread for his children's meal, if that bread could only be bought at the price of the achievement of his task. He would hesitate, for he would feel himself to be, of a certainty, an accomplice of a future homicide –'

'Yes, that is true,' Lord Ewald interrupted; 'but how does this concern you, professor? You are not making bullets.'

'But I am in the position of that workman,' was the grave response. 'I am fashioning heated metal on the forge, and just now, in thinking of your temperament and your disillusions, I seemed to see the wound before my eyes.

'This is what troubles me: the thing about which I want to speak to you might be good for you, while, on the other hand, it might prove more fatal to you than a mortal wound. So, I hesitate.

'We are both going to take part in an experiment which may, in reality, prove more dangerous for you than it at first appears. A most horrible peril will menace you, and you are certainly already in a dangerous mood, since yours is the nature that a fatal passion almost always leads to a desperate end.

'I know, on the other hand, that there is a great chance that I can save you. But if the cure is not what I expect, it will be far better to remain as you are.'

'Since you speak in such a serious manner,' said Lord Ewald, with an effort, 'I can only tell you one thing: I intended to put an end to my intolerable existence this very night!'

The professor gazed at the young man in consternation.

'To-night!' he exclaimed.

'Yes. So, you see, you need hesitate no longer on my account,' affirmed Lord Ewald quietly.

'The die is cast,' murmured the professor to himself. 'Who would have thought it – he is to be the one!'

'Again I ask you to be good enough to tell me what you are hinting,' said Lord Ewald.

A deep silence followed, and in that pause it seemed to Lord Ewald that he could feel the breath of the Infinite pass swiftly over his forehead.

'Then,' cried the inventor, drawing himself up to his full height, his eyes blazing, and his speech becoming rapid and assured, 'since I feel myself defied in this manner by the Unknown – so be it!

'Here is what I am driving at, my lord. I am going to realize for you what no man has dared to attempt for another. I owe my life and all that I have to you, and I seize this opportunity to show you my great gratitude.

'You say that your happiness, your very being, is held prisoner by a human presence – the presence only. You are held prisoner in the glory of a smile, the beauty of a face, the sweetness of a voice.

'A living being has brought you to this, her unusual attractions have brought you to the very threshold of death. I shall remake her own image and presence.

'I will show you, immediately, in a cold and calculating manner perhaps, but indisputably, how, with the actual and formidable resources of science, I can reproduce the grace of her movements, the ring of her voice, the perfume of her flesh, the lines of her form, and the light of her eyes.

'I will show you the spring of her step, her carriage, her

personality, her facial expression, her features, even her shadow, the reflection of her identity, on the ground. I will destroy her insipid animality. I will annihilate her selfish frivolity.

'At first I will reincarnate all this exterior, which is so exquisitely vital to you, in an apparition whose resemblance will far surpass your hopes and all your dreams.

'Then, finally, in place of the soul, which so repels you in this living woman, I will instil another soul, less conscious of itself, perhaps – and yet, how do we know that it will be, and what does that matter? – but suggestive of impressions a thousand times more beautiful, more noble, more elevated, a soul reclothed in its character of eternity, without which life is but a comedy.

'I will duplicate this woman with the sublime aid of light. And, projecting it on her radiant matter, I will illuminate from your idealized melancholy the imaginary soul of this new woman who will be capable of astounding even the angels.

'I will bring the illusion down to earth. I will imprison it. I will force into this phantom your ideal. You shall be the first to gaze upon her, for she will be your ideal woman, palpable, audible, materialized.

'I will seize, at the height of its sublimity, the first hour of this enchanted mirage which you follow in vain. I will seize it and enshrine it securely, almost immortally, in the one and only form where you have seen it. I will duplicate the living woman and fashion her new being according to your desires.

'I will give to this spirit all the songs of Antonio, of Hoffman; all the passionate mysticism of Poe's Lygeia; all the ardent seductions of the Venus of that master musician, Wagner! I will prove in advance that I can positively bring through human science a being made in our own likeness, out of the mire of actuality – a creation which, consequently, will be the same in effect as if it were actually created by nature.'

The great engineer, the light of genius shining in his eyes as he uttered these words, raised his hand in a solemn oath.

## VIII.

Lord Ewald turned pale. The proposition that the great physician had just made was so astounding, so fantastic, that he

was not sure that he had understood him, or that he wished
to understand him. After a stupefied pause he murmured, for
lack of anything decisive to say:

'But such a creature would be an insensible doll, with no
intelligence whatever!'

'My lord,' declared the professor gravely, 'I swear that I can
do what I have promised. You must be on your guard that in
the juxtaposition of this Andraiad and the living model, and in
listening to them both, you do not mistake the one for the
other; that you do not believe the living woman to be the doll.'

A faint, scornful smile played about Lord Ewald's lips as he
recalled Alicia Cleary's unmistakable, empty, frivolous manner-
isms, but he forced himself to reply politely:

'Your conception is indeed prodigious, professor – but let
us say no more about it. The work would always smell of the
mechanism. You will excuse my smiling, dear friend, but you
cannot *make* a woman. I wonder, as I listen to you, if your
genius –'

'One moment,' interrupted the professor calmly. 'I swear to
you that, at first, you will not be able to tell one from the
other, and again I assure you that I am now in a position to
prove my assertions.'

'Impossible!' Lord Ewald asserted.

'Again, for the third time, I pledge you my word to furnish
you presently, no matter how little you desire it, with the
most positive demonstration, not of the possibility of the fact,
but of its mathematical certitude.'

Lord Ewald, still incredulous, exclaimed: 'You, born of a
woman – you can reproduce the identity of a woman!'

'Certainly – and what is more, the reproduction will be
more identical than the woman herself, for there is not a day
that passes without bringing some change to the human form,
even altering some lines.

'Physiology shows us that our body renews its atoms entirely every seven years. That being true, how can one ever
wholly resemble oneself?

'This young lady about whom we are speaking, and you
and I – we have all changed, all aged one hour and twenty
minutes, since we began our discussion this evening.'

'You say that you will reproduce her in all her beauty, her
voice, her walk – her exact appearance, in fact?'

'Positively. I will do it with electromagnetism and radiant matter. I could even deceive a mother, so I am sure that I can fool a lover.

'I will duplicate Miss Cleary in such a way that if in a dozen years from now she should look upon her idealized double, who will have remained unchanged, she could only do so with tears of envy – and terror.'

There was a pause.

'But,' murmured Lord Ewald thoughtfully, 'to undertake the creation of such a being seems to me sacrilegious.'

'The matter is entirely in your hands,' said the inventor simply.

'But could you put a sort of intelligence in this being?'

'I will give her intelligence itself.'

This impressive declaration fairly stunned Lord Ewald. He stood before the inventor as if petrified. They stared at each other silently.

A desperate game had been proposed, and the stakes were a spirit.

Lord Ewald broke the silence with a rallying laugh.

'A wonderful dream, my dear genius,' he said, 'a very wonderful dream. I see that you have great faith in the outcome, but it is a dream that is as frightful as it is impossible.

'However, dear friend, your sympathy and your desire to help me have touched me deeply. I cannot thank you enough.'

'My dear fellow,' the professor protested, 'I can see that you secretly feel that it is not an impossible dream, for you hesitate!'

Lord Ewald wiped the beads of perspiration from his brow.

'I don't believe that Miss Cleary would ever consent to it,' he said, 'and, I admit, I would hesitate myself to let her do so.'

'That part of the problem concerns me only,' his host declared. 'I give you my word that your dear friend will suffer in no way. My work would be incomplete otherwise.'

'Well, how about me?' Lord Ewald demanded. 'Do I not count for something in my love for her?'

'Yes, certainly, and you will count for something much more than you could ever imagine.'

'Yes, but do you suppose for a moment that you will be

able to convince me of the reality of this new Eve, even if you do succeed? What formidable subtleties will you employ to do that?'

'Oh, that is merely a question of immediate impression where reason enters only as a secondary adjunct. Does one ever reason with the charm to which one submits? But, just wait – the presence of the vision, of the phantom coming to life, will answer your question for you.'

'I suppose that I can dispute,' Lord Ewald suggested, dubiously, 'that I can put up an argument during the course of the experiment?'

'Certainly, and, mark you, if only one of your objections exists, just one, we will both agree to stop the experiment and go no farther.'

'I must warn you that I have very keen eyes.'

'Your eyes?' the professor remarked, smilingly. 'Tell me, can you clearly see this drop of water? Yet, if I place it between these two sheets of crystal and then place the pieces of crystal before the reflector of this solar microscope, and then submit it to the exact refraction which I threw on to the white sheet over there, where you beheld your fascinating Alicia, you would be no less astounded at what you would see revealed than you were when you beheld her picture transplanted there.

'If we were to think of all the indefinite, the occult realities, which this liquid drop conceals we should understand that the power of our eyes, which is only a sort of a visible crutch, is insignificant. The relative difference between what we discover under the microscope and what we see without its help is almost infinite.

'And, in turn, we may well surmise that what we cannot discover with its magnifying aid is also beyond apprehension. Let us then remember that we can only see the things that suggest themselves to our eyes, and we can conceive of them only after we have beheld their mysterious entities.

'We only possess what we can feel according to our nature. Man, imprisoned in his moving self, struggles in vain to evade the illusion or to captivate his mocking senses.'

'In truth, my good Mr Wizard,' Lord Ewald observed, 'one would think that you seriously believe me capable of falling in love with your phantom.'

'If you were an ordinary person I should have that to fear. But your confessions have reassured me.

'Did you not say just now – did you not swear that your feelings for your beautiful, living friend were merely platonic? Well, then, you will only love Hadaly as she deserves, which is a far more beautiful sentiment than feeling an earthly love for her.'

'So you think I shall love her then?' demanded Lord Ewald, with a sceptical smile.

'Why not?' retorted the professor, in real surprise. 'Will she not be a perpetual incarnation in the only form where you can conceive love?'

'Yes, that is true. But one can only love an animated being. The soul is the unknown quantity.'

The professor smiled this time pityingly, but he made no comment on his lordship's dictum.

'Will the vision know who she is? I mean, what she is?' Lord Ewald persisted.

'Do you know so well yourself what you are? Do we know what we are? Why, then, do you demand more of the copy than the Creator thought right to grant to the original?'

'Will this creature of your creation be able to feel any sentiment herself?'

'Without a doubt,' replied the professor, casually.

'Eh! What do you say?' cried Lord Ewald in amazement.

'Without a doubt,' the scientist repeated. 'This will depend entirely on you. It is upon you alone that I count for this phase of the miracle to be accomplished.'

'Well, then,' said Lord Ewald, 'be so kind as to inform me where I shall draw the spark of sacred fire which will enable us to achieve the spirit. My name is not Prometheus, but simply Ewald, and I am only mortal.'

'Nonsense,' replied the professor, 'each man is a Prometheus within himself without knowing it. My lord, I assure you that a single one of those divine sparks with which you have so often tried, in vain, to animate the negative personality of your adored one will suffice to put life into this shadow.'

'Prove it to me!' cried Lord Ewald. 'And perhaps –'

'As you will!' replied the professor. 'You have told me that the being that you love, and which, for you alone is real, does not exist in this human form, but only in your desires. This being then does not exist, or, better, you know that it does not exist. You have then neither been deceived by yourself nor by this woman.

'But, still, you close your eyes, rather the eyes of your spirit; and you close the demands of your conscience by seeking to find in this woman the phantom which you desire. Her true personality is to you the illusion which you seek, and which has been raised in your whole being by the brilliance of her beauty.

'It is this illusion alone which you try to bring forth, even to create, to call to life in the presence of your beloved, in spite of the incessant disillusionments which you suffer from this mortal – this frightful – this wretched emptiness of the real Alicia.

'It is then only a shadow that you are in love with, and it is for this shadow that you would die. It is this shadow that you would recognize absolutely as real.

'It is this vision conjured up by your desires, which you have called forth, which you have created in your living being, and this vision is nothing more than a double of your own soul which you have transplanted into her. Behold, then, your love is nothing else, you can plainly see, than a perpetual and always fruitless effort at redemption.'

For a few moments there was a profound silence between the two men.

'And now, then,' continued the professor, 'since it has been shown that it is only a shadow to which you have been lending so fictitiously and warmly a being, I am offering you a chance to try the same experiment upon a creature which will be a copy, externally realized, of your own shadow. It is an illusion for an illusion.

'The being of this mixed-presence, which we call Hadaly, will depend upon the free will of the person who will dare to conceive it. By "being," I mean soul.

'Why should you not be the one? Why should you not endeavour by means of your living faith to project some of your ideals into Hadaly in the same manner in which you strive to project them into your living friend?

'Try it. Breathe upon this ideal forehead of Hadaly and

suggest to her your idealized being, and you will see how the Alicia of your dreams will be realized, unified, and animated in this phantom.

'Try it, if your last hope tells you so to do. And then, ask yourself in the depths of your conscience if this auxiliary phantom-creature, which shall draw forth in you anew the desire to live, is not truly more worthy to bear the name of a human being than the living one – the living one which has only given you the desire for death.'

Deeply perplexed, Lord Ewald murmured:

'Your deduction is truly most specific and profound, but I am sure that I should always feel somewhat alone when in the company of your unconscious Eve.'

'You will feel less alone with Hadaly than you will with her model,' the professor announced. 'Besides, my lord, that will be your fault and not mine. One must feel that one is a superman before one dares to attempt what we have in question here.

'Besides all this, let us take into account the novelty of the impression that you will experience when you hold your first conversation with this Andraiad – this idealized Alicia – walking beside you with the sun's full rays falling upon her exquisite beauty, looking up at you with all the naturalness of the living woman.'

A smile spread over Lord Ewald's face.

'Ah, you doubt,' said the great electrician. 'You think that your senses would soon discover the change that I would substitute for nature. Well, then, listen to me: have you or Miss Cleary a dog?'

'Yes, she has a little black terrier that is devoted to her.'

'Good. Now, a dog has a keen scent – and I want you to make a wager with me.

'A dog could very easily recognize its mistress in the dark, even though she were in a crowd of a thousand persons. I will make you a bet that if we transform Hadaly into the living being, and have her call this dog, it will rush toward her and recognize her merely by the scent of her gown.

'I will even go farther than that. I will wager that if Miss Cleary and the phantom should call that dog simultaneously, that it would be the phantom, and the phantom only, that he will obey. Will you take the wager?'

'Haven't you stretched that point just a little bit?' asked Lord Ewald, greatly disconcerted.

'I only promise what I can perform,' stated the scientist briefly. 'The experiment has already been carried out most successfully. If, then, the scent of a lower animal, whose organs are superior to ours in keenness, can be deceived, why should I not dare to defy the control of the human senses?

'I want to say this,' the inventor went on; 'although Hadaly is a mystery, you must not look upon her in an exalted manner. Be natural with her. You must just think of her as being slightly more animated by electricity than her living model, that is all.'

'Why should she be more animated?'

'Well,' said the professor, 'have you ever seen a beautiful young brunette combing her hair before a large bluish mirror, in a room that has been darkened and in which the curtains are all drawn, on a stormy day? Have you ever seen the sparks fly out of her hair on the points of her tortoise-shell comb, like little diamonds sparkling on a black wave in the sea at night?

'But if you have never seen Miss Alicia like that, you can see Hadaly. Brunettes have a great deal of electricity.'

There was a pause.

'Are you agreed that we shall make the attempt at this incarnation?' asked the professor finally. 'Hadaly, in this golden flower, has offered to save you from the wreck of your love.'

'This is the most frightful proposition that was ever made to a desperate man,' Lord Ewald replied in almost a whisper, 'and yet, in spite of myself, I find the greatest difficulty in the world to take it seriously.'

'Seriousness will come,' declared Professor X; 'that is Hadaly's affair.'

'I suppose,' said his lordship, 'that any other man would accept this copy that you offer me very quickly, if only out of curiosity.'

'But I should not propose it to every man,' the inventor exclaimed, smiling. 'If I were to bequeath the formula to humanity there are those who would abuse the help that it is intended to give.'

'Could the experiment be suspended after it was started?'

'Yes, even after the work is completed, it can always be destroyed, if it seems the best thing to do.'

'But that would not be the same,' declared Lord Ewald. 'After it had been completed it would not be the same thing; one would feel as if a life were being taken.'

'Well,' said the scientist, 'remember that I am not urging or advising you in the slightest manner to accept this. You are suffering, and I have told you of a remedy. But the remedy is as dangerous as it is efficacious. You may refuse it – you are free to do so.'

Lord Ewald appeared still more perplexed.

'Oh, as to the danger,' he said with a shrug of his shoulders, 'you may forget that.'

'If it were only a physical danger,' said the professor, 'I would urge you to accept.'

'Do you think that it is my reason that is threatened?'

The professor did not answer at once.

'Lord Ewald,' he said at length, 'yours is the noblest nature that I have ever known. It was a very bad star that threw its light over you and led you to the realms of love. Your dreams have vanished, your wings have been clipped by a deceiving woman whose discordant nature constantly fans the flame of a sorrow that is consuming you, and which evidently will be fatal.

'Yes, you are one of the few remaining great lovers who would not deign to survive this sort of a test, in spite of the example of those all around you who are struggling against sickness, poverty, and love. You despise to become resigned to live under the lash of such a destiny.

'Your disease is in its worse stage. You told me just now that it is only a matter of hours. There is not even a doubt as to the issue of the crisis. It is obvious that when you go over the threshold of this house you are going to your death – your very bearing testifies to this.

'Now I am offering you life again; perhaps it will be at a great price, but who can tell the value of it at this moment? The ideal has lied to you. "Truth" has destroyed all desire. A woman has frozen the love in your heart.

'Why not say farewell to the pretended reality, the everlasting deceiver, and accept the artificial and its novel incitements that I offer you?

'If you would like to be the master of this situation, the dominator, let us make a pact. I will represent science with all its powerful mirages, while you – you shall represent humanity and its lost paradise.'

'Then choose for me,' said Lord Ewald calmly.

The professor was startled.

'That is impossible, my lord.'

'Well, then, what would you do in my place? If you had reached this state of mind that I am in, what would you do? Would you risk this absurd but disturbing adventure?'

The inventor looked at his young guest fixedly, his usually placid features twitching slightly, as if he had some secret thought that he could not express.

'I would not dare to express an opinion,' he said. 'I would have more of a motive in expressing one than most men.'

'Very well,' said Lord Ewald; 'which course would you choose if you had no alternative?'

'My lord,' said the professor gravely, 'do not doubt the deep attachment which I have for you, but with my hand on my heart –'

'What would you choose, professor?' his lordship persisted, inflexibly.

'Between death and the temptation in question?'

'Yes.'

The master electrician bowed to his guest. Then he said quietly:

'I would blow out my brains first.'

## IX.

Lord Ewald made no reply for a moment. Then taking out his watch he glanced at the time and said, with a sigh:

'And now, this time we must part forever. I choose to die!'

The ringing of a bell was heard.

'You are a little late,' the professor announced. 'After your first words of resignation I commenced action.'

While speaking he started the phonograph, that spoke in his stead.

'Well?' cried its voice into the telephone.

The bass tones of the distant messenger were clearly audible in the laboratory. Their agitated intonations showed plainly that the speaker was somewhat out of breath.

'Miss Cleary was in box number seven at the opera. She will take the eleven-ten train,' said the messenger.

Lord Ewald, when he heard Miss Cleary's name shouted so boisterously and tensely, listened to the information.

'Very well,' he said, in cool acceptance of the pact, 'but what about getting back to the city? It will be very late.'

'Oh, I will attend to all that,' said the professor.

He placed a square of blank paper on the Morse receptor, which a few minutes later shot out of the frame.

'Here,' he remarked, calmly looking at the now printed sheet, 'is a charming little villa about twenty minutes from here. The lady who owns the place will expect Miss Cleary any time to-night.

'I can put you up here, but perhaps you would rather be near the villa. There is a very good inn close to it.'

'Oh, thanks very much,' said Lord Ewald, 'but I will go to the inn.'

'That's settled then,' continued the professor. 'Now I have this picture of Miss Cleary, and I will give it to my man and send him with the carriage to meet her train. He will easily recognize her from this. There will only be a few persons coming down at this hour, so you need not be anxious.'

While speaking he had taken a paste-board card from an object plate. He threw it into the receiver of a pneumatic tube after hurriedly writing a few words on the card.

The receiver corresponded with the transmitter of a pneumatic tube. In a moment a little bell, rung near by, announced that the order had been received and would be carried out.

Returning to the Morse apparatus, the professor continued to telegraph. When he had finished he turned suddenly to his guest and said:

'My lord, it goes without saying that it will be better not to speak to any one of this matter in which we are interested.'

'That is understood,' Lord Ewald said, simply. 'And I wish to say, professor, that I no longer hesitate after accepting your proposition. Please consider this my final decision.'

The professor bowed his head gravely.

'Then I shall expect that your lordship will do me the honour to live twenty-one days. I also have a word to keep.'

'Agreed, but – not one day more,' said the young man stoically.

'I, myself, will offer you the pistol at nine o'clock in the evening of the day agreed upon, if I do not win your life,' Professor X agreed. 'And now, since we clearly understand each other, and are about to make a dangerous journey, I must kiss my children good-by.'

He took up the telephone transmitter and spoke two names into it.

The sound of a bell could be heard from the other side of the grounds.

'Here's a hundred kisses for you two,' said the inventor in a fatherly tone, as, with his mouth to the telephone, he sent a caress.

Then a strange thing happened.

Around these two men, searchers of the unknown – these two adventurers who were about to enter the realms of the shades, there suddenly broke out on all sides a vocal shower of kisses from the little children, who cried out in their sweet voices:

'Papa! Papa!' Send us some more!'

The professor had held the receiver gently against his cheek as it brought him the caresses.

When the good nights were over he turned to Lord Ewald and said:

'Now, my lord, I am ready.'

'No, professor,' the young man objected sadly, 'you must not go. I have no one dependent on me. It would be better for me to go alone on this trip, if it is possible.'

'We go together,' declared the engineer calmly.

Taking down two bear-skin coats from a panel in the wall, the professor handed one to his guest, saying:

'It is very cold where we are going. Wear this.'

Lord Ewald accepted the heavy coat and inquired:

'Would it be indiscreet for me to ask – to whose house are we going?'

'To Hadaly's, of course – in the midst of thunder, powerful electrical currents, and vast flashes of light.'

'Let us go then,' said the young man.

'Just a word. Before you go, have you no last questions, no last words that you would like to say to me?'

'No. Nothing. I must admit that I am rather in a hurry to have a talk with this pretty veiled creature whose nothingness has a call on my sympathy. As for the rest, the frivolous observations or questions which come to my mind, there will be always time –'

At these words the professor turned and stopped the younger man.

'Eh, what's that!' he cried. 'Do you forget, my dear fellow, that I call myself electricity, and that I, myself, have to struggle against your thoughts. If you have anything to say, you must speak at once.

'Tell me, now, of those frivolous anxieties and questions, or I shall not know what I am fighting against. It is not such an easy thing to match body for body with an ideal such as yours, I can tell you. Now, say all that you have to say to the physician who proposes to lighten your sorrow.'

'Oh, these ideas have no weight,' said Lord Ewald. 'They are just trivial thoughts on nothing.'

'Ah,' cried the professor, 'how you go on! "On nothing" – but a nothing can assume tremendous proportions! Who was it that said: "Not so long ago a kingdom was lost by the wave of a fan at the wrong moment. If Cleopatra's nose had been a trifle shorter, the face of the world would have changed"?

'Do you imagine that I do not appreciate the nothings? Now, if there is anything that makes you the least bit anxious, let us have it out. We will have it out before we start.

'We will go after you have told me, but let us begin, for we have only just time to make this visit and return before the living one arrives.'

'I wondered, first of all, why you questioned me so closely about the intellectual character of our feminine subject?' Lord Ewald explained.

'Because I was obliged to know what was the principal aspect under which you, yourself, conceived intelligence,' replied the engineer. 'The difficulty is in the physical reproduction. There is a question, at first, of imbuing Hadaly with the paradoxical beauty of your living subject.

'It is most important that the phantom, instead of disenchanting you as her model has, should be worthy in your eyes of the sublime form into which she will be incarnated. Unless we can do that it would not be worth while to make a change from the living to the phantom.'

'Very well. Now, how are you going to persuade Alicia to lend herself to this experiment?'

'This evening, when we are at supper, it will take me only a few minutes to persuade her to do what I want. You will see, even if I have to employ suggestions to decide her. But I am sure that I can persuade her.

'Then it will only be a matter of a few sittings, and a rough clay model will effect the change. She will not even see Hadaly, and she will not have the slightest knowledge of the work upon which we are engaged.

'Now, in order to incarnate Hadaly, to bring her forth from the almost supernatural atmosphere where the fiction of her identity is realized, this Valkyrie of science must be reclothed. If she is to come into our midst, she must have the fashions, the usage, and the aspect of the women of the present day.

'While the sittings are going on, dressmakers, glove-makers, lingerie-makers, corsetières, milliners, and bootmakers – I will give you the mineral substance for the insulation of the soles and the heels – will make exact copies of all the things worn by Miss Cleary, without her knowledge.

'These things will be given to her beautiful phantom as soon as she has come into the world. Once we have the measures all taken, you may have hundreds of duplicates made in different styles without its being necessary to try them on.

'It goes without saying that the Andraiad will use the same perfumes as her model, having, as I have said, the same emanations.'

'How will she travel?'

'Why, like any other person. There are travellers more strange than she. Hadaly, if warned of a voyage, will be quite irreproachable.

'She may be a little drowsy and irritable perhaps, speaking only at rare intervals and to you only, in a low voice, but she will be seated beside you and it will not be even necessary for her to lower her veil. She will defy all human observation.'

'Would she know how to act correctly if any one should address her?'

'In such a case you would simply have to state that the lady was a foreigner and did not know the language of the country. That would close the incident.

'In the matter of equilibrium even a good many living men and women have difficulty. Hadaly will not be able to take a rough sea voyage, but many men and women remain in their berths on a trip, because they become shaken by seasickness and look ridiculous.

'Hadaly's serenity should not be ruffled; she should not be humiliated by the sight of the defective organisms of her human companions. She will travel on sea in the same manner as a corpse.'

## X.

'What; in a coffin?' cried Lord Ewald, aghast.

The professor nodded casually.

'Yes; in a coffin.'

'But not sewn up in a shroud, I hope?'

'No. This living object of art, not having known our bandages, will make her own winding sheet.

'This is how it will be done: Hadaly, among other treasures, possesses a heavy ebony casket, upholstered in black satin. The interior of this symbolic casket will be the exact mould of the feminine form that she is destined to take.

'This is her dowry. The upper sides of the casket open by the aid of a little gold key, in the form of a star, the lock of which is placed under the head of the sleeper.

'Hadaly knows how to enter this alone, either unclothed or entirely dressed. She lies down at full length and she knows how to arrange the linen sheets which are firmly attached to the interior in such a way that they do not even touch her shoulders.

'Her face is veiled; her head remains resting on a cushion; and around her brow is a band which helps to hold her in position. If it were not for her gentle, regular breathing, she would be taken for Miss Cleary, who had died that morning.

'On the closed door of this prison casket is nailed a plate inscribed with the name "Hadaly". This name signifies the ideal. The plate will be surmounted with your coat-of-arms, which will consecrate this captivity.

'The beautiful casket should be placed in a cedar case entirely lined with cotton wool. This should be square in shape in order not to arouse any suspicion. All of this will be ready in three weeks. On your return to London, a word to the director of customs will be all that is necessary to permit your mysterious luggage to enter.

'When Miss Cleary gets your last message of farewell, you will be in your castle at Athewold where you can awaken your heavenly vision.'

'In my castle,' murmured Lord Ewald, as if to himself, in a most profound and melancholy manner. 'Truly – there it will be possible.'

'Yes. There, in your solitary domain, surrounded by forests, lakes, and great rocks, you may in all security open Hadaly's prison. You have, I believe, in that castle some spacious rooms with furniture that dates back to the time of Elizabeth.'

'Yes,' agreed Lord Ewald, cynically, 'and I have enriched it with marvellous works of art. The old drawing room breathes the spirit of the genius of the past.

'The one great window in it is of stained glass draped with hangings ornamented with floral garlands of burnished gold. It opens on to an iron balcony, the balustrade of which was wrought in the reign of Richard the Third. The moss-covered steps lead down to a long avenue of oak trees which extends the full length of the park.

'It is a beautiful place. Yes, this beautiful home was destined for my wife, if I could have met her.'

A shiver passed over him and he continued:

'What is to be, will be. I will take this illusory apparition, this galvanized hope, to my castle. As I am not capable to feel or have any desire for the other, I hope that this phantom form will brighten my days – my last dreams.'

'Good,' said the professor. 'I think that your castle will be just the place for this Andraiad. Hadaly will be like some mysterious somnambulist wandering around the lakes and over the heaths. In this far off castle where your old servants, your books, your hunting trophies, your paintings, and your musical instruments, are awaiting you, this newcomer will soon take her place.

'Respect and silence will make her stand surrounded in an isolated halo. The servants must receive orders from you never to speak to her. You can explain this by saying that having been saved, as by a miracle, from a terrific danger which threatened you, your companion had made a sacred vow never to speak to any one but you.

'There, in your castle, the beautiful voice which is so dear to you will sing to you the airs you love. You can accompany her on the organ, or with the soft note of the harp, or with the piano.

'Her exquisite notes will enhance the charm of the summer twilights, they will blend with the beauty of a sunlit day, and harmonize with the songs of the birds. In the autumn and in the winter nights her voice will rise above the sighing of the wind and the roar of the waves beating against the rocks.

'As she walks alone under the trees and through the old paths with her long gown trailing, a legend will soon be woven about her. The curious will have seen her strolling alone in the pale moonlight.

'She will be a terrifying sight, and none will know the secret but yourself.

'One day, perhaps, I shall come to visit you in your semi-solitude where you have agreed to run two continual dangers – madness – and retribution.'

'You will be the only guest whom I shall receive,' declared Lord Ewald. 'But as only the preliminary possibility of this adventure is now established, let us see if the prodigy itself is possible. First of all, why is Hadaly enclosed in armour?'

'It is the plastic apparatus which is superimposed on the unity of the electric fluid that will correspond to the fleshy being of your ideal love. It contains, mounted within it, literally what corresponds to the interior organisms common to all human beings.'

'Will she always speak in the same low voice that I heard just now?'

'No. Decidedly not! She does not, even now, use that voice all of the time. Was Miss Cleary's voice always as it is now?

'Hadaly spoke, just now, in a soft, childish voice – spiritual, somnambulistic. No, she will have Miss Cleary's voice, just as she will have all her other attractions. Her singing voice and her speaking voice all remain, forever, just as it is indicated to her.

'In fabricating a woman, you must note, I have made use of

the rarest and most precious substances, a compliment to the fascinating sex,' added the scientist gallantly. 'But I was obliged to use iron in the joints.'

'Ah! Isn't iron one of the constituents of our own bodies? Why have you used it only in the joints?'

'Because the force which holds the joints together is magnetic, produced by electrical currents. As iron is the metal which magnetizes and attracts best – it is much better than nickel or cobalt – I have used it in the form of steel.'

'But steel oxidizes. Won't her joints rust?'

'I have prepared against that. Here I have a large bottle of oil of roses, scented with amber. This is the lubricant for her joints.'

'Oil of roses?' queried Lord Ewald.

'Yes. It is the only one prepared in this manner that will always keep its exquisite aroma. Perfumes belong exclusively to the feminine world. Every month you will have to put a small spoonful of this oil in Hadaly's mouth while she is dozing.

'You see, it is all very human, just as if one were giving medicine to a child. The subtle perfume will diffuse in the magnetized metal organisms. This bottle will be sufficient for a century or more – and, my dear friend, I do not think that there will be any need for us to repeat the quantity!'

'You say that she will breathe?'

'Of course, the same as we do. But she will not burn oxygen as we do. We are chockful of it, like steam engines.

'Hadaly inhales and breathes air by the pneumatic movement of her chest which rises and falls like that of a woman in good health. The air, which passes between her lips and which makes her nostrils palpitate, is perfumed and warmed by electricity – an effluvia of amber and roses.

'The future Alicia's most natural attitude will be seated with her cheek on one hand and her elbow resting on something, or else reposing on a sofa, in the attitude of any graceful woman. She will maintain these attitudes without any other movement than her breathing.

'To awaken her from her phlegmatic existence, you will only have to take her hand. That will agitate the fluid in one of her rings.'

'One of her rings?' asked Lord Ewald, in surprise.

'Yes. The one on her forefinger. It is her wedding ring.'

Lord Ewald stared at the scientist in amazement.

'Do you know why that hand there responded to your pressure just now?' asked the professor, pointing to the object on the ebony table.

'No.'

'It was because, when you tightened your clasp, you pressed the ring. I don't know whether you have noticed it or not, but Hadaly has rings on all her fingers, and the various precious stones are sensitive.

'You need not bother her when she is in one of these extra-terrestrial attitudes; but if you wish to ask her anything you will be quite at liberty to do so.

'All you will have to do at a time like this, whether she is lying down on a couch or sitting up, is to take her hand and stroke the sympathetic amethyst in the ring on her forefinger, and she will get up gently, if you say to her: "Come, Hadaly." She will obey you better than the real woman.

'The touch of the ring should be slight and natural, as when you touch the hand of your living model. You may even do it with a slight fervour, in the interest of the illusion.

'Hadaly will walk straight before her and alone, at the request of the ruby which she wears on the middle finger of her right hand; or she will hold your arm and lean languishingly towards you; or she will follow wherever you wish to lead her, not merely as any woman would, but exactly as Miss Cleary would.

'You must not permit the fact that her human walk is controlled by means of these rings to shock you. Think how much more humiliating are the prayers and entreaties to which men have to resort, in order to bring the feminine graces to a semblance of obedience!

'In response to a persuasive touch on the turquoise on the ring finger, she will sit down, and in addition to these rings, she wears a three row necklace, each pearl of which has a corresponding action that will respond to its pressure.

'Here you have a fairly explicit manuscript – quite a conjuror's book – the most extraordinary ever seen, for it gives you a key to her habits and character. With a little practice – one must study women, you know – everything will become quite natural.'

The professor's gravity, as he made these statements, was quite imperturbable.

'Now,' he continued, 'about her food, she –'

'By Jove! Does she eat?' interrupted Lord Ewald.

'That seems to surprise you, my lord. Is it possible that you had contemplated, for a single instant, allowing this marvellous creature to die for lack of nourishment? Why, that would be worse than homicide.'

'But, pray, Mr Wizard, what do you mean by her food?' asked Lord Ewald. 'I must admit that, this time, you have gone beyond the most fantastic dreams.'

'Here is the nourishment that Hadaly must take two or three times a week,' said the professor. 'In this old chest I have some boxes of lozenges and certain tablets which she will assimilate very well. The strange girl will do it all alone. You will only have to place a dish on a stand or a table which will be always at a fixed distance from her habitual sleeping place, and indicate it to her by merely touching one of the pearls of her necklace.

'She will be quite a child in everyday, ordinary matters. She does not know, and you must teach her. We were all at that stage once, ourselves. But she will scarcely seem to remember – what of that, we, ourselves, often forget many things.

'She will sip from a thin goblet of jasper made especially for her. She will drink in precisely the same manner as her model. The goblet will be filled with filtered water.

'The lozenges are of zinc and the tablets are of bichromate of potassium, a few are of peroxide of lead. There is nothing strange in that. Nowadays, many of us take a variety of things which have been borrowed from chemistry.

'You will have to give her nothing more. She will not take any more than she will require. She will be very temperate. It would be a good thing if many of us would follow her example. But if she does not find her nourishment at hand when she needs it she will faint, or, rather, she will die.'

'She will die,' murmured Lord Ewald.

'Yes, so as to give her chosen one the divine pleasure of restoring her to life.'

'A very delicate attention,' said Lord Ewald, now smiling.

'Yes. When she remains motionless, with her eyes closed,

you must restore her. All that you will have to do will be to give her a little clear water and a few of these tablets.

'But, as she will not have the strength to take them herself at such a time, you must touch the tourmaline on her middle finger – this stone communicates with a battery. That will be sufficient.

'As soon as she opens her eyes her first words will be to ask for water. Now, you must not forget to do this according to the directions given you in the manuscript. It is quite explicit.

'A few minutes after you have done this, our beautiful Hadaly will blow light fumes of pale smoke, faintly white in colour, from between her half closed lips, and then, there she is again living, as you and I, ready to obey all the rings and all the pearls, just the same as we accede to our own desires.'

'Do you mean to say that she blows clouds of smoke from her lips?'

'Just the same as we are continually doing,' said the professor, indicating the cigars which both he and his guest were holding. 'Only she does not hold an atom of metallic dust or smoke in her mouth. The fluid consumes and disappears in a moment. She has her cigarette, however, that is, if you –'

'I noticed that she has a dagger in her belt,' interrupted Lord Ewald.

'Yes. She would use that to defend herself if, while she is away from her chosen one, a trifler should dare to intrude upon her privacy. She would not tolerate the slightest familiarity. A blow from that dagger would be fatal. She is loyal to only one person, she will recognize one only – her master.'

'But she cannot see?'

'Who knows? Do we ourselves see very clearly? At any rate, she can guess or feel objects visible to you and me.

'Hadaly, I repeat, is a somewhat sombre young lady. She is indifferent to fate, and she would not hesitate to send a man to his death.'

'Then, a casual stranger could not take that weapon away from her?' asked Lord Ewald.

'I defy all the Hercules of the earth to do that,' declared the professor, laughing.

'How is that?'

'Because, enclosed in the dagger handle there is a most

formidable power. A tiny opal on the little finger of the left hand connects the blade with a very powerful current. The carnelian alongside would deaden the noise of the electrical report.

'It is a veritable streak of lightning, so powerful that the first thoughtless fellow, who thought that he could steal a kiss from the sleeping beauty, would roll to the ground with his face blackened, and his limbs twisted, destroyed by the silent avenger. He would fall dead at Hadaly's feet before he had even time to touch her garment. She will certainly be a faithful, loyal friend.'

'I see,' Lord Ewald said. 'The kiss would form a conductor.'

'Here is a glass rod which has a beryl in it. This will neutralize the opal and, when you touch it with this, the dagger will drop, harmless. The formula for this tempered glass had been lost since the days of the Emperor Nero, but I found it.'

As he spoke, the professor struck the ebony table violently with the long gleaming switch of glass which had been lying near him. The radiant switch appeared to bend, but it did not break.

Then Lord Ewald asked, jokingly:

'Does she ever bathe?'

'Naturally – every day,' replied the professor, as if he were astonished at the question.

'But how does she do that?'

'Well, you know that all photochromatic proofs have to remain in a specially prepared water for several hours. This strengthens them.

'The photochromatic action which I have mentioned is indelible; you understand that the skin is entirely saturated with it. It has been subjected to a process of light which gives it an impervious glaze.

'A small pink pearl on the left of the three-row necklace which Hadaly wears brings together an interior interposition of stones, the adherence of which hermetically prevents the water in the bath from penetrating the mechanism of this nymph. You will find the names of the perfumes in the manuscript which must be used in the baths.

'I will register the magnificent head of hair which Miss

Cleary has upon the cylinder of movements. It will be reproduced exactly.'

'The cylinder of movements?' echoed Lord Ewald,
questioningly.

'You will have to see it to understand. From what I have
told you, you can apprehend that Hadaly, primarily, is a
superb mechanical vision, almost a human being, a brilliant
*facsimile*.

'The faults which I have given her out of courtesy to
humanity consist only in that there are several types of woman
in her – the same as there is in every woman. But the supreme
type which dominates her is, if I may say it, perfect.

'She only plays the other types. She is a wonderful actress,
with greater and even more serious talent than Miss
Cleary.'

'And yet she is only a counterfeit being,' Lord Ewald
remarked, with profound regret.

'Oh, as for that, the biggest minds have always wondered
what the being in ourselves really is. Hegel, in his great work,
says that the pure idea of the being, that is the difference
between the being and nothingness, is only a simple matter of
opinion. Hadaly herself will clearly resolve the question of her
being, I can promise you.'

'How?'

'By words.'

'But if she is not a soul, will she have a conscience?' asked
the younger man.

'Pardon me,' the professor said admonishingly, 'but isn't
that precisely what you demanded? Didn't you cry out:
"Who could put a soul into that body?"

'You have called for a vision precisely identical with your
friend Alicia, without the conscience which has caused you so
much sorrow. *Hadaly has come in answer to your call.* That
is all.

'And I do not think that it will be a very great loss if
Hadaly is lacking the kind of a conscience that her model has
– do you? It will be to her advantage not to have it, at least,
in your eyes, since Miss Cleary's conscience seems to be
deplorable, a blot on the masterpiece. The conscience of a
worldly woman – bah!'

'Even though a woman has caused me great sorrow,' Lord

Ewald demurred gently. 'I think that you speak of the sex with much severity.'

# XI.

Lord Ewald arose. He threw his bearskin coat over his arm, put on his hat and gloves, and adjusted his eyeglass. Then he said:

'It is useless to argue with you about a woman's conscience, my dear doctor. You would have a crushing reply for everything that I could say. I am ready to go on our little adventure when you are.'

'Then we will be off right now,' the professor agreed, rising briskly from his seat. 'One hour has already passed, and the train from the city will start in an hour. We have only an hour and a half for our little enterprise.

'The abode which Hadaly inhabits in underground. Of course, you can understand that I could not leave the ideal in reach of every one.

'I have spent years working upon her mysteries. Night after night I have sat up experimenting and, up to this day, I have kept my achievement a secret.

'Some time ago I discovered, near this very spot, two large subterranean halls, burial places of an ancient, vanished tribe. I have done over the walls of the largest vault with a coating of basalt. The mummies and the powdered bones I confined to the inner vault, which I have blocked up – let us hope for eternity.

'The larger vault I have converted into a sort of fairyland for Hadaly. She has her songbirds. You may think me a trifle superstitious, but I really did not want to leave an intellectual creature down there all alone. Everything is worked by electricity.

'Our bear coats will protect us from penumonia, for we have to go through two long, damp underground passages. We shall go like arrows. Indeed, it is most fantastic.'

The professor preceded his young friend on their journey. They walked to the shadowy spot in the wall at the end of the laboratory where Hadaly had made her appearance.

'I confess to you,' said the scientist, 'that when I visit this enchantress I take her all my anxieties. And my problems are usually solved before I come back to earth.'

While making this confession, the professor had turned a screwhead in the wall. The panels of the walls slid back.

'Come,' he said jocularly, 'in going into the realm of the ideal, we must first pass through the kingdom of the commonplace. We will now leave the earth's surface.'

The two men passed over the lighted threshold.

'Hold on to that,' said the professor, indicating an iron ring, which Lord Ewald seized. Then, taking firm hold of a twisted cord of metal concealed in the hangings, the scientist gave a pull.

The white slab of marble under their feet began to glide downward. The light above grew smaller. They soon found themselves going from humid shadows into utter darkness where there were chill odours that were foreign to Lord Ewald.

The slab continued to descend. The light above them was now only a tiny star. Soon the last light of the world above had vanished. Lord Ewald felt that he was in a profound abyss.

'What an amazing manner in which to search for an ideal,' he thought, but he said nothing, for the professor seemed to prefer silence.

Lord Ewald suddenly became all attention. For, above the rumble of the mechanism he thought he heard the sound of laughter.

Gradually their speed diminished, there was a slight jolt, and they found themselves standing before a lighted porch. An odour of amber and roses floated enchantingly on the air.

Lord Ewald saw before him a spacious subterranean hall such as might have intrigued the fancy of the caliphs under the city of Bagdad.

'You may go in,' said the professor. 'You have been introduced.'

Lord Ewald went forward, walking on the skins of wild animals which covered the floor. A clear blue light lit up the vast hall with the brilliance of a radiant summer day. Tremendous pillars, placed at intervals, supported the interior circuit of a dome of basalt, and formed a gallery to the right and left of the entrance, running back to the half circle of the hall.

This abode was gorgeously decorated in Syrian fashion. Large sheaves and garlands of silver were entwined on a bluish background. In the centre of the vault, suspended from a long golden chain, was a cluster of powerful electric lights shaded with blue globes.

The arched roof, which was of extraordinary height, was absolutely black. Against this background the light cluster appeared like a fixed star. It was a representation of heaven as it might appear – black and sombre outside of all planetary atmosphere.

The half circle which formed the end of the hall opposite the entrance was occupied by a tropic scene. Picturesque waterfalls flowed and cascades bubbled, and under the caress of an imaginary breeze wonderful flowers of the Orient grew in profusion. Birds from southern climates warbled gaily in this garden of artificial flora.

Near a pillar, her elbow leaning on a modern piano, which was lighted with electrical candelabra, stood Hadaly. She was still wearing the long black veil. With youthful grace she gave a slight inclination of her head to welcome Lord Ewald. An artificial bird of paradise was perched on her shoulder, balancing its jewelled aigrette, and apparently talking to the Andraiad in an unknown tongue.

Under a vermilion lamp stood a long table of pink marble. At one end of this was fastened a violet silk cushion like the one in the laboratory which held the flesh-like arm.

On a small ivory table near at hand a case filled with crystal instruments stood open, displaying its gleaming contents. In a distant corner there was an electrical heater, reflected to all sides by silver mirrors.

There was no furniture except a sleeping couch covered with black satin, and a small table placed between two lounge chairs. A great ebony frame covered with a sheet of white silk surmounted by a golden rose leaned against a part of the wall.

When Lord Ewald had taken a few steps forward all the birds turned their heads and looked at him. After a moment's silence they all burst out simultaneously into a chorus of laughter in which was blended the shrill ring of feminine voices. This was so lifelike that Lord Ewald felt as if he were in the presence of human beings, and he stopped short.

The inventor, who had remained behind, in the darkness of

the tunnel, to fasten the slab, came slowly forward towards Lord Ewald and said:

'My lord, I had forgotten. They are welcoming you with a serenade. If I had known in time what we were going to do this evening, I would have spared you this racket by interrupting the current of the battery which animates these birds you see here.

'In these birds I have tried to reproduce the words of old-fashioned songs and some human laughter as I thought thus to express the real spirit of progress. Real birds repeat so poorly what one tries to teach them.

'So I have found it rather amusing to catch some fine phrase or odd statement from a casual visitor in my laboratory by the aid of the phonograph and transmit it to these birds – they are really winged condensers – this is one of my secrets which I have not made known.

'Pay no attention to them. Hadaly will make them stop. I will be with you in just a moment, but I must fasten our elevator securely. I don't want it to go back to earth without us.'

Lord Ewald looked with interest at Hadaly, whose calm breathing raised the pale silver of her breast.

The piano suddenly began playing, alone, a beautiful melody. The notes lowered and raised as though they were operated by invisible fingers. The soft voice of the Andraiad began to sing to this accompaniment:

> Hail! O fond youth, what can you gain?
>   The tears of hope shall be my dower;
> Love's curses on my head doth rain.
> Flee, then! Hasten! Your eyes refrain;
>   I'm no more than a dying flower.

Then, from the garden of flowers, there came an almost deafening noise, shouting, harsh voices of human beings, cries of admiration, foolish questions, the sound of applause, offers of money, *et cetera*. But, at a sign from Hadaly, all this stopped immediately.

The silence was broken again by the singing of a nightingale. The beautiful song, so perfect, so natural, seemed strange in this artificial place.

'A beautiful voice, is it not, Lord Ewald?' the phantom inquired softly.

'Yes,' replied the young man, both chilled and thrilled by speech from this semi-living form. 'That is the work of God.'

'Then admire it, but do not try to find out how it is produced.'

'What risks would I run if I did try?'

'God would take away the voice,' murmured the phantom. The professor now came towards them.

'Ah,' he said, 'I see that you already seem to understand each other. Don't pay any attention to me; I don't wish to interfere; just go ahead.'

'We were talking about the nightingale,' Lord Ewald explained. 'It was a strange idea of yours to give a real nightingale to an Andraiad.'

'That is because I am a lover of nature. I liked the plumage of the bird very much, and his death, which occurred two months ago, made me very sad.'

'What! The nightingale has been dead two months?'

'Yes. I took a record of his last song. The phonograph which reproduced it is twenty-five miles away from here, in a room in my apartment in the city.

'I have attached a telephone to the wires passing over my laboratory, and a branch comes down to these vaults. It ends right over there by that cluster of flowers; in fact, it is this flower right here that is singing.'

As he spoke the professor lit his cigar at the heart of a pink camellia.

'Really,' murmured Lord Ewald sadly, 'can it be that the bird whose song I heard is dead.'

'No,' the professor replied, 'not entirely dead, since I have been able to record his song, to register his soul. I did that by electricity.'

He touched the bird, and shrugged with annoyance at the tinkle of broken crystal that followed.

Suddenly, Lord Ewald felt a light touch on his shoulder. He turned. It was Hadaly.

'Ah,' she said, in a voice so sad that it made him tremble, 'that is what I feared – God has taken away the song.'

## XII.

'Hadaly,' said Professor X, 'we have just come from the earth, and the trip made us thirsty.'

The phantom drew near to Lord Ewald. 'My lord,' she said, 'will you take ale or sherry?'

'I'll take sherry, if you please,' he murmured.

Hadaly took from a stand a plate on which stood three beautiful Venetian glasses, and a bottle of wine, still wrapped in straw. Beside the wine was a box of Havana cigars.

She poured the wine into the three glasses and offered two of them to her callers. Then she raised her glass high above her head and said:

'Lord Ewald, I drink to your loves.'

The tone in which the toast was given was so exquisite that it was impossible for Lord Ewald to take offence at the sentiment.

After she had toasted Lord Ewald, Hadaly threw the contents of her glass towards the astral lamp. The old Spanish wine fell in sparkling drops on the floor.

'Thus,' said she gaily, 'I drink, in spirit, to the light.'

Lord Ewald turned to the professor.

'Tell me, Mr Wizard,' he said, 'how is it that Miss Hadaly can reply to what I say to her? It is an impossibility for such a being to foresee my questions, or for you to have had foresight enough to have recorded beforehand the correct replies on records.'

'Please permit me to keep Hadaly's secret – at least for the time being,' Professor X pleaded.

Lord Ewald bowed to his host. Then, like a man who is surrounded by marvels, and who has decided not to be astonished at any thing he sees, he drank his sherry and placed the empty glass back on the stand.

Throwing away his cigar, which had gone out, he took another from the box on Hadaly's stand, and, following the professor's example, he lighted it at an illuminated flower.

'Do you see this swan?' asked the scientist. 'I have put the voice of Albani in that. Once, on a trip to Europe, I made a record of the great diva's singing of the "Casta Diva," the great prayer from Norma. I only regret that I did not live in the time of Malibran.

'That bird of paradise over there can render for you, through all the voices and instruments imprisoned in him, the whole of Berlioz's opera, "The Damnation of Faust." That other bird over there can recite the whole of Shakespeare's "Hamlet."'

'I have only respected the voice of the nightingale, as he alone seemed to have the right; all the others are singers, musicians, and comedians to amuse Hadaly. Since she lives so far beneath the earth, she must have some distractions. What do you think of the aviary?'

'It makes the wildest imagination of the Arabian Nights pale into insignificance,' said Lord Ewald.

'Yes; the world has not begun to realize what electricity can do. We have just commenced. Soon there will be no need for cannons, or dynamite, or armies –'

'Oh, that's just a dream,' Lord Ewald objected.

'We have no more dreams!' said the master electrician, in a low voice.

He was thoughtful for a few moments, then he went on:

'Now, I am going to show you, seriously, the organisms of the new electric human creature – *The Future Eve* – which, aided by the artificiality which has been in vogue for a long time, seems to meet in full the secret wishes of our race –'

'Will you let me ask you one thing more, professor? Some thing perhaps to me more interesting than the examination you are about to make. What was the motive that caused you to create this incomparable creature?'

Lord Ewald looked straight into the eyes of the inventor, as he waited for his reply.

'That is a secret, my lord.'

'You may trust me with it,' said Lord Ewald urgingly. 'You know I had a secret and I told it at your request.'

'So be it then. Hadaly's exterior is the result of the intellectual ideal which preceded her in my mind. After you know the sum total of the reflections from which she emanated, you will be better able to understand the anatomy of this electrical being when I explain it to you later.

'Hadaly,' said the professor, turning abruptly, 'will you be good enough to leave us for awhile. I wish to say something to this young gentleman in private.'

The Andraiad, without replying, walked slowly to the end

of the vaulted hall, holding her bird of paradise high in the air on her silver fingers.

'I once had a friend, a friend of my childhood; an inventor; a splendid fellow in every way,' Professor X began. 'In a few years he rose from comparative poverty to riches. He married a girl he had loved for a long time.

'Two years passed. One day he was in the city attending a business meeting. After the conference, his friends suggested a music hall.

'Anderson, that was my friend's name, was a model husband. He was seldom away from home for any length of time. However, that same morning, a foolish little domestic scene had occurred.

'Mrs Anderson, without any reason, had asked her husband not to attend the meeting. He argued with her, and, because she would not give him her reason, he went.

'At the music hall, dazzled by the lights, excited by the music, his eyes wandered vaguely to a girl with red-gold hair who was dancing in a ballet. He put up his glasses and found that she was very attractive, but he gave her no more thought.

'Later, his friends went behind the scenes and he went with them. It was all a novelty to him. There he met Evelyn Habal, the pretty red-haired girl. Anderson gazed around him absent-mindedly, without paying any attention to the dancer.

'His friends proposed for all of them a champagne supper at a restaurant, but Anderson refused to go. And then he thought of the little scene that he had had at home that morning. The affair still rankled and he decided not to return home until his wife was asleep. He went to supper fully decided to leave as soon as the meal was over.

'Piqued by Anderson's lack of attention, Miss Habal set out to captivate him. And after he had imbibed several glasses of champagne, he began to think her very delightful.

'Anderson was a strait-laced man. He adored his wife. Yet he became gradually enamoured of the charms of the dancer. The place, the wine, and the laughter were responsible.

'Mrs Anderson, conforming to traditions, sat up all night waiting for her husband. One glance at him was enough for her. It was as though an icy hand had touched her heart.

'She asked him what had happened. He explained to her

that the banquet had lasted longer than he had expected, and that he had thought it better to remain with one of the party.

'Mrs Anderson turned as pale as a corpse, and said: "My dear, let this first lie be the last." She went to her room and wept.

'Poor Anderson suffered cruelly. His love for his wife was real. But from that day, his home was changed. He had a chill reconciliation with his wife, but his home soon became intolerable.

'After some weeks of misery, he returned to Miss Habal. His downfall began. He lavished his money upon her. When it was all gone, she refused to see him any more.

'Anderson changed physically and morally. He shunned his friends. Finally, he took his life. Poor Anderson!'

The professor paused for a moment as he thought with regret of his dead friend. Then he continued:

'Well, when I thought of poor Anderson and the woman who had caused his downfall, I told myself that all women are complex. They are all illusive. We are attracted to them by their beauty, wit, or other charms. They are not only illusive, but illusions.

'So I bethought: Why not build a woman who should be just the thing that we wanted her to be? Why not supply illusion for illusion?

'So Miss Habal became the subject of my observations – for I was about to try out a new and curious experiment. I went to study her.

'It is now several years since she died, but I can make her come back now as if nothing had happened. See, she will dance for you.'

The professor arose and pulled a cord.

On the large white silk sheet stretched on the ebony frame suddenly appeared the figure, lifelike, of a woman, a pretty red-haired woman.

In front of the powerful light of the great lamp was hung a long strip of gummed material covered with tiny glasses of transparent tints. These had begun to move, wound by a clock movement, and to pass through the bell-shaped lens of a powerful reflector.

It was the light from this reflector which fell upon the silk sheet. The vision with the transparent skin was a woman's photograph.

She began to dance. The movements were produced by the passing of successive photographs at a high rate of speed in front of the powerful light thrown by the reflector.

The professor touched a fluting on the ebony frame. Suddenly a flat, dull voice was heard – the dancer was singing to her fandango.

The movements, the looks, the twisting gestures, the play of the eyes and the eyelids, the very meaning of her smile, were reproduced.

'Is she not a fascinating creature?' asked the professor. 'My poor Anderson!

'See her beautiful red hair, truly that is burned gold, and her exquisite complexion, and her strange, almond-shaped eyes, her pretty fingers with the rose-coloured nails, her smile and her dazzling crimson mouth. In spite of all, nature is very beautiful.'

'Yes,' said Lord Ewald, 'you can joke at nature all you like. But I'll wager your friend found this young woman very delightful.'

'Wait!' cried the professor, bitterly.

He slipped the cord. The ribbon of photographs in front of the lamp, the living image, disappeared. A second ribbon began to unwind rapidly.

On the sheet was thrown the vision of a little, bloodless being, vaguely feminine, with stunted limbs, hollow cheeks, toothless jaws, almost without lips, the head nearly bald, the eyes sunken, and the face wrinkled.

The wretched apparition sang a coarse song in a drunken voice, and danced in grotesque imitation of the figure that had preceded it

'What do you think of it now?' asked the professor.

'Who is the old witch?'

'The same girl. Only this is the real girl. All this was there under the semblance of the other. The other was the illusion. Art can work wonders, my dear fellow.

'Here is the real Evelyn Habal, shorn of her exterior attractions, her fine rags and tinsel.

'Can you imagine any man dying for that? How could a man be inspired with a noble passion for that?

'Now, what do you think of simple nature? We could never compete with this, could we? I ought to despair? I ought to bow my head? What do you think of it?

'Don't you think that if Anderson had seen her for the first time like this, he would still be sitting by his fireside with his wife and children? After all, that is worth everything in the world.

'What are exterior attractions? Women have fairy fingers, and once the first impression is produced the illusion is tenacious. It even feeds on the most odious faults, one clings to the chimera with one's very nails, and, often, they come to what my friend did – an untimely death.'

'Did you say that both those figures were produced by the same woman?' Lord Ewald demanded.

The scientist looked thoughtfully at his young friend.

'Ah, young man,' he said, 'you indeed have the ideal very deep in your heart. Alas, that I must disillusion you.

'Look, my lord, here in reality is what destroyed poor Anderson's body, fortune, soul and life.'

Pulling out a drawer from the wall, while the wretched figure was still performing its sinister dancing, he added:

'You will now see the spoils of the charmer, the arsenal of the sex. Will you have the kindness to light up for us, Hadaly?'

The veiled figure of the Andraiad came forward promptly.


## XIII.


'Here,' said Professor X, 'we have most of the charms of Miss Evelyn Habal. If you found them natural in the first aspect, Lord Ewald, you will have to correct your impression. She was only counterfeit.'

Hadaly raised a lighted wand above her head and stood close to the sombre drawer – like a statue beside a sepulchre – while the professor called out like an auctioneer:

'First of all, we have the wonderful hair of Herodias, gleaming like the rays of the sun in the autumn foliage; the souvenir of Eve, golden hair, eternally glorious!'

He shook out a horrible switch of discoloured hair, in which one could see that the grey hairs had been dyed.

'Here is the lily complexion, the blush of innocent modesty, the colour of the tempting lips!'

He pulled out boxes of cosmetics, creams, powders, and beauty patches.

'Here is the calm splendour of the magnificent eyes, the arc for the eyebrows, the shadow and the languor of passion, the pretty veins of the temples, the pink of the nostrils, which dilate with joy as she listens to the footsteps of her beloved.'

He threw out the curling tongs, blackened with smoke; the blue pencil, the rouge.

'Here are the dazzling teeth, so pretty and white, which in the magic of a smile provokes the first kiss.'

He touched the spring of a set of false teeth, making them click together.

'Here is the beauty of the velvety throat, the clinging arms, the alabaster shoulders.'

He lifted up, one after another, the instruments for enamelling.

The scientist threw all the things back into the drawer pell mell, and letting the lid fall as he would on a coffin, he pushed it back into the wall.

'I think, my dear fellow, that you are more enlightened now,' he said. 'Of course, I don't mean that all women are like that, but most of those who bring men to a desperate end are, more or less. But what I want to say is, that in the end all will resemble that spectre on the screen.'

Lord Ewald was silent and saddened. He looked at Hadaly thoughtfully.

'Yes,' said the professor, 'one could kneel before a tomb, but it would be very difficult to bow before the contents of that drawer, would it not?'

He pulled the cord, the spectre disappeared, the funeral oration was ended.

'It is really not worth while,' he continued, 'to break one's home ties and to spring headlong into suicide. All for the contents of that drawer. Bah!

'With proof that my poor friend had been held by such chimeras as these, I said to myself: "This is nothing but an artificial living illusion. In Europe and America every year there are thousands of reasonable men who forsake splendid wives and allow themselves to be destroyed by an absurd illusion –"'

'Well,' interrupted Lord Ewald, 'we will say rather that your friend's case was an exceptional form of madness that should have been treated by a physician. There are not enough charming destroyers for us to establish a general law from this adventure.'

'I have commenced by establishing it very well,' said the professor. 'You forget that you, yourself, found the first aspect of Evelyn Habal quite natural. In reality it was all artificial.

'All women who bring about such catastrophes are artificial. Very well, chimera for chimera. Let us spare the woman the trouble of being artificial.

'Let us try to obtain from science an equation of love. It will save thousands and thousands of lives.

'And by the aid of a clairvoyant named Sowana, of whom I will speak later, I discovered the formula that I dreamed of. Then, suddenly, from out of the shadows, I created – Hadaly.

'Since her creation in these subterranean vaults, I have been waiting for a man whose intelligence I could depend upon, and who was in such a hopeless, despairing state as to be willing to brave the first experiment.

'It will be to you that I shall owe the realization of my masterpiece. You have loved the most beautiful woman, and she has brought you to such a mood that you are willing to die.'

Having finished his argument, he turned to Lord Ewald and indicated the fascinating, veiled creature.

'Now,' asked the professor, 'do you still wish to know how the phenomenon of this future vision was accomplished? Do you feel sure that your voluntary illusion will be strong enough to withstand this explanation?'

'Yes,' declared Lord Ewald, glancing at the phantom, who now appeared to be suffering from a sudden fear. 'What is wrong with her?' he asked.

'Nothing. It is a natural action. It is a child's attitude. She is hiding her face from the world.'

There was a tense moment. Then the inventor cried:

'Come, Hadaly!'

The veiled figure walked slowly, like a shadow, towards

the marble table. 'My lord,' said the soft voice, 'be indulgent for my humble unreality, and, before disdaining the dream of it, remember the human companion who forced you to resort to a phantom to draw you away from a destroying love.'

As these words were uttered there was a flash, and a flood of electricity animated the metal armour of the Andraiad. The professor touched the figure with a piece of wire held between two long glass pincers. The pulsing flame died out, and it was as though the soul of this humanlike thing had disappeared.

Then, with an irregular movement, the mechanical figure settled onto its back on the table with its head resting on the violet silk cushion.

The inventor leaned over and, taking two metal leashes from the slab, slipped them over the feet of the figure, which was now laid out like a patient on a surgical table.

He touched one of the phantom's rings. The metal armour slowly opened.

Lord Ewald started and turned pale. His nausea was more spiritual than physical.

Until now, despite all evidence, he had been assailed with doubt. It had been impossible for him not to think that there was a human, living creature enclosed in the armour.

Instead, here was revealed this entirely fictitious creature, born of science and of the patience of genius.


## XIV.

The professor loosened the black veil which draped the figure.

'An Andraiad,' he said, impassively, 'is divided into four parts.

'First: The vital system, the internal part, which includes equilibrium, walking, the voice, gesticulation, the senses, the future expression of the countenance, the secret regulation of movement – or better expressed – the soul.

'Second: The plastic mediator – that is to say, the metallic envelope, separated from the epidermis and the flesh, a kind of armature with flexible joints, in which the internal system is firmly fixed.

'Third: The incarnation – or, properly expressed, the artificial flesh – superimposed on the mediator and adherent to it, and which includes the features and the outlines, together with the bony skeleton, the venous network of the musculature, and the various proportions of the body.

'Fourth: The epidermis, or human skin, which includes and implies the complexion, the pores, the features, the smile, the subtle changes of expression, the accurate labial movements in speech, the hair of the head, the ocular apparatus, with the individuality of the glance, the dental system.'

The scientist had uttered these words as impassively as if he were stating a theorem in geometry. His young listener felt from the voice that Professor X was on the point of furnishing the proof.

Lord Ewald felt his blood congeal.

'My lord,' the professor continued in a voice strangely grave and melancholy, 'you are about to witness the birth of an ideal creature, in listening to the explanation of the internal organisms of Hadaly. What Juliet could undergo such an examination without causing Romeo to faint?

'But this Andraiad, even in her beginnings, causes at no moment the frightful impression called forth by the vital process of the human organism. In her everything is affluent, ingenious and impressive. Look!'

With this, he pressed with his scalpel upon the central apparatus, which was split at the cervical vertebra.

'This is the central point of life in man,' he went on. 'It is the region of the vertebra, the point where the marrow is formed. The prick of a needle here, as you know, is sufficient to extinguish life instantly.

'Let us examine, first of all, at a glance, as it were, this organism as a whole. I will explain the details to you later.

'Thanks to the power which resides in these metal discs, heat, movement and power are distributed throughout the body of Hadaly by the network of these shining wires, reproduction of our nerves, arteries and veins. Owing to these discs of hardened glass interposed between the current and the network of wires, movement begins or ceases in one of the members or in the entire body. Here you see the electromagnetic motor.

'This spark, a legacy from Prometheus, produces respiration by animating this magnet placed vertically between the breasts.

I have even given thought to those deep sighs that reflect the sadness of a woman's heart.

'Hadaly, being of a gentle and taciturn character, is not ignorant of them, nor is their charm absent from her personality. Women will all tell you that the imitation of these melancholy sighs is easy. Actresses sell them by the dozen.' The professor interrupted himself with a short laugh.

'Here are the two golden phonographs, inclined at an angle towards the center of the breast, which serve Hadaly as lungs. Through them pass, one by one, the harmonious, I might say celestial speeches, somewhat as the sheets pass through a printing press.

'A single metallic sheet contains words sufficient for seven hours; these words are the product of the greatest poets, the most subtle metaphysicians and the profoundest romancers of this century. For this reason Hadaly substitutes general intelligence for an individual intelligence.

'You see here two delicate rods of steel, trembling on fluted bases; they await only the voice of your friend, Miss Cleary. They will seize it at a distance while she is reciting, as an actress, scenes incomprehensible to her. Hadaly will incarnate herself forever in these rôles.

'Below the lungs we have a cylinder for the gestures, the walk, the visual expression, and the postures of the adored being. It is a copy of the cylinders of the highly perfected street organs. The inductor of this cylinder is, so to speak, the great sympathetic control of our marvellous phantom.

'The cylinder governs the expression of about seventy general movements; that is, approximately, the number which are at the disposal of a well bred woman.

'Our movements, except in the case of neurotic and highly nervous individuals, are nearly always the same; only the varying situations of life lend shade to them and make them appear different.

'I have calculated, by analysing their components, that twenty-seven or twenty-eight movements, as a maximum, constitute a rare personality. Moreover, what is a woman who gesticulates a great deal? An insufferable creature! One should encounter here only harmonious movements, the others being useless or shocking.

'Now, the two lungs and the great sympathetic control of

Hadaly are united by this unique movement, of which the electric fluid furnishes the impulse. Twenty hours of conversation, inspiring, captivating, are inscribed on these sheets, ineffaceable, thanks to galvanoplasty, and their corresponding expression is likewise fixed in the roughness of this cylinder, encrusted, in turn, in the micrometer.

'I am able to read the gestures on this cylinder as readily as a type-setter reads a page of type backwards – it is a question of habit. I shall correct, let us say, this proof sheet according to the mobility, or changeableness, of Miss Cleary. This operation is not difficult, thanks to successive photography, of which you have just seen an application –'

'But,' interrupted Lord Ewald, 'a scene such as you imagine presupposes an interlocutor.'

'Well,' replied the professor, 'will you, yourself, not be this interlocutor?'

'How will it be possible for you, professor, to foresee what I shall ask or reply to the Andraiad?'

'Everything may serve as an answer to anything, my lord; it is the great kaleidoscope of human speech. Given the colour and the tone of a subject in the human mind, it is indifferent what word may be used in discussing it in the infinity of human conversation. There are many vague, shadowy words, of strange intellectual elasticity, whose charm and depth depend entirely on that to which they respond.

'Let us suppose a detached word – say the word *already* – as the one to be uttered by the Andraiad at a given moment. You will expect this word, which will be uttered in the soft and grave voice of your charming young friend.

'Ah! Think of the number of questions and thoughts to which this one word may furnish an apt response. It is for you to create its depth and beauty by your very question.

'This is what you try to do in real life, with a living woman; only, when it is this very word that you expect, hope for, when it would be in such sweet harmony with your thought that you long to prompt its utterance, so to speak, never does she utter it. There will always be a harsh dissonance; another word, in fact, which her natural caution will suggest, and that will stab your heart.

'With the future Alicia, the real Alicia, the Alicia of your dreams, you will never be subjected to these sterile disappointments. It will be the expected word, the beauty of which will depend on your suggestion, that your dream-woman will utter.

'Her conscious utterance will no longer be the negation of yours, but will become the semblance of the soul that responds to your melancholy. You will be able to evoke in her the radiant reality of your exclusive love, without fearing, this time, lest she repudiate your dream.

'Her words will never disappoint your hopes. They will always be sublime – provided your inspiration serves to arouse them.

'Here, at least, you will have no fear of being misunderstood, as with the living woman; you will need only to give heed to the pauses indicated between the words. It will not even be necessary for you to articulate your words yourself – hers will be the reply to your thoughts and your silences.'

## XV.

'My dear professor,' said Lord Ewald, 'do you expect me to play a continual farce? I may as well tell you, at this point, that I shall be obliged to refuse the offer.'

'Nonsense, my dear fellow,' Professor X expostulated. 'Were you not always playing a farce with the original? From all you have told me, I know that it was necessary for you to keep your inner thoughts hidden out of politeness.

'Every man plays a comedy – he deceives himself. We are none of us sincere, for we don't even know ourselves.

'Now, since Miss Cleary is an actress, and is only worthy of your admiration in that rôle, why should you ask more of the Andraiad? She will also have a great fascination in her acting.'

'That is very specious,' said Lord Ewald sadly, 'but always to hear the same words, to have them forever accompanied by the same expression, no matter how wonderful and beautiful that expression, and how beautiful that acting might be, would be tiresome.'

'Do you think that we are alway improvising?' scoffed the professor. 'Why, we are always reciting. For nearly two thousand years all our prayers have been only weak dilutions of those which were bequeathed to us.

'In every day life nearly all our phrases are repeated. You won't always think that you are having a conversation with a phantom when you talk with Hadaly, I assure you.

'Each human trade has its particular phrases, and every man therein turns around and around in this circle. A man's vocabulary, which he thinks is great, is reduced to about one hundred phrases constantly repeated.'

'Very well,' said Lord Ewald, 'you seem to have a winning argument for all my questions and objections. Proceed with the dissection of your beautiful corpse.'

The professor again took up his glass pincers.

'It is getting late,' he said, 'and I have scarcely time to give you a general idea of Hadaly's possibilities. But if you get an idea that will be sufficient. The rest is only a question of workmanship.

'See here, she has silver feet, the beautiful silver of moonlight; they are only waiting for the pink nails and the delicate veins of the living Venus. But I must tell you that, if the footsteps seem light when walking, they are not really so. These feet are filled with quicksilver. The lower limbs are filled with a liquid metal which ascends and becomes restricted at the beginning of the calf, so that the feet bear all the weight. These two little boots are of fifty pounds weight. The Andraiad, after it is covered with the flesh I have manufactured, will have the walk which is so charming in a lively woman.

'I wish you to notice that the swan-like neck is united to these impressionable wires. They control the movements of the head.

'Note the delicate finish of this ivory bone work. Isn't it delightful?' the master inventor said with just pride. 'This charming skeleton is fastened to the armour by these crystal rings, in which each bone plays with the exact value of the movement required.

'All this is controlled by the central current, according to the swaying movements of the torso, which dictates to them their personal inflections, after these have been registered on the motor cylinder.'

Lord Ewald leaned forward so as to get a closer view of the

mysteries. It appeared to him as though he were looking at a friend being operated on for his amusement. He could not repress a shudder.

But the professor, totally oblivious of his young friend's feeling, gave a jerk or two to the body to illustrate his point. He appeared to have forgotten that not so long ago he had been talking, with almost human friendliness, to the figure before him.

'And here,' he went on, 'are the wires which control the gait. You can see that, when she is in this position, the insulator interposes between the generating wires and the magnet. In her upright position, the limb which receives the spheroid on its target is the one that bends.'

Lord Ewald felt hollow in the pit of his stomach. He bravely tried to smile.

'Now, we will suppose, my lord, that you have pressed the amethyst on Hadaly's finger, because you want her to walk; then, the order to move is immediately transmitted electrically; the spheroid will move to the nearest disc, as it may chance, and the limb connected with that disc will move.

'The weight of the body thrown forward gives an impetus to the heavy boot and the foot. This causes the foot to come to the ground, in a step measuring forty centimetres. Do you understand me clearly?'

The young Englishman nodded without any enthusiasm.

The professor began again.

'Once the Andraiad's foot is on the ground, she will remain immobile in this position. But if the tension of the knee is increased and it is pulled up about three centimetres, it comes in contact with the gold target. This exerts the crystal globe and it moves toward the other target and begins the movement all over again.

'This is how the phenomenon of the Andraiad's pace is procured. It moves forwards or backwards, as the case may be, as many steps as are inscribed on the cylinder, or until it is checked by a counter order from a finger ring.'

## XVI.

Great beads of perspiration stood out on Lord Ewald's forehead, and some ran down his face like tears, as he looked at the calm countenance of the master inventor. He felt the whole thing to be unreal, unbelievable.

Meanwhile, the professor had touched a small urn in the Andraiad's chest. There came a peculiar odorous mist in the air.

'Now, my lord, this perfumed smoke is nothing to be alarmed at. It is nothing but a vapour thrown off by the battery.'

As he spoke the professor lifted the Andraiad's hand. An almost blinding flash ran through the thousands of sensitive wires.

'You see,' said the professor triumphantly, 'she is an angel. If theology informs us aright, angels are creatures of fire and light, and that is what Hadaly is made of.'

The professor looked at Lord Ewald with a satisfied expression.

'This Andraiad was difficult because she was the first. Since I have written out the general formula, it will only be a matter of detail and of perfection. I hardly think that, at first, they could manufacture thousands of them, for, the first thing they will have to open will be a factory of ideals. This form is perfection.'

Lord Ewald, whose nerves were keenly on edge, began to laugh. The professor's words appeared to him an unseemly joke told at an inopportune time.

He began his merriment lightly at first, but, as the scientist joined in, the strangest feeling of hilarity came over him. The place, the hour, the subject of the experiment, the very idea itself, seemed to grow horribly ridiculous.

For the first time in his life, he found himself overcome with an attack of hysterical laughter, which echoed and re-sounded in this sepulchral Eden. It was some minutes before he could control himself sufficiently to speak.

'What a terrible man you are!' exclaimed Lord Ewald, hoarsely. 'What a gruesome, frightful joker!'

The professor, who was smiling to himself at the uncontrolled laughter which his young friend had permitted himself, replied: 'My lord, it is you who jests. We must hurry. Our time is up.'

At a touch on its arm, the armour of the phantom began to close. At another, the marble table began to rise. Then Hadaly stood up beside her creator. Motionless, veiled, silent, she seemed to be looking at them from beneath the shadows which hid her face.

The impression of disillusion that had somewhat come over Lord Ewald, during the professor's detailed explanation, began to disappear. His half dreamy attitude came back to him.

'Are you resurrected?' asked the professor calmly of the Andraiad.

'Perhaps!' replied the dream voice of Hadaly, coming from under the black veil.

## XVII.

At the sound of the phantom's voice Lord Ewald felt a prophetic sensation, as if a greater marvel was to come. And suddenly Hadaly turned to him.

'My lord,' she said, 'will you grant me a favour, in return for all the trouble that I have undergone for your instruction?'

'Why – er – certainly,' he murmured.

Hadaly, instead of voicing her plea as the young Englishman had expected, turned away from him and moved towards the bank of flowers at the end of the hall. A large velvet bag was hanging by a cord from one of the bushes. The phantom went directly towards this and removed it from its place, then she retraced her steps to where he was standing.

'My lord,' she said, 'I believe that in the land of the living it is considered good to do some worthy deed each day. This serves to pay for the blessings and pleasures which have been enjoyed.

'It is fitting that this deed should be performed before the close in order to complete the action for that period of time. So, will you let me ask, in the name of a very estimable widow – a young woman – alms for her and her two children? Just a little contribution.'

'What does this mean?' demanded Lord Ewald of the professor.

'I have not the slightest idea,' declared the scientist, who was quite as astounded as the young man. 'But, my dear fellow, it is not the first time that she has given me a surprise.'

'It is nothing unusual,' went on the phantom. 'I am asking alms for this poor young woman who has nothing in the world to live for but her two children. If it were not that it is her duty to provide for them, she would not deign to live another day.

'A terrible misfortune has crushed her so that, even in the face of this duty, she longs for death. But a sort of perpetual ecstasy lifts her soul outside of this world and renders her powerless to earn her bread. She is indifferent to her own painful privations, but she suffers untold tortures mentally when she thinks that the children are in want.

'She is in such a state that her mind only permits her to distinguish eternal things – she has even forgotten her earthly name – she calls herself by another, which she says was given to her by some strange voices in a dream.

'Will you grant my request? It is my first. You have come from the world of the living. Will you please join your offering to mine?'

After she had spoken, Hadaly went to a stand close by and took up some pieces of gold, which she dropped into the bag.

'Of whom do you speak, Miss Hadaly?' asked Lord Ewald.

'Of Mrs Anderson, my lord, the wife of that unfortunate man who died for the love – oh, well, you know – for the love of all those things in there.'

The veiled figure pointed to the drawer in the wall which held the gruesome objects – the relics of the woman who had wrecked the life of the professor's friend.

Lord Ewald could not refrain from taking a step backward when the Andraiad leaned toward him with the black velvet purse in her outstretched hand. He felt that her conversation was weird and her imagination sinister, but the sentiment concerning the offer appealed to the humanity in him. He reached in his pocket and pulled out a handful of bank notes and dropped them into the black purse.

'Well, professor,' he inquired, 'what is the explanation of this? Your creation questions me, answers me, and talks rationally about matters which happen down here and in the world which she has never seen.

'You don't mean to tell me that a phonograph can speak before a human voice has had a chance to make a record. You can not have invented a cylinder motor which will dictate to the phantom, which can translate thought into speech before it has been uttered by a human voice?'

'I can realize,' Professor X replied with a smile, 'that all this must seem strange, but I assure you the peculiar characteristics which you have mentioned are, relatively, the easiest to produce. I give you my word that I will prove this, and I know that the simplicity of my explanation will astonish you.

'However, I think that it would be wiser to defer the revelation of the secret for a short while, as there is something else to which I wish to draw your attention.

'Do you realize, my dear fellow, that you have never asked me any questions about the nature of Hadaly's face. Have you not felt any curiosity about its present nature?'

'The truth is that, since she is veiled, I thought it would be very indiscreet to ask,' his lordship explained.

The scientist looked at his young benefactor with a grave smile, as he said:

'The beautiful face of Miss Cleary, which remains fixed in your memory, will always reappear in the phantom's features which you are hoping to see in the future.

'I am glad that you have voiced no wish to see Hadaly's face, for I want you to retain the single imprint of that other face uppermost in your mind. It is for the same reason that I have not divulged to you the other secret – of which I have spoken.'

'Let it be as you wish, my friend,' declared Lord Ewald. 'Is it your idea to give the phantom the identical appearance of Miss Cleary?'

'Yes. So far, you may have noticed, we have not spoken of the epidermis, or the outer coating. We have only spoken of the flesh.

'You know how the touch of the arm and hand in the laboratory surprised you? I am employing the same substance now.

'The flesh of a living person is composed of certain parts of graphite, nitric acid, water, and various other chemical bodies which can be easily recognized in the microscopic examination of the sub-cutaneous tissues. These cohere in life under a great pressure.

'Now, in the construction of the Andraiad's flesh these elements are compounded in a similar manner. They are coagulated by the use of the hydraulic press. It is just the same as the flesh of the living.

'You cannot imagine to what a point of fineness iron has been powdered for this incarnation to make it very sensitive to electric action. The flesh transmits the orders of the current to the epidermis. These orders are, of course, those which are inscribed upon the cylinder of movements.

'Now, throughout the flesh there are what might be termed regulators or resistances. By these we can produce the subtle shadings of smiles, laughter on the cheek, and the other intricate and delicate embellishments of expression which will give the Andraiad the identity of the model.

'In order to produce the softened brilliancy of true flesh, the compound, which in its original state is snow white, is shaded with colouring matter like smoked amber and pale pink. The indefinite sparkle is produced by a mica-like powder, and this is set by means of a photo-chromatic compound. There you have the illusion.

'Now, we must experiment from another angle. I will take it upon myself to persuade Miss Cleary this evening to agree.'

At the sound of this name Lord Ewald locked up, startled.

'Don't excite yourself, my lord,' said the professor. 'I assure you it will be without her knowledge of our true purpose, and I guarantee that she will be complaisant. Her vanity will be flattered.

'Everything will be conducted in the most conventional manner. A great sculptress, a woman whom I know well, will commence work to-morrow in my laboratory. I shall ask Miss Cleary to sit for her.

'At these sittings Miss Cleary will have no other companion than this artist, who is called "Sowana." She will not idealize Miss Cleary. She will counterdraw her. She will seize the exact lines of her subject's statuesque form.

'Under my watchful eye, with instruments of the greatest precision, she will take the exact measurements of the form, the height, the breadth, the hands, the face, the feet, the features, the limbs and arms, and the exact weight of the living being.

'Hadaly will be standing there unseen. She will remain motionless, in readiness for her incarnation.

'We will apply the carnal substance, dazzling and perfect,

to the armour of the Andraiad according to the thickness of her beautiful counterpart. The substance lends itself admirably to carving, with the aid of very fine tools. The features at first will appear without any tint or shadings.

'We will then have the statue awaiting the order of the Pygmalion creator. The head alone requires more work than all of the rest of the body, because we must fashion the lobes of the ears, the gentle dilation of the nostrils when breathing, the transparency of the veins in the temples, the folds of the lips, and the play of the eyelids. The lips, on account of their delicacy and flexibility, are made of finer substance than the rest of the features.

'Can you imagine the tiny magnets that are necessary to bring an entire correspondence of the imperceptible inductors when the Andraiad smiles? Look at the thousand luminous points indicated by the vast photographic proofs of that smile.

'As soon as we have attached the flesh,' continued the scientist, 'we will then proceed to reproduce exactly the features and the lines of the body. Do you know the results obtained in photo-sculpture? Thus, one can get an accurate transposition of aspect.

'Miss Cleary will be photo-sculptured on Hadaly. In a flash, as it were, we will have a microscopic duplicate – a thing so perfect that Miss Cleary, if she beheld it, would think that she were looking at herself in a mirror. When all this has been done, another great artist, to whom I have imparted my enthusiasm, will give the final touches.

'Everything will be perfection. There will be a perfect flower of a skin, as velvety and satiny as it is transparent. Er – my lord, do you know has Miss Cleary all her own teeth?'

Lord Ewald looked up in amazement at this question; but, seeing that the inventor's face was serious, he nodded.

'That is good,' said the professor. 'With an anæsthetic of my own composition we will put her to sleep. We will then take an imprint of her teeth, tongue, and cavity of the mouth, the exact doubles of which will be transposed into her twin's mouth.

'You have spoken of the light on her teeth when she smiles – the marvellous effect. Well, you will not be able to distinguish the one from the other when the adaptation is made.'

When Professor X had ceased his exposition Lord Ewald

was overcome with another attack of hysterical laughter. The young man exclaimed, between bursts of laughter:

'Don't mind me, professor. Do go on, for Heaven's sake! It is marvellous. Skeletons! Incarnations! Epidermis! Perfumes! It all is too funny for words. It really – ha, ha! – it really makes me laugh and laugh and laugh. Go on, my dear fellow! Ha, ha –'

'I understand how you feel, my lord,' said the inventor. 'It is amusing, taken from that point of view, but life itself is made up of just such small nothings. Just imagine to what small nothings love itself clings.

'Nature changes, but this Andraiad will never change. She will not know life or sickness or death! She is the supreme beauty of a dream. In her magic words there will be the thoughts of several geniuses.

'Her heart will never change, because she has no heart. So, then, it will be your duty to destroy her at the hour of your death.

'A small cartridge of some high explosive will be all that is necessary to blow her to atoms to the four winds of heaven.'

## XVIII.

At this moment Hadaly moved forward from the end of the great vault, threading her way through the ever-blooming plants which brightened her sumptuous abode.

Wrapped in the clinging black folds of her veil-like mantle, with her bird of paradise perched on her shoulders, she gracefully approached her earthly visitors. When she reached the stand she again filled the glasses with wine and offered them to her guests.

They thanked her with a gesture of their heads, and drank.

'It is after midnight,' observed Professor X. 'We must hurry. However, I have a question to settle.

'In regard to your future eyes, Hadaly – tell me, can you see Miss Alicia Cleary from here with your present orbs?'

The phantom appeared to shrink into herself for a moment.

Lord Ewald started as if he had received an electric shock. He sat upright awaiting, with breathless interest, the figure's reply.

'Yes,' the dream voice murmured.

'Tell me how she is dressed and where she is.'

'She is alone, in a train,' Hadaly replied. 'She is holding your telegram in her hand. She is glancing at it; she leans nearer to the light. But the train is moving very fast, and she leans back in her seat again.'

As Hadaly spoke the last words she laughed lightly. Her laugh was echoed by the bird of paradise on her shoulder.

Lord Ewald suddenly realized that the phantom could laugh as well as if not more sweetly than human beings.

'Well, then, Miss Hadaly,' the young nobleman said, 'since you have second sight, will you be good enough to tell us how Miss Cleary is dressed.'

'She is in evening dress,' the Andraiad replied. 'It is a beautiful dress – a pale blue creation. It is of such a pale colour that under the light it looks almost green. She has on a cloak. It is open. She must be very warm, for she is using a fan that has carved ebony sticks and black flowers. On the material of the fan I see a statue –'

'This is astounding!' Lord Ewald interrupted excitedly, turning to the professor. 'It passes all imagination. What she is saying is true.'

'Of course!' said the professor, casually. 'Please talk with Hadaly, while I select some samples of eyes.'

So saying, the professor went to the far corner of the room. Lord Ewald turned to the figure.

'Miss Hadaly, will you be kind enough to tell me what that instrument on the stand over there is used for?' he inquired. 'It looks very complicated.'

'Oh, that instrument, Lord Ewald,' said Hadaly, turning around as if to look at the object from under her veil, and then turning back. 'That is also an invention of our friend, Professor X. It is a calorimetre, and is used to measure the heat in the sun's rays.'

'Oh, yes,' said Lord Ewald, with fantastic calmness, 'I have read of that in our magazines.'

'That is it,' affirmed Hadaly. 'You know, of course, that long before the earth was even nebular some stars had been shining, let us say, from a sort of eternity; but, alas, they were so far away that their radiant light, which travels at the rate of one hundred and eighty-six thousand miles a second, has only recently reached the place that the earth occupies in the heavens.

'It appears that some of these stars have even been extinguished since then, long before their inhabitants could extinguish the earth; yet the rays that came from these stars have survived them, and continue their irrevocable march through space. It is only to-day that the light from these stars, or rather from the ashes of these stars, has reached us.

'The astronomer who contemplates the heavens often admires worlds which no longer exist, but which he can see just the same because of this phantom ray in the illusion of the universe.

'Well, this instrument is so sensitive that it not only can measure the heat in a ray of light, that we might call a dead ray, because it comes from a star that no longer lives, but it can weigh the heat of this sort of star. It is very remarkable.

'Do you know that sometimes, on a very beautiful night, when the grounds are deserted, I take this instrument out on the lawn, and there, all alone, I find great pleasure in weighing the rays of the dead stars.'

Lord Ewald began to feel dizzy. He grasped the back of the seat to assure himself that he was awake. He was beginning to assimilate the idea that what he had heretofore considered the impossible – judging from what he had seen and heard on this night – was quite ordinary and very natural. He felt a dryness in the throat which prevented him from speaking.

'Here are the eyes, my lord,' cried the scientist, now hurrying towards them with an iron box in his hands.

Hadaly, appearing to realize that she would not be required to take any part in the conversation, went over to the sleeping couch and stretched out on it.

'Here are the eyes,' the inventor repeated. 'You see the difficulties which the being of an electro-magnetic creature presents in its manufacture are quite easy to solve. It is only the result that is the mystery.'

'Right, professor!' exclaimed the younger man. 'You have spent quite some time this evening explaining the means employed in obtaining this result, and yet, to me, the result appears to be a thing entirely apart from the means which you have so kindly described.'

'Yes, my dear fellow,' agreed the scientist, 'but you must

remember that I have not given you any definite or conclusive explanations of the physical enigmas of Hadaly. I have, however, told you that, presently, some phenomena of a superior order will present themselves in her. Among these there is one which I will not be able to explain. I will only be able to show you the surprising manifestations.'

'Do you mean the electric fluid?' asked Lord Ewald.

'No; it is another fluid, and Hadaly finds herself under its influence at this very moment. One can only submit to this spirit without being able to analyse it.'

'But, really, professor,' expostulated the young man, 'I don't believe in these invisible spirits.'

'Well, that may be,' the scientist observed, 'but I will swear to you that the things that Hadaly sees from behind that veil of hers are caused by such phenomena. I have not yet been able to produce sight by means of an electric current, although such a thing may be possible. No! Hadaly's vision is not my work!'

Lord Ewald felt his blood run cold; goose flesh stood out on him. But he mastered his confusion, and asked:

'May I know something about it?'

'No! It is not for me to explain. Hadaly, herself, will elucidate the mystery to you some evening, under the stars, in the beautiful silences of the night.'

'Very well,' said Lord Edwald, 'but her conversation seems unreal. What she says seems like the shadows of thoughts to which spirits listen in dreams, but which are dispersed at the awakening. Do you think that I shall understand her?

'Just now, for instance, when she was reasoning about some stars which are called in science "bags of coal," she was rather inexact, according to my schooling. Her reasoning appeared to be guided by a different logic from ours.'

'As for that, my dear fellow,' said the professor, 'rest assured that her astronomy is better than mine.'

'One would think,' said the bewildered young man, 'to hear you speak, that Hadaly had a notion of the infinite.'

'Well, I can also assure you that she has. In fact, she has little else but that. But, to assure yourself of it, you will have to learn to question her according to the oddity of her nature.

'I don't mean in a solemn sort of way. Just lightly – in an everyday manner.'

'Will you give me an example of the questions that I should put to her?' asked Lord Ewald. 'Prove to me that she can really hold in her personality – if we can call it that – in some sort of a way, a notion of the infinite.'

The professor called to the figure. She immediately arose and came towards them, but at a sign from her master she resumed her seat on the couch.

'Hadaly,' said Professor X, 'suppose that a mythological god, quite tremendous and out of proportion, should suddenly spring out of the trans-universal ether and dart across the earth's orbit in a flash of lightning – the same impulse as that which animates you, but of undreamed-of power – so that it could make solar systems spring up from the great abyss in its passage – where do you think this power would end after it had been set in motion?'

Hadaly replied at once in her grave voice, swinging her bird of paradise to and fro upon the tip of her finger.

'I think it would pass into the infinite without more importance being accorded to it than you give to the sparks that flash and fall on the grate at a peasant's fireside.'

Lord Ewald looked at the Andraiad without saying a word.

'You see,' said the professor, turning back to his guest, 'Hadaly sees and understands certain notions, the same as you and I, but she expresses herself differently. She leaves a sort of picture in one's mind after she has spoken.'

'Well,' declared Lord Ewald, 'I give up trying to puzzle the thing out.'

'Then,' said the scientist, 'let us look at these eyes.'

He opened the iron box. Its interior seemed to dart a thousand looks at the young Englishman.

'Observe these,' continued the professor; 'see how pure the sclerotic is; note what a remarkable depth there is in the pupils. They positively disturb one, don't they?

'The action of this coloured photograph adds the personal shade to them. But it is on the iris that we must transmit the exact individuality of the look. Just a question of accuracy. Have you seen many beautiful eyes, my lord?'

'Indeed I have!' asserted Lord Ewald, 'and the most beautiful were in Abyssinia. That is, excepting Miss Cleary's eyes – the eyes that you will see soon.

'When she is looking at anything in an absent-minded

fashion, her eyes are of radiant beauty. But, when she is interested they change, and the expression in them makes you forget the eyes.'

'Then that will simplify my difficulty,' declared the professor, evidently pleased, for the expression of the human look is increased by a thousand exterior incidents – by the imperceptible play of the eyelid, by the immobility of the eyebrow, by the shape of the eyelash, and especially by what one happens to be talking about, and where one happens to be. The surroundings cast a reflection. All these things reënforce the natural expression.

'Now, in this experiment, we must catch both the expression of attention and the expression of vagueness – or, in other words, both the interested and the abstract look. I believe you said that Miss Cleary always looks from under her lashes.'

'She usually does.'

'Well, I will now explain to you how we will reproduce both these looks. We now have those eyes; they are merely spheroids – the inside air of which has been submitted to a very great temperature. The moving of an object passing over one of these will be revealed on this emptiness as abstract as possible – an impression is made, but not retained, for there is no life in the eye.

'But, if we take the same eye and solder an induction wire to the sides of the spheroid with their ends set slightly apart in this emptiness, and we turn on the current, the spark will be vibrating, and you can well imagine that you are witnessing the commencement of life. The physical movement is there.

'See how clear these samples are. They are truly beautiful orbs. We can surely find here a pair that will match the eyes of our Venus di Milo.

'Once the visual point is revealed in their pupils – I suppose that you know that each person's eyes differ in the place of the visual point – once I have located this in Miss Cleary. I will put a spark of electricity in the centre. This will supply the iris with that marvellous flash, that dazzling radiance, that illusion of personality.

'The mobility of the eye is easily arranged; merely a matter of suspension in a socket which will be under the control of the central cylinder.

'When I have finished with these eyes they will have quite

as much emptiness or vacancy in them as Miss Cleary, but the dazzling beauty of her personality will be there. You will have her at her best.'

Lord Ewald smiled nervously. The professor replaced the eyes carefully back in the iron box.

'Of course, it is very easy to imitate the hair,' he said. 'All I need is a lock of Miss Cleary's tresses, and it will be scrupulously imitated.

'As for her skin and the nails on her hands and feet –'

'Professor!' cried the young man. 'Must you go on? Good heavens, to hear the things you love discussed like this is infernal!'

'Ah, but these are not the things that one loves,' the scientist protested; 'they are only the things that one is in love with.'

He pointed to a long box of camphorwood against the wall.

'In that box over there,' he said, 'is an exact imitation of the human skin. Shall I tell you of what it is composed?'

Lord Ewald arose and stamped his feet, which had become numb from his nervous tension.

'No, professor,' he said. 'I do not care to have any more glimpses of the promised vision until the vision itself is complete. I have agreed to enter into this mysterious adventure with you. You assure me that you will soon be able to reveal its marvellous results to me. I believe you.'

The professor bowed.

'Thanks, my lord,' he said. 'I ought not to expect more.'

A bell rang. It was a call from the surface of the earth.

Hadaly arose from the couch on which she had been reclining. She moved slowly, as if she were in a daze.

'There is your beautiful living one, Lord Ewald!' she exclaimed. 'She is just arriving. The carriage is turning in at the gate.'

'Thank you! Good-by, Miss Hadaly,' he said gravely.

The professor shook hands with his creation.

'To-morrow, my dear,' he said, 'you shall have life!'

The phantom silently bowed her head.

All the fantastic birds in the green arbours seemed to waken. The fountains began to play, and the gay flowers nodded their heads.

Hadaly made a low curtsy to both her visitors, and said in a low voice:

'Good-by, Lord Ewald; or, rather, *au revoir!*'

'Now for the earth!' exclaimed the professor, pulling on his bearskin coat.

Lord Ewald also wrapped his fur garment around him.

'We shall be back in the laboratory just in time to greet her,' said the scientist. 'Steady now.'

As soon as they had stepped on the stone slab, it started up rapidly, leaving the realm of shadows for the world of human beings. A few moments later the two men entered the brilliantly lighted laboratory. They were not a moment too soon.

'Here she comes!' Professor. X exclaimed in an excited tone of voice.

## XIX.

He flung open the door of the laboratory. A tall and very beautiful young lady was coming up the steps. Miss Alicia Cleary, the living incarnation of the Venus di Milo.

Her resemblance to the immortal statue was, at the first glance, incontestable. Her aspect gave the two beholders a mysterious clutch at their hearts. Here in the flesh was the woman whose photograph had gleamed in the electrical frame a few hours previously.

She remained standing on the threshold as if surprised at the strange look of the place. Alicia, the usually poised actress, was plainly amazed.

She was beautiful. Over her shoulders was thrown a wonderful sable cloak. Beneath it could be seen a pale blue clinging gown which looked almost green under the lights. Diamonds were sparkling on her throat and hanging pendent from her ears.

'Come in, Miss Cleary,' said Professor X cordially. 'My young friend, Lord Ewald has been waiting most impatiently for you, and, permit me to say, I do not wonder at it.'

'Sir,' replied the beautiful creature, with the intonation of a middle-class saleswoman – but, at the same time, her voice had an exquisitely clear ring, like a ball of gold knocking against crystal. 'Sir, you see, I have come straight here from the opera. As to you, my lord, your telegram upset me terribly – I thought – in fact, I don't know what I did think.'

She swept into the room.

'Whose place is this?' she demanded. 'Where am I?'

'This is my home,' said the professor. 'I am "Mr George Thomas".'

The radiant creature's smile appeared to cool somewhat.

'Indeed!' she remarked.

'Yes,' continued her host obsequiously. 'Mr George Thomas. Have you never heard of me? I am the general representative of the greatest theatres in Europe and America.'

Miss Cleary started, and a smile even more radiant overspread her face.

'Oh, really,' she said, in a little nervous gush. 'I am pleased to make your acquaintance.'

Then, moving nearer to Lord Ewald, she murmured:

'Why did you not tell me this was going to happen? Thank you for taking this step; I shall be celebrated – but this sort of an introduction is not regular, you know. It shouldn't be done this way. I don't want the people who live in this house to think that I'm middle class.'

Then, as Lord Ewald stood looking down at her very camly, she exclaimed:

'Are you still up in the stars, my lord?'

'Alas, yes,' replied the nobleman, bending courteously over the beautiful creature to remove her wraps.

While these two were talking in this aside, the professor had given a violent pull to the ring of steel hidden in the draperies. A heavy, magnificent stand, lit up with candelabra, and bearing an exquisitely served meal, came up through the floor.

It was like a scene in a pantomime – a supper for fairies. The lights flashed, the silver gleamed, and the rays were reflected from the beautiful Saxe porcelain upon which the game and the rare fruit were placed. A little trellised cellarette contained a half dozen old, dusty bottles. Decanters of cordials were within easy reach. There were three seats set about the table.

'Well,' Lord Ewald observed gravely. 'I will have to make a formal introduction. Alicia, this is Mr George Thomas, the noted theatrical producer. Mr Thomas, this is Miss Alicia Cleary, the young lady of whose talents I have already spoken.'

The professor bowed.

'I do hope,' he said, in an impersonal tone, 'that I shall be able to hasten your glorious début at one of our principal theatres. But come, supper is ready, and we can talk while we have some refreshment. The air down here is very keen and gives one a good appetite.'

'That is true, and I am going to eat enough for two people,' Alicia remarked, so frankly that the professor glanced at Lord Ewald in astonishment. Then, Miss Cleary, fearing that she had said something foolish before the manager she wished to impress, said:

'I know that that's not very poetical, gentlemen, but one has to come down to earth sometimes.'

The professor smiled inwardly. Lord Ewald had been right in his analysis.

'You are charming!' the host cried, with assumed good nature. 'Now, let us have supper.'

He preceded his guests to the table, and motioned them to their places. A cluster of tea roses lightly laid, as though by fairy fingers, indicated the place for the young lady.

They took their places. But before they had tasted a morsel, Miss Cleary returned to the subject on which she was interested by saying:

'What shall I have to pay you, Mr Thomas, if, through you, I can make a début in London?'

'Oh,' replied the pseudo Mr Thomas, 'I am delighted to launch a star.'

'I have already sung before crowned heads.'

'Ah, a diva!' exclaimed her host, in ecstasy. He poured wine in their glasses.

'But, sir,' said Alicia, affecting an air of gentle reproof, but, withal, greatly flattered, 'the divas, we all know, have light habits. I am not a bit like that. However, I have to resign myself to a professional career as an actress. But, then, I suppose I shall be able to make a lot of money?'

'Undoubtedly,' he agreed. 'I drink to your success.'

He raised his glass.

'Why, how sympathetic!' cried Alicia.

Lord Ewald looked appealingly at the professor whose face appeared a smiling mask.

Miss Cleary touched her host's glass with her own. The guests drank the golden wine.

All around them there was light, on the mysterious cylinders, on the large glass disks, and on the angles of the reflectors; the rays from the lamps trembled. An impression of great solemnity, even of the occult, abruptly seized the diners. All three were pale. The great wings of Science had brushed them for an instant.

Miss Cleary continued to smile. The diamonds on her fingers flashed aggressively.

The professor was gazing at her with a look at once piercing and speculative. It was the mien of the entomologist who at last encounters on a clear night, the wonderful 'night butterfly' which will repose on the morrow in the case of the museum with a silver pin through its back.

'Miss Cleary,' he asked, 'what do you think of our opera? Do you like the scenery, the singers? They are very good, are they not?'

'Oh, some of them are all right – but a trifle worn.'

'Yes, that is so,' agreed her host, laughing, 'and the costumes are those of olden times – rather foolish. But what did you think of "*Freischutz*"?'

'Who, the tenor? I didn't think much of his voice. He looked distinguished, that's all.'

'Well, all great men – Napoleon, Dante, Homer, Cromwell – had distinction, so history tells us. They owed their success to that. But I was speaking of the play itself.'

'Oh, yes, the piece,' exclaimed Miss Cleary, with a disdainful little grimace. 'Between ourselves, it was a trifle – rather – well –'

She picked up her roses between her hands and began to smell them.

'Yes, I think so, too,' agreed her host, raising his eyebrows with an understanding look, 'and that it is out of date.'

'In the first place,' continued Miss Cleary, 'I don't like them to fire a revolver on the stage. It makes you jump. And this piece began with three shots. Making a noise it is not Art.'

'I heartily agree with you,' declared the professor; 'and the accidents follow so quickly, one after the other. I thoroughly believe the opera would be improved if they would eliminate the firing.'

'Yes,' Miss Cleary went on, 'but the thing is altogether too fantastic. And the music is awful. I came out before that forest scene that every one raves over. The whole thing is too fantastic.'

'Yes,' said her host, 'the day of the fantastic is over, I suppose. We are living in an epoch when only the most positive things have a right to our attention. The fantastic no longer exists.'

Alicia Cleary continued to comment disdainfully upon the opera and the singers. And, as she spoke, the graceless words were uttered in a voice so rich, so pure, so heavenly, that to an eavesdropper she would have seemed a sublime phantom, disclaiming by the light of the stars, a passage from the Song of Songs.

Lord Ewald, who had been chagrined by his friend's facetious discourse, became oblivious to the girl's words, and only listened, dreamily, to the sound of her beautiful contralto.

The professor stopped suddenly in his conversation with his beautiful guest. He had just caught a glance which Lord Ewald, in his dreamy abstraction, had cast at one of the young woman's rings.

Evidently he was thinking of Hadaly and her controls.

'And now,' said the scientist, turning back to Miss Cleary, 'let us speak of the début. We have forgotten a very important thing – the gratuities that you will require –'

'Oh!' she cried, interrupting him. 'I am not mercenary. I am not out for the money. But I must have it, for a singer is only measured by the amount of money she earns. And, then, I want to owe all to my profession – my art.'

'A delicate sentiment. It certainly is praiseworthy. What a heart of gold you have!' exclaimed the professor.

'Well, to begin with,' said Miss Cleary, 'what do you think of twelve thousand?'

The professor frowned slightly.

'Or six,' she amended.

His face brightened a little.

'Well, let us say something between five and ten thousand

pounds sterling a year,' she said, with a divine smile. 'I would be pleased, because there would be a lot of glory.'

'How modest you are!' cried the professor, his face now quite bright. 'I thought you were going to say guineas.'

A shadow, a slight look of regret, passed over the face of the exquisite woman.

'Yes,' she said, 'I ought to get guineas, but, at a début, I suppose one can't be too exacting.'

'Well, we will arrange it,' he suggested, 'and, now, let me give you a little of this Chartreuse.'

Alicia roused herself and began to look around the room.

'Where am I?' she asked. 'This is a funny sort of place. Where in the world am I?'

'You are now in the studio of the greatest sculptress in the country. Her name is Sowana. I rent this outer building from her. She is very famous, and it would give you quite a lot of prestige to have a statue of yourself done by her.'

'When I was in Italy I saw some statues, but they were not like anything here.'

'She has an entirely new method, Miss Cleary. One has to be up-to-date in all things nowadays. Sowana is wonderful. You must have heard of her.'

'Yes, I believe I have – I – I am sure I have,' stammered Miss Cleary.

'Yes, I am sure you have,' said the professor. 'This wonderful sculptress of marble and alabaster has an absolutely new method. A recent discovery. In three weeks she can reproduce, with exact faithfulness, animals or human beings.

'Of course you know, Miss Cleary, that all society women and the great actresses are now having statues made instead of portraits. Marble is the fashion of the day. Sowana is absent this evening because she has gone to finish a full height of the charming Princess –'

'Oh, really!' exclaimed Miss Cleary, duly impressed.

'So it is *the thing*, then, with society folks.'

'Oh, yes, and in the world of Arts. Have you never seen the statues of Jenny Lind, Cleo de Merode, and Lola de Montes?'

'I ought to have seen them,' she said, trying to search her memory.

'And Princess Borghesa?'

'Oh, yes, I remember that one. I saw it in Spain, I think. Yes, when I was in Florence,' she added thoughtfully.

'Oh, yes; princesses, and even queens, are following the rage. When a woman has such great beauty as you – I have no doubt that your statue has been made and shown in some London exhibition, and yet, I am ashamed to say that I have never seen it, or even read about it.'

Miss Alicia lowered her eyes.

'No,' she said, as if ashamed, 'I have only a marble bust and some photographs.'

'Oh, but that is a crime. No wonder you are not on the top rung of the ladder of fame. Can't you realize what an advertisement it is?'

'Well, if it is the fashion, I'm sure that I would like it,' Alicia admitted.

'Yes, it must be done, and it will only take three weeks – it will be all done by then. You must stay here with Sowana, and, while you are here, we can go over your repertoire. Then I will give you the leading rôle in a new dramatic production which I shall order. Everything will go ahead very quickly, I assure you.'

'That will be fine!' Miss Cleary exclaimed enthusiastically. 'Let us begin tomorrow. How shall I pose?'

As she spoke she lifted her glass of wine to her marvellous red lips.

'Ah,' said Professor X admiringly, 'you are a woman of the world. Now, right at the start, we will crush all rivals. We must strike the public one of those audacious blows which will resound through the two hemispheres.'

'I ask nothing better,' Miss Cleary assured him. 'I must do all I can to get to the top of the ladder quickly.'

'You have the right spirit. It will be the beautiful statue of a glorious singer. It must be something that will take the great theatrical managers right off their feet. What about "The Future Eve"?'

'Eve, did you say, Mr Thomas? Is that a new rôle in a new piece?'

'Yes. The great art will justify the statue, and your exquisite beauty will disarm the most severe critics. You know the three "Graces" in the Vatican?'

'Er – yes! Then everything is settled,' Miss Cleary announced. 'Have you anything to say, Lord Ewald?'

'Nothing,' his lordship answered, with a slight shake of his head.

'The great Sowana will return to-morrow at midday,' said the professor. 'At what time shall I expect you?'

'At two o'clock, if that –'

'Two o'clock will do very well. Now, it is to be a great secret. If it were to be noised about that I am preparing to launch you in a début, I should be pestered to death on all sides by others.'

'Oh, don't worry,' said Miss Cleary. 'I won't say anything.'

Professor X began to pencil some figures on his cuffs, and Miss Alicia took the opportunity to whisper to Lord Ewald.

'Do you think he means it?' she demanded. 'Is he really serious?'

'Certainly. That is why the telegram was sent.'

At this moment Miss Cleary's glance fell on the sparkling flower which Hadaly had given Lord Ewald, and which he had absent-mindedly placed in his button-hole.

'What is that?' she asked, putting down her glass of wine and stretching out her hand.

The professor, at this moment, arose and went over to the large open window which looked out upon the park. The moonlight was beautiful, but he turned his back to the stars and looked upon his guests.

Lord Ewald, at the question and at Miss Cleary's movement toward him, made an involuntary movement to safeguard the strange flower.

'What!' she exclaimed, noticing his movement. 'Isn't that beautiful artificial flower for me?'

'No, Alicia,' he said simply. 'You are too real for this.'

Suddenly, at the end of the room, in the mysterious corner, on the steps of the magic threshold, Hadaly appeared. With a dazzling arm she slowly lifted the draperies of velvet. Then, motionless, in her armour and under the black veil, she stood.

Miss Cleary, sitting with her back to the corner, could not see the Andraiad.

Hadaly had evidently heard the last words of the conversation, for she kissed her finger tips to Lord Ewald, who got up abruptly.

Miss Cleary was startled by his unexpected movement. She half arose in her seat, and asked anxiously:

'What is it? What's the matter with you? You make me afraid!'

She turned around sharply to see what he was looking at, but the draperies had fallen into place again and the phantom had disappeared.

Profiting by this absorbed moment of Miss Cleary's, Professor X came quickly forward and, from behind her, stretched out his hand over her beautiful forehead.

Her eyelids gradually closed. Her arms, which now appeared like marble, remained still, one hand touching the table, the other holding the bunch of roses.

She was more than ever the statue of a goddess. Transfixed in this attitude, the loveliness of her face seemed recast with a celestial aura.

Lord Ewald bent over and took her hand in his. He found it as cold as ice.

'Well,' said the professor, turning to the young nobleman, 'I believe everything will be in readiness to-morrow at two o'clock. It was very easy, wasn't it? No one will be able to prevent this lady, without putting her in danger of death, from coming here onto that platform, and doing her best to further the experiment.

'Now, my lord, we have gone far, but there still is time to stop. It is up to you. Just say the word! We will forget all the fine plans we have made. You can speak freely. Miss Cleary cannot hear us.'

During the moments of silence which followed this declaration Lord Ewald stood gazing on his beautiful companion. Then, as suddenly as before, Hadaly reappeared, drawing back the lustrous black draperies. She stood motionless, but attentive, under the shadow of her veil, with her silver arms folded on her bosom.

Lord Ewald looked from the exquisite but earthbound being who was unconscious beside him to the elusive and lilting creation standing at the end of the room.

'My dear professor,' he said steadily, 'you have my word, and I never go back on it.'

'So be it,' Professor X rejoined.

'It is sworn,' added the melodious voice of the phantom.

The draperies again fell together. A spark flashed. The heavy sliding of the stone slab was heard as it was precipitated into the bowels of the earth. The vibrations lasted for a few seconds, then gradually ceased.

The professor made several swift movements with his hands over the head of the somnolent young beauty. Then he took his place again at the window.

Lord Ewald leaned back in his chair and tranquilly smoked his cigar as if nothing had happened.

Alicia Cleary came out of her coma with no knowledge of having been hypnotized, and took up her conversation at the point here she had left off.

'I should like to know why you do not answer me, Lord Ewald?' she demanded peevishly.

Lord Ewald looked at her with a sad little smile of pity. He forbore to answer her in kind, merely saying:

'Excuse me, Alicia, I am a little tired, that is all.'

The window had remained open. The moon was declining and the light of the stars had already paled. Carriage wheels came crunching on the gravel of the drive through the park.

'Ah, here is the carriage come for you, my lord,' the professor explained. 'The lady and gentleman to whose house you are going, Miss Cleary, are quiet, simple people, and I am sure that they will do everything they can to make you comfortable, and the inn which I have recommended for you, Lord Ewald, is one of the best.'

In a few minutes Miss Cleary and Lord Ewald had put on their things and were ready to start.

'Good night, Mr Thomas,' called out Miss Cleary, as the carriage started. 'I'll be here to-morrow, never fear.'

When alone, Professor X stood for a few minutes deep in thought, then he began to walk up and down and to soliloquize, as was his habit.

'What an evening!' he murmured. 'What an experience! This mystic female child and this charming young fellow. Poor boy! Poor, foolish boy! He does not see that her resemblance to the statue of Venus is only sickly, a contagion. He does not realize that it must be caused by some malady in her blood, some mysterious thing that she was born with, the same as some persons come into the world webfooted, or others inherit birthmarks.'

'It is a remarkable likeness – a phenomenon. But it is only a sort of elephantiasis, a pathological deformity; in her case a beautiful one. Alas, that mentally she is so common!

'No matter, it is strange that this sublime monstrosity should have come into my possession just when I needed her for my first Andraiad. What a magnificent experiment!

'Now to work! Let the phantom live!'

Advancing to the centre of the laboratory, he called out commandingly:

'Sowana!'

At this summons the feminine voice which had been spoken in the earlier hours of the evening, replied in a clear, grave manner:

'I am here, dear master. What have you to say?'

The voice came from the middle of the room, but, as before, no one was visible.

'Sowana, the result surpasses my wildest hopes. It is magic!'

'Oh, it is nothing as yet,' said the voice. 'After the incarnation it will be supernatural.'

The professor stood nodding his head, as though he were trying to convince himself of the truth of the words which the invisible one had spoken. His hands were clasped tightly before him, and his lips moved, but uttered no sound.

Then, with a sudden movement, he pulled himself together. Pressing a button, he extinguished the three flaming arcs that illumined the room. Only a small night light remained aglow, the one on the ebony table.

Its rays shone on the velvet cushion, lighting up the mysterious arm, the most brilliant spot of which was the wrist encircled by the golden snake, whose green, glittering eyes seemed to look piercingly at Professor X.

## XX.

During the fifteen days which followed that memorable evening the sun shone brightly on the grounds surrounding the laboratory. Autumn was advancing, however, and the leaves of the great oak trees in the park were turning to purple.

A great mantle of peace seemed to hang about the park and grounds. It was a serenity which was only broken by the rustle of the leaves falling and the chirp of the desolate birds.

But if peace reigned in the grounds, it stopped at the gates. Outside, the whole countryside was buzzing and bustling with curiosity.

Professor X had suspended all social intercourse and functions during Lord Ewald Celian's visit. And the world beyond his grounds was agog to find out what the great scientist was about.

The scientist remained immured in his laboratory with his assistants. He never went outside the building.

Reporters, sent in haste by their newspapers, found the iron gates closed and barred. The editors became excited. Night and day their faithful writers remained outside the grounds waiting for some item of news.

The one sign of life the reporters could see was a beautiful young woman, usually dressed in light blue or some other pale colour, walking and picking flowers on the lawn at different times during the day. But the newspaper men thought this was a trick of the professor's to throw them off the scent of his real activities.

For, what could this beautiful girl, gowned in fashionable clothes, have to do with the experiments of the great scientist?

Excitement and curiosity reached their height when it was discovered that Dr Joseph Saunderson, the famous physician, had been sent for in great haste; and that, a few hours later, the fashionable dentist, Dr William Peyton, also had been hurriedly summoned.

The rumour that Professor X was dying spread so rapidly, that it seemed as though the word had been disseminated by a flash of lightning. It varied somewhat – he was dying – no, he was not dying, but he was seriously ill, raving night and day – he had brain fever – he was a doomed man!

The stockholders of a large electric company of which the scientist was one of the founders and a director, almost went into a panic, for the stock issue on the market went tumbling downward. The price dropped until the shares were no longer worth one tenth of their original value.

But when both Dr Saunderson and Dr Peyton declared that

the vital spirits of the great experimenter had never been in better condition, and that they had been called to minister to a very beautiful young lady, the stock jumped so fast that several incautious brokers were forced to suspend their activities.

One fine night, a large package was delivered to the laboratory. The reporting sleuths traced out the fact that it had been sent from the city to the depot by rail and then carried to the grounds by a truck, but they could not discover what it contained.

But the package only contained a new blue silk evening dress; slippers of the same shade; silk stockings to match; a box of gloves, exquisitely perfumed; an ebony and black lace fan; fashionable corsets; delicate negligees; very fine handkerchiefs embroidered with the initial 'H;' bottles of perfume, and a jewel case containing diamond earrings, bracelets, and finger rings. It was a complete feminine trousseau.

But before the reporters could discover this fact, they were called away to hunt up the facts in a high-life scandal which had begun to agitate the country, and the gates of Professor X's park became deserted.

A few days after the trousseau arrived, the professor sent a trusty messenger to the city. This man delivered to a prominent wigmaker a photograph of a coiffure of large size. He also gave him some samples of hair, and measurements indicating size to the millimetre and the weight to the milligram, and a package of tissue in which the hair was to be set.

As it was an order from the famous scientist, the wigmaker began work on it at once. He weighed and boiled the hair, and set it in a form. But when he came to open the package which contained the tissue, he started back in alarm.

It was a human scalp, apparently freshly peeled off, and preserved by some new method! It fell from his hands to the floor and, almost panic-stricken, he sought the waiting messenger.

'But it is a scalp!' he cried. 'It is human leather!'

'Oh,' said the messenger calmly, 'it is nothing to be alarmed about. It was specially prepared for a very fashionable society woman, who has lost her hair in a fever.

'You must hurry with it. Here is the hair dressing and perfume which she uses. Make a masterpiece. The price is immaterial. Get your best men together and weave the hair in the tissue to duplicate nature.

'Don't overdo it. Make it exactly like the photograph. I will give you just four days to finish it.'

The wigmaker protested at the brief time given for such an important work, but on the fourth day the messenger took the now beautifully adorned scalp from his place to the professor's laboratory.

Meanwhile, although the reporters had been withdrawn, there was still much curiosity rife in the neighbourhood, and among those who were on the alert word was passed that each morning a closed carriage arrived at the wall of the garden and stopped at a door that was seldom used. A young lady usually descended from the carriage and spent the day alone with the professor and his assistants.

It was she who walked about on the lawn at different times. What could it mean? Who could she be?

Then it also was discovered that there was a distinguished-looking young Englishman staying at the inn. He knew the young lady. He had been seen calling on her at the pretty little cottage which was owned by some friends of the inventor. She was evidently visiting at the cottage, for it was from here that the carriage took her each morning and returned her each evening.

What could the secret be? Was the scientist having a romance?

Their questions and surmises were in vain. They found no reply to the riddle. But, having nothing better to do, they waited.

At evening, on the last day of the third week, a brown autumnal day, Lord Ewald Celian sprang from his horse at the door of Professor X's abode, and, being announced, he hastened down the path in the garden which led to the laboratory.

A short time before, while he had been scanning the newspapers and waiting to receive word that Alicia Cleary had returned from her sitting, he had received the following note:

DEAR LORD EWALD:
　　Will you grant me a few minutes? I wish to see you.
　　　　　　　　　　　　　　　　　　　　　　　　　HADALY.

He had immediately given orders for his horse to be brought and had started out. It had been a stormy day, as though nature was in accord with expected events.

Not only had the weather been inclement, but there had been an eclipse of the sun. It was still twilight and the rays of the aurora borealis stretched their sinister fan over the sky. The horizon appeared to be enveloped in the dying, smouldering flames of a destructive fire.

The air was vibrating. Gusts of wind blew the leaves in a swirl along the ground. From south to north great clouds rolled onward, looking like blankets of purple bordered with gold.

The young nobleman glanced at the sky. It seemed to him that the heavens at that moment were almost a photograph of his mental state, a reflection of his thoughts.

He hurried down the path and reached the door of the laboratory. There he hesitated for a moment. But just then he caught sight of Alicia Cleary, who had evidently finished her final sitting. He entered.

Professor X was sitting in his big armchair. He was wearing his loose lounge coat, and he held some manuscripts in his hands.

At the opening of the door, Miss Cleary turned around.

'Ah!' she cried. 'Here is Lord Ewald.'

This was the first time that he had been in the laboratory since that first terrible night, and he glanced about in real dread of the surroundings.

'You are welcome, Lord Ewald,' the professor said, extending his hand.

'The message which I received just now seemed so concise and so eloquent that I came immediately,' his lordship explained.

Then turning to Miss Cleary, he said:

'How are you, Alicia? I see that you have been rehearsing.'

'Yes,' she replied, 'but it is finished now. We were just giving it a final reading, that is all.'

The professor drew his young friend to one side.

'Tell me!' exclaimed Lord Ewald, impatiently, but in a low voice. 'Have you finished? The electrical ideal – our masterpiece, or rather yours – has it come into the world?'

'Yes,' the inventor answered simply. 'You will see the result after Miss Cleary has gone. Try to get her away, my dear fellow, and then come back here. We must be alone for this.'

'Already!' murmured Lord Ewald wonderingly.

'I have kept my word,' said the professor.

'And Miss Cleary has no suspicions?'

'None whatever. A simple rough draft of clay was all that was necessary, as I told you. Hadaly was hidden behind the impenetrable mantle of my object glasses, and Sowana has proven herself to be the genius that I maintained she was.'

'And your men – do they not suspect?'

'No. They simply saw an experiment in photo-sculpture, that is all. The rest remains a secret from them. Besides, it was only this morning that I connected the interior apparatus and made the respiratory spark function. It was most astonishing.'

'I must admit that I am very impatient to see what your creation looks like,' said Lord Ewald.

'You will see her this evening. You won't recognize her. I tell you the result is more stupendous – more marvellous – than I could have dared to believe.'

'Well, gentlemen, what conspiracy are you hatching?' the actress asked. 'Why are you conversing in such low tones?'

'My dear Miss Cleary,' the professor replied, returning to her side, 'I am telling Lord Ewald how satisfied I am with you, with your talents and your magnificent voice. I was confiding to him that I had the highest hopes in regard to the future which awaits you.'

'Well, you could have said that aloud, Mr Thomas. There is nothing in that that could hurt my feelings. But,' she continued, lighting up her words with her radiant smile, and shaking her finger threateningly, 'I also, have something to say to Lord Ewald. I am very glad that he has come.

'I have been thinking over some of the things which have taken place during the last few weeks, and there is something which weighs heavily on my mind. Just by a word, I have learned that a most ridiculous scheme has been afoot.'

She spoke with an air intended to be dignified, but, somehow, it did not seem in keeping with her true character. Then she turned away from the professor, and addressed Lord Ewald:

'Please take me for a stroll in the garden. It is important. I want you to remove a doubt from my mind on a certain subject.'

'Very well,' he agreed, after exchanging a quick glance with the professor which indicated that neither man was over-pleased with the situation. 'I hope it will not take very long, as there are some matters which I must return to take up with our friend here. You know that his time is very valuable, and he had made an appointment with me for this time.'

'Oh, what I want to say won't take very long,' said Alicia Cleary, 'and I think that it will be best for all concerned if I do not say it before Mr Thomas!'

## XXI.

Miss Cleary and Lord Ewald strolled out into the grounds, down the darkened avenue, and into the park.

As soon as the two visitors had left the room, Professor X's face took on an expression of deep anxiety. He evidently feared that the actress, in her foolish manner, might betray some confidence.

He hurriedly pulled aside the heavy curtains and, pressing to the window, followed them with his eyes. When he could no longer see them with his naked gaze he snatched up a sort of fieldglass, a microphone of a new system, and an induction coil attached to a manipulator.

The professor connected these to some wires which ran out through the walls and became lost in the network of others that crossed and intercrossed between the trees. He probably expected a quarrel between the two strollers, and wanted to keep himself informed before giving Hadaly into Lord Ewald's hands for safe keeping.

The young nobleman, in the meantime, was impatient for Alicia to begin her discourse. He thought of the enchanted subterranean abode where Hadaly awaited him – where, in a brief time, he would be face to face with the new Eve.

'What is it that you wish to say to me, Alicia?' he asked. 'I think that we are far enough out of sight and hearing. You know, I must return presently.'

Miss Cleary was walking along with her arm resting confid-ingly in that of her companion.

'Oh, I'll tell you very soon,' she replied. 'Just as soon as we get to the end of this path. It is dark there, and no one will see or hear us.

'I am very anxious about something. I can assure you that this is the first time that this thought has occurred to me. I will tell you all about it soon.'

'As you wish,' said Lord Ewald, in a resigned manner.

The evening sky was still disturbed. Long lines of red fire shot up from the boreal arcs toward the horizon. Some tiny stars, which seemed to have been in a hurry to make their appearance, had pierced their way through the dark clouds, and sprinkled themselves in the spots of clear blue ether.

The leaves rustled ominously in the park, like weird voices. In contrast, the odour of the grass and the flowers was keen, damp and delicious.

'What a magical evening,' murmured Miss Cleary.

Lord Ewald was so immersed in his own thoughts that he scarcely heard her.

'Yes it is,' he said, and in the tone there was a faint mocking ring. 'But, Alicia, tell me – what is it that you wish to say?'

'What a hurry you are in this evening, my lord. Come, sit on this bench. We can talk there – and I really am a little tired.'

She leaned on his arm.

'Are you ill, Alicia?'

She did not reply.

Lord Ewald thought it very strange that she should be so quiet. He wondered what was wrong. Did she have a woman's instinct of impending danger?

It was not at all like her. This hesitancy to speak was a new phase of her character.

She bit the stalk of a scented flower which she had picked as they had strolled along the path. All her being was resplendent with beauty. Her long, clinging gown swept the daisies which grew in the grass – belated memories of summer.

Her beautiful face was close to Lord Ewald's shoulder. Her lovely hair was a bit blown about, but this only added to its charm, as it escaped here and there from under the black short scarf she had thrown over her head. But her whole demeanour was pensive.

When they reached the bench she was the first to sit down. Lord Ewald stood looking at her, waiting for her to begin. He was inwardly impatient, as he expected to be forced to listen to a string of platitudes and commonplace arguments.

Nevertheless, an odd thought came to him. Suppose the all-powerful professor had found the secret – suppose he had found a means to dissolve the thick mist which had obscured the mind of this beautiful creature. She was silent. That was already a great step.

He sat down beside her.

'My dear boy,' she said at last, 'I have just come to realize in the last few days how unhappy you are. Have you anything to say to me? I am a much better friend to you than you think.'

Lord Ewald, at the moment when she began speaking, was a long distance from Miss Cleary. He was thinking of an enchanted floral hall where Hadaly was, no doubt, awaiting him. And, when he heard her first speech, when he listened to her first words, he began to feel annoyed, because he thought that the professor must have, inadvertently, said too much to her.

Something within him, however, denied this. He felt confident of the scientist's judgment. And, as he thought of the manner in which Professor X had managed Miss Cleary on the first evening they met, and pondered on the fact that three weeks of more or less close association with her must have given him a better knowledge of her true self, he put the idea away from him.

What, then, could be the meaning of this new, this unlooked for, development?

Another simpler and more reasonable thought came to him. The poet in him awakened.

He came to the conclusion that the wonderful evening must have had this effect on Alicia Cleary. In such an atmosphere it would not be difficult for two human beings, in the fullness of youth, to be filled with a greater sensitiveness, greater refinement of sentiment.

The heart of a woman is so mysteriously responsive that sometimes even the most shallow must submit to influences that are sweet and serene. Probably some great light had cast a ray into Alicia's soul.

Lord Ewald decided to make one more supreme effort to awaken the spark in this beauteous, but heretofore soul-dead creature whom he loved so deeply, so sadly. He drew her gently to him.

'Dearest Alicia,' he said, 'I have something to tell you. And what I have to say comes from joy and out of the depths of silence, but a joy drawn from silence even more wonderful than this which now surrounds us.

'You know I love you, dear. I do not live except in your presence. Oh, do you not feel all this which is immortal about us? Can you not divine the sensations throbbing through it all?

'My love for you is so great, so strong, one full moment of it would be worth more than a century of other emotions. What would I not give to be worthy of this great happiness!'

Alicia was silent.

Lord Ewald felt rebuffed.

'But, there,' he added, smiling sadly, 'this is just like so much Greek to you, isn't it Alicia? Why then do you question me? What words can I say? After all, what are words – what would all words mean in comparison to one real kiss from you.'

This was the first time in a long while that there had been any talk of caresses between them. And, Alicia Cleary, undoubtedly impressed by the splendour of the on-coming night and the ardour of the youth, appeared to abandon herself more gracefully, more fervently, to his embrace.

He felt a sudden, fierce throb of the heart. Her yielding gave him a breathtaking thrill, half joy, half fear. Could she have understood the tender meaning of his passionate words? A tear welled to his eye and, rolling down his cheek, fell onto her hand.

'Are you suffering?' she asked, almost in a whisper. 'And through me? I am very sorry.'

At this emotion, at these unexpected words, he was transported into exquisite amazement. An intense delight swept over him.

All thought of the other Alicia – the terrible one of commonplaces – went from him. These few words of kindness had been sufficient to shake his very soul – to awaken it to vast heights of hope, the apex of which he knew not.

'Oh, my love – my love,' he murmured, almost desperately.

Then his lips touched hers and he was comforted. He forgot the long hours, the days of disillusion through which he had passed. His love was resurrected.

He was reborn. Hadaly and her vain mirages were now gone from his mind.

They remained silently clasped in each other's arms for some moments. Alicia's breast arose and fell in a sweet panic, as if she, too, half feared. He pressed her closely, protectingly, against his heart.

Above the heads of the two lovers the sky had become clear. The blue heavens were filled with stars visible between the scant foliage of the trees. The shadows had grown deeper and more comforting.

The dazed soul of young Ewald was again attuned to the beauties of the world. But at this moment there came to him a horrible thought, piercing his happiness like a knife thrust. He remembered that Professor X was awaiting in his vaults to show him the black magic of his Andraiad.

'Ah!' he murmured remorsefully, thinking aloud. 'Was I mad? An Andraiad! How could I have dreamed of such a sacrilege – a plaything, whose appearance alone would have made me laugh – an absurd, insensible doll.

'As if any mechanical thing made of hydraulic pressures and cunning cylinders could ever bear the semblance to one so beautiful as you, my Alicia. I will go and thank the professor presently without betraying any inquisitiveness as to his make-believe beauty. Disillusion must, indeed, have cast a shadow over my thoughts for me to have considered such a terrible project.

'Oh, my beloved! I recognize you now. You exist. You are no longer an icicle, but flesh and blood like myself. I can feel your heart beating against mine.

'You have wept. Your lips have trembled under the pressure of mine. You are a woman whom love can make ideal. Alicia – I love – I adore you – I –'

He did not finish his vocal adoration.

His eyes shining with the tears of his new-born happiness, he found Alicia's lips once more. The ecstasy of the kiss brought in its train a half breathed, subtle odour, which for the moment he thought an illusion. Somehow it daunted him; a chill of doubt flashed over him from head to foot.

It was a vague perfume of amber and roses. Yet he did not understand why it shook his inner being in this terrible manner.

His companion arose to her feet and gently put her hands on his shoulder. *Her pale fingers were laden with sparkling rings.*

Then she spoke.

Her voice was a caress – a golden toned benediction – but it was not Alicia Cleary's. It was the unforgettable dream voice which he had heard that first night at Professor X's home.

'My lord, do you not recognize me?' she asked, sadly. 'I am Hadaly!'


# XXII.

At Hadaly's words, Lord Ewald felt as though all the powers of darkness had gathered their united strength to strike him one overpowering blow. He was scorched, as if he had been hurled into a fire.

If Professor X had appeared at this moment the young nobleman would have murdered him in cold blood. Everything before his eyes was in a sombre red mist.

A molten fluid rushed madly through his veins. His life of twenty-seven years appeared to him only a moment of time.

But in the complexity, the unreal horror, of the moment he could not keep his gaze off the Andraiad. His heart, gripped vicelike in a terrible rancour, seemed a dead thing in his breast.

Mechanically he contemplated Hadaly from head to foot. He took her hand. It was the hand of Alicia.

He looked at her neck, her shapely shoulders – this was, indeed, Alicia.

He stared into her eyes. They were the eyes of Alicia – but the expression was ethereal.

The dress, the shoes, even the handkerchief with which she was silently drying two tears from her ravishingly beautiful cheeks, were the usual accessories of Alicia.

It all was, in truth, Alicia! But it was Alicia transfigured.

She had become worthy of her great beauty – she had realized the beatitudes of her true identity.

He closed his eyes and wiped away great beads of perspiration from his temples with the open palms of his hands. His sensation was that of the mountain climber who hears his guide shout, hoarsely: 'Take care! Don't look to the left!' and who turns perversely in the forbidden direction to find himself standing on the brink of an abyss.

He tried to pull himself together, cursing inwardly. His cheeks were blanched and he was mute with misery.

His first palpitation of tenderness, his newborn hope, and his ineffable love, had been extorted from him under false pretences. He owed that one moment of ecstasy to this terrifying resemblance – this mechanical representation of the thing he loved. He was a dupe, humiliated, utterly crushed.

His glance swept the landscape, the sky and the earth, and he broke into a nervous, mocking laugh. It was as though he were hurling back to the great unknown the undeserved insult which it had offered to his soul.

Gradually this laughter gave him relief.

Then there sprang from the depths of his intelligence a thought which was even more astonishing than the phenomenon itself. The living woman whom this electrical doll represented had not the power to thrill him. It was through this electro-dynamic being, this photomicroscopic copy of his ideal that he had realized supreme joy.

The touching voice of Hadaly had used the words of the real actress without understanding their true meaning. The phantom was only playing a part, but the soul of Alicia had passed into the rôle. The false Alicia was more perfect, more natural, than the the living personage.

He was drawn from his groping thoughts by hearing in wine-like tones:

'My lord, are you sure that I am only playing a part? Are you quite sure that I, myself, am not really here?'

'No!' cried Lord Ewald, agitatedly. 'I am not. Who are you?'

The phantom moved nearer, and gazed at him tenderly. Then, speaking with the voice of the living Alicia, she asked:

'Do you remember, Ewald, back there in England after a day of hunting, when you had been very tired, and wished to sleep, a confusing vision would come and disturb you? Sometimes you would see a face looking at you fixedly.

'You tried to explain to yourself what you saw, but you were unable to do so, and anxiety prolonged into your waking hours the dream that had been broken. To drive away the troublesome thoughts, you would arise and light up your room, and then would come the assurance that what you had dreamed had been caused by shadows cast by the old furniture, or by the flapping of the hangings at the windows. Then you would go back to bed with a smile, and drop off into peaceful sleep. Do you remember?'

'Yes,' replied Lord Ewald thoughtfully.

'I thought you would remember. Yet, I think that if you had pondered on the recurrence of these semivisions, you would have come to the conclusion that they must have been something more than dreams. At times we reach a state whereby we may receive impressions, or project our own ideas from or into another world – I mean into the infinite.

'Well, then, when one is in this fluid state of the spirit, it is given to us to realize and behold what we only imagine when we are not in that condition.

'Often it is permitted us to behold during these periods the forecastings of events which will happen to us in real life. These things, then, are not dreams, as I have said, but actually visions of the future which are projected upon the screen of our transported souls.'

At this point Hadaly reached over and took Lord Ewald's hands in hers.

'You know, dear friend, these dreams are but the supreme effort of our souls to reach out from their incarnate bodies into the illimitable realms beyond, and grasp the truths of nature.

'But when you have put these dreams away, when you dispel the vision and drop off to sleep, you have brought the spirit back to earth and lost your opportunity of solving these secrets.'

Lord Ewald pondered deeply over this discourse of the Andraiad. He could not see how its metaphysical trend could answer his question, but he listened patiently, waiting for her to reveal her actual identity.

But the radiant Hadaly continued, and it was as though she suddenly lifted a veil from the face of unseen things:

'That probably is why we know so little of the other world, because when it is given to you in your living bodies to reach this state, when you might be able to communicate with it, you voluntarily put it aside and choose to forget. So you have gone on from forgetfulness to forgetfulness.

'You have been more than fortunate. For, although you refused to investigate these foreshadowings and allowed yourself to reach a region of black despondency and despair, from where you were willing to take that last fatal step – suicide – your dream forecasts have become a reality.

'You ask who I am. Behold in me the realization of your dreams – the phantom foreshadowed in your dreams, which you so lightly put aside. I have come to you.

'I am the messenger sent from those regions which man can only enter in that state of half dream, half vision. I am from out there where there is no time or space, where all illusions vanish.

'I am a creature of dreams that you have called to being in your own imagination, and who may be lightly dismissed by some of those common sense thoughts which will leave you nothing but an aching void in my place.

'Oh, do not banish me from your thoughts! Send me not away because of that traitor, reason. Let me live in your thoughts!

'You have lived in a dream with the living. Attribute to me, then, some of the qualities of that being. Reinforce me from within yourself and I shall become alive.

'I shall be the woman of your dreams – all that you would have me be. Your dream of the living has offered you nothing but the grave; permit me, then, to offer you the happiness of heaven.'

Hadaly, swept on by the fervour of her words and the passion of her plea, pressed Lord Ewald's hands to her bosom.

The young nobleman was almost in a stupor of admiration for this wondrous phantom.

'Are you afraid of interrupting me?' she asked. 'Do not forget that it is only at your pleasure that I may live or be animated, and that your fears about me may be fatal – for your fears may destroy the ideal.

'You must choose between me, the dream, and reason. If I have spoken to you of strange things, if I seem too grave or too serious, it is because my eyes have seen things beyond the eyes of mortals.

'See, I am talking to you like a woman, and I must become a woman – I must not remain a dream creature only.

'Oh, take me away with you; take me to England to your old castle! I long to start. I long to enshroud myself and enter my casket to prepare for the journey.

'Let us hasten! Once there, in the shadow of your great walls, you may awaken me with a kiss, if you will.'

At the end of her entreaty, Hadaly bent over and imprinted a caress on the young man's forehead.

Lord Ewald was not only brave, but fearless. The motto of his ancestral house was: 'Let others fear; not I!' and this had been instilled into the blood of his race for generations, yet at Hadaly's last words he hesitated, shudderingly. Then he resolutely set out to reason with himself.

'Ah,' he mused, 'what miracles are made to frighten the souls of men as well as to console them! What could have made Professor X imagine that this figure, which utters these thoughts inscribed on a metal cylinder, could sway me or help to dispel my gloom?

'Since when has the Divine Power permitted machines to speak? What foolish, laughable pride has conceived this phantasm in the form of a woman controlled by electricity, and hope that it would be able to introduce itself into the existence of real mortals?

'Ah, but I forget! It is only a thing of the theatre, and I should applaud it. Bravo, professor, you are indeed a genius!'

Smiling at his own thoughts, Lord Ewald leisurely lighted a cigarette.

'After all,' he thought, 'Hadaly is an infinitely superior copy of an actress. For me to pass up the sport would be an act of folly.'

However, in spite of these thoughts, he realized that he had entered into an experiment quite frightful.

While he was wrapped up in his thoughts, the Andraiad had bowed her head, and, hiding her face in her hands, was weeping silently. Then she raised her head, showing the sublime countenance of Alicia, and said, her voice trembling with tears:

'So, my lord, you refuse me! You have called me out of the dream world only to banish me to it again. Just one little thought from you could have invested me with life, but, all powerful though you be, you have disdained to use the power. You prefer a conscience which causes you grief. You scorn the divine, and the ideal in captivity intimidates you!'

And, turning away from him, Hadaly, bowed in grief, moved away. The rising moon was shining gently through the tree tops, and raising both her arms toward it, she cried:

'Oh, moon, you that brings so much of hope, I had so longed to live that I might know of love beneath your tender light. But all is lost, I must relinquish life, and return to death.'

Then, wiping her tears away, she suddenly faced Lord Ewald, and said:

'Good-bye, my lord. Go, leave me, and rejoin the realities of the world. You may think of me as merely a curiosity upon which you have looked. You are quite sensible in your choice.

'Go! Forget me if you can. But I warn you that it will be impossible. He who has looked upon an Andraiad as you have upon me can never forget her. You have killed your ideal and the memory will ever remain with you as a constant punishment for the indignity offered to the divine.

'I will return to my beautiful cavern. Farewell to you who will know no more of joy in life!'

She walked towards the path and on in the direction where Professor X was keeping vigil. Sobbing, she pressed her handkerchief to her lips.

Her blue form slowly passed among the trees. The light of the moon, falling upon it, gave her the aspect of a spirit. Then she turned and, with a graceful movement, silently raised her hands to her lips and tossed Lord Ewald a double kiss. It was her final gesture of despair.

And now, literally in spite of himself, Lord Ewald rushed down the path and rejoined her. Drawn by an irrestible force, he threw his arm about Hadaly.

'Spirit, phantom, Hadaly, it is settled!' he exclaimed. 'It is true that I do not deserve to have your sweet presence in place of that other earthly one, but I accept it. I wish you to live, for I realize that in comparison the living one is the phantom, and that you are real.'

Hadaly put both her rounded arms around Lord Ewald's neck and permitted him to press her closely to him.

An infinite grace, languid and ravishing, emanated from her like a magnetic radiance. She rested her head on his shoulder and looked at him from under her lids with a beatific smile.

She seemed to be welding her soul with his in their enchained eyes. Finally, she placed on his lips a kiss that was entirely virginal.

'At last!' Hadaly said in a voice that was more spiritual flame than sound. 'At last I am born!'


## XXIII.

A few moments later Lord Ewald entered the laboratory with Hadaly on his arm.

Professor X was standing, his arms crossed before him, in front of a long ebony coffin. The two sides of the box were open, showing black satin upholstering. The interior was moulded in the form of a woman.

One might have thought it an Egyptian casket perfected by modern methods, for it was worthy of Cleopatra herself. On the right and left sides a dozen strips of metal were fastened and in the interior of the box could be seen a papyrus roll, a manuscript and the crystal wand.

Withdrawing her arm from her protector's, Hadaly stepped to one side and stood motionless, while Lord Ewald advanced to the professor and said:

'My friend, this Andraiad is a present that only a semigod could offer. Never in the bazaars of Bagdad could such a slave have been found for the Caliphs.

'No other enchanter could have created such a vision. Never did Scheherazade imagine such a vision in her tales of the Thousand and One Nights.

'No money could persuade me to part from this masterpiece. If, at first, I was dismayed, admiration has triumphed over that.'

'You accept her then?' the professor inquired, smilingly.

'I would be mad to refuse her,' the young man replied, offering his handclasp as a pledge of agreement.

'Will you have supper with me, both of you?' asked the scientist. 'If you will, we will take up the conversation where we left off on that first night. You will see, my lord, that Hadaly's replies will be entirely different from those of her model.'

'No, thanks,' Lord Ewald objected. 'I am in a great hurry to become the guardian of this divine enigma.'

'Farewell then, Hadaly,' the professor said. 'When you are over the seas, you must sometimes think of your subterranean vault where we have often talked of the one who would come to awaken you to the pale existence of a human being.'

'Ah, my dear master,' replied the Andraiad, bowing humbly before the great electrician, 'my resemblance to the mortals and my place among them will never go so far as to make me forget my creator.'

'That is fine, Hadaly, I thank you.'

Professor X then turned to Lord Ewald and asked: 'And what about the living one?'

'On my word, I had forgotten her!' the young nobleman exclaimed ruefully.

'She went away in a very bad frame of mind this evening,' the professor said. 'You had scarcely gone for the walk with Hadaly when she returned here, absolutely herself, and free from all influence.

'Well, you should have heard her flow of words! It made it impossible for me to hear what you two were saying out there in the park; and I had just placed instruments in position so that I might listen.

'However, I see that Hadaly, even in her first moments of life, has shown herself to be worthy of our expectations. Goodness knows what we may expect of her in the years to come.

'Miss Cleary informed me in very strong terms that she renounces the new rôles which I had prepared for her, because the prose was too difficult for her to memorize. She declared that the words ossified her brain. Her modest wish now is to enter vaudeville, for which she has a sufficient repertoire. She believes that she will have a rapid success.

'As for the statue, she told me to speak to you about

forwarding it to London, as you were making preparations for your departure to-morrow. She instructed me to ask a stiff sum for it, as she knew that you would not bargain with an artist. Then she bade me good-by, and told me that if you should come here by chance that she would see you later about the arrangements.

'Now, my dear fellow, once you are in London you will have nothing further to do than to see that she is started in her chosen profession. Then a letter, accompanied by a substantial gift, will be all that is necessary.'

Hadaly, who had been listening attentively, now said to the scientist:

'You will come to see us at Athelwold, dear master, will you not?'

Lord Ewald could not repress a start when he heard her express these natural words. Then he noticed a strange thing. Professor X had been more amazed at Hadaly's words than he, himself, had been.

'What is the matter, professor?' asked Lord Ewald.

Professor X put his hands to his forehead for an instant, then, drawing aside the hem of the Andraiad's gown, he pressed his fingers heavily on the heels of her slippers.

'I am unchaining Hadaly,' the inventor explained. 'From now on she belongs to you. In the future it will be only the rings and the collar on the neck that will animate her.

'While we are on this point, you will find the manuscript in the casket. After reading it you will understand into what mysteries you will be able to delve during the sixty hours inscribed on the cylinder. Hadaly will be a continual surprise.'

'My dear professor,' said Lord Ewald, 'as far as I am concerned you may destroy the manuscript. I believe that Hadaly is a real phantom, and I no longer wish to know what it is that animates her. I hope that I shall even forget what you have already told me about her.'

At these words, Hadaly tenderly pressed the young man's hands and, leaning nearer to him, while the scientist was still kneeling at her feet, whispered:

'Don't tell him what I told you out there just now. That was for your ears only!'

The professor arose with two small brass buttons which he had unscrewed from the heels of Hadaly's slippers. She trembled throughout her whole being until he touched a pearl in her collar.

'Help me,' she said simply, leaning her head on Lord Ewald's shoulder.

The young man supported her gravely, and when she regained her composure she walked to the casket and smilingly drew aside the cover. Then, without hesitation, she reclined in the sable mould.

After having wound the thick linen bandage round her forehead, she tightly hooked the lengths of silk about her body, arranging herself in such a manner that no shock could disturb her.

'My friend,' she said, addressing Lord Ewald, 'after the crossing, you will awaken me. Until then as of old, we will see each other in the world of dreams.'

She closed her eyes, as if in sleep.

Professor X closed the coffin tightly. A silver plate inscribed with Lord Ewald's coat of arms was fastened on the top, bearing the name *Hadaly* engraved in Oriental characters.

'Now,' said the professor, 'the sarcophagus will be placed presently, as I have told you, in a large square crate with sides well padded. We are taking this precaution to avoid any suspicions. Here is the key of the casket, and the invisible lock which permits the spring to unbend is this tiny black star directly above the head of the Andraiad.'

'Now,' he added, pulling a chair forward for his guest and one for himself, 'let us have a drink.'

The scientist pressed a crystal knob, and instantly several flaming arcs flashed their light over the room, creating the effect of a sunlit day. Handing a glass to Lord Ewald he exclaimed:

'I drink to the impossible!'

Lord Ewald touched glasses as a sign of acquiescence.

'There is one question which I must ask,' the young nobleman said. 'You told me that a woman, an artist, helped you in your work. I believe you said that her name was Sowana. It was she who helped to measure and weigh and to calculate, limb for limb, the living model.

'Miss Cleary told me that she was a very pale creature, of uncertain age, who spoke little, was always dressed in black, and once must have been very beautiful. She said that this strange woman kept her eyes always half closed, but saw clearly, and that she moved as if mesmerized. Alicia also told me that sometimes this woman worked with a live electric torch as if she intended to design her statue with the flashing light.'

'What do you want to know about her?'

'I wanted to know who she is. From what I have heard she must be a marvellous woman.'

'Sowana is Mrs Anderson,' the professor replied, gravely. 'The widow of my dead friend. She was penniless, and I did all that I could to help her. After his death she became very ill. She had an incurable disease called sleeping sickness.

'I went to see her occasionally, and I was surprised to find that during her trances she was able to talk and reply to all my questions. I determined to try to cure her.'

'To cure her!' exclaimed Lord Ewald. 'You mean transform her?'

'Well,' admitted the professor, 'perhaps you are right. You may have noticed that when I used my power over Miss Cleary the other evening it was very easy. You have seen hypnotism before, so you will not doubt that there is existent a nervous current or fluid exactly corresponding to electricity.

'I do not know how the idea came to me to resort to magnetic action. I worked upon her almost every day for about two months. I learned the surest methods, and gradually the known phenomena were produced one after the other.

'At the present day they remain still unexplainable, but in the near future they will not appear strange. Then Mrs Anderson began to have spells of clairvoyance, absolutely enigmatical, in these deep sleeps. She became my great secret. Owing to the state of intensified torpor in which the patient had fallen, I had the chance to develop this hypnotic attitude of mine to an intense degree.

'Between Mrs Anderson and myself there became established a current so subtle that I was able to penetrate metal with it. I magnetized a piece of metal with this fluid or current, and then fashioned it into two rings – this sounds like mere magic, doesn't it? – and it sufficed to estabish a communicating current between us. If Sowana had on one ring, and I had on the other, even though she were asleep twenty miles away, we could converse.

'This savours of the occult, but I cannot tell you how many times I have been able to make her hear and obey me, how many times she has spoken to me, just holding the ring, in a very low voice, when she was far away.

'In one of her trances she told me that, although her name on earth was Annie Anderson, her real self for a long time had been called Sowana.

'Not only her name, but her whole nature, was changed. Mrs Anderson had been a dignified, fairly intelligent woman; but, after all, her intelligence had been limited. However, in her sleep, with her name changed, she suddenly became a person of great talent and unknown powers. This vast knowledge, this strange eloquence, this being penetrated with a new personality of Sowana, are things that cannot be explained, for Mrs Anderson is, physically, the same woman. The duality is an astounding phenomenon, but this duality has been seen – in lesser extent – in persons under the influence of hypnotizers.

'There came a time when I decided to reveal the relics of Miss Evelyn Habal, the woman who destroyed her husband. When I showed them to her I gave her a rough idea of my conception of Hadaly. You cannot imagine with what sombre joy Mrs Anderson seized upon this novel idea. She encouraged me in my scheme. She insisted that I should get to work at once.

'So I put all my other work aside to devote my time to this experiment. When the complexities of the Andraiad's organisms were executed, I assembled them and showed them to her.

'At this sight Mrs Anderson became strangely exhilarated. She insisted that I must explain to her the most secret of the mysteries, so that she could familiarize herself with them against the day when she might be able to reanimate herself in the Andraiad and to incorporate herself in her supernatural state.

'Impressed with this vague idea, I taught her all that I knew by building for her instruction a set of apparatus similar to that of Hadaly's movements. When Sowana had completely mastered it, one day, without warning, she sent the Andraiad here to me while I was at work.

'I declare to you that its appearance gave me the most frightful shock I ever had in my life. The completed work terrified the workman!

'Then came to me the daring idea of incorporating the phantom in the double of a woman. Thenceforth I calculated all my steps with the utmost precision, so that I could offer a finished product to any one daring enough to accept.

'You must notice that there is nothing chimerical in the creature. It is indeed an unknown being. It is Hadaly, the ideal who, under the veils of electricity – in the silver armour simulating feminine beauty – has appeared to you. Although I thoroughly know Hadaly, I swear to you I do not so know Mrs Anderson – Sowana – or her powers.'

Lord Ewald was startled at the grave tone of the wizard, who continued thoughtfully:

'Down there, hidden among the shadowy leaves and the floral lights of the subterranean cavern, Sowana, with closed eyes herself, incorporated in some marvellous manner the power of sight into Hadaly. In her icy hands Sowana held the wires which controlled the Andraiad, and, although she was in the flesh like a corpse, she has through Hadaly walked and spoken in that strange, far-off voice.

'Sometimes she did not speak aloud – she merely vibrated her words on her lips; nor was it necessary for me to do more. But even more wonderful yet was her ability to understand what we were thinking about.'

While the professor was speaking, Lord Ewald kept leaning nearer and nearer towards him, drawn by his interest in the subject. But here he interrupted with a sudden gesture:

'From where does this creature hear? From where does she speak? In fact, with whom are we dealing?'

'As I have told you before,' Professor X replied, 'there are many things which so far cannot be explained, but I will refresh your memory and give you an example of what I mean.

'Do you remember how Hadaly looked at Miss Cleary's photograph when I projected it on the frame? It was perfectly natural, wasn't it? Then, do you remember her strange explanation of the apparatus in the cavern, and her accurate description of Miss Cleary on the train? Do you know how this mystifying clairvoyance was brought about?

'Well, I can explain that. Because of your great admiration for Miss Cleary, her personality has made a permanent impress upon you – magnetized you, so to speak – in the same way that I magnetized the metal for the rings which I have described.

'Do you remember that Hadaly took your hand before describing Miss Cleary? That was because it was necessary for her so to do in order to establish contact with the magnetism with which you are imbued. As soon as this was done it was perfectly easy – just the same as between Sowana and myself.'

'Is it possible?' breathed Lord Ewald.

'Yes,' replied the scientist; 'and there are many, many other "impossible" things which daily materialize around us. I can well say that I am never surprised, as I am one of those who never forget that the universe was created out of a quantity of nothingness.

'But, of course, we have here something to marvel at. Sowana, lying helpless and sightless on a cushion, has been able to project her feelings, speech, and powers of reasoning into Hadaly – to create in her a veritable other woman. This is a phenomenon of superclairvoyance.'

'One moment,' interrupted Lord Ewald. 'What you have said interests me greatly. Since I have been here I have seen you transmitting messages through the medium of space without any wires. Is it possible that electricity alone can transmit its messages to distances and heights without limit, as long as there are established contacts at those distances? How can that be done?'

'It is very simple,' declared the professor. 'In the first place, distance is, in truth, only a sort of illusion. Then, experimental science has already established many fundamental facts, such as the power of hypnotism, thought transference by personal magnetism from one human being to another, *et cetera*. These are all recognized and utilized by some of our leading physicians.

'Then, we have certain metals and chemicals which give off currents and act upon bodies – even at a great distance away – and electric magnets exert great powers of attraction, such as the lines of magnetism between the poles; and all things that pass between these lines or enter the paths of these currents are affected by them.

'Now, I believe that in the case of Sowana we have found a demonstration of a new fact. It has been possible for her, while in these spells of clairvoyant sleep, to project her magnetism upon Hadaly to such an extent that the phantom has become permanently imbued with it – or, in other words, she has become animated by it – an incarnation of Sowana herself.'

'An incarnation!' murmured Lord Ewald in surprise.

'Yes. Let us say an incarnation of idealized humanity. Now, when you have arrived at your castle, and you have given to Hadaly her first glass of water and her pastilles, you will be surprised to see what a really accomplished phantom she will be.

'As soon as her habits and presence have become familiar to you, you will have a very interesting interlocutor, for if I have furnished physically a terrestrial and illusory body, Sowana has superimposed and injected into my creation a soul which is unknown to me.

'So you have incorporated forever a being from the other world. There is centralized in your Andraiad forever, irrevocably, a mystery that it would be impossible for us to imagine.'

## XXIV.

The scientist abruptly arose and walked about, as if to quiet the sinister suggestions which had come to his mind. Lord Ewald watched him with a half dreamy expression.

Professor X suddenly pointed to the clock. It was 9 P.M.

'And now, my lord,' he said, 'I have kept my word. My work is done, and I believe that my creation is more than a common copy of a human being. Tell me truly, in comparison between the illusion and the reality, do you think the illusion is worth living for?'

Lord Ewald drew his pistol and handed it to the scientist.

'My dear wizard,' he said, 'allow me to offer you this pistol as a souvenir of our second meeting. I have no use for it, and you well deserve it as a trophy. My dear friend,' Lord Ewald continued, 'I am afraid that you have made a great sacrifice for me. I am robbing you of a superhuman masterpiece – stealing your greatest treasure.'

'Not so,' replied the inventor, forcing a smile. 'You see, I still have the formula. But,' he added sadly, 'I shall not fabricate any more Andraiads. My subterranean halls will serve to hide me when I am trying other less dangerous experiments. And now, my lord, a toast! You have chosen the land of dreams. Carry your phantom there. I am destined to be chained to the realities of life.

'Some of my trusted men will escort you and your precious luggage onto your ship, the *Britannia*. The Captain is a friend of mine, and has already been notified. Perhaps some day we may meet at your castle. Write to me. Now, farewell!'

The two men clasped hands fervently.

A few moments later Lord Ewald rode slowly down the path, where he was joined by a closed truck guarded by three men. The strange procession soon disappeared in the direction of the depot.

Left alone in his laboratory, Professor X began to pace up and down, muttering to himself. Something seemed to be troubling him, for he stopped once, rubbed the ring on his finger, and then began to stride again.

He shook his head wonderingly, and then walked quickly to the black, concealing hangings. He pulled the curtains back on their rings.

Stretched out, all robed in black, and apparently asleep on a large red sofa placed on huge disks of glass, was the form of a slender woman, no longer young. Her beautiful black hair was streaked with gray. Her fine cut features and the pure oval form of her face seemed set with an unnatural calmness. Her hand, dropping to the carpet, still held a sort of mouthpiece.

'Ah, Sowana,' the professor murmured. 'we have at last done the impossible. This is the first time that science has been able to prove that she can cure man – of love.'

As the figure made no reply, Professor X hurriedly bent and lifted her hand. Its icy touch startled him. He leaned closer to the prostrate form.

The pulse had stopped. The heart was still.

Forcefully, desperately he made magnetic signs over her forehead; but it was in vain.

At the end of an hour of furious, tireless efforts he was forced to concede that she who seemed to be asleep had passed forever from the land of the living.

He bowed his head in grief. Inexorable fate had taken its toll, a soul for a soul.


## XXV.


A week later, when Professor X was alone in the laboratory, his glance fell upon the glaring headlines in an evening newspaper, which shrieked:


### GREAT DISASTER AT SEA!
### S.S. BRITANNIA LOST!!
### SEVENTY-TWO PERISH!!!


Aghast, the scientist perused the account of the sad happening, his prophetic glance leaping here and there among the paragraphs:

Fire broke out in the stern about two o'clock in the morning, presumably in the hold where there was a large store of mineral oils and highly inflammable essences, from some unknown cause.

It was a very rough sea. The steamer, since leaving sight of land, had run into a series of gales. Tremendous waves towered high above the liner, which at times seemed to have sunk into the depths of the ocean, and crashing down upon her decks wrought havoc.

The steamer fought her way bravely through the waves, but the sheet of flames quickly spread over her and into her baggage hold. There was such a high wind that the captain soon saw that the vessel was doomed.

Terrible scenes took place. The women and children shrieked in despair as they retreated before the advancing flames.

The captain ordered the lifeboats to be lowered, and this

was done in five minutes, but there was such a terrific rush for them that many persons were injured.

The women and children were lowered first.

But, during these scenes of horror, a strange event took place. A young Englishman, Lord Ewald Celian, tried to force his way into the baggage hold through the midst of the flames. He fought bravely against those who tried to keep him from entering, and after he had knocked down two of the crew, it took five men to hold him from rushing to his death into the fire.

While struggling with those who sought to detain him, he offered his entire fortune to any one who would help him to save a crate which enclosed some precious object. It was quite impossible to do this. The crate, which was stored in the hold where the fire was raging, could not have been taken off the steamer, as the lifeboats were more than crowded with passengers.

After a great struggle, for he showed extraordinary strength, the young man was at last bound hand and foot and put aboard the last lifeboat.

The boat he was in was rescued by the French steamship *Le Redoutable* about six o'clock in the morning.

The first lifeboats with the women and children were upset by the rough sea. So far, it is learned seventy-two were drowned.

Afterward came the list of those who had perished. The first name was that of Miss Alicia Cleary, actress.

Professor X reread every detail of the terrible disaster and the dreadful ordeal that Lord Ewald had gone through in his attempt to save Hadaly.

When he had finished reading, his eyes wandered to the ebony table. He put out the lights.

Again the moon was shining, and its rays fell upon the rounded arm and the white hand with its sparkling rings, and once more the green, ominous eyes of the snake glittered at him.

With a feeling of intense sadness he gazed through the window, and for some time listened to the wind whistling amid the branches of the trees.

Then he raised his eyes to the starry skies – to the infinite mystery of the heavens – and he shuddered – with the cold, no doubt. His was the terrible heartbreaking silence of a strong man in utter loneliness.

# The Incubated Girl

## By FRED T. JANE

*Ten years after the appearance of De L'Isle Adams' The
Future Eve, a British writer, Fred T. Jane, published another
story of an artificially created female, The Incubated Girl —
but it is unlikely he had read or even heard about the
Frenchman's novel. Jane's story has likewise become virtually
forgotten in the intervening years, although the author's name
lives on in the titles of the annual books of which he was the
first editor, Jane's Fighting Ships and Jane's All The World's
Aircraft, plus the later editions dealing with everything from
weaponry to (appropriately) space travel.*

*Frederick Thomas Jane (1865–1916), a Victorian journalist
and illustrator, apparently became interested in ships when he
was a child and used to stage mock naval actions on a village
pond with his brother. Quite where his interest in fantasy and
science stemmed from is less easy to determine, although he
did provide the illustrations for a number of prophetic 'Future
War' stories for magazines in the 1890s which may well have
fired his interest. He was, in fact, a contemporary of H.G.
Wells and wrote several books — now extremely rare — which
explored similar themes to Wells. In 1897, for instance, he
published To Venus In Five Seconds, one of the earliest books
to feature a non-humanoid race of intelligent beings living on
another planet, at the same time that Wells' War of the
Worlds was being serialised in Pearson's Magazine. (Wells
is, of course, credited as having created the malevolent, bug-
eyed monster theme in his novel.) The following year, Jane
produced The Violet Flame which has been described by
sf historian George Locke as 'the ultimate in mad scientist yarns, abounding with wild theories and ending with a
world catastrophe'. He provided the pictures for both of these*

*volumes himself, revealing the skill which he would employ in the ensuing years to illustrate and describe the fighting ships and aircraft of the world's forces. Once these publications had become successful and provided Jane with a steady annual income he never wrote another word of fiction.*

The Incubated Girl *in which an ancient Egyptian papyrus (Egypt again) provides the secret for creating an artificial girl by chemical means, was apparently issued by the Tower Publishing Company of London just before the imprint collapsed, which doubtless explains its great rarity today. Here, though, is the opening chapter from the story in which Stella, the 'incubated girl', is given life, and it is followed by a later episode in which she reveals herself to be a passionate campaigner against scientific experiments on animals – a concern still very much in the news today. Even though Fred T. Jane has earned his small piece of immortality on the covers of the maritime and aeronautical books which still bear his name, it would be nice to think he might also be given a little more credit in the annals of Science Fiction.*

To one used to such places, there was but little in the laboratory to claim or arrest attention. Its appurtenances were, mostly, usual and ordinary enough: rows upon rows of great glass-stoppered bottles, retorts, stands of test-tubes, pipes, thermometers, taps, Bunsen burners, and electrical machines, all ranged round the room in a prodigal confusion, so plentifully that, save for a large cleared space in the middle, the whole seemed to be an inextricably crowded and jumbled chaos. Only in the centre of the place, where beyond the zone of light two men bent eagerly over something upon a massive, marble-topped table, was the collection of material curious and strange, of a sort to make the most indifferent pause and wonder. Here were things unusual, indeed: a mysterious engine in the form of an immense incubator; and below it, beyond where bowls of steaming liquid gave forth a wall of vapour that rose as a mystic intangible curtain, stood, strangest thing of all, a cradle ready for an infant child!

Neither of the men heeded it; the attentions of both were given to the extraordinary contrivance that towered along the whole length of the table. The elder of the two, a man verging upon fifty, seemed to be an onlooker rather than aught else, for every now and again he turned his head to gaze idly round the room, as though weary of watching; and as he did so, the distant lamps lighting up his face, showed it white and fearful, as of one who is embarked upon an enterprise from which, if he could, he would fain withdraw.

The other, Blackburne Zadara, professor of Egyptology, fellow of many a learned society, a man some fifteen years the other's junior, was wrought up to an equal tension, for he paused occasionally to wipe the sweat from his heated brow, and as he did so his steel-grey eyes glittered with suppressed excitement; yet such relapses were but momentary and occasional; for the most part he steadily and coolly went on with his task. Before him, a little to the left of a row of gauges and thermometers, was a large vessel of quaint workmanship, rudely egg-shaped in form, and this was in a continual state of slight oscillation, as though it held some pent-up force; while through its semi-transparent sides, dimly visible, were faint white forms moving aimlessly to and fro like the tentacles of a sea-anemone at the set of the tide.

Zadara was now busily engaged in scraping off the clay that sealed the mouth of this vessel, and at last, after some forty minutes of arduous labour, the greater part of it had been removed. Then, while he yet laboured, gently and cautiously, there came a violent explosion, the clay floated off in an impalpable dust; and a strange, pungent, all-pervading odour of some unknown gas filled the room. So strong was it that he reeled where he stood, clutching at the table for support, as, faint and dizzy, he sought to control his senses.

'The solution, numbered three,' he hoarsely whispered.

The other, with trembling hands, passed him a jar, the contents of which he presently poured into and over the Egg; then, hastily glancing at a sheet of paper that was pinned up in front of him, he took a mallet, steadied himself for a moment, and struck the Egg one sharp, short blow with it. Immediately the shell split asunder, the pieces falling this way and that; and before him, living and breathing, there lay a female child!

'Thank God!' ejaculated the elder man, as he heard the infant's cry, and saw its little perfect limbs, 'you have not created a Frankenstein monster as I feared you would.'

'I never expected to, my friend,' returned the other shortly, as he wrapped the wailing baby in a blanket. 'Hand me that bottle of water and asses' milk; we must feed the brat.'

'Aye; but you, Zadara, knew nothing of the stranger.'

'What stranger, man? You speak in riddles,' said the professor, as he busied himself over the infant, washing and dressing her in some sort of fashion.

'I did not tell you of it before, for various reasons. First, I have often thought that it may have been but a hallucination; secondly, I did not wish to have the experiment delayed while you began it all over again, as you would have done had you believed my tale; thirdly, I –'

'Never mind your reasons, Wilson; tell me, rather, what it was that you saw, or think you saw.'

'It was nearly seven months ago now, you had gone out about something, leaving me here on watch; and as I sat in the big chair yonder, I became conscious that I was not alone; I felt that there was someone in the room with me. It was in the darkening of the twilight, and as I rose to look about me, I saw, standing over the incubator, a man, one whose face I could not see. He had opened the frame, and was doing something to the Egg, but what, I could not, in the darkness, discern. "Hold!" I cried to him; "leave that alone." He made no answer, nor any sign that he had heard, and presently, fearing to approach him, I lit the gas to see him the better ... Zadara, when I looked again, there was no one there!'

'He had gone out of the door while your back was turned, I suppose?'

'He had not; the door was locked from the inside.'

'Then, my dear fellow, you may take it that you were dreaming; I, too, have had my hallucinations ... However, here is the child; that is a fact, and facts are all we have to deal with.'

'You are a sceptic and materialist, Zadara; I am a –'

'Overwrought fool, perhaps, just at present,' interrupted the other. 'Let us get out of this place, to where we can discuss the future quietly ... Pah! this gas that was in the Egg is like champagne mixed with chloroform: no wonder your fancies run riot.'

He picked up the cradle as he spoke, and together they went into an adjoining room, which, with a bright fire burning in the grate, contrasted cheerfully with the dismal place that they had just quitted.

The professor pressed a button in the wall, and presently a middle-aged woman appeared in the doorway. He signed to the sleeping babe, rapidly said a few words on the deaf and dumb alphabet; in reply to which, she, with a vacuous nod of response, lifted the cradle and carried it and the child away.

'Now,' said Zadara, 'we can rest and think ... Let us first, however, look over the papyrus, to make sure that nothing has been omitted; though, faith, I think that I know every word by heart ... Here we are: I will read you the portion that refers to to-day's proceedings ... I have kept the translation pretty closely to the original – as closely as I could, that is.'

He paused a moment, while he found the place then read: –

'*Thereafter shalt thou nurture her upon the cakes that be within the casket. Also thou mayest give her of the milk of she-asses, or of cows, or of she-goats: yet, nurture her not upon the milk of any woman, lest thereby she take the nature of the woman.*

'*And when she shall be of an age to be weaned, then shalt thou feed her upon bread and upon corn and upon fruits of every sort, but neither flesh nor wine shalt thou give unto her.*

'*Yet, beware, in these days of her tender years that she be brought up in the fear of the gods. Behold she shall be a woman that is a woman, not as other women that be but the part of a man.*

'*And so long as she remain a virgin undefiled so shall she neither grow old nor fade in her beauty that is more than the beauty of the daughters of men. In the likeness of Isis, the earth-form of Isis, till the day long appointed shall dawn on the world. She shall not die nor suffer sickness, nor shall she be weary. And coming the day long appointed then shall –*'

*

He stopped reading, and folded up his translation, saying as he did so: – 'That is about enough of that sort of rubbish.'

'I consider it interesting,' said Wilson, 'and would be glad to hear more. What we have already witnessed is so astounding, so miraculous, that I am prepared to believe anything and everything that the papyrus may say. Let me hear the rest.'

'There is very little more; and what there is, I have not yet succeeded in translating,' replied Zadara, as though annoyed at the request.

'We had better, I think, select a name for her,' he added hastily, changing the subject. 'You can choose it … I thought myself of Protoplasma.'

'I should prefer Stella; it is prettier and shorter.'

'Stella be it, then,' assented the professor, much as though the name of a dog were under discussion.

'And now,' said Wilson, 'let us think about the girl's upbringing. You, of course, will have her registered and baptized.'

'I shall, of course, do nothing of the sort. She is an animal, so needs no registration; as to baptism, that is, in any case, a silly waste of time.'

'Unless the Sacrament of Baptism is administered she will be unregen –'

'Nonsense !'

'Well – you are, perhaps, right; I forgot that Stella is not of the race of men. She will, of course, be therefore free from "original sin," and –'

'Original fiddlesticks; remember our compact, Wilson, not to discuss religion.'

'I have not forgotten; but, Zadara, I cannot let you bring her up as a heathen without a word of protest. I firmly believe that this child has been vouchsafed to you for some divine purpose – unless, indeed, it is some new and terrible device of the Evil One. I believe that the man that I saw was no creature of earth, that he was a being from another world, that –'

'And I,' interrupted the professor, as was his wont, 'believe nothing of the sort; for I believe in neither God nor devil … However, my friend, we can, each of us, experiment in his own fashion; you have your son Meredyth, train him up in your theories; I, adopting this Stella as my daughter, will educate her in mine; then we shall see what we shall see.'

'But consider, the injustice that you will do the girl; for, too well, I know the sort of training you will give. By a judicious course of education – she being free from original sin – you might make of her an earthly angel, a guiding beacon to all suffering women; a type impossible, perhaps, to imitate, yet one to follow from afar; a very –'

'A truce to what I might do. Listen, and you shall hear what I really feel and hope in the matter, for I have a scheme before me, already mapped and planned ... Women, as you know, have of late grown aggressive and insufferable in their views of their own importance, and as regards their relations with men; at the present rate, some forty years hence they will have attained such influence, that, either the race of men will become a collection of effeminate, emasculated entities, or else women will, one and all, be practically harlots. You may take it that "free love" will, if it ever comes into general use and custom, if it ever becomes orthodox, be simply prostitution under another name. Plenty of women are naturally immoral, because they like to be, that is neither here nor there; but a far greater number are so because there is money in it. At present, these sort marry for money where they can, the pay is greater that way, the future, so hopeless to the street-women, is assured to the "honourably married" strumpet, unless the divorce court intervene; but, with "free love" as their watchword, women will sell themselves, or remain virgins ... You follow me?'

'Perfectly; go on, I am all attention.'

'Well, I, as you know, pretend to no sentiment; to me, virtue and chastity, as sentiments, are all rubbish; but when they are viewed from a practical, logical standpoint, things assume a very different complexion; then, I have views, and strong ones. Wilson, I tell you that women *must* be chaste; or else the race must degenerate.'

'I am with you there, though I confess that such a sentiment from you astonishes me.'

'Well – to continue my monologue – women being on this downgrade, Stella, and others like her that I shall make, will come most opportunely. The present race of women, unmarried, will die out; the Stellas will replace them. So I shall train her strictly in the paths of virtue; not, let me tell you, in the path the "new woman" would have girls brought up in, knowing everything of all the vices and diseases, knowing everything of their anatomy and the causes of sensations; for, faith, such a girl is far worse than the woman of the streets, no matter how chaste her wisdom may keep her. Innocence is better than chastity that is such merely to increase the ultimate market value of the woman. The street woman, at least, is an essential of civilisation, a protectress – unmeaningly, no doubt, but still a protectress – to the women yet unfallen; but the modern virgin is a miasmic fungus, a loathsome, useless parasite, an abscess in our civilisation. Of such as these, Stella shall be the direct antithesis. There now, you have my views *in toto.*'

'There are women, thousands of good, pure women,' – began Wilson; but Zadara would hear no more, and presently the former bade goodnight, and went home to dream excited and distorted versions of the extraordinary birth of which he had that night been a witness.

Left alone, the professor turned once more to the papyrus document, reading it carefully and slowly, pausing long over the concluding sentences, the same that he had denied knowledge of to Wilson earlier in the evening.

'Yes,' he said to himself slowly, 'there is no doubt that that is what it says and means, though, whence came the idea?'

He went over his translation yet again, frowning and pursing up his thin, eel-like lips as he did so.

'Yes,' he murmured once more, 'no other reading is permissible or even possible ... Well, it is an interesting proof of the antiquity of a certain superstition; though, faith, it has more plausibility here than have some of later growth. Not that I am going to credit it; but Wilson would ... Oh, Wilson!' he continued, apostrophising his absent friend, 'what would you not have said, what would you not have done, had you only been able to read this? ... What a precious ass you would have made of yourself! ... As things are, I see that you'll be trouble enough; but if you only knew of these few lines that I have withheld; ah, what then? ... No, my friend, you shall not know; the little creature in the next room will have other and more practical uses than those to which your superstitions would bring her ... Yet, I am half sorry that you will not learn; it would be interesting to see how this claim – if you believed it – would affect your Christianity!'

Then his thoughts wandered back a couple of years, to when he and Wilson, touring in Egypt, had made the strange find that, to-day, had had such a marvellous development. He could picture it to himself as well as though it were yesterday; the great ruined temple, the pitiless sun beating down upon the sand-covered stones, the blazing up-cast light driving the two Englishmen to seek shelter where the inviting shadows lay so deep and cool and blue.

'How hot the stones are, even in the shade,' he had remarked, as he idly tapped his fingers upon the age-worn masonry.

Even as he spoke there had come the hoarse creak of an axis untouched for countless centuries, as a great stone started from its socket, to hang projecting and motionless from the temple wall.

There had been no more thought of the heat, as they and their guides struggled for hours to shift it this way and that, till at last as, worn with useless effort, they had been about to desist, the huge mass swung suddenly downward with a crash, leaving a wide black cavity in the temple wall; and in that opening, upon linen folds that crumbled into nothingness at their touch, stood a strange stone casket carved with many hieroglyphics, coloured vermilion, and green, and black.

That same night he had made out the inscription; and that once deciphered, he could find no rest from his longing to look inside and learn all.

The legend on the casket, when translated into approximate English, ran: –

· HERE-IN · IS · THE · SECRET ·
· OF · LIFE ∴ LET · HIM · THAT ·
· IS · WORTHY · TO · KNOW · ALONE ·
· OPEN · AND · LEARN ∴ LET · HIM · THAT ·
· IS · NOT · WORTHY · BEWARE ∴ THE · DIS- ·
· COVERY · OF · PIANCHI : THE · SON · OF · MERHU ·
· SETI : PRIEST · OF · ISIS · HATH · PLACED · WITHIN ·

After an investigation extending over several days, a period during which he had grudged himself the time for food or rest, he had found the upper face of the stone to be cleverly devised into a quaint many-sided form, which followed the design of the top so cunningly that a man might look a thousand times and not perceive how the mechanism acted.

This once discovered, the rest had proved easy; the lid revolved slightly, so that it could be lifted out, to reveal a large bronze vessel inside, while in one corner were laid a number of small squares of some unknown composition that had a peculiarly sweet pungent odour.

Inside this second casket he had found the papyrus already referred to, and a few tiny specks, that might have been dust or anything else, and which he narrowly escaped overlooking. As it was, he had closed the vessel after removing the scroll; nor did he open it again until many weeks had elapsed.

The papyrus was headed by an inscription that prepared him somewhat for the startling nature of the document itself. This set forth, at great length and with many details, the means whereby a child could be chemically constructed; it was, in fact – or practically claimed to be – a solution of that great problem – how to evolve the organic from the inorganic. In the nature of things, it – being Egyptian – had a good deal of mysticism wrapped around it; many, too, of the chemical formulæ were puzzling in the extreme; but, as though anticipating future difficulties of this sort, the papyrus went on to state that the essentials for the experiment had already been combined and solidified, so that the directions could be followed without let or hindrance.

As for the mysticisms involved, he smiled to himself now as he thought of them; had he credited them, the experiment, in all probability, would never have been attempted; yet now, as he sat alone in the firelight, he could not help thinking of the stranger of whom Wilson had told him. He looked round, half expecting to see someone watching him, he seemed to feel a Presence; so strong was this impression, that he lit a candle and went into the next room, where the baby was. The child was sleeping peacefully in its cradle, the mute dozed in a chair near by; nothing else, nothing of the supernatural, clung about the place.

'Faith!' he exclaimed, using his favourite expression, 'I

must be overstrung indeed; what did I expect to see? Truly, I shall be in for a brain fever if I think of that preposterous claim any more; what an ass I am, to give it a second thought.'

Nevertheless, he set to work to erase the final sentences from his translation; then sat down again to think about the child whose wonderful destiny he, materialist and sceptic as he was, had decided to warp even while he utterly denied it credence. Somewhere in his nature Zadara had a grain of faith, of credulity, of superstition; like many another atheist, he discarded all beliefs, only to be thrust into the dilemma of fearing to find some truth-germ in things he discredited; he dreaded to believe, dreaded to disbelieve, and so his mental state became chaotic, confused, a charnel-house of the might-have-been.

Whatever were Zadara's views about Wilson's stranger, he kept them to himself, and expressed no opinion on the matter, utterly refusing to be drawn into conversation about it. After a time he started to manufacture some more children in incubators similar to that which he had used for Stella, but his efforts were unsuccessful; at the most he merely produced a low form of vegetable life; and presently, after a long study of the papyrus, he destroyed his creations, broke up the incubators, and settled down to other pursuits, morosely and sourly, as one who has struggled unavailingly against the inevitable.

Stella meanwhile grew and flourished, a strange and wonderfully beautiful child ...

\* \* \*

The much-advertised Sunday came at last; and Stella, when she went on to the platform, was pleased to find the big room full of people. Many of them were sympathisers with the Prevention of Cruelty to Animals movement, but there was also a fair sprinkling of folk who had been drawn thither by curiosity after reading all that the newspapers had surmised; there was, too, quite a small army of reporters.

She was dressed in a quaint, white, Egyptian-like costume, and it was curious to note how well it became her, despite the seeming inappropriateness of her fair complexion. Very beautiful she looked, this priestess of the new religion, as she stood, statue-like, before that vast concourse, hushed into silence by the weird loveliness of the eyes that looked down upon them all so scornfully. It was this that they had come for, to see and gaze upon the woman of whom all London was babbling – the woman who claimed, said some, to be more than mortal woman, around whom so many mysteries and vague romances hung, she whose mere name was already a synonym for the *outré* and the quaint. For a while she stood thus, saying nothing, but slowly scanning the faces of the crowd below her. They were all there – Harding, Susie, Catesby, Wickham, Warwick, Mrs Kennedy, ay, even Professor Zadara himself, nearly everybody with whom she had come into contact during the last few months; but one, Wilson, whom of all men she had most wished should behold her in this her hour of triumph, she could not see, though she looked for him long and anxiously.

'I shall speak to-night,' began Stella, in her usual voice, without a tremor or sign of nervousness, 'of many things. I shall put my words in no regular order or sequence, since I am well assured that it is not by logical sequences that one can speak to the hearts of men. The world is all dogma, lives on it, worships it; dogma alone commands respect, so dogma you shall have.

'I will speak first of animals. They are better and truer than most of mankind, and the day of their emancipation is long overdue; science can perform all that is now done by wretched beasts; the employment of the horse as a beast of burden is a disgrace to your time and century, a disgrace to you, to every one of you. Were I going to trend in the direction of logic, I would point out the absurd fallacy of the position, the rank hypocrisy of those who have yelled themselves hoarse for freedom to slaves, yet still enslave the helpless animals. Bah! you hypocrites, it is only because you see no way to use their votes! Ay; could they only vote for the great party of Progress, then would you shed blood in rivers to set them free; but they are dumb, so you do not care: yet, you can shriek because a few Armenian malcontents get served by the Turks in the same fashion that the Turks get treated by them when the occasion serves; your Dissenting Demagogues can weep their eyes out over that – it brings in votes, so you can all be fools or knaves about it.

'The animals would be free, too, had you not rebelled

against the Appointed Order of Things; else it had been you that toiled, with none to care for your misery; and that, indeed, is your proper lot. All of you here that are of the lower orders – and you are mostly of that sort – should even now be slaves and beasts of burden; you have it in your blood, you are born to it, made for it, slavery is your hereditary portion. Think you that you escape from it by calling yourselves free? Why, did not I, who am by rank and birth your ruler, drive a dozen of you from a 'bus-top but a few weeks since? Ah! you knew the whip, and fell to it; ay, and the day is coming when you will have to fall to it again; that is the day I live for, and whose coming I foretell.'

She paused for a little space, but no one, as yet, sought to interrupt her; some smiled, some looked sad, but all were alike interested in this novel lecture, and waited expectantly to hear more.

'Therefore,' cried Stella, continuing, 'these are the dogmas that I give to you as law.

'Firstly. "That it is a crime to employ animals for duties that, unless done by machinery, should be performed by men and women."

'Secondly. "That any men or women torturing animals whether with the excuse of science, or of pleasure, or of sport, shall themselves be treated in like fashion."

'Thirdly. "That those bestial ones, lower than the horse, the cow, and the sheep, who feed themselves upon the flesh of animals that they have murdered, and from which through long-acquired use they cannot abstain, shall hereafter be made to kill and eat each other, drawing for the same by lot, till the filthy breed be self-annihilated."

'These are propositions – dogmas, if you will – to which no honest man, no true woman, can do aught but accede.'

The audience may have acceded, but they gave no sign of it. She went on –

'I shall speak more upon this at another time; now, I have other things also to say, and the like of you soon weary of hearing things that are for your good.

'See, I am a woman, of the same similitude as you women now before me, though perchance I am fairer than you that are but daughters of men. I have seen and watched and heard you; I have seen you, women, flaunting in the daylight, puffed out with your own conceit, proud to say that you have virtue; I have seen others of you at night, flaunting still, proud of your shame: and so you drive each other to vice or virtue and put the blame upon your God. I have seen you reeling drunken in the streets, making coarse noises that any animal would scorn to make, horrible sounds that you call singing and laughter. I have even seen you in your places of amusement, where you shame yourselves to make glad the hearts of men that are lower than beasts; what beast, indeed, would care to watch such a thing? I have read your books, wherein they among you who are too old or too ugly to expose your persons and prance upon the stage, seek the same end and say the same thing, and more, and worse. Knew you ever a beast or an animal that did any such thing?'

Some of the women in the room blushed at these remarks, some only smiled, as also did all the men.

'What of the men?' called out a woman, sitting far down in the hall, a veritable member of the shrieking sisterhood. 'Granting for a moment that we are what you say, what of the men who made us so?'

'I hear what you say,' replied Stella, when the cheers and laughter had died down, 'but I come not here to reform your woes. If men *will* choose you, and such as you, it were better that you were grateful and not complaining. I have no mission to men, nor care I what they do; which among them, indeed, is worth the caring? Mostly they are lower than the beasts, yet are they well mated with you. A little less virtue on the one side, a little less honour on the other, well are you mated and well do you sort. But of men I cannot speak much, seeing that I have not troubled to note them, save a few that have forced themselves upon my society. These were mostly artists, and nearly all men of the common class,' – (here Harding and his friends began to exchange glances and wish that they had stayed away) – 'none of whom benefit by living.

'Yet, since for one good and honest woman, one who is now sitting in your midst, I have found three good and honest men, of whom two are not here, and the other, my secretary, is on the platform beside me,' – (here Manton blushed, and thinking of the past, blushed yet deeper) – 'I will say no more about them. I could have said much that was bitter, yet having read the women's books and found therein all that can be written against men, I will say no more. But of you, women, and your woes, I am very weary and tired.

'For the last few months I have been studying your religion, and of a truth I find it as good as any, did you but practise a tithe of that which you preach. But I find that, preaching charity to each other, you show none in your thoughts; telling of love, you have none save lust; speaking of faith, you show none save in yourselves. I have probed the writings of those who would expound your six hundred creeds; some of you dissent so that you may thus be held greater in a smaller circle, some of you hold to the Established Faith that you may be honoured for the same, holding it more respectable. Many of you believe in nothing save your own selves, and why indeed should you? Is it meet that in the Scheme of Things such dross as you should continue, after this earthly existence in the land of darkness, and should enter into the land of light? It were no heaven, no land of light, if such as you were there. You eat, and drink, and sleep, you make merry and you mourn, but of a higher life than that you know nothing. Therefore you are well advised to live as you do, seeing that when you die the most of you shall perish utterly and have no more existence.

'I have probed your religions that have come out of Egypt, whence you have stolen them and forgotten: Osiris is forgotten; Pthah and Thoth you have railed at and forgotten; yet before the Pyramids were built, or ever the Israelites came into Egypt, Osiris was God. Born in the likeness of men, they killed Him; but He lived again to help them. Osiris was; He has passed away; Isis is no more. You have had many a god since then, and your own Christ was killed by the hand of men. Which was the true One? Were they Both true?'

She paused a moment, wrought up to a pitch of excitement, foreign to her and strange. Then in a voice that penetrated every nook and cranny of the hall, she cried –

'They were, They were not, and They were; then after a space you forgot Them, and worshipped none save your own selves; for a while you lived thus and were content.

'And now, now that you must worship, and have not what to worship, to whom will you bow? The world has ever needed something tangible to bow to, and thus are the Roman Catholics wise in their Virgin worship and the images that represent her; for this is the worship of Isis, dishonoured and disgraced, yet still the copy of the old creed. What a copy too! Verily, there is no proof of the Christian religion so great as the existence of the Roman Catholic faith, or, at least, no proof so great of all such parts as need belief in a personal devil. Read history, read of Spain, read how a mighty empire was scattered by the aid of that religion. The empire has been long dead, but the effect of the teaching remains. Were there ever such cowardly brutes as the Spaniards of to-day with the inherited taint of the Inquisition in their blood, men who, since they cannot have men and women to torture, do worse, and torture innocent animals, horses and cattle, in their bull-fights, while their dainty women look on and smile.

'Think well, any of you here who may be Papists, you, with your celibate priests, your chaste and virgin nuns, your auricular confessions. Are your priests all gods; your nuns, goddesses? Are not they human like you yourselves? Have you never heard tales of your convent schools? If it be worth the while for your women to be chaste, will all this help them to virtue?

'Ah, well, perhaps, since It has brought Its imitators to such a pass, in this has the Old Faith triumphed.

'And when some of you rebelled, and said, "We will worship God alone, and the priests shall no more have to keep their women in the nunneries, but shall marry them openly even as other men do," what else did you do, but put your Bible in the place of the image, and worship that till you tired of such an inanimate God. And for your father-confessors you have substituted the editors of weekly papers that may be bought at a penny or so, men who in their "Answers to Correspondents" advise you how to marry, how to live, how to dress, how to eat, and every other thing: they answer all things, do these new Bibles – and the less that they know the more do they arrogate to themselves the position that you once assigned to the Deity.

'To-day, gold is your god; but gold is a sorry deity, material and sordid: the world needs something higher and more beautiful than metal to bow to.

'Young men seek to worship women, seek to think them an image of eternal goodness. Honour to them for the weak attempt; but it is a passing mood, a fragile idol, and one whereof they are their own iconoclasts in the end.

'Who would worship, who would love, who would marry a woman, could he see her as she will be but ten years hence, stupid and commonplace when her beauty has fled?

'Your great writers say that religion must be founded upon Love, which is Sacrifice; yet not, I think, upon sacrifices made after this fashion, for he who thus sacrifices himself, does it but for his own ends of the moment, thinking not of the future. If he did, he would not marry!

'Therefore, of all foolish and pernicious things, love is the very worst, and virtue, which is but a buttress built to the edifice, is of small account. Women, I take it, make after chastity merely because it suits the whim of men that they should do so; so that whether she be chaste or no, whether in heart or act, every woman pretends so to be, if she in any way can, and thus is the seeking after virtue but an engine for hypocrisy, and the cause of many troubles.

'I have not gone into this matter so far as I would, there being difficulties in the way; nor can I, I confess, understand that which you call love. Yet I am well assured that it is but a word meaning many things, and that the world were better could this love be done away with altogether ...

'Therefore, that the world may be rid of this trouble, I think I would have it that you bred men even as now you breed animals, setting aside the healthiest women for breeding the race, not allowing the others to marry save they might care, or be able, to rise to a union free from lust, living together in platonic friendship. Then would the world be higher and better, then would women be fit for to worship, and the feeble and delicate would cease to be born.

'Yet, I doubt if this shall be, save that there be one to lead you; for men must have to worship a woman all pure and all lovely; one above all earthly women. Such a one am I; therefore if you would worship – and you must worship something – then bow and worship me!

'I was not born as you were; worship me, and I will be your goddess.'

She ceased. More she might not have said. On every hand, from all that vast assemblage, rose voices of protest, loud and continued, a roar of execration and of scorn, as the people sprang to their feet calling out this thing and that. Here, one cried, 'Blasphemy,' while another answered him that it was time to have a new creed, since the old were worn so threadbare, and the most shouted out that she was mad.

And while they yet wrangled, cheering and blaming, Stella passed swiftly behind the great black curtains that overhung the back of the platform, and vanished from their sight.

# The Surgeon's Experiment

## By W.C. MORROW

The Surgeon's Experiment *which appeared in a popular American periodical,* The Argonaut, *on October 15, 1887, has been described as the first short story to utilise the same theme as* Frankenstein *without the actual name. This tale about a scientific experimenter who revives the headless corpse of a suicide by affixing a steel head, was certainly gruesome reading for the magazine's refined readership, and there is evidence that a number of readers complained, while others actually cancelled their subscriptions on the grounds that if this was what the editor was planning to print in the future they wanted no more of it. Certainly, nothing so horrid appeared again in the pages of* The Argonaut.

*The author of the story, William Chambers Morrow (1853–1923), probably enjoyed this furore for he was a man with a sense of fun and was a much travelled writer and journalist. Apart from books on widely differing topics like* Bohemian Paris of Today *(1900) and* Lentala of the South Seas *(1908) he also penned a number of weird tales including* The Hero of the Plague, The Inmate of the Dungeon *and* The Resurrection of Little Wang Tei, *all of which were collected into a now rare volume entitled* The Ape, The Idiot and Other People, *published in Philadelphia in 1897. In the following story, W.C. Morrow builds an atmosphere of mounting suspense and presents a final dénouement that has since been imitated frequently by the makers of horror films – not least of all, those producing sequels to the* Frankenstein *saga ...*

A young man of refined appearance, but evidently suffering great mental distress, presented himself one morning at the residence of a singular old man, who was known as a surgeon of remarkable skill. The house was a queer and primitive brick affair, entirely out of date, and tolerable only in the decayed part of the city in which it stood. It was large, gloomy, and dark, and had long corridors and dismal rooms; and it was absurdly large for the small family – man and wife – that occupied it. The house described, the man is portrayed – but not the woman. He could be agreeable on occasion, but, for all that, he was but animated mystery. His wife was weak, wan, reticent, evidently miserable, and possibly living a life of dread or horror – perhaps witness of repulsive things, subject of anxieties, and victim of fear and tyranny; but there is a great deal of guessing in these assumptions. He was about sixty-five years of age and she about forty. He was lean, tall, and bald, with thin, smooth-shaven face, and very keen eyes; she kept always at home, and was slovenly. The man was strong, the woman weak; he dominated, she suffered.

Although he was a surgeon of rare skill, his practice was almost nothing, for it was a rare occurrence that the few who knew of his great ability were brave enough to penetrate the gloom of his house, and when they did so it was with a deaf ear turned to sundry ghoulish stories that were whispered concerning him. These were, in great part, but exaggerations of his experiments in vivisection; he was devoted to the science of surgery.

The young man who presented himself on the morning just mentioned was a handsome fellow, yet of evident weak character and unhealthy temperament – sensitive, and easily exalted or depressed. A single glance convinced the surgeon that his visitor was seriously affected in mind, for there was never a bolder skull-grin of melancholia, fixed and irremediable.

A stranger would not have suspected any occupancy of the house. The street door – old, warped, and blistered by the sun – was locked, and the small, faded-green window-blinds were closed. The young man rapped at the door. No answer. He rapped again. Still no sign. He examined a slip of paper, glanced at the number on the house, and then, with the impatience of a child, he furiously kicked the door. There were signs of numerous other such kicks. A response came in the shape of a shuffling footstep in the hall, a turning of the rusty key, and a sharp face that peered through a cautious opening in the door.

'Are you the doctor?' asked the young man.

'Yes, yes! Come in,' briskly replied the master of the house.

The young man entered. The old surgeon closed the door and carefully locked it. 'This way,' he said, advancing to a rickety flight of stairs. The young man followed. The surgeon led the way up the stairs, turned into a narrow, musty-smelling corridor at the left, traversed it, rattling the loose boards under his feet, at the farther end opened a door at the right, and beckoned his visitor to enter. The young man found himself in a pleasant room, furnished in antique fashion and with hard simplicity.

'Sit down,' said the old man, placing a chair so that its occupant should face a window that looked out upon a dead wall about six feet from the house. He threw open the blind, and a pale light entered. He then seated himself near his visitor and directly facing him, and with a searching look, that had all the power of a microscope, he proceeded to diagnosticate the case.

'Well?' he presently asked.

The young man shifted uneasily in his seat.

'I – I have come to see you,' he finally stammered, 'because I'm in trouble.'

'Ah!'

'Yes; you see, I – that is – I have given it up.'

'Ah!' There was pity added to sympathy in the ejaculation.

'That's it. Given it up,' added the visitor. He took from his pocket a roll of banknotes, and with the utmost deliberation he counted them out upon his knee. 'Five thousand dollars,' he calmly remarked. 'That is for you. It's all I have; but I presume – I imagine – no; that is not the word – *assume* – yes; that's the word – assume that five thousand – is it really that much? Let me count.' He counted again. 'That five thousand dollars is a sufficient fee for what I want you to do.'

The surgeon's lips curled pityingly – perhaps disdainfully also. 'What do you want me to do?' he carelessly inquired.

The young man rose, looked around with a mysterious air, approached the surgeon, and laid the money across his knee.

Then he stooped and whispered two words in the surgeon's ear.

These words produced an electric effect. The old man started violently; then, springing to his feet, he caught his visitor angrily, and transfixed him with a look that was as sharp as a knife. His eyes flashed, and he opened his mouth to give utterance to some harsh imprecation, when he suddenly checked himself. The anger left his face, and only pity remained. He relinquished his grasp, picked up the scattered notes, and offering them to the visitor, slowly said:

'I do not want your money. You are simply foolish. You think you are in trouble. Well, you do not know what trouble is. Your only trouble is that you have not a trace of manhood in your nature. You are merely insane – I shall not say pusillanimous. You should surrender yourself to the authorities, and be sent to a lunatic asylum for proper treatment.'

The young man keenly felt the intended insult, and his eyes flashed dangerously.

'You old dog – you insult me thus!' he cried. 'Grand airs, these, you give yourself! Virtuously indignant, old murderer, you! Don't want my money, eh? When a man comes to you himself and wants it done, you fly into a passion and spurn his money; but let an enemy of his come and pay you, and you are only too willing. How many such jobs have you done in this miserable old hole? It is a good thing for you that the police have not run you down, and brought spade and shovel with them. Do you know what is said of you? Do you think you have kept your windows so closely shut that no sound has ever penetrated beyond them? Where do you keep your infernal implements?'

He had worked himself into a high passion. His voice was hoarse, loud, and rasping. His eyes, bloodshot, started from their sockets. His whole frame twitched, and his fingers writhed. But he was in the presence of a man infinitely his superior. Two eyes, like those of a snake, burned two holes through him. An overmastering, inflexible presence confronted one weak and passionate. The result came.

'Sit down,' commanded the stern voice of the surgeon.

It was the voice of father to child, of master to slave. The fury left the visitor, who, weak and overcome, fell upon a chair.

Meanwhile, a peculiar light had appeared in the old surgeon's face, the dawn of a strange idea; a gloomy ray, strayed from the fires of the bottomless pit; the baleful light that illumines the way of the enthusiast. The old man remained a moment in profound abstraction, gleams of eager intelligence bursting momentarily through the cloud of sombre meditation that covered his face. Then broke the broad light of a deep, impenetrable determination. There was something sinister in it, suggesting the sacrifice of something held sacred. After a struggle, mind had vanquished conscience.

Taking a piece of paper and a pencil, the surgeon carefully wrote answers to questions which he peremptorily addressed to his visitor, such as his name, age, place of residence, occupation, and the like, and the same inquiries concerning his parents, together with other particular matters.

'Does anyone know you came to this house?' he asked.

'No.'

'You swear it?'

'Yes.'

'But your prolonged absence will cause alarm and lead to search.'

'I have provided against that.'

'How?'

'By depositing a note in the post, as I came along, announcing my intention to drown myself.'

'The river will be dragged.'

'What then?' asked the young man, shrugging his shoulders with careless indifference. 'Rapid undercurrent, you know. A good many are never found.'

There was a pause.

'Are you ready?' finally asked the surgeon.

'Perfectly.' The answer was cool and determined.

The manner of the surgeon, however, showed much perturbation. The pallor that had come into his face at the moment his decision was formed became intense. A nervous tremulousness came over his frame. Above it all shone the light of enthusiasm.

'Have you a choice in the method?' he asked.

'Yes; extreme anaesthesia.'

'With what agent?'

'The surest and quickest.'

'Do you desire any – any subsequent disposition?'

'No; only nullification; simply a blowing out, as of a candle in the wind; a puff – then darkness, without a trace. A sense of your own safety may suggest the method. I leave it to you.'

'No delivery to your friends?'

'None whatever.'

Another pause.

'Did you say you are quite ready?' asked the surgeon.

'Quite ready.'

'And perfectly willing?'

'Anxious.'

'Then wait a moment.'

With this request the old surgeon rose to his feet and stretched himself. Then with the stealthiness of a cat he opened the door and peered into the hall, listening intently. There was no sound. He softly closed the door and locked it. Then he closed the window-blinds and locked them. This done, he opened a door leading into an adjoining room, which, though it had no window, was lighted by means of a small skylight. The young man watched closely. A strange change had come over him. While his determination had not one whit lessened, a look of great relief came into his face, displacing the haggard, despairing look of a half-hour before. Melancholic then, he was ecstatic now.

The opening of the second door disclosed a curious sight. In the centre of the room, directly under the skylight, was an operating-table, such as is used by demonstrators of anatomy. A glass case against the wall held surgical instruments of every kind. Hanging in another case were human skeletons of various sizes. In sealed jars, arranged on shelves, were monstrosities of divers kinds preserved in alcohol. There were also, among innumerable other articles scattered about the room, a manikin, a stuffed cat, a desiccated human heart, plaster casts of various parts of the body, numerous charts, and a large assortment of drugs and chemicals. There was also a lounge, which could be opened to form a couch. The surgeon opened it and moved the operating-table aside, giving its place to the lounge.

'Come in,' he called to his visitor.

The young man obeyed without the least hesitation.

'Take off your coat.'

He complied.

'Lie down on that lounge.'

In a moment the young man was stretched at full length, eyeing the surgeon. The latter undoubtedly was suffering under great excitement, but he did not waver; his movements were sure and quick. Selecting a bottle containing a liquid, he carefully measured out a certain quantity. While doing this he asked: 'Have you ever had any irregularity of the heart?'

'No.'

The answer was prompt, but it was immediately followed by a quizzical look in the speaker's face.

'I presume,' he added, 'you mean by your question that it might be dangerous to give me a certain drug. Under the circumstances, however, I fail to see any relevancy in your question.'

This took the surgeon aback; but he hastened to explain that he did not wish to inflict unnecessary pain, and hence his question.

He placed the glass on a stand, approached his visitor, and carefully examined his pulse.

'Wonderful!' he exclaimed.

'Why?'

'It is perfectly normal.'

'Because I am wholly resigned. Indeed, it has been long since I knew such happiness. It is not active, but infinitely sweet.'

'You have no lingering desire to retract?'

'None whatever.'

The surgeon went to the stand and returned with the draught.

'Take this,' he said, kindly.

The young man partially raised himself and took the glass in his hand. He did not show the vibration of a single nerve. He drank the liquid, draining the last drop. Then he returned the glass with a smile.

'Thank you,' he said; 'you are the noblest man that lives. May you always prosper and be happy! You are my benefactor, my liberator. Bless you, bless you! You reach down from your seat with the gods and lift me up into glorious peace and rest. I love you – I love you with all my heart!'

These words, spoken earnestly in a musical, low voice, and accompanied with a smile of ineffable tenderness, pierced the old man's heart. A suppressed convulsion swept over him; intense anguish wrung his vitals; perspiration trickled down his face. The young man continued to smile.

'Ah, it does me good!' said he.

The surgeon, with a strong effort to control himself, sat down upon the edge of the lounge and took his visitor's wrist, counting the pulse.

'How long will it take?' the young man asked.

'Ten minutes. Two have passed.' The voice was hoarse.

'Ah, only eight minutes more! ... Delicious, delicious! I feel it coming ... What was that? ... Ah, I understand. Music ... Beautiful! ... Coming, coming ... Is that – that – water? ... Trickling? Dripping? Doctor!'

'Well?'

'Thank you, ... thank you ... Noble man, ... my saviour, ... my bene ... bene ... factor ... Trickling, ... trickling ... Dripping, dripping ... Doctor!'

'Well?'

'Doctor!'

'Past hearing,' muttered the surgeon.

'Doctor!'

'And blind.'

Response was made by a firm grasp of the hand.

'Doctor!'

'And numb.'

'Doctor!'

The old man watched and waited.

'Dripping, ... dripping.'

The last drop had run. There was a sigh, and nothing more.

The surgeon laid down the hand.

'The first step,' he groaned, rising to his feet; then his whole frame dilated. 'The first step – the most difficult, yet the simplest. A providential delivery into my hands of that for which I have hungered for forty years. No withdrawal now! It is possible, because scientific; rational, but perilous. If I succeed – *if*? I *shall* succeed. I *will* succeed ... And after success – what? ... Yes; what? Publish the plan and the result? The gallows ... So long as *it* shall exist, ... and *I* exist, the gallows. That much ... But how account for its presence? Ah, that pinches hard! I must trust to the future.'

He tore himself from the reverie and started.

'I wonder if *she* heard or saw anything.'

With that reflection he cast a glance upon the form on the lounge, and then left the room, locked the door, locked also the door of the outer room, walked down two or three corridors, penetrated to a remote part of the house, and rapped at a door. It was opened by his wife. He, by this time, had regained complete mastery over himself.

'I thought I heard someone in the house just now,' he said, 'but I can find no one.'

'I heard nothing.'

He was greatly relieved.

'I did hear someone knock at the door less than an hour ago,' she resumed, 'and heard you speak, I think. Did he come in?'

'No.'

The woman glanced at his feet and seemed perplexed.

'I am almost certain,' she said, 'that I heard foot-falls in the house, and yet I see that you are wearing slippers.'

'Oh, I had on my shoes then!'

'That explains it,' said the woman, satisfied; 'I think the sound you heard must have been caused by rats.'

'Ah, that was it!' exclaimed the surgeon. Leaving, he closed the door, reopened it, and said, 'I do not wish to be disturbed today.' He said to himself, as he went down the hall, 'All is clear there.'

He returned to the room in which his visitor lay, and made a careful examination.

'Splendid specimen!' he softly exclaimed; 'every organ sound, every function perfect; fine, large frame; well-shaped muscles, strong and sinewy; capable of wonderful development – if given opportunity ... I have no doubt it can be done. Already I have succeeded with a dog, – a task less difficult than this, for in a man the cerebrum overlaps the cerebellum, which is not the case with a dog. This gives a wide range for accident, with but one opportunity in a lifetime! In the cerebrum, the intellect and the affections; in the cerebellum, the senses and the motor forces; in the medulla oblongata, control of the diaphragm. In these two latter lie all the essentials of simple existence. The cerebrum is merely an adornment; that is to say, reason and the affections are almost purely ornamental. I have already proved it. My dog, with its cerebrum removed, was idiotic, but it retained its physical senses to a certain degree.'

While thus ruminating he made careful preparations. He moved the couch, replaced the operating-table under the sky-light, selected a number of surgical instruments, prepared certain drug-mixtures, and arranged water, towels, and all the accessories of a tedious surgical operation. Suddenly he burst into laughter.

'Poor fool!' he exclaimed. 'Paid me five thousand dollars to kill him! Didn't have the courage to snuff his own candle! Singular, singular, the queer freaks these madmen have! You thought you were dying, poor idiot! Allow me to inform you, sir, that you are as much alive at this moment as ever you were in your life. But it will be all the same to you. You shall never be more conscious than you are now; and for all practical purposes, so far as they concern you, you are dead henceforth, though you shall live. By the way, how should you feel *without a head*? Ha, ha, ha! ... But that's a sorry joke.'

He lifted the unconscious form from the lounge and laid it upon the operating-table.

About three years afterwards the following conversation was held between a captain of police and a detective:

'She may be insane,' suggested the captain.

'I think she is.'

'And yet you credit her story!'

'I do.'

'Singular!'

'Not at all. I myself have learned something.'

'What!'

'Much, in one sense; little, in another. You have heard those queer stories of her husband. Well, they are all nonsensical – probably with one exception. He is generally a harmless old fellow, but peculiar. He has performed some wonderful surgical operations. The people in his neighbourhood are ignorant, and they fear him and wish to be rid of him; hence they tell a great many lies about him, and they come to believe their own stories. The one important thing that I have learned is that he is almost insanely enthusiastic on the subject of surgery – especially experimental surgery; and with an enthusiast there is hardly such a thing as a scruple. It is this that gives me confidence in the woman's story.'

'You say she appeared to be frightened?'

'Doubly so – first, she feared that her husband would learn of her betrayal of him; second, the discovery itself had terrified her.'

'But her report of this discovery is very vague,' argued the captain. 'He conceals everything from her. She is merely guessing.'

'In part – yes; in other part – no. She heard the sounds distinctly, though she did not see clearly. Horror closed her eyes. What she thinks she saw is, I admit, preposterous; but she undoubtedly saw something extremely frightful. There are many peculiar little circumstances. He has eaten with her but few times during the last three years, and nearly always carries his food to his private rooms. She says that he either consumes an enormous quantity, throws much away, or is feeding something that eats prodigiously. He explains this to her by saying that he has animals with which he experiments. This is not true. Again, he always keeps the door to these rooms carefully locked; and not only that, but he has had the doors doubled and otherwise strengthened, and has heavily barred a window that looks from one of the rooms upon a dead wall a few feet distant.'

'What does it mean?' asked the captain.

'A prison.'

'For animals, perhaps.'

'Certainly not.'

'Why?'

'Because, in the first place, cages would have been better; in the second place, the security that he has provided is infinitely greater than that required for the confinement of ordinary animals.'

'All this is easily explained: he has a violent lunatic under treatment.'

'I had thought of that, but such is not the fact.'

'How do you know?'

'By reasoning thus: He has always refused to treat cases of

lunacy; he confines himself to surgery; the walls are not padded, for the woman has heard sharp blows upon them; no human strength, however morbid, could possibly require such resisting strength as has been provided; he would not be likely to conceal a lunatic's confinement from the woman; no lunatic could consume all the food that he provides; so extremely violent mania as these precautions indicate could not continue three years; if there is a lunatic in the case it is very probable that there should have been communication with someone outside concerning the patient, and there has been none; the woman has listened at the keyhole and has heard no human voice within; and last, we have heard the woman's vague description of what she saw.'

'You have destroyed every possible theory,' said the captain, deeply interested, 'and have suggested nothing new.'

'Unfortunately, I cannot; but the truth may be very simple, after all. The old surgeon is so peculiar that I am prepared to discover something remarkable.'

'Have you suspicions?'

'I have.'

'Of what?'

'A crime. The woman suspects it.'

'And betrays it?'

'Certainly, because it is so horrible that her humanity revolts; so terrible that her whole nature demands of her that she hand over the criminal to the law; so frightful that she is in mortal terror; so awful that it has shaken her mind.'

'What do you propose to do?' asked the captain.

'Secure evidence. I may need help.'

'You shall have all the men you require. Go ahead, but be careful. You are on dangerous ground. You would be a mere plaything in the hands of that man.'

Two days afterwards the detective again sought the captain.

'I have a queer document,' he said, exhibiting torn fragments of paper, on which there was writing. 'The woman stole it and brought it to me. She snatched a handful out of a book, getting only a part of each of a few leaves.'

These fragments, which the men arranged as best they could, were (the detective explained) torn by the surgeon's wife from the first volume of a number of manuscript books which her husband had written on one subject – the very one that was the cause of her excitement. 'About the time that he began a certain experiment three years ago,' continued the detective, 'he removed everything from the suite of two rooms containing his study and his operating-room. In one of the bookcases that he removed to a room across the passage was a drawer, which he kept locked, but which he opened from time to time. As is quite common with such pieces of furniture, the lock of the drawer is a very poor one; and so the woman, while making a thorough search yesterday, found a key on her bunch that fitted this lock. She opened the drawer, drew out the bottom book of a pile (so that its mutilation would more likely escape discovery), saw that it might contain a clue, and tore out a handful of the leaves. She had barely replaced the book, locked the drawer, and made her escape when her husband appeared. He hardly ever allows her to be out of his sight when she is in that part of the house.'

The fragments read as follows: '... the motory nerves. I had hardly dared to hope for such a result, although inductive reasoning had convinced me of its possibility, my only doubt having been on the score of my lack of skill. Their operation has been only slightly impaired, and even this would not have been the case had the operation been performed in infancy, before the intellect had sought and obtained recognition as an essential part of the whole. Therefore I state, as a proved fact, that the cells of the motory nerves have inherent forces sufficient to the purposes of those nerves. But hardly so with the sensory nerves. These latter are, in fact, an offshoot of the former, evolved from them by natural (though not essential) heterogeneity, and to a certain extent are dependent on the evolution and expansion of a contemporaneous tendency, that developed into mentality, or mental function. Both of these latter tendencies, these evolvements, are merely refinements of the motory system, and not independent entities; that is to say, they are the blossoms of a plant that propagates from its roots. The motory system is the first ... nor am I surprised that such prodigious muscular energy is developing. It promises yet to surpass the wildest dreams of human strength. I account for it thus: The powers of assimilation had reached their full development. They had formed the habit of doing a certain amount of work. They sent their products to all parts of the system. As a result of my operation the consumption of these products was reduced fully one-half; that is to say, about one-half of the demand for them was withdrawn. But force of habit required the production to proceed. This production was strength, vitality, energy. Thus double the usual quantity of this strength, this energy, was stored in the remaining ... developed a tendency that did surprise me. Nature, no longer suffering the distraction of extraneous interferences, and at the same time being cut in two (as it were), with reference to this case, did not fully adjust herself to the new situation, as does a magnet, which, when divided at the point of equilibrium, renews itself in its two fragments by investing each with opposite poles; but, on the contrary, being severed from laws that theretofore had controlled her, and possessing still that mysterious tendency to develop into something more potential and complex, she blindly (having lost her lantern) pushed her demands for material that would secure this development, and as blindly used it when it was given her. Hence this marvellous voracity, this insatiable hunger, this wonderful ravenousness; and hence also (there being nothing but the physical part to receive this vast storing of energy) this strength that is becoming almost hourly herculean, almost daily appalling. It is becoming a serious ... narrow escape today. By some means, while I was absent, it unscrewed the stopper of the silver feeding-pipe (which I have already herein termed "the artificial mouth"), and, in one of its curious antics, allowed all the chyle to escape from its stomach through the tube. Its hunger then became intense – I may say furious. I placed my hands upon it to push it into a chair, when, feeling my touch, it caught me, clasped me around the neck, and would have crushed me to death instantly had I not slipped from its powerful grasp. Thus I always had to be on my guard. I have provided the screw stopper with a spring catch, and ... usually docile when not hungry; slow and heavy in its movements, which are, of course, purely unconscious; any apparent excitement in movement being due to local irregularities in the blood-supply of the cerebellum, which, if I did not have it enclosed in a silver case that is immovable, I should expose and ...'

The captain looked at the detective with a puzzled air.

'I don't understand it at all,' said he.

'Nor I,' agreed the detective.

'What do you propose to do?'

'Make a raid.'

'Do you want a man?'

'Three. The strongest men in your district.'

'Why, the surgeon is old and weak!'

'Nevertheless, I want three strong men; and for that matter, prudence really advises me to take twenty.'

At one o'clock the next morning a cautious, scratching sound might have been heard in the ceiling of the surgeon's operating-room. Shortly afterwards the skylight sash was carefully raised and laid aside. A man peered into the opening. Nothing could be heard.

'That is singular,' thought the detective.

He cautiously lowered himself to the floor by a rope, and then stood for some moments listening intently. There was a dead silence. He shot the slide of a dark-lantern, and rapidly swept the room with the light. It was bare, with the exception of a strong iron staple and ring, screwed to the floor in the centre of the room, with a heavy chain attached. The detective then turned his attention to the outer room; it was perfectly bare. He was deeply perplexed. Returning to the inner room, he called softly to the men to descend. While they were thus occupied he re-entered the outer room and examined the door. A glance sufficed. It was kept closed by a spring attachment, and was locked with a strong spring-lock that could be drawn from the inside.

'The bird has just flown,' mused the detective. 'A singular accident! The discovery and proper use of this thumb-bolt might not have happened once in fifty years, if my theory is correct.'

By this time the men were behind him. He noiselessly drew the spring-bolt, opened the door, and looked out into the hall. He heard a peculiar sound. It was as though a gigantic lobster was floundering and scrambling in some distant part of the old house. Accompanying this sound was a loud, whistling breathing, and frequent rasping gasps.

These sounds were heard by still another person – the surgeon's wife; for they originated very near her rooms, which were a considerable distance from her husband's. She had been sleeping lightly, tortured by fear and harassed by frightful dreams. The conspiracy into which she had recently entered, for the destruction of her husband, was a source of great anxiety. She constantly suffered from the most gloomy forebodings, and lived in an atmosphere of terror. Added to the natural horror of her situation were those countless sources of fear which a fright-shaken mind creates and then magnifies. She was, indeed, in a pitiable state, having been driven first by terror to desperation, and then to madness.

Startled thus out of fitful slumber by the noise at her door, she sprang from her bed to the floor, every terror that lurked in her acutely tense mind and diseased imagination starting up and almost overwhelming her. The idea of flight – one of the strongest of all instincts – seized upon her, and she ran to the door, beyond all control of reason. She drew the bolt and flung the door wide open, and then fled wildly down the passage, the appalling hissing and rasping gurgle ringing in her ears apparently with a thousandfold intensity. But the passage was in absolute darkness, and she had not taken a half-dozen steps when she tripped upon an unseen object on the floor. She fell headlong upon it, encountering in it a large, soft, warm substance that writhed and squirmed, and from which came the sounds that had awakened her. Instantly realising her situation, she uttered a shriek such as only an unnameable terror can inspire. But hardly had her cry started the echoes in the empty corridor when it was suddenly stifled. Two prodigious arms had closed upon her and crushed the life out of her.

The cry performed the office of directing the detective and his assistants, and it also aroused the old surgeon, who occupied rooms between the officers and the object of their search. The cry of agony pierced him to the marrow, and a realisation of the cause of it burst upon him with frightful force.

'It has come at last!' he gasped, springing from his bed.

Snatching from a table a dimly-burning lamp and a long knife which he had kept at hand for three years, he dashed into the corridor. The four officers had already started forward, but when they saw him emerge they halted in silence. In that moment of stillness the surgeon paused to listen. He heard the hissing sound and the clumsy floundering of a bulky, living object in the direction of his wife's apartments. It evidently was advancing towards him. A turn in the corridor shut out the view. He turned up the light, which revealed a ghastly pallor in his face.

'Wife!' he called.

There was no response. He hurriedly advanced, the four men following quietly. He turned the angle of the corridor, and ran so rapidly that by the time the officers had come in sight of him again he was twenty steps away. He ran past a huge, shapeless object, sprawling, crawling, and floundering along, and arrived at the body of his wife.

He gave one horrified glance at her face, and staggered away. Then a fury seized him. Clutching the knife firmly, and holding the lamp aloft, he sprang towards the ungainly object in the corridor. It was then that the officers, still advancing cautiously, saw a little more clearly, though still indistinctly, the object of the surgeon's fury, and the cause of the look of unutterable anguish in his face. The hideous sight caused them to pause. They saw what appeared to be a man, yet evidently was not a man; huge, awkward, shapeless; a squirming, lurching, stumbling mass, completely naked. It raised its broad shoulders. *It had no head*, but instead of it a small metallic ball surmounting its massive neck.

'Devil!' exclaimed the surgeon, raising the knife.

'Hold, there!' commanded a stern voice.

The surgeon quickly raised his eyes and saw the four officers, and for a moment fear paralysed his arm.

'The police!' he gasped.

Then, with a look of redoubled fury, he sent the knife to the hilt into the squirming mass before him. The wounded monster sprang to its feet and wildly threw its arms about, meanwhile emitting fearful sounds from a silver tube through which it breathed. The surgeon aimed another blow, but never gave it. In his blind fury he lost his caution, and was caught in an iron grasp. The struggle threw the lamp some feet towards the officers, and it fell to the floor, shattered to pieces. Simultaneously with the crash the oil took fire, and the corridor was filled with flame. The officers could not approach. Before them was the spreading blaze, and secure behind it were two forms struggling in a fearful embrace. They heard cries and gasps, and saw the gleaming of a knife.

The wood in the house was old and dry. It took fire at once, and the flames spread with great rapidity. The four officers turned and fled, barely escaping with their lives. In an hour nothing remained of the mysterious old house and its inmates but a blackened ruin.

# Some Experiments
# With A Head

## By DICK DONOVAN

*Two years after the publication of* The Surgeon's Experiment, *an English writer effectively reversed the theme by concentrating on the idea of keeping a disembodied head alive with the aid of electricity. The author, Dick Donovan, a prolific contributor to Victorian magazines and newspapers, distilled a lifetime of travel in India, Asia, America, Canada, Russia and Europe into over 150 books ranging from travel guides and historical romances to spy stories and detective thrillers. He was also a very proficient writer of supernatural and horror tales, the best of which were collected in volumes such as* Stories Weird and Wonderful (1889) *and* Tales of Terror (1899).

*Donovan, whose real name was Joyce E. Preston-Muddock (1842–1934), actually lived for five years in Switzerland as correspondent to the* Daily News *in London. Apart from editing and publishing* Muddock's Guide to Switzerland *during his residency, he also wrote at least two articles about the lives of Byron and the Shelleys while they were living on Lake Geneva – collecting personal recollections from a number of the oldest inhabitants. It is hardly surprising, therefore, that he should have been drawn to the* Frankenstein *theme and written his own variation,* Some Experiments With A Head *– subtitled, 'Being a Record from the Papers of a Late Physician' – published in the* Cornhill Magazine *in 1889. Interestingly, the theme was to be taken a step further by one of the leading American twentieth century writers, Kurt Vonnegut, Jr. – as the reader will discover in Section III . . .*

The following notes have reference to a time, now far off, alas! when I was a very young man, and imbued with an unquenchable desire for knowledge. I was an enthusiast, I freely admit; and there were some who called me a dreamer; but, if that is to be interpreted as meaning a visionary, I decline to admit that the term was applicable. I had a profound love of science in all its branches, and in those fields of research which the scientist must conscientiously explore if he wishes to be accepted as a trustworthy guide, I diligently sought for demonstrable facts. Scientists may be divided into two very distinct classes, your men of theory and your men of practice. I preferred to fall into the latter category, and asked for proof of all that was advanced. It was this very trait in my character which led to the extraordinary incidents related in this paper.

Let me at once state that at the time to which I refer I was a medical student, studying at the College de France in Paris. My father before me had been an eminent member of the medical profession, and from the very earliest period of my existence I evinced a strong desire to follow in his footsteps. The consequence was that, by the time I was twenty, I was studying hard in the French capital. I had already passed several examinations with flying colours, and was looking forward to obtaining my diploma within the next two years.

Now, there was one subject that had always possessed for me almost fascinating interest, and I am free to confess that it absorbed a very great deal of my attention. It was whether in cases of decapitation death was instantaneous. My professional brethren will know that opinions on the subject have been much divided, but 'instantaneous' is an elastic term. The coming and going of a flash of lightning is said to be instantaneous, and yet it occupies an appreciable space of time that is capable of being accurately measured. Now, the question that suggested itself to my mind was whether though life was extinguished in a space of time no longer than a flash of lightning takes to manifest itself, that is, in the blinking of an eye, there was still time for introspection, retrospection, and speculation? I was fully aware that the point involved was a peculiarly delicate one, and might be said to belong more to the domain of psychology rather than physiology. But in considering the subject one could not ignore the experiences of those who had come within an ace of losing their lives by drowning. In well-authenticated instances the drowning person had in an incredibly brief space of time traversed the whole record of his life; had recalled incidents of childhood long ago forgotten, and had even worked out speculatively what his friends would think of his death, how his affairs would be settled, and what would be the careers of his children – if he had any – in the far-off future. In such brief moments the mind is capable of grasping an extraordinary range of subjects, past, present, and to come; and yet the duration of consciousness in such cases can hardly exceed, in the extremest limit, five minutes.

In dwelling upon these facts I asked myself whether the brain of a decapitated person was not capable of thought for a period as correspondingly long as that experienced by a drowning man. I was, of course, aware that some of the most eminent anatomists affirmed that the entire severance of the jugular vein, the carotid arteries, especially the internal carotid supplying the brain with blood, and the spinal cord (or main nerve track of the body), must produce absolutely instantaneous death. But I had the boldness to answer to this that 'instantaneousness' was capable of being measured as a space of time, and such a space of time, to a dying man, was filled with potentialities that could not be ignored by the inquirer who had a due regard for minutiæ. Nor could I forget the well-authenticated case of an unfortunate victim of the Reign of Terror, whose head was seized by the executioner as soon as the guillotine had severed it, and as the man was in the act of holding it up by the hair to the view of the crowd he saw the eyes turn upon him with such a look of anguish and unspeakable reproach that, with a cry of horror, he let the head fall and fled.

The professorial chair of anatomy in the College was filled by the celebrated Doctor François Grassard, who had been a friend of my father, and took a great interest in me. He was pleased at times to discuss my favourite subject with me, but his opinion was that cessation of thought and power of reflection was absolutely coincident with the severance of the neck, which, as every one knows, in the case of the guillotine is as quick as the blinking of the eye. But then I took my stand upon that elasticity of the term instantaneous, and which, as I have already urged, while counting for nothing in an ordinary way, might be much to a dying person, that is, a person dying by sudden and violent means.

On one occasion, after an argument with Doctor Grassard, I ventured to suggest that it might be possible to make some practical experiments with a view to substantiating or disproving my argument. The doctor reflected for a little time, and then said:

'Yes, I think it is possible, and such experiments can hardly fail to be deeply interesting, and even scientifically valuable.'

It was not until nearly a year after this that the opportunity for the suggested experiments occurred. It happened that about this time Paris was startled by a wholesale butchery of a peculiarly atrocious character. In one of the wretched dens of the Rue des Cascades a man named Gaspard Thurreau hacked his wife, his mistress, and four children to pieces. The Rue des Cascades is situated in the neighbourhood of St Denis, which is perhaps one of the foulest spots to be found in any city in the world.

It is not necessary to dwell upon the details of the crime, which, however, were peculiarly horrible even for Paris; but the criminal himself was altogether a most remarkable man. He had formerly been an analytical chemist, and was a man of high intellectual attainments. In direct opposition, however, to the wishes of his friends and relations, he married a woman much below him in social rank and one of very indifferent character. Such a mésalliance was, of course, bound to bring misery and unhappiness. Madame Thurreau had a violent temper and a most jealous disposition. The result was, the ill-matched couple led a cat and dog life for years. At first the man struggled against his misfortunes; then he gave way to drink, and that brought the inevitable concomitant train of evils. He lost his position, his business, his honour; went from bad to worse; was deserted by all his relations; committed forgery, and served a long term of imprisonment. On his release, he sank down to the lowest stratum of society, and, together with his wife and four children, found shelter in the dreadful Alsatia of St Denis. Here he formed a *liaison* with a woman who lived under the same roof. For a time the wife tolerated her rival, then the two women began to fight like wild cats until the feud ended in the awful tragedy. Thurreau, inflamed with wine, went to his den one night, when both the women reviled and reproached him until, excited into a fit of frenzy, he slew them and his children.

His history, such as I have sketched it in outline, was gradually unfolded at the trial, and, although he found some sympathisers, the weight of public opinion was decidedly against him. There never was from the first a shadow of a doubt about his being the culprit. The only question was whether, to their verdict, the jury could not append the 'extenuating circumstances' of which French juries are so fond, and which invariably saves the murderer's head. But Thurreau's crime was so revolting and barbarous that the 'extenuating circumstances' were left out, and the criminal was condemned to death without hope of reprieve. As soon as Doctor Grassard heard of the sentence, he said to me:

'Well, young gentleman, I think we shall at last be able to try our experiments, and, what is more, we shall have an unusually good subject.'

I knew what he meant by 'an unusually good subject.' Thurreau was a man of striking physical mould. From an anatomical point of view he was perfect, with a well-shaped head, firmly set on massive shoulders. He was under forty, and had never had any disease, so that in such a man vitality would be very strong, and there would be a corresponding tenacity of life. Apart from sheer physical attributes he was endowed with a keen intelligence and mental powers of a high order, though he had shown himself weak in one respect – that was in his inability to rise superior to his misfortunes.

Doctor Grassard's position as one of the first anatomists in France gave him great influence, so that he had no difficulty in obtaining permission from the authorities to visit the condemned man. He found Thurreau callous as to his fate, and holding views with regard to a future state which rendered him deaf to the voice of spiritual consolation. As a matter of fact, he absolutely and determinedly refused to receive the prison or any other chaplain, though a day or two before his execution he so far relented as to consent to see a priest, to whom he made confession.

It will be readily comprehended in what respects such a man was about as good a subject as could have been selected for our purpose. With tact and delicacy, Doctor Grassard led

up to the purpose that had induced him to visit him; telling
him that in the interest of science it was desired to make
certain tests, with a view to endeavour to establish the precise
moment when the death of the brain ensued after decapitation.
With a grim smile Thurreau said that as a chief actor in the
experiments, he was perfectly willing to do all that he possibly
could to further the ends of science. But he wanted to know
what part he was to play after he was beheaded. He was told
that what was desired of him was that at the moment when
he was laid upon the plank with his neck under the knife, he
should concentrate all his thoughts upon four questions that
would be spoken into his ear. These questions were:

1. Are you in pain?
2. Do you recognise those about you?
3. Do you remember what you have been guillotined for?
4. Are you happy?

The affirmative answer to these questions was to be a single
blink of the eyelids, the negative two. Now, if consciousness
remained for any appreciable space of time, there was no
reason why this motion of the eyelids should not be made,
because the *palpebræ* or eyelids are dependent for their action
on certain muscles known as the *orbicular* or circular muscles
and the *levators, palpebræ superiores*, the muscles used to
raise the upper eyelids, which would be quite uninjured struc-
turally. The same remark applies to the muscles of the eye
known as the *recti*, which are six in number, so that the eye
might also be moved if the will was there. On that the whole
question turned. *Would* the will be there? By will I mean
consciousness. These preliminaries having been settled, it now
remained to make arrangements for carrying the experiments
out, and in this we were aided in every possible way by the
authorities, the matter, of course, being kept strictly secret. In
discussing these arrangements with Professor Grassard I took
the liberty to express myself to the effect that if the brain
could be kept at its normal temperature by the blood, consciousness might be retained for many seconds if not minutes,
and what we had to consider was how to prevent the tremendous drain of the vital fluid as soon as the severance was
accomplished. Naturally, with the cutting through of the great

veins and arteries the blood flowed away as water would flow from a reservoir if the banks were to burst, and what we had to do was to dam this flow. After some consideration Professor Grassard suggested that by plunging the bleeding surface into a basin of softened wax the end aimed at would be attained.

The month was November, and the morning of the execution was as dismal as could be imagined. All night long a drizzling rain had been falling, and a searching, biting wind made the streets unbearable. To this fact, no doubt, was due the comparatively small crowd that had assembled in the Place de la Roquette, where the guillotine was erected. The hideous machine of death had been placed within three yards of the door of the prison through which its victim would have to pass on this his last journey. A corridor had been formed from the door to the steps of the guillotine by putting up a canvas screen on each side. This had been done for our special convenience. It had also been arranged that, instead of the basket which was to receive the head being placed on the scaffold in the usual way, some of the planks were cut, forming, as it were, a trap door, the basket being on the ground under the trap. Consequently, after the execution the head could be taken out without the spectators having any knowledge of what was being done. The authorities were also good enough to place at our disposal an ante-room just inside of the corridor of the prison, so that we had no difficulty whatever in completing our preparations, and being quite ready for the exciting moment.

As is well known, culprits condemned to death in France are never informed of the day of their execution until the very morning, and only then about an hour before the time. It was six o'clock when the prefect, the governor of the prison, various officials, and a priest entered Thurreau's cell, and, arousing him from a sound sleep, informed him that he had but an hour to live. The wretched man received the announcement with the most perfect *sang froid*. Then turning to the priest, who had approached him with a crucifix, he bowed, and said, politely but firmly:

'Monsieur, pardon me if I say I can dispense with your services. I have never attempted to deny that I committed the crime, and now in this supreme hour, in your presence and the presence of these gentlemen, I confess that my hand, and my hand alone, killed the women and the children. I am perfectly aware that by the laws of my country my life is forfeited, and the perfect justness of my sentence I freely admit. But if such crimes as mine are to be visited with the wrath of heaven, I cannot hope to turn aside that wrath by a hurried prayer now that I am all but dead. Therefore, monsieur, I pray that you will leave me to my own reflections during the brief time left to me, for, as a matter of fact, I have pledged myself, so far as I can, to aid certain experiments that Professor Grassard is desirous of carrying out.'

This speech at such a time will show that the culprit was no ordinary man. The priest, however, did not retire, but remained with the prisoner and accompanied him to the scaffold, and there Thurreau consented to press his lips to the crucifix that the good priest extended to him.

As soon as ever the mournful procession had passed through the doorway, one of our hospital assistants followed with a tin bowl half full of heated wax. A cordon of gendarmes was drawn round the guillotine, and beyond them, again, was a double line of mounted soldiers, so that the crowds of people were kept a long way off.

Exactly three minutes after Thurreau had crossed the threshold of the door he was lying on the plank. Daylight had scarcely yet begun to assert itself. From the murky sky the drizzling rain still descended, and away to the east there was an angry flush of red. The boom of the bell of Notre Dame, as it slowly tolled the hour of seven, fell on our ears as the gleaming and fatal knife flashed down the wooden uprights in which it worked, and Thurreau's head fell into the basket on the pavement. With extraordinary dexterity and coolness the assistant caught it up, and set it with the neck downwards in the basin of wax, and then with agile movement he rushed into the room where we waited for him. The face of the culprit was then perfectly natural in its colour and expression, but we noted that there was a slight twitching of the muscles of the mouth.

The basin was set on a table all ready prepared, and in the full rays of a strong light. Then the Professor placed his lips close to the right ear, and in a clear, deliberate, resonant voice asked:

'Are you in pain?'

Instantly there were two distinct blinks of the eyelids.

'Do you recognize those about you?' was next asked.

This time there was one blink.

'Do you remember what you have been guillotined for?'

One blink again, but now the muscular motion of the eyelid was perceptibly slower.

The last question was then put:

'Are you happy?'

With the utterance of the word 'happy,' Professor Grassard straightened himself up, and instantly the eyes, which were full open, and also quite natural in colour and expression, turned upon him. The effect of this was thrilling, and certainly would have unnerved men who had not been braced up by an enthusiastic love for science. The Professor moved round the table slowly, describing the segment of a circle in his movement, and as he did so the eyes followed him. Then suddenly we saw a film come over them, and the lids drooped, while the face assumed a bluish white tint, and there was a dropping of the lower jaw.

From the time that the head was taken out of the basket to this change setting in, exactly three minutes eight seconds had elapsed, as measured by a chronometer watch, so that there was consciousness of the brain for that period after the head was severed from the body. The proofs of this were beyond all question of possible doubt. It may of course be stated with positiveness that this in a great measure, if not entirely so, was due to the hermetically sealing of the ends of the cut vessels by means of the wax. We regretted exceedingly that an answer by the sign of negation or affirmation, which had been agreed upon, had not been given to question number four. It seemed probable that the question was understood, but instead of the motion of the eyelid, the eyes themselves turned, following the movements of the Professor, and on discussing this subsequently we came to the conclusion that it was due to Doctor Grassard rising from the bent position he had assumed while speaking into the ear, and naturally he regretted that he had altered his position so quickly. The change in the face that then set in was probably due to the congesting of the sinuses, which would at once deprive the brain of all sensibility. In other words, the brain there and then died. This was the conclusion we arrived at, but nevertheless we resolved to try what effect an electric current might have, though we were actuated more by curiosity than any absolute idea of results.

We had provided ourselves with a small battery, and, laying bare the *ganglion cervicale superius*, a nerve centre in the neck, we sent a current through it, but the only effect produced was some twitching of the nerves of the face. We therefore made a deep incision down on to the optic nerve behind the eye, and connecting the nerve with the positive pole of the battery, while the negative pole was applied to the base of the anterior lobe of the brain, we turned on the current. In a few seconds the face seemed to lose its bluish, waxen appearance, and become suffused with a warm flush as in life; the eyes lost their glassiness, and the eyelids their droop.

As we watched these phenomena with breathless interest we saw with amazement the eyes move in a perfectly natural way from right to left and left to right. Then Professor Grassard drew with his finger an imaginary line on a parallel axis to the eyes of the head, and the eyes slowly followed the motion of the finger.

Speaking for myself, I confess to being positively startled by this unlooked-for result; for anything more weird or awful than the bodiless head rolling its eyes in counterfeit presentment of actual life could hardly be imagined by brain of man. But the climax had not yet been reached; for the next moment the Professor brought his lips on a line with the right ear of the head, and in a clear, distinct voice said:

'If you are conscious of what is being done, make that known to us by blinking your eyelids.'

I had been looking at the face intently as this was said, and I was now absolutely horrified to observe that the eyelids actually did blink. I could endure no more. I seemed to be suffocating. I staggered to the door, flung it open, and, reaching the passage, fell down in a swoon.

When I recovered consciousness, Professor Grassard conveyed me to my residence in his carriage. I saw that he was very grave and thoughtful.

'I think,' he said quietly, as we neared our destination – 'I think our experiments went a little beyond what we intended, for we seem to have brought the dead to life again.'

'Yes,' I answered with a shudder, 'and we have substantiated my theory, that the head of a human being may live for some minutes after its severance from the body; but nothing would ever induce me to undertake such experiments again.'

# The New Frankenstein

## By E. E. KELLETT

The Victorian era saw the rise of a number of popular monthly magazines that printed an ever-increasing amount of well-illustrated weird and horror stories, including The Strand (which, of course, first introduced Sherlock Holmes to the public), Windsor, Pall Mall and Pearson's – the latter playing a major role in promoting the embryo genre of Science Fiction by serialising H.G. Wells' most famous novels. Pearson's, in fact, developed a policy of running fantasy fiction and published a variety of stories of this kind, all superbly illustrated by artists like Dudley Tennant, Murray Smith, Stanley L. Wood, Cyrus Cuneo and Sidney Paget – who earned even greater fame as the first illustrator of Sherlock Holmes' cases.

Among the regular contributors to Pearson's was Ernest Edward Kellett (1860–1933), another prolific journalist and fiction writer, who could turn his hand to any current public interest. Among his tales of fantasy were Self Haunted, Intimations of Immortality and A Corner in Sleep which provided the title for a collection of the best of his stories published in 1900. The New Frankenstein (not to be confused with the earlier parody by William Maginn) in which an eccentric man of science creates a perfect woman who then becomes the object of desire of two implacable rivals, appeared in Pearson's in May 1899. Its enthusiastic reception made it very clear that the appeal of the Frankenstein theme to both writers and readers was all set to continue flourishing into the twentieth century.

'Yes,' said Arthur, 'I feel very much inclined to try it.'

The speaker, Arthur Moore, was a man whom I was proud to call my friend. Early in life he had distinguished himself by many wonderful inventions. When a boy he had adorned his bedroom with all sorts of curious mechanical contrivances: pulleys for lifting unheard-of weights, rat-traps which, by cunning devices, provided the captured animal with a silent and painless euthanasia; locomotives, which when once wound up, would run for a day, and numberless other treasures, which, if hardly useful or even ornamental, had yet the effect of inspiring the housemaid who made the bed, with a mortal terror of everything in the room. As he grew older he lost none of his skill. At the age of fifteen he had successfully emulated most of the feats of Vaucanson; his mechanical ducks gobbled and digested their food so naturally that even the famous scientist, the Rev. Henry Forest, was for a moment taken in. He had been to Oxford, but after a year of University life, he had wearied of the dull routine, and had begged his father to let him start life on his own account. His father need have had no fear for the result. Within a year the young Moore's automatic chess-player, that had played a draw with Morphy himself, had attracted the awe-struck attention of the civilised world by the simplicity and daring of its mechanism. The chess-player was followed in two years by a whist-player, still more simply and boldly conceived; and after that time scarcely a year had passed without being signalised by the appearance of new wonders from Moore's fertile brain and dextrous hand. His last achievement had been a phonograph so perfectly constructed that people began to think that even Edison must soon begin to look to his laurels, or he would be eclipsed by the rising fame of this young man of thirty.

I had known him since he was a boy; and had kept my acquaintance with him in spite of the ever-widening difference between our paths and our beliefs. I had chosen the medical profession, and after a year or two of early struggles, was at last beginning to see my way to an assured reputation, and a fair competency. In fact, I was already a fashionable doctor, pretty well known by the public, and I hope pretty well esteemed by the profession.

It was just after the new phonograph had appeared that I

had with Arthur the memorable and unfortunate conversation which I shall regret to the very end of my life.

'Well,' I said, 'a new and great success again. You will be one of the greatest benefactors of the century in a few years.'

'Yes,' he answered, for he had no false modesty. 'I believe the phonograph is about as perfect as I can make it. Suppose we listen to it now.'

He produced the instrument, and I had the pleasure of listening to a speech of Mr Gladstone's, with the familiar tones and inflections of the great orator reproduced to the life. I could have believed I saw the Grand Old Man before me, as I had seen him so often.

'Wonderful,' said. 'It is indeed perfect. What a strange, almost uncanny thing it is! We shall soon have to be very careful what we say; for a bird of the air shall carry the voice, and that which hath wings shall tell the matter. Fancy what a preventive of crime a phonograph fastened on every lamp-post would be! It would be a kind of Magic Flute, forcing people to tell the truth whether they would or no. Jones might say, "I said this," but the phonograph would say, "You said that." Mere human fallible creatures will soon be banished from the witness-box; judges and juries will content themselves with taking the evidence of unerring, unlying phonographs!'

'Heaven save us!' Moore replied; 'all of us say many things that will hardly bear repeating; and if they are all to be recorded, how dreadful it would be.'

'Yes; you see you are after all but a doubtful benefactor of the human race; it is not everybody who, like Job, can wish that his words were now written.'

'Nor Job himself at all times,' he answered: 'perhaps he would hardly have wished to have recorded the words he used when he cursed his day.'

'In fact,' I said, 'what is a phonograph after all but a tattling old woman, repeating whatever it hears without discrimination or tact?'

'Exactly,' he said; 'but with this difference, that the phonograph repeats what it hears without alteration or addition, whereas the old woman repeats it just as it suits her.'

At this moment the fatal idea struck me, which now I would give worlds to have forgotten or suppressed before it came to the birth. Alas, we know not the results of our least words.

'Why,' I said, 'don't you try to make a kind of complement of a phonograph?'

'What do you mean?'

'Why, this. Your phonograph only repeats what it hears. Why not make an instrument which should, not *repeat* words, but speak out the suitable answer to them? If, for instance, I were to say to it "Good morning, have you used Pears' Soap?" then why should it not answer, "No, I use Cleaver's," instead of merely reiterating my words? At present, your machine is nothing but an echo; glorious, I grant; a triumph of civilisation; but what an achievement it would be to contrive a sort of anti-phonograph, that should give the appropriate *answer* to each question I like to put!'

'Why, a thing that could do that would be nothing less than man.'

'Well,' I said, 'what *is* man but a bundle of sensations – a machine that answers pretty accurately to the questions daily put to it?' For I was, or pretended to be, a full-blown materialist.

'It may be so,' he answered; 'yet it seems to me that he is a very complex machine for all that. He has taken thousands of years to evolve, if what Darwin says is true; you ask me to make him in at most a year or two.'

'Listen to me,' I said, half in irony, half in earnest. 'When you made your whist-player, what did you do but calculate on a certain number of actions, all theoretically possible, and arrange that the machine should give the proper answer to them?'

'True.'

'And with your chess-player, was it not the same?'

'Exactly.'

'Well, then, the principle is granted. Allow that a certain number of phrases may be used; let your machine give the proper answer to them. Don't you see the analogy? Had it been impossible for the machine to speak, I should have been satisfied with your disclaimers; but your phonograph has settled that.'

'The number of sentences is infinite.'

'A detail, my friend. Are there not, practically, infinite

varieties of hands at whist? Yet your automaton never made a mistake. Are there not infinite varieties of number? Yet did that puzzle Babbage's calculating machine?'

'You may be right, Phillips,' he said, smiling at my earnestness. 'I will think of it.'

I took my leave, little dreaming that I had set in motion a mighty force which would bring misery to more than a few. Indeed, I completely forgot the whole conversation. It was not till several months later that, happening to meet Moore in the street, I was suddenly startled by hearing the words I have already mentioned.

'Yes, I feel very much inclined to try it.'

'To try what?' I said, completely bewildered.

'Why, the thing we were talking of some months ago.'

'Do you mean to say you have been thinking of it?' I said. 'Why, I had utterly forgotten it.'

'Thought of it, yes; and worked at it, which is more. I see my way to something very like it, at any rate.'

'Go on,' I said, becoming interested. 'This is the most wonderful thing you have done yet, if –'

'Listen,' he interrupted. 'Words are nothing but air-vibrations, are they?'

'Nothing,' I answered.

'Well, then, it follows that words, if put in the proper positions, can generate motion.'

'I follow you; a molecular windmill.'

'Well,' he said, 'this is the idea of my machine. Words are spoken into the ear of my automaton. Passing through the ear they enter a machine you would call an anti-phonograph, and set in motion various processes which in a very short time produce the words constituting the proper answer.'

'Wonderful,' I said, 'if true.'

'Come and see then,' he rejoined, 'if you will be so sceptical.'

I followed him to his workshop, and saw a small instrument, in its main external details exactly like a phonograph.

'This,' said Moore, 'is the centre of my automaton. Try it yourself. Ask it a question – anything you like.'

Wondering, I did as he suggested. There was a tube on each side of the instrument, communicating with its centre, which I supposed would form the 'ear' of the automaton when finished. I was at a loss how to begin the conversation; but, being an Englishman, called the weather to my aid.

'A very cold day,' I remarked.

A sweet and beautifully modulated feminine voice answered:

'Yes; but hardly so cold as yesterday.'

I started, as though I had seen a ghost. Had I not been a doctor, old as I was, I should have precipitately fled. But it takes a good deal to shake the nerves of a physician. In an instant I recovered myself.

'Moore,' I said, 'you can't play with me. You are ventriloquising.'

He was very indignant.

'What do you think of me?' he said. '*I* to go playing the tricks of a strolling mountebank! What the devil!'

'I beg your pardon,' I replied. 'But you must acknowledge that on the Baconian principle one must acknowledge no new cause until the possibility of all known causes has been eliminated. Now ventriloquism, vulgar or not, is a known agent; your principle, whatever it be, is perfectly new. So that you can hardly blame me.'

'I swear,' he said, 'that I have had nothing to do with the thing since you came into the room, and that while you were speaking to it I never opened my mouth.'

'Never mind, I believe you fully.'

'You shall take it with you,' he replied, 'and try it in your own rooms, if you doubt me.'

'Not a bit,' I replied. 'Still, I will take it, in order that the outside world may be convinced.'

'You shall; but try it again here, and see for yourself again. I will not open my mouth.'

I tried again, a certain uncanny feeling still possessing me. Oh, for the inventive powers of a Frenchman, in order to begin the conversation naturally!

'That was a fine speech of Mr Gladstone's yesterday evening.'

'Yes,' the delicate feminine voice again replied; 'I didn't read it all, but the beginning and the end were very good, weren't they?'

Again the same eerie feeling came over me, followed as before by the conviction that some trickery must be at the bottom of this most unparalleled experience. I looked at Moore. He was sitting in his arm-chair by the fire, a smile playing on his face; but his lips were set fast.

I tried yet a third time, determined to watch Moore's face during the whole operation.

'Mr Gladstone must be old now,' I said rather inanely.

'Seventy-nine last birthday,' replied the voice, *precisely at the same moment as Moore was saying,*

'By Jove, eighty-five if he is a day!'

I was convinced by that. No human being ever spoke two sentences precisely at the same instant. Either there was somebody else in the room, or Moore had succeeded, marvellously succeeded. He had made an instrument that could not only imitate the tones of the human voice, but could keep up a conversation as constantly, if not as wittily, as Miss Notable and Mr Neverout in Swift's *Polite Conversation*.

'Satisfied, old fellow?' said Moore, rising from his chair and coming toward me.

'Are you sure there is no one else in the room?' I said.

'Search,' he replied, a little contemptuously, as though half amused, half wearied by my recurring scepticism.

But I was too well acquainted with Moore's earnest and honourable nature to doubt him any more.

'My dear fellow,' I said, 'I know you are incapable of deception. I take your word. On anything else I would take your nod or shake of the head. But this is extraordinary, very extraordinary. I never heard anything like it.'

'No more did I,' he replied with pardonable vanity, 'until a week or so ago. I had tried all kinds of devices to make the thing answer sensibly; she would answer, of course, long ago, but I wanted her to behave like a lady, not like a lunatic.'

'So you mean your automaton to be a lady, do you?'

'Yes,' he replied, drawing closer. 'And I want her to be a lady that would deceive the Queen herself. Not a thing that can only act when lifted into a chair, or stuck up on a platform; but a creature that will guide herself, answer questions, talk and eat like a rational being, in fact, perform the part of a society lady as well as any duchess of them all.'

'Moore,' I said, 'you must be mad.'

'Mad or not, I mean to try it. See here. Here is another automaton, that can walk, eat, turn its head, shut its eyes.

That is common enough. Here is the brain power, the "anti-phonograph" that can speak and hear, indeed do anything but think. What is wanted but that the two should be combined?'

'My dear fellow,' I answered, 'it is easy to talk like that. I am a materialist, and would grant you more than most; but even in my view the brain is more than a mere machine. A man guides himself; *you* have to guide this automaton. How are you to get inside her and make her do all these things together at the proper time? Take a very simple example; your thing has to be sure to open its mouth when it speaks. How are you to ensure that the process which causes it to open its mouth, and the process which causes certain words to be uttered, shall take place simultaneously? Suppose the thing were to say, "I will sit down;" how are you to ensure that, at the proper moment, she shall go through the proper motions involved in sitting down? Remember, an error of half a second in your mysterious clockwork may make all the difference between your duchess occupying a dignified position in a chair and sprawling ingloriously on the floor. Why, think of the actions of but five minutes. She rises from a chair, she avoids the toes of the ladies and gentlemen in the room, she bows to a gentleman, she smiles – more or less hypocritically – at a lady, she makes a *bon-mot*, she laughs at somebody else's *bon-mots*; she even blows her nose. What countless simultaneous processes, not one of which must go wrong!'

Moore heard me through.

'Plausible enough,' he said, when I had finished; 'we shall soon see who is right. But tell me, should you not have said, a year ago, that the anti-phonograph was an impossibility?'

'Certainly I should.'

'Then a year hence you may alter your opinion on this point, as you have on that.'

'Hardly.'

'Who was it,' he asked, 'who lectured so vigorously on the folly of certain women of our time, and talked so largely about their utter inanity? Why, I remember your exact words. "The Society woman of our time," you proclaimed, "what is she but a doll? Her second-hand opinions, so daintily expressed, would not a parrot speak them as well? Her motions, her poses, which she thinks so statuesque, how affected, how mechanical they are! Is she a woman, this creature of the nineteenth century, or a puppet dressed up to go through a number of motions on the stage of London life, an automaton obeying the wire-pullings of the showman Fashion?" You meant all that for metaphor and eloquence, old fellow; and yet you object to my proving that it is all literal truth!'

'Prove it first,' I said.

'Only give me time,' he answered. 'But before you go,' he said, with a sudden impulse, as he saw me nearing the door, 'for God's sake not a word of this until I give you leave.'

'Make your mind easy,' I replied; 'a doctor knows how to keep a secret. When your lady goes out of order, send for a bottle of my emulsion, and I'll engage she'll trouble you no more!'

During the next few months I often thought of Moore and his hallucination; the picture of the poor fellow engaged on a hopelessly mad task often rose before my mind. I pitied him greatly. 'Another fine brain wasted,' I used to say. 'A man that more than rivalled Edison, spending the best years of his life over a mad chimera!' For I often visited him, and found him now despondent, now enthusiastic, but always dogged and impenetrably determined. I urged rest, a sea-voyage, anything to cure him of his brainsick folly. But he met me always with one reply: 'Rest *then;* not before.' Rest in the grave, poor fellow, I thought, as I noted his hectic cheek and staring bones. His fiery soul was fretting his body to decay.

At last, more than a year after our last conversation, amid the heap of letters lying on my table at breakfast, I came upon one that startled me. It was from Arthur Moore: short, but to the point.

'Success at last; come when you can.'

As soon as my round of visits was finished, I drove to his rooms. Mounting the stairs, I was ushered into the room by the most beautiful girl I had ever seen: a creature with fair hair, bright eyes, and a doll-like childishness of expression.

'Can he have married?' I thought, as I looked at her. 'How is Mr Moore?' I said aloud.

'Poorly to-day,' she replied. 'He will be here in a moment.'

Where and when had I heard that voice before? I seemed to know it, and yet I could not associate it with anybody. But I had no time to be perplexed; for in two or three seconds Moore appeared, looking ghastly and deathlike in his pallor.

'You are ill,' I said, when the first greeting was over. 'You have been overstraining yourself. You must really rest, or you will kill yourself.'

'Yes, I must,' he replied; 'and I think I shall. It has been toilsome work. But I think it was worth it, don't you?'

'How should I know?' I answered, 'I haven't seen it yet.'

'Yes, you have,' he said, smiling in spite of the pain that he must have been feeling.

I looked around, bewildered. I could see nothing but the same old room, and the strange girl sitting in an easy chair in the corner.

'You are mysterious,' I said, wondering not only at his words, but at the fact of his not having introduced me to the girl. 'Perhaps she is a nurse,' I thought; though no nurse in all my experience had ever looked like that.

'Wait a moment,' said Moore. Then, turning to the girl, he spoke a little louder.

'Mr Gladstone must be getting old now,' he said.

Again those clear, distinct, delicate tones, as the answer came,

'Eighty last birthday.'

I saw it all now. That beautiful, lady-like girl, that had ushered me into the room, whom I had taken for his wife, was an automaton! That doll-like expression was due to the fact that she *was* a doll. I was utterly astounded, and felt as if I were dreaming. The impossible had taken place. Moore sat by, enjoying my bewilderment; for a moment his weakness left him.

'Watch,' he said.

'Come here,' he said to the automaton.

The lady arose, after one second of apparent indecision, and approached him.

'Let me introduce to you Dr Phillips,' he said.

The lady smiled approval. (To this day I have never understood how Moore had managed to produce that smile – that fatal, monotonous, fascinating smile.)

'Dr Phillips, Miss Amelia Brooke.'

The lady bowed, and extended her hand.

'I am most happy to meet one of whom I have so often heard,' she said.

Could it be a reality? I felt more and more staggered. The

lady stood perfectly still, her hands clasped before her. This fair creature not of flesh and blood? Impossible!

'You may go,' said Moore.

The thing moved back to her place, and sat down.

'What do you think of her?' he said aloud.

Before answering, I looked round to see where she was.

'Don't mind,' he said, laughing; 'she can't hear. I often have that feeling myself. You may discuss her as you please, and she won't be offended. She has one merit other women haven't, she is not touchy; but she has a failing the best of them have not, she can't blush. On the whole, however, I prefer her.'

'I am still almost incredulous,' I replied; 'indeed, until I have dissected her, and found pulleys instead of a liver, and eccentrics instead of a spleen, I shall hardly believe she isn't a woman in reality.'

'You can easily do so,' he said. 'Come here, Amelia.'

The creature rose, and came forward.

'Let Dr Phillips see your arm,' he said.

The lady showed me her arm, and turned up her sleeve. It did not need a moment's inspection to show me that this was not an arm of flesh and blood. What it actually was made of Moore would not tell me.

'Better than Madame Tussaud's, isn't it?' he said.

'Much better,' I replied. 'Might deceive anyone but a doctor.'

Passing my hand down to her wrist, I noted an exactly-moving pulse. So wonderfully was the human pulse imitated, that I believe anybody but one, like myself, trained to accurate discrimination, would have been deluded. I could not refrain from expressing my admiration.

'Yes,' said Moore, 'she will often have her arms bare, and there may be a good deal of hand-pressing and that sort of thing; so that I thought I ought to have everything right.'

'Does her heart beat too?' I asked.

'No,' he said; 'I wanted the space for other mechanism, so she has to do without a heart altogether. Besides,' he added, smiling, 'I wanted her to be a Society lady.'

'The thing will be worth thousands to you,' I said, when I had finished the examination of the creature's cutaneous covering. 'It is uncanny enough, and I can't say I like it, but it will draw. What a pity Barnum has gone! He would have given you a million dollars for it.'

Moore rose angrily.

'Do you think I will sell my own life-power for money?' he cried. 'That thing has cost me at least ten years of my life, and she shall never be exhibited like a two-headed nightingale, or a creature with its legs growing out of its pockets! She shall walk drawing-rooms like a lady, or I will break her to pieces myself!'

'My dear fellow,' I said, 'you are over-excited and ill. Surely you cannot know what you are saying?'

'I know well enough,' he answered doggedly. 'I have made a lady, you can't deny it; and a lady she shall be.'

'You have made a marionette,' I said, 'a very wonderful marionette, but nothing more. Never mind,' I went on, seeing him getting more passionate, 'all in good time. For the present you must rest and lie still.'

'Phillips,' he said, all the force of his character coming out in his face, 'I am determined that she shall be the beauty of the season. She shall eclipse them all, I tell you. What are they but dolls? And she is more than a doll, she is *Me*. I have breathed into her myself, and she all but lives; she understands and knows! Come, promise me you will not betray me!'

'Of course I will not,' I said; 'but you must give up this mad scheme. Consider, as an automaton she will make you for life; as a lady she will be found out in five minutes, and you will be laughed at. For your own sake pause!'

'Listen,' he said fiercely, all the veins in his forehead standing out like cords. I saw then how his own creation had possessed him till he was no longer master of himself.

'Listen,' he repeated. 'You call her an automaton. I tell you she is alive. See!'

He called the thing to him.

'Amelia,' he said, 'I have made you, and you are mine. Are you grateful?'

The creature smiled – the one smile she possessed, which she had, as I knew afterwards, for prince or peasant, man or maid.

'I can never forget what I owe you,' she replied.

'Kiss me then,' he said.

The thing bent down and kissed him obediently.

'You see,' he cried; 'is *that* an automaton?'

I felt sick and disgusted. I was already beginning to feel that hatred of this creature which afterwards filled me to overflowing.

'No,' I said, 'she is no automaton for *you*.'

'Then,' he replied, ignoring the implication of my words, 'will you introduce her to Society as a lady?'

'Never!' I answered. 'Moore, you are beside yourself.'

'Very well,' he rejoined; 'I will find somebody to do it instead. Remember, you have promised not to betray me, or to breathe a syllable of all this to anyone.'

Things had evidently gone far. As a doctor, I knew well how the constant brooding on a fixed idea often unhinges the strongest brain; but I confess that never in all my experience had I seen anything like this. It seemed to me like a possession of the devil. Would to God the accursed automaton were burnt to ashes, or had never been made! Again and again I wished I had never uttered the thoughtless words which had set all this in motion. But it was useless crying over the irremediable past. Something must be done, and done quickly, or poor Moore would make himself the laughing-stock of all London.

'Arthur,' I said, 'you must take a little time to rest before you do anything. Your physical nature is completely overwrought. Take my advice, and go to bed.'

'Will you help me?' he said obstinately.

'No,' I answered, losing patience at his confirmed stupidity.

'Then,' he said, 'I give –' What he would have added remains a secret, for at that moment his strength, tried too long, gave way, and he fell at my feet in a swoon.

Forgetting everything, save only that he was my friend, and that he was helpless, I applied the usual restoratives, and soon brought him round. I then rang the bell; a woman appeared.

'Your master is ill,' I said. 'Help me to put him to bed.'

The woman was a rough and rather dirty creature, without a trace of beauty in her, but she applied herself with alacrity to the task. We soon had poor Moore comfortably lying in bed; I gave the woman the proper directions, and left, promising to call again in the morning.

During all this time the automaton had remained motionless in the corner. I afterwards ascertained that Moore had concealed her more extraordinary powers from the other immates of the house, thinking they would be frightened; only letting them fancy she was a doll of the kind of Mr Maskelyne's Psycho. She had made no motion to assist her maker, 'grateful' as she was to him. I noted this with a sort of angry satisfaction.

'Moore,' I thought, 'said he preferred her to other women; on the whole *I* prefer the ugliest and dirtiest of them all to that beautiful but unfeeling creature.'

In a week care, and his own indomitable energy, restored Moore to something that did for health. He rose from his bed silent, impenetrable. He thanked me for my attention in polite terms; too polite, I thought, for the friend of so many years. Of his purpose, not a word. Had he forgotten it? Alas, no!

If there is any quality on which, more than on others, I fancy I have a right to plume myself, it is that of a firm will. What else, indeed, than an unflinching resolution could have brought me through the innumerable difficulties and struggles of my early life to the position I occupy at present? My enemies, indeed, have called me obstinate; but no one, not even a caricaturist, has ever represented me as flabby and pliable. Strong-willed I know I am; I have proved it over and over again – and yet there was one man before whom I was as wax, or as one of his own automata. That man was Arthur Moore. Years have gone by since he died; yet such is the spell his very memory casts over me that I feel even now that were he to come again and tempt me I should yield again, and yield almost willingly. Let those sneer who have never been tried as I was, who have never met the man of adamant, the King of Men, and who fancy themselves strong because they have always lived among the weak.

Shortly after his recovery, Moore called on me. There was a look of fixed resolve upon his face before which I quailed. It was the look of the monomaniac, that look which only comes after long brooding upon one idea.

'For the present she is perfect,' he said. 'I have taught her French – drawing-room French, I mean – and three songs. She can enter a room, bow, smile, and dance. If with these accomplishments she can't oust the other dolls and turn them green with jealousy for one season, I am much surprised. Now will you help me?'

'No,' I said. I was still struggling with the omnipotence of his will.

'You shall,' he replied. 'Others would do it if you refused; but it is my whim that you shall be the one to share my glory. Oh, what a time we shall have – how we shall laugh when we see it all, and think what fools men are!'

Again I tried to enter a feeble protest, but he overbore me. You ask how: I cannot tell. One thing I know, that if the thing were to happen again I should yield again. Call it magic, call it the force of personality; call it anything you like; but it overbore me. I yielded; I promised my assistance. We sat like two mischief-making children far into the small hours of the night, plotting how we could carry out the plan best, and arranging every detail so as to assure success and evade detection. Excuses and palliations coursed in undercurrents through my mind. I was a scientist, conducting a psychological experiment. I was a mere toy-maker, introducing into the world a rather elaborate toy. I was a Maskelyne, exposing the spiritualists. But on the whole I gave little heed to these thoughts. Moore had enslaved me, body and mind; I was carried away in a kind of drunken enthusiasm, and almost as feverishly excited as Moore himself. Nothing would now have stopped me. Would Frankenstein have paused the very hour before his creature took life? As for Moore, I believe he would have gone on with his designs in the very midst of the thunders of the Judgment Day itself.

Why should I linger over the early triumphs of our Phantasm? I was a fashionable doctor: I brought Miss Amelia Brooke out as a niece of mine. The Countess of Lorimer, one of my patients, undertook to pilot her through the first shoals of real life. Never shall I forget that first evening. Scarcely had she entered the room – it was at Lady Vandeleur's – when the eyes of all seemed, as if by magic, to be turned towards her. Exquisitely dressed, with a proud demeanour, with the step of a queen, she swept into the ball-room. She was my niece; I ought to have been proud of her; but I hated her with an intense loathing. Moore could do much with me, but he could not make me like this creature. Yet I was bound in nature to do all I could for her.

'Who is she?' said young Harry Burton to me. 'By Jove, she looks like a born queen.'

'You flatter me,' I replied. 'She is my niece. Good God,' I went on to myself, 'would that she were a born anything, instead of a made doll!'

'Oh,' rejoined Burton, 'lucky man that you are! Introduce me, will you?'

'With pleasure,' I answered.

I took him up and introduced him. During the ceremony I watched the creature carefully. No, there was no doubt about it. Such acting would deceive the Master of the Ceremonies in the court of Louis XIV himself. Every motion, every word, was exactly as it should be. How on earth had Moore managed it? I was almost deceived myself. Could this be after all a real creature of flesh and blood, substituted for the Phantasm? No; that detestable, beautiful smile was there – a smile which no woman ever wore, yet which none the less would be the bane of more than one man's existence.

Harry Burton danced many dances with her that night. When it closed, he was head over ears in love.

'Phillips,' he said in a brief interval, 'she is divine.'

'Devilish, rather,' I thought. 'Yes,' I said aloud, 'I think she is good-looking.'

'Good-looking!' he cried. 'What are all these painted dolls to her? *They* have nothing to say for themselves, *they* are mere bundles of conventionality; but *she* – she is all soul.'

'My boy,' I said warningly, 'you are evidently all heart. Be careful. Don't do anything rash. Dance with her, talk to her – do anything but fall in love with her.'

'Who talked of falling in love?' he said, astonished at my earnestness. 'I said nothing but that she was the finest girl in the room, and so she is, by Jove!'

'Nevertheless,' I said, 'it doesn't follow that she's worth falling in love with. Many a person *looks* all right, that's unsound within.'

'Why, here you are running down your own niece!'

'Not running her down; merely warning you. Besides,' I added smiling, 'she's only my niece by marriage.'

At this moment a new dance began, and Burton ran off to claim his partner. I remained, absorbed in not very pleasant reflections. Things were getting involved already. Moore had only told me he was making a woman; I had never calculated that he would make a coquette. What would come of it? I sat and watched her as she danced, dancing beautifully but a little mechanically, I thought, saying always the right things, answering questions always in the same way, and wearing at pretty regular intervals the same detestable smile. If I hated her before, I hated her tenfold now. I would speak to Moore, and put an end to it. A sudden cold – ordered to the South of France – and never let her come back. Good heavens, this creature never had a cold, never had a headache, never felt out of sorts: yet Moore said he had made a woman!

Slowly the evening dragged to its close – the most wearisome evening I had ever spent. The creature did not seem to tire; one dance or twenty was the same to her. The monotony of it all became at length intolerable to me. At the earliest decent opportunity I took my leave.

Moore had never been a Society man. Even to witness his own triumph he had refused to be drawn out of his retirement. Perhaps indeed he was afraid that his nerves might prove unequal to the strain of watching the creature that he had made rivalling the creatures that God – and the milliner – had made; perhaps he feared he might be tempted to betray all. At any rate, he stayed away; and it was with a feverish eagerness that he waited for the story of her successes from my lips.

'How did it all go off?' he said anxiously, as I made my promised call to tell him.

'As an experiment, very well,' I answered. 'There was no hitch, no failure. The success was only too monotonous. Human beings sometimes put their foot in it; she never. Would to God she might show now and then a little proneness to error!'

'You are queer,' Moore answered. 'Why should you grudge her her victories?'

'Arthur,' I said, 'the joke has gone quite far enough. Put a stop to it. Why go further? Think of the chances of detection – no, think of the far worse chances of success! Can't you see that the more skilful the deception the more dangerous will its consequences be? Already more than one young fellow has fallen head over ears in love with her. It is horrible to think of!'

'The fools!' he said, with a rather cynical smile. 'That is just the way with young fellows – never looking below the surface, looking only at the face. Why, Phillips, if they are taken in in that way they deserve to be taken in! *I* shall do nothing.'

He fixed his eyes upon me in conscious power. He knew that I could not resist him. Weakly, but inevitably, I gave way. I should do so again, with all the consequences as clearly before me as they are now.

So the thing went on, new developments constantly arising. I shall not stay to repeat them. The story is too painful to me; it is the story of my own insensate folly, and I do not care to dwell upon it. I hasten to the fatal ending.

Among the many deserters from the shrines of other goddesses, who thronged to pay their court to this new and strange divinity, two seemed to hold the divided first place in her favour. One was my young friend, Harry Burton; the other was handsome, impulsive, universally liked Dicky Calder. These two had been firm friends before, in spite of the fact that they had often flirted with the same girl. But it was impossible for two young fellows to love Amelia and continue to love each other. I watched the gradual change of their affection into distrust, jealousy, and hate; first with unutterable sorrow, and then with a sort of fatalistic shame. It was *my* fault, certainly; I could not hide that even from myself; but I seemed to be bound to go on in the path I had begun, committed to a course which knew no turning. Did I hesitate? A glance from Moore's commanding eyes impelled me onward. I repeat it, I am a strong-willed man; but Moore was the stronger.

To do Amelia justice, she was rigidly impartial between Burton and Calder. For both she had the same silvery tones, for both the same fascinating smile. To both, if they asked the same questions, she returned identically the same answers. To both she sang the same songs, with the crescendo in the same passages, and both, at the conclusion of the songs, received the same languishing, irresistible smile over the right shoulder, which made them her slaves on the spot.

At times the irony of the situation overcame me, and I could not restrain a laugh. 'Philosophers look forward to the time when men shall have automata as their slaves; but here are two young fools in willing, absurd slavery to an automaton, who bends them to her will as she pleases. Her *will!* I suppose she has no will, but she looks uncommonly like it.

Let us call it caprice, then.' Then I would go off into a reverie.
'Are we all automata? Are we all mere chess-men on the
board of life, moved hither and thither by a fate we cannot
control? Well, if we are, then Amelia is the queen, and Burton
and Calder are two knights of opposing colours.'

One evening, a curious incident happened. Burton and
Calder were as usual basking in the rays of their divinity,
when by some mischance Amelia's brooch fell to the ground.
Both the swains stooped to pick it up, but Burton was
successful. Delighted at his triumph over his rival, he solic-
ited the honour of re-fastening it. Calder watched him with
jealous eyes. Suddenly a clumsy pair of waltzers, not looking
where they were going, came hard into Burton. The
brooch-pin was driven deep into the fair throat of Amelia.
Burton started in horror; he began a savage oath, but stopping in time he pulled out the pin. Amelia had not uttered
a sound.

Burton, speechless with dismay, was taking out his handkerchief to staunch the blood; Calder was holding the girl up as
though she were fainting; a little crowd was gathering round
them; when I, suddenly recollecting myself, rushed in. With
the speed of lightning I whipped out my handkerchief and tied
it round Amelia's neck.

'Stand back, all of you!' I said in a tone of command. Even
Burton and Calder fell back a little.

My niece is very sensitive,' I said. 'The hurt is not great,
but it would be as well that she should go home at once.' A
terror had possessed me; an overmastering fear of detection
held me as in a vice.

'I assure you, uncle, that I am not hurt at all,' said Amelia.

'Come along,' I said sternly.

I hurried her off, finding just time to bid my adieus to my
hostess, and to console the dumbfounded Burton by saying
there was no danger.

We drove, not home, but direct to Moore's lodgings. Hurriedly we went upstairs. Moore was still up. He seemed
surprised to see us.

'What do you want?' he said.

'Fools that we are,' I answered. 'Why, we were within a
hair's-breadth of detection. *The creature can't bleed.*'

'Why, what need has she to bleed?' he said.

'Every need,' I answered. 'Doesn't a girl bleed when a pin is driven a good inch into her throat?'

'What do you mean?'

I explained the circumstances, and how I hoped I had for this once staved off discovery. I had been just in time.

'No,' he said, when I had finished. 'I never thought she would need to bleed. Strange that I should have forgotten that! They say that murderers always forget just one thing, just one little thing! But *they* take pains to get rid of the blood, and I ought to take pains to have it there.'

'Give it up, Moore,' I said.

'Give it up! Never!' he shouted. 'Give it up for a few drops of blood! Rather would I drain my own veins into hers! Rather go out and kill somebody. What does Mephistopheles say? "Blood is a very peculiar sort of juice." But I will make it.'

Did I not know that no difficulties would deter him, that obstacles were in his eyes only incentives to further effort? If ever any man was ignorant of the word impossible, Moore was that man.

Miss Brooke was 'ill' for a few weeks from 'shock to the system.' At the end of that time I saw Moore again. He and the Phantasm were in the room together. He gave me a pin.

'Prick her,' he said.

I obeyed, not unwillingly; and to my horror something very like bleeding began.

'Yes,' said Moore, 'I have done it. I have looked up Shakespeare. Do you remember what Shylock says, to prove that a Jew is, after all, a man? "Hath not a Jew eyes? hath not a Jew hands, organs, dimensions, senses, affections, passions? fed with the same food, hurt with the same weapons, subject to the same diseases, healed by the same means, warmed and cooled by the same winter and summer, as a Christian is? If you prick us, do we not bleed? if you tickle us, do we not laugh? if you poison us, do we not die?" Now every one of these marks my Amelia has; so I say she is a genuine woman. Why, if you tickle her, she will laugh.'

'No one is likely to tickle her,' I said.

'No; but after our last experience it is well to be prepared for all emergencies.'

In this case, however, I did not make an experiment.

Moore's word was enough. If the creature's smile was so detestable, what must her laugh be like?

After her time of seclusion, Amelia again appeared in Society, and was again the cynosure of all eyes, chiefly, however, of the four owned by Burton and Calder. These latter had never ceased to make inquiries after her health. I had often wondered whether Burton had noticed that the scratch of the pin had drawn no blood; but his conduct afterwards set me at ease. If he had seen it, he had probably thought that his Venus was too ethereal to bleed even the thinnest celestial ichor. The infatuation of youth can account for or put up with anything. At any rate, the young fellow admired her still; and Calder was equally possessed. In vain I assured them that she had no feeling; but this, though the literal truth, was met with derisive incredulity; and naturally I disliked to speak too often or too strongly against my niece. Blood, after all, even Amelia's manufactured blood, is thicker than water.

Though Amelia certainly could not feel, yet there was no doubt that in the future she would bleed if pricked, and I was free from anxiety on that score. But there was one thing which caused me considerable uneasiness. She was a girl of originality – indeed, I venture to think that there has never been a girl quite like her – yet there was a sameness, an artificiality about her which puzzled and alarmed me. To the same question she always and inevitably returned the same answer. On topics of the day she always had the same opinion, expressed in the same words. My rival, Sir John Bolus, who didn't like her for some reason or other, used to say that in her company he always felt as if talking to a very well-trained parrot. She uttered her opinions as if they had been learnt verbatim from someone else. Now there is nothing a true woman ought to do so frequently as to change her mind. Everybody should hear from her lips something different from what everybody else hears. It was on this point that I felt that Moore had failed; and it was from this that somehow or other I vaguely anticipated disaster. My apprehensions were but too well founded.

The time drew near for Calder and Burton to declare themselves. I need not say that, closely as I watched the doings of Amelia, I was not present on these auspicious occasions. But I can distinctly assert, nevertheless, from my knowledge of human nature, that the language of Calder, who came second, was almost precisely the same as that of Burton, who had the first chance. Hence it followed, with mathematical certainty, that Amelia's reply would be the same to both. Here was a pretty predicament! What I had blamed in her was her unwomanly constancy; but this very constancy had led – as I was sure both *a priori* and from the happy faces of the two young men – to a display of fickleness unparalleled in the whole history of womankind. Within an hour after accepting Burton the faithless creature accepted Calder in almost identically the same terms! Even the most heartless of coquettes had surely never been guilty of such conduct as this.

All this, however, was for the present merely a plausible conjecture, based upon a more or less certain knowledge of character. To make sure of it, I determined to ask. The result but too sadly confirmed my fears. Burton was almost delirious with joy.

'She is mine,' he said; 'and that beast Calder was never in it with her. To think that I should ever have been afraid of a cad like that!'

I congratulated him as in duty bound, and spent an hour with him which may have been pleasant to him, but became very tedious to me: so difficult was it to get him off his one eternal topic and induce him to talk like a rational being. At last, however, I managed to effect my escape, and made my way to Calder. He also received me very graciously.

'Old man,' he said, 'I have good news to tell you. Amelia has just consented to be engaged to me.'

'Indeed!' I replied; 'I am very pleased to hear it. You are a happy man, Dick.'

'Yes,' he said, 'happier than I deserve. But what delights me almost as much as having won her is that she never gave a thought to that fellow Burton. If I had had any sense I must have seen that a girl like her could never be taken in by a wretched fellow like him; but somehow I managed to be jealous of him. Well, *that's* all over, thank goodness. I really believe I shall get to like him now I'm sure he can do me no harm.'

And so the young fellow chattered on, cutting me to the

heart with almost every sentence that he uttered. What a dreadful awakening I was preparing for him! For of course the awful truth must be told him, that he and his rival had fallen in love with a sham. It would be an awkward moment for both of us. Should I tell him now, and get it over? On the whole I preferred to put it off, and consult Moore first. His fertile brain would suggest a way out of the difficulty. Perhaps he would make a second automaton that would do for one of the rival suitors, while the other kept to Amelia. At any rate, I preferred to get his advice before acting. He had made the Phantasm bleed; might he not get us out of this still more unpleasant position?

I told him of the new complication. To my surprise he made light of it.

'Well?' he said when I had finished my recital.

'Well?' I replied, 'I should think that was enough.'

'Why,' he said, 'I can see nothing wonderful in that. The wonder would be if they *hadn't* proposed to her. Women have had offers before now.'

'But you can't intend to let things go on as they are?' I cried.

'That's exactly what I *do* intend,' he answered. 'Why should I interfere?'

'But think of it for one moment,' I said. 'Two men in love with the same automaton: two men in the position of accepted lovers at the same moment! Think of even *one* man in that position! How awful it is – why, it is too dreadful to think of!'

'Then I shan't think of it,' he answered coolly. 'My dear fellow, what is there so strange in it all? Men have been in love with stone-like women before this. Men have given themselves up to heartless and soulless abstractions before this. Anyone who gets my Amelia will get *something*, at any rate, not a mere doll.'

The plain fact dawned on me that Moore's extraordinary success had turned his brain. He had put so much of himself into his automaton that he had positively begun to regard her as a real living being, in whose veins flowed his own blood, in whose nostrils was his own breath. Eve was not more truly bone of Adam's bone than this Amelia was part and parcel of Moore's life. There was a mysterious union between them which gave me an uncanny feeling of sorcery. Could it be that by some unholy means Moore had succeeded in conveying some portion of his own life to this creature of his brain? I tried to dismiss the thought, for I am a man of science; yet it recurred again and again.

Moore was monomaniac on this point; yet, strange to say, my conviction of his lunacy did not lessen the influence he had acquired over me. His intellect was as keen, his will as powerful, as ever; and in spite of the utter monstrosity of his plans, and their inhuman cruelty, I lent myself to their fulfilment, and went desperately on to the bitter end. Let me hasten to the final catastrophe.

Burton and Calder were engaged to Amelia. It may be easily understood that now and then they came into collision. Sometimes things looked strange to them. Calder once demanded an explanation of his *fiancée* as to the frequency of Burton's visits. She gave him an account that satisfied him, and sealed it with a smile and a kiss that made him feel like a villain for ever doubting her. People wondered at the confidence with which both the young men asserted that they were the favoured suitor, and admired the daring skill with which Amelia played off one against the other. No one warned the young men; it was none of our business to interfere with them. English people do not care for meddling. As for me, had I not done enough by giving both of them a very plain piece of advice at the very outset, to which neither of them had paid the slightest attention, beyond insinuating that I was jealous of my own niece?

In such matters one young man is remarkably similar to another. Their very modes of speech tend to become the same. In asking Amelia to fix the day, need it be wondered at that they used precisely the same terms as have been used by all young men from the day when that nameless suitor of 'pretty Jane' promised to buy the ring for his beloved? The result may be easily foreseen. Amelia, by some hidden law of her being, for which not she but perhaps Moore was to blame, could not help fixing the same day for both. Had a third candidate appeared on the scene, she would have fixed the same day for him also.

When I had heard this last fatal *dénouement*, I confess that even Moore's influence could not keep me from taking a step on my own account. I would not destroy Amelia, much as I hated her for the trouble she had caused me. Something seemed to tell me that her death would be the certain death of Moore, whose life was bound up in hers as closely as the life of Jacob was bound up in that of Benjamin. By some subtle process, every time danger threatened Amelia, Moore's spirits seemed to sink; every time she surmounted the danger his spirits rose again. He had put himself into her. I would not destroy her; but I went to Calder and I gave him a pretty plain hint as to the position of affairs between her and Burton. He would not believe me.

'If I thought she was false,' he said, 'I would stab her where she stood, were it at the very altar. But it cannot be. She has pledged herself to me, and mine she is!'

'I know it for a fact,' I answered, 'that she has promised to marry Burton on the 29th of February.'

'The twenty-ninth!' he cried. 'Why, that is *my* day, the day on which she has promised to marry me!'

'Precisely so,' I said. 'What she means to do I don't know.'

'But I know what *I* mean to do,' he answered gloomily. 'I will have it out with her.'

'No violence!'

'None at all. Don't fear me. By God, what a heartless creature! But it can't be true. You are deceiving me!'

'Too true. But find out for yourself.'

'I took my leave, and went home. I did not intend to see Moore; I knew the strange spell of his eyes, and that even now I might be unable to resist his will.

I afterwards ascertained what Calder's plan was. He made no inquiry from Amelia; he simply went and begged her to put off the day of his marriage a month, from the twenty-ninth of February to the last of March. She readily agreed. He then went off to a shop he knew, and bought a sharp Spanish dagger.

The day of the marriage drew near, and nearer. Every preparation was completed. It was to be fashionable. St George's was got ready in expectation of a large assemblage of people. At length the eventful morning dawned. I was to give the bride way to Burton, as after the postponement of Calder's wedding he was the only bridegroom left in the race. We came out and stood before the altar. As I passed along I noticed two figures in different parts of the building, both familiar to me. They were Moore and Calder. The former was untidy, evidently excited and restless. The latter was scrupulously neat; but he had a strangely determined look on his face. One hand was hidden under the breast of his frock-coat.

The service proceeded. Fancy a girl like this being told she was a daughter of Abraham, so long as she was not afraid with any amazement! Certainly a cooler, less perturbed daughter of the patriarch I never saw. She gave the responses in a clear, musical voice. They came to the fatal question – 'Wilt thou have this man to be thy husband?' Before she could answer 'I will,' there was a sudden confusion; a man rushed forward, drew forth a dagger from his breast, and shouting 'You shall not!' stabbed Amelia to the heart – or rather through the left side of her bodice. She fell to the ground, striking her head heavily as she fell against the rail. There was a whirr, a rush. The anti-phonograph was broken. I bent over her, and opened her dress to staunch the wound. Moore had made no provision for her bleeding *there*. As I drew out the dagger, it was followed by a rush of sawdust.

In the confusion of the strange discovery, no one noticed that a real death was taking place not twenty feet away. As the sexton was clearing out the church, be noticed a man asleep in one of the pews, leaning against a pillar. He went up and touched him; but there was no answer. He shook him; but the man was as heedless as Baal. It was Arthur Moore, and he was dead. He had put his life into his masterpiece; his wonderful toy was broken, and the cord of Moore's life was broken with it.

And as for me, why, I am no longer a fashionable physician. As I write, there are men about me, who talk of me as a *patient*.

# The Man Who
# Made A Man

## By HARLE OREN CUMMINS

*America, too, had its range of popular monthly illustrated magazines which flourished in the decades either side of the dawn of the twentieth century. Harper's Monthly, The Century, Scribner's and McClure's Magazine were just four that sold extremely well in America and also published special English editions. These publications similarly developed their own excellent illustrators including Howard Pyle, Maurice Griffenhagen, Rollin Kirby, Andre Castaigne and Frederick Dorr Steele – America's pre-eminent interpreter of Sherlock Holmes. A similar band of prolific and adaptable writers kept these publications supplied with stories, including Harle Oren Cummins (1859–1931) whose work is to be found in all of the magazines I have listed.*

*Cummins, who lived in Boston, Massachusetts, wrote a wide range of fantasy tales from such out-and-out ghost stories as The Fool and His Joke to the ingenious Science Fiction yarn of The Space Annihilator. A selection of his best short stories, rather curiously entitled Welsh Rarebit Tales, was issued by the The Mutual Book Company in his native Boston in 1902, and is now something of a rarity. The Man Who Made A Man which Cummins contributed to McClure's Magazine in December 1901, is a curious little story in which a certain Professor Holbrok creates a man and animates him by electricity. But it is the inevitable end of the creature that provides the reader with a puzzle – for just how or by whom was it destroyed . . .*

When Professor Aloysius Holbrok resigned his chair as head of the department of Synthetic Chemistry in one of the famous American colleges his friends wondered; for they well knew that his greatest pleasure in life lay in original investigations. When two weeks later the papers stated that the learned chemist had been taken to the Rathborn Asylum for the Insane, wonder changed to inordinate curiosity.

Although nothing definite was published in the papers, there were hints of strange things which had taken place in the private laboratory on Brimmer Street; and before long a story was current that, as a result of dabbling in the mysteries of psychology, a man had been killed while undergoing one of Professor Holbrok's experiments.

It is to clear up this mystery and to refute the charges of murder that I, who served for ten years as his assistant, am about to write this account, which, to the best of my knowledge and belief, contains the facts of the case.

I had noticed for the year previous that Professor Holbrok was much preoccupied; but I knew that he was working over some new experiment. Many times when I came to his door at five o'clock to clean up as usual for the next day, I found a notice pinned on the door telling me that he was in the midst of important work and would not need me again that day. I thought nothing about it at the time; for when he was experimenting with Dr Bicknell, performing operations with hypnotism instead of anæsthetics, there were weeks at a time when I was not allowed even a glimpse of the inside of the laboratories. One day, however, as I came in to report, the professor called me aside and told me that he wanted to have a talk with me.

'You know, Frederick,' he began, 'that I have been working and experimenting for a long time on a new problem, and I have not told you or anyone else the object of my toil. But now I have come to a point where I must take some one into my confidence. I need an assistant; and I know of no one I can trust more than you, who have been with me now nearly a dozen years.'

I was naturally flattered.

'Frederick,' he continued, rising and placing his hand on my shoulder, 'this experiment is the greatest one of my life. I am going to do what has never been done in the history of the world, except by God himself – I am going to *make a man*!'

I did not realize at first what he meant. I was startled, not only by his wild statement, but also by the intense tone in which he had spoken.

'You do not understand,' he said; 'but let me explain. You know enough chemistry to realize that everything – water, air, food, all things which we use in every-day life – are merely combinations of certain simple elements. As you have seen me, by means of an electric current, decompose a jar of pure water into its two component parts, – two molecules of hydrogen to every molecule of oxygen – so you can bring these same elements together in the gaseous state; and if the correct proportions are observed, when an electric spark or flame is brought into contact with the mixture, you will obtain again the liquid water. This is only a simple case; but the chemical laws which govern it hold equally well for every known substance found in nature. There are only about seventy-five known elements, and of these less than thirty compose the majority of the things found in every-day life.

'During the last six months I have been working with these elements, making different substances. I have taken a piece of wood, decomposed it with acids, analysed it quantitatively and qualitatively, finding the proportions in which its elements were combined. Then I have taken similar elements, brought them together in the same proportions, and I have produced a piece of wood so natural you would have sworn it grew upon a tree.

'I have been analysing and then making again every common thing which you see in nature, but I was only practising. I have had an end in view. Finally, I took a human body which I obtained from Dr Bicknell, at the medical college; and I analysed the flesh, the bones, the blood, in short, every part of it. What did I find? Of that body, weighing 165 pounds, 106 pounds was nothing but water, pure water, such as you may draw at the tap over yonder. And the blood which in the man's life had gone coursing through his veins, bringing nourishment to every part – what was that? Nothing but a serum filled with little cellular red corpuscles, which, in their turn, were only combinations of carbon, oxygen, sulphur, and a few other simple elements.

'I have taken the sternum bone from a dead man's chest, analysed it, then brought together similar elements, placed them in a mould, and I have produced a bone which was just as real as the one with which I started. There were only two things in nature which I could not reproduce. One was starch, that substance whose analysis has defied chemists of all ages; the other was flesh. Though I have analysed bits of it carefully, when I have brought together again those elementary parts flesh would not form.

'Chemists all over the world have been able to resolve the flesh into proteids, the awesome proteids, as they are called. They form the principal solids of the muscular, nervous, and granular tissues, the serum of the blood and of lymph. But no man on earth except myself has ever been able to create a proteid. They have missed the whole secret because they have been working at ordinary temperatures. Just as the drop of water will not form from its two gases at 4,500 degrees Fah., nor at its own lower explosion temperature, unless the spark be added, so will protoplasm not form except under certain electric and thermal conditions.

'For the last two months I have been working on these lines alone, varying my temperatures from the extreme cold produced by liquid air, to the intense heat of the compound blow-pipe; and I have been repaid. A fortnight ago I discovered how it was that I had erred, and since then I have succeeded in everything I have tried. I have formed the proteids, the fats, and the carbohydrates which go to make up protoplasm; and with these for my solid foundations, I have made every minute and complicated organ of the body. I have done more than that – I have put these component parts together, and now behold what I have made.'

He lifted a sheet, which was thrown over a heap of something on the table, and I started back with a strange mixture of awe and horror; for, stretched out on that marble slab, lay a naked body, which, if it had never been a man, living and breathing, as I lived and breathed, then I would have sworn I dreamed.

The thoughts which began to come into my mind probably showed in my face, for the professor said: 'You doubt? You think that I have lost my reason, and this thing is some man I have killed. Well, I do not blame you. A year ago I myself would have scoffed at the very idea of creating such a man. But you shall see, you shall be convinced, for in the next part of the experiment I must have your help. I will show you how I have made this man, or I will make another before your eyes. Then you and I, we will go further; we will do what no one but God has ever done before – we will make that inert mass *a living man.*'

The horror of the thing began to leave me, for I was fascinated by what he said, and I began to feel the same spirit with which he was inspired.

He took me into his private laboratory, and before my eyes, with only the contents of a few re-agent bottles, a blowpipe, and an electric battery, he made a mass of human flesh. I will not give you the formula, neither will I tell you in detail how it was done. God forbid that any other man should see what I saw afterwards.

'Now, all that remains is the final experiment, and that with your help I propose making to-night,' said the Professor. 'What we have to do is as much of a riddle to me as it is to you. It is purely and simply an experiment. I am going to pass through that lifeless clay the same current of electricity which, if sent through a living man, would produce death. Of course, with a man who had died from the giving out of some vital function I could not hope to succeed, but the organs of this man which I have made are in a perfectly healthy condition. It is my hope, therefore, that the current which would destroy a living man will bring this thing to life.'

We bore that naked body, not a corpse, and yet so terribly like, into the electric laboratory, and laid it on a slab of slate. Just at the base of its brain we scraped a little bare spot not larger than a pea, and, as I live, a drop of blood oozed out. On the right wrist, just over the pulse, we made another abrasion, and to these spots we brought the positive and negative wires from off the mains of the street current outside.

I held the two bare uninsulated bits of copper close to the flesh, Professor Holbrok switched into circuit 2,000 volts of electricity, and then before our starting eyes that thing which was only a mass of chemical compounds *became a man.*

A convulsive twitching brought the body almost into a sitting position, then the mouth opened and there burst forth from the lips a groan.

I have been in the midst of battles, and I have seen men

dying all around me, torn to ribbons by shot and shell, and I have not flinched; but when I tore the wires from that writhing, groaning shape, and saw its chest begin to heave with spasmodic breathing, I fainted.

When I came to myself I was lying half across the slab of slate, and the room was filled with a sickening stench, an odour of burning flesh. I looked for the writhing form which I had last seen on the table; but those wires, with their deadly current, which I tried to tear away as I fainted, must have been directed back by a Higher Hand, for there remained on the slab only a charred and cinder-like mass.

And the man who had made a man could not explain, for he was crawling about on the floor, counting the nails in the boards and laughing wildly.

# Frankenstein II

## By LEONARD MERRICK

*Leonard Merrick (1864–1939), the author of this next story, had a more personal reason than most writers to have been inspired to create a piece of fiction on the theme of Franken-stein – for during his career as an actor he had briefly appeared in a stage version of Mary Shelley's novel playing the experimenter's assistant. Merrick, who was actually born Leonard Miller in Belsize Park, London had to cut short his education when his father suffered severe financial problems. He was sent to South Africa, where he worked in a solicitor's office for two years and nearly died of camp fever. Returning to London, he was already stage-struck and managed to obtain a job with a repertory company who toured England playing 'sensational melodramas' in the major towns and cities. It was while he was appearing as an actor that he changed his surname to Merrick, and continued to use this when, two years later, he abandoned the stage for writing.*

*Merrick later produced a string of successful plays and novels, several of which were based on his theatrical experi-ences, including* The Actor Manager *(1898) and* While Paris Laughed *(1918). The theatre was also the setting for a number of his most ingenious short stories like* Frankenstein II *concern-ing a young playwright and the script which becomes his monster. H.G. Wells was a great admirer of Merrick, writing in a critique of his work, 'He stands for something that has not been done in fiction before, and he has done it so well that he must necessarily become a type in our memories.'*

I was at the Throne Theatre to see Orlando Lightfoot's comedy. Entering the buffet, in the first interval, I met Orlando Lightfoot.

'Hallo, old man!' I said. 'Congratulations in large quantities.'

'Thanks,' said the new dramatist. 'Have you seen it before?'

'No; but I saw in the papers that it was an "emphatic success." How beautiful Elsie Millar is in the part!'

We induced one of the personages behind the bar to notice that we were present, and removed our glasses to a table. Orlando sighed heavily.

'What's your trouble?' I inquired.

'My "emphatic success,"' he said. 'But it's too long a tale to tell you now – I suppose you want to see the second act?'

The vindictiveness with which he pronounced the last two words was startling. I stared at him. 'My dear Orlando –' I began, but he cut me short.

'Call me "Frankenstein"!' he groaned. 'Like Frankenstein, I've constructed a monster that's destroying me. Before I created this accursed comedy I was a happy man.'

'It must have been a very long while before,' I said. 'When I had the misfortune to share your rooms, you used to remark casually at breakfast that you wished you were dead.'

'Anyone is liable to express dissatisfaction in moments; but on the whole I was cheerful and buoyant, especially when you were out,' he insisted. 'I frequently had as much as five pounds at the time. I'm not boasting; you know it's true. Five pounds at the time is prosperity, if a fellow hasn't got a monster to support. Since I wrote the comedy, a five-pound note has been as ephemeral as a postage stamp. I pinched and pawned to start the monster in life. What it cost me in typewriting alone would have kept me for a month. It has gorged gold. It has devoured my All. And now, by a culminating stroke of diabolical malice, it's breaking my heart.'

'There's nearly a quarter of an hour before the act,' I said. 'Give me a cigarette and the story – I want one badly; an appreciative editor is eager to send a cheque.'

'Halves?' asked the author of the 'emphatic success.'

'Halves,' I agreed.

'Well,' said Orlando, 'the devil tempted me in the pit of the

Vaudeville one night. Elsie Millar was in the cast; she had very little to do, but, as usual, she did it exquisitely. I had always admired her, wished I knew her, and that night I thought, "By Jove, wouldn't I like to write a big part for her! Wouldn't she make a hit if she only got the chance!" I came out after the performance imagining her in the sort of part she's playing in the monster. A plot was beginning to put its head round the corner, and I wandered out of the Strand on to the Embankment trying to get hold of it. The Embankment was deserted, and the river –'

'Yes,' I said. 'Cut that kind of thing – I can put it in when I do the writing. I don't want to miss any of the second act.'

'Well, I went to bed about three o'clock with a plot that enraptured me. When I woke up and saw it in the daylight, it didn't look quite so fetching – as is the way of plots et cetera; still, it had good features, if it wasn't a Venus, and I curled its hair, and titivated it generally, till it was fascinating again. The dialogue was the most interesting work – especially the love scene; I enjoyed that. It was like making love to a nice girl myself, and saying the right things at the time instead of thinking of 'em afterwards. I ought to have been turning out stuff for the papers, but I let them slide, and at last the play was finished. It sounds as rapid as filling your pipe, told like this; when you do the story you should stress the alternate ups and downs of the business: the nights when I wrote epigrams and felt like Pinero, and the mornings when I read 'em and felt like cutting my throat. Don't forget that. It's real.'

'I'll remember,' I said. 'I'll have a paragraph on it.'

'Well, I had two copies of the thing typewritten at Miss Becks's, in Rupert Street; and pretty they were, tied up with pink bows – till I put in all the improvements I had thought of after I posted to her. The improvements I had thought of after I posted to her made such a mess of the copies that I had to have two more typewritten. However, I couldn't pretend she was dear, and I paid and looked pleasant. Guilelessly, I imagined my expenses were over.

'Sonny, they were just beginning! Miss Becks's bill was only the preface. A man who knew the ropes told me I should be a fool to have the scrip hawked about before it had been copyrighted. "How do you do it?" I said. "Oh," he said, "it's very easy. You give a private performance of the piece in a building licensed for public entertainments. There are a few details to be observed." When I grasped the details I knew I had committed a reckless extravagance in writing a play. I examined my belongings, and doubted if they would run to luxuries like this. Still I had constructed the monster, and it had its claims. I did my duty by it.

'I hired a hall in Walthamstow for an afternoon. I invented two columns of Fashions for Men to pay for the hall in Walthamstow. Whipping a tired brain, I invented them – and then they fetched eighteenpence short of the rent. I posted one of the nice, clean copies of the monster to the Lord Chamberlain to read. *I* didn't want him to read it – especially since I had learnt the compliment was to cost me guineas – but that was one of the "details to be observed." I had to pawn my watch for the Lord Chamberlain. And he didn't even send the nice clean copy back – he buried it in archives. More typewriting expenses! After that I had to have the parts typewritten. My dress clothes paid for the parts. Then I had to advertise for artists to read them. I got my "artists" cheap – a half-crown a head, but my watch-chain went after my watch, and the monster began to attack my library. "Any more 'details'?" I asked. "One or two," said the man; "you must have a couple of playbills printed, and don't forget to register your title." Well, I won't dwell on the drinks, but by the time I was through with the Walthamstow hall, and Stationers' Hall, the monster had left nothing in my wardrobe except a mackintosh, and had consumed a complete set of Thackeray bound in calf!'

Orlando groaned again, and I murmured sympathy. I also reminded him that the second act must be drawing near.

'All right!' he said testily. 'Listen. The monster was now my legal property – it was about the only property I did have now, but anyhow, the monster was mine. I was informed that an official licence for it would reach me in due course. Admire my next move! An average intellect might have been shattered by the sacrifices I had made for the beast; *I* was still brilliant. Did I send the thing to a theatre uninvited and wait six months to see it expelled? Not Orlando! I realized that I was an outsider. I realized that I needed someone to take me in. Elsie Millar was playing at the St James's then. She had never heard of me, but I wrote to her; I said I had written a comedy with her in my mind, and that I'd like her to read it before I offered it to a management.'

'What for?'

'"What for"? Because I thought she might be so enamoured of her part that she'd move mountains to get the piece produced.'

'My prolix friend,' I said, 'I perfectly understand your inward reason; but what was the reason you gave to the lady?'

'Oh!' said Orlando, 'I borrowed from a letter that I once knew an actress received from a full-blown dramatist; I wrote that I was "desirous of hearing whether she would care to play the part if an opportunity arose." Suggestive?'

'For an amateur who had never been through a stage-door it was consummate impudence,' I admitted. 'And she replied?'

'She replied that she would be pleased to read the piece if I sent it to her private address. It departed to her, registered, the same day. And I wish you wouldn't keep interrupting me! ... Well, a fortnight went by, a fortnight of suspense that I can't describe to you.'

'I don't want you to describe it!' I exclaimed. 'For heaven's sake, remember that the act 'll be starting directly. *I'll* describe your feelings when I write the story.'

'If you don't write it better than you listen to it, there's a poor show of a cheque,' he complained. 'I say a fortnight went by. Then she wrote that she had read my comedy and was "delighted with it." Look here! if you don't undertake not to speak another word till I've finished, I shan't tell you any more. Is it understood?'

I nodded. And for a spell Orlando had it all his own way.

'She wrote that she was "delighted with it," and asked me to call on her one day about half-past four. I could hardly believe my eyes. Really, it looked as if the monster's rancour had worn itself out. I felt tender towards the beast again, my affection revived. I said that it was like a monster in a fairy tale, transformed to a benevolent presence by the heroine. I thought that a pretty idea; I hoped I should get a chance to mention it to Miss Millar when I went.

'Of course, I meant to go the next afternoon – weather permitting – and I was so eager to see what sort of weather it was in the morning that I trembled when I pulled up the blind. Thank Heaven! it was raining. I breakfasted gratefully, and my only fear was that the sun might come out later on. Fortunately it didn't. The drizzle continued, and all was well. By your idiotic expression it's evident you've forgotten that the only decent garment remaining to me was a mackintosh. My suit was socially impossible; if it had been a fine day I couldn't have gone.

'She lives with her mother in a top flat in Chelsea. When I was shown in, she was alone. Her voice was just as sweet as it was on the stage. She isn't a bit like any other actress I've met; she talks rather slowly, and she's very quiet. Even when she enthused about the piece she spoke quietly.

'"I think it's beautiful," she said. "I'm glad I asked you to let me read it. I nearly didn't, because –"

'"Because you didn't know my name?" I said.

'"Well, yes," she said. "So many people write to one, and their pieces are generally so impossible. Is this your first, Mr Lightfoot?"

'"My first, and it has threatened to be my last," I said. "I've been copyrighting it, and the complications have nearly ruined me. I had begun to feel myself another Frankenstein with a monster – and then you turned the monster into a prince of light, like Beauty in the fairy tale."

'It didn't "go" so well as I had expected, but she smiled a little. "You'll let me give you some tea?" she said. "Won't you take off your mackintosh?"

'"No, thanks," I said; "it isn't very wet."

'Then we had tea and cake, and got a bit forrader. She said she wished she had a theatre to produce the thing, and *I* said *I* wished I had an agent to place it for me. She asked me if I'd like her to show it to Alexander, and *I* said the English language would be inadequate to express the gratitude I'd feel. Of course, I added, she mustn't do all that for nothing, and she said she'd find it reward enough to play the part. I said "Pickles!" then, quite naturally, because she was an exceedingly nice girl, and I liked her. I told her she should have any share of the fees she chose to ask for. "Oh, nonsense!" she said. "No, it isn't nonsense!" I said; "it's only fair." "Oh, well, then," she said, "if I get the piece done for you anywhere, you shall give me the usual agent's commission. Does *that* satisfy you?" We were talking quite chummily by this time. And I had another cup of tea.

'Before I went, her mother came in. Her mother didn't treat the commission so airily – her mother wanted the girl to have a contract. But that was all right; I put it on paper for her when I got home.

'There was nothing for me to see her about again for two or three months. I had heard from her that Alexander had no use for the piece, and that "Sir Charles Wyndham had promised to read it on Sunday." Then she wrote that she was going on tour – and I called to say "good-bye" to her. There wasn't a cloud in the heavens, and I was still dependent on the mackintosh, but it couldn't be helped. I stayed longer that time. I could have stayed to supper if it hadn't been for the mackintosh!

'Of course she went on working at the business while she was away, and she used to write me what she was doing about it. She was a regular trump, and I liked getting her letters and answering them, though the prospects never came to anything. At last she wrote that she was coming back – and I called to say "How do you do?" to her. It still hadn't run to a new suit, and – I attribute a great deal to that mackintosh! it curtailed all my visits, I haven't had a fair chance with the girl.

'I had never loved before – so quickly; I was fond of her already. I hope, when you write the story, you'll bring her charm out strong; you had better send the manuscript to me, and I'll put in some of the things she has said – loyal, womanly things, without any grease paint on 'em. As I sat there that afternoon, sweltering in the infernal mackintosh, I knew I'd like to marry her; I knew that if the comedy ever caught on, I'd try to make my agent my wife.

'Well, when a production looked as far off as Klondyke, there came this offer for the piece from Cameron, who had just taken the Throne. She was as excited about it as *I* was.

'"The Throne isn't quite the house I'd have chosen," she said, "but you'll get a beautiful cast; Cameron will take pains with the smallest detail, you'll be pleased with everything – Oh! I mustn't answer for your leading lady."

'I laughed. There was no need for me to tell her I had faith in my leading lady.

'"You *have* given me a chance!" she said. "It'll be the best part I ever played. If this engagement makes me, I shall owe it to *you*." There was one of the things without any grease paint on 'em. Wasn't it sweet? She'd have had every excuse for reminding me all the time what a service she had done me.

'We talked it over like pals. She said that, of course, Cameron would play the Colonel himself, and that he wanted to get Fairfax for the lover.

'"Who's Fairfax?" I said; "I don't know him. The lover is an important part — all that pretty scene of yours in the Orchard Act will go for nothing if your lover's not good."

'"Oh, Fairfax is a very clever young actor!" she said; "we've never played together, but he has just made a great hit at the Imperial; I saw him there; he was very good indeed."

'Well, things couldn't have looked more promising. Cameron was enthusiastic — he didn't pay any money on account, but he gave me a cigar — the percentage he agreed to was satisfactory, and the girl I loved considered me her benefactor. Making a discount for disappointment, I hoped for a hundred a week from the Throne; besides that, there'd be the provincial tours, and there were the American and Colonial rights. I had visions of a house in Sloane Street, and a motor car.

'Then the expenses began again. I couldn't attend daily rehearsals through August in the mackintosh, so I managed to raise a pony on the agreement. The interest was iniquitous, but I was bound to have decent clothes, and on the threshold of a fortune I didn't fuss. I went to a tailor, and I bought a two-guinea panama, and had eighteen pounds left.

'Fairfax turned out to be a plain young man with a big head, and I didn't think so much of his reading as Miss Millar seemed to do. However, he improved. She, of course, was divine, and Cameron was all right. On the whole I was satisfied with the rehearsals — dramatically; financially they were a shock. The luncheon adjournments upset my calculations. I always had to adjourn with Cameron — though I'd rather have taken Miss Millar — and Cameron lunched extensively. If a man stands you Bollinger one day, you can't offer him Bass the next. I had expected to enjoy the rehearsals, but the eighteen pounds were vanishing at such a rate that I thanked Providence when the last week came.

'Well, by dint of missing a rehearsal or two; I had contrived to cling to a fiver; and I shook hands with myself. I counted on it to keep me going till I got the first fees. Vain dream! They decided to "try the piece" in Worthing for three nights – and I had to pay fares and an hotel bill! Old chap, when I walked here to the Throne, on the night of the London production, I possessed one shilling – and that went on a drink for the acting manager. In the morning I hadn't the means to buy newspapers with the notices of my own play. Penniless, I read them in a public library among the Unemployed!

'Of course, the notices bucked me up. With an "emphatic success," I could smile at being stone-broke till the hundred a week came in. But it didn't come. The box-office sheets gave me the cold shivers when I saw them, and the queues at the pit and gallery doors were so short that the buskers gave up playing outside. The piece always went very well, but there was never any money in the house; the audience always looked very nice, but none of them had ever paid. They look very nice this evening, don't they? Paper! Paper in rows! Paper in reams!

'A hundred a week? By the first Saturday night I reckoned my week's royalties would about cover the cost of my Worthing trip! And *then* I was optimistic.

'Cameron sent for me; he said:

'"I'm afraid I must take this piece off at once."

'The dressing-room reeled. I muttered that the notices had been good.

'"It's more than the business is. Look at the booking!" he said.

'I hinted feebly that the best people hadn't come back to town yet.

'He said, "Well, I'll give it a chance to pick up if in the meantime you like to waive fees."

'I waived! I heard him in a kind of stupor ... "I've never had a bob!"

Orlando paused; his head drooped sadly. I ascertained that the barmaids weren't looking, and pressed his hand.

'It's hard lines,' I said. 'We must have another talk after the show. You won't mind my bolting now? The bell rang ever so long ago; the second act must be half over.'

'A curse upon the second act!' he burst out. 'Why did I ever write the second act? Don't see it!'

'But I must see it,' I urged. 'I want to see it. What's the matter with it?'

The dramatist was silent again; I saw that he was struggling with strong emotion. At last he said in a low voice:

'The rest of the story – so far as it has gone – is more painful still. Perhaps you suppose that, now it had stripped me of all and involved me in the meshes of a money-lender, the monster's malignity was appeased? Not so! Pecuniarily it could harm me no more, but through my affections I was still vulnerable; the monster's most insidious injury you've yet to hear.

'I noticed during the rehearsals that Fairfax was struck with Miss Millar; and lately Miss Millar has shown an unaccountable interest in the big-headed Fairfax. I call it "unaccountable" because Fairfax, in his proper person, can't be said to account for it. She's always saying how "tender he is in the part." The *part's* tender! I own the man can act, but *I* gave him the lines to speak! *I* invented the tender things for him to do. She doesn't remember that.

'Consider what happened when I wrote the piece! I imagined a charming girl in an orchard; I imagined myself in love with her. She had Elsie Millar's face; she answered me with Elsie Millar's voice. With all the tenderness, all the wit, all the fancy I could command I tried to make this charming girl fond of me. Materially, I was producing half a dozen pages of dialogue; psychologically, I was lending my own character to any man who played the lover's part.

'It fell to Fairfax – and it's all "Fairfax" with her. Oh, she has been very sympathetic about my failure, we're still friends, but – there's another man now! She talks more of his performance than of my comedy. It's natural, I suppose – she understands his work better than mine – but I detest the second act; you shan't see the second act, the second act's the other man's glamour to her! She's falling in love with the part, and thinks it's with him. The monster gave him his opportunity – and *he's stealing her from me with my own words!*"

'Talk to her as you've talked to me,' I said, 'and hope still.'

'I can't help hoping,' he answered, 'but –'

An attendant entered the buffet with a note: 'Mr Lightfoot, sir?'

Orlando tore it open – and passed it to me mutely. I read:

'DEAR MR LIGHTFOOT – I hear you are in front to-night. I've been waiting to tell you something all the week. Mr Fairfax and I are engaged to be married – and we owe our happiness to your play. Will you come round afterwards to let us thank you? – Yours always sincerely, ELSIE MILLAR.'

'Poor devil!' I exclaimed ... 'Well, the monster has finished with you now, at any rate! You know that you're disappointed in love, and you know that the last of the expenses is over.'

'Y-e-s,' he said ... 'You think your editor *will* send a cheque for the story?'

'In overdue course,' I told him. 'Why?'

'Well,' he moaned, 'how am I to find the money to buy her a wedding present?'

# The Composite Brain

## By ROBERT S. CARR

*There is a special association between the writer of this next story and his theme. For Robert Spencer Carr (1909–1984) began his working life in a biological research laboratory before literary success lured him to Hollywood and a very lucrative career as a screenwriter for Walt Disney and several of the other major film studios. Robert was the younger brother of John Dickson Carr, the famous American writer of 'impossible crime' novels, and shared with him a love of sensational fiction. The younger Carr was only fifteen when he sold his first horror story to the legendary pulp magazine, Weird Tales; and thanks to the editor, Farnsworth Wright, not only received encouragement but also guidance on the manuscript of his first novel, The Rampant Age (1928). This powerful story about rebellious youngsters at high school predated the famous James Dean movie on the same theme, Rebel Without A Cause, by almost a quarter of a century. The success of Carr's book – which he gratefully dedicated to Farnsworth Wright – led to his becoming a full-time novelist, writer for the Saturday Evening Post and the Blue Book, and to his screen contracts.*

*Robert Carr later admitted that Frankenstein had been one of the books which had fired his initial enthusiasm to write horror stories like Spider Bite, Soul Catcher and Phantom Fingers for Weird Tales between 1925 and 1927. Indeed, he was still younger than Mary Shelley when he wrote The Composite Brain in which the influence of her novel, as well as his work on biological research, will quickly become apparent to the reader ...*

Professor Hurley leaned forward tensely and added a drop of a sparkling red liquid to the jelly-like grey mass in the jar before him. He placed the tips of his long white fingers together and narrowed his eyes to mere slits, while his high, pale, intellectual brow wrinkled in a slight frown as he mused.

His repose was interrupted by the entrance of Leroy, the young student who was studying under him.

'Sorry to bother you, professor, but I wanted to finish that plating test I started this morning.'

Leroy eyed the jar on the professor's desk.

'New experiment?' he inquired, lifting his eyebrows quizzically.

'Yes, it is,' said the professor. 'Sit down, I want to talk to you.'

There was a moment of silence as Leroy drew up a chair. Then the professor spoke.

'Leroy, do you believe it possible to make living protoplasm?'

The young man smiled.

'Well, I don't believe it is impossible, but so far no one has done it.'

'Suppose someone were to do it. Would that not be wonderful?'

'In the abstract, yes, but I fail to see where it would affect anybody or anything, save the fame of its discoverer. A mass of simple protoplasm would be useless.'

'But not if made up into tissues!'

'Now you are talking fantasies, professor, for you know that protoplasm is but the filling, as one might say, of a cell, and must be surrounded by a cell wall and contain a nucleus before it is really active.'

'Suppose we could eliminate the nucleus and supply the cell wall; then should we not have living cells to build muscles and tissues with?'

'But would it be possible to do away with the nucleus and to make a cell wall?'

'The mesoglea of a sponge is living tissue, and yet it has no nucleus. You know that such a simple thing as a cell wall *could* be created.'

'Exactly what is the point of all this questioning, professor?'

'Only this, Leroy,' said the old scientist, leaning eagerly forward with a strange light burning in his pale grey eyes: 'in this jar is living protoplasm! Before the night is over it will have formed itself into cells, un-nucleated, imperfect and weak, to be sure, but living cells, nevertheless, which, with proper care, can be developed into living flesh!'

For a moment complete silence reigned in the great laboratory. The last rays of the afternoon sun shone through the tall, barred windows in long, slanting, golden beams, accentuating the gloom within and bringing out the figures of the two men in startling relief. At last Leroy gasped:

'Living flesh? Why, professor, surely that is impossible! The evolution of the single cell to the complex tissue took millions of years!'

'See this?'

The professor took from a drawer the bottle of red liquid he had been using.

'This greatly hastens the development of the protoplasm. Within two weeks we shall have workable tissue, but of course there are many complicated procedures we must go through which will involve some time, but I believe eventually we shall be able to say that we have *chemically created a living organism!*'

'How?' asked the young student, excitely.

'Leroy,' said Professor Hurley, slowly, leaning back in his chair and shaking his head thoughtfully, 'men have not yet devised words that can adequately describe what has been revealed to me. By working with me on this discovery, you may learn, but it is too stupendous for mere words. It is the *secret of life itself!* Using chemically constructed tissue as a base, and grafting various organs into it, the possibilities are unlimited.'

He took a bit of the grey, semi-transparent substance from the jar and placed it on a microscope slide. The two men bent their heads over the instrument and conversed in low, earnest tones until far into the night.

More than three years later, James Hurley, Professor Hurley's nephew, returning from abroad, bounded up the steps to his uncle's home. The old family servant greeted him at the door and took him to the laboratory where the professor and Leroy were working.

The young man rushed in to greet the kindly old uncle he had known a few years before, but drew back aghast at the white-haired, deathly pale old man with deep-set, burning eyes, who confronted him.

'Why, uncle, have you been sick?' he exclaimed.

'No,' replied the old professor in hollow tones. 'just working hard on a big experiment.'

'You've been working too hard, I'm afraid. What is the experiment?'

'Come with me and I shall show you.'

Leroy led the way down into the basement of the big house. He switched on the light and touched a concealed button. A portion of the wall slid slowly and silently back, revealing a dark and sinister-looking cell, or rather pit, for its floor was some eight or ten feet below that of the cellar.

As the three men lined up at the brink, the professor turned on a strong light in the roof of the cell, which illuminated the interior brightly. His nephew gave an exclamation of horror, for there, in the centre of the floor of the foul, sweaty pit, was the product of the two scientists' work.

It lay a shapeless mass, clothed in matted, jet-black hair, the kind of hair one sees on sewer spiders. Along the lower parts of its sides protruded two rows of the blotched, grey-green tentacles of the octopus, which dragged limply as the thing rolled slightly on its four short stubby legs.

The face on the stocky, low-hung protuberance that was its head, was a repulsive, hairy mask in which two lidless eyes rolled slowly and hideously from side to side. There was no sign of a nose, while a great, gaping mouth with formidable fangs occupied the entire lower quarter of its face. Its most startling feature was the pair of naked human arms that protruded from either side of its forward half. Occasionally a low sucking sound escaped it, as it lay in its slime and water like some ancient monster in a subterranean cavern.

For several minutes the men stood silently. Then the professor's nephew burst out:

'Great God! that's a horrible thing! Where did it come from?'

'We made it,' replied his uncle.

'Made it?'

'Yes,' said the professor. 'Several years ago I stumbled upon the secret of making living protoplasm. After a great deal of experimenting, I was able to build up simple flesh, not the complex, nerve-filled flesh you know, but a flesh that contains only a few nerves and the very simplest circulatory system possible. Using this as a base, I grafted various parts of various animals on to it. The creature was constructed exactly as you would build a house, using only what you want and selecting only the sturdiest and most essential things. Lying there it requires but little nourishment, as it moves but seldom. Its heart, transferred alive from a bull, beats about twice a minute when the beast is not active, but is strong enough to force the blood all over its body.'

James' horror had by this time lessened enough for him to become interested. 'But, uncle,' he inquired, 'how could you get one kind of blood to nourish organs from different animals?'

'That was simple. I prepared a saline solution that was adaptable to all and was even more life-sustaining than blood, although it requires a stronger heart to pump it. The beef heart in there is the best and strongest that could possibly be obtained.'

James looked again at the human arms, showing dead-white against the black hair of the creature, and shuddered to think of the lengths to which his uncle might have gone. The professor continued:

'The simple but efficient digestive system is the best I could construct, and it is protected from injury by a sheathing of strong cartilage. The idea of using the tentacles of an octopus was Leroy's. They are singularly efficient,' he added with an evil smile.

'The jaws and teeth are from a monster bulldog, as is also the fore part of the skull. A clever little thought of mine was to graft the poison sacs, ducts and fangs of a huge swamp rattlesnake into the jaws of the living dog, after filling the sacs with a poison of my own manufacture. It is an albuminous poison much the same as the natural venom of the snake, but with much different effect. It paralyses its victim completely until the antidote is applied, and it has no bad after-effects. As to those arms you eye so fearfully: a late-walking pedestrian obligingly stepped in front of my auto one night in a dark little side street, so I brought him along.'

James looked at his uncle askance.

'As I said before,' he went on, 'there is no highly complicated circulatory or nervous system, but only the trunk nerves
to carry the message from the brain to the muscle. There are
but few blood vessels. Because of this fact, and because the
beast is made up mostly of the lower animals, it has practically
no feeling. I could pump a hatful of bullets out of this
automatic into it with very little effect. Of course, if one of
the trunk nerves or a leader were severed, that part alone
would stop functioning; but since there is only one nerve for
each part, and those nerves are well covered and protected,
you would almost have to chop the creature to bits with an
axe before he would die. The sluggish circulation prevents
rapid bleeding to death.

'Yes, the body is cleverly enough constructed, but the brain
is my masterpiece. Since only the arms of a human being were
used, only that part of a human brain that governs the arms
was put into my composite brain. So it is with the octopus'
tentacles: only the portion of an octopus' brain that controls
its tentacles was used.

'Practically all of the bulldog's brain was left in, so the
creature has nearly all of the simple instincts of a bulldog,
such as use of its jaws, fighting, and avoiding objects when it
walks. All of the native pugnacity of a bulldog is present.

'But the most important thing of all is: *this composite brain
is controlled by my own*! When I transmit the thought of
the action of walking, the beast's brain reacts. When I
think killing, it fights with almost inconceivable ferocity and
abandon. Remember, I think the action, not the word; in
fact, it is nothing more nor less than an extremely simple
form of hypnotism, so simple that it is practically thought-
transference, for I have no personality to overcome. I have so
trained myself that I can direct the thing almost as well as my
own body. I will give you a little demonstration.'

The professor stood quietly and gazed fixedly at it. Under his
direction, it went through various gyrations, snapped its jaws,
rolled over, and at length began to climb the opposite wall of
the pit.

With a slowness more horrible than speed, it progressed
straight up, the tentacles making uncanny little noises on the

sweaty walls, while the naked hands in front clutched frantically at little cracks and projections.

Now the thing halted and hung, like a huge spider, directly opposite them. James could see that under the fingernails of the hands the flesh was dead-white, and he knew, without touching the grafted arms, that they were cold with the clammy, creepy cold of a week-old corpse.

The professor's voice broke the silence:

'To show you how complete my power is, I will give the command "relax".'

He looked at the hanging body. All holds let go simultaneously and it fell with a terrific thud to the bottom of the pit, where it lay limply, as if dead.

'Now watch!'

Again the professor directed his thought waves at the inert mass. As if touched by a galvanic battery it sprang into action. The professor's nephew realized how immensely powerful the misshapen thing was as it lumbered rapidly about the pit. As it passed beneath him he could see the great thews rolling under the tough hide.

'Could anyone's brain direct it?' he asked.

'Yes, with simple thoughts such as "relax," "move forward" or "kill". Another extremely important fact is that I can detect its mental reactions, or, to use the term broadly, read its mind. Of course, its mental processes are very few and simple; in fact, the word "impression" describes them better than "thought". They are very elemental and embrace such subjects as extreme heat or cold, great hunger, and a kind of confusion, met with when the beast encounters a blank wall or an abrupt drop. In this way I can direct it even when it is out of my sight.

'Do not get the impression that it is unconscious except when under the direction of thought waves. It occasionally crawls about in the pit and will fight anything, any time, for the mere pleasure of killing, sometimes coupled with hunger ... I wonder what it is thinking about at present?'

A moment's silence, then he said: 'The brain registers the impression "very hungry".'

The professor spoke the last words with peculiar emphasis. James shot a sidelong glance at his uncle, and started when he saw the wild light of sheer insanity gleaming in his eyes ...

His uncle made a move towards him, and James took a step backwards ... The old scientist stopped and made a horrible grimace, which was intended for a smile but failed of its purpose. He resumed his subject:

'You see what a powerful engine of destruction I have here. With it' (the light of insanity glowed from his cadaverous eyes once more) 'I can do anything I will. I am all-powerful, I can kill whom I wish, I can depopulate the earth!'

He shrieked out the last words in a frenzy. Then his manner changed suddenly.

'Come,' he said, beckoning with a clawlike finger, 'come here. My secret is not safe with you. You belong down there.'

He pointed down into the pit. Suddenly he leapt forward and grasped James by the arm. James looked at him dumbly a moment before he fully realized the significance of the movement.

With a scream he tried to break away, but his uncle held him with the rigid grip of a madman, and drew him closer to the pit. Again he screamed and struggled nearly out of the professor's hold. Leroy leapt forward suddenly; there was a short scuffle at the brink, and with another horrible scream James pitched forward into the pit.

The two men stepped back. Leroy touched the button that operated the door; the heavy slab slid in place; and the insane scientists smiled at each other as the muffled screams below ceased abruptly.

'Bulldog instincts working,' remarked the elder, calmly.

'Professor,' said Leroy after they had once more seated themselves in the laboratory, 'don't you think that the addition of a portion of a good human brain to our beast's headpiece would render him more efficient?'

'Yes, I had thought of that, but where can we obtain a live man to get a brain from? The man from whom we obtained the arms was only knocked unconscious, luckily, but occasions like that are rare and that young fool, James, is in shreds by now. What a pity we didn't think of it then!'

'Well, I don't think that fellow was much of an intellectual giant, anyhow; we want the most highly developed brain we can get.'

Professor Hurley was silent a moment. Then:

'I know the very brain we want,' he said, 'and it happens that I have a personal score to settle with this man. You know Dr Forrester of the university? He was the cause of my removal from the chair of surgery some years ago, and I swore vengeance. It would be my moment of triumph to have him in my power and let him know that I intend to use his brain in an experiment of mine.'

'But how shall we lure him here?'

'I have a plan in which we can utilize our tentacled little friend down there in the pit to good advantage.'

'Let's hear it.'

Within an hour the two madmen had formulated their plans.

The far-off university tower clock faintly tolled the hour of midnight, as in the basement of the laboratory the professor and Leroy finished feeding their hideous ward a generous amount of a nourishing, gruel-like mixture. This done, the professor mentally directed it up the steps and out on the driveway, where their machine waited.

The springs creaked as the misshapen monster clambered in and lay on the floor in the rear of the car. A blanket was flung over it; the two men got in; and the automobile plunged off into the night.

Fifteen minutes later it coasted to a silent halt in front of Dr Forrester's elm-shaded residence. The professor pointed to an open window near the corner of the house, on the second floor.

'That is where our man sleeps. Now watch our little friend get him.'

So saying, he seated himself on the running board and began the task of mentally piloting the creature.

Under his direction it lumbered across the lawn, reached the house and began the long climb up the water spout and vines. Once it sprang into sharp silhouette in a splash of moonlight, only to blend back into the shadows again when the moonlight dimmed, as if to blot out a sight that was unpleasant in the eyes of God.

At last it swung itself to the window-ledge of the doctor's room, and Professor Hurley breathed a sigh of relief as the creature disappeared inside.

'Bulldog instincts will do the rest, though I had better direct it to bite and not to kill, or our brain will not be alive when we get it,' he said with a low chuckle.

Dr Forrester awoke from uneasy dreams at the gentle shaking of his bed. He rolled over and opened his eyes, then sat bolt upright as his startled eyes fell upon the hideous thing that was slowly creeping over the foot of his bed.

Absolutely paralysed by terror, unable to make a sound, he sat rigid until a slimy tentacle brushed against his naked forearm. Then he bounded out of bed, still soundless, seized a chair and struck a savage blow at the horror now lying on his bed. The blow rebounded as if he had struck a resilient piece of rubber. Under a shower of blows the beast slid off on to the floor and backed the doctor into a corner, where the still soundless man fought frantically against the foul-smelling, clammy embrace until the paralysing effect of the poison brought merciful unconsciousness.

Scarcely had Professor Hurley withdrawn the needle of the hypodermic syringe that administered the antidote, than the mists of oblivion began to lift from the young doctor's brain.

He found himself bound to a post in an underground laboratory, where Leroy and the professor were busily engaged in preparing an operating table. As his eyes swept the room, they fell upon the shapeless mass of the thing. A shudder of horror shook his body as he gazed upon the handiwork of his captors. His observations were interrupted by the voice of the professor, taunting him.

His old enemy came and stood before him, laughed at him, tantalized him, tortured him, showered him with curses as he stormed and raged before his captive. He dwelt on his fancied wrongs, told him how and why he had brought him there, and screamed his vengeance until he fell back into his chair exhausted, a suggestion of foam about the corners of his mouth.

During the long silence that ensued, Dr Forrester looked again at the black-furred huddle in the corner. Something in its absolutely inert appearance fascinated him. He wished that it would make a movement of some kind, rather than sprawl so limply on the floor.

He looked again at the elaborate preparations being made so that his brain might be alive to be put into that frightful thing. The fast-crumbling throne of sanity in his head tottered and nearly fell. Oh! if that beast would only move. If that single tentacle would only move an inch, what a relief it would be! He fairly shrieked it mentally.

To his surprise it did move. A moment later he wished it would open its mouth. It did. Then the swaying throne of reason in his brain became steady, and for the next thirty seconds his brain spun in one of those lightning-like thought processes that sometimes come to men in the face of death.

His eyes glowing, he mentally commanded the thing to flex the arms that hung limply at its sides. They flexed, then, at his order, unflexed. He looked at the operating table ... The professor was pouring ether on an anaesthetizing cone ... He looked back at the thing ... It was a desperate chance, but he must take it.

Slowly, and with beads of perspiration standing on his forehead, he urged the creature noiselessly across the floor towards the professor.

As it crouched behind the old man, the captive closed his eyes and directed all his faculties on the mental command of 'kill'.

There was an instant of scuffling, a piercing shriek, and the doctor opened his eyes to see his enemy borne to the floor by the weight of his attacker.

Somewhere in that bit of grafted bulldog brain had lain dormant the little group of cells that snap when the dog goes mad and attacks his master. This instinct took full possession of the huge body and the results were horrible to see.

The doctor closed his eyes again. When the sounds of the struggle ceased he reopened them and saw the thing sprawling motionless over what had been Professor Hurley.

He glanced at Leroy, who had stood motionless during the grim tragedy.

'Cut these ropes quickly, or I'll send that creature at you!' he commanded.

Like one in a trance, and keeping his eyes steadfastly fixed upon the thing, the student obeyed.

Freed, Dr Forrester strode across the room, where he halted abruptly at the sight of a wicked automatic lying on the desk. Slowly he picked it up. He shot a sidelong glance at Leroy, still staring dumbly at the repulsive sight before him. He deliberated a moment; would it not be best to erase all evidences of such a travesty of nature? Suddenly he stepped forward and emptied the contents of the gun pointblank into Leroy's body. Without a sound the youth crumpled to the floor, his fast-glazing eyes still fixed upon the thing.

A short search in an adjoining room brought to light a large can of kerosene. Dr Forrester dashed it over the furniture and shelves, saturated the clothing of the corpses with it, ignited it in several places, locked the door to the underground laboratory, where the thing still lay, and fled from the house.

Many blocks away, on the university hill that overlooked the town, he glanced back and smiled grimly at the ruddy glow in the distance that marked the funeral pyre of so awful a secret. The old building was blazing fiercely.

# Demons of the
# Film Colony

## By THEODORE LEBERTHON

Weird Tales *was only one of the American horror pulp
magazines of the Twenties and Thirties which published short
stories inspired by the* Frankenstein *theme. Inside the gaudy
covers of pulps such as* Strange Stories, Terror Tales, Astounding *and* Fantastic – *with their ravening monsters and terrified,
nearly naked girls – could be found a plethora of yarns about
mad scientists trying to create life of one sort or another and
amateur experimenters building robots or artificial men and
women. Some of these like* Frankenstein's Twenty Cousins *by
R.S. Lerch (*Strange Mysteries, *January 1940) and* Test-Tube
Frankenstein *by Wayne Robbins (*Terror Tales, *May 1940),
capitalised on the allure of the name but actually had little to
do with either Frankenstein or his creature. While others such
as* The Extraordinary Experiment of Dr Calgroni *by Joseph
Faus and James Bennett Wooding (in the very first issue of*
Weird Tales, *March 1923),* Doctor Grant's Experiment *by
H.A. Noureddin Addis (*Strange Stories, *October 1929) and* A
Madman's Experiment *by Jack Andrews (*Terror Tales, *February 1939) were almost all derivative, repetitive and generally
abysmally written. There was the imaginative exception or
two, of course, especially after Hollywood had produced the
first great* Frankenstein *movie with Boris Karloff in 1931. The
success of this now classic film not only excited the imagination of the world's cinema-goers to the appeal of horror
pictures, but demonstrated to readers and writers just some of
the potential uses to which the theme could be put. This fact
has, indeed, continued to be developed ever since.*

Demons of the Film Colony *by Theodore LeBerthon*

*(1898–1975) is perhaps the best and certainly the most unusual
short story to be found in the horror pulps, which draws on
the* Frankenstein *legend in general and Boris Karloff's role
in particular. LeBerthon, a Hollywood journalist, screenwriter
and author, published the story in the October 1932 issue of*
Weird Tales *and remained silent for the rest of his life as to
just how much of it was fact and what was fiction. It also
undoubtedly serves as an appropriate bridge to Part II of this
book which features the most outstanding of the variations of
Mary Shelley's tale on stage and screen ...*

For ten years I have been writing stories about the activities of
the motion picture colony for what are known as the 'fan'
magazines; and, in strict justice to the movie people in and
about Hollywood, I never before had an experience such as
the one that befell me recently – for there is nothing weird,
preternatural or otherwise affrighting about most motion
picture people, from the child Jackie Cooper to the more
elderly Marie Dressler. There have been, it is true, curious
legends about Greta Garbo, but she stays away from interview-
ers. Whatever her secret, she keeps it.

Obviously, I could not relate the experience I had in the
pages of a 'fan' magazine. The readers of these magazines are
too accustomed to sunshine to relish shadows. So I decided to
submit to the readers of WEIRD TALES the ghastly details of
the gigantic hoax perpetrated on me by Bela Lugosi, star of
the films *Dracula* and *Murders in the Rue Morgue*, and Boris
Karloff, who played the monster in the film *Frankenstein*.

Candidly, for reasons which the reader may surmise before
he finishes reading. I have hesitated considerably about writing
of just what happened, but now I feel I should make what
happened public.

I was just leaving Universal City one rainy, dreary morning
when John Le Roy Johnstone, Universal publicity director,
called to me:

'Ted, don't go away. I just happened to think that our two

demons, "Dracula" Lugosi and "Frankenstein" Karloff, are coming here in a few minutes. A demons' rendezvous ought to interest you. I might add that they're hastening here from opposite directions, to meet for the first time. They actually have never met. You see, *Dracula* and *Murders in the Rue Morgue*, in which Lugosi starred, were made here at different times than *Frankenstein*, in which Karloff played the ghastly, man-made monster. And that's why they've never met professionally. Nor have they ever met socially, although both have been in Hollywood, on and off, for several years. But you know the film colony. All split up into little groups and circles.'

I didn't mind sticking around. For one thing, a murky drizzle had begun to fall outside. The mammoth Universal stages, seen through a window, seemed, in the greyness, to be enormous squat tombs, unadorned sarcophagi in which giants five hundred feet tall, stretched in death, could be laid. It might not be a bad idea, I concluded, to wait around a little, if only to give the rain a chance to stop.

'Doggoned if it isn't just the kind of a morning for a couple of monsters to meet,' laughed Johnstone. 'And do you know something, I've a queer hunch something funny'll happen when they meet. Not that there's any professional rivalry between them in the demon field, as far as I know; but there's been a lot of banter going around the studio about the weird possibilities, you know, the things that could happen, when Dracula meets the Frankenstein monster! Candidly, I wouldn't be surprised if they try to frame each other.'

'What do you mean?' I chuckled nervously.

'Well,' he countered, 'it's natural that this meeting should strike them both as funny. And you know what actors are for pulling gags on each other.'

The rain, increasing, muttered against the ground outside.

Boris Karloff was first to arrive – and, fantastically enough, in evening clothes, worn under a rain-flecked overcoat which he tossed off with a mischievous, almost boyish fling.

We were introduced. And I learned, from his accent, then from his admission, that his name is not Karloff, but that he is an Englishman with a most unfortunate name. But we won't go into that.

He is slender, debonair, graceful, with powerful shoulders and large strong hands, smooth iron-grey hair, darkly tanned skin, and lucent, deep-set brown eyes. A witty, casual, well-bred fellow, with one of those strong-boned, hollow-cheeked countenances that seems carved out of hickory, and is characteristic of so many well-travelled, weather-beaten, distinguished-appearing Britishers.

He joked waggishly, this Englishman from God knows where, whose name is *not* Karloff, about his coming meeting with Bela Lugosi.

As he was talking, and Johnstone and I were absorbed in his high spirits, the door leading to the studio outside evidently opened. No one saw it open. In fact, we did not see anything until Karloff, who faced the door as he chatted with us, suddenly looked up and asseverated startlingly, 'Oh my God!'

Johnstone and I looked around and I don't know what he thought or felt. I do know I became visibly disconcerted, to put it lightly.

There stood Lugosi, filling the doorway, quiet as death, and smiling in his curiously knowing way. It is the smile of a tall, weary, haunted aristocrat, a person of perhaps fallen greatness, a secretive Lucifer who sees too clearly and knows too much, and perhaps wishes it were not so, and would like to be a gracious chap. He, too, was in evening clothes – on a rainy morning! He advanced with a soft, springy tread.

Karloff stood up as if galvanized by some sudden irrevocable plan of action. Then he turned on the advancing Lugosi a cold, unbelieving stare that would have riveted another man in his tracks. But the tall, tapering-fingered Hungarian, drawing himself erect, continued to smile with unmistakably ghastly knowingness.

It was Lugosi's hand which was thrust forward first.

As they shook hands they seemed to lock horns with their eyes. Only for a moment, however; for both broke into ear-to-ear grins.

'I hope I didn't scare you to death,' Lugosi smiled, narrowing his eyes, and seeming to look right through the quondam monster.

'I hope I didn't scare *you*,' parried Karloff mirthfully.

I could not be certain, but I thought Lugosi bristled, as if his demoniacal prowess had been challenged by a tyro in demonism.

Finally he said slowly:

'I think I could scare you to death.'

Karloff struck a match, lit a cigarette, puffed a couple of times, and retorted with an air of whimsical scorn:

'I not only think I can scare your ears right off, Mr Dracula, I'll bet you that I can.'

Within the next few minutes a wager of a hundred dollars had been made. They would go onto a deserted set, within one of the vast, empty, tomb-like stages squatting in the rain outside. No lights would be turned on. They would tell each other stories – such stories of darkness, terror and madness that one or the other would either faint or cry out for the other to stop. The other would then be pronounced victor.

Publicist Johnstone, grinning a bit unconvincingly, as if he were somehow ill, protested:

'There should be a referee. You go along, LeBerthon, and decide which one out-scares the other. And, I'll tell you what. Take Ray Jones, the photographer, along. He can get incontrovertible evidence.'

'I don't want to oppose your wishes,' put in Lugosi, his eyes widening like wrathful alarm signals, 'but I would rather be alone with Mr Karloff. You won't need any evidence. All you may need is a doctor, a nerve and heart specialist. You see, only one of us will walk off that stage. The other will be ... er ... carried off.'

He said this with some heat, yet with a growing twinkle in eyes which gradually narrowed again. But Johnstone was obdurate.

And so, two tall actors in evening clothes, a photographer, and a writer walked with bowed heads and hunched shoulders in the rain to reach the stage building with its unfortunate resemblance, for me, to a colossal sepulchre.

We entered a small door in the side, nearly tripping over cables that coiled like lifeless serpents about the floor in the dank, dusky atmosphere. Photographer Jones lit a match. We found our way to a set where, among other articles of furniture, there was a davenport. It was then agreed that

Jones could take photographs if he and I would stand twenty-five feet away in a dark corner, and if he would use only noiseless flash powder.

The tall actors in evening clothes sat on the davenport. In the obscure gloom we scarcely could discern their figures. But soon we were to hear a mournful voice, Lugosi's.

'Boris,' he began, in a gloating sonority, 'what would you say if this set, this stage, this studio, suddenly vanished, and you found that in reality you and I were sitting at the bottom of a pit? Ha! That would be inconvenient for you, wouldn't it? But of course I might provide some charming company – I might drag down into this pit an exquisite young woman. And I should indulge in a curious experiment that would cause your hair to turn white – and your stomach to turn inside out.

'Boris,' he went on in a ghoulish, sickeningly exultant tone, 'women are thrilled by Dracula, the suave one. Women love the horrible, the creepy, more than men. Why does a woman always tell the story of her husband's death so often and with such relish? Why does she go to cemeteries? Tenderness? Grief? Bah! It's because she likes to be hurt, tortured, terrified! Yes, Boris! Ah, Boris, to win a woman, take her with you to see *Dracula*, the movie. As she sees me, the bat-like vampire, swoop through an open casement into some girl's boudoir, there to sink teeth into neck and drink blood, she will thrill through every nerve and fibre. That is your cue to draw close to her, Boris. When she is limp as a rag, take her where you will, do with her what you will. Ah, especially, Boris, bite her on the neck!

'The love-bite, it is the beginning. In the end, you too, Boris, will become a vampire. You will live five hundred years. You will sleep in mouldy graves at night, and make fiendish love to beauties by day. You will see generations live and die. You will see a girl baby born to some woman, and wait a mere sixteen to eighteen years for her to grow up, so that you can sink fangs into a soft white neck and drink a scarlet stream. You will be irresistible, for you will have in your powerful body the very heat of hell, the virility of Satan. And some day, of course, you will be discovered – a knife, after long centuries, will be plunged into you, you will groan like a dying wolf, and you will drop like a plummet into the bottomless sulphurous pit. Yes, Boris, that's the end – for you! For us! For, look at me, Boris ...'

'Ha! Ha! Ha! You fool, Bela,' came Karloff's scornful, pealing laugh in the darkness, 'why try that kindergarten stuff on me? You ask me to look at you, Bela. Well, look at me! Look ... look ... look ... and take an occasional glance upward, Bela. These two hands of mine, clenched together above my head, could descend at any moment, in a second, ay, even before I finish this sentence, if I wanted them to, and they'd bash your distinguished head in as if it were an egg. Your brains would run out like the yolk of an egg, and spatter your pretty tuxedo.

'Bela, a monster created by Frankenstein is not worried by your stories of sucking blood from beauties' necks. But did *you* see the movie *Frankenstein*, Bela? Did you see *me* take an innocent little girl, a child playing among flowers, and drown her? Some sentimentalists said I did it unknowingly. Bosh! I have done it a thousand times, and will do it a thousand times, again. Bela, it's dark in here, but you know me. You know it was no accident or chance, but significant, that I – the Englishman from God knows where whose name is *not* Karloff – was called upon to play that monstrous role! You know me, Bela, you know me. Why that bosh about five hundred years old? You know that both of us are nearly six thousand years old! And that we've met many times before, the last time not more than two hundred years ago ... And you shouldn't have made that foolish wager. Admit it, Bela!' Karloff's voice shook with deep agitation.

'I wonder,' came Lugosi's reply, dreary as a fog-horn in the semi-darkness.

In the meantime, Photographer Jones in his convenient corner kept snapping pictures. The noiseless powder recurrently rose in puffs, so that – spookily enough – the scene resembled the laboratory of a mediæval alchemist.

'Come, Bela – let's go. Er ... Jones, LeBerthon,' Karloff shouted hoarsely, 'are you ready to go? Bela and I have found we're members of the same – well, suppose we say lodge. We're therefore, quite unable to scare each other to death, for reasons you might not understand, even to oblige you. You'll just have to call it a draw.'

'All right, we're ready to go,' responded Jones, nervously

enough for that matter. 'And – say – I've used up my last match. Will one of you fellows strike one?'

I shall never know whether it was Lugosi or Karloff who struck the match. All I do know is that when the match was struck it apparently revealed, not Lugosi and Karloff on that davenport, but two slimy, scaly monsters, dragon-like serpents, with blood-red, venomous eyes. The apparitional things flashed before me so suddenly that I became sick to my stomach and made a rush, on buckling legs, for the exit – and the cool air.

Just as I reached it and noted fleetingly that the rain had stopped, and that my heart was pounding to the bursting-point, and that I was strangely weak and giddy, Jones and the two tall actors in evening clothes came through the door. Jones was rather sober and unconcerned, but Lugosi and Karloff were laughing heartily over something or other.

'Will you have lunch with us?' Lugosi asked me, still grinning but with something of a physician's tender concern.

'No, thank you,' I replied, scarcely looking either at him or Karloff, 'I have to hurry away.'

And I did hurry away.

I am, of course, now convinced that what happened was their idea of a practical joke, that the slimy, scaly things I had seen, the things which had so frightened and sickened me in that fleeting moment, were either the imaginings of my over-wrought nerves – or some mechanically contrived illusions in which Jones had some share.

There are, of course, some who will wonder if I do not merely prefer this simple, comforting explanation to one that might cause Hollywood hostesses to fear to invite Lugosi and Karloff to social functions – and fear not to invite them!

Many people, deep down, still are superstitious. And there are many things in life we do not fully understand, such as why it is the destiny of certain human beings to portray certain roles – whether in real or 'reel' life.

# II
# *The Films*

# Frankenstein;
# or, The Man and the Monster!

## By H. M. MILNER

Less than five years after its publication, Frankenstein made
its first move into a new medium: the theatre. It was to prove
the first of several transitions – for, in time, the story would
also be adapted for the cinema, the radio and television.
Sadly, it was only this theatrical version of her book that
Mary Shelley lived to see and it had, of necessity, to be
considerably altered from the original to meet the demands of
the stage. Mary was, in fact, in Paris when she heard of these
plans, as a letter to her friend, the poet and essayist, Leigh
Hunt, dated August 14, 1823, indicates: 'I have just had a visit
from Horace Smith who does not know much English news,
except that they brought out Frankenstein at the Lyceum and
vivified the monster in such a manner as caused the ladies to
faint away and a hubbub to ensue – however, they diminished
the horrors in the sequel and it is having a run.'

Such a sensational début – not to mention a dramatic finale
in which the monster plunged into a volcano – no doubt
brought the public flocking in to see the play; at the same
time inaugurating a tradition that has come to be associated
with many later dramatisations. It was not until the end of
the month, however, that Mary was back in London and able
to see a performance for herself on the evening of Friday,
August 29. The wait had been worthwhile, for as she again
told Leigh Hunt on September 9: 'But lo and behold I found
myself famous! Frankenstein had prodigious success as a
drama and was about to be repeated for the 23rd night at the
English Opera House.' Mary also gave her impressions of the
actors: James Wallack 'looked very well' as Frankenstein, she

*said, but it was Thomas Potter Cooke as the monster who really caught her eye. (Cooke, a former naval seaman who was shipwrecked in 1804 and thereafter decided to remain on dry land as an actor, played many villainous roles, but as a result of making over 350 appearances as the creature became as thoroughly identified with the role as Boris Karloff was to be a century later.)*

*'The stage represents a room with a staircase leading to Frankenstein's workshop,'* Mary wrote, *'he goes to it and you see his light at a small window, through which a frightened servant peeps, who runs in terror when F exclaims, "It lives!" Presently F himself rushes in horror and trepidation from the room and while still expressing his agony and terror, the unnameable throws down the door of the laboratory, leaps the staircase and presents his unearthly and monstrous person on stage. Cooke played the part extremely well – his seeking as it were for support – his trying to grasp at the sounds he heard – all indeed he does was well imagined and executed.'*

A rare surviving copy of this two-act *'peculiar, romantic melodrama'* by the prolific London playwright, H.M. Milner, who specialised in literary adaptations, also included a description of Cooke's make-up consisting of lashings of yellow and green grease-paint as well as details of his costume: *'Close vest and leggings of a very pale yellowish brown, heightened with blue, as if to show the muscles. Greek shirt of very dark brown, and broad black leather belt.'* The success of this version of the story ensured many more theatrical presentations in the years to follow, not a few of which drew on Milner's concept. The creature's appearance, however, was to change drastically over the ensuing years – and no more so than when it entered its second reincarnation on the cinema screen . . .

# ACT I.

## SCENE I.

*The Gardens of the* Prince del Piombino's *Villa. – At the back a River, beyond which, Picturesque Country. On the* P.S. *side, the Entrance to the Villa. On the* O.P. *side, a small Pavilion.)*

    *Enter* QUADRO, STRUTT, *and* LISETTA, *from the Villa, meeting male and female Villagers.*

LIS: And you think yourself a vastly great man, Mr Strutt, I suppose.

STRUTT: Philosophers are not content with thinking, I know it. My master's a great man, and I'm like the moon to the sun, I shine with a reflected brightness.

QUAD: Great man, indeed! I should like to know what there is great about either of you. A couple of adventurers, whom my poor silly dupe of a master, (Heaven help him!) has brought from that beggarly place, Germany; and I suppose you'll never leave him whilst he has got a ducat.

STRUTT: Pooh, for his ducats! We want his ducats, indeed! when we could make gold out of any rubbish – your worthless head, for instance, Signor Quadro. My master is the most profound philosopher, and consequently the greatest man that ever lived. To tell you what he can do is impossible; but what he cannot do, it would be still more difficult to mention.

QUAD: Yes, his way of making gold, I fancy, is by conveying it out of other people's pockets. He may make gold, but he'd much rather have it made to his hand, I've a notion.

STRUTT: Signor Quadro, it is fortunate for you that my master does not hear you, and that (considering the choice bottles of Catanian wine that you have from time to time been pleased to open for me) I'm too discreet to tell him; – for, oh! signor Quadro, his power is terrible; – he could prevent you from ever passing a quiet night again!

QUAD: When I've got three quarts of good Rhenish in my skin, I'll give him leave, if he can. Your master is a water-drinker, sir, he keeps no butler; I never knew any good of a man that drank water and kept no butler.

STRUTT: At all events, Master Quadro, that's an offence which you cannot lay to my charge; I have the most philosophical principles upon the subject – I drink water, Signor Quadro, only when I can't get any thing better.

QUAD: And that's generally the case, I fancy, when you can't find some good-natured simpleton, like the Prince del Piombino, to keep you and your master together. Instead of board-wages, he billets you upon the kitchen of any body that's fool énough to take you into it.

STRUTT: Be assured of this, Signor Quadro, I am not ungrateful; when any kind friend has the goodness to take me in, I do the best in my power to return the compliment.

QUAD: The devil doubt you.

STRUTT: But for my master, Signor Quadro, don't think that all the wine in Sicily is any object to him; he could turn that river into wine if he thought proper, – I've seen him do it, sir, and convert a quart of simple water into a bottle of prime Burgundy.

QUAD: Can he? Can he do that? Then he has an easy way of making me his sworn friend for life. Only let him turn – I won't be unreasonable; I won't say a word about the river – only let him turn the pump in our stable-yard into a fountain of claret, and I'll never purloin another bottle of my master's, so long as I'm a butler.

LIS: And pray, Mr Strutt, has all this philosophy and learning quite driven the thoughts of love out of your head? I suppose you fancy yourself now quite above us poor weak women?

STRUTT: Not at all, my dear creature; for the man who has the impudence to fancy himself above the fairest half of human nature has sunk immeasurably below it.

QUAD: Egad! philosophy has not made quite a fool of the fellow. But pray now, my good Mr Strutt, amongst all this transmuting of metal, and converting of water, can you inform us what it is that this wonderful master of yours is doing in that pavilion, where he remains constantly shut up, day and night, and into which no mortal but himself is ever permitted to penetrate?

STRUTT: You would like to know, would you?

QUAD: Yes I should, very much indeed.

LIS: Oh yes, I'd give the world to know, I should so like to find out the secret.

STRUTT: (*after a pause*) And so should I.

QUAD: What then, you can't tell us?

LIS: Or perhaps you won't.

STRUTT: Why you see – I'm not exactly certain – but I partly guess – (*they cling to him with eager curiosity*) – that is, I suspect – that it is – something that will astonish your weak nerves, one day or another.

QUAD: Pshaw!

LIS: A nasty, ill-natured fellow – see how I'll serve you, the next time you try to kiss me. (*Music without.*)

QUAD: But hark! his highness approaches with his lovely sister, the lady Rosaura. Back! back! all of you, show him proper respect.

(*They are joined by other domestics, male and female, who form in order. A Gondola approaches the shore, from which the* Prince, Rosaura, *and* Attendants *land. As the* Prince *advances, all salute him.*)

PRINCE: Enough, enough, my friends, hasten to the villa, and busy yourselves in preparations for the festival I wish to give in honour of the illustrious genius, who honours my house with his presence.

QUAD: (*aside*) A festival, too! for a man who drinks no wine. Well, there's one consolation; there'll be more for those who do – and I'll do my best to make up for his deficiencies, he may depend on't.

STRUTT: (*to* Lis.) If there's dancing, may I claim the honour –?

LIS: Will you try to find out your master's secret for me? –

STRUTT: It is positively against his orders, to pry into his concerns; and do you know, there is but one person in the world whose commands could induce me to disobey those of my master.

LIS: And who may that be, pray?

STRUTT: My mistress, you jade. (*takes her under his arm, and exeunt with* Quadro, Domestics, &c. *into the Palace.*)

PRINCE: I feel most deeply that rank and opulence can never do themselves greater honour, than by protecting and assisting talent and genius.

ROS: And never, surely, did genius clothe itself in a more enviable guise, than in the person of Frankenstein. How different is the unassuming modesty of his demeanour, his winning gentleness, from the harsh pedantry and formal solemnity of schoolmen in general.

PRINCE: Theirs is the solemn mockery of mere pretension, which genius, such as Frankenstein's, despises. – The Universities of Germany have all bent to his prodigious talent, and acknowledged his superiority: – the prince who, conscious of his merit, rewards, assists, and forwards it, not only reaps the fruit of his sublime discoveries, but becomes the sharer of his immortality.

ROS: Oh! may virtues and talents such as Frankenstein's, ever receive the patronage and protection of such men as the Prince del Piombino.

PRINCE: I rejoice that my dear Rosaura's admiration of this illustrious foreigner almost equals the enthusiasm of her brother's. Has her penetration ever hinted to her that last, that best, inestimable reward with which I meditate to crown my favours towards this Frankenstein?

ROS: (*Turning away*) Ah, my brother!

PRINCE: That blush, that downcast look, assure me, that should my admiration of his merit induce me to confer on him a gift so precious as my sister's hand, I should not in her heart find an opposer of my generosity: – I will not tax your delicacy for a frank avowal, but in your silence read your acquiescence. This night, amidst the joyous mirth that fills our halls, will I hint to our philosopher, the dearer pleasure that I have in store for him.

ROS: My dear, dear brother! – A heart like yours will ever find the secret of making all around it happy.

[*Exeunt into Palace.*

## SCENE II.

*A Nearer View of the Outside of the Pavilion, appropriate as Frankenstein's study; practicable door, and transparent window above.* (*dark.*)

*Enter Frankenstein, from the Pavilion.*

FRAN: It comes – it comes! – 'tis nigh – the moment that shall crown my patient labours, that shall gild my toilsome studies with the brightest joy that e'er was yet attained by mortal man. – What monarch's power, what general's valour, or what hero's fame, can rank with that of Frankenstein? What can their choicest efforts accomplish, but to destroy? 'Tis mine, mine only to create, to breathe the breath of life into a mass of putrefying mortality; 'tis mine to call into existence a form conceived in my own notions of perfection! How vain, how worthless is the noblest fame compared to mine! – Frankenstein shall be the first of men! – And this triumph is at hand; but a few moments and it is accomplished. Burst not, high swelling heart, with this o'erwhelming tide of joy!

*Enter* JULIO. O.P.

JU: Ah! my dear sir, I have not seen you before, to-day; I am so glad to meet with you.

FRAN: (*Abstractedly*) 'Tis well, boy. – Good even to you.

JU: There are such doings in the palace; such feasting, and such merry-makings, and all, as they say, for you.

FRAN: Why that is better; 'tis as it should be. Doubt not, I will be with ye. Let the full bowl high sparkle, let the joyous note swell loud; I will be there, exulting in my triumph.

JU: Aye, but moreover than all that, I could – but I don't think I shall, because it was told to me as a very great secret – I could tell you of something that would make you so happy.

FRAN: I shall, I must be happy; the secret is my own. Leave me, boy, leave me.

JU: Nay, now, you do not love your poor Julio; I'm sure I know not how I have offended you; but you never spoke to me thus harshly before.

FRAN: (*embraces him*) Nay, my pretty pupil, my affectionate Julio, I must love thee, ever. I am disturbed by intense study, and for a few moments I would be alone.

JU: If you are sure you love me, I will leave you; but if I had offended you, I would not leave you till you had forgiven me, I would not, indeed; we shall see you anon. I shall know where to find you, by my pretty aunt Rosaura's side. Oh, if you did but know what I could tell you!

[*He runs off.* O.P.

FRAN: The time is come, the glorious moment is arriv'd. Now, Frankenstein, achieve the mightly work, gain that best of victories, a victory o'er the grave!

[*Exit into the Pavilion.*

*Enter* STRUTT, *with a Ladder,* – *and* LISETTA.

STRUTT: Well now, do you know, Lisetta, I'm going to do a great deal more for you, than I dare to do for myself. I'm dying to know what my master is about yonder, but if he should catch me peeping, what a jolly thump o' the head I shall get, to be sure; and then, Lisetta, you have it in your power to break my heart, and that's a great deal worse.

LIS: Well, now, without any more ado, you put the ladder against the window, and hold it fast, whilst I mount up and see what he is about.

STRUTT: Fie, for shame, Lisetta, what are you thinking about? I'll get up the ladder, and I'll report all that I see, to you below.

LIS: Well, just as you please, only I'd rather peep myself, because, you know, seeing is believing. (Strutt *places the Ladder against the window of the Pavilion, mounts it, and peeps in; a faint glimmering of light is seen through the window*.) Well, now, what can you see?

STRUTT: Why, I can see a little fire, and a great deal of smoke.

LIS: And I suppose all your boasted discoveries will end in smoke.

STRUTT: Oh! now I can see better; – and would you believe it, Lisetta, from all I can see, I really do think, at least it seems so to me, that my master is making a man.

LIS: Making a man! – What, is not he alone?

STRUTT: Yes, quite alone. (*A strong and sudden flash of light is now seen at the window*; Strutt *slides down the Ladder*.) Oh, Lord! that's too much for me! – he's raising the devil – he's blown off the top of the pavilion! – Run, run, Lisetta, or the old gentleman will have you!

LIS: Nay, then the devil take the hindmost, I say!

[*They run off*. O.P.

## SCENE III.

*The Interior of the Pavilion – folding Doors in the Back. On a long Table is discovered an indistinct Form, covered with a black cloth. A small side Table, with Bottles, and Chemical Apparatus – and a brazier with fire.*

FRANKENSTEIN *is discovered, as if engaged in a Calculation.*

FRAN: Now that the final operation is accomplished, my panting heart dares scarcely gaze upon the object of its

labours – dares scarcely contemplate the grand fulfilment
of its wishes. Courage, Frankenstein! glut thy big soul with
exultation! – enjoy a triumph never yet attained by mortal
man! (*Music.* – *He eagerly lays his hand on the bosom of
the figure, as if to discover whether it breathes.*) The breath
of life now swells its bosom. – (*Music.*) As the cool night
breeze plays upon its brow, it will awake to sense and
motion. (*Music.* – *He rolls back the black covering, which
discovers a colossal human figure, of a cadaverous livid
complexion; it slowly begins to rise, gradually attaining an
erect posture,* Frankenstein *observing with intense anxiety.
When it has attained a perpendicular position, and glares
its eyes upon him, he starts back with horror.*) Merciful
Heaven! And has the fondest visions of my fancy awakened
to this terrible reality; a form of horror, which I scarcely
dare to look upon: – instead of the fresh colour of humanity, he wears the livid hue of the damp grave. Oh, horror!
horror! – let me fly this dreadful monster of my own
creation! (*He hides his face in his hands; the* Monster,
*meantime, springs from the table, and gradually gains the
use of his limbs; he is surprised at the appearance of*
Frankenstein, – *advances towards him and touches him;
the latter starts back in disgust and horror, draws his
sword and rushes on the* Monster, *who with the utmost
care takes the sword from him, snaps it in two, and throws
it down.* Frankenstein *then attempts to seize it by the
throat, but by a very slight exertion of its powers, it throws
him off to a considerable distance; in shame, confusion,
and despair,* Frankenstein *rushes out of the Apartment,
locking the doors after him. The* Monster *gazes about it in
wonder, traverses the Apartment; hearing the sound of*
Frankenstein's *footsteps without, wishes to follow him;
finds the opposition of the door, with one blow strikes it
from its hinges, and rushes out.*)

## SCENE IV.

*Outside of the Pavilion, as before.* Frankenstein, *in great
agitation, rushes from the Pavilion locking the door after him.*

FRAN: (*After a pause of much terror.*) Have all my dreams of
greatness ended here? Is this the boasted wonder of my
science, – is this the offspring of long years of toilsome

study and noisome labour? Is my fairest model of perfection come to this – a hideous monster, a loathsome mass of animated putrefaction, whom, but to gaze on chills with horror even me, his maker? How how shall I secrete him, how destroy –? Heaven! to think that in the very moment of fruition, when all my toils were ended and I should glory in their noble consummation, my first, my dearest, only wish, is to annihilate what I have made! Horrible object, wretched produce of my ill-directed efforts! never must thou meet another eye than mine – never must thou gaze upon a human being, whom thy fell aspect sure would kill with terror! (*A tremendous crash is heard, the* Monster *breaks through the door of the Pavilion*) Ah! he is here! I have endued him with a giant's strength, and he will use it to pluck down ruin on his maker's head. (*Music. – The* Monster *approaches him with gestures of conciliation.*) – Hence! avoid me! do not approach me, wretch! thy horrid contact would spread a pestilence throughout my veins; touch me, and I will straightway strike thee back to nothingness!

*The* Monster *still approaches him with friendly gestures – Frankenstein endeavours to stab him with his dagger, which the* Monster *strikes from his hand; – whilst the* Monster *is taking up the dagger, and admiring its form,* Frankenstein *steals off. – The* Monster, *perceiving him gone, rushes off, as if in pursuit, but in an opposite direction.*

## SCENE V.

*The heart of a gloomy and intricate Forest. – Tremendous Storm, Thunder, Lightning, Rain, & c.*

*Enter* RITZBERG, – *and* EMMELINE, *bearing the* Child.

EM: The thunder's awful voice, and the fierce tumult of the wildly raging storm, have drowned thy plaintive wailings, my poor babe, and thou art hushed to silence. Sleep on, my babe, let thy mother's throbbing bosom shelter thee. We shall find him soon, – yes, I am sure we shall. – And when he sees thy ruddy smiling cheek, and marks his Emmeline's wan and haggard features, his heart will turn to us, he will again be all our own.

RITZ: I don't believe a word of it. Talk of his heart, indeed!

He has no heart: if ever he had any, it has evaporated in the fumes of his diabolical preparations. He loves and protect you! – all his affections are in the bottom of a crucible; and in the wild chimeras of his science, and the dreams of his mad ambition, all his human feelings are lost and annihilated.

EM: Oh, no! my father; the enthusiasm of knowledge, the applauses of the powerful, may for a time, have weaned him from us, but my own kind, gentle Frankenstein, can never be inhuman.

RITZ: Can't he? Well, I don't know what you may call it; but to deceive and trepan a young, innocent, confiding creature, as you were, and to leave you and your child to poverty and want, whilst he went rambling in the train of a prince, after his own devilish devices; – if that is not inhuman, I don't know what is.

EM: Ah, my father; I have heard that the Prince del Piombino has an estate in this beautiful island; that he has, attached to his household, a wonderful philosopher – I am confident 'tis he – and oh! my heart tells me, that he will shortly bless us with his returning love.

RITZ: Yes, and with this fine tale; and because I could not bear to see you pining away in hopeless sorrow, have you lured me to quit my quiet, peaceful abode in Germany, and come wandering over here to Sicily. And today you must march out on a pretty wild-goose chase, to endeavour to trace him in the household of this prince; till we have lost our way in the mazes of this forest, and can't trace a path back again to the hovel I have hired. And it's my belief, that if you found him in the Prince's palace, you would be driven away from the gate like a common beggar.

EM: Oh, say not so, my father; do not destroy my hope, for in that consists the little strength that now remains to me.

[*Storm rages furiously.*]

RITZ: And a pretty night this for a young, delicate creature like you, with your helpless infant, to be out in. – Curses, a thousand curses on the villain –!

EM: Oh, no, my father, no! – Do not curse him. – Curse not the husband of your Emmeline, – the father of her child!

RITZ: Well, well, I won't – the damn'd good-for-nothing vagabond! – I daren't stir a step in this plaguy forest, for all the storm keeps such a beautiful hubbub about us, for fear of straying further out of the way; and I am sure you have no strength to waste. – But here, I have it. You stay here, exactly where I leave you; give me the child, for you must be tired of carrying it, and I'll endeavour to find the path. – When I have traced it, I'll return for you. – There, stay here, just under this tree; it will afford a partial shelter. I warrant me, that with the assistance of the lightning, which keeps flashing so merrily, I shall soon discover the path. – I think I've got an inkling of it now. (*Takes the* Child *from* Emmeline, *and goes out as if endeavouring to trace the path.*)

EM: My spirits fail me, and my strength is exhausted. Whilst I bore the child, nature gave me powers, and I could not sink beneath the grateful burthen. – Ah, what a peal was there! – Heaven itself joins in the persecution of the hapless Emmeline. – Father, father! come to me! – I sink – I die – oh, Frankenstein! Frankenstein! (*She falls on the ground – the storm still continues to rage. The* Monster *enters in alarm and wonder, stares wildly about him; at length perceives* Emmeline *extended on the ground – is struck with wonder, approaches and raises her; is filled with admiration; expresses that the rain occasions inconvenience, and that the lightning is dreadful, his pity for* Emmeline *being exposed to it, his wish to procure her shelter; at length takes her up in his arms, and bears her off.*)

*Re-enter* RITZBERG, *with the* Child.

RITZ: Come, Emmeline, I think I have found it at last, and we shall be snug at home before the thunder can give another growl at us. – (*Perceives that she is gone.*) Merciful Heaven! not here! Where can she be gone? Surely no danger can have approached her. – She has wandered on, endeavouring to overtake me, and has mistaken the path, and so increased our troubles. Imprudent girl! – Emmeline, my child, my girl, my Emmeline.

[*Exit with the* Child, *calling aloud.*

## SCENE VI.

*The Inside of* Ritzberg's *Cottage. – Entrance Door in Flat; in some part of the Scene, a Fire-place.*

(*The* Monster *dashes open the door, and enters, bearing*

Emmeline; *he places her in a chair, and looks round for some means of assisting her; perceives the fire, discovers by touching it, that it yields heat; removes the chair with* Emmeline, *to the fire, and remains watching her. The* Child *enters, on perceiving the* Monster *utters a shriek of terror, and runs across the stage, exclaiming,* 'Mother! – mother!' Ritzberg *then enters, is likewise alarmed at the appearance of the* Monster. *The* Monster *observes the* Child *with admiration and beckons it to approach him which the* Child *refuses to do; he then softly approaches the* Child *with gestures of conciliation, the* Child *endeavouring to escape from him.* Emmeline *utters a piercing shriek.* Ritzberg *snatches up his gun, fires at the* Monster, *wounds it in the shoulder. The* Monster *puts down the Child, who rushes to his mother's embrace; expresses the agony occasioned by the wound; the rage inspired by the pain! would rush on* Ritzberg, *who keeps the gun presented; it is deterred by fear of a repetition of the wound; rushes out of the hut;* Ritzberg *remaining on the defensive; whilst* Emmeline *thanks Heaven for the preservation of her child.*

## SCENE VII.
### *A Landscape.*
#### *Enter* JULIO.

JU: I can't conceive what has happened to Mr Frankenstein. When I spoke to him this evening, he was so cross, and so abstracted, and so mysterious; and now here my father, the Prince, has given a grand festival, expressly to do him honour, and he is no where to be found. I wish I could meet with him. I think he loves me, and I would coax him out of his gloomy humour, and lead him smiling and good-natured to my aunt Rosaura, or I'd know the reason why, I am determined. (*Music. – The* Monster *furiously rushes on.*) Ah! what dreadful gigantic creature is this? (*The* Monster *approaches and seizes him.*) Oh! – help, – mercy, – spare me, – spare me!

(*The* Monster *expresses that his kindly feelings towards the human race have been met by scorn, abhorrence, and violence, that they are all now converted into hate and vengeance; that* Julio *shall be his first victim; he snatches him up and bears him off,* Julio *crying* 'Mercy! – help help!')

## SCENE VIII.

*Splendid Banqueting Hall in the Palace, open in the back upon the Garden, and giving a View of the Lake. Banqueting Tables, & c.*

*The* PRINCE *and* ROSAURA *discovered on a Throne under the centre Arch. Company of both sexes,* Attendants, & c. A *BALLET is performed, after which the* Prince *and* Rosaura *advance.*

PRINCE: I know not why it is, that he in whose honour this entertainment was expressly given, should so long absent himself from our revels. Surely, for one night he might have relaxed from his deep studies.

ROS: I think he scarce will tarry longer, for I have sent Julio in search of him. – Ah! he is here.

   *Enter* FRANKENSTEIN, *in great agitation.*

PRINCE: At length you are arrived. Be assured, my friend, your absence has been both felt and regretted.

FRAN: Accept my humble and sincere apology. I was engaged, most intently engaged, in the solution of a Problem, on the result of which I had much at stake. (*aside*) My every hope depended on it, and the solution has stamped me a wretch for ever!

PRINCE: A truce to study, now, and moody thoughts. – Let the grape's sparkling juice chase from your brain all dark chimeras; partake the joy that smiles around you : – anon, I have a proposal to make to you, that will not damp your mirth, I trust.

FRAN: Aye, let me be joyous; let me seek joy even at the bottom of the maddening bowl; I cannot find it in my own heart. – Give me wine; – quick, let me drain a flowing goblet, perchance it may chase – oh! no, no, it can never drive from my remembrance that form of horror that exceeds conception.

ROS: From my hand will the cup bring less of joy? – Dear Frankenstein – I would say, learned sir, what means the dreadful wildness that gleams on your countenance?

FRAN: Dear and most lovely lady, 'tis the intoxication of high swelling mirth, of gratitude, of animating hilarity. Fair lady, permit the humblest of your slaves to pledge you. (*He is raising the cup to his lips, when* Quadro *hastily rushes in.*)

QUAD: Oh, my lord, my lord! – such intelligence of horror: – the young prince, Julio, has been murdered!

FRAN: (*Dashing the cup from him.*) Eternal Heaven! – that fiend has perpetrated it!

ROS: Julio murdered!

PRINCE: My boy! my pretty, innocent, affectionate boy! say where, how, by whom?

QUAD: He was found in the pavilion where Mr Frankenstein pursues his studies, the door thrown from its hinges: from the mark on his neck, he appears to have been strangled.

FRAN: (*aside.*) Then my worst fears have proved too true!

PRINCE: How could that lovely child provoke his fate? Robbery was not the object. Who could have the heart to harm that unoffending, darling child!

QUAD: Can your highness doubt?

PRINCE: Speak, what mean you? On whom do your suspicions fall?

QUAD: Who should it be, but this foreign adventurer, this Frankenstein?

ROS: Oh, Heavens!

QUAD: Has any one else access to the pavilion, or ever presumes to enter it, or would have done now, except in eager search for the young prince?

PRINCE: I scarcely can believe it possible; but yet his lengthened absence from the festival at the very hour, his palpable agitation when he entered. – Frankenstein, what say you to this dreadful accusation?

FRAN: I say that I am guilty, guilty a thousand times!

ALL: Ha!

FRANK: Not of the crime of murder. I could not lay a finger in the way of violence on that lovely Child. Mine is a guilt a thousand times more black, more horrible. I am the father of a thousand murders. Oh! presumption, and is this thy punishment? has my promised triumph brought me but to this?

PRINCE: Frankenstein! for mercy's sake explain. What horrid mystery lurks beneath thy words?

(*Shots and noise of pursuit heard without – the* Monster *rushes in through the archway in the back, pursued by* Peasants *variously armed – all shriek with horror – he rushes up to* Frankenstein, *and casts himself at his feet, imploring protection.*)

FRAN: Hated, detested fiend! now reeking with the blood of innocence – fiend of malice and destruction – here on thy hated head, I now invoke a father's and a prince's vengeance. Die, monster, die! and quit the life thou hast disgraced by blood and slaughter. – (*He seizes on the* Monster – *the guards close round – the* Monster *dashes* Frankenstein *to the earth, and by an exertion of his immense strength breaks through the opposing line – the* Prince *gives the word to fire – the* Monster, *snatching up the* Officer, *holds him as a target before him – he receives the shots and falls dead – the* Monster *rushes up the steps of the throne and laughs exultingly – a general picture is formed, on which the* Drop *falls.*)

## ACT II.

### SCENE I.

*A Cellar belonging to the Villa, entered only by a ladder from a small Trap-door above.*

STRUTT: (*discovered*) Well, my master has done a nice job for himself, it should seem, with all his machinery and magic; the making of a man has rendered him a made man for life, and I seem destined to share all his advantages. Because his hopeful bantling chose to amuse itself with strangling a child, much in the same way, I suppose, that our ordinary brats do kittens, out of pure kindness, they have seized hold of me and popped me into this underground apartment, to keep me out of mischief; as if they thought I shared my master's propensities, and had a *penchant* for making of men and strangling of children. – And so, after having taught me philosophy, my master has left me here to practise it. Now, if this were a wine cellar, there would be some kind of consolation; I might, by the magic of a butt of good liquor, convert this dungeon into a fairy palace, and when I could stand no longer, fancy these hard stones were silken cushions. But every thing now has the appearance of a cursed uncomfortable reality. Ha! I think I hear some one coming. I suppose it's old Quadro, who is about to set me at liberty, or at least to afford me the consolation of a flaggon of his best. (*The trap-door above opens, a ladder is put down, and* Quadro *descends, followed by* Lisetta.) Ah! how d'ye do; I'm so glad to see you. I hope you are come to bring me comfort in one shape or the other.

QUAD: Oh, yes! the best of all possible comfort, the news of a speedy termination to all your miseries; you will very shortly be exalted, my fine fellow, elevated, tucked up, dance upon nothing.

STRUTT: Don't mention it. I assure you such allusions are altogether unpleasant to my feelings; for though you may consider my master a bit of a mountebank, I assure you that I have never been accustomed to dance on a tight-rope; and as to hanging – (*to* Lisetta) oh! you dear little creature, I have dreamt of nothing but hanging round your neck – whilst for tucking up, I had hoped we should have been both tucked up together in the bridal bed, before this.

LIS: Oh! for shame, sir!

QUAD: Oh! you did, did you? I can tell you that there is a very narrow bed in preparation for you, where you will find it most convenient to lie alone, and where you will be tucked up with the sexton's shovel.

STRUTT: I am surprised at your mentioning such indelicacies before a young lady.

QUAD: In the confusion occasioned by the appearance of his delectable companion, your pretty master effected his escape; but I took care to grapple you. I considered the nabbing of such a fellow as you to be in my department, and so I popped you into this cellar.

STRUTT: It would have been much more handsome of you to pop me in the cellar where you keep the liquor.

QUAD: And you will be hanged for having aided, abetted, and assisted your master in the formation of a monster, and as an accessory in the young Prince's murder.

STRUTT: Signor Quadro, you shock me. Me accused of assisting to make a man! Let me tell you I was never before suspected of such an offence; not even by the beadle of our parish, and he was a sharp chap at nosing out such matters, I warrant ye.

QUAD: But now, sir, you are in my clutches, you won't get off so easy you may depend on it.

STRUTT: Oh, Mr Frankenstein! Mr Frankenstein! this is a pretty mess you have got me into, to stand god-father to your monster. (*He sits down in the back.*)

LIS: Now, my dear father, how can you be so harsh to this poor young man? I don't really believe he had any hand in it; in my opinion, he would not be concerned in the making of anything half so ugly.

QUAD: Did not I say it from the beginning; did not I always insist that they were a brace of vagabonds, and that no good would come of harbouring them?

LIS: But now my own good, kind, dear father, seeing that what is done cannot be undone, and that hanging this young man would only make bad worse, could not you contrive to let him go?

QUAD: Let him go, indeed! and what for?

LIS: Why just to oblige me, father; for really he is a tolerably well-behaved young man enough, and not so much amiss to look at.

QUAD: Oh! you think so? And then, I suppose, the next thing is that you must go with him, eh, you minx? Go and see him hanged if you like.

LIS: Now my dear, beautiful father, you don't know, though you are rather old, how well you look when you are doing a good-natured action. (*She makes signs behind his back to* Strutt, *to take advantage of the opportunity and run up the ladder.*)

QUAD: You coaxing Jezebel! But don't think to wheedle me out of my duty.

LIS: Now look in my face. (*places one hand on each side of his face, as if to turn it towards her;* Strutt *watches his opportunity and silently ascends the ladder*) Look in my face, and frown a refusal if you can. Will you let him go?

QUAD: No, I won't.

LIS: You are sure you won't?

QUAD: No, I'll be damned if I do. (Strutt *has now gained the top of the ladder.*)

LIS: Then I'd advise him to do as I shall, to be off without asking your leave, and let you enjoy the comforts of this place by yourself. (*She runs to the ladder, and with* Strutt's *assistance hastily ascends it, after which they quickly draw up the ladder.*)

QUAD: Why, you jade, you vixen, you undutiful hussey, what do you mean?

LIS: Only to let you stay there, father, till the young man is out of your reach; for I could not bear that you should have his death upon your conscience, father, I could not, indeed.

QUAD: Go, both of you, and people the world with monsters, if you will; you can produce none worse than an unnatural daughter.

STRUTT: Good bye, old gentleman!

(Strutt *and* Lisetta *disappear with the ladder,* Quadro *rushes out in a rage on the opposite side.*)

## SCENE II.
### *The inside of* Ritzberg's *Cottage, as before.*

FRANKENSTEIN: *rushes in, in great agitation.*

FRAN: Where am I? Let me a moment pause and collect my distracted thoughts – compose, if possible, this tumult of the brain. I have fled! and wherefore fled? Had not death been welcome? But then to perish on a scaffold – loaded with infamy – branded with a crime my very soul abhors – the murder of an innocent I would have died to save. No, no, it must not be – not yet. My life has been devoted to the fulfilment of one object, another now claims the exertion of its short remainder, to destroy the wretch that I have formed – to purge the world of that infuriated monster – to free mankind from the fell persecution of that demon. This, this is now my bounden duty, and to this awful task I solemnly devote myself.

### *Enter* EMMELINE *and* Child.

EM: A stranger here! Ah! can I believe my senses – am I indeed so blest, does he come to seek his Emmeline? My lord, my life, my Frankenstein!

FRAN: What do I behold? Emmeline Ritzberg! Lost, guilty, cursed wretch! thy cup of crime and misery is full. Hell yawns for thee, and all thy victims now surround thee, calling down Heaven's vengeance on thy head.

EM: And is it thus? Is Emmeline's presence, then, a curse? Farewell, then, hope. – But we'll not persecute thee, Frankenstein, for with my child I'll wander where thou shalt never more be punished with remembrance of us, and where death will soon end our sorrow.

FRAN: Emmeline! Emmeline! tear not my heart with words like those. What to a guilty wretch can be a greater curse than the presence of those he has injured? Now at thy feet behold me, Emmeline, in humble agony of heart, I plead for thy forgiveness. Oh! that I ne'er had quitted thy peaceful blest abode – ne'er let into my bosom those demons of ambition and fell pride, that now, with ceaseless gnawing, prey upon my soul.

EM: Not at my feet, but in my arms, dear Frankenstein, lose all the memory of sorrows past. Oh! if thy heart still owns thy Emmeline, all shall be well, be happy. – One fond embrace of thine repays an age of sorrow; in thy smiles and those of this sweet cherub, I shall again awake to joy.

FRAN: Oh, Emmeline, since we parted, all has been crime; crime of so black a dye, that even to thy gentle forgiving spirit, I dare not confess it. Crime, whose punishment will be unceasing, will be eternal.

EM: Oh, no, my Frankenstein, guilt, to be absolved needs but to be abjured. Returned to virtue and domestic peace, thy Emmeline shall soothe thy every woe, and on her bosom thou'lt forget thy griefs.

FRAN: I dare not hope it. But in this land I cannot hope a moment's ease. Quick, let us fly – far, far from this accursed spot, the bane of all my peace. There, to that calm retreat, where first thy angel charms awoke my soul to love, there let us quick repair. Oh, that in former and in happier scenes, I could forget the guilt, the misery that I have since been slave to.

*Enter hastily* RITZBERG, *through door in Flat.*

RITZ: Ha! Frankenstein here! but 'tis no time to parley; the cottage is on fire! That fierce gigantic figure of terrific aspect, waves aloft his torch, as if in triumph at the deed. (*a coarse yelling laugh is heard.*)

FRAN: Ha! 'tis that hideous voice! Quick, quick, let us fly! His hellish malice still pursues me; and but with his death or with mine, will this fierce persecution cease. Could I but place you beyond his power –! (*With* Ritzberg *he attempts to open the door, they find it barricaded from without; the laugh is repeated – the conflagration has enveloped the whole building – Frankenstein rushes off as if in search of some other outlet – Part of the building breaks – the* Monster *enters at the chasm, seizes on* Emmeline *and the* Child, *and bears them through the burning ruins, followed by* Ritzberg. Frankenstein *returns, perceives that* Emmeline *and her* Child *are gone, and in despair rushes after them.*)

## SCENE III.
### *A Landscape.*
#### *Enter* STRUTT *and* LISETTA. (P.S.)

STRUTT: Well, Lisetta, and now having by your assistance, escaped from the clutches of that cantankerous old father of yours. What is next to be done?

LIS: Why, as I have got out of his clutches at the same time, and so lost my natural protector, what do you think you ought to do next?

STRUTT: Why, I suppose you think I ought to marry you?

LIS: Whilst you, perhaps, are of a very different opinion.

STRUTT: Not in the least, my angel; but then my poor master, he perhaps is in trouble, and requires my assistance; and to desert him in the hour of need, I could not do it, Lisetta, no, not to possess such a treasure as yourself.

LIS: And if you could I should despise you for it. But suppose, Mr Strutt, we were both to go and assist him. Two heads, they say, are better than one, and so are two pair of hands: and instead of having one faithful follower he would have a couple, that's all.

STRUTT: What, no, you don't mean it do you? Will you really take me for better for worse, and go with me in search of my poor dear master? Well, I always thought you were a good creature, but now you're a perfect divinity, and I'll adore you.

LIS: Who knows, perhaps Mr Frankenstein may get married too, and then he'll have better employment than making monsters.

STRUTT: Oh, that monster! don't mention him, Lisetta. If he should be with my master now, do you think you would have the courage to face him? I'm not quite sure that I should.

LIS: Oh! never doubt me; if I take him in hand, I'll bring him to his senses, I warrant me; for if a spirited woman can't tame him, he must be a very fierce ungovernable devil indeed. – (*a scream is heard without.*)

STRUTT: Ah! what means that shriek? See, yonder, where the demon comes, he bears with him both a woman and a child. She does not seem to have made much of a hand of him, at any rate. Here, back, back, conceal yourself, Lisetta, I would not have him come within arm's length of you, for the world. (*he pulls her behind a tree.*)

(*The* Monster *enters, exultingly bearing* Emmeline *and her* Child, *crosses and exit.* Frankenstein *follows him with a staggering step, almost overcome with fatigue and terror.* (P.S.) *to* (O.P.)

STRUTT: (*coming from his concealment.*) What, ho! Sir! master! Mr Frankenstein! 'Tis Strutt, your faithful servant! He hears me not, but madly still pursues the fiend he cannot hope to master.

LIS: And will you, too, Strutt, be mad enough to follow him?

STRUTT: Why not singly, because I think it would be to little purpose; but I'll tell you what I'll do – I'll first bestow you in a place of safety, and then I'll summon together a few stout-hearted fellows, and we'll see if we can't settle his monstership; for sooner than he should harm that poor woman and her infant, damn, he shall kill and eat me – but I'll endeavour to give him a bellyfull.

[*Exeunt.* (O.P.)

## SCENE IV.

*A tremendous range of craggy precipices, near the summit of Mount Etna. On the* P.S. *a conspicuous pillar of rock stands on a lofty elevation. The only approach is from the depths below.*

(*The* Monster, *with gigantic strides, ascends from below with* Emmeline *and the* Child *– she is so overcome with fatigue and terror as to be unable to speak – the* Monster *gains the elevation, and with a cord that is round his waist, binds* Emmeline *to the pillar of rock – He returns to the* Child *–* Emmeline *sinks on her knees in supplication –* Frankenstein *with great difficulty ascends from below – he perceives his* Child *in the* Monster's *power – he is about to rush on him; the monster defies him – and* Frankenstein, *recollecting his* *former defeats, abandons his threatening gestures and assumes one of entreaty.*)

FRAN: Demon of cruelty, art thou still insatiate with the blood of innocence? How many victims does it require to contest thy rage? I do implore thee, I, thy creator, who gave thee life, who endued thee with that matchless I cannot hope to master, I, on my knees, entreat thee but to spare that innocent. If fury and the thirst of blood be in thy hellish nature, on me, on me glut thy fell appetite – but, oh! if in thy human frame there dwells one spark of human sympathy or feeling, spare, spare that unoffending child!

(*The* Monster *points to his wound – expresses that he would willingly have served* Frankenstein *and befriended him, but that all his overtures were repelled with scorn and abhorrence – then, with malignant exultation seizes on the* Child, *and whirls it aloft, as if about to dash it down the rock –* Emmeline *screams,* Frankenstein, *with a cry of horror, covers his eyes – at this moment a thought occurs to* Emmeline *– she pulls from under her dress a small flageolet, and begins to play an air – its effect on the* Monster *is instantaneous – he is at once astonished and delighted – he places the* Child *on the ground – his feelings become more powerfully affected by the music, and his attention absorbed by it – the* Child *escapes to its father –* Emmeline *continues to play, and* Frankenstein *intently to watch its effect on the* Monster. *As the air proceeds his feelings become more powerfully excited – he is moved to tears: afterwards, on the music assuming a lively character, he is worked up to a paroxysm of delight – and on its again becoming mournful, is quite subdued, till he lies down exhausted at the foot of the rock to which* Emmeline *is attached.*)

(Strutt *now rushes on with* Ritzberg, *and a number of* Peasants *variously armed, and furnished with strong cords.*)

STRUTT: There he is! that's him! that's my gentleman! and luckily for us, he seems in a bit of a snooze – now's our time or never. On him, my lads, and bind him fast, and then we shall be all right.

(*With* Ritzberg *and others, he immediately falls on the* Monster, *and they bind him stoutly with cords –*

Frankenstein *has meantime released* Emmeline – *the* Monster *makes prodigious exertions of strength to burst his bonds, but he is overpowered by the number of his adversaries.*)

STRUTT: Away, away, sir, and place the lady and child in safety. I'll take care and accommodate this gentleman with snug quarters, and return immediately to attend your commands.

FRAN: Faithful creature! Eternal Providence, receive my thanks; and if it be thy pleasure to inflict on me an added punishment, oh! on this guilty head alone direct thy wrath; spare those who are most dear to me, those whose innocence may challenge thy compassion! (*With* Emmeline *and the* Child *he commences the descent, and disappears.*)

STRUTT: Now I think the best thing we can do is to fasten my gentleman to this pinnacle of rock; the cool air of this exalted region may give him an appetite; but he will stand very little chance of getting it gratified, unless the lava should flow from the volcano, and that may be a kind of cordial for him. (*They are binding him to the rock, the* Monster *making a furious resistance, in the course of which he hurls one of the* Peasants *to the depths below.*) – That's right, make a tight job of it, whilst you are about it; for if he once gets loose, he'll play the devil with you all; he'd crack you like so many walnuts. There, I think he'll do now; there's not much fear of his troubling us again for one while. If he gets away from here, and finds his way down to terra firma again, I'll give him leave to drink hob-and-nob with me, in the cup I have filled to celebrate his overthrow.

(*They descend the precipice by means of ropes and ladders, leaving the* Monster *attached to the pinnacle of rock – when they are gone, he redoubles his efforts to escape from his bonds, and at length succeeds – he surveys the chasm, and is afraid to venture down it – he firmly attaches to the pinnacle one end of the cord by which he was bound – and by means of this lowers himself down the chasm.*)

## SCENE V.
*A Subterranean Passage hollowed in the Mountain.*
*Enter* STRUTT *and* Peasants. (P.S.)

STRUTT: Faith, my lads, it's cold work this, climbing so near the summit of Etna, in a chill evening breeze – yes, and fatiguing work too – catching such game as we've been after is no boy's play. Lord, what a chap my master must be, to be sure, when he was making a man – he thought he might as well have a wapper at once, I suppose. Now I say, a little and good for my money. But, however, we have quieted my gentleman, and I think we have done a much better job than my master did in making him. And now I can tell you a secret. This passage leads to the hermitage of father Antonio; that you all know, so that's no secret; but what you perhaps do not know is, that old Quadro, the Prince's servant, whenever he visits the holy father to confess, always brings a bottle or two of prime old wine, which is involved by the hermit in lieu of penance; and so he makes his master pay for all his sins, and purchases absolution for one by committing another. Now do you know, I really think, that we better deserve this wine than the reverend father, and my proposal is, that we adjourn to his cave and drink to the future prosperity of the heroes who subdued the monster.

[*Shout, and exeunt,* (O.P.)

## SCENE VI.
### *Interior of the Hermit's Cave.*
STRUTT *and* Peasants *discovered seated round a table.*

STRUTT: Well, upon my soul, it's a monstrous pleasant retreat. And now for the little store of choice Falernian.

PEAS: (*who has been hunting about the cave*) Here it is, master Strutt; here's his reverence's holy water.

STRUTT: Out with it, then, and in with it. If his reverence should miss it when he comes home, he knows where to get more. Old Quadro's sins will always keep his cellar well stocked. So now my lads, charge your cups – (Peasants *have meanwhile placed on the table several flaggons of wine, horns, &c.*) Now for it, fill all, and mind it's a bumper. (*all fill*) Here's confusion to any creature that would harm a defenceless woman and a helpless child; for be their shape what it may, they must be monsters indeed.

PEAS: Bravo! with all my heart! (*all drink.*)

STRUTT: And now I'll give you another. Here's our noble

selves, and may all our future enterprises be crowned with as complete success, as that which we have now so gloriously achieved.

(*They have their cups raised to their lips, when the* Monster, *still lowering himself by his rope, descends from an aperture in the roof of the cavern, and stands on the table in the midst of them – they all shrink back in terror with loud cries – the* Monster, *with one blow, dashes the table in pieces – all fly in extreme fear – the* Monster *in rage dashes about the seats –* Strutt *takes an opportunity to stab him in the back, and flies leaving the dagger in the wound – the* Monster *extracts it, and roaring with pain rushes off.*)

### SCENE VII.

A *narrow rocky Path-way, leading to the summit of Etna. Enter* STRUTT *and* Peasants *rapidly retreating from the* Monster *– the* Monster *follows in pursuit. –* Frankenstein *enters with* Emmeline *– they are followed by a party of* Soldiers, *whom* Frankenstein *encourages to the attack of the* Monster.

[*They all go off in pursuit, from* P.S. *to* O.P.

### SCENE VIII.

*The Summit of Mount Etna – the Crater occupies the middle of the stage – near it is the Path-way from below – in very distant perspective are seen the sea and towns at the foot of Etna – the Volcano during the scene throws out torrents of fire, sparks, smoke, &c. as at the commencement of an eruption.*

(*The* Monster *ascends from below, faint from loss of blood and overcome by fatigue – he is followed by* Frankenstein, *whom he immediately attacks and stabs with the dagger he had taken from his wound – as* Frankenstein *falls,* Emmeline *rushes in shrieking and catches his lifeless body – the* Monster, *attempting to escape, is met at every outlet by armed* Peasantry *– in despair he rushes up to the apex of the mountain – the* Soldiery *rush in and fire on him – he immediately leaps into the Crater, now vomiting burning lava, and the Curtain falls.*)

### FINIS.

# *Frankenstein:*
# *The Man Who Made A Monster*

## By GARRETT FORD &
## FRANCIS FARAGOH

*It is one of the most extraordinary facts of the* Frankenstein *legend that only a strange twist of fate enabled Boris Karloff to create what remains the most enduring image of Mary Shelley's creature in the classic 1931 Universal movie. The picture was not – as some accounts have insisted – the first attempt by film-makers to bring the novel to the screen. As early as 1910 the Edison Stock Company had made a ten-minute silent version starring Charles Ogle as a grotesque monster, and this had been followed five years later by an hour-long feature film – also silent – produced by the Ocean Film Corporation with Percy Darrell. Retitled* Life Without Soul, *this picture was very different from its predecessor in that Darrell played a very human-looking monster who was 'awe-inspiring but never grotesque'. Neither of these versions appears to have made much of an impact on cinema-goers, however, but this changed dramatically in 1931 immediately after Universal had scored a huge box office hit with an adaptation of Bram Stoker's vampire classic,* Dracula, *starring Bela Lugosi. What could be more obvious to follow one horror classic with another, and to cast Lugosi in* Franken-stein? *Initially, the Hungarian-born actor was visualised as playing Dr Frankenstein, but the studio felt Lugosi was more associated in the public mind with horror roles and decreed he should star as the creature. Legend has it that Lugosi was very reluctant to take the part and hated the grotesque make-up devised for him by Jack Pierce, Universal's head of* make-up. Even after shooting some sequences on one of the old Dracula sets, he remained unhappy with the casting. However, when James Whale, a new English director recruited by Universal, was assigned to the picture and decided to recast the part of the monster, Lugosi left with an audible sigh of relief. He had no way of knowing that he had probably made the biggest mistake of his life, for his career was never to reach the heights of Dracula again. Instead another Englishman with the unlikely name of William Pratt – which he had changed to Boris Karloff in the hope of getting some better roles – suddenly found himself on the verge of creating screen history.

'I was making a picture at Universal when the director of Frankenstein, James Whale, saw me in the commissary,' Karloff was to recall years later, 'and he asked me if I'd like to try for the part of the monster. At the time, I didn't nurse much private hope for the picture, but things had not been so brisk for me that I could afford to turn it down. James Pierce experimented with me for several weeks before the screen test and it was his artistry as much as anything I did that clinched the decision. Looking back, if I hadn't been eating my lunch that day when Whale came in, my whole career might have been different.' So, indeed, might the Frankenstein story – the rest, as they say, is history.

The screenplay for the film was the handiwork of two of the studio's most experienced writers, Garrett Ford and Francis Faragoh, who loosely based it on Mary Shelley's novel with the introduction of several new elements including Frankenstein's placing of a criminal brain into the creature's body – a factor that has been reworked in a number of the sequels. To heighten the impact of his picture, James Whale gave a nice acknowledgement to the furore which had greeted the first stage presentation by inserting an opening scene in which Edward Van Sloan appeared through some curtains to warn the audience, 'What you are about to see may shock you ... it might even horrify you!' What it did in fact do was to prove that the story of Frankenstein could be just as exciting on the screen as on the stage – and thereby set another enduring tradition into motion.

The weeping mourners huddle around the open grave. Sad-faced, black-clad old women in peasant dresses and old men, their faces lined from hard work and a long life, bow their heads as the priest finishes the final blessing and sprinkles the grave with earth.

Two men watch the ceremony from behind a headstone. One is pale and dark; his wan skin seems to be lit from within as if he were being burned by some intense flame. His bright eyes are almost black in contrast to his skin. Everything about him implies a life of study, enrichment of the mind and some intense passion that is consuming him.

The other man is very small. He turns and we see that his spine is bent into a grotesque hump. He has thick, stupid features framed by ragged brownish locks that hang down to his brows. His eyes peer out from under them – burning orbs of fire staring from pits of carbon black. He watches the funeral with wide-eyed interest.

The priest, having finished the blessing, leads the procession from the graveyard. One of the mourners stays, takes off his jacket, picks up a shovel and proceeds to fill the grave. The rattle of earth on the hollow wooden coffin fills the cold grey twilight. Finally the man thrusts the shovel into the earth, lifts his jacket to his shoulder and trudges home.

'Now!' says the intense man to the hunchback, quietly but commandingly. The two hurry out onto the still-soft mound. 'The moon's rising! We've no time to lose!' Quickly the two uncover the coffin.

'Here it comes!' cries the hunchback. They hoist the coffin to the edge of the grave.

The pale dark man strokes the pine-wood box like a mistress's limb. 'It's not dead, just resting.'

Dr Henry Frankenstein and his assistant lift the box from the grave.

High in the mountains, overlooking a rocky valley, there stands a crude wooden gallows. A corpse swings at the end of a rope. 'Look,' says Fritz the hunchback, softly, 'it's still here …' The rope creaks in the wind and the body swings grotesquely, as if still alive. Fritz watches the ghastly pendulum with a dreadful fascination.

'Climb up and cut the rope,' commands Frankenstein, holding the lantern aloft.

The dark, stupid features of the hunchback blanch. 'No-o-o-o!'

'Go on!' says the doctor coldly, taking no heed of the other's discomfort. 'It can't hurt you. Here's a knife.'

Slowly, with great effort, the hunchback climbs the rough wood of the scaffold. Drenched with sweat, he reaches the top. He crawls along the crossbar and, holding tightly with one hand, severs the rope. The corpse falls stiffly. The hunchback leaps down, anxious to be free from the grim structure.

'Is it all right?' asks the assistant in hushed, reverent tones.

Dr Waldman, a brisk, white-haired old man who has not yet lost his brain to senility, and who speaks with a youthful zest for his own words, is lecturing to his anatomy class. On the table before him are two glass jars, slippery with moisture on the outside and clouded with saline solution within. He is unconscious of Fritz's wide-eyed face peering in at the window and watching the lecture ghoulishly.

'And in conclusion, ladies and gentlemen, here we have one of the most perfect specimens of the human brain ever to come to my attention here at the university.' He points to the other jar. 'And here, the abnormal brain of a criminal. All the degenerate characteristics check amazingly with the case history of the dead man, whose life was one of brutality, of violence and murder. Both of these jars will remain here for your further inspection. Class dismissed.' And he strides from the room.

The students herd out and the lights are turned low: the room is left dark and empty. The skulls and skeletons hanging from the ceiling move in the breeze of an opened window.

Fritz scrambles down between the rows of desks to the floor of the lecture hall. He turns and backs into one of the rattling skeletons hanging from the ceiling. Then, stumbling in his nervousness and haste to get out of the room, he goes to the table and lifts the jar containing the normal brain from its place.

The ring of a bell startles Fritz, and the slippery jar falls from his hands and shatters on the floor. The brain lies in the spilled solution and glass splinters; it is useless now. Fritz's face contorts with fear at the thought of his master's wrath. With one darting motion he snatches the criminal brain from the table and leaves the room.

Elizabeth, Dr Frankenstein's fiancée, paces her parlour. She looks at the paper she holds in her hand then looks back up, her eyes concerned and worried.

Sir Victor Moritz is announced. He is a tall, handsome man – Elizabeth's former suitor and Henry's rival for her hand. 'You've heard from Henry?' he asks.

'The first word in four months. Oh, Victor, I'm afraid! Listen,' and she reads: '"You must have faith in me, Elizabeth. Wait. My work must come first – even before you. At night the wind howls in the mountains. There is no one here. Prying eyes can't peer into my secrets. I'm living in the abandoned watch-tower close to the town of Goldstadt. Only my assistant is here to help me with my experiments."'

'That's what frightens me. The day we were engaged he told me of his experiments,' she goes on. 'He said he was on the verge of a discovery so terrific he doubted his own sanity. There was a strange look in his eyes – some mystery. His words carried me right away. Victor, have you seen him?'

'Yes, I met him walking in the woods. He spoke to me of his work, too. When I asked if I might visit his laboratory he just glared at me and said he'd let no one go there. His manner was very strange.'

Victor thinks a moment then adds, 'But don't worry. I'll go to Dr Waldman, Henry's old professor at the medical school. Perhaps he can tell me more.'

Elizabeth accompanies him and the two go out into the night.

Dr Waldman leans over his desk to observe more closely the faces of his callers. 'Yes,' he continues to the two in his study, 'Herr Frankenstein was a most brilliant student – yet so erratic.'

Elizabeth interrupts him. 'Why has he left the university? He was doing so well and seemed so happy with his work.'

Waldman continues delicately. 'His researches in the field of chemical galvanism and electro-biology were far in advance of our theories here at the university. In fact, they had reached a most advanced stage and were becoming ... dangerous.' He puts ominous accents on the last word. 'Yes, Herr Frankenstein is greatly changed. Changed by his insane ambition to create life.'

'How ... *how*?' Elizabeth pleads. 'Please tell us everything, no matter what it is.'

'The bodies we used here in the dissecting classes were not perfect enough for his experiments, he said. He wished us to supply him with other bodies – and we were not to be too particular as to where and how we got them. I said that his demands were unreasonable, so he left the university to work unhampered,' Waldman concludes matter-of-factly. Then he adds, 'He got what he needed elsewhere.' Victor forces a laugh that dies quickly. 'Oh, the bodies of animals. What are the lives of a few rabbits and dogs?'

'You do not understand what I mean,' says Waldman quietly, leaning forward. 'Herr Frankenstein was interested only in ... human life; first to destroy it, then recreate it. That was his "mad dream".'

'Do you think we can go to him?' asks Elizabeth.

'You will not be very welcome.'

'Oh, what does it matter? I must see him. Dr Waldman! You have influence with Henry. Won't you come with us? He respects you.'

Tiredly Dr Waldman puts a coat over his jacket and the three leave for 'an abandoned watch-tower close to the town of Goldstadt'.

It is the tower laboratory of Frankenstein. Lights that mount the mammoth machines flicker like the lightning that flashes outside the open skylight high above the laboratory floor. Cathodes crackle and the thunder from the rising storm outside roars down on the ancient tower. Flasks and test tubes reflect a montage of dials and levers and electrodes. A white-coated figure hurries across the room.

Frankenstein fusses over a huge sheet-covered form on a silver table directly below the skylight. He checks the bandages covering the form, rechecks the connections and secures thick wires to two bolts on a discoloured neck. Then he pulls the sheet back over the humanoid's head.

He cranes his neck at the skylight. 'Fritz!'

'Hel-lo!' Fritz peers wide-eyed over the edge.

'Have you finished making those connections? Well, hurry and come down; we've lots to do!' The assistant, bent in body and mind, scurries down the single rope hand-over-hand, like an ape. He shudders as he comes close to the sheeted body.

Frankenstein watches him, half-amused. 'Fool, if this form develops as I hope, you'll have plenty to be afraid of before the night's over! Come on – attach the electrodes!' Frankenstein strides to the barometer on the wall. 'Ah! The storm will be magnificent. All the electrical secrets of nature – and this time we're ready, eh Fritz?' he exults. 'Ready!'

Huge, scarred and discoloured, a hand falls from beneath the sheet covering the body on the table. 'Oh, look!' says Fritz, horrified.

Tenderly Frankenstein lifts the hand. 'Why? What's the matter?' He quietly scans his handiwork. 'There's nothing to fear. No blood, no decay ... just a few stitches. But look,' he beams, 'the final touch!'

He pulls the sheet away from the head, hidden in a layer of bandages. 'Here's the final touch: the brain *you* stole, Fritz.' Fritz looks up at the doctor guiltily. Frankenstein goes on, unheeding. 'Think of it! The brain of a dead man ... waiting to live again in a body I made – with my own hands, Fritz! With my own hands ...' He sinks into silence.

He starts from his reverie. 'Let's have one final test. Throw the switches!' The instruments of life hum and crackle impatiently. 'Good. In fifteen minutes the storm will be at its height – and we'll be waiting.'

A knock resounds through the watch-tower.

'What's that?'

The knocking grows louder, more insistent. 'There's someone at the door,' says Fritz in wonder.

'Send them away! No one must come here! Help me cover this!' They shroud the body once more. Frankenstein hands Fritz a lantern. 'Whoever it is, don't let them in!'

'Leave it to me!' Fritz assures him.

Fritz scrambles down the wide, stone steps. The lantern in his hand barely pierces the centuries-old gloom around him. The cold stone walls magnify his thoughts. 'I'm coming, I'm coming! ... can't come in now ... coming around this time of night ... got too much to do!' The knocking threatens to shatter the iron-braced door. 'All right! All right!'

The three visitors huddle together in the doorway, barely protected from the driving rain by a stone ledge over the door. Waldman pounds the door once more, louder than before.

A gargoyle peers out at them through a hole in the door. It speaks, 'You can't see him! Go away!' and Fritz slams the opening in their faces.

The pounding starts again but Fritz pays no heed. They then turn to the lighted window above the door. 'Henry! Henry Frankenstein! Open up!'

Frankenstein's figure blocks the square of light. 'Who is it?'

'It's Elizabeth!'

He turns from the window.

The shouting resumes and he returns. 'What do you want? Leave me alone!'

'At least give us shelter!' they beg.

He vanishes once more and in a moment opens the door.

'Elizabeth,' he pleads tiredly, 'won't you please go away?'

'There's something wrong,' cries Elizabeth, alarmed at the steel-white face of her fiancé. 'You're ill!'

'I'm quite all right. Can't you see that I mustn't be disturbed? You'll spoil everything. My experiment is almost completed.'

'Wait a moment,' she says gently. 'I understand ... I believe in you ... but I cannot leave you tonight!'

'Henry, you're inhuman! You're crazy!' Victor shouts.

The tiredness vanishes from the doctor's face. 'Crazy, am I?' he says quietly. 'We'll see who's crazy. Come on up.'

He leads them up the stairs to the heavy oaken door of his laboratory. 'Are you sure you want to come in? Very well.'

He unlocks the door. It opens onto a many-levelled stone room with a high Gothic ceiling that dissolves into darkness as it rises. On the floor is a nightmare of electrical equipment; huge machines dwarfing Frankenstein as he stands beside them; a metal table on which lies a sheet-covered – body?

Frankenstein goes to the door and relocks it. 'Forgive me, but I am forced to take unusual precautions. Sit down, please,' and he motions Victor to a chair on one of the raised stone platforms dividing the floor. Victor stands, unhearing, staring at the body on the table. 'Sit down!' Victor sits. Then, in a softer tone, to Elizabeth, 'You too, Elizabeth. Please.' Unnoticed, Dr Waldman wanders over to one of the huge machines.

'A moment ago you said I was crazy,' begins Frankenstein. 'Tomorrow we'll see about that.'

Waldman reaches for a lever. '*Don't touch that!*' Fritz shrieks at him. The doctor backs away from the hunchback, warily.

'I'm sorry, doctor, but I insist,' says Frankenstein, motioning Dr Waldman to a third chair. Waldman seats himself.

'Dr Waldman,' Frankenstein begins, 'I learned a great deal from you at the university – about the violet ray, the ultra-violet ray, which you said was the highest colour in the spectrum. You were wrong.' Frankenstein leans closer to the doctor. 'Here in this machinery I have gone beyond that. *I have discovered the great ray that first brought life into the world.*'

Waldman smiles slightly, curiously. 'And your proof?'

'Tonight you shall have your proof. At first I experimented only with dead animals; then with a human heart, which I kept beating for *three weeks*. But now, *I am going to turn that ray on that body and endow it with life!*'

Waldman is more serious now. 'And you really believe you can bring life to the dead?'

'That body is not dead. It has never lived. *I made it.* I created it – from bodies I took from the graves, the gallows; anywhere! Go and see for yourself!' He swirls the sheet from the body on the table and turns to stare into their horrified eyes. 'Quite a good scene, isn't it? One man *crazy*; three very *sane* spectators!'

The thunder has grown louder, more ominous and frightening. Frankenstein turns to Fritz and at a sign they man the huge machines – great monolithic mechanisms covered with a maze of dials and switches. Frankenstein grasps one of a row of levers and pushes it down. All the wondrous electrical elements of creation stir to life! Generators and transformers hum with power; electrodes start to crackle; the wires connected to two silver knobs on the body's neck start to smoke. As another lever is thrown, the huge table with its burden rises on a steely column of metal – rises high above the heads of the wide-eyed spectators below – rises to the open skylight, where it stands, silhouetted against the blue-white lightning that fills the skies.

Frankenstein moves to the lever – a single huge and heavy lever set apart on the fantastic machine. With a slow, sure motion he pulls it down – and *all the life-giving forces of nature are channelled into the corpse!* Then, slowly, the table is brought down to rest on the cold stone floor.

Frankenstein rushes to the side of the body. One hand, limp, lifeless, hangs over the table's edge. All stare as the hand, weakly, hesitantly, *lifts itself away from the floor!*

'It's moving ... it's alive. It's alive ... it's alive!' exults Frankenstein. 'It's alive, it's alive! It's alive! It's *alive!* IT'S ALIVE!'

'Henry – in the name of God!' It is Victor who cries out.

'In the name of God, now I know what it feels like to *be* God – !' And every atom in Henry's body trembles in a paroxysm of triumph, vindication, the ecstasy of creation.


In the library of Castle Frankenstein, Victor and Elizabeth are being confronted by Baron Frankenstein, Henry's father. He demands petulantly, 'Why does he go messing about in an old ruined windmill when he has a good house, good food and drink, and a darned pretty girl to come home to?'

They offer unsure explanations, suggesting 'experiments'.

'There's another woman, isn't there? Hah! Pretty sort of *experiments* these must be!'

The burgermaster, a fat pompous man, is announced. Self-consciously he enters the room and greets the three already there.

'Well, what do *you* want?' the baron demands impatiently.

'Well ... when will the wedding be, if you please?'

'Unless Henry comes to his senses there'll be *no* wedding!'

'But the preparations have been made for weeks!' protests the burgermaster.

'Then let them be unmade!'

Insulted, the burgermaster leaves.

The baron turns to Elizabeth and Victor and states, 'Henry *will* come home, if I have to fetch him myself! There *is* another woman, and I am going to find her.'

*

Back in the tower laboratory, Waldman paces the stone floor. Frankenstein watches him coldly, gloating over his success. 'Come and sit down, Doctor. You *must* be patient. Did you expect perfection at once?'

Waldman turns angrily. 'This creature of yours should be kept under guard. Mark my words, he may prove dangerous.'

'"Dangerous!"' Frankenstein scoffs. 'Poor old Waldman, have you never wanted to do anything that was "dangerous"? Where would we be if nobody ever tried to find out what lies beyond? Haven't you ever wanted to look behind the clouds and the stars? To learn what causes the trees to sprout, or what changes the dark to light? But if you talk like that, they say you're crazy. Well, if I could discover just *one* of these things, I wouldn't care if they *did* think I was crazy.

'You're young, my friend; your success has intoxicated you. Wake up!' pleads Waldman. 'Look the facts in the face! Here we have a creature whose brain ...'

'Whose brain must be given time to develop,' asserts Frankenstein confidently. 'It's a perfectly good brain, Doctor. You ought to know: it was stolen from your laboratory.'

'The brain that was stolen from *my* laboratory was a *criminal* brain,' says Waldman with deadly revelation.

Frankenstein is stunned for a moment, at a loss for words. 'Oh, well ... after all, it's only a piece of dead tissue,' he says uncertainly.

'Only evil can come of it. You will ruin your own health if you persist in this madness.'

'I'm astonishingly sane, Doctor,' retorts the former student coolly.

'You have created a monster and *it will destroy you!*'

'Patience, patience. I believe in this monster, as you call it. If you don't, then you must leave me alone. I've got to experiment further.'

He walks over to a huge, heavy door braced with a wooden timber. He contemplates it a moment, then turns back to Waldman. 'He's only a few days old, you know. He has been kept in total darkness. Now I'm going to expose him to the light.'

He lifts off the massive oaken bar that braces the door and silently steps away.

Noiselessly, excruciatingly slowly, the door swings open on

its hinges. A mammoth figure backs out of the blackness. It senses the light behind it and slowly, awkwardly turns ... Beneath the thick, bulging forehead, from under heavy, immobile eyelids, peer blank, watery eyes, childlike in their innocence. The face of the monster is grotesquely thin, like a single layer of skin stretched over a huge, misshapen skull. The flesh is green, dead-looking, framed by the dank, black hair that hangs over the monster's high forehead.

A livid purple scar slashes its way across the forehead, like a streak of the lightning that gave the monster life. The jaw is split by another scar and beneath the scar, on the neck, are two silver electrodes. The mouth is a dark gash across the blankness of the skin. The eyes peer out from blackened hollows; shy, trusting eyes, doe-like eyes; no fear or hate in the windows of the soul or on the face that frames them: the monster has no reason yet to fear.

Frankenstein moves towards his creation slowly, warily, so as not to frighten his giant 'child'. The creation observes him, and awkwardly approaches this small thing before him. He dwarfs his creator, this huge creature with the mind of a child.

Slowly Frankenstein backs away from his creation, beckoning it to follow. With clumping, hesitant steps, the monster obeys. It is led to a chair on one of the stone platforms above the floor. Frankenstein motions downward and says gently, 'Sit down.' The monster looks down on him blankly, and collapses into the chair.

Frankenstein, elated, turns to Waldman. 'You see – it understands! Watch.' He turns from the monster and strides over to a covered window. Slowly he lifts the blind and the sunlight flows into the room and rests on the monster's face. The monster's eyes shine with wonder and delight. Smiling dumbly, he rises, and paws the air, trying to catch, to hold these beams of delight ...

The blind is dropped. The golden rays are cut off, the source of delight is gone. The monster's arms drop to his side and he looks at his creator mutely.

Frankenstein gestures anew, 'Sit down.' The monster collapses once again into the chair. 'He understands this time! Isn't it ...'

Fritz stumbles in carrying a torch, looking about feverishly.

The torch, held in wildly gesticulating hands, comes too close to the seated monster. The creature strikes out in fear, animal panic, at the fire! He leaps to his feet and with one swing of his mammoth arm dashes Fritz to the floor.

As Fritz crawls from the fury of the advancing demon, Frankenstein throws him a chain; then the two rush in to bind the growling, angry beast. Waldman helps them thrust him back into his cell and bar the door before he can escape.

Waldman turns to the deathly-white Frankenstein and says, '*He is a monster. You must destroy him!*'

The monster, chained to the wall, howls its misery to the cold confines of its cell. Fritz, torch in hand, lurches in. 'Quiet – quiet!' He pulls a whip from his belt and lashes the helpless creature. 'You'll have the whole countryside down on us!'

Hearing shrieks of pain, Frankenstein rushes in. He commands, 'Come away, Fritz, for heaven's sake – you're upsetting him!' Fritz cowers under Frankenstein's words and gets too close to the monster . . .

The huge scarred hands clutch him and again Fritz feels the creature's strength. Screaming, twisting, he squirms from the deadly grasp. The monster howls his rage and pain at the hunchback and strains against his chains, trying to catch his tormentor once again.

Frankenstein, sickened by his creature and by his assistant, turns away. 'Oh, come away, Fritz. Leave it alone. *Leave* it alone!' he cries, stumbling from the scene of violence and pain.

But Fritz, glaring at the monster, rubbing the bruises left by the huge hands, remains behind. Suddenly he smiles twistedly and takes the torch from the wall. He looks evilly at the monster and advances menacingly, pushing the torch before him . . .

Frankenstein, head in hands, sits at his laboratory table listening – listening to the pitiful shrieks of the monster that tear the air within the tower. Suddenly there is a growl – then an entirely different shriek; one that rises in fear, pain; one that rises from a throat held by powerful, hating hands, Fritz! Frankenstein leaps from the table and Waldman follows him as he bounds down the stairs to the monster's cell.

The door swings open at their touch. The torch on the

floor within the cell reveals the monster, grinning hideously. The door opens farther – and shows Fritz, hanging by his neck, dead.

The monster sees them. He growls and charges!

The two slam the door shut and bar it, just as the monster's bulk crashes against it. The monster screams, and thunders at the door, pounding and kicking and threatening to break through.

Frankenstein leans against the door and says, shakily, 'Poor Fritz. He always tormented the monster. He hated Fritz.' He appeals to his former teacher, 'What can we do?'

'*Kill it!* But we must overpower him first. Get me a hypodermic needle.'

'That's murder!'

'It's our only chance! In a few moments he'll be through that door! Hurry!'

A second later Frankenstein returns and hands the needle to the professor. 'Very good,' says Waldman. 'Now you stand here,' and he hands Frankenstein a torch. 'When he comes toward you, I'll jab his neck with this.' The two take places on either side of the door and Waldman kicks the bar off its rests.

The pounding on the door stops. Slowly the door swings inward and the monster looks out. He sees the torch and lurches toward it, growling, his face contorted with hate for the burning brand and its carrier. Frankenstein waves the torch in the monster's face, which drives him back – and Waldman jabs the needle into the back of his neck!

The monster, infuriated, charges his creator and strikes the torch from his hands. They grapple and Frankenstein is hurled to the floor. The creature falls on him, wraps his hands around his maker's neck and begins to choke the life from him. Waldman pounds on the beast's back, trying to distract him, but to no avail. The creator is at his creation's mercy; and it is clear from the monster's twisted mask of hate that he feels no mercy.

A sudden spasm of shock passes over the brute's face – he is bewildered, helpless before the attack from within his body; the drug is taking effect. He whimpers, then collapses, senseless.

A knock sounds at the door and Victor rushes in. He stops,

amazed, before the scene of violence and says, 'What's happened here? Elizabeth and your father are coming to see you and I ran ahead to warn you!'

Waldman takes command.'Quick! Help me drag this in here.' The unconscious creature is locked in his cell once more. 'Henry – you'd better hurry upstairs and get that blood off your face before your father and Elizabeth get here.' Ashen, and dazed from the battle, Frankenstein stumbles up the stairs.

'Pretty sort of place for my son to be in,' grumbles Baron Frankenstein as he surveys the crumbling face of the watchtower. He and Elizabeth climb the rocky path to the ancient wooden door. 'Oh well, here goes.' He hammers at the door with his cane, waits a moment and crashes again. Victor, his face betraying barely concealed emotion, opens the door.

The baron blusters in and sees the torch, still burning on the floor where it was thrown by the monster. 'What's this? Are you trying to burn the place down?' He looks at Victor a moment, then adds, 'And what's the matter with you? You look as if you'd been kicked by a horse. Where's Henry?'

Victor says apologetically, 'He can't be disturbed just now.'

The baron still suspects Henry of having an affair. 'Oh, he can't? I'll soon settle this nonsense.' He swaggers forward and nearly collides with Dr Waldman. 'Who are you?'

'I'm Dr Waldman.'

'Perhaps you know what all this trouble's about. I'll be hanged if I do.'

Waldman confides, 'I advise you to take Henry away from here at once.'

'What do you think I'm here for – pleasure?' He turns to Elizabeth. 'Come, my dear, let's see what's up those stairs.' The two climb the stone steps. Waldman holds Victor back.

'Leave them alone.'

Elizabeth knocks on the door at the top of the stairs. From the other side Henry's voice comes faintly, 'Come in.'

She rushes to him. 'Henry ...'

'Elizabeth.' Pale and worn, he rises from his chair to meet her – and collapses at her feet, unconscious.

'Victor – Dr Waldman! Come quickly!' They rush in.

Henry is brought round with some brandy. His father informs him, 'I'm going to take you home with me, Henry.'

'I can't! My ... my work! What'll happen to the records of my experiments?'

'We will preserve them,' promises Waldman soothingly.

'And he ...?'

'I will see that he is painlessly destroyed. Just leave it all to me.'

Henry moans. 'Poor Fritz. It was all my fault ...'

Elizabeth breaks in quickly, 'There, Henry, you can't do any more now. You must come home until you are well again. You'll soon feel better when you're out of here.'

On a sheet-covered operating table in Frankenstein's laboratory the monster lies, inert. Waldman, in a surgeon's smock, hovers over the table, watching it. He turns and wheels a table laden with surgeon's instruments close to the operating table. He lifts a worn, black notebook and writes, 'Increased resistance makes necessary stronger and more frequent injections.' The monster's body is building a resistance to the anaesthetic. Waldman writes more, 'However, will perform dissection at once.' Waldman puts the notebook back on a shelf. While his back is turned, the monster's huge heavy eyelids. flutter open. The creature watches Waldman for a moment, then stealthily closes his eyes once more.

Waldman selects the longest of the scalpels on the instrument-tray. He bends over the apparently dormant monster and for a second contemplates his student's handiwork. The monster's great hand rises behind the doctor's back and clamps down on his neck with fingers like steel. The other hand rises to meet it and the two choke the life from the doctor. The creature sits up on the table and loosens his grip on the doctor, allowing the lifeless body to fall to the floor.

The monster climbs from the table and lurches through the inside of the tower, looking for his creator. But the tower is now empty of human life. With a growl the monster opens the huge door to the outside and steps into the light.

The reign of terror has begun.

Henry Frankenstein sits with Elizabeth's head on his lap beneath the flowery branches of the orange trees in the

Frankenstein groves. He is no longer deathly pale and speaks no more with the fire of a fanatic but with the warmth of a lover. He looks from Elizabeth and shudders. 'My work. Those horrible days and nights. I couldn't think of anything else.'

'You promised not to think of those nights any more,' she protests.

'Dearest, when will our wedding be?' he asks.

'Let's make it soon.'

'As soon as you like.' They embrace.

The church bells ring out grandly for the wedding in the house of Frankenstein. Dancing fills the streets of the village and songs fill the air.

In the Frankenstein manor, the baron hands Henry a garland of orange blossoms and says, 'For three generations these orange blossoms have been worn at our weddings. Thirty years ago I placed this on your mother's head, Henry. Today you'll make me very happy by doing the same for Elizabeth. And I hope that in thirty years a youngster of yours will carry on the tradition.'

A toast rings through the halls: 'A son to the house of Frankenstein!'


A small house nestles against a shady forest; a lake lies near by, dark blue in the shade of the trees; in a sunny spot a little girl plays with a kitten. Her father, a strong man in peasant dress, walks toward the forest. He turns to his child and says lovingly, 'You stay here, Maria. I'll go into the woods and have a look at my traps, then we'll go into the village and have a grand time, eh?'

'Won't you stay and play with me a while?' she pleads.

'I can't now, darling, I'm too busy. You stay here and play with the kitten.' He kisses her and strides off.

''Bye, Daddy!'

A little later, the bushes at the edge of the clearing rustle. Maria leaps up to meet her father – and comes face-to-face with Frankenstein's huge, misshapen creation. Innocent and unafraid, she smiles up at him. The creature towers above her and stares at her in wonder for here is one who doesn't beat him or torment him or hate him.

'Who are you? I'm Maria. Will you play with me?'

These are the first words of kindness the monster has heard. In his way he loves the child immediately and allows her to take his hand and lead him to the grassy edge of the lake where the deep water flows quietly and slowly.

She kneels down. 'Would you like to play with my flowers?'

Stiffly, the monster kneels across from her.

She picks some of the bright valley daisies that grow on the bank and gives them to the monster. His face lights with joy at the gift and he looks up at her, smiling expectantly.

She tosses one of her flowers onto the water where it floats, a spot of brightness on the dark surface of the lake. 'I can make a boat! See how mine floats?' She drops the rest in, one by one.

The monster drops one of his in. It joins the tiny floral fleet on the water and floats there prettily. Whimpering with pleasure he drops the rest in, delighted with the play and his playmate.

The flowers are gone and he must do something in return, something to show his affection for the girl. He sees how nicely and serenely the flowers float on the lake's surface; how they brighten the dark water. He looks up at Maria – and sees another fresh spot of colour to brighten the lake. Smiling innocently and whimpering with anticipation, he reaches out to her, lifts her off the ground and gently places her on the lake's smooth surface.

Wildly kicking, and waving, she sinks.

The monster looks on in horror – where has she gone? Why doesn't she float like the others? He realises she will not return! He paws wildly at the water's surface and then, screaming wordlessly, runs into the forest.

Elizabeth, in full white bridal glory, meets Henry in the hall of the Frankenstein manor. 'Henry, I must speak to you.' Without a word he follows her into the chamber.

She turns to him, 'Oh, I'm so glad you're safe!'

'Of course I'm safe,' he says, surprised. 'But you look worried. Is anything wrong?'

'No,' she stammers; then, 'Forget my foolishness. It's just a mood.' She whirls on him. 'Henry, I'm afraid. Terribly afraid! Where is Dr Waldman? Why is he so late for our wedding?'

Frankenstein smiles. 'He's always late. He'll be here soon.'

'Something is going to happen,' she says nervously. 'I can't get it out of my mind.'

'You're just nervous,' says Henry soothingly.

'No, no – I've felt it all day. Something's come between us. I know it – I know it! If only I could do something to save us from it!'

'From what, dear; from what?'

'I don't know! If I could just get it out of my mind!'

She turns to him, calm once more. 'I'd die if I had to lose you now, Henry.'

'But I'll always be with you.'

'Will you, Henry? Are you sure?'

There is a knock on the door and Victor rushes in. 'Henry! Dr Waldman . . .!'

Despite Elizabeth's cries, Henry pushes Victor out into the hall and locks her door.

'Waldman's dead!' cries Victor.

'And the monster?'

'He's been seen in the hills, terrorising the mountainside!' A deep, threatening growl is heard. 'He's in the house!' shouts Frankenstein. 'Upstairs!' They speed up the stairway.

Elizabeth sits nervously on the edge of her settee. Silently the window behind her is opened.

Noiselessly the monster comes up behind her.

Still not aware of him, she rises and goes to try the locked door.

The monster follows. He growls.

She turns to be confronted by Frankenstein's creation, and screams!

Frankenstein, upstairs, hears her cry and rushes back down.

The monster reaches for Elizabeth, trying to still her cries. She dodges his slow, heavy hands – but is caught! His grip tightens around her throat.

The creature hears the commotion outside the door and drops Elizabeth. He escapes through the window and just as the doctor enters, he turns. He growls his hate and disappears from sight.

Frankenstein rushes to Elizabeth and tries to calm her as she screams 'Keep him away! Don't let him come near me!'

*

Through the suddenly hushed gaiety of the celebrating villagers, the woodsman dazedly carries a wet, limp form. His face is numb and he stares straight ahead, oblivious of the crowd.

A child's voice calls out, 'Look ... it's Maria!'

As he passes, the music stops and they follow him, silently.

The crowd calls out for the burgermaster and he steps before them. 'Silence! What is it?'

'Maria!' cries the woodsman. 'She's drowned!'

'My poor man,' says the burgermaster sympathetically, 'why do you bring her to me?'

'But ... but she has been murdered!' he cries. The crowd scream for revenge.

'I'll see that justice is done!' shouts the burgermaster. 'Just tell me – who did it?'

The crowd screams back at him, 'The Monster!'

Henry sits before the fire in Castle Frankenstein. He says to Victor. 'She's still in a daze – she just stares and says nothing. It's maddening.'

'She'll be all right soon. The wedding will only be postponed a day at most.'

'There can be no wedding while this creation of mine is still alive. I made him with these hands and with these hands I shall destroy him!' He turns to Victor. 'I leave Elizabeth in your care – whatever happens. You understand?' And he leaves.

The burgermaster stands before a sea of waving torches, pitchforks and clubs. 'Ludwig,' he shouts, 'you take to the woods. Those are your group. Herr Frankenstein will take to the mountains. Those are yours. I will lead the third group by the lake.' He gives them last instructions: 'Remember – get him alive if you can, but *get* him! Search every ravine, every crevice! The fiend *must* be found!'

The dogs are released, barking along the various trails, their masters close behind.

The lake party in their boats poke through the reeds. Their torches are held high, for the sun is setting and it is dim.

The party in the woods spreads out, covering every inch of ground. The mountain party divides, half taking the slopes, the others the rocky plateaux.

The setting sun paints the mountains blood-red – and the monster glares down at the dogs from high above them, clearly outlined against the crimson heavens.

The mountain searchers find a barely living man lying crushed and broken. 'Which way did he go?' demands Frankenstein. The victim groans and points to the high ground.

They swarm up the mountain. One of the dogs catches a scent, but Frankenstein is the only one to see. He follows and is separated from the rest of the party. They miss him and, realising the danger he is in, call him desperately. 'I think he's up here! Quick!'

Frankenstein stands upon a plateau of rock and pauses in his search to watch the progress below. Deliberately the monster steps from behind a boulder. Frankenstein turns at the noise and two pairs of eyes meet. For a moment they stand, hating each other. Then Frankenstein lifts his torch.

'Back! Back!' The beast tears the torch from his hand and hurls it down. He grasps the doctor and grapples with him. 'Help! He ...' The cry is cut off.

His cry is heard and the party below hurry to his aid.

The growling monster, his face twisted into a mask of hate for the baying hounds and villagers, carries the unconscious Frankenstein under one arm. He is driven by his pursuers to the top of an old abandoned windmill. He drops the unconscious form and leans over the rail, watching the gathering mass of villagers and barking dogs at the base of the mill. He growls with fury and paws the air, as if trying to wipe away the tormentors.

Frankenstein, lying on the floor, awakes and staggers to his feet, trying to escape. He tries to climb through the trap in the floor but the monster sees him and hurls him to the other side of the room. They stare at each other through the whirling spokes of the mill-wheel for an eternity – then Frankenstein makes a dash for the railing, the monster close behind him.

The creature catches him and with a scream of fury hurls him to the ground below. The doctor's long fall is broken by one of the wings of the windmill and he drops to the ground, unconscious.

As Frankenstein is now out of the mill, the villagers set their torches to it. The monster watches from the railing and howls with rage – and then terror, as the flames lick hungrily up the old timber of the mill. The mob watch as the monster, in a frenzy of fear, lurches through the flames, beating at their fiery tongues, trying to escape. He shrieks his pain and despair as he is pinned beneath falling timber and pounds the floor, trying to free himself.

But the timber is too heavy and the monster cannot escape. The villagers look on as the burning mill collapses, cremating the hated creature within it. Dr Frankenstein's dream has turned to dust.

Ashes to ashes.

# The Bride
# of Frankenstein

—————

## By JOHN L. BALDERSTON &
## WILLIAM HURLBUT

Frankenstein *proved to be just as big a box office triumph for Universal as* Dracula *had been, and within a year plans were being made for a sequel with the working title* The Return of Frankenstein. *Pre-publicity announced that the script would be 'based on events in the 1818 novel by Mary Wollstonecraft Shelley', and that James Whale would direct Boris Karloff in the role of the creature with Colin Clive again playing Dr Henry Frankenstein. In truth, though, the only important facet of the novel to be used in the film was the idea of creating a bride for the monster who wanted a companion – and the terrible consequences which resulted from Franken-stein's decision. To play the bride, James Whale cast Elsa Lanchester, the beautiful English wife of the actor, Charles Laughton. He also had her 'double' as Mary Shelley in an ingenious prologue to the picture in which the young authoress explained how she had come to create her famous story.*

*Like Boris Karloff, Elsa Lanchester always remembered how the make-up which made her famous had been created by Jack Pierce. 'It was actually my own fuzzy, untidy hair,' she revealed. 'They brushed it and combed it and made four little braids, and then they put a sort of little house on top – a wire cage, really – and anchored it with pins. Then they added two white hairpieces, one at my upper temple, another at my lower temple. It took two hours to draw in the little scars and go over them in red. The make-up man thought he was some kind of god because he created* The Bride of Frankenstein!'

*James Whale filmed his second epic on a number of huge, Gothic-like interior settings and utilised his camera in a series of panning and travelling shots which thrust the viewer into the very heart of the drama. The result was 'a rare instance of a sequel being better than the original,' according to critic George Perry – a view shared by several reviewers in 1935 and still argued today. According to Radu Florescu in his authoritative survey,* In Search of Frankenstein *(1975), 'Whale gave the world the best of all the Frankenstein sagas in which all the elements of film-making meshed together to form a nearly perfect feature.' Although the picture itself inspired a number of immediate sequels –* The Son of Frankenstein *(1939) and* The Ghost of Frankenstein *(1942) being perhaps the two most notable – none quite achieved the standards of the first two movies. Indeed, a whole decade would pass before another studio – on the other side of the Atlantic – would set new standards of excellence in a new interpretation of the original story . . .*

*Such was the interest in* The Bride of Frankenstein *when it was released, that a special adaptation was written for the English magazine,* Pearson Weekly *(a stable-mate of* Pearson's Magazine*) by a prolific British horror story writer named Guy Preston who was familiar to many readers for a pair of highly acclaimed blood-curdlers,* The Inn *(1932) and* The Way He Died *(1933). The publication coincided with the opening of the picture in London on September 28, 1935 and represented another new development in the history of motion pictures – the use of the 'tie-in' novelisation to attract audiences – as well as one more landmark in the Frankenstein legend.*

# PROLOGUE

Have you forgotten how the Monster 'died' – or what the Monster was? Perhaps you never even heard the prologue to this hideous tale?

Read then, that you may better understand the most fantastic history in the world – and remember that to-day men are still striving for the same goal that Frankenstein achieved, and with similar, if not yet equal, success.

Frankenstein, the brilliant young scientist, had defied the laws of nature. He had unravelled the very secrets of Heaven. He had made – a man!

Man? – well, perhaps that term was generous. Nevertheless it was by that name that he hailed his creation in the first flush of his success.

For months he had worked in secret. Everything had been thrust aside while he slaved for the fulfilment of his dream – to create a living man from the bodies of the dead. Even Elizabeth Lavenza, his betrothed, had been forced to endure his neglect while her lover remained behind the locked doors of his great laboratory.

Gradually, rumours began to spread through the surrounding villages. There were whispers of ghouls at work in the churchyards. Body snatchers. Vampires.

A frightened peasant ran screaming to the mayor with a fantastic story of a newly opened tomb, and a dead man who sat propped inside a coach while a cloaked figure with glaring eyes urged on his horses as though all the devils in Hell were after him.

Corpse after corpse was stolen from the grave before Frankenstein's horrible experiment was completed. His handsome face grew white and lined under the terrific strain. But at last the moment came when with a trembling hand he pressed the vital lever – and only *he* knew with what feelings he watched the result of his handiwork rise moving from the operating-table.

Afterwards had followed a period of terror. This was no Man – but a Monster! True, it was fashioned in the semblance of a man, but there the likeness ended. Turning on its creator it broke loose, transforming the peaceful countryside into a shambles.

Night after night came tales of a monstrous shape that stalked the lanes; a giant frame reeking of the tomb, whose rags but ill-concealed the grave-worms crawling in their folds. It moved and gibbered – so said report – for it could not speak. Its yellow skin scarcely covered the muscles and arteries beneath, and its dun-hued watery eyes bleared sullen murder.

Sweethearts wives, honest yeomen and innocent children, all had fallen lifeless beneath its steely fingers. Frankenstein's Monster spared none. Grateful indeed was the scientist that nobody outside his one immediate circle knew that he was responsible for the death-dealer's existence.

Then, just before this tale commences, the strangest piece of irony occurred. On Frankenstein's own wedding day the Monster appeared. As he and Elizabeth left the church together, the creature struck him down, and trampling all who got in its way, fled roaring out of the village. Emboldened by their numbers the villagers set out in pursuit, trapping the creature in a deserted windmill. With oil-soaked rags they fired the place.

And as the flames roared upward, they saw the Monster, overcome by the fumes, fall back into the fire.

Thus rises the curtain on this most horrid sequel.


# ONE

Night was casting her shadows over the little village of Ingolstadt – *and the Monster was dead!*

Around the smouldering ruins of the old mill the villagers still shrieked their hate, but mingled with their shouts were cries of joy. At last it would be possible to sleep in peace. The terror had been destroyed.

At the side of the little hillock topped by the glowing wreckage, an old man and woman were standing. They had been there all day, waiting for the end. Now, his eyes crazed with pain as those of a maddened bull, the old fellow stared dumbly at the Monster's pyre.

A charred beam fell with a crash on to the smoking heap. The embers stirred and glowed, and a new flame leaped skyward. The old man's lips moved, and he shook off the woman's detaining hand fiercely.

His words came in a groan of anguish: 'Maria! My daughter – my little girl! IT killed her!'

Tenderly his wife put her arm about him. Her own grief

was forgotten in her fear for his reason.

'Come home, Hans,' she urged him. The Monster is dead now. Nothing could live through that furnace. Why stay here longer?'

He shook his head. A shower of sparks spat venomously up at the night sky from the crackling beam lying athwart the ruin. Once more his lips parted.

'I must see him with my own eyes,' he muttered, as one who spoke to calm his own soul. 'If I can but see his blackened bones – I may sleep at nights.'

Slowly he made his way towards the ruins.

One by one the villagers were departing, urged homeward by the burgomaster. They went in little groups, for few could summon the courage to walk alone at night so soon after the nightmare had passed. Soon only the woman was left to watch the smouldering pile and the stumbling, halting figure of her good man.

With faltering footsteps the old fellow made his way to the edge of the burned-out mill. The villagers had done their work well. The heat was terrific. Hans felt the dense smoke slewing on the breeze, prick at his old eyes till the tears came. For his child he could not weep. Some sorrows cut too deep.

A sudden fear came to the woman on the hillside.

'Come back!' she called. 'You will be burnt yourself.'

For a moment Hans hesitated. Did he hear her? Or was he but searching for a firm foothold?

Gingerly, he placed one foot on an ashen pile. It seemed safe enough. He leaned his weight upon it and peered for the brute's remains.

His wife's warning scream came too late.

A pile of blackened bricks fell with a crash beside him, and the ground seemed to open under his feet. With a startled cry the old man flung up his arms and plunged forward – forward and *downward!*

A shower of red-hot debris sparked all about him. A rush of cold air raced past his ears. With a mighty splash Hans struck the icy water of the mill's underground cistern. He was trapped.

Coughing and spluttering, he came up to the surface and

began to swim. If only he could keep up until his wife came
or brought help.

An iron bar projected from the side of the well. He made
for it with the heavy, deliberate strokes of an ageing man. If
he could cling to that ...

A sudden swirl in the water brought his head round with a
jerk It was dark down here. Only the glow of the smoking
timbers up above illuminated the dank moss-strewn walls.

He screwed up his eyes with the effort to see.

*Splash!*

There it was again! Nearer this time. Something slithering
in the darkness. Over to his left. He drew himself up by his
bar and peered.

Something was heaving up out of the water beside him.
It seemed as though it would never stop. Higher and higher
it grew until it loomed gigantic over him. IT turned its
head.

With a shriek he loosened the bar and struck out. The
Monster was alive – *alive!*

Like a streak a giant paw clamped on the withered neck,
thrusting it down – down. There was a feeble struggle, a
gurgle, the splash of beating limbs against water – and Hans
lay still. Then with a wordless roar of animal fury, Frankenstein's Monster lifted the drowned body in its arms and
hurled it blindly at the wall.

The skull cracked and the corpse slipped out of sight; and
at the same moment from the ruins above there sounded the
voice of the dead man's wife.

'Are you there, Hans? Hans, where are you? Hans!'

The Monster's lips parted in a crack of fiendish glee and an
unholy light gleamed from behind its loathsome eyes. The red
glow from the embers illumined its face as it groped – upward,
upward –

Raising itself still higher it reached a paw through a crack
in the ruins. The woman grasped it.

'Oh, thank God, Hans!' she gasped. 'There you are. Wait,
and I'll pull you up.'

Back in the Schloss von Frankenstein there was rejoicing.

Young Baron Frankenstein had regained consciousness for the first time since the Monster's murderous assault.

He looked up with gratitude in his eyes as he saw his wife bending over him, and guessed that it was thanks to her nursing that he was better.

Elizabeth Frankenstein and Minnie, her maid, guarded him jealously, and soon he was well on the way to recovery.

Naturally enough, feeling his strength return, he hankered to go on with his experiments. But on one point Elizabeth was firm. There was to be no more ghoulish tampering with the dead.

'Forget all that horror,' she implored him. 'It was never meant that we should know those things – the secrets of life and death.'

Her husband looked at her fondly. Heaven knew that he loved her – that he would do most things in his power to please her. But to abandon research just now, when he had achieved the superhuman? Ah, no, he argued, it was unfair of her to ask.

'I dreamed of being the first to give to the world the secret of which God is so jealous,' he told her, sitting in the great panelled room which was his favourite. 'I yearned for the formula for Life.' A light came into his eyes, and he went on eagerly: 'Think of the power it gave me – to create a man! And I did it! Who knows, in time I might have trained him to do my will. I could have bred a race!'

Gently Elizabeth smoothed his brow, smiling when she saw the wrinkles melt. But there was an undercurrent of fear in her voice as she warned him.

'Henry, don't say those things. Don't think them – as you love me.'

She knew that Frankenstein had ever longed for power. Now that he had achieved the warped ambition on which he had set his heart, she dreaded the overwhelming brilliance of his brain.

Many times they talked together like this, and frequently she urged Frankenstein to yield to her wish to go abroad far from the scene of his vile creation.

But late one night, when the wind howled like a thousand tortured devils round the tall battlements of the castle, there came a knock at the heavy oak door which shattered forever the hope that was dawning in Elizabeth's heart.

It was Minnie who answered the summons. A queer, tall man smiled down at her. There was that in his glittering eyes which struck terror as she backed involuntarily before him. Somehow she knew instinctively that he had come for no good purpose.

'Tell the Baron Frankenstein that Doctor Pretorius is here on a secret matter of grave importance,' said the stranger, not unmusically. 'Tell him that I must see him alone – to-night.'

Minnie's scared glance flickered up and down the long black cloak which wrapped the stranger. It reminded her of the pall which had covered her father's coffin. She shivered.

'The master's a-bed,' she quavered, flinching despite herself under the tall man's gaze. 'That's where all decent folk should be at this time of night.'

'So?' Pretorius' long teeth gleamed wolfishly in the moonlight as he grinned at her discomfiture. 'Nevertheless he will see me.' And with a thrust of his hand he was past Minnie and in the hall.

Pretorius was right. Frankenstein knew him well. He was a Doctor of Philosophy who had been dismissed his University for dabbling in Black Art.

He saw him at once. In the world of science in which he moved there were many less creditable persons with whom he had had to do business.

Pretorius came straight to the point. He knew all about Frankenstein's monster and complimented him upon its creation. But, he added, he had also succeeded in producing Life – though by a vastly different method. If the Baron would accompany him he would be delighted to show him the results of his experiments.

'What is behind all this?' asked Frankenstein at last. It was plain that the doctor was wrestling with some secret excitement.

Pretorius' lips parted in their wolfish grin.

'Don't you see?' he said. 'We must work *together*. Together we may reach a goal undreamed of.'

Again he urged him to accompany him back to his laboratory.

Feebly Frankenstein clung to his promise to Elizabeth.

'No, I'm through with it all. I'm going away,' he said.

His tone transformed the other.

Savagely Pretorius clutched him by the arm. The mask came off and he showed himself in his true colours as a threatening blackmailer.

'Do you know that your monster is still at large?' he challenged. 'That it has already done two more murders since its resurrection?'

Frankenstein stared aghast, and the doctor went on:

'Luckily, few apart from your wife and myself know that you are responsible for its existence. But there are penalties, I would remind you, for killing people. If I were to tell the law who made this roving instrument of death —'

Frankenstein paled and frowned.

'Are you threatening me?' he asked haughtily.

Again came that wolfish grin.

'Ah, no! Don't put it so crudely. Say rather that I am reminding you it were better that we work — *together*!'

For a moment there was silence, then Frankenstein rose to his feet and rang the bell. To the man who came he gave orders for his carriage to be made ready. Then he turned to Pretorius.

'Damn you!' he muttered. 'I have no choice. Let us go.'

He soon found that the doctor had not exaggerated. He had produced Life as he had claimed, and in his laboratory were some half-dozen pigmy men and women — all living and imprisoned in flasks.

'While you were digging in your graves,' Pretorius explained, 'and piecing together dead tissues — I went to the source of Life. I grew my creatures.'

'They are perfect!' exclaimed Frankenstein, scientifically enthusiastic in spite of himself. 'But what a pity they are so small.'

Pretorius nodded encouragingly.

'Ah, there I give you best. You *did* achieve size. But don't you agree, my friend, that we should make an astonishing collaboration?'

For some tense moments love of science and love for his wife warred within Frankenstein's breast. Pretorius guessed that the battle needed but one more thrust to turn the way he wanted.

'Think,' he whispered eagerly. 'Our dream is but half realised. Alone you have created a man – now, together we shall make him a mate.'

'You mean –?'

Pretorius nodded slowly.

'Yes – a woman.'

The light of fanaticism gleamed in Frankenstein's eyes.

Even as they were discussing this unholy partnership the Monster was stumbling over fields and pasture land. It was thirsty and famished.

Hitherto, Life had shown it only brutality, so that it lived by the code of Fear. If it could frighten, it had soon learned that it could take what it wanted. If in its turn it could be made to fear – it fled.

Somehow the blood pumping through the long-dead tissues of its body was bringing back feeling to its nerves. Dully, like a clogged engine, its brain was learning to work – to think. Dimly it realised that it was an outcast – a horror to other men, for the meaning of stray remarks was permeating its befogged mind.

The sun rose over the hills, lighting the tree-tops with a golden sheen. The monster, weary, paused in its path. It needed drink. The sound of sheep bleating floated towards it, and it ambled slowly in the direction of the sound. There was blood in the bodies of sheep.

Suddenly, rounding a bend, it saw her – a woman-thing. She was standing on a rock by the side of a stream and about her her sheep were scattered. A stream! – Water! The creature quickened its pace.

The shepherdess did not see the Monster until it was almost upon her. Her first intimation of its presence was the strange snarl which served it for speech. She turned – then aghast at the horrid spectacle mowing and posturing before her, she screamed in abject terror and fainted dead away.

How could she tell that the queer noises it made were a pathetic attempt to reassure her?

Angrily the Monster bent over her. This faint was something

it had not seen before. It did not understand it. It struck irritably at the inanimate girl …

*Crack!*

From the distance came the sound of a shot. The Monster uttered a growl of pain and clasped its arm. Then, drawing back its taut skin above its yellow fangs, it roared its fury.

The two huntsmen who had seen it strike the girl conferred hastily. Again a gun was raised. Instinct or intelligence was awakening in the Monster. It ducked and fled incontinent into a nearby wood.

'Well, well, what is it?'

The burgomaster looked up irritably from his desk as a man, panting and dishevelled, burst unceremoniously into his room. Behind him, mouthing startled protests, stood the burgomaster's servant.

The intruder gulped for breath. He swayed, exhausted with his long run.

'The Monster!' he gasped, clutching blindly at a chair for support. 'He's in the woods. A friend and I were out shooting – we saw him attacking a girl. My friend fired. I think he hit him.'

'The Monster, you say? Excellent!' It was the moment for which the pompous old burgomaster had been waiting. For years he had been longing to show the good people of Ingolstadt the kind of stuff of which he was made. He turned to his servant.

'Stop gibbering, man! Get out the bloodhounds. Raise all the men you can. Lock the women indoors and wait for me.' Fuming, he reached for his gun on the wall.

Outside the house he could hear his servant shouting the news. In a minute the narrow street was packed with a jostling throng of excited villagers, all armed haphazard with guns, pitchforks, crowbars and anything else to which they could lay their hands.

Headed by the burgomaster, they trooped out of the village.

They came to the spot where the other huntsman stood supporting the frightened shepherdess in his arms.

'Which way did he go?'

Even before he could answer the burgomaster's question the bloodhounds were baying and straining at the leash.

'That way. Hurry!'

Howling threats, the rabble plunged into a neighbouring thicket.

The hounds nosed the ground, their breath coming in quick, eager sniffs. They moved silently, swiftly, leading the mob off the rough cart track and up a steep, pine-covered slope.

Suddenly from the ranks of the crowd there came a cry.

'There he is!'

'Faster, faster!'

The burgomaster shaded his eyes. Ahead, just breasting the top of the hill, a vast, misshapen figure was loping. It ran awkwardly, as though its man-made limbs were unequal to the task. They moved ponderously like primitive metal pistons.

In a trice the hounds had reached it, and stood round baying while the rest of the human pack came up.

Snarling, the great creature faced them, its pallid lips drawn back above huge yellow fangs. It lunged out savagely, grunting and squealing like a tormented pig. Fœtid green froth dripped from its gaping mouth.

But there were too many this time for Frankenstein's creation to tackle. Someone slipped behind it. A thwack from an iron bar struck it on the head. It screamed with the pain. A well-aimed stone brought it to its knees.

One, more daring than the rest, stepping forward from the throng, slipped a rope about its neck. Striking, stabbing, kicking, the crowd closed in. The memory of murdered wives and children banished all pity.

'Bind him securely!' bellowed the burgomaster from a safe distance. 'Tie his feet first – then lash him to a pole. There are plenty of fallen pines about here.'

Groaning and writhing, the Monster was subdued, lashed to a fallen tree and carried down the hill. There he was thrust into a farm wagon and brought back in triumph to Ingolstadt.

In the dungeon of the prison a small gang of men had stayed to make the place proof against the Monster's gargantuan strength. A gigantic chair had been prepared with rings of iron, into which its feet and hands were now thrust. An immense iron collar was welded about its neck, and a steel chain twisted about its body secured it to staples driven into the wall.

At last the burgomaster stepped back satisfied.

'That will hold him. What a pity I can't act further without orders from my superiors!' He looked round for his secretary. 'Heinrich! – Where the devil's he got to?' The man came forward. 'Ah, I want you to take a letter to Geneva.'

With a smirk of triumph the burgomaster went out. Behind him he heard the shock of the heavy bolts of the dungeon thudding into place.

Each side of the metal-studded door two guards stationed themselves. Both were armed.

The burgomaster smirked again. Yes, it was a clever capture. It should mean the mayoral chain for him – that is, if these fool villagers had any gratitude!

Scarcely had he begun to dictate his letter, however, when a terrific uproar in the street outside called him to the window. He called down angrily:

'Ungrateful wretches! What is it now?'

A fusillade of shots scattered the crowd before they could answer him, and a screaming woman fell wounded in the roadway. The burgomaster thrust his head farther out and withdrew it hurriedly.

Down the centre of the road, roaring with shrill animal fury, came the Monster. About its neck, wrists and ankles were rough abrasions where the shackles had clasped its flesh. Its eyes glared wildly and its teeth gnashed as it raced after the scared villagers who had so lately been its captors.

Stooping, it swooped upon the prostrate woman, snapping her spine in its two hands as easily as a man might break a twig. It shook the body venomously before flinging it brutally down on to the cobbles. The skull split open and the Monster trampled viciously upon the dead white face until its leaden boots were spattered with vivid gouts of blood.

'Shoot!' screamed the burgomaster helplessly from his window. The red-tape which had prevented him from having the creature killed on sight vanished. With it fled his hopes of the mayoralty. His natural pomposity was forgotten in the sudden wave of horror which overcame him. Cursing, he ran to the wall where he had just replaced his gun.

When he returned it was in time to see the Monster lumbering over the fields beyond the village, and in a corner of the street a little group huddled over the still body of a child.

Terror was loose again!

One by one from outlying hamlets reports came in. There was Frau Neumann wantonly and horribly murdered. A gipsy family completely wiped out. The burgomaster railed at his guards and called on Heaven, but to no purpose. No bonds could have held a creature possessing such colossal strength; and now few could be found with the courage to go after it again. Perhaps, they argued, somewhat belatedly, if they left it alone it would leave them in peace.

It was after its third murder that the Monster, wounded by a random shot and exhausted by the chase, came to a tiny hut set in the heart of a coppice.

Night was falling, and the earthy smell of the dewdrenched bracken beckoned the creature to rest awhile.

Furtively, for it had learned to fear all men, the Monster moved towards the lighted window of the hut. Then it paused, startled.

From within the little dwelling came a strange, sweet sound. Another. And another. Someone was playing a violin.

Music was a new sensation to the Monster. It was pleasant. It drew near, fascinated.

Within the hut a hermit, who was blind and old, played on unaware of the hideous face pressed close to the pane. For fully a minute the Monster watched. Then it saw the old man turn – turn and stare mildly at him through sightless eyes that saw not the watcher's aspect and were, consequently, unafraid.

The Monster moaned faintly. It was nearly spent.

The playing ceased. As often happens when one sense is lost, another develops acutely. So it was with the blind man. The sound the Monster made struck loudly on his ears. He went to the door.

'Who is there?' he called, gently.

# TWO

For a space Monster and man faced each other. The moment was tense with foreboding. What would the Monster do?

Slayer of innocents, would it strike down the helpless blind figure before it, or would it mistake the violin in his hand for an instrument of destruction and stagger away into the darkness?

The hermit came closer. He could sense where the other was standing. Gently he spoke.

'You are welcome, my friend, whoever you are. Forgive me, but I cannot see you. I am blind.'

Slowly he stretched out a hand and touched the Monster. A tense growl caused him to start back in alarm, then a sticky sensation at the tips of his fingers made him utter a low cry of concern. *Blood!* – the stranger was wounded!

Blind and unafraid, he slipped an arm about the creature and guided it into the hut. And there he tended the Monster's hurts.

That night the hermit prayed. He had long wanted a companion in his loneliness.

'Dear Father, I thank Thee,' he murmured, 'that out of the silence of the night Thou has brought two of Thy lonely children together and sent me a friend to be a light to mine eyes and a comfort in time of trouble. Amen.'

From then onward, a queer friendship sprang up between them. The hermit believed the Monster to be dumb, and the affliction gave them a mutual bond. Blindness and dumbness – each could supply a want to the other.

And the Monster? No longer hounded, stoned and treated as an outcast, it responded to the hermit's kindness with the gratitude and devotion of an injured animal.

It learned to speak.

Painfully, it struggled with the sounds the hermit taught it.

'Bread – drink – good!' These words were pleasant, happy words. They were words which brought comfort and helped to supply bodily needs. But the greatest word of all, the word which sowed the seed of a soul in the Monster's vast carcase was – *'friend.'*

'Friend,' it repeated over and over again, touching the hermit's sleeve with grateful humility. 'Friend – good!'

And here it might have stayed harmlessly for ever but for a certain happening.

There had been peace in the countryside for some months now and people were beginning to venture abroad again. The Monster was supposed to be dead. Some even claimed to have seen its giant body lying at the foot of a precipice. A great cloud seemed to have been rolled back from above the village of Ingolstadt.

One night, two strangers called at the hut. They had been out after wild duck and lost their way in the wood. With his usual courtesy, the hermit asked them in to rest and eat. They entered.

Suddenly one of them uttered a low cry and pointed to a huge shape that sat hunched in a corner.

'Look!' he gasped. 'It's the Monster!'

With an oath the other leaped to his feet and raised his gun. But he was not quick enough.

Association with the hermit had sharpened the Monster's intelligence. Though as yet it could talk but little, it understood all that was said. And it knew that the word 'Monster' was never applied to it by a 'friend.'

With a hideous cry it sprang, wresting the gun from the startled man and hurling him back against the wall. The next instant it had sent the weapon flying through the window.

Bewildered, the poor hermit raised his voice.

'What are you doing?' he cried anxiously. 'This is my friend.'

The men turned on him furiously.

'Friend? Why this is the fiend which has been murdering half the countryside. Good Heavens, can't you see?'

Then, looking closer, they realised what had happened. The hermit was blind. He did not know.

But there was no time now for explanations. The Monster, roused from its feeling of security, meant to remove the two strangers who had blundered out the truth in the only way it understood. Lifting the table as easily as a matchbox, it flung it savagely across the hut.

It caught the second man as he was shifting his gun from his shoulder, knocking him back against the door. The impact brought the swinging lamp down from its staple in the roof and a wave of flame shot up. In three seconds the hut was ablaze.

Both men tugged at the hermit, dragging him out of harm's way. Then they, too, leaped for the open door. Within the hut the Monster battled frenziedly with the flames, hurling himself again and again at the wall in the attempt to break it down – anything to get out of the furnace which was raging all about it.

At last with a crash a board gave. Another and another. Screaming with pain and fury, the creature plunged through the opening and out into the wood. The hunt was on again.

A black shape stood silent by the gaping mouth of a tomb. It was tall and gaunt, and the pallid moonlight shining from above, gleamed on a row of yellow teeth set in a wolfish grin.

All about it, like stark fingers pointing to the sky, rose countless headstones, while here and there a monument to some noble family towered grimly remindful above its neighbours. It amused Doctor Pretorius to think that even in death there was snobbery.

The graveyard was deserted, as a graveyard should be at dead of night, save for this solitary figure who waited motionless beside the crypt.

Somewhere an owl hooted. The Doctor turned his head, then his lips snapped with an exclamation of annoyance as he noted the glimmer of a light moving over the graves. Of what use all this secrecy when the fools gave their presence away in this idiotic manner?

Cupping his hands, he uttered an answering hoot and waited until the two men came up.

'Put out that light,' he hissed, as they stood together awkwardly before him. 'We want no witnesses for what we have to do.'

Reluctantly, for the men he had hired were superstitious peasants, they obeyed him. One of them blew out the lantern and the three figures stood listening intently.

No sound, however, fell upon their ears, save the moan of the night breeze in the tall trees fringing the cemetery and the occasional creak of their branches.

Satisfied at last that they were unobserved, Doctor Pretorious led the way down the narrow stone steps to the bowels of the crypt.

To-night was an important one for Pretorius. He had threatened, wrangled, cajoled and pleaded with Frankenstein for his co-operation in the experiment which was to make a woman fit to mate with the Monster. But it had all been to no purpose. Just when he had believed that Frankenstein was ready to yield, that his enthusiasm and love of science would compel him to throw in his lot with him, Elizabeth had entered the room.

The few words that she had heard as she entered the door had been sufficient to enlighten her as to what was proceeding, and she had immediately forbidden her husband to countenance the thought of another such experiment. What was more – she had shown the Doctor the door and given orders for the Schloss to be closed while she and Frankenstein undertook a long trip abroad together.

It was necessary, therefore, that Pretorius should conduct his experiment alone, and it was to procure a suitable body for the attempt that he was here in this crypt to-night.

At the foot of the steps he paused and re-lit the lantern. The pale light flickered fitfully, dimmed and glowed. Like a great crow, draped in his long black cloak, Pretorius lifted the lantern on high and sniffed. The rank earthy smell of the grave assailed his nostrils. He grinned appreciatively. He was in his element.

He looked about him. Behind him his assistants shivered apprehensively.

The coffins were arranged in tiers. Some of them were incredibly old. Mildewed and rotting, they had warped with the damp, and where they had warped they gaped, disclosing yellow bones or torn and fibrous shrouds.

Into one of these Pretorius thrust his hand. When he withdrew it, it clasped a woman's skull. He chuckled softly, patting the bony cheek with insolent familiarity. Then he tossed it playfully at the shrinking men, deriding their horror as it smashed to pieces like an egg on the cold stone floor.

'She's no use to me,' he muttered, tearing down a huge

festoon of cobwebs which hung from the ceiling with his bare hands. 'Too old. Too small.'

A fat spider scuttled across his foot. He stamped upon it. It squelched, and he wrinkled his nose with distaste as he thrust its remains aside with his boot.

'I want someone young,' he continued, peering at the inscriptions on the coffin lids. 'A girl – beautiful, supple, recently dead – and unmarked from any injury.'

The two men stirred uneasily.

Taking a wall each, they began to inspect the coffins. Presently one of them called out, his voice booming strangely beneath the vaulted ceiling.

'Will *she* do?'

Pretorius hurried to his side.

'Read the inscription. How old was she?'

Stooping, the man began to read.

'Madeline Ernestine, beloved daughter of –'

'Skip that.' Pretorius' voice was sharp. 'How *old* was she?'

'Aged nineteen years and three months.'

'Good! That's the one. Break open the coffin.'

The two men hesitated and glanced at each other. A sudden glint came into the Doctor's eyes. It was a glint akin to madness. His fingers worked.

'Well, what are you waiting for?' he asked in a dangerously soft tone.

The two men shivered and crossed themselves. Their fear was abject. Pretorius grinned wickedly.

'Do you want me to send you to the gallows – where you belong?' he reminded gently. 'Do not forget that I know who murdered Julius Steinberg.'

The hold he had over them had its effect. Muttering, they bent over the girl's coffin, hacking and prising, until a few moments later with a rending sound the lid came away.

Gloating, Pretorius leaned over the still form within.

'Pretty little thing,' he chuckled, cutting the winding sheets from about her face. 'I hope her bones are firm.'

Caressingly he ran his fingers over the dead limbs.

The two men picked up their tools, and, at a sign from the Doctor, made their way out of this abode of death. The lantern they left burning on the bottom step. It was enough for them to breathe once more the pure fresh air of the world above, and with all haste they flitted gratefully across the graveyard, leaving their erstwhile employer with the corpse.

Alone, Pretorius seated himself upon the coffin, while he raised the slender body in his arms. She was not heavy, despite her dead weight. He propped her up against a wall while he lit a cigar and awaited the arrival of his own servant. Between them they would convey the corpse to his laboratory. There was half an hour at least to wait.

The lantern burned lower.

Pretorius was alone now, save for the silent occupants of the shelves about him. His isolation did not trouble him in the least. Cynical, indifferent to life and death, he was enthusiastic only in the matter of research. This subject, however, whipped his imagination to the point of madness, and he was entirely at a loss to understand how it was that Frankenstein, who had succeeded so far, could fail to pursue his crazy dream to the limit.

If only he could think of a way to force his hand!

Musing, Pretorius puffed out dense volumes of cigar smoke. They assumed strange shapes in the failing light.

'Alone – I am still a pioneer,' he muttered to the corpse that faced him. 'I may fail at any turn. But with Frankenstein, whose creature still walks somewhere on this earth, to help me, ah, my pretty morsel, what a nuptial I could arrange for you!'

As though it heard and understood, the head of the corpse dropped forward. The Doctor's eyes narrowed, then he laughed softly as he noted the cause.

A giant rat falling with a soft plop from the ceiling had struck the body on the shoulder in its passage, slightly dislodging it. Glancing malevolently at the Doctor with beady eyes, it scuttled across the flagged floor and disappeared.

Chuckling to himself, Doctor Pretorius sat back and blew another smoke-ring. Then he delved into his pocket for his watch. What a devil of a time the fellow was in coming, to be sure!

A creak sounded at the far end of the crypt. Surely that was he?

Pretorius prepared to rise, when suddenly it dawned upon him that the noise emanated from that part of the crypt farthest from the entrance. It could not, therefore, be his servant. It must be *someone else!*

For a moment his heart leaped, and a thousand superstitious fears inherited through the ages came to plague him. The next instant reason conquered, and he was his emotionless self again.

The sound was repeated. It was louder this time.

To the Doctor's straining ears it sounded like a heavy weight being cautiously lowered to the floor. It dragged slightly.

Slowly he turned his head. Then, with an exclamation of complete surprise, he sprang to his feet.

There, close behind him, its body almost completely out of a coffin, was the Monster. It had obviously lain hidden there all the time the two men had been working in the crypt. Slowly it swayed to its feet and lurched towards the Doctor.

It was to Pretorius' credit that, after the first shock of surprise was over, he was unafraid. He regarded the creature coolly but warily. Indeed, a certain studied insolence crept into his voice as he addressed it.

'Oh, I thought I was alone,' he said airily. 'Good evening.'

The flickering light from the dying lantern picked out the bones on the creature's face. They gleamed yellow-white under the taut skin. Pretorius watched it guardedly as it drew a step nearer. For weeks it had been missing – who knew what subtle changes might have taken place in the man-made creature. Its next action sent the hair rising up on the Doctor's prosaic head. It spoke.

'Friend?' asked the Monster. Its voice was harsh and sepulchral.

Pretorius took a grip on himself. After all, it was all perfectly normal. The Monster had been in the world some while now. It was natural that it should have learned to imitate human speech.

'Indeed, I hope so,' responded the Doctor, his brain beginning to work rapidly. He indicated a seat beside him. 'Have some refreshment?'

Avidly the Monster swallowed the wine and food that Pretorius had brought for himself. It was a wise move on the Doctor's part. It put the creature in a good humour.

Peering about it with curiousity, its gaze lighted on the corpse of the girl. It turned to Pretorius.

'You make man, like me?' it asked. There was a pathetic eagerness in its harsh notes.

Pretorius shook his head.

'No,' he replied, playing up. 'Woman – friend for you.'

The Monster nodded, gratified.

'Woman? Friend? I want friend, like me,' it said.

The idea which had been simmering in the Doctor's brain from the moment he set eyes on the Monster and learned that it could speak, suddenly fructified. Stroking his chin, he rose to his feet.

'I think you can be very useful, my friend,' he smiled. 'You can add a little force to my argument, if necessary.'

For a moment he hesitated, then: 'Do you know who Henry Frankenstein is?' he asked. 'And who you are?'

The Monster nodded.

'Made me – from dead. I love dead – hate living.'

Pretorius chuckled.

'You are wise in your generation,' he answered. 'Well, we must have a long talk, you and I. And then I have an important call to make. Perhaps Baron Frankenstein will not, after all, be so selfish as to refuse my request – when he sees you face to face.'

There and then in the blackness of the tomb – for the light had gone out long before they finished – Pretorius told the Monster about his plan to make a mate, emphasising Franken-stein's refusal and appealing for the creature's co-operation. And when at last he stumbled up the steps into the graveyard above, it was with the knowledge that the Monster understood its part in his plan and could be relied upon to do its share well.

Immediately Pretorius made his way to the Schloss von Frank-enstein. Despite the lateness of the hour, Minnie was awake.

'I must see the Baron,' declared the Doctor, pacing the hall. 'Immediately.'

Protesting that her master and mistress were unable to see anybody, Minnie left him. But the clangour of the great door bell had alarmed Frankenstein.

'What is it?' he called from the library.

'It's that Doctor Pretorius again. He wants to see you,' Minnie answered.

Frankenstein groaned and turned to his wife.

'Then I knew it. Shall I never have any peace from the man?' He went to the door and addressed Minnie. 'Send him away. I won't see him.'

Minnie turned, then she gasped. Silently the Doctor had come up behind her.

'Good evening, Baron,' he said pleasantly.

For the moment Frankenstein was too aghast at the man's effrontery to say anything. His wife took command.

'Dr Pretorius,' she said icily. 'I don't know what your business at this time of night may be – but whatever it is it will have to wait. My husband and I are leaving almost immediately.'

Pretorius refused to be ruffled. He bowed with mock courtesy and turned to Frankenstein.

'I think you know why I have come, Henry,' he said with meaning. 'If the Baroness will leave us a moment –'

Elizabeth and Frankenstein exchanged glances. He nodded and she gathered her wrap about her.

'I will await you in my room,' she told him, then beckoned to the waiting maid. 'Come, Minnie.'

Alone, the two men faced each other. 'I have completed by my method a perfect human brain,' announced the Doctor. 'It is living, but dormant. Everything is ready – for *us*.'

Frankenstein shook his head.

'No!' he said. 'I won't do it – that's my final word!'

Pretorius smiled. Again there was a hint of the wolf in his expression. Slowly he crossed the library to the french window and beckoned.

'I expected this,' he said. 'So I have brought my other assistant, who may persuade you to change your mind.'

As if hypnotised, Frankenstein stared at the french window, which was gradually opening. Then, with a cry of fear, he fell back, hands out-stretched.

The Monster, hideous creature of his own making, stood before him. With one massive paw it pointed to a chair. Its harsh voice filled the room.

'Frankenstein – sit down!' it said.

Pretorius began to chuckle.

'Yes, there have been developments, you see. He can talk.'

Something in the creature's malevolent leer as it gazed at him chilled the man who had made it. He called out piteously.

'What do you want?'

The Monster came closer.

'You know,' it said.

Pretorius intervened.

'He wants a woman – a friend – a mate. You'll help us make one now, won't you, Frankenstein?'

Dumbly the scientist shook his head. The Monster growled. It advanced threateningly.

'Yes – *must!*' it ordered.

Frankenstein cowered under the upraised fist. To think that he had made this Thing – which was now commanding him as if *It* were master!

He appealed to Pretorius.

'Get him out!' he cried. 'I won't even discuss it till he's gone.'

Ponderously the Monster turned its head until it looked squarely at the Doctor. Back in the recesses if its brain it knew that there was something it had to do – something pre-arranged between them. Pretorius gave the sign. Stiffly the creature turned and marched back the way it had come. The french window swung wide as it passed through into the moonlight, its tattered rags flapping in the breeze – and with it went the stench of the tomb.

Ashen pale, Frankenstein wiped the sweat from his brow.

'Now,' said Pretorius with a grin, 'let me explain my method and benefit from your experience.'

Frankenstein sat as though carved in stone, while the Doctor talked. Elizabeth meant more to him than anything in the world, and she had extracted his promise. If he agreed to this devilish proposal, he knew that he might be loosing yet another murderer upon the world – who knew, if not in time – a race of murderers? Yet if he refused?

Pretorius was speaking.

'I have, my friend,' he was saying, 'an excellent laboratory installed within a ruined tower high on a hill. It is not far from here. There we can conduct our mutual experiment in seclusion. I can assure you there will be no dearth of fresh bodies, for I have in my employ –'

He broke off, and his mouth slowly widened into that terribly wolfish grin. From somewhere above them a terrible scream had rung out. It reverberated down the castle corridor.

It came again. And again.

Frankenstein leaped to his feet, his face suddenly grey.

'My God!' he muttered. 'That's Elizabeth's voice.'

The next instant he was racing up the great stone stairs.

At the head of the stairs he met Minnie. She was shaking with terror. Fear glared from her eyes and for a moment she could not speak. He seized her roughly.

'What's happened! Quickly! Tell me!'

The grip of his fingers brought back her courage, and she moistened her frozen lips. Then:

'My lady!' she moaned. 'Oh, my lady – the Monster's got her!' With a trembling finger she pointed out of the window. They crowded round it.

Scaling the wall of the courtyard as easily as if it were a ditch was the Monster. Even as they watched, it began to lope down the hill. The light of the moon threw its grotesque shadow after it like some great black demon dancing with fiendish glee. And from Frankenstein's throat there rasped a despairing cry as the moon showed something else across the Monster's shoulder – the body of a woman, slender and white and limp – the body of Elizabeth, his wife!

'Now, perhaps, you will do what he asks,' whispered Pretorius in his ear. 'It is the only way to save her.'

## THREE

It was true – and Frankenstein knew it. The only way to save Elizabeth was to throw in his lot with Pretorius and accede to the Monster's demands.

The Monster wanted a mate. Very well, it should have one.

There was but one thing for which Frankenstein stipulated before he set to work, and that was to hear his wife's voice that he might know she was safe and unharmed. To this Pretorius agreed.

Together they went to the ruined tower on the hill where the doctor had his laboratory. There Frankenstein was allowed to speak to his wife by means of a kind of telephone.

'Elizabeth,' he cried eagerly into the mouthpiece. 'Are you safe?'

He could scarcely speak for the relief when he recognised her beloved voice answering him.

'Henry! – Yes, darling I'm quite safe – but oh! the dark and this dreadful –'

There was a noise at the other end of the wire. Frankenstein held his breath, straining his ears to listen. Her voice came again.

'I'm quite near – in a cave. Come for me –'

It broke off with a gasp. Then, shrilling in his ear he heard the words: 'Oh, God, it's here! It's here! – Henry!' Silence followed.

Distracted, Frankenstein shouted down the instrument. There was no reply. Impotent to do anything, he looked up and found Doctor Pretorius smiling sardonically at him.

'My dear friend,' murmured the doctor, 'you surely did not believe Elizabeth's gaoler would be so foolish as to permit her to betray her whereabouts? But rest assured, so long as you do what is asked of you she will come to no harm.'

Frankenstein knew when he was beaten. Subdued at last, he bent himself to his task.

It was not long before the scientist in him rose uppermost and he was working day and night at a bench littered with strange apparatus. Test-tubes, retorts, queer metallic globes and intricate dials, all had their part in fashioning what was to be the heart of this man-made woman.

And over him all the time, urging, encouraging threatening, stood the Monster.

A queer place was this ruined tower where Pretorius had his laboratory. It was shaped like a tall cone some hundred and fifty feet in height.

The laboratory itself occupied the ground floor, and the hollow tube of the tower leading to the starlit vault overhead formed a kind of lift-shaft. Strange and complicated machinery hung suspended from beams in the wall, or stretched trellis-like up to the castellated top of the building. The only lights were flares or arc-lamps.

Came the time when the current was applied and the mechanical heart began to beat. Pretorius bent his head exulting over the glass container, watching while the blood pumped steadily up and out. Suddenly, the heart fluttered and stopped.

With a curse, Frankenstein flung the contents of a bubbling crucible on to the stone floor and slumped into a chair.

'We need another heart!' he cried. 'A human heart. It must be sound and young. Where can we get it?'

The doctor and the Monster exchanged glances, then Pretorius went to the door.

'Karl!' he called.

A loutish misshapen brute appeared. Frankenstein recognised him as the doctor's most trusted servant. He began to explain.

'What we need is a female victim of sudden death. Can you do it? There are always accidental deaths occurring.'

For a moment Karl hesitated, then the doctor spoke and there was that in his eyes which made his meaning clear.

'Yes, Karl,' he nodded. 'There are always *accidental* deaths occurring.'

The man withdrew.

And that night a youth was mourning his sweetheart and a new heart – a human heart – beat strongly in Frankenstein's glass container.

For nine hours the small heart beat with the regularity of the normal. Excitement ran high. Taking it in turns, Pretorius and Frankenstein watched the indicator rising and falling; saw the blood began to flow simply and easily through the valves.

At last it was decided that the time had come to transfer the organ to the waiting corpse. The vital stages of the excitement had arrived.

It was an occasion when the slightest slip might mean the undoing of all their work. The Monster had served its purpose. It had kept Frankenstein from prowling in search of his wife. It was now in danger of becoming something of a nuisance.

Accordingly Pretorius drugged the creature and left it lying on its great straw bed.

What was needed for the successful completion of their task was a terrible thunderstorm. Then, claimed Frankenstein, the air would be full of electricity, which could be imparted to the corpse by means of a wire attached to two kites and passing through an electrical diffuser.

Pretorius looking out of the window noted with satisfaction that such a storm was brewing this night.

'We must work quickly!' he cried, wheeling the stiff body under the bright lights of the arcs. Together they bent over it, cutting away the surgical bandages which swathed the entire figure. Soon it was ready to receive the heart.

Poising a scalpel above the breast the doctor made a swift incision and, his fingers working with all thé deft skill of which he was capable, Frankenstein inserted the beating organ.

They worked in a tense silence until the deed was finished. The atmosphere grew clammy.

'The storm is almost overhead,' announced Pretorius presently, peering out of the window. 'It will break soon.' He turned almost affectionately to the figure lying still upon the operating table. 'To think that within that skull,' he murmured, 'is an artificially developed human brain – each cell waiting for the life that is to come.'

A low rumble of thunder brought his sentence to a close. He glanced up the funnel of the high tower.

'Are the kites ready?' called Frankenstein.

'Yes.'

'Then send them up as soon as the wind rises. They must reach their zenith before they are struck.'

For some minutes longer they worked together, connecting the wires of the cosmic diffuser to the body on the table. Up on the battlements of the high tower, their shadows dancing grotesquely in the light of the paraffin flares, two men wrestled with the giant windlass which was to hold the kites when they cast off. A blue wave of lightning flickered over the mountain ridge to the south. Thicker and thicker grew the atmosphere. It felt like an immense blanket pressing down upon the world beneath.

Then came the first assault of the storm. A terrific clap of thunder which shook the valley. A vivid fork played wildly up and down the sky, and at the same time the rain began to fall.

Up the dark funnel of the hollow tower glared the white face of Frankenstein. Faintly his voice reached the men above the din of the storm.

'Stand by the kites! – Are you ready? – Let go!'

Guessing his meaning more by his gestures than by his words, they let the wires run out. The kites streamed steadily up in the wind which had mysteriously arisen to whip the raindrops fiercely into their faces.

*Crash!*

With a hideous crackle the lightning stuck the kites. A beam of fire zipped down the wires holding them, down the eerie funnel of the tower to the cosmic diffuser suspended above the body. A shower of sparks played over the long-dead face and the hands of a dial began to jig rapidly.

With eyes glued to this dial Frankenstein waited while the storm raged louder and fiercer overhead. Pretorius joined him, rubbing his thin hands together nervously. He was grey with excitement, sweat dripped from his forehead, and his queer, pale eyes glinted malevolently.

Shock after shock passed through the diffuser and entered the body. The indicator on the dial rose. Forty – fifty – sixty.

Overhead the white faces of the waiting men peered down the shaft. Both had had their orders.

Suddenly Frankenstein stepped back and touched a lever.

'Ready?' he yelled. 'Stand back! It's coming up.'

There came a steady thumping from the floor below. It was the hydraulic lift at work. The table maintaining the body lurched, steadied and began to rise. Higher. And higher.

It reached the top of the tower.

Like a thousand demons let loose the storm concentrated its fury upon it. It seemed to be lit by a constant stream of lightning. Great flashes of combustible gas illuminated the shaft, jagging the darkness with flickering light.

Suddenly from one of the men on the battlements came a yell of terror.

'The Monster! It's loose! It's after me!'

Together Pretorius and Frankenstein peered upward. A

gigantic shape loomed over the narrow opening far above. It picked up the screaming man, shaking him as if he had been a rat and threw him bodily over the parapet. Maddened by the sound of the storm it was running amok high up there in the battlements.

The sound of its roars reached them far below. There was no mistaking it.

'How much drug did you give him?' shouted Frankenstein in the doctor's ear.

'Enough to keep ten men under for a couple of hours more.'

Frankenstein groaned.

'Damnation! He'll ruin everything!'

But even as he spoke, a faint luminosity began to spread over the table containing the corpse above. Both noticed it together.

'Thanks Heaven! We're in time, Pretorius. Pull over that switch.'

The doctor obeyed, and with a strange hissing sound the whole devilish contraption descended.

Together they stared at the still swathed body on the table. Forgotten now was the raging Monster overhead. They were grimed with dirt and exhausted with their efforts, but their greatest moment was yet to come. Had the experiment been a success?

Slowly, almost awfully, Frankenstein bent over the corpse. With shaking fingers he loosened the bandages covering its face. He took them off. Then he fell back gasping.

A pair of vivid blue eyes looked up at him. Strange eyes. Eyes that had in them the questing wonder of a child's and yet were filled with terror.

He turned to Pretorius.

'She lives!' he cried, triumphant. 'She lives! She *lives*!'

It was the culmination of the wildest dream. A mate had been made for the Monster.

As Pretorius and Frankenstein watched the slender figure of the girl they had created move gracefully, if a little unsteadily, across the floor of their laboratory they envisaged all that this triumph might mean.

A new race of creatures to be born in the world. Offspring

of once-dead bodies. What would they be like? It was a staggering speculation.

Unlike the Monster, this girl was nearly perfect in appearance. The Monster had been the pioneer creation. It was crude and unprepossessing. All that Frankenstein had learned while making it had been utilised to this second creature's benefit. As yet, of course, she could not speak. Moaning faintly, and staring about her in terror like one barely awakened from a nightmare, she sat on a ledge by the wall of the laboratory, enduring the critical glances of her creators.

Suddenly with a queer little jerky gesture, she threw up her head and a shrill cry escaped her lips.

Following the direction of her gaze, Frankenstein gave vent to a low exclamation.

The Monster was standing in the doorway. Its face was cracked in a hideous grimace which the scientist recognised was meant to be a smile. In spite of himself, Frankenstein shuddered.

Pretorius gripped his arm.

'Sh! my friend. Watch!'

Ponderously the Monster heaved its huge bulk down the steps and into the room. Its mouth worked spasmodically. It walked straight to the staring girl.

'Friend,' it said.

The staring blue eyes grew wider. She shrank back. The two scientists watching could see fear make way for panic in the small, drawn face.

A note of anger crept into the Monster's voice.

'Friend?' it said again, reaching for the girl's hand with one gigantic paw. There was a note of command in the voice.

Something about this ghastly travesty of love sickened Frankenstein.

'Stop!' he cried.

The Monster turned with a snarl and caught the girl fiercely to him. Her mouth snapped wide and a high metallic scream rang forth. It maddened the Monster. It began to croon reassuringly to the girl, but its harsh notes only terrified her the more. She screamed again.

Swiftly Frankenstein crossed the room and took her from it. A bellow of fury escaped it.

'She hate me – like others!' mouthed the Monster. Once more it made for the girl.

At that moment there came an interruption. The door of the laboratory was flung wide and Elizabeth appeared. Finding herself unguarded, she had managed to escape.

'Henry!' she called.

Frankenstein motioned her back.

'Get out,' he cried, 'as you value your life!' He knew, none better, the temper of the Monster when roused. She shook her head.

'Not without you.'

A terrific crash told of the shattering of a trayful of glass apparatus. Smashing its way towards him, the Monster reached out once again for the girl. One paw fell for an instant on the electrical control lever.

'The lever! Look out for that lever! You'll blow us all to atoms!' shrieked Pretorius, flinging everything within reach at the raging creature.

The meaning of his words clicked in the Monster's slow intelligence. With a trumpeting roar of triumph it seized the control with both hands.

'Henry,' screamed Elizabeth again, 'you *must* come! I won't go without you.'

For a moment Frankenstein hesitated.

'I can't leave them,' he stammered. 'Don't you see –' But his hesitation gave the Monster the chance it had sought. Like a flash one huge paw shot out and seized the girl from the scientist's arms. Then it gestured savagely towards the door.

'You live!' it cried. 'Go! Go!'

Frankenstein waited no longer. And as the door slammed behind him and his wife, and the Monster saw them running madly down the hill, it caught the shrieking girl in a close embrace and threw itself flat across the lever.

'We – belong – dead!' it cried as the first shudder shook the building.

And the white, gibbering face of Dr Pretorius was the last thing it saw, before there came a blinding flash, a terrific explosion, and the whole tower thundered down in ruins.

# The Workshop of
# Filthy Creation

---

## By ROBERT MULLER

*Television was still very much in its infancy – most pro-*
*grammes were screened live and all sets had black and white*
*pictures – when the story of* Frankenstein *made its début in*
*1952. At least three adaptations of the novel had been broad-*
*cast on BBC Radio in the years on either side of the Second*
*World War, and perhaps twice that number in America in the*
*same period, all underlining the effect the story was capable*
*of having on the imaginations of listeners. It was in the*
*United States, however, that* Frankenstein *first appeared on*
*television in the autumn of 1952 in a 30-minute ABC series*
*entitled* Tales of Tomorrow. *Because the series was transmit-*
*ted live from New York, nothing exists to commemorate this*
*landmark show, although the star is known to have been the*
*famous Hollywood horror actor, Lon Chaney, whose make-*
*up apparently consisted of a bald head with stitched gashes*
*on his cheeks and skull. Rumour has it that Chaney's perform-*
*ance in this much-condensed version of the novel was a*
*mixture of the bizarre and the unpredictable as the actor*
*believed for much of the transmission that he was taking part*
*in a camera run-through and not a live broadcast! The rival*
*network, NBC, put out the first colour version of* Franken-
*stein five years later in their* Matinée Theater *series with the*
*famous boxer Primo Carnera playing the monster. Perhaps*
*worried about the reaction of viewers to this early evening*
*presentation, an announcement preceded the transmission*
*warning that it might prove too frightening for children.*
*Shades of the impact of the first stage and film adaptations*
*once more!*

*The first major television production that was faithful to Mary Shelley's story was undoubtedly that screened on British TV by Thames Television in November 1968, adapted by one of the country's leading TV scriptwriters, Robert Muller (1925– ). Muller, who had escaped from Nazi Germany as a child, served as a journalist and critic before starting to write for television and there demonstrated a particular talent for Gothic horror. He approached the task of bringing the novel to the small screen with a very clear vision: 'We decided, rightly I think, not even to attempt to compete with the film, but to go right back to the book – the original images that must have raged in Mary Shelley's mind as she was writing it.' The result was a highly acclaimed production that was well served by its talented cast of Ian Holm as Frankenstein and Ron Pember as his creature. The image of* Frankenstein *indeed continued to haunt Robert Muller, and in 1977 when he was masterminding a TV series of horror stories for the BBC entitled* Supernatural *about a group of storytellers who assemble at The Club of the Damned to try and terrify one another, he wrote an outstanding episode featuring a writer who is researching a biography of Mary Shelley and unexpectedly discovers a relative of the Frankenstein family still obsessed with creating life. The stars of this Grand Guignol production were Gordon Jackson as the writer and Vladek Sheybal as the heir to the Frankenstein legacy.*

What on Earth was this?

The members of the Club of the Damned did not respond with enthusiasm to the idea of a writer joining their secret establishment. A writer liked to gossip. A writer invented things. A writer was unreliable.

Was he trying to hoodwink them, this scholarly, myopic gentleman who now stood by the fireplace waiting to begin his tale of horror? Was he possibly even a spy sent out by some unscrupulous publisher to discover new sources for gruesome tales of the supernatural?

*It would never do to be careless about the choice of new members. What was said, what was done, at the Club of the Damned was not for the curious, the ordinary, the uninitiated.*

*Howard Lawrence, for that was the author's name, purported to be a writer of biography, though few members could ever remember having read a work by a person of that name. Sir Francis, as he watched the face of the speaker, fussed with his snuff-box and made a mental note to ask for a list of his works – if indeed there were any.*

*Sir Francis' rheumy eyes focused on the figure by the fireplace. Howard Lawrence had an ascetic face, narrow and bony, and there was a possibly deceptive mildness about his eyes. So mild indeed was his general demeanour that Sir Francis felt certain that the alleged author was under sedation.*

*'There is one story,' the speaker was saying, 'without doubt the most startling and the most original I have ever written, which will never be published ...'*

*'Indeed?' Sir Francis exclaimed, 'and why not? Is it not a work of biography? Is it perhaps libellous?'*

*'It could be said to be both,' Howard Lawrence said, the crooked smile around his mouth contradicting the spirituality behind his eyes ...*

In 1882, flushed with the critical success of my *Life of Shelley*, and accompanied by my wife and daughter, I sailed from England in an endeavour to follow as exactly as I could the footsteps of the poets Byron and Shelley in their tours abroad during the early years of this century. My purpose was a simple one: to gather and ascertain facts that would provide the material for further scholastic works, biographies of two men whose intellectual passions stood so closely to my own precise manner of thought. You may be familiar with some of my early writings, notably the biographies of Wordsworth and Coleridge, besides that of Percy Bysshe Shelley and his tragically charmed circle. Without undue modesty, I can safely assert that these works are not traditional learned monographs, sterile literary mausoleums founded solely on arid fact; for I insist that only a sensitive understanding of the creative spirit behind the master-works of genius can give us a true perspective of their aesthetic splendour. Though they are no longer with us, to me the vital essence of these men lives on – not only in the words and thoughts they have bequeathed us, but in the places they visited and the very dwellings they inhabited. It is as though the power of their remembered genius enables dead stones to live again.

Throughout my investigations into the hidden lives of these dead poets, the patience and solicitude of my dear wife Elsbeth had been of the utmost satisfaction to me; but on this latest expedition a further charming companion was to lighten my days of travel and study – our daughter Mary. Our only child, she was entranced at the prospect of celebrating her nineteenth birthday while actively journeying along the more secret literary byways of Europe. It was a delight to be shared by all of us, for not only would she be a tender companion to her mother, but also an eager vessel into which I could pour the distilled experiences of my continuing research. Shy, even stilted in the presence of strangers, my dear child almost glowed with bright curiosity behind her trim spectacles whenever the opportunity arose to discuss the discoveries of the day. I was pleasurably aware of her restless desire to grasp and appreciate new vistas of truth and knowledge that I gladly opened before her; if only she had been a son, what even greater affinities we might have shared! Even so, she was very dear to me; the blossoming of her mind, moulded by my discreet parental guidance, was an added and continuous delight.

By way of Belgium, then of France, we came at last to Switzerland and the environs of Geneva, where we were to remain for several weeks at the Villa Diodati. Does the sound of that darkly familiar name reverberate uneasily within your mind? The Villa Diodati ... sinister, disquieting, a place haunted by the shadows of unanswered minds questioning the unknown. Here it was that Byron played host to his fellow fallen angel, Shelley, whose eighteen-year-old mistress Mary Godwin was soon to marry him after the suicide of his first wife, Harriet. Here, revolutions of the soul were born, shibboleths cast down by thunderbolts of intellect and passion, and new concepts of creation brought forth like dragons' teeth sown by vengeful cherubim. It was all there still, a grim miasma echoing that distant, dismal summer of 1816. Then, to pass the long rainfilled evenings, Byron and his mysterious secretary Polidori, Shelley, and the child he had liberated into womanhood, amused themselves by competing to invent a story based upon some supernatural occurrence. It was not to prove easy; long hours filled by discussing Erasmus Darwin had filled their minds with the grand theme of Man's challenge against the gods – the legend of Prometheus, no less. But out of those nights' amusement came a moment of nightmare imagination penned into literature by the girl soon to become Mary Shelley: its title – *Frankenstein*.

The strangely intense atmosphere at the Villa Diodati, added to the hours of long study that I undertook there, eventually took their toll; I was quite exhausted. It was at this point that my dear wife, ever concerned for my well-being and welfare, suggested that before proceeding along our chosen route to Italy, we should attempt to restore our health and calm our nerves by spending a few idle weeks in a friendly Alpine inn or guesthouse. The idea of a brief period of contemplation, exercise and rest appealed to me, and I agreed. As to why I chose the somewhat remote Gasthof Ritterhof, I can give no logical reason. Could it have been the inevitability of fate, or sheer chance? Or had the sinister spirit of the Villa Diodati mesmerized my subconscious into fortuitously selecting what appeared to be at first sight such an exceptionally tranquil and inviting establishment? Such questions are useless now; when we first saw that simple inn, nestling by the lonely mountain road, brightly picturesque amongst the serenity of sunlit snow we felt only an enormous sense of ease and imminent contentment. Here was a location so pleasant, so open, so unlike the brooding villa we had left behind us, that we each openly smiled in expectation of the homely welcome we were sure awaited us; in that, we were not to be disappointed.

Inside the inn, all was simplicity and rustic comfort. Although there seemed to be no windows, the plain white walls, punctuated by plain wooden doors and stairways leading to the upper and lower recesses of the house, imbued the atmosphere of the place with a soft light all their own. Through the open door leading to the 'Stube' stood a black stove, stark against yet more white walls, and rough wooden tables –

scrubbed, like the floors, spotlessly clean. This limpid whiteness was brightened constantly by flowers set on tables and in
alcoves. Heartening though this scene was, a moment of
puzzlement crept into my mind: something was missing, something that should be there ... and wasn't. In an instant, the
thought had passed – we were confronted by our host, a
person of remarkable friendliness waiting anxiously to attend
to our every requirement.

'Our modest house is honoured, sir,' announced the innkeeper. His voice was kindly and courteous, his bow of
welcome almost a parody, more suited to the theatre, perhaps. Mary, I could see, was as taken with our host's appearance just as much as I was, but she managed to control the
smile that threatened to broaden into girlish laughter. As
my wife addressed the innkeeper, I studied him more
closely.

'We should like two rooms,' declared Elsbeth crisply. 'One
for my husband and myself, and one for our daughter.' Our
host listened as though hanging on each trivial word, his thin,
arched eyebrows raised at the alert, and in stark contrast to
the almost unnatural whiteness of his skin. His mouth, too,
though thin, stood out boldly and surprisingly red, while the
final touch of artificiality was supplied by his crop of hair –
deep black, and obviously dyed. Vanity, perhaps? An unusual
display for a venue so off the beaten track, I told myself. Not
far behind our host stood a once-handsome but now emaciated
Frau. Worn out by work, white-haired, she made no concessions to the passing of time over her ageing face. Like the
innkeeper she smiled a gentle welcome, adding to this a
simple, open-handed gesture that invited our trust and a
warm response; but for a moment, when her eyes fell upon
Mary, her anxious gaze flicked almost instantaneously away,
troubled and furtive. The furs that Elsbeth and Mary wore
made it quite clear that we were travellers of no little worth, a
rare and welcome source of custom in this remote valley. It
crossed my mind that the Frau was anxious that we might
consider the inn not suited to our tastes, and I hastened to
reassure her.

'Your situation here is both charming and secluded ... just
what we require ...'

The woman curtsied slightly, obviously pleased, but it was

her husband who replied. The near-perfection of his English added a quaintness to his dignified speech.

'We are simple people, but everything we have is placed at your disposal. Your rooms will be homely and warm, just as is our hospitality. Our name, sir, is Hubert ...' A fond gesture drew his wife shyly to his side, and she half-curtsied again as he introduced her to us. 'Frau Minna ... my good wife.' He smiled jovially at her, and she blushed as he spoke. 'You will never forget her cooking for as long as you live ...'

These formalities concluded, our luggage was deftly collected to be taken upstairs, and we prepared to follow the sturdy fellow – Hans by name – who was to lead us to our rooms. We were still not free of Herr Hubert's hospitality, however.

'Some refreshments, sir?'

'Some tea, perhaps ...' interjected Frau Minna, thoughtfully. 'Or some warm wine – it is cold now, even during the day ...' The sleigh journey – we could still hear the departing jingle of bells – had been most invigorating, and the thought of a steaming beverage was to all our tastes.

'Tea ...' cried Elsbeth happily, '... how splendid. In our room, please. I cannot wait to change my clothes ...'

'Oh, please,' trilled Mary, 'but I should like some of your "warm wine" ... if it is red, that is ...'

The eagerness of her response both amused and disarmed any mild disapproval that Elsbeth or I might have voiced, had the occasion been less indulgent; accordingly, I confirmed our request for tea and a little Glühwein, and was thanked effusively by our host as he handed me the keys to our rooms. While Hans gathered up our various items of luggage, we looked about us; in the whole establishment, there was only one other guest – a cheery old peasant seated in the far corner of the Stube, drinking and watching all that went on with twinkling interest. We had barely started to follow Hans across to the stairs, with Mary chattering gaily to her mother, when the old peasant nimbly rose and intercepted us, glass in hand.

'Prost!'

I replied in kind, but without encouragement; I had no mind for this sort of confrontation, but the peasant was not to be put off.

'*Engländer?*' he beamed upon me. 'I am Otto! How-do-you-do! Button-my-shoe! Mixed-pickles-on-board! Ahoy!' Following which display of verbal dexterity, he cheerfully raised his glass, maintaining the bravado gesture until we were finally out of his sight upstairs. Elsbeth, ever prepared to admonish such impropriety, was about to put the fellow in his place, but I urged her on quickly. To have addressed the man would have meant running the danger of being perpetually buttonholed whenever we met again, and made to suffer the ordeal of Herr Otto's linguistic talents *ad nauseam*. Mary, less aware of the more regrettable aspects of such a person, made no attempt to hide her amusement.

'Papa – they are so quaint ...! We shall be happy here, I know it. It's so different from that dreadful Villa Diodati –'

'There are many strange things *here*, my pet ...' observed her mother, pausing wearily on the stairs.

I glanced at Elsbeth, surprised that she too had noticed that missing element that had nagged at the back of my conscious-ness ever since we'd arrived. But as so often before, I had miscalculated her powers of observation.

'Didn't you notice too, Howard? The innkeeper – Herr Hubert – how badly his hair was dyed ...!'

'Perhaps it's a wig ...' suggested Mary, her eyes full of mischief. 'Perhaps he comes from a long line of waiters ...!' Elsbeth, though tired, joined in Mary's girlish laughter.

'Switzerland is full of surprises!' she smiled.

We were on the landing now. Hans was well ahead, opening doors and depositing luggage in each room.

'The surprises are not only concerned with people,' I re-marked. 'Perhaps you will have observed that there are no crucifixes to be seen – not anywhere. Nor even the small portraits of saints, as is the usual custom ...'

'How odd ...' dutifully echoed Elsbeth. 'Could our inn-keepers be extreme Protestants, do you think, Howard ...?'

'Or even Israelites?' teased Mary.

'Swiss Israelites ...?' Elsbeth half-stifled a giggle. 'Surely that's not so ...?

'Oh, Mama –' laughed Mary out loud, '– what fun we're going to have! Unleavened bread and Swiss cheese for supper, even!' It was good to see them both so content with our new surroundings. While my darling Mary opened the window of her room and stared enchanted at the dancing fall of snow-flakes against the gathering darkness outside, her mother solicitously unpacked the child's valise, prior to dealing with her own.

I left them there, and entered the adjacent bedroom alone. Suddenly I felt very weary, and laid myself upon the massive double bed that shared domination of the room with an ancient but efficient iron stove. My mind refused to rest; for some reason, the shadowy figures I had hunted so assiduously at the Villa Diodati insisted on peopling not only the deeper crannies of my consciousness, but almost, it seemed, corners of the room itself, despite all my attempts to turn my thoughts from them. That episode of our expedition was past, ended; for Elsbeth's sake, we were here to indulge in harmless relaxation, to free myself from the intense, secretive and irritable mood that had increasingly come to dominate my normal affability. I knew she dreaded the continuation of our journey onwards to Italy, with all the pressures it would bring, and I was determined that this brief sojourn at Gasthof Ritterhof should be an idyllic one. Yet the sensation of unease persisted. Without reason, unbidden questions began to form in my weary mind. Why did I feel such an instinctive bond between this simple inn and the sinister Villa Diodati? A homecoming ... for whom? For Shelley – no, for Mary – but why? The confusion, far from clearing, intensified into a sharp, throbbing headache. My work is set aside, I told myself – I am free of them all: Shelley, Mary, his Lordship – all!

'My dear, you really mustn't talk to yourself like that. And remember what we agreed – no work!'

It was Elsbeth, returned from Mary's room; I could see she was upset. I should have shown concern, some sign of sympathy, I know – but for a few moments longer the only questions in my mind rejected all reality other than my dark obsession. I barely comprehended or acknowledged her tight-lipped complaints as, brusquely, she set about transferring our belongings throughout the room.

'I'm afraid Mary is a little over-tired. I have had to speak to her quite sharply ...' She paused, waiting for me to question her about what had happened. But I was lost; in my mind's eye, I saw only the looming silhouette of the Villa Diodati, that treasury of dark knowledge. I had searched out everything of use there, picked every secret clean ... and yet ... could there be something more ... ?

'Howard –' my wife's brittle impatience invaded my mood at last. 'Did you know that Mary keeps a hidden diary? So secret that I am not permitted to have sight of what it holds?'

'Really, my dear ... ?' She was in no mood to be reminded that such a personal confidant was virtually a romantic necessity in a girl of Mary's age; Elsbeth herself must have kept a similarly discreet journal when young – just as did Mary Godwin throughout her rootless wanderings with ... him. Suddenly, I grew angry with myself; why did these ridiculous thoughts persist!

'It is no concern of mine – none at all!'

Elsbeth froze, shocked by the intensity of my outburst. Before I could even attempt to explain the impossible, Herr Hubert appeared silently at the door and announced that dinner was served.

The dining-room was at once picturesque and intimate, bright curtains drawn against the snow-filled night, bold red table-cloths, meticulously laid for our meal, soft shadows delineated by mellow candlelight. We sat and waited. I was uncomfortably aware of Herr Otto, seated as ever in his familiar corner, observing us shrewdly from behind the emissions of his ornate but to me noxious meerschaum pipe. Catching my glance, he waved – a small wriggle of his fingers, palm flat, a gesture I found intensely impudent. Inevitably, it was Elsbeth who ignored my muttered warning, and addressed the peasant eccentric.

'Do tell us,' she trilled, placing him firmly in the order of things crass, 'are we the only guests ... ?'

'Please?' came the guttural reply; his face showed a genuine surprise at her question.

'My mother was wondering,' explained Mary with innocent patience, 'if we were the only people staying here at the Gasthaus ... ?'

The surprise seemed to drain only slowly from Otto's face: such a question to be asked! 'No other people here, no –' he affirmed, indicating the emptiness of the room with his meerschaum. 'No other people on board – only family Hubert. No guests, oh no – never ...!'

'Never?' laughed Mary, certain that she was being teased and willing to enjoy such a game. Her mother looked no further than the immaculate tableware on which to base her own comment. 'Extraordinary. It's very well kept, for so little custom ...'

I had to speak in spite of myself; naked curiosity steeled me to face Otto's rheumy blue eyes through the drift of pipe smoke.

'But how on earth do the Huberts manage?'

He looked towards me, old eyes squinting a shrewd appraisal of my purpose in asking, but with no reply. I was forced to explain, as to a dullard child. 'There appears to be no farm here – no livestock, even. How do they manage to exist on so little, the Hubert family ...?'

His watery eyes grew huge with astonishment; here were such innocents, they did not *know*?

'*Die Marionetten* ...!' he finally exclaimed in a whisper, as though this revelation would explain all. Then he slumped back in his seat, chuckling quietly and shaking his head incredulously at the ways of foreigners.

Before we could question Otto further, Herr Hubert had entered bearing the soup terrine and had begun to serve us with such style and dexterity that we were totally engrossed in his performance.

'You do that most wonderfully well, Herr Hubert ...' complimented my wife.

'And with such panache,' Mary twinkled mischievously, 'just like a circus balancing trick ...!'

Hubert acknowledged their remarks with a polite smile and the merest tilt of the head. 'I have served soup for many years,' he said, 'and before that, I was indeed part of the world of the circus. It is in the blood, you understand ...'

I said nothing, but I could picture him in my mind's eye – that travesty of a face, those impossibly gauche movements, so deliberately artificial ... and inhuman.

'Really?' bubbled Elsbeth. 'How fascinating!'

'A juggler?' Mary laughed, her eyes wild as she pushed her spectacles more firmly on to the bridge of her pert nose. 'I know – a lion-tamer!'

Hubert smiled, thinly, and I sensed his distaste at our clumsy hilarity. With an easy, almost comic movement, he drew back from the table and in that moment I knew what he had been, once.

'A clown!' I declared, flatly.

He bowed, smiled, and then was gone.

Made happy by this brief moment of serendipity, we turned to our soup – only to find that Herr Otto had scurried to the adjacent table and was leaning his ripe face towards us, eager with explanation.

'*Die Marionetten*' he blurted out, his pipe happily set aside. 'It is the Huberts who work the marionettes!' Intrigued, we had stopped eating, and the soup grew cold.

'They hold puppet shows *here*?' queried Elsbeth gently.

'Punch and Judy with alpenhorns!' teased Mary, her eyes wondering why I appeared so sober-faced. 'When does it happen?' It was to be this coming Saturday, Otto assured us, his face still showing surprise that we did not already know. Surely this was why we had come to Gasthof Ritterhof? Always people came – from far away, by horse and sled, great long journeys, just to see the Huberts give a performance.

A pause, as Otto looked at us shyly, convinced we were teasing an old man. 'Ach – I can see it in your eyes!' He chuckled, and poked his meerschaum at me, playfully. 'You *have* heard! It is for the *Marionetten* you have come ...! Eh?'

Soberly, I assured him that our visit was purely accidental. His face grew shadowed, and he edged back as though aware that he had said too much. But Elsbeth had not yet finished.

'Truthfully – are you saying that nobody ever stays here at the inn except to see this ... puppet show? There must be other visitors, surely ...?'

If Otto had ever intended to reply, he had no further chance. Eva, the plump maid of all work who now advanced to clear our soup plates, observed that they had hardly been touched, and immediately knew the cause. With a flurry of skirts, she advanced fiercely on Otto and despatched him from the room with a volley of brisk, guttural yelps, none of them friendly.

'*Weg! Weg! Weg! Alter Trotte! Weg!*'

We sat in silence as, with Otto gone, Eva smiled rosily upon us, cleared away our dishes, and departed with the sweetest of smiles. It was Mary, her girlish sense of humour ever alert, who bravely broke the still moment.

'I do believe it really *is* a circus, Papa ...!' She giggled, tossing her dark ringlets. 'Hubert the clown, followed by Eva and her dancing bear ...! What next, I wonder?'

That night, sleep was impossible. A shifting kaleidoscope of sounds and images flowed through and over me as gently yet as insidiously oppressive as the snowfall settling outside the inn. Elsbeth slept, though uneasily, and for that I was thankful. I could neither succumb to her persistent solicitude and dismiss my imaginings, nor admit and explain them to her shallow mind. A map of Europe hovered before my eyes; lines crawled maggot-like across its frontiers, charting the progress of Shelley and Byron's restless, aimless journeyings. But there were gaps ... many breaks in their itinerary that we knew nothing of – such as where, after the Villa Diodati, did they go? Could it be ... why should it *not* be ... here? There *was* a link, a bond, I knew it. Could I have come – by sheer chance, or by even a darker thread of fate – to the very wellspring of my quest, the heart of the labyrinth? Desperately I struggled to consider the logic of such an intuitive possibility – but the sounds, the sounds inside my head, the sounds all about me cobwebbed the clarity of my thought. A quietly mad but relentless orchestration of keening wind, clattering shutters, distant angry voices, countered by a vile percussion of banging, hammering, and stamping, choreographed a monstrous dance inside my head that ended only at dawn's first light. It was then at last, that I came to the truth. Not *after* their stay at the Villa Diodati ... before they visited Byron – *before*! Shelley and Mary. Here, in this house. In a room just such as this ... *before* ...! And, as always, Mary writing up the day's events, her every thought, in that small, immaculately kept diary. It would all be there ... everything. Suddenly, all was peace. I *knew* ... and now I could sleep. One last deceptively gentle vision drifted across my darkening eyelids: Mary, my own sweet child, writing in her treasured little book. The vision pleased me and I smiled, as I slipped into deep oblivion.

*I cannot sleep. There are so many mysterious sights and sounds in this strange little inn. Poor father is greatly disturbed, I can sense it. He is too obsessed by the bizarre occurrences that he investigated so unflinchingly at the Villa Diodati, they haunt him. It is as if, far from pursuing the ghosts of Byron and of Shelley, we have somehow angered them, so that now they are pursuing us, in the mind if not in the flesh ...*

Next morning, I discovered Mary in the Stube, waiting patiently for us to join her for breakfast. Elsbeth had woken to find me already working at my notes, and had objected bitterly; but I was not to be dissuaded from my task by a woman and the ensuing quarrel had left her close to tears. Knowing she would join us when she had sufficiently composed herself, I had gone downstairs, taking my precious book with me. Greeting Mary, however, I found my dream broken; she had not slept at all well, and with good reason.

'Those dreadful sounds, Papa –!' she exclaimed. 'It was as though we were lodging in a Yorkshire factory!' Carefully, I pointed out that since we were here out of season, perhaps the Huberts were forced to carry out their annual repairs in secret. Mary could hardly be expected to believe such a lame explanation, and said so with bright candour.

'It sounded more like a drunken clog dance. Surely you heard it too?'

'Dancing ...' I agreed, about to sip my coffee – then, like Mary, I froze, listening intently. The sound was there again, furious and demented. But this time we could see the perpetrator and his purpose; in the hallway, Hans was nailing up a poster announcing details of the forthcoming puppet show. At last he finished, and we laughed, just as Elsbeth entered. She paused, puzzled and not a little put out until we cheerfully explained, our dark imaginings of the night quite swept away. The strange berserk hammerings must have been nothing more than the Huberts preparing for the show – scenery, the stage itself – it was only too obvious. Elsbeth was not amused, and complaining of a headache, called for a jug of Glühwein instead of morning tea. She cast a quick, disapproving glance at the book beneath my hand, but said nothing. Mary noticed too, and read the title aloud, mischievously.

'*Frankenstein* ... by Mary Wollstonecraft Shelley ...' She frowned, but her eyes showed interest, not disapproval. 'Really, Papa – you're supposed *not* to be working, you know ...' I chose to say nothing, and her next words surprised me. Indeed, I felt a flicker of pleasure at so acute a question.

'How could she write such a strange story, Papa ...? A girl of only eighteen years – my own age, in fact –'

'Nineteen, my dear,' Elsbeth corrected her. 'Tomorrow *is* your birthday, after all ...'

'Dear Mama ...' cooed Mary, and kissed her mother's brow; all the while her eyes were on mine – serious, questioning, demanding answers. But how could I even discuss with her the dark omens coursing through my mind? What strange secrets did that girl of eighteen comprehend nearly seventy years ago, that I could make clear to a child of today, my own daughter? Somehow, I knew the hideous answer was there to be grasped, but I could not speak it.

'Then I see I must find out for myself,' smiled Mary, as though she understood, perfectly. She took the book from me and I made no move to prevent her. The truth was, I wanted her to know, to understand ... for herself ...

Mary retired to bed early that night, giving the excuse that she needed adequate rest in order to face the imminent excitement of tomorrow's anniversary. Of course, I realized her true intent; the book which had been denied her all day long now lay waiting by her bedside, ready to feed her eager mind. Elsbeth, herself pleading indisposition and finding a genteel solace in increasingly frequent sips of aromatic Glühwein, also went to bed early and quickly fell into a fitful slumber. The opportunity that offered itself was not to be wasted. As night deepened, those sounds of nightmare issued forth again – the hammering, the stamping, the elusive, angry voices. My purpose was plain: to search them out, discover their fearful reason, and confront the terrible truth, face to face. Candle in hand, I advanced bravely through the shadows guarding the stairs and landing above; the sounds were louder now, yet without a precisely identifiable source. Door after door opened to my touch, only to reveal empty, uninhabited rooms. Then, just as I came to the final bedroom on that seemingly deserted floor, every sound ceased – utterly. I wheeled about, sensing some evil presence behind me in that terrible silence – and there, crooked and ancient as a fire-blasted tree, stood a wild-eyed, dishevelled creature reaching out its trembling, claw-like hand towards me! In the fragmentary moment before the candle flame guttered into darkness, I saw an incredibly old, deep-furrowed face framed by snake-like wisps of white, white hair, above a body enveloped in a long, greasy apron. Then the void swallowed us both, and I bolted for the stairs in ridiculous, mindless panic.

Stumbling and half-falling downwards to the safety of the landing below, I found Mary standing there, candle in hand, her eyes round and questioning behind her glinting spectacles. I gripped her, holding her fast, unable to say anything coherent. Her alarmed glance flicked past me towards the darkness of the landing above.

'The sounds, Papa – I had to come and see ...'

'No!' I commanded hoarsely. 'Go back to your room at once, child ... quickly!' I pulled her along with me, desperate to find sanctuary from I knew not what.

'But what is it?' she begged me. 'What did you see? Tell me. Is it the graveyard at the back of the inn?'

Only when I had shut the door firmly behind us did I realize that she had no fear; the terror was all mine. Our abrupt arrival had brought Elsbeth sitting up in bed, bemused and complaining.

'That dreadful banging ...' She huddled the bedclothes about her, shivering. 'It really is too much to bear, Howard. How am I to get any rest ...' Her voice slurred and faded as she fought against sleep and lost. Mary helped me settle her mother back on to the rumpled pillows. In the half-darkness, she probed my scattered defences with a tense, whispered excitement.

'It is so like the book, Papa. A waking nightmare ...!' She looked at me across the bed, and as she softly quoted that other Mary's words, I suddenly knew she was closer to understanding than I had dreamed possible in one so young.

'*My imagination, unbidden, possessed and guided me ...!*' I ordered her to cease, but she would not. '*Was* it her imagination, Papa ...? Or was it something more ...?'

'For your mother's sake,' I managed to blurt out, 'we must leave this place – tomorrow!' I knew her answer even before she spoke; it was inevitable, and could not be denied.

'No, Papa – we have to stay. We have to find out the truth,

you and I – together. Besides –' her voice commanded me lightly but completely '– tomorrow *is* my birthday ...!' And kissing me fondly, she slipped away to her own room, leaving me to face the night alone.

The next day was not only Mary's birthday, it was also to be the occasion of the marionette theatre, in the evening. The pleasure of celebrating our intimate family anniversary alleviated to some extent the unreasonable foreboding I felt at the prospect of the public show; but I had said nothing to Elsbeth or Mary about my eerie encounter of the night before. However, the coincidence of the two celebrations at least gave me an excuse to further my enquiries. Despite Mary's declared enthusiasm, I was determined not to involve her physically in my investigations. When I made my way to the inn's kitchen, I went alone. Frau Minna was there, preparing vegetables with Eva. They responded with sympathy and delight to my request that they might prepare a suitable cake for our birthday child – but when I tried to question them about the other subject on my mind, their attitude changed completely.

'The old man –' I enquired pleasantly enough, '– perhaps you can inform me of his whereabouts? I wish only to talk to him ...'

'I know nothing of an old man,' replied Frau Minna, stonily. I turned to question Eva, but she had gone. 'I cook,' stated the innkeeper's wife, bluntly, 'and I will be pleased to bake the cake you ask for. That is all.'

There was nothing to be gained by defying this honest dismissal; I thanked her and left, but her very evasion intrigued and tortured me. What *was* the true mystery of this place?

In the afternoon I played Mary at chess, but I could not bring my mind to concentrate. Elsbeth, comfortably sipping wine against the chilling threat of the snow outside, smiled with benign vagueness as Mary deftly brought me into check again and again, happy in the belief that I was allowing her a birthday victory. My undoing was the distractions that I suffered – firstly the comings and goings of Eva and Hans, carrying benches into the room beyond, and more insidiously, by a growing sensation that I stood on the verge of a precipice. The others were blithely unaware of my secret apprehensions.

Between moves, Mary took a girlish delight in slyly observing Hans clumsily manoeuvre items of scenery into the adjoining room, soon to be used as a miniature theatre.

'It is all so amateur and naive ...' complained Elsbeth mildly. '*Must* we attend, Howard ...? I simply cannot abide Punch and Judy shows ...'

'We do not perform for children, madame ...'

It was Herr Hubert who had answered. He advanced towards us, skilfully balancing Mary's candlelit cake, and presented it to her with a gauche flourish. Mary gasped with delight and applauded prettily, but my own gaze was fixed firmly on the bland white face of the innkeeper.

'This drama of yours, Herr Hubert –' I indicated the poster in the hallway – 'I hope it is not too coarse or unsuitable ...'

'It is perhaps a little primitive, sir,' he replied, quite unperturbed. 'But our audiences demand old favourites. Please see it as they do – a fairy tale for adults ...' He gestured gallantly towards Mary. 'What could be better, to celebrate such a very special occasion ...?'

'Charming ...' cooed Elsbeth, sipping more wine. Mary spoke more to the point. 'These puppets,' she queried innocently, – 'do you work them yourselves? You – and your family?'

The innkeeper did not answer immediately, but watched her unsmiling now, across the candle flames of the prettily decorated cake. 'We have not always been innkeepers,' he said carefully. 'Our little drama was first created ... many years ago. By relatives ... now deceased, you understand.'

'The old man,' I interjected quickly, 'the one who lives upstairs, your father perhaps – is *he* a puppetmaker also – ?'

'You must be mistaken, sir,' retorted Herr Hubert politely. 'It is our sincere hope that you will be adequately entertained this evening. Until then ...' He bowed ingratiatingly, and was gone.

That evening, summoned by the clamour of an iron hand-bell, we entered the rustic, makeshift auditorium – somewhat gingerly, for the small crowd that bustled all about us was little better than a peasant rabble, poorly dressed, ribald and vociferous. The seats were rough wooden benches, the stage no more than a small raised platform fronted by simple curtains; the garish lighting came from red and green lanterns hung from wall brackets set all about the room. The almost childlike excitement of the audience subsided at last in response to 'the knocks' – two ominous raps of a stave on the wooden floor. The curtains were then pulled apart, clumsily ... and the play began. But the first, unbelievable assault on our senses was the stench; sweetish, sickening, corrupting ... something I knew, yet could not – dared not – identify. Elsbeth immediately complained of feeling faint, and I offered her my kerchief with which to cover her mouth and nose – a device used also by the ragged audience, casually, as though it was an accepted hazard, cheerfully undergone without complaint. Like them, Mary was too enthralled by the sights on stage, to overtly register that awful, enervating smell. I too watched, incredulous, appalled, yet fascinated. The settings, if that they could be called, were crudely painted in black and white and grey, punctuated violently by great daubs of lurid scarlet. The awkward-limbed marionettes, when they appeared, quite numbed my every sensation; not only were they extraordinarily lifelike, they were, startlingly, *life-size*. The total effect at once mimicked yet mocked reality; it was a nightmare come to life. *Her nightmare ...!*

The story told by the play was as Herr Hubert claimed, primitive to the point of melodrama, and quickly stated.

Scene One: A Bedroom. A female marionette – The White Princess – struts on stage, and after taking in the audience, lies down upon the bed. At the window, the leering face of the marionette to be known as the Magician appears, made more hideous by the Japanese mask he wears. The curtain falls, to cries of frightened enthusiasm from the childlike audience.

Scene Two: A Cell. The third marionette – The Black Murderer – reclines, lifeless, in a coffin. The Magician enters, and with weird, expressive gestures, mesmerizes the Black Murderer into life. Rising from his tomb, the hideous zombie staggers, club-footed and with outstretched arms, first towards the shrieking audience, then offstage. Curtain.

Scene Three: The Bedroom. The White Princess is asleep, as the Black Murderer stares in at her from the window. She sits up as the Black Murderer enters, and is drawn by him into an obscene Dance of Death – for at its climax, the bride-like sacrifice is strangled and flung sprawling limply upon the bed. Just as the Black Murderer is about to stalk away, he is confronted by the Magician, who, enraged with grief, grapples with the vile destroyer and finally stabs him to death, urged on by the rabid cries of the now almost hysterical audience. Thus the play ended; but their rapture continued like the baying of wild beasts.

Elsbeth, Mary and I sat transfixed, petrified amongst that sickening pandemonium. For what we had witnessed, we dared not believe ... the eyes, the very mouths and painted lips of those supposed wooden puppets – *had moved*. Not only that: when the Magician's knife struck home, *blood flowed*! Was this the unholy ritual that these crass, ravening animals had come to see: *marionettes that bled?* Whimpering, Elsbeth sought out a tiny concealed flask and raising it to her pallid lips, drained it. She shuddered, white-faced, her eyes shut tight against the dream that howled and stamped its feet all about us. Mary clung tightly to me, face averted, but her bright, feverish eyes still looked eagerly towards the stage. I could feel the mounting excitement of her tense body, the rapid flutter of her breath – and then, simultaneously, we both gasped aloud. The remaining puppet – The Magician – had stepped forward to acknowledge the orgiastic applause and with a flourish, removed his mask. The face revealed was not that of any puppet: *it was Hubert* ...

Somehow, we left that amphitheatre of dread, and between us Mary and I brought Elsbeth to our room, where we laid her fully clothed upon the bed. Fatigue, shock, and the effects of the heady wine had brought her to a state of waking coma; she seemed almost totally unaware of who we were or where she was – a merciful though temporary amnesia. Leaving my wife safely at rest, I now escorted Mary to her room, bidding her to lock her door until morning. We had seen enough and I was determined we should leave as early as possible the next day. But the unquestioned silence that lay between us could not endure.

Regarding me with a brave, tremulous smile, Mary held out the book that we both knew now by heart.

'Everything is here, Papa ...' she murmured. 'Enriched,

embroidered ... but only an echo of what we have seen tonight. Is it not so ...?'

I could not deny it. The evil centre of those dark imaginings existed here in this simple, terrifying country inn. *This was the source!*

'Herr Hubert – the Magician, the Prometheus firemaker – he has to be the model for the Baron!' She spoke with growing excitement, each thought providing fuel for further speculation. I could only agree with her, our minds were so finely in accord.

'Some other family ancestor,' I corrected her. 'Who knows for how many tens of years this vile ritual has been performed ...'

'And the White Princess –' Mary continued keenly – 'is Elizabeth ... Frankenstein's dear bride, destroyed on her wedding night by his own vengeful creation –'

'A creature without a name ...' I shuddered at the memory of what we had seen, but looking into her face, I saw the feverish glow of excitement rising there again. I sensed that this child would dare anything to know the truth, and the challenge I expected, even hoped for, came.

'If the source is here ... then so is a most terrible secret ...' Mary insisted.

'Those sounds ...' I had not her courage; I dared only to whisper the thought. 'The making of those hideous puppets ...'

'*The workshop of filthy creation ...!*'

The words she uttered were from the book, Mary Shelley's own; and we had seen for ourselves the product of that nightmare. Still she continued quoting, relentlessly. '*I succeeded in discovering the cause of generation and life, nay – more: I became myself capable of bestowing animation upon lifeless matter ...*'

The words came readily to me now, stirred by her eager prompting: '*... bodies deprived of life, which from being the seat of beauty and strength, had become food for worms ...*' My throat choked with the memory of that first opening of the curtain and the wave of sickeningly sweet putrefaction that had greeted us.

'*Who shall conceive the horrors of my secret toil, as I dabbled among the unhallowed damps of the grave, or tor-*

*tured the living animal to animate the lifeless clay ...'* She paused, breathlessly, my shining angel of truth. 'Papa – what *is* it that they do? If *she* saw that, then surely so can we!' Her spirit consumed me, and I lost all fear. Taking her hand, I led the way on to the landing, and together we trod the shadowed stairway upwards.

Hubert was standing there, half-hidden by the eerie darkness, as though long awaiting our coming.

'Can I help you, Mr Lawrence ...?' His arrogant civility took me aback, and tongue-tied, I could not frame a question. It was Mary who spoke, bravely.

'The poet Shelley – and his mistress, Mary Godwin –'

'I was never privileged to meet them, miss,' Hubert interrupted blandly.

'The old man – your father –' I demanded hoarsely. 'He was the puppetmaster when they came here, just as he is now – admit it, man!' Such was my confidence that I would brook no more evasion. Hubert's face brooded, cruelly, before speaking – harshly now, without any trace of servility.

'My father does not merely work the marionettes, sir – he creates them! See for yourselves!' With a savage gesture, he wrenched open the door at his side, and Mary and I clung together, rendered dumb by what we saw in the room beyond. Standing there was the old man, grim, dignified and commanding. He said nothing, but stared out at us with eyes so old, so infinitely weary that even in my fear I felt compassion. All about him a thick, sulphur-yellow vaporous mist coiled and swirled like an aetherial snakepit. In his hand was a butcher's blade, bright with fresh blood; on the bench at his side was something that had once been made of flesh and bone, from which now arose that awful, familiar stench of corruption; and behind him, the hulking, inhuman figure of the Black Murderer, grotesquely erect. In that same split second, as its yellow, ghoulish eyes registered and fixed on Mary, Hubert slammed the door to, shutting out that hideous vision. Still we could not move, fixed by the malice of Hubert's thin, ghastly smile.

'Does it satisfy you, Mr Lawrence, now that you have seen our "workshop of filthy creation"?' His dry, strangely aristocratic voice commanded us grimly. 'You will ask no more questions. And you will leave early tomorrow, of course. For now ... sleep well ...' As he returned to the monstrous room from which he had come, the spell of fear was broken, and we fled.

We regained Mary's room, and there I would have stayed to guard her, but she was adamant: we should both rest before leaving the next morning. I left her fondly; yet as I went I observed again that bright flush of fever in her eyes and even as she closed and locked the door after me, her diary was already at hand, open for use. Sweet, brave girl – to be so composed that she could commit the night's bizarre experiences to paper! But she was never to delineate the final horror that concludes my tale.

I did not expect to sleep, but my mind was utterly drained. Oblivion washed over me almost as soon as my head touched the pillow, and I slipped into a velvet deep of sheer exhaustion. It was Elsbeth who woke me. She had cried out, only once, but in such deep and genuine alarm that I was fully alert to the unseen danger.

'Mary – my child!' She was sitting bolt upright. Flinging herself at our bedroom door in a fit of desperation, she cried out again. 'She is in terrible danger – I know it!' She struggled with the locked door, frantically. 'Howard – for pity's sake – *quickly*!'

I opened the door and we came to Mary's room. The rest was nightmare. Her bedroom door, smashed from its hinges, hung loosely open. Inside lumbered the vile form of the Black Murderer; held in his arms, swooning but not afraid, was Mary – her white nightgown clinging to her loose-limbed body, clasped tightly to that noxious creature in a bridal *danse macabre*. On the floor, crushed by those massive brute feet, were my child's delicate spectacles, alongside the open, unfinished diary. Elsbeth choked and fainted against me; my nerveless hands could not support her collapsing body, and she fell unconscious at my feet. I reached out, mute and helpless, knowing I was unable to prevent the ultimate act of horror. But suddenly I was thrust aside; I recall only the dark, urgent figures of Hubert and the Old Man mastering the monstrous creature, dragging him and his needless, trailing strings out of that ravaged room to I know not where. One final image forever haunts me – the living but mindless face of a doll that was once my own sweet child, delivered into damnation and madness by her father's corrupting ambition. For all the knowledge I had gained, I had lost my very soul: and will I ever find forgiveness ...?

*The speaker paused and asked for a glass of water.*

'Are you saying,' Sir Francis mumbled, first clearing his throat noisily, 'my dear sir, are you saying that the Frankensteins really existed? That their heirs exist still?'

'For all I know,' the author replied with surprising blandness. 'The Huberts as they call themselves may even now be at work manipulating their puppets.'

'Manipulating? Do you mean there lives an inn-keeping family in Switzerland which fashions marionettes out of corpses, the corpses of murdered guests, and imbues them with some kind of damned life?'

'I have no evidence that the Huberts have ever killed anyone at all,' Howard Lawrence said. 'There was ... is no need ...' He paused and sipped water. 'The proximity of the graveyard ...'

There was silence then. Sir Francis looked about him. The members seemed duly impressed.

'I have one further question.' A member at the far end of the room raised a limp arm. 'What happened to your own family? How did mother and daughter survive their appalling ordeal?'

'As patients,' the author replied in a gentle voice, and for the first time that night Sir Francis registered the fact that the middle-aged writer's hair was white, totally white, and that his skin was that of an old man.

'Professor Lawrence,' came the voice from the back, and Sir Francis realized that it was that of the Chairman. 'In our opinion, your story is a pack of lies. The whole world knows that the book *Frankenstein* is an invention, a novel based on the nightmares of a wretched, over-imaginative young girl ...'

Once again, the teller of the tale grinned.

'What my poor daughter and I have seen, we have seen,' he said in a hollow voice. 'What we have heard, we have heard.' He paused and his smile vanished.

'What we have dreamed, we have dreamed ...'

# The Dead Man

## By FRITZ LEIBER

As in the theatre and cinema before, Frankenstein *quickly proved to have a continuing appeal to each new generation of television audiences, and adaptations of the original novel as well as stories inspired by the concept have been regular features on the medium ever since the Fifties. There have been at least three feature length versions of the book:* TVM's Frankenstein: The True Story (1973) *with Leonard Whiting and Michael Sarrazin as experimenter and creature;* Yorkshire TV's *dramatization in 1984 with Robert Powell and David Warner; and* Frankenstein – The Real Story (1992) *with Patrick Bergin and Randy Quaid. Amongst the anthology series which have drawn on the idea with commendable success have been* Suspense, Thriller *and* Night Gallery – *while the same cannot be said for a trio of spin-offs:* Frankenstein Jnr and the Impossibles, *a dreadful cartoon series from Hanna-Barbera in 1966;* Struck by Lightning, *an unfunny comedy series screened in 1979 with Jeffrey Kramer as a descendant of Dr Frankenstein and Jack Elam as the monster; and* Dr Franken (1980) *an unsuccessful attempt to transplant the story to New York with Robert Vaughn and Robert Perrault.*

The Dead Man *from a story by Fritz Leiber which was adapted for the prime time* Night Gallery *series in December 1970 is undoubtedly the most memorable of all the television variations. The series had been devised by Rod Serling, creator of the famous* Twilight Zone, *and ran for a total of 95 episodes. It also achieved a little piece of Hollywood history as the show which gave Steven Spielberg his directorial début. The stories which were featured in the series ranged from tales of atmospheric suspense to some quite grisly horrors –*

*few more so than the walking cadaver seen in Fritz Leiber's contribution. Leiber (1910–) who came to prominence writing for* Weird Tales *– which happened to be based in his native Chicago – says he first read* Frankenstein *when it was serialised in the magazine: and as a writer who enjoyed putting his fantasies into modern settings, this gave him the basic idea for* The Dead Man. *Appropriately, therefore, the story first appeared as the lead item in November 1950. Douglas Heyes adapted and directed the television version which starred Carl Beitz as Dr Max Redford and Michael Blodgett as the unhappy soul over whom he has power of life and death. It was Rod Serling's practice to introduce each episode of* Night Gallery, *and he described the following story in his unmistakable dry whisper as 'An interesting meeting between flesh and bone, between that which walks and that which* (you should excuse the expression) *gets buried ...'*

Professor Max Redford opened the frosted glass door of the reception room and beckoned to me. I followed him eagerly. When the most newsworthy doctor at one of America's foremost medical schools phones a popular-science writer and asks him to drop over, but won't tell him why, there is cause for excitement. Especially when that doctor's researches, though always well-founded, have tended towards the sensational. I remembered the rabbits so allergic to light that an open shade raised blisters on their shaved skins, the hypnotized heart patient whose blood-pressure slowly changed, the mould that fed on blood clots in a living animal's brain. Fully half my best articles with a medical slant came from Max. We had been rather close friends for several years.

As we hurried along the hushed corridor, he suddenly asked me, 'What is death?'

That wasn't the sort of question I was expecting. I gave him a quick look. His bullet-shaped head, with its shock of close-cropped grizzled hair, was hunched forward. The eyes behind the thick lenses were bright, almost mischievous. He was smiling.

I shrugged.

'I have something to show you,' he said.

'What, Max?'

'You'll see.'

'A story?'

He shook his head. 'At present I don't want a word released to the public or the profession.'

'But some day – ?' I suggested.

'Maybe one of the biggest.'

We entered his office. On the examination table lay a man, the lower half of his body covered by a white sheet. He seemed to be asleep.

Right there I got a shock. For although I hadn't the faintest idea who the man was, I did recognize him. I was certain that I had seen that handsome face once before – through the French windows of the living room of Max's home, some weeks ago. It had been pressed passionately to the face of Velda, Max's attractive young wife, and those arms had been cradling her back. Max and I had just arrived at his lonely suburban place after a long evening session at the laboratory, and he had been locking the car when I glanced through the window. When we had got inside, the man had been gone, and Max had greeted Velda with his usual tenderness. I had been bothered by the incident, but of course there had been nothing I could do about it.

I turned from the examination table, trying to hide my surprise. Max sat down at his desk and began to rap on it with a pencil. Nervous excitement, I supposed.

From the man on the examination table, now behind me, came a dry, hacking cough.

'Take a look at him,' said Max, 'and tell me what disease he's suffering from.'

'I'm no doctor,' I protested.

'I know that, but there are some symptoms that should have an obvious meaning even to a layman.'

'But I didn't even notice he was ill,' I said.

Max goggled his eyes at me, 'You didn't?'

Shrugging my shoulders, I turned – and wondered how in the world I could have missed it at the first glance. I supposed

I had been so flustered at recognizing the man that I hadn't noticed anything about him – I had been seeing the memory image more than the actual person. For Max was right. Anyone could have hazarded a diagnosis of this case. The general pallor, the hectic spots of colour over the cheek bones, the emaciated wrists, the prominent ribs, the deep depressions around the collar bones, and above all the continued racking cough that even as I watched brought a bit of blood-specked mucus to the lips – all pointed at an advanced stage of chronic tuberculosis. I told Max so.

Max stared at me thoughtfully, rapping again on the table. I wondered if he sensed what I was trying to hide from him. Certainly I felt very uncomfortable. The presence of that man, presumably Velda's lover, in Max's office, unconscious and suffering from a deadly disease, and Max so sardonic-seeming and full of suppressed excitement, and then that queer question he had asked me about death – taken all together, they made a peculiarly nasty picture.

What Max said next didn't help either.

'You're quite sure it's tuberculosis?'

'Naturally I could be wrong,' I admitted uneasily. 'It might be some other disease with the same symptoms or –' I had been about to say, 'or the effects of some poison,' but I checked myself. 'But the symptoms are there, unmistakably,' I finished.

'You're positive?' He seemed to enjoy drawing it out.

'Of course!'

He smiled. 'Take another look.'

'I don't need to,' I protested. For the first time in our relationship I was wondering if there wasn't something extremely unpleasant about Max.

'Take one, just the same.'

Unwillingly I turned – and for several moments there was room in my mind for nothing but astonishment.

'What kind of trick is this?' I finally asked Max, shakily.

For the man on the examination table had changed. Unmistakably the same man, though for a moment I questioned even that, for now instead of the cadaverous spectre of tuberculosis, a totally different picture presented itself. The wrists, so thin a minute ago, were now swollen, the chest had become so unhealthily puffy that the ribs and collar bones were lost to view, the skin had a bluish tinge, and from between the sagging lips came a laboured, wheezy breathing.

I still had a sense of horror, but now it was overlaid with an emotion that can be even stronger, an emotion that can outweigh all considerations of human personality and morals: the excitement of scientific discovery. Whoever this man was, whatever Max's motives might be, whatever unsuspected strain of evil there might exist deep in his nature, he had *hit* on something here, something revolutionary. I didn't know what it was, but my heart pounded and little chills of excitement chased over my skin.

Max refused to answer any of the questions I bombarded him with. All he would do was sit back and smile at me and say, 'And now, after your second look, what do you think's wrong with him?'

He finally badgered me into making a statement.

'Well of course there's something fishy about it, but if you insist, here's my idea: heart disease, perhaps caused by kidney trouble. In any case, something badly out of order with his pump.'

Max's smile was infuriatingly bland. Again he rapped with his pencil, like some supercilious teacher.

'You're sure of that?' he prodded.

'Just as sure as I was the first time that it was tuberculosis.'

'Well, take another look ... and meet John Fearing.'

I turned, and almost before I realized it, my hand had been firmly clasped and was being vigorously shaken by that of one of the finest physical specimens I have ever seen. I remember thinking dazedly, 'Yes, he's as incredibly handsome and beautifully built as he seemed to me when I glimpsed him kissing Velda. And along with it a strange sort of smoothness, like you felt in Rudolph Valentino. No wonder a woman might find him irresistible.'

'I could have introduced you to John long ago,' Max was saying. 'He lives right near us, with his mother, and often drops over. But, well ...' he chuckled, '... I've been a little jealous about John. I haven't introduced him to anyone connected with the profession. I've wanted to keep him to myself until we got a little further along with our experiments.

'And, John,' Max went on, 'this is Fred Alexander, the

writer. He's one science popularizer who never strays a hairs-breadth into sensationalism and who takes infinite pains to make his reporting accurate. We can trust him not to breathe a word about our experiments until we tell him to. I've been thinking for some time now that we ought to let a third person in on our work, and I didn't want it to be a scientist or yet an ordinary layman. Fred here struck me as having just the right sort of general knowledge and sympathetic approach. So I rang him up – and I believe we've succeeded in giving him quite a surprise.'

'You certainly have,' I agreed fervently.

John Fearing dropped my hand and stepped back. I was still running my eyes over his marvellously proportioned, athletic body. I couldn't spot a trace of the symptoms of the two dreadful diseases that had seemed to be racking it minutes ago, or of any other sort of ill health. As he stood there so coolly, with the sheet loosely caught around his waist and falling in easy folds, it seemed to me that he might well be the model for one of the great classical Greek statues. His eyes had something of the same tranquil, ox-like, 'all-body' look.

Turning towards Max, I was conscious of a minor shock. I had never thought of Max as ugly. If I'd ever thought of him at all in regard to looks, it had been as a man rather youthful for his middle age, stalwart, and with pleasingly rugged features.

Now, compared to Fearing, Max seemed a humped and dark-browed dwarf.

But this feeling of mine was immediately swallowed up in my excited curiosity.

Fearing looked at Max. 'What diseases did I do this time,' he asked casually.

'Tuberculosis and nephritis,' Max told him. They both acted pleased. In fact, mutual trust and affection showed so plainly in their manner towards each other that I was inclined to dismiss my suspicions of some sinister underlying hatred.

After all, I told myself, the embrace I had witnessed might have been merely momentary physical intoxication on the part of the two young and lovely people, if it had been even that much. Certainly what Max had said about his desire to keep Fearing a secret from his friends and colleagues might very well explain why Fearing had disappeared that night. On the other hand, if a deeper and less fleeting feeling did exist between Max's pretty wife and protégé, Max might very well be aware of it and inclined to condone it. I knew him to be a remarkably tolerant man in some respects. In any case, I had probably exaggerated the importance of the matter.

And I certainly didn't want any such speculations distracting my thoughts now, when I was bending all my mental efforts to comprehend the amazing experiment that had just been conducted before my eyes.

Suddenly I got a glimmer of part of it.

'Hypnotism?' I asked Max.

He nodded, beaming.

'And the pencil-rappings were "cues"? I mean, signals for him to carry out instructions given to him in an earlier stage of the trance?'

'That's right.'

'I seem to recall now,' I said, 'that the raps were different in each case. I suppose each combination of raps was hooked up with a special set of instructions you'd given him.'

'Exactly,' said Max. 'John won't respond until he gets the right signal. It seems a rather complicated way of going about it, but it isn't really. You know how a sergeant will give his men a set of orders and then bark out "March!"? Well, the raps are John's marching signals. It works out better than giving him the instructions at the same time he's supposed to be carrying them out. Besides,' and he looked at me roguishly, 'it's a lot more dramatic.'

'I'll say it is!' I assured him. 'Max, let's get to the important point. How in the world did John fake those symptoms?'

Max raised his hands. 'I'll explain everything. I didn't call you in just to mystify you. Sit down.'

I hurriedly complied. Fearing effortlessly lifted himself onto the edge of the examination table and sat there placidly attentive, forearms loosely dropped along his thighs.

'As you know,' Max began, 'it's a well-established fact that the human mind can create all sorts of tangible symptoms of disease, without the disease itself being present in any way. Statistics show that about half the people who consult doctors are suffering from such imaginary ailments.'

'Yes,' I protested, 'but the symptoms are never so extreme,

or created with such swiftness. Why, there was even blood in the mucus. And those swollen wrists –'

Again Max raised his hands. 'The difference is only one of degree. Please hear me out.'

'Now John here,' he continued, 'is a very well adjusted, healthy-minded person, but a few years ago he was anything but that.' He looked at Fearing, who nodded his agreement. 'No, our John was a regular bad boy of the hospitals. Rather, his subconscious mind was, for of course there is no question of faking in these matters, the individual sincerely believes that he is sick. At all events, our John seemed to go through an unbelievable series of dangerous illnesses that frightened his mother to distraction and baffled his doctors, until it was realized that the illnesses were of emotional origin. That discovery wasn't made for a long time because of the very reason you mentioned – the unusual severity of the symptoms.

'However in the end it was the extraordinary power of John's subconscious to fake symptoms that gave the show away. It began to fake the symptoms of too many diseases, the onsets and recoveries were too fast, it jumped around too much. And then it made the mistake of faking the symptoms of germ diseases, when laboratory tests showed that the germs in question weren't present.

'The truth having been recognized, John was put in the hands of a competent psychiatrist, who eventually succeeded in straightening out the personality difficulties that had caused him to seek refuge in sickness. They turned out to be quite simple ones – an overprotective and emotionally demanding mother and a jealous and unaffectionate father, whose death a few years back had burdened John with guilt feelings.

'It was at that time – just after the brilliant success of the psychiatrist's treatment – that I ran across the case. It happened through Velda. She became friends with the Fearings, mother and son, when they moved into our neighbourhood, and she visited with them a lot.'

As he said that, I couldn't resist shooting a quick glance at Fearing, but I couldn't see any signs of uneasiness or smugness. I felt rather abashed.

'One evening when John was over at our place, he mentioned his amazing history of imaginary illnesses, and pretty soon I wormed the whole story out of him. I was immediately struck with something about his case that the other doctors had missed. Or if they had noticed it, they hadn't seen the implications – or the possibilities.

'Here was a person whose body was fantastically obedient to the dictates of his subconscious mind. All people are to some degree psychosomatic, to give it its technical name – you know, *psyche* and *soma*, mind and body. But our John was psychosomatic to a vastly greater degree. One in a million. Perhaps unique.

'Very likely some rare hereditary strain was responsible for this. I don't believe John will be angry with me if I tell you that his mother used to be – she's really changed herself a great deal under the psychiatrist's guidance – but that she used to be an excessively hysterical and emotionally tempestuous person, with all sorts of imaginary ailments herself, though not as extreme as John's, of course. And his father was almost exactly the same type.'

'That's quite right, Dr Redford,' Fearing said earnestly.

Max nodded. 'Apparently the combination of these two hereditary strains in John produced far more than a doubling of his parents' sensitivities.

'Just as the chameleon inherits a colour-changing ability that other animals lack, so John has inherited a degree of psychosomatic control that is not apparent in other people – at least not without some kind of psychological training of which at present I have only a glimmering.

'All this was borne in on me as I absorbed John's story, hanging on every word. You know, I think both John and Velda were quite startled at the intensity of my interest.' Max chuckled. 'But they didn't realize that I was on to something. Here, right in my hands, was a person with, to put it popularly, only the most tenuous of boundaries between his mental and material atoms – for of course, as you know, both mind and matter are ultimately electrical in nature. Our John's subconscious mind had perfect control of his heart-beat and circulatory system. It could flood his tissues with fluids, producing instant swellings, or dehydrate them, giving the effect of emaciation. It could play on his internal organs and ductless glands as if they were musical instruments, creating any life-time it wanted. It could produce horrible discords, turn John into an idiot, say, or an invalid, as it tried to do, or perhaps an acromegalic monster, with gigantic hands and head, by stimulating bone-growth after maturity.

'Or his subconscious mind could keep all his organs in perfect tune, making him the magnificently healthy creature you see today.'

I looked at John Fearing and realized that my earlier impression of the excellence of his physique had, if anything, fallen short of the mark. It wasn't just that he was a clear-eyed, unblemished, athletically built young man. There was more to it than that – something intangible. It occurred to me that if any man could be said to radiate health, in the literal meaning of that ridiculous cliché, it was John Fearing. I knew it was just my imagination, but I seemed to see a pulsating, faintly golden aura about him.

And his mind appeared to be in as perfect balance as his body. He was wonderfully poised as he sat there with just the sheet pulled around him. Not the faintest suggestion of nerves. Completely alive, yet in a sense completely impassive.

It was only too easy to imagine such a man making love successfully, with complete naturalness and confidence, without any of the little haltings and clumsinesses, the jarrings of rhythm, the cowardices of body, the treacheries of mind that betray the average neurotic – which is to say, the average person. Suddenly it hit me, right between the eyes as they say, that Velda *must* love John, that no woman could avoid becoming infatuated with such a man. Not just a football star or a muscle maniac, but a creature infinitely subtler.

And yet, in spite of all this, I was conscious of something a shade repellent about Fearing. Perhaps it was that he seemed too well-balanced, too smooth-running, like a gleaming dynamo say, or a beautiful painting without that little touch of ugliness or clashing contrast which creates individuality. In most people, too, one senses the eternal conflict between the weak and indecisive tyrant Mind and the stubborn and rebellious slave Body, but in Fearing the conflict seemed completely absent, which struck me as unpleasant. There was a kind of deep-seated toughness about him, a suggestion of indestructibility. One might have said, 'He'd make a nasty ghost.'

Of course all this may just have been envy on my part for

Fearing's poise and physique, or some sort of jealousy I felt on Max's account.

But whatever the sources of my feeling of revulsion, I now began to believe that Max shared it. Not that Max had slackened in his genial, affectionate, almost fatherly manner toward John, but that he was so effortful about it. Those elephantine 'our Johns,' for example. I didn't get the feeling that he was concealing a jealous hatred, however, but that he was earnestly fighting an irrational inward aversion.

As for Fearing, he seemed completely unaware of any hostile feeling on Max's part. His manner was completely open and amiable.

For that matter, I wondered if Max himself were aware of his own feeling. All these thoughts didn't take much time. I was intent on Max's story.

Max leaned across the desk. He was blinking excitedly, which, with his glasses, gave an odd effect of flashing eyes.

'My imagination was stirred,' he went on. 'There was no end to the things that might be learned from such a super-psychosomatic individual. We could study disease symptoms under perfect conditions, by producing them in controlled amounts in a healthy individual. All sorts of physiological mysteries could be explored. We could trace out the exact patterns of all the nervous processes that are normally beyond the mind's reach. Then if we could learn to impart John's ability to other people – but that's getting a bit ahead of my story.

'I talked to John. He saw my point, realized the service he might render mankind, and gladly agreed to undergo some experiments.

'But at the first attempt a snag appeared. John could not produce any symptoms by a conscious effort, no matter how hard he tried. As I said before, you can't consciously fake a psychosomatic illness, and that was what I was asking John to do. And since he'd undergone psychiatric treatment his subconscious mind was so well behaved that it wouldn't yield to any ordinary blandishments.

'At that point we almost gave up the project. But then I thought of a way we might be able to get around the snag:

suggestions given directly to the subconscious mind through hypnotism.

'John proved a good hypnotic subject. We tried it – and it worked!'

Max's eyes looked bright as stars as he said that.

'That's about how matters stand today,' he finished off, sinking back in his chair. 'We've started a little special work on arterial tension, the lymphatic glands and their nerve supply, one or two other things. But mainly we've been perfecting our set-up, getting used to the hypnotic relationship. The important work still lies ahead.'

I exhaled appreciatively. Then an unpleasant thought struck me. I wasn't going to voice it, but Max asked, 'What is it, Fred?' and I couldn't think of anything else to say, and after all it was a thought that would have occurred to anyone.

'Well, with all this creation of extreme symptoms,' I began, 'isn't there a certain amount of –'

Max supplied the word. 'Danger?' He shook his head. 'We are always very careful.'

'And in any case,' Fearing's bell-like voice broke in, 'the possibilities being what they are, I would consider almost any risks worth running.' He smiled cheerfully.

The double meaning I momentarily fancied in his words nettled me. I went on impulsively, 'But surely some people would be apt to consider it extremely dangerous. Your mother, for instance, or Velda.'

Max looked at me sharply.

'Neither my mother nor Mrs Redford knows anything of the extent of our experiments,' Fearing assured me.

There was a pause. Unexpectedly, Max grinned at me, stretched, and said to Fearing, 'How do you feel now?'

'Perfectly fit.'

'Feel up to another little demonstration?'

'Certainly.'

'That reminds me, Max,' I said abruptly, 'out in the corridor you mentioned something about –'

He shot me a warning glance.

'We'll go into that some other time,' he said.

'What diseases are you going to have me do this time?' Fearing queried.

Max wagged his finger. 'You know you're never told that.

Can't have your conscious mind messing things up. We'll have some new signals, though. And, Fred, I hope you won't mind waiting outside while I put John under and give him his instructions — acquaint him with the new signals. I'm afraid we still haven't got far along enough to risk the possibly disturbing presence of a third person during the early stages of an experiment. One or two more sessions and it should be all right, though. Understand, Fred, this is just the first of a large number of experiments I want you to witness. I'm asking a great deal of you, you see. The only tangible compensation I can offer you is exclusive rights to break the story to the public when we feel the time is ripe.'

'Believe me, I consider it a great honour,' I assured him sincerely as I went out.

In the corridor I lit a cigarette, puffed it a moment, and then the tremendous implications of Max's experiments really hit me.

Suppose, as Max had hinted, that it proved possible to impart Fearing's ability to other people?

The benefits would be incalculable. People would be able to help their bodies in the fight against disease and degenerative processes. For instance, they could cut down the flow of blood from a wound, or even stop it completely. They could marshal all the body's resources to fight local infections and stop disease germs before they ever got started. Conceivably, they could heal sick organs, get them working in the right rhythm, unharden arteries, avert or stifle cancers.

It might be possible to prevent disease, even ageing, altogether.

We might look forward to a race of immortals, immune to time and decay.

A happy race, untroubled by those conflicts of body and mind, of instinct and conscience, that sap Mankind's best energies and are at the root of all discords and wars.

There was literally no limit to the possibilities.

I hardly felt I'd been in the corridor a minute, my mind was soaring so, when Max softly opened the door and beckoned to me.

Again Fearing lay stretched on the table. His eyes were

closed, but he still looked every whit as vibrantly healthy as before. His chest rose and fell rhythmically with his breathing. I almost fancied I could see the blood coursing under the fair skin.

I was aware of a tremendous suppressed excitement in Max.

'We can talk, of course,' he said. 'Best keep it low, though.'

'He's hypnotized?' I asked.

'Yes.'

'And you've given him the instructions?'

'Yes. Watch.'

'What are they this time, Max?'

Max's lips jerked oddly.

'Just watch.'

He rapped with the pencil.

I watched. For five, ten seconds nothing seemed to happen.

Fearing's chest stopped moving.

His skin was growing pale.

There was a weak convulsive shudder. His eyelids fell open, showing only the whites. Then there was no further movement whatever.

'Approach him,' Max ordered, his voice thick. 'Take his pulse.'

Almost shaking with excitement, I complied.

To my fumbling fingers, Fearing's wrist felt cold. I could not find a pulse.

'Fetch that mirror,' Max's finger stabbed at a nearby shelf. 'Hold it to his lips and nostrils.'

The polished surface remained unclouded.

I backed away. Wonder gave place to fear. All my worst suspicions returned intensified. Once again I seemed to sense a strain of submerged evil in my friend.

'I told you I would show you something with a bearing on the question, "What is death?"' Max was saying huskily. 'Here you see death perfectly counterfeited – death-in-life. I would defy any doctor in the world to prove this man alive.' There was a note of triumph in his voice.

My own was uneven with horror. 'You instructed him to be dead?'

'Yes.'

'And he didn't know it ahead of time?'

'Of course not.'

For an interminable period – perhaps three or four seconds – I stared at the blanched form of Fearing. Then I turned to Max.

'I don't like this,' I said. 'Get him out of it.'

There was something sneering about the smile he gave me.

'Watch!' He commanded fiercely, and rapped again.

It was only some change in the light, I told myself, that was giving Fearing's flesh a greenish tinge.

Then I saw the limp arms and legs stiffen and the face tighten into a sardonic mask.

'Touch him!'

Unwillingly, only to get the thing over with as swiftly as possible, I obeyed. Fearing's arm felt stiff as a board and, if anything, colder than before.

*Rigor Mortis.*

But that faint odour of putrescence – I knew that could only be my imagination.

'For God's sake, Max,' I pleaded, 'you've got to get him out of it.' Then, throwing aside reserve, 'I don't know what you're trying to do, but you can't. Velda –'

Max jerked as I spoke the name. Instantly the terrifying shell that had gathered around him seemed to drop away. It was as if that one word had roused him from a dream. 'Of course,' he said, in his natural voice. He smiled reassuringly and rapped.

Eagerly I watched Fearing.

Max rapped again: three – one.

It takes time, I told myself. Now the muscles were beginning to relax, weren't they?

But Max was rapping again. The signal printed itself indelibly on my brain: three – one.

And yet again. Three – one. Three – one. THREE – ONE.

I looked at Max. In his tortured expression I read a ghastly certainty.

I wouldn't ever want to relive the next few hours. I imagine that in all history there was never a trick conceived for reviving the dying that Max didn't employ, along with all the modern methods – injections, even into the heart itself, electrical stimulation, use of a new lightweight plastic version of the iron lung, surgical entry into the chest and direct massage of the heart.

Whatever suspicions I had had of Max vanished utterly during those hours. The frantic genuineness and inspired ingenuity of his efforts to revive Fearing couldn't possibly have been faked. No more could his tragic, rigidly suppressed grief have been simulated. I saw Max's emotions stripped to the raw during those hours, and they were all good.

One of the first things he did was to call in several of the other faculty doctors. They helped him, though I could tell that from the first they looked upon the case as hopeless, and would have considered the whole business definitely irregular, if it hadn't been for their extreme loyalty to Max, far beyond any consideration of professional solidarity. Their attitude showed me, as nothing else ever had, Max's stature as a medical man.

Max was completely frank with them and everyone else. He made no effort whatsoever to suppress the slightest detail of the events leading up to the tragedy. He was bitter in his self-accusations, insisting that his judgment had been unforgivably at fault in the final experiment. He would have gone even further than that if it hadn't been for his colleagues. It was they who dissuaded him from resigning from the faculty and describing his experiments in such inaccurately harsh terms as to invite criminal prosecution.

And then there was Max's praiseworthy behaviour toward Fearing's mother. While they were still working on Fearing, though without any real hope, she burst in. Whatever reforms the psychiatrist may have achieved in her personality, were washed out now. I still can close my eyes and visualize that hateful, overdressed woman stamping around like an angry parrot, screaming the vilest accusations at Max at the top of her voice and talking about her son and herself in the most disgusting terms. But although he was near the breaking point, Max was never anything but compassionate towards her, accepting all the blame she heaped on his head.

A little later Velda joined Max. If I'd still had any of my early suspicions, her manner would have dissipated them. She was completely practical and self-possessed, betraying no personal concern whatsoever in Fearing's death. If anything, she was too cool and unmoved. But that may have been what Max needed at the time.

The next days were understandably difficult. While most of the newspapers were admirably reserved and judicious in reporting the case, one of the tabloids played up Max as 'The Doctor Who Ordered a Man to Die,' featuring an exclusive interview with Fearing's mother.

The chorus of wild bleats from various anti-science cults was of course to be expected. It led to a number of stories that crept into the fringe of print and would have been more unpleasant if they hadn't been so ridiculous. One man, evidently drawing on Poe's story, 'The Facts in the Case of M. Valdemar,' demanded that a 'death watch' be maintained on Fearing and, on the morning of the funeral, hinted darkly that they were interring a man who was somehow still alive.

Even the medical profession was by no means wholly behind Max. A number of local doctors, unconnected with the medical school, were severe in their criticisms of him. Such sensational experiments reflected on the profession, were of doubtful value in any case, and so forth. Though none of these criticisms were released to the public.

The funeral was held on the third day. I attended it out of friendship for Max, who felt it his duty to be present. Fearing's mother was there, of course, dressed in a black outfit that somehow managed to look loud and common. Since the tabloid interview there had been a complete break between her and our group, so that her wailing tirades and nauseous sobbing endearments could only be directed at the empty air and the bronze-fitted casket.

Max looked old. Velda stood beside him, holding his arm. She was as impassive as on the day of Fearing's death.

There was only one odd thing about her behaviour. She insisted that we remain at the cemetery until the casket had been placed in the tomb and the workman had fixed in place the marble slab that closed it. She watched the whole process with a dispassionate intentness.

I thought that perhaps she did it on Max's account, to impress on him that the whole affair was over and done with. Or she may conceivably have feared some unlikely final demonstration or foray on the part of the wilder anti-science groups and felt that the presence of a few intelligent witnesses was advisable to prevent some final garish news item from erupting into print.

And there may actually have been justification for such a fear. Despite the efforts of the cemetery authorities, a number of the morbidly curious managed to view the interment and as I accompanied Max and Velda the few blocks to their home, there were altogether too many people roaming the quiet, rather ill-kempt streets of the scantily populated suburb. Undoubtedly we were being followed and pointed at. When, with feelings of considerable relief, we finally got inside, there was a sharp, loud knock on the door we had just closed.

Someone had thrown a stone at the house.

For the next six months I saw nothing of Max. Actually this was as much due to my friendship for him as to the press of my work, which did keep me unusually busy at the time. I felt that Max didn't want to be reminded in any way, even by the presence of a friend, of the tragic accident that had clouded his life.

I think, you see, that only I, and perhaps a few of Max's most imaginative colleagues, had any inkling of how hard Max had been hit by the experience and, especially, *why* it had hit him so hard. It wasn't so much that he had caused the death of a man through a perhaps injudicious experiment. That was the smaller part. It was that, in so doing, he had wrecked a line of research that promised tremendous benefits to mankind. Fearing, you see, was irreplaceable. As Max had said, he was probably unique. And their work had been barely begun. Max had obtained almost no results of a measured scientific nature and he hadn't as yet any ideas whatever of the crucial thing: how to impart Fearing's ability to other people, if that were possible. Max was a realist. To his clear, unsuperstitious mind, the death of one man was not nearly so important as the loss of possible benefits to millions. That he had played fast and loose with humanity's future – yes, he'd have put it that way – was, I knew, what hurt him most. It would be a long time before he regained his old enthusiasm.

One morning I ran across a news item stating that Fearing's mother had sold her house and gone for a European tour.

Of Velda I had no information.

Naturally I recalled the affair from time to time, turning it over in my mind. I reviewed the suspicions I'd had at the time, seeking some clue that might have escaped me, but always coming to the conclusion that the suspicions were more than wiped out by Max's tragic sincerity and Velda's composure after the event.

I tried to visualize the weird and miraculous transformations I had witnessed in Max's office. Somehow, try as I might, they began to seem more and more unreal. I had been excited that morning, I told myself, and my mind had exaggerated what I had seen. This unwillingness to trust my own memory filled me at times with a strange poignant grief, perhaps similar to what Max must have felt at the breakdown of his research, as if some marvellous imaginative vision had faded from the world.

And occasionally I pictured Fearing as I'd seen him that morning, so radiantly healthy, his mind and body so unshake-ably knit. It was very hard to think of a man like that being dead.

Then, after six months, I received a brief message from Max. If I were free, would I visit him at his home that evening? Nothing more.

I felt a thrill of elation. Perhaps the period of thraldom to the past was over and the brilliant old mind was getting to work again. I had to break an engagement, but of course I went.

It had just stopped raining when I swung down from the interurban. Remnants of daylight showed a panorama of dripping trees, weed-bordered sidewalks, and gloom-invested houses. Max had happened to build in one of those subdivi-sions that doesn't quite make the grade, while the unpredict-able pulse of suburban life begins to beat more strongly farther out.

I passed the cemetery in which Fearing had been interred. The branches of unpruned trees brushed the wall, making sections of the sidewalk a leafy tunnel. I was glad I had a flashlight in my pocket for the walk back. It occurred to me that it was unfortunate Max had this unnecessary reminder almost on his doorstep.

I walked rapidly past houses that were more and more

frequently separated by empty lots, and along a sidewalk that became progressively more cracked and weed-grown. There popped into my mind a conversation I had had with Max a couple of years ago. I had asked him if Velda didn't find it lonely out here, and he had laughingly assured me that both he and Velda had a passion for being alone and liked to be as far away as possible from spying neighbours.

I wondered if one of the houses I had passed had been that belonging to the Fearings.

Eventually I arrived at Max's place, a compact two-storey dwelling. There were only a few more houses beyond it on the street. Beyond those, I knew, the weeds reigned supreme, the once hopeful sidewalks were completely silted and grown over, and the lamp-posts rusted lightlessly. Unsuccessful subdivisions are dismal spots.

In my nostrils, all the way had been the smell of wet cold earth and stone.

The living room lights were on, but I saw no one through the French window where I had once glimpsed Velda and Fearing. The hall was dark. I rapped at the door. It opened instantly. I faced Velda.

I haven't described Velda. She was one of those very beautiful, dignified, almost forbidding, yet quite sexy girls that a successful, cultured man is apt to marry if he waits until he's middle-aged. Tall. Slim. Small head. Blonde hair drawn tightly across it. Blue eyes. Compact, distinguished features. Sloping shoulders, and then a body that a cynic would call the main attraction. And perhaps with partial inaccuracy, because an alert, well-informed, quite courageous mind went with it. Exquisite manners, but not much apparent warmth.

That was Velda as I remembered her.

The Velda I faced now was different. She was wearing a grey silk dressing gown. In the dim light from the street lamp behind me, the tight-drawn hair looked, not grey, but brittle. The tall beautiful body somehow seemed sterile, weedlike. She crouched like an old woman. The distinguished features in the face she lifted towards mine were pinched. The blue eyes, white circled, were much too staring.

She touched a finger to her thinned lips, and with the other hand timidly took hold of the lapel of my coat, as if to draw me away to some place where we could talk secretly.

Max stepped out of the darkness behind her and put his hands on her shoulders. She didn't stiffen. In fact, she hardly reacted except to softly drop her hand from my coat. She may have winked at me, as if to say, 'Later, perhaps,' but I can't be sure.

'You'd better be getting upstairs, dear,' he said gently. 'It's time you took a little rest.'

At the foot of the stairs he switched on the light. We watched her as she went up, slowly, holding on to the rail.

When she was out of sight Max shook his head and said, rather lightly, 'Too bad about Velda. I'm afraid that in a little while – However, I didn't ask you out here to talk about that.'

I was shocked at his seeming callousness. A moment later, however, he said something which gave me a hint of the philosophy that underlay it.

'We're so mysteriously fragile, Fred. Some slight change in a gland's function, some faint shadow falling on a knot of nerve tissue, and – pouf. And there's nothing we can do about it, because we don't know, Fred, we simply don't know. If we could trace the thoughts in their courses, if we could set their healing magic radiating through the brain – but that's not to be for awhile yet. Meanwhile, there's nothing we can do about it, except to face it cheerfully. Though it is hard when the person whose mind goes develops a murderous hatred of you at the same time. However, as I said, I don't want to talk about that, and you'll please me if you don't either.'

We were still standing at the bottom of the stairs. Abruptly he changed his manner, clapped me on the shoulder, steered me into the living room, insisted that I have a drink, and busied himself starting a fire in the open grate, all the while chatting loudly about recent doings at the medical school and pressing me for details of my latest articles.

Then, giving me no time whatever to think, he settled himself in the opposite chair, the fire blazing between us, and launched into a description of a new research project he was getting started on. It concerned the enzymes and the mechanisms of temperature-control of insects, and seemed to have far-reaching implications in fields as diverse as insecticide manufacture and the glandular physiology of human beings.

There were times when he got so caught up in his subject that it almost seemed to me it was the old Max before me, as if all the events of the past year had been a bad dream.

Once he broke off momentarily, to lay his hand on a bulky typescript on the table beside him.

'This is what I've been keeping myself busy with these last few months, Fred,' he said quickly. 'A complete account of my experiments with Fearing, along with the underlying theories, as well as I can present them, and all pertinent material from other fields. I can't touch the thing again, of course, but I hope someone else will, and I want him to have the benefit of my mistakes. I'm rather doubtful if any of the journals will accept it, but if they don't I'll publish it at my own expense.'

It really gave me a pang to think of how much he must have suffered pounding out that typescript, meticulously, of course, knowing that it wasn't his job any more or ever could be, knowing that it was the account of a failure and a personal tragedy, knowing that it wouldn't be at all well received by his profession, but feeling duty-bound to pass on information that might some day kindle another mind and prove of scientific value to mankind.

And then the tragedy of Velda, which I hadn't yet been able to properly assimilate, with its faint, last-twist-of-the-screw suggestion that if Max had continued his research with Fearing he might conceivably have learned enough to be able to avert the cloud shadowing her mind.

Yes, I thought then, and I still think, that Max's behaviour that night, especially his enthusiasm about his new research project, into which he'd obviously thrown himself wholeheartedly, was an inspiring and at the same time heart-rending example of the sort of unsentimental courage you find in the best scientists.

Yet at the same time I had the feeling that his new project wasn't the real reason for his summoning me. He had something very different on his mind, I felt, and as an unhappy person will, was talking himself out on other subjects as a preliminary to getting around to it. After a while he did.

The fire had died down somewhat. We had temporarily

exhausted the topic of his new project. I was conscious of having smoked too many cigarettes. I asked Max some inconsequential question about a new advance in aviation medicine.

He frowned at the crawling flames, as if he were carefully weighing his answer. Then abruptly he said, without looking towards me, 'Fred, there's something I want to tell you, something I felt I must tell you, but something I haven't been able to bring myself to tell you until now. I hated John Fearing, because I knew he was having a love affair with my wife.'

I looked down at my hands. After a moment I heard Max's voice again. It wasn't loud, but it was rough with emotion.

'Oh come on, Fred, don't pretend you didn't know. You saw them through the window that night. You'll be surprised to know, Fred, how hard it was for me not to avoid you, or pick some quarrel with you, after that happened. Just the thought that you knew...'

'That's all I did see or know,' I assured him. 'Just that one glimpse.' I turned and looked at him. His eyes were bright with tears.

'And yet you know, Fred,' he went on, 'that's the real reason I picked you to sit in on our experiments. I felt that knowing what you did, you would be better able than anyone else to check on my relationship with John.'

There was one thing I had to say. 'You are quite certain, Max, that your suspicions of Velda and Fearing were justified?'

One look at his face told me I needn't press that line of questioning any further. Max sat for a while with his head bowed. It was very quiet. The wind had died which earlier had splattered a few drops from nearby branches against the windowpanes.

Finally he said, 'You know, Fred, it's very difficult to recapture lost emotions, either jealousy or scientific zeal. And yet those were the two main ones in this drama. For of course it wasn't until I had begun my experiments with Fearing that I found out about him and Velda.' He paused, then went on with difficulty. 'I'm afraid I'm not a very broadminded man, Fred, when it comes to sex and possession. I think that if John had been some ordinary person, or if I had found out earlier, I would have behaved differently. Rather brutally, perhaps. I don't know. But the fact that our experiments had begun, and that they promised so much, changed everything.

'You know, I really try to be a scientist, Fred,' he went on, with the ghost, or cadaver rather, of a rueful smile. 'And as a scientist, or just as a rational man, I had to admit that the possible benefits of our experiments infinitely outweighed any hurt to my vanity or manhood. It may sound grotesque, but as a scientist I even had to consider whether this love affair wasn't necessary to keep my subject cooperative and in a proper state of mind, and whether I shouldn't go out of my way to further it. As it was, I didn't have to vary my routine in order to give them plenty of opportunities, though I think that if that had been necessary, I might even have done it.'

He clenched his fist. 'You see, so very much depended on those experiments of ours. Though it's awfully hard for me to remember that now. The feeling's all gone ... the tremendous vision ... this typescript here is just dead stuff ... an obligation ...

'I feel differently about a lot of things now. About Velda and John, too. Velda wasn't exactly the girl I thought I was marrying. I've realized lately that she had a tremendous need to be adored, a kind of cold lust for beauty and ecstasy, like some pagan priestess. And I cooped her up here – the old story – and tried to feed her on my enthusiasms. Not exactly the right diet. And yet, you know, Fred, my life's work was inspired by Velda to an extent that you might find hard to believe. Even before I'd met Velda. The expectancy of her.

'And John? I don't think anyone will ever know the truth about John. I was only beginning to understand him, and there were sides to his nature I couldn't touch. A remarkable creature. In one sense, a true superman. In another, a mindless animal. Astonishing weaknesses, or blind spots. The influence of his mother. And then the way his instincts and conscience went hand in hand. I feel that John may have been completely sincere both about his desire for Velda and his desire to help me aid mankind. It may never have occurred to him that the two desires didn't exactly go together. It's quite possible he felt that he was being very nice to both of us.

'Yes, and if John and Velda's affair were something that could happen now, I think I would feel very differently about it.

'But then —? God, Fred, it's so hard to think truthfully about *them*! Then there existed in me, side by side, every moment of the day and night, the highest pinnacles of scientific excitement and the deepest pits of jealous rage. The one strictly subordinated!' A note of passionate anger came into his voice. 'For don't think I was weak, Fred. Don't think I ever deviated so much as a hairs-breadth from the course that was scientifically and humanistically right. I kept my hatred for John in absolute check. And when I say that, I mean that. I'm no ignoramus, Fred, I know that when one tries to suppress feelings, they have a way of bursting out through unsuspected channels, due to the trickery of the subconscious mind. Well, I was on the watch for that. I provided every conceivable safeguard. I was fantastically cautious about each experiment. I know it may not have looked that way to you, but even that last one — heavens, we had often done experiments twice as dangerous, or as seemingly dangerous, testing every step of the way. Why, Soviet scientists have had people technically dead for over five minutes. With John it couldn't have been one!

'And yet ...

'That's what tormented me so, don't you see, Fred, when I couldn't revive him. The thought that my unconscious mind had somehow tricked me and opened a channel for my all-too-conscious hatred, found a chink in the wall that I'd neglected to stop up, a doorway unguarded for a second. As he lay there dead before my eyes, I was tortured by the conviction that there was some little thing that would revive him at once if only I could remember what it was.

'Some little mistake or omission I'd made, which only had to be thought of to be corrected, but which my subconscious mind wouldn't let me remember. I felt that if only I could have relaxed my mind completely — but of course that was the one thing I couldn't do.

'I tried every way I knew to revive John, I reviewed every step I'd taken without finding a flaw, and yet that feeling of guilt persisted.

'Everything seemed to intensify it. Velda's frozen, suicidal calm, worse than the bitterest and most tempestuous accusations. The most childish things — even that silly occultist with his talk of a deathwatch on John.

'How John must hate me, I'd tell myself irrationally. Commanded to be dead, tricked into dying, not given the faintest hint of what was intended.

'And Velda. Never a reproachful word to me. Just freezing up, more and more, until her mind began to wither.

'And John. That miraculous body rotting in the tomb. Those magnificently knit muscles and nerves, falling apart cell by cell.'

Max slumped in his chair exhausted. The last flame in the grate flickered out and the embers began to smoke. The silence was deadly.

And then I began to talk. Quietly. Nothing brilliant. I merely reviewed what I knew and what Max had told me. Pointed out how, being the scientist he was, he couldn't have done anything but what he did. Reminded him of how he'd checked and double-checked his every action. Showed him that he hadn't the shred of a reason for feeling guilty any longer.

And finally my talk began to take effect, though, as Max said, 'I don't think it's anything you've said. I've been all over that. It's that at last I've unburdened myself to someone. But I do feel better.'

And I'm sure he did. For the first time I truly sensed the old Max in him. Battered and exhausted of course, and deeply seared by a new wisdom, but something of the old Max, nevertheless.

'You know,' he said, sinking back in his chair, 'I think I can really relax now for the first time in six months.'

Immediately the silence settled down again. I remember thinking, queerly, that it was dreadful that a place could be so silent.

The fire had stopped smoking. Its odour had been replaced by that seeping in from the outside – the smell of cold wet earth and stone.

My taut muscles jerked spasmodically at the sudden grating of Max's chair against the floor. His face was ghastly. His lips formed words, but only choking sounds came out. Then he managed to get control of his voice.

'The cue! The cue for him to come alive again! I forgot I changed the signals. I thought it was still –'

He tore a pencil from his pocket and rapped on the arm of the chair: three – one.

'But it should have been –' And he rapped: three – two.

It is hard for me to describe the feeling that went through me as he rapped that second signal.

The intense quiet had something to do it. I remember wishing that some other sound would break in – the patter of raindrops, the creaking of a beam, the hollow surge of the interurban.

Just five little raps, unevenly spaced, but imbued with a quality, force, and rhythm that was Max's and nobody else's in the world – as individual as his fingerprint, as inimitable as his signature.

Just five little raps – you'd think they'd be lost in the walls, gone in a second. But they say that no sound, however faint, ever dies. It becomes weaker and weaker as it dissipates, the agitations of the molecules less and less, but still it goes on to the end of the world and back, to the end of eternity.

I pictured that sound struggling through the walls, bursting into the night air with an eager upward sweep, like a black insect, darting through the wet tangled leaves, soaring crazily into the moist tattered clouds, perhaps dipping inquisitively to circle one of the rusted lamp-posts, before it streaked purposefully off along the dank street, up, up, over the trees, over the wall, and then swooped down toward wet cold earth and stone.

And I thought of Fearing, not yet quite rotted in his tomb.

Max and I looked at each other.

There came a piercing, blood-chilling scream from over our heads.

A moment of paralysed silence. Then the wild clatter of footsteps down the stairs in the hall. As we sprang up together, the outside door slammed.

We didn't exchange a word. I stopped in the hall to snatch up my flashlight.

When we got outside we couldn't see Velda. But we didn't ask each other any questions as to which direction she'd taken.

We started to run. I caught sight of Velda almost a block ahead.

I'm not in too bad physical condition. I slowly drew ahead of Max as we ran. But I couldn't lessen the distance between myself and Velda. I could see her quite plainly as she passed through the pools of light cast by the street lamps. With the grey silk dressing gown flying out behind her, she sometimes looked like a skimming bat.

I kept repeating to myself, 'But she couldn't have heard what we were saying. She couldn't have heard those raps.'

Or could she?

I reached the cemetery. I shone my flashlight down the dark, leafy tunnel. There was no one in sight, but almost halfway down the block I noticed branches shaking where they dipped to the wall.

I ran to that point. The wall wasn't very high. I could lay my hand on its top. But I felt broken glass. I stripped off my coat, laid it over the top, and pulled myself up.

My flashlight showed a rag of grey silk snagged on a wicked barb of glass near my coat.

Max came up gasping. I helped him up the wall. We both dropped down inside. The grass was very wet. My flashlight wandered over wet, pale stones. I tried to remember where Fearing's tomb was. I couldn't.

We started to hunt. Max began to call, 'Velda! Velda!'

I suddenly thought I remembered the lay-out of the place. I pushed on hurriedly. Max lagged behind, calling.

There was a muffled crash. It sounded some distance away. I couldn't tell the direction. I looked around uncertainly.

I saw that Max had turned back and was running. He vanished around a tomb.

I hurried after him as fast as I could, but I must have taken the wrong turning. I lost him.

I raced futilely up and down two aisles of tombstone and tomb. I kept flashing my light around, now near, now far. It showed pale stone, dark trees, wet grass, gravel path.

I heard a horrible, deep, gasping scream – Max's.

I ran wildly. I tripped over a headstone and sprawled flat on my face.

I heard another scream – Velda's. It went on and on.

I raced down another aisle.

I thought I would go on for ever, and forever hearing that scream, which hardly seemed to pause for inhalation.

Then I came around a tangled clump of trees and I saw them.

My flashlight wavered back and forth across the scene twice before I dropped it.

They were there, all three of them.

I know that the police have a very reasonable explanation for what I saw, and I know that explanation must be right, if there is any truth in what we have been taught to believe about mind and body and death. Of course there are always those who will not quite believe, who will advance other theories. Like Max, with his experiments.

The only thing the police can't decide for certain is whether Velda managed to break into the tomb and open the casket unaided – they did find a rusty old screwdriver nearby – or whether tomb and casket hadn't been broken into at an earlier date by some sort of cultists or, more likely, pranksters inspired by cultists. They have managed to explain away, almost completely, all evidence that tomb and casket were burst from the inside.

Velda can't tell them. Her mind is beyond reach.

The police have no doubts whatsoever about Velda's ability to strangle Max to death. After all, it took three strong men to get her out of the cemetery. And it is from my own testimony that the police picked up Max's statement that Velda hated him murderously.

The odd position of Fearing's remains they attribute to some insane whim on Velda's part.

And of course, as I say, the police must be right. The only thing against their theory is the raps. And of course I can't make them understand just how tremendously significant those raps of Max, that diabolic three – two, seemed to me at the time.

I can only tell what I saw, in the flashlight's wavering gleam.

The marble slab closing Fearing's tomb had fallen forward. The tomb was open.

Velda was backed against a tombstone opposite it. Her grey silk dressing gown was wet and torn to ribbons. Blood dribbled from a gash above her knee. Her blond hair streamed down tangledly. Her features were contorted. She was staring down at the space between herself and Fearing's tomb. She was still screaming.

There before her, in the wet grass, Max lay on his back. His head was twisted backward.

And across the lower part of Max's body, the half-fleshed fingers stretching towards his throat, the graveclothes clinging in tatters to the blackened, shrunken body, was all that was left of Fearing.

# The Curse of Frankenstein

## By JIMMY SANGSTER

One projected Frankenstein TV series with a notable pedigree that should have had great potential but, curiously, never got beyond the pilot episode, was Tales of Frankenstein *which was made in 1958 by Britain's Hammer Films in conjunction with Columbia Pictures' Screen Gems. The pilot was filmed in the immediate wake of Hammer's huge box office success the previous year when they had revived the original story for the cinema as* The Curse of Frankenstein *starring Peter Cushing and Christopher Lee. Though the same scriptwriter, Jimmy Sangster, had been assigned to write four episodes for the TV series, new actors were cast: the German-born Anton Diffring to play Baron Frankenstein and the American strong-man, Don Megowan, as the monster. As it turned out, only the one episode,* The Face in the Tombstone Mirror, *in which Frankenstein revived the creature using a sick man's brain, was ever shot, and this failed to find a sponsor on either side of the Atlantic. It has remained forgotten in the vaults of Hammer Pictures ever since.*

*The film* The Curse of Frankenstein *proved a very different proposition indeed. Michael Carreras at Hammer had made the decision to revive the creature who had been lying dormant since the demise of the Universal series a decade earlier and, almost at a stroke, Hammer assumed the mantle of the world's leading makers of horror films. During the years which followed, they repeated the formula just as frequently and successfully as the American studio had done earlier. However, the formula which Carreras and Jimmy Sangster devised differed fundamentally from that of Universal in that greater emphasis was now placed on Frankenstein instead of his creation, and the restrained horror of the earlier pictures was replaced by lashings of blood and gore as well as plenty of violence and sexual titillation. It proved hugely successful with the public and made a star of Peter Cushing who went on to play Frankenstein in half a dozen sequels. He has, in fact, become as thoroughly identified with the role as Karloff did with the monster, and confessed to one interviewer a few years ago, 'I have a tremendous amount of affection for Baron Frankenstein. I based the original character on Mary Shelley's novel, which I'd never read until I knew I was doing the film. Later on I used Dr Robert Knox, the famous anatomist who went to terrible trouble trying to get the medical profession to allow him to use cadavers.'* (The Curse of Frankenstein *also made a star of Christopher Lee as the creature, though he never repeated the role – instead becoming famous as Hammer's Dracula.)*

*The author of that landmark script, Jimmy Sangster (1927–) has been described as one of the most important influences behind Hammer Films in the Fifties and Sixties. He actually began his career with the company as a clapper boy, and at 19 became the youngest assistant director in the British film industry. In 1955 he broadened his activities to include script-writing, and a year later produced the storyline which made his reputation. He wrote several of the sequels, too, including* The Revenge of Frankenstein *(1958) and* The Horror of Frankenstein *(1970) which he also directed, before deciding to move to Hollywood where he continues to work on television specials. Appropriately, in this adaptation of Jimmy's script, the events are also recounted by Frankenstein himself...*

I

Today the priest came to my cell to offer what he considered comfort and to see if I was in repentant mood. The impertinence of it! Of what should I repent? I was glad to see him, but not because of any hopes he might hold out to me of the next life. It is this life in which I am interested. I am in no hurry to leave it. I wanted understanding and practical help from him, not pious platitudes. To him I would tell the whole story and ask him to pass it on. People trusted him: they listened to what he told them.

He was a drab, unimaginative little man. It was appalling that the survival of a mind such as my own should be at the mercy of a creature like this. Yet I had to try. Tomorrow they propose to execute me. It is monstrous, unthinkable. I am Baron Frankenstein, and there is still so much work which I must do.

'I'm sorry if you think my word will carry any authority,' he bleated at me. 'I'm afraid you're mistaken.'

I insisted that he should listen, and listen most carefully. Unless I could convince him that what I was about to tell him was the absolute truth, in the morning I would die. Yet how could anyone so fixed in his ways understand a word of the complexities for which I and I alone was responsible? He was as limited as the old fool who had been my teacher in Geneva.

Geneva in those early years of the nineteenth century was a lively city, a forum for brilliant debate and philosophical argument. Even as a boy I was a keen student of natural philosophy, and I think I may say without undue pride that I had a bent for research and logical analysis of problems. It was unfortunate that my mother, who knew little of such things, should have sent me for tuition to a bumbling old idiot who knew even less. He had been teaching the same dreary rubbish for thirty years. I doubted whether he had read a new book or considered a new idea for at least twenty of those.

The studies which counted were those I carried out on my own. While my friends – and I had few of them, for I found most of my contemporaries dull – were out carousing, I worked late into the night. With the few resources at my disposal I carried out small experiments which one day would have to be done on a larger scale. I read voraciously. I imbibed scientific theories in the way that my acquaintances imbibed wine. They thought that I was the dull one, and laughed at me for not knowing how to live. But what they meant by life and what I meant were two very different things. If they imagined I was not interested in life, they were absurdly mistaken. Life was just what interested me most – life, and how to create it.

It was something I didn't speak of to others. There were too many sceptics, and too many bigots anxious to suppress every manifestation of true progress.

When my mother died I inherited the Frankenstein fortune. This would enable me to begin the work and life I had always planned. I went back to the great house on the slopes above the pretty, trivial little village which had for centuries provided servants for the Frankenstein family and labourers to work in its fields; and here I endured the irritating formalities of the funeral, the condolences, and the family ritual before I could be left alone to concentrate on things which mattered.

My uncle from Basle commiserated with me and offered his assistance should I ever need it in my financial affairs. He thought I was rather young to be handling everything myself. If I wished to return to Geneva to continue my studies, he would make himself personally responsible for the estate. I was sure that he would – but I was not too happy about the possible future of the estate in such hands.

My Aunt Sophie had a delicate matter which she wished to broach. It was indeed so delicate that she could not bring herself to speak of it outright, and after some movements on her part as stately as a minuet but less conclusive, I was forced to say bluntly:

'You are concerned about the allowance my mother made you?'

'Oh. Victor, I would not wish to –'

'You need have no fears, Aunt Sophie. I shall continue to pay it.'

'You're a good boy, Victor. Your mother would have been proud of you. The dignity with which you have handled everything . . .'

'Yes,' I said. I wanted her off the premises so that I could relax and savour my new freedom and the taste of my riches.

But Aunt Sophie had every intention of declaring her overwhelming gratitude and at the same time of insinuating another possibility into my mind. Her daughter Elizabeth had been waiting demurely in the background. Now she was brought forward.

'Elizabeth, thank your cousin.'

'There's really no need,' I said.

She was adamant. 'Come along, Elizabeth, say thank you properly.'

The poor girl curtsied, blushing most becomingly as she did so.

'She's a good girl, Victor,' said Aunt Sophie in what she supposed to be a confidential aside. 'She'll grow into a fine woman one day.'

'I'm sure she will.' This at least I could say with conviction, for Elizabeth already had the makings of that fair, smooth-skinned, graceful woman she was soon to become.

'She'll make someone a fine wife.'

I held out my hand. 'Goodbye.'

Aunt Sophie herself almost contrived a curtsy. It was amazing that so gauche and insensitive a creature should have produced such an attractive daughter.

I was glad when at last they had all gone. The house was mine. The future was mine. All the resources of the Frankenstein estate were mine. At the back of the house were servants who would look after my every need without ever obtruding themselves. In the real sense of the word I was alone; and delighted to be so.

These pleasant musings were interrupted by the deep thud of the knocker on the main door. I was still not accustomed to having a full staff to attend to such matters, and instinctively I rose from my chair and went to the door. A serving girl, little more than a child, was already coming up the steps from the basement. She stopped when she saw me. She had bold dark eyes and a strangely impertinent, inscrutable little smile that was older than her years. I hesitated, not wanting to seem foolish by turning back and leaving her to answer the door. Then I waved her away and went to open it.

A young man stood on the step gazing out over the magnificent panorama of the valley. He turned to face me and made a polite bow in which there was no undue subservience.

'Good morning. My name is Paul Krempe. I have an appointment with Baron Frankenstein.'

I had been ready to dismiss the newcomer without delay, but now I stood back to let him in. He had come more swiftly than I had expected in answer to my summons. This was a good sign. I liked his shrewd, inquiring expression – I needed a man with a mind as relentlessly inquiring as my own – and I approved the speed with which he had got here.

'You must be Victor,' he said as he entered the hall and looked frankly around. 'I'm to be your tutor.'

I led him towards the salon in which my mother had once received visitors in that eternal round of courtesies and conventions which I proposed to abolish. 'Surely it isn't settled yet?' I said. 'I thought this was just an interview to decide whether you were suitable for the position.'

'I have had some correspondence with the Baron, and he seemed quite satisfied with my qualifications.'

'That's right.' I was deriving some amusement from this. 'He did, didn't he?'

Paul Krempe gave me a swift sidelong glance. He was trying to assess just how difficult a charge I was likely to be.

He said: 'Will you tell your father that I'm here.'

'My father is dead.'

This took him aback. 'But that's ridiculous. I had a letter from him . . .'

'He has been dead for many years. It was I who advertised for a tutor. It was I who wrote to you.'

'You are the Baron?'

'And have been since I was five years old.' I smiled.

'Yet you wrote to me saying that you wanted a tutor for your son.'

I had thought it would save a lot of explanation if I made the man come for a personal interview. In a letter he might have read things awry and been dubious about dealing direct with one as young as myself. He might have decided that the long journey was not worth while merely to satisfy what might be a rich young idler's whim. Now that he was here we could talk frankly.

We did talk, and at great length. I admired the way in which he reacted to what must at first have been a somewhat disturbing situation. He had a wry sense of humour and a keen appreciation of most of the points I made about my education so far and my requirements for the future. We talked as equals, yet he paid just the appropriate respect to my position, while I found it easy to defer to the wider range of his knowledge.

I had no intention of leaving this house and the estate in the hands of any of my relatives. I had no intention of completing my studies in Geneva, since I was convinced that under such conditions they never would be completed. What I wanted was a man like Krempe, a scientist and a scholar, who would live here and fill in the lamentable gaps in my knowledge. A general education was not what I sought: I was happy enough with my general background, and wished to concentrate now on the specialized work for which I felt I was destined.

'You were engaged as my tutor,' I said at the end of our long discussion, 'subject to the Baron's approval.' We both smiled: it had now become an agreeable joke between us. 'I may tell you that the Baron approves. Do you still want the position?'

'I shall be honoured, Herr Baron,' said Paul with a trace of respectful mockery which I found most refreshing after the hypocrisies and servility of my relatives.

And so we began.

There were times when I grew impatient. Paul turned out to be an admirable tutor, and in two years I had learned all he had to teach. But those two years dragged abominably. Of course, the groundwork was essential; but I wanted to move on to the subjects which really obsessed me.

It was Paul who taught me patience. Now, when he has forsaken me and repudiated all that we worked on together, I wonder if he realizes just how much of my doggedness and unwearying application can be attributed to his personal example? We spent the days, the weeks, the months together, probing into the unknown, investigating, recording, searching ... always searching, until gradually the great sweep of our research began to narrow down to a single direction.

To this we finally turned all our energies. We had explored biological byways, had even studied alchemy in the hope of finding grains of truth in the dross; but now we saw how recent discoveries in the field of magnetism opened up possibilities of a stimulus which might provoke the reaction we sought. It took us years of unrelenting work to approach even the fringe of what we longed to find.

During those years Paul lived in the house and rarely went out. We needed no outside distractions. He paid a few visits to some ageing uncle many miles away, but was always eager to return. Sometimes he went down to the village and I refrained from asking what entertainment he found there. For myself, I observed with a by no means dispassionate interest the development of the young serving girl on my staff, and when I fancied some frivolous relaxation I coaxed her into my bed. She required little coaxing. For all the splendid firmness of her body and the burning promise of those restless eyes, there were few in the neighbourhood who could satisfy her, and we spent some rewarding hours together. Justine was her name, and I will confess that there were many times when I murmured the syllables lovingly into her ear in such a way as to persuade her that she meant everything to me. There is little point in pursuing any pleasure, however fleeting it may be and however easily discarded it may later be, unless one is wholehearted about it at the moment of its consummation. There would come a time when I regretted the romantic glibness of my tongue.

Justine, after all, was merely a diversion. I summoned her when I was in the mood for her, and if she had understood the responsibilities and limitations of her employment in my household there would never have been any trouble. I was Baron Frankenstein, and my life was consecrated to life itself.

Of the activities of Paul and myself she knew nothing. Or so we believed. Our efforts were applied out of sight and sound of the rest of the house. Nobody was allowed into the laboratory. When the place required cleaning we cleaned it ourselves. When there were things to be disposed of – things better concealed from the prying eyes of ignorant servants – we destroyed them in various ways.

And at last, after years of application, we were rewarded.

We had been experimenting on a dog which Paul had lured away from the village. There had been a small outcry about its disappearance as it was a great pet with the family to which it belonged, but nobody suspected that it had found a resting place in the Frankenstein home. They ought to have been honoured. Possibly one day, when the whole story is told, they will indulge themselves in some petty pride: their dog made history, though the history is still to be written for the world to see.

I had killed the animal painlessly and then lowered it into the tank. It floated for two days in the viscous fluid with which we had already dosed or injected some hundreds of rats, mice, and birds. At the end of two days we began to apply the magnetic charges which jolted through the system and beat out an imperious rhythm in the animal's heart. A hundred minor adjustments were necessary. The frequency of the heartbeats and the intensity with which these could be simulated were delicate matters.

We reached the crucial stage late one night. There had been so many failures that I was not unduly optimistic. The most I allowed myself to hope was that we should learn something, some tiny additional piece of knowledge, that would make the next step clearer. I opened the tank and drained it. Paul, as engrossed in the task as myself, was impatient to reach in and take out the dog but I waved him away. The body needed thoroughly washing before we could allow ourselves to touch it. I drew on my gloves and sluiced the dog down until I was sure it was safe to approach the final investigation.

The dog lay as it had lain the day I killed it. Its eyes were open but glazed and unseeing. The paws lay flat and lifeless. There was no sign of breathing.

Paul stood beside me as I applied the stethoscope. He, too, might well have been lifeless: he was afraid to breathe or make a move. I listened, and he watched me.

The throb might be in my own head. I wanted so much to hear it that I could be cheating myself.

But no – there could be no mistake. I stood upright and tried to control my trembling exultation.

'Paul ... it's alive!' I scooped the dog up in my arms. It was a limp weight, but I laughed madly over it and felt a wild desire to give it a pet name because it had behaved so well. Good dog ... good dog! I said: 'We've done it.'

2

There was a considerable lag between the cardiac reaction and the first visible signs of life. Paul took the dog from me, wanting to share in my jubilation just as he had so devotedly shared in my work, and carried it downstairs to the sitting room. He laid the dog on the floor, and we drank a glass of brandy while waiting for it to get up on its feet. I was alarmed by its continuing stillness, but Paul pointed out that some time would be necessary for the first heartbeats to circulate life through the body once more.

'In itself,' he said eagerly, 'this opens up magnificent possibilities. Suppose that we could delay or prolong that period in which the body presumably remains dead while the heart is alive – then we'd have a living body with only the barest life spark present. Think what that would mean when it came to performing major surgery! It would save hundreds of lives, reduce shock to a minimum ... no loss of blood ...' He was beside himself with joy. 'Victor, the medical federation meets in Berne next month. Can we have our paper ready by then?'

At our feet the dog stirred. It shuddered along its whole length and then lazily lifted its head. As we watched, it thumped its tail twice. Then it began to stagger to its feet.

'Do you think we can?' Paul persisted.

'We could,' I said, 'but we're not going to.'

'But why not? There isn't another meeting of this scale for another year. Why wait that long?'

I was conscious of a twinge of disappointment. He had been a faithful ally and had shirked nothing, but now that success was within our grasp he showed himself too naïve in his enthusiasm. What we had done so far was nothing to what we could yet do. We had only just started. The door was open: now was the time to go through and find what lay beyond. I had had my own moments of impatience, but these were now conquered. I knew what came next and I knew that it required care and concentration. We had discovered the source of life itself and had used it to restore a creature that was dead. It was a tremendous discovery which was not ready to be shared. We must move on to the next stage.

'It's not enough just to bring a dead animal back to life,' I said. The dog sniffed at me and then went to Paul, who patted it affectionately as though he had owned it for years. 'We must create from the beginning. We must build up our own creature – build it up from nothing, if necessary. Otherwise we have accomplished only half the task we set ourselves.'

'Build?' He was baffled. 'Build what?'

'The most complex thing known to man,' I said. 'Man himself. Let's not concern ourselves with side issues such as operational techniques. We must create a human being.'

'Victor, this has gone to your head. Let's talk tomorrow and –'

'A man with perfect physique,' I said. 'With the mature brain of a genius. Everything planned and perfect. We can do it. Don't you see?'

In all these years I had seen no indication that he was anything but a devoted man of science. Now he revealed unsuspected doubts – the doubts of an ordinary superstitious mortal.

'What you're saying is madness – a revolt against nature. Such a thing can end only in evil.'

'Come now, Paul.' I forced myself to be patient with him. 'You haven't shown any scruples up to now. As for revolting against nature, haven't we done so already and succeeded? Isn't a thing that's dead supposed to be dead for all time? Yet we brought it back to life.'

The dog confirmed this by licking his hand. Paul looked down. The rasp of that rough tongue seemed to convince him more than my words did. He nodded to himself.

I went on: 'We hold in the palms of our hands such secrets as have never been dreamed of. Nature puts up her own barriers to confine the scope of man, but over and over again these barriers have been surmounted or thrust farther back. We have pushed them back. We are in a great tradition, Paul. There's nothing to stop us now.'

With that wry smile I knew so well, admitting rueful defeat, he asked: 'What do you want to do?'

'First,' I said, 'we need the framework – the body. Whatever adaptations may be necessary, that basic material is our starting point. Last week they hanged a man in Inglestadt. He was a highwayman who'd been terrorizing the countryside for months. As a warning to others his body has been left on a gibbet just outside the town. It'll stay there until it rots ... or until it's stolen.'

For a moment I thought Paul was about to protest again. Then he raised his glass. We were partners again in our splendid enterprise.

It would have suited me very well to ride out at once and claim the body of the robber, but we had worked deep into the night and were both exhausted. Paul made up a comfortable bed for the dog from an old blanket in the corner of the laboratory, and then we made our own way to bed. I lay awake for a long time, too tired and, at the same time, too ecstatic to sleep.

The following day my thoughts were occupied entirely by the next crucial step. Rising late, I checked that the dog was still alive and healthy, and decided that in a day or two it must be turned loose. Let it go back to its startled owners if it wished! Having a dead dog concealed in my house was no great problem; having a live one padding about the place would certainly arouse some conjecture. I wondered, with excitement rather than apprehension, how we would cope with the problem of a newly created man when that arose.

Justine tried to fondle me as I passed along the first-floor landing during the course of the afternoon. I brushed her off. She was growing much too forward for my liking. She belonged to the darkness and to the hours of my choice: I was disturbed to see signs of a brash familiarity and even arrogance in her manner.

The rebuff brought a dark frown to that usually pert, provocative face. Then she laughed none too agreeably.

'You'll be more friendly tonight, I'll be bound.'

'Tonight I'm busy,' I said.

'Busy?' She was alert at once. 'You and your friend are bringing village girls into the house – is that it?'

'No, Justine,' I said. 'No. We shall be working. And now go and do the same.'

The sulky pout of her lower lip, so entrancing at the right moment, now had the sinister quality of a threat. But she still knew the sound of an order when she heard it in my voice. She flounced away.

She was beautiful – yet not, deplorable as it may seem to some, as beautiful in my eyes as the corpse that swung from the gibbet by the roadside that night.

Paul and I took a horse and cart by a roundabout route to the scene of the execution. We had a ladder in the cart, and it was a matter of minutes to set this up and for me to climb up and cut through the rope from which dangled the robber, twisting gently in the cool night breeze. The body fell neatly into the cart, where Paul straightened it out and covered it with sacking. We drove back to the house.

In the brightness of the laboratory the dead rogue was not

an attractive sight. I was delighted to have him, but far from impressed by his appearance. The birds hadn't wasted any time: they had started on his eyes and then demolished one side of his face.

The head was of no use anyway. My idea was to create a perfect human being, and it had never been part of the plan that we should use the defective head and brain of a subnormal personality. I reached for a knife and turned the body over on the table.

'What are you going to do?' asked Paul.

I showed him. Our recent experiments had given me some surgical skill, and it was a comparatively simple matter to cut off the head of the corpse. Once I glanced up to see if Paul was interested in my anatomical knowledge, and caught him with a mixture of horror and amazement on his face.

With the same knife I sheared off a piece of sacking and wrapped the head in it. I held it away from me so that blood would not seep through and drop on to my clothes, and then I crossed the laboratory and dropped the head into the acid tank. The empty eye sockets yawned at me as the head rolled over and settled on the bottom.

It would not take long before skin and bone were eaten away. Less time than it would have taken the birds. In a few minutes there would be no trace.

'Now, Paul' – I had to jar him out of his trance – 'a hand with his clothes, if you please.'

I was eager to see the condition of the rest of the body. Paul was rather fastidious about it all, and I sensed his reluctance as we stripped the filthy rags from the stinking cadaver. To me this was still a glorious object, not because of its present deplorable state but because of its potentialities.

Together we washed down the body and then wrapped it in bandages from head to toe ... or, rather, from neck to toe. As we lifted it into the specially prepared tank, I could not help shuddering. My shudders were different from Paul's: his were those of a squeamish sentimentalist; mine arose from aesthetic considerations. The brute's hands were really too coarse to be contemplated. With such clod-hopping hands he could hardly have been anything other than a robber, except perhaps a gorilla.

We lowered the swathed form into the fluid and I studied

the splayed fingers and venous discoloration with mounting distaste. This was not how I had visualized my creation. But I had been prepared for deformities and the need for alterations. A head, new limbs – carefully chosen, they would contribute to the final unity of which I would be master.

Paul said: 'Victor, I don't think we should continue with this. We should wait and discuss our findings with the Federation. If anything –'

'Hands,' I said. I wanted him to concentrate on the essential things and forget his ludicrous scruples. 'Where shall we find the right hands?'

'Listen to me, Victor.'

But I had no intention of listening. I was not to be deterred. After so many frustrations, everything was going well for us now. Only a coward would turn back. I hurried him out of the laboratory and sent him off to bed with instructions to lie awake and think about the difficulties presented to us by this unsuitable corpse. I tried to make a joke of it, but his usual reluctant smile was not forthcoming.

In the morning I still knew that I was right. And among my correspondence was an item which I could take only as an omen. It was the printed announcement of the death of Bardello, the world's greatest sculptor, in Dresden. He had been a great friend of my father, who had helped him with two or three commissions early in his career. A memorial service was to be held tomorrow. It would undoubtedly be a magnificent affair, complete with florid eulogies, and I decided that I would not go; then, after a brief reflection, I decided that I would go.

It would be a tragedy should the hands of the most gifted sculptor of our time be left to rot below ground.

There was another communication announcing a death. This was less formal. It was a letter from my cousin Elizabeth telling me that her mother, my Aunt Sophie, had passed on. To this funeral ceremony I was also invited. I could not combine the two of them, and I knew which was the more important to me. I therefore wrote to Elizabeth before I set out for Dresden, expressing my grief at my aunt's death and regretting that it would be impossible for me to attend the interment, dearly as I should have loved to do so. I also invited Elizabeth to come and stay with me. It would be a good thing to have her in the house: it had been taken for granted from our childhood that we would one day marry, and if this were made tactfully clear to Justine it would go some way to diluting that arrogance of hers. Besides, it was time I married. With so many more absorbing problems in my mind, I devoted little time to the running of the household, and it would be a good thing for the staff to have a woman in the place organizing such matters.

Now I was in a hurry to leave. There was no time to explain every detail to Paul, and in any case I felt it would be wiser not to tell him too much in advance.

'Better not touch our friend in the laboratory while I'm gone,' I said. 'Let him rest in peace while he can.'

And then I left. Paul was bewildered by the speed of all this. If he thought to ask why I was going to Dresden, it was not until after I had gone.

The business took me longer than I had anticipated. I had to proceed from one little bit of bribery to another – and the more protracted the operation, the more danger there was of someone talking. The pomp surrounding the occasion did not help. One might almost have thought that a reigning monarch had died. At last, however, when the fuss had died down and the attention of the public turned from the dead Bardello to some new fad, I was able to accomplish my mission. At dead of night two men went out and returned with the hands of Bardello.

I hurried back to Switzerland.

I tried to imagine Paul's face when I broke the news to him. But more than that, I tried to imagine the corpse in the tank and how very different it would look when these magnificent, sensitive hands had been grafted to its arms.

The last mile was the longest. I urged the coachman on. With a tiring journey behind me I was nevertheless eager to get to work at once. If it meant staying up all night I wanted to set things in train.

With the precious parcel under my arm I marched across the hall and threw open the door of the salon. I was very nearly tempted to unwrap the parcel and throw the hands down triumphantly before Paul. I was glad I had restrained myself, for he was not alone. A beautiful young woman was sitting by the window. As I burst in she was saying:

'Yes, I've come to live here. This is to be my home.'

'Live here?' gasped Paul. 'But that's . . .'

Then they both turned towards me.

'Victor.' Elizabeth rose and crossed the room. She was as graceful as I had predicted she would be. Her beauty had the fragile yet firm quality of fine porcelain, but whereas porcelain is fixed, set, hard-surfaced, she was alive and volatile.

'I'm glad you got here safely,' I said. We shook hands very formally. I fancy she expected me to kiss her cheek, but I was already thinking and moving beyond her. 'Paul, you must come and see what I've got. A treasure, I assure you – a real treasure!'

Elizabeth fell back a step, disappointed. I gave her a quick smile and she tried to seem at ease. My social graces had perhaps suffered in the years of seclusion and devotion to the task in hand. With Justine I had needed no social graces. For this reason as well it would be good to have my cousin here. With Elizabeth I could learn again: she would, I flattered myself, find me a charming companion when I chose to be so.

But now there were more urgent demands on my time.

'We'll see you at dinner, my dear,' I said.

Paul glanced at her as though unsure of his own responsibility – whether to stay and provide her with social chit-chat or whether to come with me.

I left him in no doubt. I said: 'Shall we go to the laboratory, Paul?'

With an apologetic smile he left Elizabeth and followed me up the stairs. When we were in the laboratory I indicated that he should lock the door, and then I unwrapped the parcel.

'What about these? Have you ever seen anything so beautiful?'

He started as the long, powerful fingers were revealed. yet even as he stared at them there was a certain remoteness in his manner. He appeared to have something more important on his mind. But what could be more important than this?

'Where did you get them?' he asked abstractedly.

I told him, without giving too circumstantial an account of the methods I had employed. When I had finished he said:

'Victor, do you realize what this means?'

'It means,' I said, 'that our friend in the tank will be reborn with the finest hands ever possessed by any man.'

'I was referring to the arrival of your cousin. We can't continue with this experiment – not here, anyway.'

'What are you talking about?'

'Elizabeth. She might find out.'

'What if she does?' I could see no cause for alarm in this.

'She's young. Her mind will be incapable of standing up to such a shock. Victor, you don't realize the horror of what you're doing. At first I was blind to it myself.'

'And now?'

'While you were away I decided that I would not continue with this experiment. I hope I can convince you that I'm right, and make you change your mind, too.'

His chance of doing that was small. I tried to make him see reason. 'In six months' time you'll rejoice in the fact that you helped me present this achievement to the world. You'll become as famous as I will.'

'No, Victor,' he said. 'Infamous. I won't help you any more. And I beseech you to give this up – if not for your own sake, then for the sake of that girl.'

It was evident that my delightful cousin had made a strong impression on him. I had not realized that he could be so susceptible. In an endeavour to shake him out of this mood I said:

'Come along, Paul – help me to graft these hands on. It will be fascinating to see how they take.'

He made no move to follow me to the tank. 'Can't you understand, I'm not going to help you any more. And I shall try to make Elizabeth leave here.'

He was really disappointingly naïve. With his bourgeois background, he could, of course, not understand how such matters were arranged in families like ours. Elizabeth would listen to me rather than to him, and she would certainly not leave here. There were some explanations which would soon have to be made to Paul; but at this moment I was in no mood for dissertations of that kind. I said:

'If you really mean that you're not going to help me, you'd better leave me alone.'

He went to the door, then hesitated.

'Victor ...'

'If I'm to work on my own,' I said, 'I shan't have time to spare for dinner. Every hour that's wasted means a possible deterioration in these hands. Make my excuses to Elizabeth, will you?'

He went out. I took off my jacket and turned towards the bandaged shape in the tank. I half expected Paul to return. How could he possibly resist? But he didn't come back.

I wondered what he and Elizabeth would find to talk about.

3

It took me the better part of two hours to make the first attachment and submerge it in the tank. The speeded-up revivification of the tissues brought about by the fluid would now establish a firmer growth, and in due course the magnetic process would stimulate the entire organism. But that must wait: there were many faults yet to be corrected in this body.

Letting myself sink on to the laboratory stool after that concentrated effort over the tank, I realized that I was dizzy with exhaustion. If I was to go on working into the night, I needed coffee. I could go for a long time without food, but not without the stimulus of black coffee.

Elizabeth and Paul should have finished dinner by now. If I went down I would be in time to take a cup from the tray. And perhaps when he saw the gleam in my eyes Paul would, after all, find himself making excuses to follow me back to the laboratory.

I went along the landing and down the stairs. The door of the dining room was open and I could hear the murmur of voices as I descended. Suddenly Paul's rose in a plea that brought me to a halt.

'Leave this house at once. It won't be safe here.'

'Not safe?' came Elizabeth's quiet but surprised response. 'But Victor will be here.'

'It's because of Victor I'm asking you to leave. He is conducting a series of experiments which could be extremely dangerous.'

I was on the verge of hastening down the rest of the flight and into the dining room to cut short this disloyalty. Then I heard Elizabeth's calm voice, and noted with approval the tinge of reproach in it.

'I don't think Victor would have invited me here if he had thought I would be in any danger.'

'He doesn't realize himself just what risks he is taking.'

'What are these experiments?'

'You wouldn't understand them.'

'I'm sure I would. I could try, anyway. Please tell me.'

'I can't.'

'Then I shall have to ask Victor. If I am to marry him –'

'Marry him!' Paul's reaction was an absurd shout.

'We are engaged,' said Elizabeth coolly. I foresaw that she was going to make an admirable wife. Her dignity and tranquillity would suit me very well. 'It was agreed years ago between Victor and my mother.'

'But ... you've hardly seen him in recent years. You can't know anything about him.'

'It has always been my dearest wish to marry him,' she said, 'and I shall do all that is in my power to be a worthy wife to him.'

There was a silence. Paul broke it with an appeal that had lost all its force. 'I still say that you must leave here ...'

He heard footsteps along the passage just as I did. Justine walked into the dining room. I stayed where I was, now more gratified than angered by what I had just overheard.

'Shall I take the master's dinner up, do you think, sir?' Justine asked.

'He may be ready for something by now,' Paul agreed. 'Leave it outside the door.'

'Of course, Herr Krempe. I always do.'

I turned and went swiftly back to the laboratory. When Justine came to the door some minutes later, she rapped twice, but I refused to answer. She stood there for a few minutes. It was not the first time she had done this. Whether she expected me to come out to her or whether she wanted a glimpse into the laboratory I could not tell: whichever it might be; she obtained no satisfaction.

That night I worked until dawn and then stole a few hours' sleep. With some reluctance I forced myself to spend part of the afternoon with Elizabeth discussing our future. The reluctance faded somewhat after I had confirmed my original opinion that she was a serious, intelligent, well-balanced young woman. She made no stickily romantic protestations, and expected none in return. In her face I read both affection and respect, mingled in what I considered the ideal proportions. We had no need to discuss family or financial problems since we were both familiar with all the ramifications of the Frankenstein lineage and estates. We were two sensible adults: it had been established years ago that we should marry and we had no quarrel with this arrangement. A decent period would be allowed after her mother's death, and then we would have a simple ceremony to which, unfortunately, it would be necessary to invite one senile uncle and two remote cousins. Elizabeth would then be mistress of the household. I made it plain that, so far from objecting to her rehearsing this role before we were married, I would take it as a favour. It would take the weight off my shoulders and enable me to concentrate on my own work.

'This work of yours,' she said tentatively: 'is it very ... unusual?'

I knew that, provoked by Paul, she had been about to use another word, but was too noble to do so.

'Very unusual,' I said.

'You are not in any danger?'

I swear that she phrased the question sincerely. It was the possibility of danger to me rather than to herself that concerned her.

'None,' I said. 'And when the work is completed, you shall be the first to share in my triumph.'

She accepted this sweetly, without demur.

Acceptance did not, however, come easily to Justine. In Elizabeth's presence she grew surly, though was never so insolent as to necessitate her dismissal. Elizabeth assumed that the girl had been used to taking many decisions for herself and was finding it difficult to adjust to a new régime. She was patient with her.

But Justine was not patient. One night when I had worked late in the laboratory and was on my way to my bedroom, she materialized suddenly from the shadows in a corner and flung her arms round me. They were strong, demanding arms. She wore only a flimsy shift, and when I touched her I felt a tremor of urgent desire run through that body which I knew so well.

She breathed: 'Victor ...'

'How many times must I tell you –'

'Baron, then,' she whispered derisively. 'Herr Baron.'

'That's better.' I had made it a rule that she should always address me this way. The last thing I wanted was for her to fall so much into the habit of using my Christian name that she would one day blurt it out when others were present.

She said: 'How much longer is this to go on?'

Her hands were digging into my neck and yet she was holding herself away from me, not so much tantalizing me as waiting until something essential was said between us.

I was in no mood for her tonight. I said: 'How long is what going on?'

'Meeting like this in dark corridors. Making love in secret. Treating me as a servant, beneath your notice, in daylight. When are you going to marry me?'

It was an outrageous question. I stifled a contemptuous laugh. She had given me many hours of pleasure and I had no wish to be discourteous. But this was really too absurd.

I tried to free myself from her arms, but she held on. 'What makes you think I would contemplate marrying you?'

'Things you have said to me. In the night. And' – now she pressed herself against me – 'this.'

Only the most strong-willed man could have resisted that woman. Her every movement was so well known to me that it immediately suggested all the following movements, and I knew from experience that my memories of her never lived up to the reality. I was helplessly drawn on. I kissed her. Our mouths fought savagely together, and she laughed. Then, with a typical change of mood, she wrenched her head away and said tartly:

'Herr Baron Victor. This woman – what is she doing here?'

'Are you jealous?' I asked.

'No.' Then she snorted and said: 'Yes, yes, I am jealous. She is not your mistress, that pale creature? No, she could not be. If I thought she was –'

'On the contrary, Justine,' I said, 'she is to be *your* mistress. It is your duty to serve my cousin Elizabeth and see to her every need just as thoroughly as you have mine.'

I expected an explosion, but what I had just said struck her as being funny, and at once she was warm and laughing.

'Oh, no,' she spluttered. 'I think not, Herr Baron.'

'In a different way, of course,' I said, bringing on further laughter.

'Of course,' she said.

And we fumbled our way to my bedroom, where she proved to me that I was not as tired as I had thought.

Elizabeth suspected nothing of this. She had led a formal, somewhat restricted life, and took it for granted that life elsewhere – in her own social circle, at least – followed the same prescribed pattern. Gently and with admirable tact she took over the reins of management. Nothing was said about her eventually ceasing to be merely my cousin and becoming my wife. This was no business of the servants. They would be told when it was appropriate to tell them. For myself, I was not looking forward to breaking the news to Justine. Whatever she might suspect, she was still mercifully conscious enough of her own position to keep her curiosity within bounds. Once or twice she began to edge towards some awkward questions, but I silenced her in the most effective way I knew – which was pleasurable for both of us.

There were no people in our own circle to whom we made any announcement or even gave any hints. This was simply because no such circle existed. Paul had left the house, still firmly refusing to assist me in any further developments, and had settled in the village. This perturbed me slightly. It was amusing that he should have a quixotic desire to watch over Elizabeth, but not so amusing that he should be, as it were, on my doorstep, ready to give away our secrets to others if the mood took him. There was nobody else to pry into my personal or working life. We visited nobody and invited nobody. I could manage happily without company. If Elizabeth felt lonely, she did not complain. Since her mother had never been able to afford to entertain lavishly, the girl was probably used to occupying herself without the need for the chatter of others.

Her only complaint was that she saw so little of me. I spent what time I could with her, but I could not have been a very gay companion. All my thoughts were wrapped up in my experiments, and of these I could not speak to Elizabeth. There must be no false alarms raised at this stage. Only when the creature was complete and I could present it as an accomplished fact, justifying all my labours, would I let her into all my secrets.

I had discovered that the robber had had a defective right ankle, and as his feet were over-large in any case this meant replacing both of them to get a decent result. I made a trip to a charnel house in a canton many miles away: I was taking no chances near home. Then there was the question of the head. It took me several weeks to find a good specimen – and a specimen which was accessible – and then the eyes were in poor condition. A lot of intensive work was still to be done.

Leaving the house for any length of time worried me. I took the most stringent precautions to ensure that no one could get into my laboratory, but at the back of my mind was always the fear that some accident would happen – there would be a fire and someone might break the door down or find traces of my work in the ruins ... and the mere idea of a fire destroying all that work was in itself a nightmare.

One day I received word from the keeper of a charnel house – whom I had promised to pay well for such a notification – that if I made haste I could claim a pair of eyes before deterioration set in. I hastily took my small bag and made ready to set out.

'You're going away again?' said Elizabeth wistfully.

'I'll be back tomorrow evening,' I assured her.

'I was hoping you would help me in checking the household accounts.'

'They're your department,' I said, wanting to make it clear that I had complete faith in her. 'I'm sure you'll handle them admirably.'

'But I'd like you to see them. I'd like your assistance with them.'

'You'll be asking soon if you can help me with my experiments.'

It was a rash thing to say. Her face brightened. 'I would,' she said. 'I'd like that more than anything in the world.'

Perhaps one day she would be the helper I needed. It was a fascinating concept. She looked so feminine and so fragile, yet there was a toughness in her loyalty and devotion that could make her worthier than Paul had been.

The mere thought of Paul irritated me. He was a coward. Petty though it might seem, there were times when I felt that

above all else I wanted to prove to him that I had been right
all along and, furthermore, that I had been able to attain my
goal without his assistance.

I went to collect the eyes.

They made a beautiful pair. The man who removed them
from the corpse had done so with skill. They were just what I
needed.

'Not often we get them perfect in here,' the keeper confided.
'Eyes is generally the first to go.' He looked at me anxiously.
'Well, sir – what do you think?'

'They'll do,' I said. He was still watching as I took coins
from my pocket. 'Ten, we said, didn't we?'

'Each,' he nodded.

I was grateful to him for finding these excellent specimens, but not so grateful that I was prepared to be
cheated.

'The pair,' I said.

He shrugged. 'The pair, just like you said.'

I packed them very carefully, and headed back to my home
and that laboratory under the roof where the miraculous was
soon to be made feasible.

It was dark when I arrived. I was glad of this. It made it
easier for me to go straight to work without having to make
polite excuses or waste time in conventionalities.

Two days later I was unable to resist the impulse to send a
message to the village asking Paul Krempe to call.

He came up at once. When he was shown in I saw that he
was prepared for some alarming news. There was possibly a
trace of disappointment in his expression when he saw that,
far from wishing to give him news of a disaster or of a change
of mind on my part, I was in a cheerful, confident frame of
mind.

'You wanted to see me?' He was curt, immediately on the
defensive.

Nothing would have given me greater pleasure than to have
us both back on our old footing. 'It's been a long time since
you've been to see us, Paul,' I said affably. 'You know you're
always welcome here.'

'I told you I wouldn't help you.' He wasn't going to give an
inch.

'Then why continue to live in the neighbourhood?' I could

not restrain the gibe: 'Do you think you're better qualified than I to keep watch over Elizabeth?'

He refused to rise to this, but said simply: 'What is it you want?'

I suggested that he came upstairs to the laboratory. It was a long time since he had set foot in it. He hesitated, but his curiosity was too great for him. Together we went upstairs.

As I opened the door and waved him in, I said: 'Haven't you found it difficult keeping away, just guessing what I was doing, never knowing how well I was getting on? I've decided to let you see my progress. You can judge for yourself whether I shall succeed or not.'

With obvious trepidation he approached the tank. He was longing to be confronted by a failure. He was scared not of scientific mysteries but of the chance that I was on the right lines. He of all people should have known how little doubt there was of this.

My robber lay in the fluid, no longer as he had been when Paul left but with a head, new hands, and new feet. His head was turned towards our side of the tank, and his eyes, perfect but still sightless, stared fixedly out at us. Soon they would be animated. Soon there would be emotion and recognition in them.

Still Paul said nothing. At last I asked: 'What do you think of him?'

'It's horrible,' he muttered.

I was surprised that he should be so unscientific about the whole affair. I had to admit that my creature's face was not very pretty yet: there had been a great deal of grafting and stitching involved, and the scars were not yet healed. But the features were not important. What mattered was that I had created a being which would live and breathe.

'Victor,' said Paul earnestly, 'I appeal to you once more to stop what you're doing before it's too late.'

'But what am I doing? Nothing wrong.'

He looked at the suspended, floating creature with revulsion. 'You see nothing wrong in that ... that *assembly*? That concoction of fragments, culled from God knows where ...'

I said: 'I'm harming nobody by robbing a few graves. What scientist or doctor doesn't? How else are we to learn the complexities of the human animal?'

'Doctors rob for the eventual good of mankind. This can end in nothing but evil.'

'Look' – I was patient with him because it was important to me that he above all others should understand and approve – 'I admit he isn't a particularly handsome specimen at present. But the facial expression is conditioned by the character which lies beneath it. A benevolent mind will gradually soften the outlines and show through. An evil mind creates an evil face. What we have here is nothing yet. But it will be something soon: something splendid. For this a brain of genius will be used, and when the brain starts to function within the frame then the features will assume wisdom and nobility. I'm at the last stage but one, Paul – the brain. A brain of superior intellect, with a lifetime of knowledge already behind it. Imagine it – my creature will be born complete with a fund of knowledge such as takes decades of arduous study to acquire.'

'Victor, where's this brain to come from?'

I saw that he was, alas, not to be trusted. At this final stage I would have welcomed his help. But it would not be offered and so I must not say too much of my plans.

I said: 'I'll get it.'

4

Elizabeth was overjoyed when I suggested that we should break our austere routine by inviting a distinguished guest for a few days' stay. She laughed when I went on to say that I was referring to Professor Bernstein, Europe's greatest living physicist, and accused me of offering this hospitality only because I wanted to drag the old man off to my laboratory and pick his brains. I thought this was a singularly unfortunate way of putting it, but did not say so: I merely assured her that I had no intention of asking the Professor into the laboratory. We worked in different fields. I wanted to talk to him on general topics, and since I had heard from many mutual friends that he had lost none of the charm and breadth of interests which I remembered from a meeting some years previously, I thought Elizabeth, too, would find him a stimulating visitor.

Professor Bernstein certainly showed no signs of age. He was a spry, twinkling little man with a massive head of spiky white hair. His conversation ranged freely and effortlessly over every subject known to civilized man, and on every topic he was both witty and profound. I also envied him his unforced courtesy: he had a gift for enchanting a woman, and Elizabeth glowed in his presence. Once or twice he shook his head enviously at me. I was pleased by this and by picturing the well-matched couple which Elizabeth and I would make.

I plied the old man with wine until his tongue wagged more and more animatedly. Elizabeth still enjoyed every word, but I saw that she was a trifle perturbed by the amount I had given our guest.

He began to make rather arch references to the joys which awaited a young couple like us. To my surprise Elizabeth neatly turned these remarks against me. The stimulus of having another man, even an elderly one, being so attentive to her had evidently given her courage.

'I fear,' she said,' 'that the only time we spend together will be times like this, when we have a guest.'

'My dear young lady –'

'Your presence at dinner tonight,' said Elizabeth, 'ensures Victor's presence. If you were not here he would be in his laboratory. He stays there for hours on end. Often he doesn't eat, and I'm sure he doesn't sleep. I for one think the world would be a better place without research – at least, my world would.' She took the edge off her words by a gentle smile in my direction, but there was no doubt that she meant them.

Professor Bernstein sat back and looked at me with owlish gravity. 'She may be right, Baron. One can spend too much of one's life locked in stuffy rooms seeking out obscure truths – searching, researching, until one is too old to enjoy life.'

Elizabeth was delighted. 'You see, Victor! The Professor is on my side.'

I had to take it in good part. 'You've let me down badly, Professor. Now I shall have Elizabeth quoting you every time she wants me to leave my work and idle away the time with her.'

'Indeed you shall,' vowed Elizabeth. 'I shall say, "Victor, you're only a *little* scientist and I'm not going to listen to you. On the authority of the greatest brain in Europe you must leave your stuffy laboratory and come out into the sunshine with me.'''

She, too, was growing somewhat light-headed. I didn't want this to go too far, but at the same time I had no wish to appear churlish.

'You see, Professor,' I said, 'how women twist our words to suit their own ends. She will be happy only if I give up my work entirely.'

'Is the world ready for the revelations her scientists make?' Seriousness struggled through Bernstein's genial manner. All at once he was very sober and very intense. 'There is a great difference between knowing that a thing is so and knowing how to use that knowledge. To use it for the good of mankind. The trouble with us scientists is that we quickly tire of our discoveries. We hand them over to people who are not ready for them because we are in a hurry to get on to the next thing – which will be mishandled in just the same way, when the time comes.'

This struck me as being an irrationally pessimistic view. Taken to its logical conclusion it would lead to the abandonment of research altogether. I hoped Professor Bernstein wasn't getting senile. I wanted a great mind, not a decaying one . . .

Gradually the conversation slowed and took on a drowsy note. Elizabeth, playing the part of hostess to perfection, knew exactly when to say: 'I feel we have exhausted the professor.'

'No, no.' It was a sleepy protest. 'I have enjoyed every minute of this delightful evening.' But – he suppressed a yawn – 'I must confess that old age does bring with it an attendant weariness.'

I got up. 'I'll show you to your room.'

The Professor said goodnight to Elizabeth. I escorted him out of the room and up the stairs. He went very slowly, holding the banister rail.

'Most enjoyable evening,' he murmured as we mounted the stairs.

'I really am most honoured to have you here, sir.'

'Most grateful to you, my boy.' He stopped for a moment, breathing hard. 'You know I'm alone in the world. To be a guest in someone's home – especially such a charming home as this ... such a wonderful atmosphere ... very precious to me.'

'You're too kind, sir.' I took his arm and helped him up the last few steps. Then I halted him, facing the painting at the top of the staircase. It had been bought half a century ago by my father, and illustrated the grisly anguish of a very early operation. I had thought it would interest the old man, and indeed he stooped and blinked to get a better view of it. 'If you step back,' I said, 'you'll see it better.'

He stepped back.

I got him firmly by the arm and flung him against the rail.

It was old, and I had ensured that it was none too secure at this point.

Professor Bernstein tried to shout, but I was already yelling. 'Look out, Professor' – my voice rose so that even at the back of the house they must have heard it – 'look out!'

The rail gave way. Bernstein seemed to hang over the drop for an interminable second, and then he plunged to the marble floor below. There was a crack as his head struck, and his arms and legs splayed out like those of a broken doll. He lay quite still as Elizabeth rushed out and moaned with horror.

I hoped the impact had not damaged his brain.

Of course we were desolated by such a ghastly occurrence. I wrote to Bernstein's more distinguished colleagues, who were most sympathetic and fully understood our grief. The least I could do was to arrange a suitably noble funeral for the great man, and as he was the last of his family, with no living relatives, I suggested that his body should find its last resting place in the Frankenstein family vault. It was a gesture which met with great approbation from the visiting mourners.

I ensured that all these famous scholars and lecturers from Dresden should be sent on their homeward way immediately after the ceremony. I spared no expense: they travelled in the greatest comfort in the finest coach my stables could provide. They were overwhelmed, poor penurious pedants. The luxury of it blinded them to the fact that they were being rushed with unbecoming haste off the premises.

That night, when all was still, I made my way to our family vault in the graveyard, complete with the tools I should need. I stood a lantern on a coffin which contained all that was left of my great-grandfather, and began to prise open the newest coffin in the vault. It came away after a couple of minutes with a shriek of nails, and I looked down on the placid face of Professor Bernstein. Whatever contortion of fear might have twisted his face as he fell, it was smoothed away now.

He could not have lived much longer in any case. Better that he should be dead and useful than alive and doddering towards senility.

I would have been able to work more efficiently in my laboratory, but I did not fancy carrying the corpse all that distance. I had come prepared for operations here, on the spot. In the steady light of the lantern I set to work with a scalpel and carefully laid bare the Professor's brain.

It was fascinating to speculate how much of the actual personality would carry over with the brain itself. So much of our character is conditioned by outside stimuli and by the limitations, great or small, of our bodies and their functions, that one finds it hard to think of the brain as a detached, separate entity. Yet here it was. I lifted it reverently from the skull — a storehouse of knowledge, a hoard of wisdom from which the body of my creature would draw all that it needed for further development, for developments so far undreamed-of.

In my bag I had brought a jar. I lowered the brain into it. It looked flabby and inanimate; but I knew what brilliant potentialities lay locked in it, and I was confident that I had the key.

As I was putting the jar and my tools back in the bag, there was the faint scrape of a footstep on the stone treads down into the vault. I reached for the lantern, but it was too late. There was nowhere I could run.

Paul Krempe came down the steps.

'I thought I'd find you here.'

'Very intelligent of you,' I said. 'Now you've found me, what do you want?'

He stared at the open coffin. I turned towards the lid and began to settle it back in place. Paul said: 'You killed the old boy, didn't you? You killed him, and now you're mutilating his body.'

'Mutilating?' I scoffed. 'I've removed the brain. There's no question of mutilation.'

'I can't prove you murdered him' – Paul took a menacing step towards me – 'but I can stop you using his brain.'

'Why? He has no further use for it. He'll be proud when –'

Paul made a grab for the bag. 'Give it to me.'

I swung away from him, protecting my precious haul. He tried to hold me with one hand while tugging at the bag with the other. Without dropping the bag I was not free to fight back adequately – and I did not dare to drop such a fragile load.

'Be careful, you fool!' I cried. 'You'll damage it.'

He was a senseless, raving vandal. He forced me back towards the wall of the vault. As I tried to beat him off with my free hand he seized me and shook me to and fro. The bag swung out, and then smacked back against the edge of a stone shelf. There was the sound of breaking glass.

I struck Paul so furiously across the face that he tottered backwards. Then I looked down at the bag. Liquid oozed through it.

'Get away from me,' I shouted. 'Get out! Leave me alone. Get off my land! And if you've damaged this ... if you've damaged it ...'

The thought was too appalling to contemplate. I let out a sob of rage. Paul Krempe backed away. He was really frightened. He stared at me fearfully as though I and not he were the irresponsible maniac.

When he had gone I finished nailing down the coffin hurriedly, and then made my way as quickly as possible back to the house. Feverishly I unpacked the bag and lifted the brain from the debris within. It was so soft and malleable that one could hope it had escaped damage. Then I found two slivers of glass embedded in it. The gashes were not deep. All I could do was trust that they had not affected essential tissue.

I worked almost until dawn on the preparatory stages, and then slept for a few hours. I was awakened by voices under my window. One of them was Elizabeth's. I could visualize her strolling as she usually did in the garden, breathing in the morning air and adding a new decorative beauty to the garden. She had ambitious plans for that garden. Perhaps even now she was giving instructions for a major reorganization here, a fresh splash of colour there.

Then I identified the other voice. It belonged to Paul Krempe.

'I've come to appeal to you to leave here.'

The insolence of the man – coming up here from the village to poison the mind of my betrothed! I got out of bed and stood by the window, debating whether to ring for a lackey to throw him off the land.

'Why should I leave here?' asked Elizabeth.

'Now – this very minute, before it's too late.'

'Paul,' she said in a troubled tone, 'we've been through this before.'

I was pleased by the way she so firmly kept him in his place; but a little less pleased by a note of what I could only describe as intimacy in her voice, as though she were fond of the man and had enjoyed many easy, pleasant hours in his company. Perhaps I had neglected her. There had been too many opportunities in the past for them to be together.

'Won't you understand you're in real danger?' the traitor was urging her. 'What Victor is doing is dangerous to everyone in this house – perhaps to the whole neighbourhood.'

'Then why do you stay in this district?' said Elizabeth. 'You're not helping him any longer.'

'I'll tell you why I stay here. I can't bear to think of you in this house with him, unprotected. When something goes wrong –'

'Paul, believe me, you're wrong about Victor.'

'Am I?' he said bleakly.

'You must be. I know him so well –'

'What do you know about his work? Have you ever been in his laboratory? No, you can't possibly conceive the dreadful thing he's proposing to do.'

'What are you trying to say to me?' she challenged him. 'That Victor is wicked ... insane?'

I looked down as they emerged from the shadow of the house and stood on the lawn. The slanting sunlight struck flecks of gold from Elizabeth's hair. She was standing very stiffly and proudly.

Paul said: 'He is just so dedicated to his work that he can't see the terrible consequences that must result.' He reached out and tried to touch her, but she drew herself away. 'I can't bear the thought of any harm coming to you. I'd do anything not to hurt you both – Victor means more to me than perhaps he understands – but he is so wrapped up in his experiments that –'

'Stop it, Paul.' There were tears in her voice. 'Please leave me. I think ... I think it would be better for you not to come here again.'

Paul, stricken, looked at her. From where I stood I could not make out his expression, but I had few doubts about what it would show. The presumptuous fool was in love with Elizabeth. His petty slurs on me were all designed to win her away from me. He understood neither Elizabeth nor myself.

Elizabeth stood quite still and watched him as he walked towards the drive and on to the main gates. When he had disappeared, her shoulders sagged and there was a dejection in her whole manner which made me uneasy. She must not let herself feel too ready a sympathy for the absurd man.

Later that morning she asked me in a roundabout way what stage my experiments had reached. I could have been annoyed, knowing what had provoked this curiosity, but she spoke in such a way that there was nothing to which one could take exception. I assured her that all was going well and that I was nearly finished. At the end of the week perhaps she would be able to see what I had been doing. I was, in fact, so exhilarated by the prospect of forthcoming success that my happiness infected her, and she laughed without quite knowing why she was laughing. The morning sunshine and my obvious cheerfulness banished the dark forebodings which Paul had so unscrupulously tried to plant in her mind.

5

In the afternoon the skies grew darker. Beyond the peaks there was a slow barrage of thunder. The threat of rain was sufficient to keep Elizabeth indoors. She occupied herself with her embroidery while I, too, did a great deal of stitching – though on somewhat different material.

I worked through most of that night and through the next day, when a sullen greyness lay on the mountains and the valley was sunk in gloom. Lightning flickered pale in the daylight, but took on a new harshness as night began to fall.

Elizabeth and I dined together by candlelight. She was glad that I was in a gay mood: really, it was touching that she should depend so much on my smiles and approval. Her only disappointment came when I said that I proposed to do several hours' work in the laboratory after coffee.

I was tempted to invite her to accompany me. She should have the privilege of watching the final stages. Then I decided against it. Without deferring to any of Paul Krempe's melodramatic accusations, I realized that an ordinary person might be shocked at first by the magnitude of what I was attempting. Better to win the victory before boasting too loudly!

There was a vast difference between those two faces – the gentle face of Elizabeth and the seamed, unresponsive face in the tank. Indeed, the contrast between the rooms themselves was a striking one. Downstairs was the graciousness of a long tradition, the panelled beauty of high craftsmanship from a bygone world; here in my laboratory was a tangle of apparatus under a sloping roof, an accumulation of litter, all the scientific brashness of the new world – but one in which craftsmanship must still count.

There was a set of controls on the side of the tank itself, and a set which governed the magnetic impulses from a sparking wheel against the outer wall of the laboratory. Originally the entire layout had been planned with a view to dual operation, but now that Paul was no longer playing a part I would have to manage on my own. Some of the finer settings would be tricky. However, I had enough confidence in my own alertness to feel that I could cope.

The creature lay there, passive, waiting. The body was strong, the hands and feet admirable, the head splendid in spite of the still unhealed scars. And in that head one of the greatest brains in Europe was about to function again.

I slowly switched on the feed pipes to the tank, and a gentle bubbling began.

There was a flash of lightning. It made me start back, fearing for a moment that there was a fault in the apparatus. A clap of thunder, so far from alarming me, reassured me. I left the tank and set the generator wheel in motion so that the electro-chemical reaction could begin.

I seemed myself to be vibrant with electric forces. Whatever new avenues are opened up in the future, whatever progress is made in the physical sciences, and whatever may come from work which I know is going on in England, for example, at this very moment, history must acclaim me as the true pioneer in the application of magneto-electricity. Without Davy's theories and demonstrations of galvanism I admit I could not have got so far in such a short time; but without my own discoveries of the relationship between the life force and magnetic force, further developments would not be possible.

Now began the delicate business of balancing the various adjustments. I darted to and fro between the tank and the controls of the sparking generator wheel. It was infuriating. A slight increase at one could mean the most minute alteration to the other. The dual controls ought to have been operated by Paul and myself, snapping instructions to and fro. Unless I could maintain a perfect balance, the experiment would not succeed.

The chemical input was surging and bubbling remorselessly now. There was no turning back. At least two hours of intense concentration lay ahead of me. The power pulses had to be injected with unfaltering regularity. I had to turn myself into an automaton – but an automaton capable of checking and rechecking, thinking fast and acting without hesitation, going from one control to the other, studying the body in the tank, pacing to and fro across the laboratory.

The fluid in the tank grew viscous, and the features were blurred. Slowly the body rolled over like a man lazily, contentedly swimming.

But the reaction was not what it ought to have been. From our work on the dog I knew that at this stage there ought to be an appreciable convulsion: there ought to be a sequence of minor jolts, as the body was stimulated by successive punches of power.

The timing was not exact enough. No, that is an unscientific way of expressing it. There was no question of being 'exact enough': it had to be *exact*.

I made a swift, anguished calculation. The process could not be reversed or stopped. But given thirty minutes – forty minutes at the outside – I could cut off the pulses and keep the chemical reaction at its lowest while I went for help. There was no other way: I had to have another pair of hands here. Once more the idea of Elizabeth crossed my mind, this time as an assistant. But even after the preliminary explanations and reassurances, I would still have to teach her the innumerable details. It would be too late. The only man who could fall into the routine with the skill of long practice was Paul Krempe. He had to be persuaded. Faced with a crisis of this kind, surely I could rely on his scientific spirit?

I cut down the input and slowed the wheel to a stop. Then I went swiftly but silently downstairs and out into the night.

The storm was drawing closer. Lightning flickered along the mountain crags, its stabs of brightness as jagged as the peaks themselves. I seized a cape and flung it over my shoulders, then hurried down the footpath to the village.

I pounded on the door of Paul's lodging with a force that should have wakened the dead. I felt that I was hammering life into that creature of mine: I wanted to pick it up and shake it, beat vitality into it.

Paul, swathed in a heavy dressing-gown, opened the door and stared.

Before he could speak, I said: 'You've got to help me.'

'You must be mad.'

'The apparatus was constructed for dual operation. You know that. I thought I could work it myself, but I can't.'

'I'm delighted,' said Paul. A flash of brightness from behind me fell across his face, etching stern lines into it. 'That means your experiment will not succeed.'

'It's got to succeed. Paul, you're going to help me. You must.'

He shook his head.

I kept my voice down although I wanted to shout to the heavens. It was intolerable that my years of application should go to waste now because of the stubbornness of this one man.

'With so much at stake ...'

He turned as though to go back into the house. I was desperate. I would have to make whatever terms I could with him.

'Paul,' I implored him, 'if you help me I promise that once I've proved my theories I'll dispose of this creature.'

He stopped. 'How long will that be?'

'A month or two at the outside.'

'And have that thing alive up there all that time? No, Victor.'

'If you don't help me' – I could not suppress my fury, in spite of my need of him – 'then I make no such promise. Somehow I'll manage on my own. However difficult, I'll do it.'

'Very well,' he taunted. 'Go back and do it.'

And then it came to me. It was my last chance. I said: 'Or else I'll train Elizabeth to help.'

'You wouldn't dare. You wouldn't be so –'

'I'll introduce Elizabeth to the world of science,' I said, 'and see how she likes it.'

If he could have killed me with a look he would have done so. 'You wouldn't be so wicked, Victor. Even a fanatic like you ... you couldn't.'

'There is nothing – do you hear me, nothing – more important to me than the success of this experiment. I'll do anything to conclude it properly. It's what I've worked for all my life.'

'Very well,' he said bitterly. 'I'll help you.'

'I knew I could rely on you,' I said.

He made an incoherent, contemptuous sound. Then he said: 'I'll get dressed. You go on ahead and set up the preliminaries. I'll be no more than ten minutes behind you.'

'I can trust you to come?' I said.

'Yes, you can trust me to come.'

That was sufficient for me. I walked briskly back up the hillside. It would have been easy to lose one's footing: the fitful lightning illuminated the path in bursts of glaring intensity, followed by a blackness more Stygian than that of an ordinary night. But I knew every inch of the way. This was my home, my property, the scene of my childhood rovings and now to be the scene of my mature triumphs.

The house was abruptly a black silhouette against the sky, and then was lost again.

I quickened my pace, eager to get back to that magic room at the top of the house.

Suddenly there was a stab of lightning so savage that I raised my arm to cover my eyes. It was followed by a crack that was not the crack of thunder. When I dared to look, I saw brightness like a malevolent will-of-the-wisp running along the eaves of my home. The window of the laboratory, high up under the roof, seemed to be lit from inside. It must have been an optical illusion, but it was terrifying in that split second of its occurrence; terrifying because of the uncanny blaze in that square, blank eye, and because of my fears for what lay inside. An electrical disturbance of that magnitude could easily affect the delicate balance of my experiment.

I hurried into the house. The whip-like crack of the lightning still stung my ears, but indoors there was tranquillity. Nobody stirred. Either none of them had heard the sound or they were all cowering in their beds, praying.

For once in my life I was trembling. My knees felt unsteady. I went into the salon and took a bottle of brandy from the wine cupboard. I poured myself a large drink and gulped it down with a haste which was unworthy of the brandy.

Then I went upstairs.

At the first landing I stopped. There was no sound from the direction of Elizabeth's room. I went on my way.

As I approached the door of the laboratory I heard an impossible sound. Faintly, through the heavy door, came the intermittent splutter of the wheel as it turned and sparked. But it had no business to be turning. I had switched it off before leaving. Nobody could have entered the laboratory in my absence.

Filled with foreboding, I thrust the key into the lock. If that lightning had somehow triggered off the process and it was working again, the whole balance could have been wrecked.

I flung open the door.

Standing erect in the middle of the room was my creature. The bandages dripped with fluid. The arms hung slackly, but as I stood there, aghast, they tightened and fought against the bandages. There was a tearing of cloth. The groping hands went up to the face.

In the flickering light cast by the madly rotating wheel, the creature bared its teeth in a snarl. It was a wide, savage grimace such as I had never seen or ever wished to see in my life. It was utter bestiality unleashed.

I still had my hand on the door. The sight had robbed me of all power to move. I could neither go in nor retreat.

Suddenly the creature lurched towards me. Its legs were still impeded by the bandages, which made its shambling gait all the more horrible. I turned to run ... and it was too late.

The heavy arm, with torn bandages drooping from it,

curled round my neck. I was jerked back into the laboratory. The smell of the chemicals which impregnated the creature and its swathing bit at the back of my throat and in my nostrils. I tried to cry out, but the pressure was tightening. I kicked vainly against the padded, well-protected figure.

The lights in the room began an insane dance. They blazed in and out of a kaleidoscope of other lights, sparking not only before my eyes but somehow inside my head. A great hammer began to pound from within my skull.

I twisted round, trying to get a grip on the creature. Its distorted face was a slavering nightmare, a few inches from my own. I struck out, but the blow was feeble and useless.

To have come so far, and now to be destroyed by what I had created ... to be killed by a grotesque mischance, a wayward jest of the elements ...!

Then suddenly I was falling sideways. The creature had relinquished its grip. As I went down, I was dimly aware of Paul springing over me and lashing out again and again. I tried to push myself up, to come to his aid, but the roaring in my ears and the pain that ran through me were too much. I saw the feet of the creature trample towards me and then stagger away at a tangent. Paul lifted one of the laboratory stools and beat the creature back into a corner.

As I finally got myself up to my knees, with the floor reeling beneath me, Paul swung the stool against the creature's head. It emitted a croaking, feral sound that rasped hideously through the room; and then it collapsed into a stained, ragged heap.

Paul dropped the stool and hurried to me. He got his arm round my shoulder and helped me to my feet. I leaned against him for a full minute, gasping and vainly retching.

And then, as the pain ebbed away, I was conscious of the most fantastic elation. It was as though, purged of irrational fear, I could see things not just as clearly as before but with an added vividness.

'Paul' – it hurt me to talk, but I was laughing the words out – 'I did it! I did it ...'

'Yes.' He was not really listening. He helped me to the only chair in the room – there had never been time for relaxation in this part of the house – and lowered me gently into it.

I put my head back. I had succeeded. The glow of

accomplishment warmed me through, driving out the memory of those few terrifying minutes when things had gone wrong. It was not my fault that they had gone wrong. Paul himself was largely to blame. Obviously there had been damage to the brain during that undignified scuffle in my family vault. That could soon be rectified. Also the process had been dangerously speeded up and my equipment had run wild after the lightning stroke. Next time there would be no such mistakes. Next time all my calculations would be strictly observed.

The important thing was that I had done it.

Paul was dragging the creature on to the bench and strapping it securely down. I neither helped him nor interfered. It was undoubtedly a good thing that the creature should be restrained until I could get to work on it.

Paul drew the last strap tight and then turned back to me.

'You must destroy it right away before it regains consciousness.'

I could hardly believe what I heard. Already I was wondering which of the seams in the head to open in order to get at the brain without involving too much further damage to the features.

'Did you hear, Victor?' Paul insisted.

'What did you say?'

'You must destroy this thing now.'

I was grateful for his intervention, but I was not going to be dictated to in this way. I tried to make him see reason. 'Don't you realize, Paul – I've succeeded.'

'You nearly succeeded in getting yourself killed. Another ten seconds and –'

'This is my creation.' I was still marvelling at it. Of course I had known that all would come right, but it was still splendid to have it proved beyond all doubt.

'Your creation,' said Paul: 'a criminal lunatic. It tried to kill you.'

'That was due to the brain damage. When you attacked me,' I reminded him, 'it was damaged. That makes the responsibility very largely yours, Paul. It's your fault that it ran wild. Your fault that it's not what I intended it to be. I can repair the brain. It's what I've done that counts: I've created a living, sentient being.'

'You promised to destroy it, Victor.'

'Never.'

'When you came to ask me for help,' he said, 'you said that once you had proved your theories you would destroy it.'

But the fool could not see that I had many more things to prove, many more things to demonstrate. This was only the beginning. I said: 'When I've finished my research.'

'Don't you see – you've created a monster.'

'I shall operate on the brain tomorrow,' I said. 'It shouldn't take too long.'

The basic principles were sound. From now on the difficulties could only be minor ones.

Paul looked from me to the prone figure strapped to the table. He touched one of the straps to make sure it was secure. Then he shook his head sadly.

'You won't listen to me?'

'When we worked together,' I said, 'I was glad to listen to you. You have contributed a great deal to this discovery, Paul. If you'll continue with me –'

'No,' he said, 'you won't listen. And you're too powerful in this district for me to have any chance of opposing you here.'

'Opposing me?'

'For your own sake, Victor, and for the sake of mankind I think you should be stopped.' He turned away. At the door he said: 'I shall pack my things and leave the village tomorrow. I can see there's nothing I can do here.'

I was sorry that we had to part in this way, but I could not let my resolve be weakened. There have always been opponents of new developments in all science and philosophy. Every great advance has been made in the teeth of ignorant opposition. Even the pioneers themselves, such as Paul might have been, often falter and turn back.

For me there would be no faltering.

It would be foolish to apply myself to the task in hand tonight, though. My body had taken a considerable battering and my fingers would lack the firmness and precision which were essential for the brain examination. I tested the straps holding the unconscious creature to the bench, disconnected the apparatus so that there should be no further mishaps, and went down to bed. I had to lie on my left side, as my right shoulder was heavily bruised, but I slept without difficulty.

The morning was clear and the storm clouds had moved

on. I awoke refreshed, and breakfasted with Elizabeth. A dull bruise along the line of my jaw attracted her attention, and I had to improvise some silly little story about walking into a door. She did not know whether to laugh or to reprove me. Once again she referred with mild but genuine disparagement to my cherished laboratory, and threatened to come up and inspect it. 'My rival,' she called it. I did not think that the sight of the creature with its torn bandages strapped to the bench would be the most edifying one to greet her.

As soon as possible I made my excuses and escaped to the top of the house. At the end of the first landing I caught a glimpse of Justine staring at me curiously. She made a move as though to intercept me – to ask me pertly, no doubt, what I was doing with my nights and why I had neglected her charms recently – but I waved her off and hurried up to the laboratory.

I hesitated briefly before opening the door. My experience of the previous night was not one which I would wish repeated.

But it was absurd. The creature could not have burst its bonds. It could not be standing there waiting for me again, ready to strike.

I opened the door.

There was no creature confronting me. There was no creature in the laboratory at all. Straps and bandages lay in a twisted pattern on the bench. The floor was sticky with fluid from a dozen shattered tubes and bottles, and there was broken glass everywhere. The window had been torn open, smashing two of the panes. When I went incredulously to look out of it, I saw a couple more torn strips of bandage caught in the heavy guttering. The way down to the ground was perilous, but the jutting masonry gave enough footholds for anyone determined enough – or mad enough – to choose such a route.

The creature had gone.

6

'He's gone,' I said. 'I've searched the house to make sure, and then gone all over the grounds. Heaven knows where he's got to.'

Once more I was standing at Paul's door. There was a certain grim satisfaction in his manner, as though he saw all his predictions coming true; but at the same time he was truly alarmed.

'We must call out the village – start a thorough search at once.'

'You had better leave that to me,' I said. 'I have the authority here. But I want the two of us to set out at once. We know the creature we are dealing with better than the villagers do. And we've got to pick up his trail before he goes too far. If he gets deep into the woods we'll never find him.'

Paul went indoors to make ready, while I walked away along the village street. I nodded to some of my tenants, and exchanged civilities with two Army officers from the garrison down the valley. I did not, however, stir up any unseemly panic. There was no reason why the villagers should know too soon about my experiments. I didn't want their clumsy hands laid on my creation; and I didn't want madly inflated stories about it to go humming along the valley.

I went back to Paul, and handed over to him one of the two rifles I had brought from my small armoury. It had been a long time since there had been any use for them in this peaceful part of the world. I hoped now that we would manage without having to fire them.

We set off into the woods.

In other circumstances it could have been a delightful morning. Working as I did at night and spending so many mornings asleep before resuming this work, I had not strolled through the woods and glades at this hour for some years. As a boy I had known every path through the trees and every clearing. Now it was all strange to me. The fresh morning air had the taste of a sparkling water, cool and tangy from the stream.

When my experiments were concluded and had been acclaimed by the world's leading scientists, I would make a new life for Elizabeth and myself. We would walk here often.

But now there was a grim duty ahead of us. I wanted to find my creature before some stupid peasant stumbled across him. He had to be recaptured and taken back to his birthplace. For that was what my home was for him: his birthplace.

Once the operation had been carried out on his brain, I was sure that I would find him a worthy intellectual companion. He and I might go on to further discoveries, blazing a trail for lesser mortals to follow.

Paul and I exchanged few remarks as we prowled through the trees. A brisk nod was enough to indicate a new direction; one hand held up brought us to a halt when some rustle in the undergrowth or the creak of a branch seemed to indicate another presence.

At the end of half an hour I was growing apprehensive. If we didn't find him soon, others would find him. He would stray into their farms or down lanes which led to other villages.

Or he would lie low in the woods, hidden for as long as he chose to remain still, a constant menace – and perhaps past salvation by the time I found him.

Then we heard a voice. It was some distance away, and came eerily through the trees like the muffled cry of an animal in a trap.

Paul glanced at me. We swung off the path and trampled over leaves and snapping twigs without further concern for the noise we were making. Once again there was a cry, causing us to veer slightly to the left. We broke out, after scratching our faces on a thin but stinging barrier of trailing branches, into a clearing. Through the trees on the far side was a faint glimmer of water, and when we came to a stop we could hear the gentle chatter of a stream.

An old man lay beside a fallen tree trunk in the centre of the glade. For a moment my breath caught in my throat. Then I saw that he was not dead. He stirred and groaned, and reached out blindly with a gnarled hand. He touched the trunk and groped over it. His hand fell back.

Paul hurried forward to help him up.

At the first touch of Paul's hands, the old man flinched and began to moan.

'No ... who are you ... what are you ...?'

Beside him lay two pieces of a stick as gnarled as himself. Clearly it had been his support, but now it was snapped clean in two.

I advanced into the clearing and stood before him. A man of his generation should recognize the Frankenstein face when he saw it. I had hoped to calm him, but he babbled on unintelligibly.

'What is it ... what are you ...?'

Then I understood his groping and the blindness of his movements. He was indeed blind.

Paul said: 'It's all right. Have no fear. We are friends. What happened to you?'

'My grandson – where is he?'

Trembling fingers clawed at Paul's sleeve.

'Your grandson?' Paul spoke as soothingly as possible, but he glanced at me urgently.

'The stream ... he left me sitting here, in the sun ... so warm ... he went to the stream. Has he wandered away? Or is it after him, too?'

'Is what after him?'

'The stream ... my grandson,' the old man raved.

Paul got to his feet. 'Stay with him,' he ordered. It was not his place to give orders, but before I could protest he had moved away and was hurrying towards the stream.

I wanted to follow, but the old man wavered on the tree trunk and once I had tried to hold him steady he gripped me and would not let go. His story came out in fits and starts. His grandson had brought him into the woods as he often did on sunny mornings. It was good to sit here and reflect. The boy was a good boy, very patient with his old grandfather. He would go off and pick mushrooms – sometimes went farther away than he ought to, but he always came back.

Today the grandfather had thought he heard him coming back much more quickly than usual. There had been footsteps – slow footsteps – and then when he had spoken to the boy there had been no reply. Only the footsteps. And all at once he had known that this was not his grandson. He could not tell who it was, and it wasn't right, it wasn't normal.

'When you're blind as I am, you get to know things – to sense things. This thing, it ... it wasn't *right*.'

He had groped for his stick and then waved it. He had struck something, and then his stick had been snatched from him and he had heard a crack. In his blind gyrations he must have fallen over the tree trunk and gone down heavily.

'And it went away. I felt it going. Something lost,' he said hesitantly. 'A pathetic thing ... a lost soul.' Then his puzzled sympathy was swept away. 'Where's my grandson – my little boy?'

The crack of Paul's rifle resounded through the woods. The old man started against me. I freed myself from that biting grip, and pulled his hands firmly down to the tree trunk so that he would know where he was. Then I raced into the woods in pursuit of Paul.

He had gone some distance along the stream. I caught a flicker of movement between the trees, and charged straight through the undergrowth.

Paul was standing irresolutely with his rifle at the ready. As I came up he said:

'I saw him. Making down that way.'

'Did you have to shoot?'

'Yes,' he snapped. 'I had to shoot. I'm taking no chances.'

'If we can take him back without harming him –'

'The villagers should be on their way by now, surely?' he said. 'Where did you tell them to make for?'

'The south lake shore. I said that if we converged on that we ought to be able to flush him out.'

Paul jerked his rifle towards a gap that had been smashed through some bushes. 'The trail ought to be easy enough to follow. But where's that boy the old man was talking about?'

We went on. The creature had certainly made no attempt to hide its tracks. It seemed to possess no cunning, no intelligence. Or else it simply did not care. In either case it was tragic: had Professor Bernstein's sensitive brain been irreparably damaged?

'There!' breathed Paul suddenly.

We stopped. Through a gap in the trees we saw the stream curling round on itself before disappearing down a shallow slope. A small boy bent over it, plucking at something on the bank. He carried a rough local basket and was filling it with mushrooms.

A larger shape moved across our line of vision. The boy was obscured. The creature, swaying slightly, began to advance through the trees.

Paul raised his rifle.

'No!' I caught at his arm. He tried to shake me off.

Abruptly the boy scuttled away. He had not even noticed

the creature plodding towards him. His basket was full and he was on his way back along the winding edge of the stream.

'Grandpa!' There was a cracked note of fright in his voice, but it was not because of what he had seen: it was simply that he had wandered farther than he realized, and was now worried about getting back. He began to run. 'Grandpa . . .!'

The creature stood still for an instant, then turned slowly as though to retrace its steps. It was facing us. A terrible rictus convulsed its mouth. The fingers flexed.

I had let go of Paul. Before I realized what he was doing, he brought the rifle up again and this time he fired.

The hands – the sculptor's magnificent hands – shot up to the face and clawed at it. The creature took a few helpless steps forward, as erratic as those of the blind man; and then it bent its head piteously back and forth and slowly, in an awful sagging surrender, rolled forward and fell to the ground.

I ran towards it.

'Be careful, Victor!'

Paul's warning was unnecessary. He was a good shot. Too good a shot. My creation, my painstaking handiwork, was dead once more after having been so laboriously brought to life.

Paul stood over me. I gazed up at him accusingly.

He said: 'I did what had to be done. We'll bury him before the villagers arrive.'

'There's no hurry,' I said. 'They won't come.'

'If you told them to meet us –'

'I didn't tell them. I didn't want them prying into my work and spreading ugly rumours. Better for them not to know.'

'You madman! You risked just two of us against this. We might have been killed.'

'We might. But we weren't.' Did it matter, now that he was dead? In my mind I was blurring the distinction between 'he' and 'it'. I wondered what kind of a man he would have been. 'It's done,' I said, 'and I hope you're satisfied.'

'I'm satisfied we were able to stop this monstrous act before it was too late,' said Paul.

I thought that I would never forgive him. Looking back, I associate all my troubles with Paul Krempe. A loyal assistant turned traitor is more dangerous and more destructive than an enemy whom you know from the start to be an enemy.

We buried the creature there in the peace of the woods. Paul scattered leaves over the newly turned ground and we made our way in silence back to the village. We were dirty and sweating from the labour: digging even a shallow grave is arduous work. Even if we had had the breath to speak, I don't think we would have had much to say to each other.

When we parted I held out my hand. He was reluctant to take it, but finally we shook hands.

He said: 'I shall leave now. You won't see me again.'

'As you wish. If you think I owe you anything in the way of fees for your services over the years . . .'

I let the remark trail away. He flushed. I could see that the reminder of our relative status hurt him. He replied stiffly: 'I think all the debts have been paid.'

'Where will you go – what are you intending to do?'

'I have no idea. But it's no longer necessary for me to stay here.'

It was on the tip of my tongue to say that his presence had not been necessary for quite some time now. Then I realized what he meant.

'Ah,' I said. 'Of course. Elizabeth – you stayed to protect her. Well, you've done what you set out to do. You can leave with a clear conscience.'

He gave one longing glance towards the path which led away from the village, up to the house. I left him there. He could take his fill. Let him look. The house and its contents were mine, and Elizabeth was mine.

When I reached the entrance hall Elizabeth was waiting for me. She had been troubled by my absence. The sight of the rifles alarmed her. I said that I had been through the woods and had thought of doing some shooting – the second gun was one which I had lent to one of my keepers.

'I like to think of you in the open air,' she said. 'You spend so much time locked away. I would like to walk with you in the woods sometime, if I may.'

I was able to tell her quite honestly that I had been thinking of just this while I was out.

My life could at this stage, I suppose, have taken a different turn. Many a man would have abandoned his researches or at least sought new channels. It was time to make plans for our wedding. Everything else could have been postponed until after the ceremony. To forget the disappointments and frustrations which had ended in tragedy, I could have devoted myself to Elizabeth and shaped a new existence, not just for myself but for the two of us.

It was not to be. I was not a man who could forget. I was not prepared to abandon all that had so far been achieved. Those years could not be discarded: it could not all be allowed to go to waste.

To Elizabeth's delight I spent my next two evenings with her. We made plans for our future. I promised that we would travel and that I would restrict my working hours to reasonable limits. This was a sincere promise. I was convinced that, in spite of all that had happened, there remained very little to do. Soon I would be able to rest on my laurels.

On a night when there was no moon I took a horse through the woods to the place where we had buried my creature. In the gloom the grave was hard to find, but I did not dare to risk going out on too bright a night. At last I found the spot, and took the creature from the earth. I carried him home across the crupper, and over my shoulder up the stairs.

Paul's shot had drilled a hole between the eyes. I foresaw further work on the brain, but that would have been essential in any case.

'I'll give you life again,' I vowed.

7

We made no grand proclamations regarding our forthcoming marriage. I wrote to the few relatives we had, and was relieved when two of them said that due to illness in the family they would be unable to attend the ceremony. The quiet, frugal life which Aunt Sophie had imposed on her daughter meant that Elizabeth had no close friends of her own, and there was a similar lack in my life due to the fact that I had shut myself away with my experiments for so long. We decided upon a simple reception after the wedding, to which we would invite those local dignitaries who would expect it. I called upon the burgomaster, who was overwhelmed to see me: my father had contributed greatly to the social life of the district, and my own seclusion had given rise to a great deal of adverse criticism. The poor man was so transparent: he was sure that my marriage to my charming young cousin would bring me out more into the world and that there would be parties up at the great house, money flowing into the village, and heaven knew what else besides. I did not disillusion him. My wife should be entertained and should build up a circle of friends if she wished, but it would not be to these parochial boors that we would turn.

One evening, two weeks before the date of the wedding, I had been working in my laboratory. The need for absolute precision in the repairs to the brain meant that for practical as well as emotional reasons I was keeping my pledge to Elizabeth. I spent less time in the laboratory because it was possible to maintain such concentration and steadiness of hand for only limited periods. I set myself a target each day, but if I found my vision growing blurred or my hands wavering, I stopped at once. This evening I had decided to finish shortly before dinner. In fact, I made better progress than I had expected, and it was with a renewal of my earlier sense of triumph that I realized the work was complete. I closed up the head. The stitches could be taken out later. I was impatient to see life pulsing through the creature again – to talk to him and explain what had happened, to test the re-created faculties under strict test conditions.

It was with a sense of impending fulfilment that I closed the door of the laboratory behind me and began to descend the stairs.

On the next landing Justine was waiting for me.

'What are you doing here?' I demanded. 'We shall want dinner served in a few minutes' time.'

I made to pass her, but she blocked my way.

She said: 'Is it true?'

'Is what true?'

'About you marrying that ... that woman.'

I would not tolerate insolence of this kind. 'You're forgetting yourself.'

'I'm not forgetting that you promised to marry me,' she said.

I looked round. Fortunately Elizabeth was already downstairs. I said: 'That's absurd. It would never have entered my head to make such a promise.'

'The things you said to me ...'

I laughed. 'Justine, my dear, we've discussed all this before. I thought you had understood the position.'

'Don't laugh at me!' she blazed. 'Stop it, or I'll ... I'll ...'

'What will you do?'

'I'll kill you.'

I was really in no mood to deal with a serving wench's hysteria. She needed the sharp slap of reality to bring her to her senses. I said:

'You stupid little fool. Did you imagine for one second that a man of my standing would contemplate marrying you?'

She raised her arm as though to strike me. I gripped it above the elbow and forced her back along the landing, away from the staircase.

'You're hurting,' she whimpered. She could change her tune very quickly, little Justine.

'Get back to your work,' I said.

'You've got to marry me. You've got to.' As I released her she fell back against the wall, panting. 'I'm going to have a child.'

I refused to believe it. It was like a glancing blow – a sudden sting that one instinctively dodges and that ceases to hurt immediately.

'Since when would this be?' I asked.

'It doesn't matter. It's true.'

'Why choose me as the father?' I said sceptically. 'Pick any man in the village. There's a reasonable chance you may select the right one.'

Hatred burned in eyes which I had seen lit with a very different fire. Even when her violence and lack of breeding repelled me as they did now, I could not help but observe what a splendid specimen of womanhood she was. But I was not going to be cajoled or intimidated, whatever variations she might play on her banal theme.

'*She* won't think much of your story about a village man,' hissed Justine. 'Not when I tell her what we've been to each other. And I'll tell her a lot more besides. I'll tell her about what you're doing in that laboratory of yours. And then I'll go to the authorities and tell them, too.'

Her threats might be idle, but I felt a chill of foreboding. She was so silent, Justine, so accustomed to slipping soundlessly along the corridors, entering my room, and leaving it: she could have seen more than she was ever meant to.

'Tell them what?' I said with all the contempt I could muster.

'Oh, I know a lot. If I care to tell.'

'What do you know?'

'You wouldn't like that, would you? Well, if you don't marry me I'll tell.'

'Tell what?' I persisted.

'You know what I'm talking about.'

'No,' I said. 'I don't know. And if you intend to make any accusations against me, you will need proof. Proof, my dear – that's all the authorities would be interested in.'

I turned and left her there. Protracting this conversation could only result in further petty attacks on my self-respect.

She cried after me: 'I'll get proof. Oh, you'll see – there's plenty of proof.'

'I want you out of this house,' I said, 'tomorrow morning.'

After dinner I told Elizabeth that I had dismissed Justine. Fortunately she was relieved. Justine's manner to her had always bordered on the impertinent, and although Elizabeth had tried to run the household smoothly she had been disturbed by this hostility. We would both be happier without the girl.

'Do you think I should have a word with her before she leaves?' she asked anxiously.

'No. I am discharging her because of her slovenliness and insolence, and if you were to speak to her at all I have no doubt that she would take the opportunity to vent her spleen. I have said all that needs to be said.'

Again Elizabeth showed that she was happy about this. She was glad that she had not had to take action and that I had settled the matter of my own accord.

Next morning I resumed work in the laboratory. The routine was a familiar one by now. I had altered the controls so that I could operate them single-handed, and had practised the sequence several times in order to win complete confidence in it. This time I intended that the creature should come gradually to life instead of being rudely jolted into it. I also intended that, whatever happened, it should not have the opportunity of running loose again until I had talked to it, reasoned with it, and, if necessary, trained it.

It or him ... in a way I was leaving the decision to the creature. Let him show himself a man, and we would talk as equals; let it be subhuman, and I would train it in whatever way was required.

I adjusted the process so that it spread over the entire day. There were no sudden shocks and no breaks in the procedure. I was confident enough to leave the equipment operating while I went down to have lunch with Elizabeth. The confidence was justified: when I returned to the laboratory, the creature was moving very gently and languidly in the tank. Everything was going according to plan. The head turned, the fingers moved slightly, and the eyes closed against the fluid.

When I lifted the creature from the tank it was like helping a man near to drowning. He appeared to be on the verge of collapse; but in point of fact the opposite was the case – he was on the verge of resuscitation.

I helped him to the one chair and settled him in it. Then, as a precaution, I strapped his arms behind him and put a heavy stick with a solid silver knob against the bench where I could seize it should I need it.

It was now late afternoon. I spent the next hour talking quietly to the creature. I wanted him to feel safe. I wanted him to speak freely – for the two of us to establish a rapport.

At the end of an hour he made a sound. His eyes had been blankly open all this time, but now I seemed to detect a gleam of understanding, and I saw the lips open and begin to work. They twisted, tried to form syllables, and then produced a long, meaningless groan.

I said: 'If you understand what I'm saying, nod.'

Slowly the head nodded, but slackly, like that of a baby who has not yet learned to control it.

'You know where you are?'

There was a pause, then another top-heavy nod.

'Are you comfortable?'

He shook his head this time and made a jerking motion with his shoulders which clearly signified that the straps were hurting. I studied that unresponsive face. There were no signs of incipient viciousness there. I thought I could risk giving him a bit more freedom. Cautiously, with the stick always in reach, I loosened his bonds. He raised his arms in a parody of a stretch, and then pushed himself to his feet. It was a painful process. I stood well back. It seemed a sensible thing to do, but in fact I would have done better to stay close to him. He took one step forward and then lost control of his legs. He floundered about the laboratory, knocking glasses over and crashing against the benches. I had to leap forward in order to steer him away from a delicate mass of equipment, and his weight almost carried me off my feet.

When I had steadied him he leaned against the wall, panting. He tried once more to speak, but produced only a sickening, gobbling noise.

Of course it would take time. I would have to be patient. The assembly of different limbs, of a new head and a new brain, would take time to settle down as an individual entity. The normal motor skills would have to be relearned, and allowances made in the brain for differences in physical sensation and reaction.

If the brain, that is, had not been so deeply damaged that it would never be able to assume full control . . .

'Slowly,' I commanded, as the creature made an attempt to move away from the wall. 'Come to me – but slowly.'

I held out my hand. He edged towards me, and the sculptor's hand took mine. At first it was as limp as a shy child's. Then the grip tightened. His hand was like iron. I tried to pull away, and at once he clamped down, in a savage automatic reaction to the sudden movement.

As gently but firmly as possible I said: 'Let go.'

For an instant he was quite still. Then his hand relaxed.

I stood back. He swayed, and once more tottered, blundering against the chair and bringing his arm round in a wide, drunken sweep that could have cleared the bench of beakers and test tubes if he had been a few inches closer.

It was not safe to allow such an unco-ordinated creature to roam freely about the laboratory. I did not want to restrict him too much, but obviously he must be kept on a leash until he was able to manage himself in a more civilized fashion.

On a leash, I thought. Yes, that was it. There was, in fact, a length of chain in the store cupboard at the end of the laboratory. It had been used at one stage for hanging dogs in various stages of dismemberment from the rafters, and had been tossed on to a shelf when we advanced beyond those preliminary experiments. Now I took it out.

There was no point in alarming the creature. He looked uncomprehendingly at the chain as I walked casually towards him. I attached one end to a hook in the wall, and hammered the hook closely over the link. He watched, swaying giddily. Then, gauging the distance and the necessary speed, I whipped the chain suddenly round his waist and secured the links behind him. He began to struggle and to beat the air, but as he turned and reached for me I said:

'Down. Keep your arms down.'

Slowly they fell to his side.

With such obedience it would not take long to train him. But to what lengths could I go? Where would I reach a full stop? This was not how I had visualized my creation: not as a massive infant incapable of coherent speech. The thought that the magnificent brain had been damaged beyond redemption nagged at me again and sickened me.

The time had slipped by. Elizabeth would be expecting to see me downstairs. I cleared a space round the creature so that he could roam in comparative freedom without damaging anything, and then went to the door. He watched me like a dog begging to be taken for a walk.

I said: 'I'll come back as soon as I can. We'll soon have you fit to show yourself to the world.' As I was about to open the door, it occurred to me to add: 'You will do as I say. As *I say* . . . and nobody else. Is that understood?'

He nodded.

'Nobody else will come here,' I said. 'Nobody else is allowed in here. And you will do nothing until I come back.'

I went out and locked the door. A cloud of depression settled on me as I walked along the creaking boards of the narrow passage. I had a premonition that things were not going to work out as magnificently as I had planned. And there was something else that made me uneasy – something I couldn't define.

It was the slightest of movements that put me on the alert. A wooden beam that rose up the entire stairwell made an alcove, always sunk in shadow, partly obscured at the top by the eccentric slant of the roof. Dust and cobwebs accumulated

there, for I allowed nobody up to this floor to clean or to pry.
As I passed it on my way to the stairs, my attention was
caught by a broken, drifting cobweb. And I realized that the
darkness was more substantial than usual. Somebody was
hiding behind the beam.

I did not falter. I went straight on, and down a few steps.
Then I paused, flattening myself against the wall, and peered
up through the banisters.

Justine emerged from the shadows and scurried along the
passage. I went back up the steps, keeping low, until I could
see her at the door of the laboratory. From her apron she
produced a key. She tried it a few times in the lock, rattling it
faintly, and then turned it.

I don't know how she came by such a key. Perhaps there
had been a duplicate key in the servants' quarters of which I
had never known. Perhaps she had stolen my only key for an
hour or so after we had been together and had persuaded one
of her young village men to make a copy – though I could not
recall ever having missed it or having given her such an
opportunity, and I could not believe that she would be so
foolish as to put it even for a short time into the hands of
some valley yokel.

Wherever the key came from, it worked. The door opened
and she tiptoed in.

I returned to the landing and made my way along to the
open doorway, treading warily so that the squeak of the
boards should not give me away.

Justine was silhouetted against the attic window, through
which the twilight cast a faint glow. She bumped against
something, and stopped. I saw her grope for the edge of the
bench, and then she lit the lantern which stood to one side –
the lantern which had accompanied me on most of my more
important nocturnal trips.

In the mellow light she looked round the laboratory. I
waited for her gaze to reach the creature, but she was distracted by a cage of mice at the end of the room. She went to
them and peered down.

The shadow of a hand fell across her back.

I started forward, then restrained myself. She had chosen to
go in there. Perhaps this was the answer to many things. She
had no business in my house after my clear dismissal, and

certainly no business in the laboratory. She intended to be a nuisance to me. Let her pay the price of her threats and this trespass.

There was a heavy thud which I identified as the sound of the creature blundering into some obstruction.

Justine spun round.

In the uncertain light I saw the shadows on her face form a pattern of terror. She rammed a fist into her mouth as though to stifle a scream – very considerate of her, I thought ironically.

The dark bulk of the creature loomed over her. The chain rattled. Justine whimpered and turned to run for the door.

I reached it before her. I pulled it shut and turned the key which she had used and which she had had no right to use.

Now she screamed. Now there was no hand in her mouth – she was shrieking like a soul demented.

She must indeed have been mad. A sane person would have realized that the creature, on his chain, could not operate in more than a restricted area. All the stupid girl had to do was stay out of range. But she must have begun to run to and fro like the mice in the cage. Suddenly there was a gasp, cutting off one of her screams. Her feet beat a tattoo on the floor. And there was a dull muttering, and a crunching sound which I did not wish to identify ... and then silence.

8

The wedding invitations, few as they were, had been sent out and the replies were coming in. At breakfast a few days before the ceremony, Elizabeth looked at me with the first sign of awkwardness I had detected in her.

Timidly she said: 'Victor ... I've invited Paul to the wedding.'

It was alien to her nature to have any secrets, and I was surprised that she should have kept this one; surprised, too, that she should have acted thus without consulting me and that she should in any case have known Paul's new address.

But of course he would have sent word to her somehow. I could imagine the florid missive. It would have been evasive but manly, in Paul's best treacherous style, telling her that if ever she needed help he would be at her service, that he wished us both well but that if she had any doubts she must be sure to consult him and lean on him.

When I said nothing, Elizabeth went on: 'He was a very good friend of yours.'

The past tense was all too appropriate. In recent times he had been anything but a friend.

'I'm sorry if I've done wrong,' she said, her head bowed. 'He hasn't accepted yet, so perhaps he won't come.'

The poor girl was so dejected that I had to reassure her. Although I had no great wish to see the man himself, there was something I wanted to show him. He should see what I had accomplished, and would know what more I could have done if it had not been for his interference.

I said: 'I hope he does come, my dear. I hope he accepts.'

This put her mind at rest. She was able to devote all her energies to the wedding preparations.

On her insistence I invited the burgomaster and his wife to dinner one evening, together with some other local worthies who would be present on the day. She was right, of course: it was better that she should meet these folk now rather than make her first acquaintance with them at the ceremony itself. I had neglected some of my duties as her betrothed. I tried to make up for this in a few sociable hours. Certainly the local dignitaries, becoming rather less dignified and more bucolic as the evening were on, had no complaints about their treatment. A large meal and a plentiful supply of wine speedily washed away any lingering resentment they might have harboured from the years of indifference which the present Baron Frankenstein had displayed towards them.

Nevertheless, I was glad to be rid of them. I was gracious to their plump wives and took their heavy jocularity in good part, but beneath this surface amiability I was deeply, miserably bored. When at last they had all gone I poured myself a glass of the brandy which had been too good to offer them, and smiled over the glass at Elizabeth.

She said: 'Gracious, how quiet it is!' She patted the couch beside her. 'Come and sit with me a moment, Victor.'

She was demure yet alluring – a gracious hostess yet also, I saw, a woman with a latent fire of her own who would be an entrancing wife. I would allocate a reasonable amount of my precious time to her. I would be well repaid. It was good to know that the tattered remains of Justine were safely buried in the woods and that there would never be any fear of her malicious tongue speaking evil of me to Elizabeth.

But I must not allow her to assume that I was going to change into a sentimental courtier and abandon all my more serious occupations.

I said: 'I think I must tidy up some loose ends in the laboratory.'

She came as near to pouting as I had ever seen her. On other women it would have been irritating; on her it was rather charming.

'Victor, I thought that for just one evening –'

'I have to conclude one or two processes before the wedding,' I said. 'I must leave everything tidy – and safe.'

She acknowledged this with a resigned sigh. Then she asked: 'May I come and watch you at work?'

'Not yet, my dear. One day very soon, I promise.'

'You've promised that before. I thought you were going to show me what you had done a few weeks ago.'

'I ran into some difficulties. When they are resolved, you shall see.' I finished my brandy and set the glass down. 'A pity we haven't heard from Paul.'

Elizabeth smiled wryly. 'If Paul were here, you'd show *him*.'

'Because he understands the technical background. He was with me during the earlier stages, remember.'

'And why didn't he want to go on?'

This was taking a turn I had no wish to follow. I said: 'Soon you'll see what it has all been about. Soon.'

I was halfway up the stairs when there was a knock at the main door. I paused on the landing. Elizabeth's new maid, a respectable little girl without pretensions and without undue curiosity, crossed the hall.

Paul Krempe stood in the doorway.

'Are the Baron and Miss Elizabeth at home?'

Elizabeth recognized his voice and came running out with an eagerness which I found unbecoming in a young woman of her station.

'Paul, how wonderful to see you. We were afraid you had forgotten us.'

'You are looking more radiant than ever,' he said.

I thought it was time for me to intervene. I went back down the stairs, saying:

'It is good of you to come, Paul.'

He reluctantly looked away from Elizabeth and up at me.

'How are you, Victor?'

I reached his level and we shook hands.

'Victor has been saying,' Elizabeth chattered gaily, 'how much he wanted to see you. He says he's got something he wants you to see – haven't you, Victor?'

Paul looked earnestly, piercingly into my eyes.

'Have you?'

'Yes.' I took his coat from him and waved towards the stairs. 'Would you like to go up and see?'

'Victor!' Elizabeth protested. 'The very moment Paul arrives ...'

'We shall not be long,' I said, moving up behind Paul so that he should not be tempted to turn back.

We went up to the laboratory. Once Paul glanced back inquiringly as though asking for some indication of what he might expect. But I intended that he should see for himself, without preamble.

At the door I took out my key.

'Still keeping the place locked?' said Paul. 'Is that necessary?'

'You can judge for yourself.'

I opened the door and stood back as he entered.

The creature was crouched in a corner, staring at the floor. When it became aware of us it turned its face to the wall.

Paul stared mutely.

'Nothing to say?' I challenged him.

'So it wasn't killed,' he said softly.

'It was. At least, life had passed from its body. But I was the one who put it there in the first place, and it was I who restored it.'

Paul turned away. He headed for the door.

'No, wait,' I said. 'I want to show you something else.'

'I've seen enough.'

'Wait!'

Grudgingly he stayed where he was. He seemed to have difficulty in facing the hunched, huddled body of the creature in the corner. In his face there was no scientific curiosity, no spark of reawakened interest; only loathing.

I stood over the creature. 'Get up.' It shivered slightly and tried to compress itself into an even tighter ball. 'Come on,' I ordered; 'get up.'

Slowly it clambered to its feet. It glanced at Paul and then quickly away at me, waiting for the next command.

I said: 'Now come here.'

It came towards me and stood a few inches away.

'Sit down,' I said.

The creature pondered this, then with an ungainly lurch it lowered itself to the floor with its knees under its chin.

'Is this your creature of superior intellect?' said Paul. 'Your perfect physical being ... this animal?' He drew his hand across his brow, and his eyes narrowed in pain. 'Ask it a question in advanced physics. It's got a brain with a lifetime of knowledge behind it. That was the theory, wasn't it? Go on, ask. It should find it simple.'

This sneer was the most monstrous thing of all. I felt anger like a burning poison in my throat.

'Do you know why it looks like that – behaves like that? There you see the result of *your* handiwork, Paul. Yours as well as mine. I gave it life ... I put a brain in its head ... but I chose a good brain – a brilliant one ...' I took a deep, shuddering breath. 'It was you who damaged it, you who put a bullet in it. This is your fault – do you understand? Your fault.'

'Yes,' said Paul sombrely, 'I understand.'

'But you won't stop me, Paul. You won't force me to stop, to despair. I'm going to carry on. I'll try further brain surgery. If that fails then I shall seek another brain –'

'No, Victor.' Abruptly he was shouting. 'No, you will not.'

'And another if necessary,' I said, 'and another and another, until –'

'No!'

He turned and tried to rush through the doorway. I was so accustomed now to anticipating the creature's erratic movements that I acted instinctively. Before Paul could escape I had grasped his shoulder and twisted him back towards me.

'What are you going to do?'

He pushed at me with all his might. I held firm, and we

staggered back into the centre of the room. He stopped and I could tell that he was trying to keep his voice steady.

'For your sake and to protect Elizabeth I've kept silent so far,' he said. 'But now I'm going to the authorities. That creature must be destroyed – and you must pay for your atrocities.'

I could have laughed if it had not been for the deadly seriousness of it. Absurdity and tragedy go so often together.

Paul flung me away with a sudden lunge, and my hip jarred nauseatingly against the bench. Before I could get my breath, he was out of the door and running along the passage.

I stumbled after him. As he raced down the stairs, Elizabeth came out into the hall.

'Paul, where are you ...'

Her question died on her lips as she saw me in hot pursuit. I followed Paul out into the open, and our feet scuffed up dust from the drive. His pace was slowing. In spite of the pain in my side I forced myself to keep going, and overtook him as he reached the path to the village.

'Paul, wait a minute.'

He swung towards me on the defensive, ready to strike if I tried to grab him.

'Paul,' I pleaded, 'what do you hope to gain by this? You're as much a part of it as I am.'

'I've had nothing to do with it for months.'

'You can't shed all responsibility for the earlier stages. And if you think that by betraying me you'll have Elizabeth for yourself, I can assure you you're mistaken.'

In the evening light it was difficult to make out his features. But he drew himself up stiffly and said: 'I want nothing more than to protect Elizabeth. But I have never tried to win her away from you. If you think that –'

'If you want to protect her,' I broke in, 'you are going the wrong way about it. How will it help her to learn that the man she is about to marry is in danger from meddling officials? How will it help her to know that his old friend and colleague is a traitor who himself worked on the preliminary stages? If we both suffer at the hands of the authorities – and don't imagine, Paul, that I shall accept all blame myself – what will she do? She can't live here alone, the butt of all the malicious tongues in the country. She has nowhere else to go.

It is nearly her wedding eve – and you propose to shatter her whole future?'

'You're falsifying it, Victor.'

'Falsifying it?' I said. 'Think of her in that house while the authorities and their booted minions stamp through, examining everything, pulling the place apart, wrecking my laboratory ...'

The same thought occurred to us both at the same instant.

'The laboratory,' said Paul. 'When we came out ... the door's still open.'

'She wouldn't ...'

'Wouldn't she?'

Elizabeth had not followed us out. The main door was still open, shedding light on the steps. She could, of course, have gone back into the salon. Or she could, wondering about our wild chase, have taken the opportunity of going upstairs. And I had undoubtedly left the door wide open.

We stared at the house.

'Victor!' Paul clutched my arm.

High up on the roof a light showed, and there was a flicker of movement. It was impossible to distinguish the outlines of the moving shape at first, but in the stillness of the night we heard the clink and rattle of a chain.

The creature had pulled its chain away from the wall. The light came from the open skylight which led out on to the roof. As we got used to the distance and the darkness, we saw the wavering head and the groping arms unmistakably.

The creature came to the edge of the parapet and looked down.

'We must get up there,' I said.

'Not this time,' said Paul. 'I'm going to the village for help.'

I seemed to have lost the will to restrain him. Everything was going wrong. As he went away down the path to round up helpers and ruin my schemes once and for all, I returned to the house. I did not even bother to hurry. I was in the grip of a bleak fatalism.

But once I was indoors my steps quickened. There was no sign of Elizabeth. She must indeed have gone upstairs.

I went up the first flight two at a time and called her name along the landing. There was no reply. I pounded on my way up to the laboratory. The door was open, and the lights were burning just as we had left them. But the skylight, which came right down to floor level, was pushed open. A faint breeze stirred the sheets of notes which had accumulated on my desk.

A lantern stood on the parapet just outside the skylight. It must be one which Elizabeth had carried to light her way up the stairs, since I had certainly not put it there. And it meant that Elizabeth had followed the creature out on to the roof.

There was only a low balustrade to save them from the drop to the terrace below.

I opened the desk drawer and took out my pistol. Then I stepped through the open skylight on to the parapet.

Faintly touched with light, almost at the end of the roof, Elizabeth stood looking away from me, looking at something round the corner of the ridge.

'Elizabeth' – I spoke softly, not wanting to alarm her in that precarious position – 'come back.'

She turned and stared at me. It was hardly the face of Elizabeth any longer. Horror was written across it – an incredulous, unconquerable horror that included me as well as the other thing she must have seen. This was not how I had meant her to see the creature for the first time. The shock must have dazed her. Coming into the laboratory just as the creature wrenched its chain free from the wall staple, she must have been hypnotically drawn to follow it, to prove to herself that it was real.

'Elizabeth . . .'

She shook her head as though to deny that I existed. I took a step out on to the parapet and she waved me back. She might have been trying to ward me off – concerned with keeping me rather than the creature at bay.

And behind her the creature appeared, clawing and rocking its way back from the edge of the roof.

I lifted my pistol. Elizabeth screamed. The creature reached out as though to embrace her, and I fired.

It was a bad, impossible target. Elizabeth jerked as though she had been struck, and even in this light I could see a dark stain begin to spread from her shoulder.

She fell back into the creature's arms.

I had another shot to fire. This time I could not afford to miss. As Elizabeth's head drooped to one side I braced myself and took careful aim. The creature stared stupidly, uncompre-hendingly at me.

I fired, and this time it was the creature's turn to flinch. Its arm slid to its side, and Elizabeth crumpled over the edge of the balustrade. She hung there, unconscious, her head swaying over the deadly drop.

The creature touched her once in a puzzled sort of way and then carefully, with a lumbering solemnity, clambered past her and began to come towards me.

'Stay where you are,' I commanded it.

It kept up its slow, steady pace.

'Get back,' I shouted. It must have heard; must know what I was saying. So far its obedience had been unquestioning. 'Get back – get away.'

It was within a few feet of me. I backed away until I was in the skylight opening. Still it did not slacken its advance.

I yelled for help, but there was nobody to hear.

I threw the pistol at the creature. It bounced off, and an eternity later I heard the rattle as it hit the ground far below.

Behind me was the laboratory. If I fled across it I could lock the door from outside and make my escape. The door was solid enough to withstand even the strength of this powerful creature. But to leave Elizabeth out there, trapped with the monster . . .

I glanced back over my shoulder in search of a suitable weapon. There was none. The silver-knobbed stick was not something I would care to trust against this solid brute force.

At my feet was the lantern. I felt the warmth of the flame against my ankle.

I stooped and picked it up.

The creature plodded towards me and raised its arms. I swung the lantern twice to give it plenty of impetus, and hurled it full at the creature.

As the spurting, flickering light was launched at it, the creature bared its teeth. If it could have sprung at me it would have done so. But it had not yet learnt such co-ordination of movements. It made one further step forward and then the lantern smacked into its chest.

There was a moment when nothing seemed to happen. A faint smear of thick black smoke hung on the air. Then flame blazed up from the lamp.

The creature was on fire. The flames licked up greedily, devouring it at a speed which appalled me. Its eyes stared out at me in agonized entreaty, and then were blotted out by crimson fury. A strangled, hideous voice screamed despairingly. The creature's head jerked back in an effort to dodge the flames, but they were too voracious. Its hands beat vainly on its face. And then, a raging pillar of fire, it came blundering on towards me again.

I stumbled back into the laboratory. The glass of the skylight crashed into splinters, spraying across the parapet and into the laboratory.

And suddenly, rearing up like a living torch, the creature hurled itself forward. In its death throes it sought a respite, something to put an end to the intolerable pain. With one wild, insane leap it plunged into the tank.

The screams went on, reverberating through the laboratory. And the screams were mine. I was yelling like a maniac, trying to stop what had already been done. The tank was no longer full of the fluid in which the creature had once lain. I had recently recharged it with acid. And into that acid plunged the burning creature.

There was an acrid smoke that billowed up and raced like some elemental fiend about the room. In the tank there was a moment of wild thrashing and churning, and acid splashed out over the floor, driving me back into a safe corner.

Then the noise abated. It died to a sizzling and bubbling that went on for some time before finally fading into utter stillness.

My life's work was destroyed. Destroyed in a moment by the same hand that brought it into existence. Within half an hour there was nothing left of my creature. The acid tank was cloudy, but that, too, would clarify in a short time and there would be no evidence that the creature had ever been in this world at all.

## 9

That is the true story of what happened. But it is a story which no one will believe. The priest shakes his head and exhorts me to repent. The executioner makes ready, and my hours are numbered.

One man could have saved me. If Paul Krempe had spoken out, then surely the verdict would have gone differently. But Paul had nothing to say. Paul, who was the cause of all that went wrong with the experiment, took Elizabeth away into the quiet countryside and left me to my fate – an undeserved fate.

When Paul brought a dozen villagers to the house that night with the story of a dangerous monster being loose, it was to find no monster. And foolishly, in my desire to suppress any further investigations and any possible scandal, I denounced him as an agitator and trouble-maker. There had been no monster such as he described. I was Baron Franken-stein, and I was shocked that my own villagers should have been seduced by this man's glib inventions. I ordered them to go home and ordered Paul to leave the district before I instituted proceedings against him.

He left the district – and took Elizabeth with him.

I have said that I acted foolishly in so firmly denying the existence of the creature. For a week later some interfering shepherd, who had no business to be on that part of my land in the first place, noticed a peculiar conformation of recently turned earth in the woods, and began to dig into it. Why it should have occurred to him to do so I cannot say: it was but the last in a long series of ironical blows dealt me by fate.

In the grave which he exposed was the mutilated corpse of Justine.

They would not believe that I was innocent of her death. When I told them how the monster of my creation had torn her apart, they shrank away from me and reminded me that I had scorned the notion of any such monster. I tried to explain, but they would not listen. In their eyes *I* was the monster. Justine had been expecting a child, and I had mur-dered her. The more I cried that it was a terrible accident for which I was not responsible, the more their detestation of me hardened.

I sent out a plea for Paul Krempe to come forward and testify. He did not appear. I implored eminent scientists to inspect the apparatus in my laboratory while I explained how it could be used to create life. I offered to demonstrate the whole sequence of experiments to them. Grimly they said I would not be allowed that much time in this world. And on all sides I was accused not merely of murder but of blasphemy.

The priest to whom I have told the story cannot make up his mind whether I am mad or wicked. He has listened, but none of it means anything to him. He will intercede on my behalf with nobody – and if he did, it would be of little use, for who would make any sense out of his meanderings?

Late today came the worst moment of all. A last hope flickered and began to burn ... but I should have known that my trust in old friendships was a vain one.

Paul Krempe came to see me. At last he deigned to show himself. The pathetic little dwarf who is my gaoler, and whom I truly think regards me with respect and a strange affection, showed him in with a flourish. I fancied I detected in the dwarf's sad little eyes the hope that my wishes would be granted and that here at last would be a reprieve.

A great weight was lifted from my heart. Paul, after all, was not going to fail me. He would tell all that he knew. The truth would come out. The rest of the world would have to accept that Justine had been killed not by me but by a creature which, admittedly, I had constructed, but for whose wayward savageries I could hardly be held responsible. Paul knew. His conscience could surely not permit him to remain silent any longer. He must have been trying to hold out, to let me be executed so that Elizabeth would be his; but now he had seen where his duty lay.

I sent for the priest so that he could be a witness to all that was said.

'I knew Paul wouldn't fail me,' I said. 'He will verify everything I've already told you.'

The priest blinked. He gave every sign of being frightened of learning that what I had said was true. Better, in his eyes, that I should be executed than that these unpalatable facts should be firmly established.

Paul was shown in by the dwarf. I put out my hand, longing to clasp his in mine. But Paul stood sternly aloof.

He said: 'I have come with a message from Elizabeth.'

'She will speak, too?' I said eagerly.

'She wishes you to know that she forgives you and that she

will pray for you. I have implored her not to think of the past,
but she would not rest content until I promised that I would
speak to you before the end.'

'Tell them, Paul. Tell the priest here – and later we will
make a declaration to the authorities.'

'Tell them what?'

He was being wilfully obtuse. 'About the creature I made,'
I said as patiently as possible. Patience was not easy with the
shadow of the scaffold darkening over me. 'Paul, you were
the only person ever to see him alive. Elizabeth caught only a
glimpse, but you *know*. You and Justine ... Justine must have
seen him, but she can't help me now, can she?'

'Justine,' he said thoughtfully; 'the girl you murdered.'

It was like a knife in my bowels. I said: 'But I didn't. You
must realize that. He was the one. He ... it ...'

'Who, Victor?' Paul's steely calmness brought fear welling
up in me again.

'The creature.' I was trying to maintain my dignity, trying
not to shout at him. 'The creature we made together. Don't
keep up the pretence any longer. You've got to tell the truth
now.'

Paul glanced at the priest and slowly shook his head. As
though this had been a signal he was expecting, the priest left
the cell.

I clutched Paul's jacket. 'You must tell them! You know
what's going to happen to me. Only you can save me. You
must tell them. I'll make you speak. I'll make you ...'

We fought in the confined space of the cell. It lasted only a
few seconds. The guards rushed in and dragged me off him.
Paul dusted himself off and gave the guards the same false,
regretful look he had given the priest.

This was the only time during these degrading proceedings
that I broke down. I began to scream.

'You must tell them, Paul. You've got to save me. You
can't let them ... can't let me ... Paul, I'll promise not to
carry out any further experiments, but *tell* them. Tell them
now!'

They held me back as he went out of the cell with his head
hypocritically bowed.

The priest was waiting outside.

Paul said: 'There's nothing we can do for him now.'

And he left, doubtless to insinuate himself even further into Elizabeth's graces.

I sobbed helplessly. I am ashamed of myself for showing such weakness, but this final betrayal robbed me temporarily of all self-control.

Now I am myself again. They shall not see me flinch. And even at this eleventh hour I feel that somehow there must be an answer. There cannot be such injustice in the world. I am Baron Frankenstein, and I cannot believe that I shall die. I cannot believe that I shall ever die. I who have created life – how can they presume to take life from me?

There must somehow be a way to cheat death.

# The Reanimator

## By H.P. LOVECRAFT

*Hammer's success with* Frankenstein *continued until the early Seventies when the well-spring of ideas finally ran dry with* Frankenstein and the Monster from Hell *(1972). The influence of theme was, however, far from over, and a decade later another story inspired by it was turned into a movie which has become a cult classic and also generated a sequel:* Herbert West: Reanimator *by the America horror writer, H.P. Lovecraft (1890–1937). Lovecraft, who lived much of his life as a recluse on Rhode Island and has posthumously been acknowledged as a master of the genre, was a prolific reader of supernatural literature and described* Frankenstein *as 'one of the horror classics of all time – it has the true touch of cosmic fear.' It is interesting to note that just as Lovecraft's work has influenced subsequent generations of writers, so* Frankenstein *shaped his early work, in particular* Herbert West: Reanimator: *the six episodes of which were first published in the curiously titled* Home Brew *magazine in 1921–2. The influence of Mary Shelley on this saga of a young experimenter, barred from medical school, who practises his unholy arts on the corpses of human beings and reptiles is immediately apparent – but when director Stuart Gordon decided to bring the stories to the screen in the mid-Eighties he initiated what has since become known as the 'splatter film' genre with its dedication to shocking viewers with blood, gore and violence.*

*The first* Re-Animator *picture released in 1986 has been described as 'one of the most memorable horror smashes of the Eighties' and apart from winning a Special Prize at the Cannes Film Festival made a number of people faint when it was screened at the Sitges Fantasy Festival in Spain. Stuart Gordon, who also co-wrote the screenplay with Dennis Paoli and William J. Norris, went to considerable lengths to make the medical background to the picture as authentic as possible, hiring two Los Angeles doctors as consultants: Dr Daniel Del Boccio of the Pathology Department at Henrotin Hospital and the appositely named Dr Robert Stein from the Cook County Morgue. In creating the remarkable special effects which were to have such a strong impact on viewers, Gordon also spent some time in Los Angeles' morgues, recalling later, 'I soon realised most films portray corpses inaccurately. They are not necessarily "deathly" white with dark rings under their eyes. People are as different in death as they are in life. They can be all colours of the rainbow, depending on how they died.'*

*The film company later claimed to have used in excess of 30 gallons of 'blood' in making the picture, which starred Jeffrey Coombs as Herbert West, Bruce Abbott as his assistant, Dan Cain, and David Gale as Dr Carl Hill the treacherous, hypocritical head of Miskatonic University. Melvin, the Re-animated Man, was played by Peter Kent. Reviewers at both ends of the spectrum enjoyed the picture as much as its audiences. 'A splatter film that's head and spurting trunk above the rest,' said New York's Village Voice, while The Times of London declared, 'It aims for cult status.' In fact, the success of the movie, like its Frankenstein predecessors, led to a sequel in 1990, which was released in some countries as Re-Animator 2 and in others [with a nice acknowledgment to the past] as Bride of Re-Animator. Brian Yuzna, who had been producer of the first picture, now assumed the role of director and also co-wrote the script with Woody Keith and Rick Fry. All the principals of the previous film re-appeared with the addition of Kathleen Kinmont playing Gloria, the bride, and Irene Forrest in the role of Nurse Mary Shelley. The special effects for the tale in which West created a woman from just a female head were the handiwork of Hollywood's gore specialist, Screaming Mad George. Like its predecessor, Re-Animator 2 has become a favourite for screening at late night horror shows, and here are Lovecraft's episodes which inspired these cult classics.*

# I. FROM THE DARK

Of Herbert West, who was my friend in college and in other life, I can speak only with extreme terror. This terror is not due altogether to the sinister manner of his recent disappearance, but was engendered by the whole nature of his life-work, and first gained its acute form more than seventeen years ago, when we were in the third year of our course at the Miskatonic University medical school in Arkham. While he was with me, the wonder and diabolism of his experiments fascinated me utterly, and I was his closest companion. Now that he is gone and the spell is broken, the actual fear is greater. Memories and possibilities are ever more hideous than realities.

The first horrible incident of our acquaintance was the greatest shock I ever experienced, and it is only with reluctance that I repeat it. As I have said, it happened when we were in medical school, where West had already made himself notorious through his wild theories on the nature of death and the possibility of overcoming it artificially. His views, which were widely ridiculed by the faculty and by his fellow-students, hinged on the essentially mechanistic nature of life; and concerned means for operating the organic machinery of mankind by calculated chemical action after the failure of natural processes. In his experiments with various animating solutions he had killed and treated immense numbers of rabbits, guinea-pigs, cats, dogs, and monkeys, till he had become the prime nuisance of the college. Several times he had actually obtained signs of life in animals supposedly dead; in many cases violent signs; but he soon saw that the perfection of his process, if indeed possible, would necessarily involve a lifetime of research. It likewise became clear that, since the same solution never worked alike on different organic species, he would require human subjects for further and more specialised progress. It was here that he first came into conflict with the college authorities, and was debarred from future experiments by no less a dignitary than the dean of the medical school himself – the learned and benevolent Dr Allan Halsey, whose work on behalf of the stricken is recalled by every old resident of Arkham.

I had always been exceptionally tolerant of West's pursuits, and we frequently discussed his theories, whose ramifications and corollaries were almost infinite. Holding with Haeckel that all life is a chemical and physical process, and that the so-called 'soul' is a myth, my friend believed that artificial reanimation of the dead can depend only on the condition of the tissues; and that unless actual decomposition has set in, a corpse fully equipped with organs may with suitable measures be set going again in the peculiar fashion known as life. That the psychic or intellectual life might be impaired by the slight deterioration of sensitive brain-cells which even a short period of death would be apt to cause, West fully realised. It had at first been his hope to find a reagent which would restore vitality before the actual advent of death, and only repeated failures on animals had shown him that the natural and artificial life-motions were incompatible. He then sought extreme freshness in his specimens, injecting his solutions into the blood immediately after the extinction of life. It was this circumstance which made the professors so carelessly sceptical, for they felt that true death had not occurred in any case. They did not stop to view the matter closely and reasoningly.

It was not long after the faculty had interdicted his work that West confided to me his resolution to get fresh bodies in some manner, and continue in secret the experiments he could no longer perform openly. To hear him discussing ways and means was rather ghastly, for at the college we had never procured anatomical specimens ourselves. Whenever the morgue proved inadequate, two local negroes attended to this matter, and they were seldom questioned. West was then a small, slender, spectacled youth with delicate features, yellow hair, pale blue eyes, and a soft voice, and it was uncanny to hear him dwelling on the relative merits of Christ Church Cemetery and the potter's field, because practically every body in Christ Church was embalmed; a thing of course ruinous to West's researches.

I was by this time his active and enthralled assistant, and helped him make all his decisions, not only concerning the source of bodies but concerning a suitable place for our loathsome work. It was I who thought of the deserted Chapman farmhouse beyond Meadow Hill, where we fitted up on the ground floor an operating room and a laboratory, each with dark curtains to conceal our midnight doings. The place was far from any road, and in sight of no other house, yet precautions were none the less necessary; since rumours of strange lights, started by chance nocturnal roamers, would soon bring disaster on our enterprise. It was agreed to call the whole thing a chemical laboratory if discovery should occur. Gradually we equipped our sinister haunt of science with materials either purchased in Boston or quietly borrowed from the college – materials carefully made unrecognizable save to expert eyes – and provided spades and picks for the many burials we should have to make in the cellar. At the college we used an incinerator, but the apparatus was too costly for our unauthorized laboratory. Bodies were always a nuisance – even the small guinea-pig bodies from the slight clandestine experiments in West's room at the boarding-house.

We followed the local death-notices like ghouls, for our specimens demanded particular qualities. What we wanted were corpses interred soon after death and without artificial preservation; preferably free from malforming disease, and certainly with all organs present. Accident victims were our best hope. Not for many weeks did we hear of anything suitable; though we talked with morgue and hospital authorities, ostensibly in the college's interest, as often as we could without exciting suspicion. We found that the college had first choice in every case, so that it might be necessary to remain in Arkham during the summer, when only the limited summer-school classes were held. In the end, though, luck favoured us; for one day we heard of an almost ideal case in the potter's field; a brawny young workman drowned only the morning before in Summer's Pond, and buried at the town's expense without delay or embalming. That afternoon we found the new grave, and determined to begin work soon after midnight.

It was a repulsive task that we undertook in the black small hours, even though we lacked at that time the special horror of graveyards which later experiences brought to us. We carried spades and oil dark lanterns, for although electric torches were then manufactured, they were not as satisfactory as the tungsten contrivances of today. The process of unearthing was slow and sordid – it might have been gruesomely poetical if we had been artists instead of scientists – and we were glad when our spades struck wood. When the pine box was fully uncovered West scrambled down and removed the lid, dragging out and propping up the contents. I reached down and hauled the contents out of the grave, and then both toiled hard to restore the spot to its former appearance. The affair made us rather nervous, especially the stiff form and vacant face of our first trophy, but we managed to remove all traces of our visit. When we had patted down the last shovelful of earth we put the specimen in a canvas sack and set out for the old Chapman place beyond Meadow Hill.

On an improvised dissecting-table in the old farmhouse, by the light of a powerful acetylene lamp, the specimen was not very spectral-looking. It had been a sturdy and apparently unimaginative youth of wholesome plebeian type – large-framed, grey-eyed, and brown-haired – a sound animal without psychological subtleties, and probably having vital processes of the simplest and healthiest sort. Now, with the eyes closed, it looked more asleep than dead; though the expert test of my friend soon left no doubt on the score. We had at last what West had always longed for – a real dead man of the ideal kind, ready for the solution as prepared according to the most careful calculations and theories for human use. The tension on our part became very great. We knew that there was scarcely a chance for anything like complete success, and could not avoid hideous fears at possible grotesque results of partial animation. Especially were we apprehensive concerning the mind and impulses of the creature, since in the space following death some of the more delicate cerebral cells might well have suffered deterioration. I, myself, still held some curious notions about the traditional 'soul' of man, and felt an awe at the secrets that might be told by one returning from the dead. I wondered what sights this placid youth might have seen in inaccessible spheres, and what he could relate if fully restored to life. But my wonder was not overwhelming, since for the most part I shared the materialism of my friend. He was calmer than I as he forced a large quantity of his fluid into a vein of the body's arm, immediately binding the incision securely.

The waiting was gruesome, but West never faltered. Every now and then he applied his stethoscope to the specimen, and bore the negative results philosophically. After about three-

quarters of an hour without the least sign of life he disappoint-
edly pronounced the solution inadequate, but determined to
make the most of his opportunity and try one change in the
formula before disposing of his ghastly prize. We had that
afternoon dug a grave in the cellar, and would have to fill it
by dawn – for although we had fixed a lock on the house we
wished to shun even the remotest risk of a ghoulish discovery.
Besides, the body would not be even approximately fresh the
next night. So taking the solitary acetylene lamp into the
adjacent laboratory, we left our silent guest on the slab in the
dark, and bent every energy to the mixing of a new solution;
the weighing and measuring supervised by West with an
almost fanatical care.

The awful event was very sudden, and wholly unexpected. I
was pouring something from one test-tube to another, and
West was busy over the alcohol blast-lamp which had to
answer for a Bunsen burner in this gasless edifice, when from
the pitch-black room we had left there burst the most appalling and demoniac succession of cries that either of us had ever
heard. Not more unutterable could have been the chaos of
hellish sound if the pit itself had opened to release the agony
of the damned, for in one inconceivable cacophony was
centered all the supernal terror and unnatural despair of
animate nature. Human it could not have been – it is not in
man to make such sounds – and without a thought of our late
employment or its possible discovery both West and I leaped
to the nearest window like stricken animals; overturning
tubes, lamp, and retorts, and vaulting madly into the starred
abyss of the rural night. I think we screamed ourselves as we
stumbled frantically toward the town, though as we reached
the outskirts we put on a semblance of restraint – just enough
to seem like belated revellers staggering home from a
debauch.

We did not separate, but managed to get to West's room,
where we whispered with the gas up until dawn. By then we
had calmed ourselves a little with rational theories and plans
for investigation, so that we could sleep through the day –
classes being disregarded. But that evening two items in the
paper, wholly unrelated, made it again impossible for us
to sleep. The old deserted Chapman house had inexplica-
bly burned to an amorphous heap of ashes; that we could

understand because of the upset lamp. Also, an attempt had been made to disturb a new grave in the potter's field, as if by futile and spadeless clawing at the earth. That we could not understand, for we had patted down the mould very carefully.

And for seventeen years after that West would look frequently over his shoulder, and complain of fancied footsteps behind him. Now he has disappeared.

## II. THE PLAGUE-DEMON

I shall never forget that hideous summer sixteen years ago, when like a noxious afrit from the halls of Eblis typhoid stalked leeringly through Arkham. It is by that satanic scourge that most recall the year, for truly terror brooded with batwings over the piles of coffins in the tombs of Christ Church Cemetery; yet for me there is a greater horror in that time – a horror known to me alone now that Herbert West has disappeared.

West and I were doing post-graduate work in summer classes at the medical school of Miskatonic University, and my friend had attained a wide notoriety because of his experiments leading toward the revivification of the dead. After the scientific slaughter of uncounted small animals the freakish work had ostensibly stopped by order of our sceptical dean, Dr Allan Halsey; though West had continued to perform certain secret tests in his dingy boarding-house room, and had on one terrible and unforgettable occasion taken a human body from its grave in the potter's field to a deserted farmhouse beyond Meadow Hill.

I was with him on that odious occasion, and saw him inject into the still veins the elixir which he thought would to some extent restore life's chemical and physical processes. It had ended horribly – in a delirium of fear which we gradually came to attribute to our own over-wrought nerves – and West had never afterward been able to shake off a maddening sensation of being haunted and hunted. The body had not been quite fresh enough; it is obvious that to restore normal mental attributes a body must be very fresh indeed; and the burning of the old house had prevented us from burying the thing. It would have been better if we could have known it was underground.

After that experience West had dropped his researches for some time; but as the zeal of the born scientist slowly returned, he again became importunate with the college faculty, pleading for the use of the dissecting-room and of fresh human specimens for the work he regarded as so overwhelmingly important. His pleas, however, were wholly in vain; for the decision of Dr Halsey was inflexible, and the other professors all endorsed the verdict of their leader. In the radical theory of reanimation they saw nothing but the immature vagaries of a youthful enthusiast whose slight form, yellow hair, spectacled blue eyes, and soft voice gave no hint of the super-normal – almost diabolical – power of the cold brain within. I can see him now as he was then – and I shiver. He grew sterner of face, but never elderly. And now Sefton has had the mishap and West has vanished.

West clashed disagreeably with Dr Halsey near the end of our last undergraduate term in a wordy dispute that did less credit to him than to the kindly dean in point of courtesy. He felt that he was needlessly and irrationally retarded in a supremely great work; a work which he could of course conduct to suit himself in later years, but which he wished to begin while still possessed of the exceptional facilities of the university. That the tradition-bound elders should ignore his singular results on animals, and persist in their denial of the possibility of reanimation, was inexpressibly disgusting and almost incomprehensible to a youth of West's logical temperament. Only greater maturity could help him understand the chronic mental limitations of the 'professor-doctor' type – the product of generations of pathetic Puritanism, kindly, conscientious, and sometimes gentle and amiable, yet always narrow, intolerant, custom-ridden, and lacking in perspective. Age has more charity for these incomplete yet high-souled characters, whose worst real vice is timidity, and who are ultimately punished by general ridicule for their intellectual sins – sins like Ptolemaism, Calvinism, anti-Darwinism, anti-Nietzscheism, and every sort of Sabbatarianism and sumptuary legislation. West, young despite his marvellous scientific acquirements, had scant patience with good Dr Halsey and his erudite colleagues; and nursed an increasing resentment, cou pled with a desire to prove his theories to these obtuse worthies in some striking and dramatic fashion. Like most youths, he indulged in elaborate day-dreams of revenge, triumph, and final magnanimous forgiveness.

And then had come the scourge, grinning and lethal, from the nightmare caverns of Tartarus. West and I had graduated about the time of its beginning, but had remained for additional work at the summer school, so that we were in Arkham when it broke with full demoniac fury upon the town. Though not as yet licensed physicians, we now had our degrees, and were pressed frantically into public service as the numbers of the stricken grew. The situation was almost past management, and deaths ensued too frequently for the local undertakers fully to handle. Burials without embalming were made in rapid succession, and even the Christ Church Cemetery receiving tomb was crammed with coffins of the unembalmed dead. This circumstance was not without effect on West, who thought often of the irony of the situation – so many fresh specimens, yet none for his persecuted researches! We were frightfully overworked, and the terrific mental and nervous strain made my friend brood morbidly.

But West's gentle enemies were no less harassed with prostrating duties. College had all but closed, and every doctor of the medical faculty was helping to fight the typhoid plague. Dr Halsey in particular had distinguished himself in sacrificing service, applying his extreme skill with whole-hearted energy to cases which many others shunned because of danger or apparent hopelessness. Before a month was over the fearless dean had become a popular hero, though he seemed unconscious of his fame as he struggled to keep from collapsing with physical fatigue and nervous exhaustion. West could not withhold admiration for the fortitude of his foe, but because of this was even more determined to prove to him the truth of his amazing doctrines. Taking advantage of the disorganization of both college work and municipal health regulations, he managed to get a recently deceased body smuggled into the university dissecting-room one night, and in my presence injected a new modification of his solution. The thing actually opened its eyes, but only stared at the ceiling with a look of soul-petrifying horror before collapsing into an inertness from which nothing could rouse it. West said it was not fresh enough – the hot summer air does not favour corpses. That time we were almost caught before we incinerated the thing, and West doubted the advisability of repeating his daring misuse of the college laboratory.

The peak of the epidemic was reached in August. West and I were almost dead, and Dr Halsey did die on the fourteenth. The students all attended the hasty funeral on the fifteenth, and bought an impressive wreath, though the latter was quite overshadowed by the tributes sent by wealthy Arkham citizens and by the municipality itself. It was almost a public affair, for the dean had surely been a public benefactor. After the entombment we were all somewhat depressed, and spent the afternoon at the bar of the Commercial House; where West, though shaken by the death of his chief opponent, chilled the rest of us with references to his notorious theories. Most of the students went home, or to various duties, as the evening advanced; but West persuaded me to aid him in 'making a night of it.' West's landlady saw us arrive at his room about two in the morning, with a third man between us; and told her husband that we had all evidently dined and wined rather well.

Apparently this acidulous matron was right; for about three a.m. the whole house was aroused by cries coming from West's room, where when they broke down the door they found the two of us unconscious on the blood-stained carpet, beaten, scratched, and mauled, and with the broken remnants of West's bottles and instruments around us. Only an open window told what had become of our assailant, and many wondered how he himself had fared after the terrific leap from the second storey to the lawn which he must have made. There were some strange garments in the room, but West upon regaining consciousness said they did not belong to the stranger, but were specimens collected for bacteriological analysis in the course of investigations on the transmission of germ diseases. He ordered them burnt as soon as possible in the capacious fireplace. To the police we both declared ignorance of our late companion's identity. He was, West nervously said, a congenial stranger whom we had met at some downtown bar of uncertain location. We had all been rather jovial, and West and I did not wish to have our pugnacious companion hunted down.

That same night saw the beginning of the second Arkham horror – the horror that to me eclipsed the plague itself. Christ Church Cemetery was the scene of a terrible killing; a watchman having been clawed to death in a manner not only too hideous for description, but raising a doubt as to the human agency of the deed. The victim had been seen alive considerably after midnight – the dawn revealed the unutterable thing. The manager of a circus at the neighbouring town of Bolton was questioned, but he swore that no beast had at any time escaped from its cage. Those who found the body noted a trail of blood leading to the receiving tomb, where a small pool of red lay on the concrete just outside the gate. A fainter trail led away towards the woods, but it soon gave out.

The next night devils danced on the roofs of Arkham, and unnatural madness howled in the wind. Through the fevered town had crept a curse which some said was greater than the plague, and which some whispered was the embodied demon-soul of the plague itself. Eight houses were entered by a nameless thing which strewed red death in its wake – in all, seventeen maimed and shapeless remnants of bodies were left behind by the voiceless, sadistic monster that crept abroad. A few persons had half seen it in the dark, and said it was white and like a malformed ape or anthropomorphic fiend. It had not left behind quite all that it had attacked, for sometimes it had been hungry. The number it had killed was fourteen; three of the bodies had been in stricken homes and had not been alive.

On the third night frantic bands of searchers, led by the police, captured it in a house on Crane Street near the Miskatonic campus. They had organized the quest with care, keeping in touch by means of volunteer telephone stations, and when someone in the college district had reported hearing a scratching at a shuttered window, the net was quickly spread. On account of the general alarm and precautions, there were only two more victims, and the capture was effected without major casualties. The thing was finally stopped by a bullet, though not a fatal one, and was rushed to the local hospital amidst universal excitement and loathing.

For it had been a man. This much was clear despite the nauseous eyes, the voiceless simianism, and the demoniac savagery. They dressed the wound and carted it to the asylum at Sefton, where it beat its head against the walls of a padded cell for sixteen years – until the recent mishap, when it escaped under circumstances that few like to mention. What had most disgusted the searchers of Arkham was the thing they noticed when the monster's face was cleaned – the mocking, unbelievable resemblance to a learned and self-sacrificing martyr who had been entombed but three days before – the late Dr Allan Halsey, public benefactor and dean of the medical school of Miskatonic University.

To the vanished Herbert West and to me the disgust and horror were supreme. I shudder tonight as I think of it, shudder even more than I did that morning when West muttered through his bandages, 'Damn it, it wasn't *quite* fresh enough!'

## III. SIX SHOTS BY MOONLIGHT

It is uncommon to fire all six shots of a revolver with great suddenness when one would probably be sufficient, but many things in the life of Herbert West were uncommon. It is, for instance, not often that a young physician leaving college is obliged to conceal the principles which guide his selection of a home and office, yet that was the case with Herbert West. When he and I obtained our degrees at the medical school of Miskatonic University, and sought to relieve our poverty by setting up as general practitioners, we took great care not to say that we chose our house because it was fairly well isolated, and as near as possible to the potter's field.

Reticence such as this is seldom without a cause, nor indeed was ours; for our requirements were those resulting from a life-work distinctly unpopular. Outwardly we were doctors only, but beneath the surface were aims of far greater and more terrible moment – for the essence of Herbert West's existence was a quest amid black and forbidden realms of the unknown, in which he hoped to uncover the secret of life and restore to perpetual animation the graveyard's cold clay. Such a quest demands strange materials, among them fresh human bodies; and in order to keep supplied with these indispensable things one must live quietly and not far from a place of informal interment.

West and I had met in college, and I had been the only one to sympathize with his hideous experiments. Gradually I had come to be his inseparable assistant, and now that we were out of college we had to keep together. It was not easy to find a good opening for two doctors in company, but finally the influence of the university secured us a practice in Bolton – a factory town near Arkham, the seat of the college. The Bolton Worsted Mills are the largest in the Miskatonic Valley, and their polyglot employees are never popular as patients with the local physicians. We chose our house with the greatest care, seizing at last on a rather run-down cottage near the end of Pond Street; five numbers from the closest neighbour, and separated from the local potter's field by only a stretch of meadow land, bisected by a narrow neck of the rather dense forest which lies to the north. The distance was greater than we wished, but we could get no nearer house without going on the other side of the field, wholly out of the factory district. We were not much displeased, however, since there were no people between us and our sinister source of supplies. The walk was a trifle long, but we could haul our silent specimens undisturbed.

Our practice was surprisingly large from the very first – large enough to please most young doctors, and large enough to prove a bore and a burden to students whose real interest lay elsewhere. The mill-hands were of somewhat turbulent inclinations; and besides their many natural needs, their frequent clashes and stabbing affrays gave us plenty to do. But what actually absorbed our minds was the secret laboratory we had fitted up in the cellar – the laboratory with the long table under the electric lights, where in the small hours of the morning we often injected West's various solutions into the veins of the things we dragged from the potter's field. West was experimenting madly to find something which would start man's vital motions anew after they had been stopped by the thing we call death, but had encountered the most ghastly obstacles. The solution had to be differently compounded for different types – what would serve for guinea-pigs would not serve for human beings, and different specimens required large modifications.

The bodies had to be exceedingly fresh, or the slight decomposition of brain tissue would render perfect reanimation impossible. Indeed, the greatest problem was to get them fresh enough – West had had horrible experiences during his secret college researchs with corpses of doubtful vintage. The results of partial or imperfect animation were much more hideous than were the total failures, and we both held fearsome recollections of such things. Ever since our first demoniac session in the deserted farm-house on Meadow Hill in Arkham, we had felt a brooding menace; and West, though a calm, blond, blue-eyed scientific automaton in most respects, often confessed to a shuddering sensation of stealthy pursuit. He half felt that he was followed – psychological delusion of shaken nerves, enhanced by the undeniably disturbing fact that at least one of our reanimated specimens was still alive – a frightful carnivorous thing in a padded cell at Sefton. Then there was another – our first – whose exact fate we had never learned.

We had fair luck with specimens in Bolton – much better than in Arkham. We had not been settled a week before we got an accident victim on the very night of burial, and made it open its eyes with an amazingly rational expression before the solution failed. It had lost an arm – if it had been a perfect body we might have succeeded better. Between then and the next January we secured three more, one total failure, one case of marked muscular motion, and one rather shivery thing – it rose of itself and uttered a sound. Then came a period when luck was poor; interments fell off, and those that did occur were of specimens either too diseased or too maimed for us. We kept track of all the deaths and their circumstances with systematic care.

One March night, however, we unexpectedly obtained a specimen which did not come from the potter's field. In Bolton the prevailing spirit of Puritanism had outlawed the sport of boxing – with the usual result. Surreptitious and ill-conducted bouts among the mill-workers were common, and occasionally professional talent of low grade was imported. This late winter night there had been such a match; evidently with disastrous results, since two timorous Poles had come to us with incoherently whispered entreaties to attend to a very secret and desperate case. We followed them to an abandoned

barn, where the remnants of a crowd of frightened foreigners
were watching a silent black form on the floor.

The match had been between Kid O'Brien – a lubberly and
now quaking youth with a most un-Hibernian hooked nose –
and Buck Robinson, 'The Harlem Smoke.' The Negro had
been knocked out, and a moment's examination showed us
that he would permanently remain so. He was a loathsome,
gorilla-like thing, with abnormally long arms which I could
not help calling fore-legs, and a face that conjured up thoughts
of unspeakable Congo secrets and tom-tom poundings under
an eerie moon. The body must have looked even worse in life
– but the world holds many ugly things. Fear was upon the
whole pitiful crowd, for they did not know what the law
would exact of them if the affair were not hushed up; and
they were grateful when West, in spite of my involuntary
shudders, offered to get rid of the thing quietly – for a
purpose I knew too well.

There was bright moonlight over the snowless landscape,
but we dressed the thing and carried it home between us
through the deserted streets and meadows, as we had carried
a similar thing one horrible night in Arkham. We approached
the house from the field in the rear, took the specimen in the
back door and down the cellar stairs, and prepared it for the
usual experiment. Our fear of the police was absurdly great,
though we had timed our trip to avoid the solitary patrolman
of that section.

The result was wearily anti-climactic. Ghastly as our prize
appeared, it was wholly unresponsive to every solution we
injected in its black arm, solutions prepared from experience
with white specimens only. So as the hour grew dangerously
near to dawn, we did as we had done with the others –
dragged the thing across the meadows to the neck of woods
near the potter's field, and buried it there in the best sort of
grave the frozen ground would furnish. The grave was not
very deep, but fully as good as that of the previous specimen –
the thing which had risen of itself and uttered a sound. In the
light of our dark lanterns we carefully covered it with leaves
and dead vines, fairly certain that the police would never find
it in a forest so dim and dense.

The next day I was increasingly apprehensive about the
police, for a patient brought rumours of a suspected fight and

death. West had still another source of worry, for he had been called in the afternoon to a case which ended very threateningly. An Italian woman had become hysterical over her missing child, a lad of five who had strayed off early in the morning and failed to appear for dinner – and had developed symptoms highly alarming in view of an always weak heart. It was a very foolish hysteria, for the boy had often run away before; but Italian peasants are exceedingly superstitious, and this woman seemed as much harassed by omens as by facts. About seven o'clock in the evening she had died, and her frantic husband had made a frightful scene in his efforts to kill West, whom he wildly blamed for not saving her life. Friends had held him when he drew a stiletto, but West departed amidst his inhuman shrieks, curses, and oaths of vengeance. In his latest affliction the fellow seemed to have forgotten his child, who was still missing as the night advanced. There was some talk of searching the woods, but most of the family's friends were busy with the dead woman and the screaming man. Altogether, the nervous strain upon West must have been tremendous. Thoughts of the police and of the mad Italian both weighed heavily.

We retired about eleven, but I did not sleep well. Bolton had a surprisingly good police force for so small a town, and I could not help fearing the mess which would ensue if the affair of the night before were ever tracked down. It might mean the end of all our local work – and perhaps prison for both West and me. I did not like those rumours of a fight which were floating about. After the clock had struck three the moon shone in my eyes, but I turned over without rising to pull down the shade. Then came the steady rattling at the back door.

I lay still and somewhat dazed, but before long heard West's rap on my door. He was clad in dressing-gown and slippers, and had in his hands a revolver and an electric flashlight. From the revolver I knew that he was thinking more of the crazed Italian than of the police.

'We'd better both go,' he whispered. 'It wouldn't do not to answer it anyway, and it may be a patient – it would be like one of those fools to try the back door.'

So we both went down the stairs on tiptoe, with a fear partly justified and partly that which comes only from the soul of the weird small hours. The rattling continued, growing somewhat louder. When we reached the door I cautiously unbolted it and threw it open, and as the moon streamed revealingly down on the form silhouetted there, West did a peculiar thing. Despite the obvious danger of attracting notice and bringing down on our heads the dreaded police investigation – a thing which after all was mercifully averted by the relative isolation of our cottage – my friend suddenly, excitedly, and unnecessarily emptied all six chambers of his revolver into the nocturnal visitor.

For that visitor was neither Italian nor policeman. Looming hideously against the spectral moon was a gigantic misshapen thing not to be imagined save in nightmares – a glassy-eyed, ink-black apparition nearly on all fours, covered with bits of mould, leaves, and vines, foul with caked blood, and having between its glistening teeth a snow-white, terrible, cylindrical object terminating in a tiny hand.

## IV. THE SCREAM OF THE DEAD

The scream of a dead man gave to me that acute and added horror of Dr Herbert West which harassed the latter years of our companionship. It is natural that such a thing as a dead man's scream should give horror, for it is obviously not a pleasing or ordinary occurrence; but I was used to similar experiences, hence suffered on this occasion only because of a particular circumstance. And, as I have implied, it was not of the dead man himself that I became afraid.

Herbert West, whose associate and assistant I was, possessed scientific interests far beyond the usual routine of a village physician. That was why, when establishing his practice in Bolton, he had chosen an isolated house near the potter's field. Briefly and brutally stated, West's sole absorbing interest was a secret study of the phenomena of life and its cessation, leading toward the reanimation of the dead through injections of an excitant solution. For this ghastly experimenting it was necessary to have a constant supply of very fresh human bodies; very fresh because even the least decay hopelessly damaged the brain structure, and human because we found that the solution had to be compounded differently for different types of organisms. Scores of rabbits and guinea-pigs had been killed and treated, but their trail was a blind one. West had never fully succeeded because he had never been able to secure a corpse sufficiently fresh. What he wanted were bodies from which vitality had only just departed; bodies with every cell intact and capable of receiving again the impulse toward that mode of motion called life. There was hope that this second and artificial life might be made perpetual by repetitions of the injection, but we had learned that an ordinary natural life would not respond to the action. To establish the artificial motion, noctural life must be extinct – the specimens must be very fresh, but genuinely dead.

The awesome quest had begun when West and I were students at the Miskatonic University medical school in Arkham, vividly conscious for the first time of the thoroughly mechanical nature of life. That was seven years before, but West looked scarcely a day older now – he was small, blond, clean-shaven, soft-voiced, and spectacled, with only an occasional flash of a cold blue eye to tell of the hardening and growing fanaticism of his character under the pressure of his terrible investigations. Our experiences had often been hideous in the extreme; the results of defective reanimation, when lumps of graveyard clay had been galvanised into morbid, unnatural, and brainless motion by various modifications of the vital solution.

One thing had uttered a nerve-shattering scream; another had risen violently, beaten us both to unconsciousness, and run amuck in a shocking way before it could be placed behind asylum bars; still another, a loathsome African monstrosity, had clawed out of its shallow grave and done a deed – West had had to shoot that object. We could not get bodies fresh enough to show any trace of reason when reanimated, so had perforce created nameless horrors. It was disturbing to think that one, perhaps two, of our monsters still lived – that thought haunted us shadowingly, till finally West disappeared under frightful circumstances. But at the time of the scream in the cellar laboratory of the isolated Bolton cottage, our fears were subordinate to our anxiety for extremely fresh specimens. West was more avid than I, so that it almost seemed to me that he looked half-covetously at any very healthy living physique.

It was in July, 1910, that the bad luck regarding specimens began to turn. I had been on a long visit to my parents in Illinois, and upon my return found West in a state of singular elation. He had, he told me excitedly, in all likelihood solved the problem of freshness through an approach from an entirely new angle – that of artificial preservation. I had known that he was working on a new and highly unusual embalming compound, and was not surprised that it had turned out well; but until he explained the details I was rather puzzled as to how such a compound could help in our work, since the objectionable staleness of the specimens was largely due to delay occurring before we secured them. This, I now saw, West had clearly recognized; creating his embalming compound for future rather than immediate use, and trusting to fate to supply again some very recent and unburied corpse, as it had years before when we obtained the Negro killed in the Bolton prize-fight. At last fate had been kind, so that on this occasion there lay in the secret cellar laboratory a corpse whose decay could not by any possibility have begun. What would happen on reanimation, and whether we could hope for a revival of mind and reason, West did not venture to predict. The experiment would be a landmark in our studies, and he had saved the new body for my return, so that both might share the spectacle in accustomed fashion.

West told me how he had obtained the specimen. It had been a vigorous man; a well-dressed stranger just off the train on his way to transact some business with the Bolton Worsted Mills. The walk through the town had been long, and by the time the traveller paused at our cottage to ask the way to the factories his heart had become greatly overtaxed. He had refused a stimulant, and had suddenly dropped dead only a moment later. The body, as might be expected, seemed to West a heaven-sent gift. In his brief conversation the stranger had made it clear that he was unknown in Bolton, and a search of his pockets subsequently revealed him to be one Robert Leavitt of St Louis, apparently without a family to make inquiries about his disappearance. If this man could not be restored to life, no one would know of our experiment. We buried our materials in a dense strip of woods between the house and the potter's field. If, on the other hand, he could be restored, our fame would be brilliantly and perpetually established. So without delay West had injected into the body's wrist the compound which would hold it fresh for use after my arrival. The matter of the presumably weak heart, which to my mind imperilled the success of our experiment, did not appear to trouble West extensively. He hoped at last to obtain what he had never obtained before – a rekindled spark of reason and perhaps a normal, living creature.

So on the night of July 18, 1910, Herbert West and I stood in the cellar laboratory and gazed at a white, silent figure beneath the dazzling arc-light. The embalming compound had worked uncannily well, for as I stared fascinatedly at the sturdy frame which had lain two weeks without stiffening I was moved to seek West's assurance that the thing was really dead. This assurance he gave readily enough; reminding me that the reanimating solution was never used without careful tests as to life; since it could have no effect if any of the original vitality were present. As West proceeded to take preliminary steps, I was impressed by the vast intricacy of the new experiment; an intricacy so vast that he could trust no hand less delicate than his own. Forbidding me to touch the body, he first injected a drug in the wrist just beside the place his needle had punctured when injecting the embalming compound. This, he said, was to neutralize the compound and release the system to a normal relaxation so that the reanimating solution might freely work when injected. Slightly later, when a change and a gentle tremor seemed to affect the dead limbs, West stuffed a pillow-like object violently over the twitching face, not withdrawing it until the corpse appeared quiet and ready for our attempt at reanimation. The pale enthusiast now applied some last perfunctory tests for absolute lifelessness, withdrew satisfied, and finally injected into the left arm an accurately measured amount of the vital elixir, prepared during the afternoon with a greater care than we had used since college days, when our feats were new and groping. I cannot express the wild, breathless suspense with which we waited for results on this first really fresh specimen – the first we could reasonably expect to open its lips in rational speech, perhaps to tell of what it had seen beyond the unfathomable abyss.

West was a materialist, believing in no soul and attributing all the working of consciousness to bodily phenomena;

consequently he looked for no revelation of hideous secrets from gulfs and caverns beyond death's barrier. I did not wholly disagree with him theoretically, yet held vague instinctive remnants of the primitive faith of my forefathers; so that I could not help eyeing the corpse with a certain amount of awe and terrible expectation. Besides – I could not extract from my memory that hideous, inhuman shriek we heard on the night we tried our first experiment in the deserted farmhouse at Arkham.

Very little time had elapsed before I saw the attempt was not to be a total failure. A touch of colour came to cheeks hitherto chalk-white, and spread out under the curiously ample stubble of sandy beard. West, who had his hand on the pulse of the left wrist, suddenly nodded significantly; and almost simultaneously a mist appeared on the mirror inclined above the body's mouth. There followed a few spasmodic muscular motions, and then an audible breathing and visible motion of the chest. I looked at the closed eyelids, and thought I detected a quivering. Then the lids opened, showing eyes which were grey, calm, and alive, but still unintelligent and not even curious.

In a moment of fantastic whim I whispered questions to the reddening ears; questions of other worlds of which the memory might still be present. Subsequent terror drove them from my mind, but I think the last one, which I repeated, was: 'Where have you been?' I do not yet know whether I was answered or not, for no sound came from the well-shaped mouth; but I do know that at that moment I firmly thought the thin lips moved silently, forming syllables which I would have vocalised as 'only now' if that phrase had possessed any sense or relevance. At that moment, as I say, I was elated with the conviction that the one great goal had been attained; and that for the first time a reanimated corpse had uttered distinct words impelled by actual reason. In the next moment there was no doubt about the triumph; no doubt that the solution had truly accomplished, at least temporarily, its full mission of restoring rational and articulate life to the dead. But in that triumph there came to me the greatest of all horrors – not horror of the thing that spoke, but of the deed that I had witnessed and of the man with whom my professional fortunes were joined.

For that very fresh body, at last writhing into full and terrifying consciousness with eyes dilated at the memory of its last scene on earth, threw out its frantic hands in a life and death struggle with the air; and suddenly collapsing into a second and final dissolution from which there could be no return, screamed out the cry that will ring eternally in my aching brain:

'Help! Keep off, you cursed little tow-head fiend – keep that damned needle away from me!'

## V. THE HORROR FROM THE SHADOWS

Many men have related hideous things, not mentioned in print, which happened on the battlefields of the Great War. Some of these things have made me faint, others have convulsed me with devastating nausea, while still others have made me tremble and look behind me in the dark; yet despite the worst of them I believe I can relate the most hideous thing of all – the shocking, the unnatural, the unbelievable horror from the shadows.

In 1915 I was a physician with the rank of First Lieutenant in a Canadian regiment in Flanders, one of many Americans to precede the government itself into the gigantic struggle. I had not entered the army on my initiative, but rather as a natural result of the enlistment of the man whose indispensable assistant I was – the celebrated Boston surgical specialist, Dr Herbert West. Dr West had been avid for a chance to serve as surgeon in a great war, and when the chance had come he carried me with him almost against my will. There were reasons why I would have been glad to let the war separate us; reasons why I found the practice of medicine and the companionship of West more and more irritating; but when he had gone to Ottawa and through a colleague's influence secured a medical commission as Major, I could not resist the imperious persuasion of one determined that I should accompany him in my usual capacity.

When I say that Dr West was avid to serve in battle, I do not mean to imply that he was either naturally warlike or anxious for the safety of civilization. Always an ice-cold intellectual machine: slight, blond, blue-eyed, and spectacled:

I think he secretly sneered at my occasional martial enthusiasms and censures of supine neutrality. There was, however,
something he wanted in embattled Flanders; and in order to
secure it he had to assume a military exterior. What he
wanted was not a thing which many persons want, but
something connected with the peculiar branch of medical
science which he had chosen quite clandestinely to follow,
and in which he had achieved amazing and occasionally
hideous results. It was, in fact, nothing more or less than an
abundant supply of freshly killed men in every stage of
dismemberment.

Herbert West needed fresh bodies because his life-work was
the reanimation of the dead. This work was not known to the
fashionable clientele who had so swiftly built up his fame
after his arrival in Boston; but was only too well known to
me, who had been his closest friend and sole assistant since
the old days in Miskatonic University medical school at
Arkham. It was in those college days that he had begun his
terrible experiments, first on small animals and then on human
bodies shockingly obtained. There was a solution which he
injected into the veins of dead things, and if they were fresh
enough they responded in strange ways. He had had much
trouble in discovering the proper formula, for each type of
organism was found to need a stimulus especially adapted to
it. Terror stalked him when he reflected on his partial failures;
nameless things resulting from imperfect solutions or from
bodies insufficiently fresh. A certain number of these failures
had remained alive – one was in an asylum while others had
vanished – and as he thought of conceivable yet virtually
impossible eventualities he often shivered beneath his usual
stolidity.

West had soon learned that absolute freshness was the
prime requisite for useful specimens, and had accordingly
resorted to frightful and unnatural expedients in body-snatch-
ing. In college, and during our early practice together in the
factory town of Bolton, my attitude toward him had been
largely one of fascinated admiration; but as his boldness in
methods grew, I began to develop a gnawing fear. I did not
like the way he looked at healthy living bodies; and then
there came a nightmarish session in the cellar laboratory
when I learned that a certain specimen had been a living body

when he secured it. That was the first time he had ever been able to revive the quality of rational thought in a corpse; and his success, obtained at such a loathsome cost, had completely hardened him.

Of his methods in the intervening five years I dare not speak. I was held to him by sheer force of fear, and witnessed sights that no human tongue could repeat. Gradually I came to find Herbert West himself more horrible than anything he did – that was when it dawned on me that his once normal scientific zeal for prolonging life had subtly degenerated into a mere morbid and ghoulish curiosity and secret sense of charnel picturesqueness. His interest became a hellish and perverse addiction to the repellently and fiendishly abnormal; he gloated calmly over artificial monstrosities which would make most healthy men drop dead from fright and disgust; he became, behind his pallid intellectuality, a fastidious Baudelaire of physical experiment – a languid Elagabalus of the tombs.

Dangers he met unflinchingly; crimes he committed un-moved. I think the climax came when he had proved his point that rational life can be restored, and had sought new worlds to conquer by experimenting on the reanimation of detached parts of bodies. He had wild and original ideas on the independent vital properties of organic cells and nerve tissue separated from natural physiological systems; and achieved some hideous preliminary results in the form of never-dying, artificially nourished tissue obtained from the nearly-hatched eggs of an indescribable tropical reptile. Two biological points he was exceedingly anxious to settle – first, whether any amount of consciousness and rational action might be possible without the brain, proceeding from the spinal cord and various nerve-centres; and second, whether any kind of ethereal, intangible relation distinct from the material cells may exist to link the surgically separated parts of what has previously been a single living organism. All this research work required a prodigious supply of freshly slaughtered human flesh – and that was why Herbert West had entered the Great War.

The phantasmal, unmentionable thing occurred one mid-night late in March, 1915, in a field hospital behind the lines at St Eloi. I wonder even now if it could have been other than a demoniac dream of delirium. West had a private laboratory in an east room of the barn-like temporary edifice, assigned him on his plea that he was devising new and radical methods for the treatment of hitherto hopeless cases of maiming. There he worked like a butcher in the midst of his gory wares – I could never get used to the levity with which he handled and classified certain things. At times he actually did perform marvels of surgery for the soldiers; but his chief delights were of a less public and philanthropic kind, requiring many explanations of sounds which seemed peculiar even amidst that babel of the damned. Among these sounds were frequent revolver-shots – surely not uncommon on a battlefield, but distinctly uncommon in a hospital. Dr West's reanimated specimens were not meant for long existence or a large audience. Besides human tissue, West employed much of the reptile embryo tissue which he had cultivated with such singular results. It was better than human material for maintaining life in organless fragments, and that was now my friend's chief activity. In a dark corner of the laboratory, over a queer incubating burner, he kept a large covered vat full of this reptilian cell-matter; which multiplied and grew puffily and hideously.

On the night of which I speak we had a splendid new specimen – a man at once physically powerful and of such high mentality that a sensitive nervous system was assured. It was rather ironic, for he was the officer who had helped West to his commission, and who was now to have been our associate. Moreover, he had in the past secretly studied the theory of reanimation to some extent under West. Major Sir Eric Moreland Clapham-Lee, D.S.O., was the greatest surgeon in our division, and had been hastily assigned to the St Eloi sector when news of the heavy fighting reached headquarters. He had come in an aeroplane piloted by the intrepid Lieutenant Ronald Hill, only to be shot down when directly over his destination. The fall had been spectacular and awful; Hill was unrecognizable afterwards, but the wreck yielded up the great surgeon in a nearly decapitated but otherwise intact condition. West had greedily seized the lifeless thing which had once been his friend and fellow-scholar; and I shuddered when he finished severing the head, placed it in his hellish vat of pulpy reptile-tissue to preserve it for future experiments, and proceeded to treat the decapitated body on the operating table. He injected new blood, joined certain veins, arteries, and nerves at the headless neck, and closed the ghastly aperture with engrafted skin from an unidentified specimen which had borne an officer's uniform. I knew what he wanted – to see if this highly organized body could exhibit, without its head, any of the signs of mental life which had distinguished Sir Eric Moreland Clapham-Lee. Once a student of reanimation, this silent trunk was now gruesomely called upon to exemplify it.

I can still see Herbert West under the sinister electric light as he injected his reanimating solution into the arm of the headless body. The scene I cannot describe – I should faint if I tried it, for there is madness in a room full of classified charnel things, with blood and lesser human debris almost ankle-deep on the slimy floor, and with hideous reptilian abnormalities sprouting, bubbling, and baking over a winking bluish-green spectre of dim flame in a far corner of black shadows.

The specimen, as West repeatedly observed, had a splendid nervous system. Much was expected of it; and as a few twitching motions began to appear, I could see the feverish interest on West's face. He was ready, I think, to see proof of his increasingly strong opinion that consciousness, reason, and personality can exist independently of the brain – that man has no central connective spirit, but is merely a machine of nervous matter, each section more or less complete in itself. In one triumphant demonstration West was about to relegate the mystery of life to the category of myth. The body now twitched more vigorously, and beneath our avid eyes commenced to heave in a frightful way. The arms stirred disquietingly, the legs drew up, and various muscles contracted in a repulsive kind of writhing. Then the headless thing threw out its arms in a gesture which was unmistakably one of desperation – an intelligent desperation apparently sufficient to prove every theory of Herbert West. Certainly, the nerves were recalling the man's last act in life; the struggle to get free of the falling aeroplane.

What followed, I shall never positively know. It may have been wholly an hallucination from the shock caused at that instant by the sudden and complete destruction of the building in a cataclysm of German shell-fire – who can gainsay it, since

West and I were the only proved survivors? West liked to think that before his recent disappearance, but there were times when he could not; for it was queer that we both had the same hallucination. The hideous occurrence itself was very simple, notable only for what it implied.

The body on the table had risen with a blind and terrible groping, and we had heard a sound. I should not call that sound a voice, for it was too awful. And yet its timbre was not the most awful thing about it. Neither was its message – it had merely screamed, 'Jump, Ronald, for God's sake, jump!' The awful thing was its source.

For it had come from the large covered vat in that ghoulish corner of crawling black shadows.


## VI. THE TOMB-LEGIONS

When Dr Herbert West disappeared a year ago, the Boston police questioned me closely. They suspected that I was holding something back, and perhaps suspected even graver things; but I could not tell them the truth because they would not have believed it. They knew, indeed, that West had been connected with activities beyond the credence of ordinary men; for his hideous experiments in the reanimation of dead bodies had long been too extensive to admit of perfect secrecy; but the final soul-shattering catastrophe held elements of demoniac phantasy which make even me doubt the reality of what I saw.

I was West's closest friend and only confidential assistant. We had met years before, in medical school, and from the first I had shared his terrible researches. He had slowly tried to perfect a solution which, injected into the veins of the newly deceased, would restore life; a labour demanding an abundance of fresh corpses and therefore involving the most unnatural actions. Still more shocking were the products of some of the experiments – grisly masses of flesh that had been dead, but that West waked to a blind, brainless, nauseous animation. These were the usual results, for in order to reawaken the mind it was necessary to have specimens so absolutely fresh that no decay could possibly affect the delicate brain cells.

This need for very fresh corpses had been West's moral undoing. They were hard to get, and one awful day he had secured his specimen while it was still alive and vigorous. A struggle, a needle, and a powerful alkaloid had transformed it to a very fresh corpse, and the experiment had succeeded for a brief and memorable moment; but West had emerged with a soul calloused and seared, and a hardened eye which sometimes glanced with a kind of hideous and calculating appraisal at men of especially sensitive brain and especially vigorous physique. Toward the last I became acutely afraid of West, for he began to look at me that way. People did not seem to notice his glances, but they noticed my fear; and after his disappearance used that as a basis for some absurd suspicions.

West, in reality, was more afraid than I; for his abominable pursuits entailed a life of furtiveness and dread of every shadow. Partly it was the police he feared; but sometimes his nervousness was deeper and more nebulous, touching on certain indescribable things into which he had injected a morbid life, and from which he had not seen that life depart. He usually finished his experiments with a revolver, but a few times he had not been quick enough. There was that first specimen on whose rifled grave marks of clawing were later seen. There was also that Arkham professor's body which had done cannibal things before it had been captured and thrust unidentified into a madhouse cell at Sefton, where it beat the walls for sixteen years. Most of the other possibly surviving results were things less easy to speak of – for in later years West's scientific zeal had degenerated to an unhealthy and fantastic mania, and he had spent his chief skill in vitalizing not entire human bodies but isolated parts of bodies, or parts joined to organic matter other than human. It had become fiendishly disgusting by the time he disappeared; many of the experiments could not even be hinted at in print. The Great War, through which both of us served as surgeons, had intensified this side of West.

In saying that West's fear of his specimens was nebulous, I have in mind particularly its complex nature. Part of it came merely from knowing of the existence of such nameless monsters, while another part arose from apprehension of the bodily harm they might under certain circumstances do him. Their disappearance added horror to the situation – of them all West knew the whereabouts of only one, the pitiful asylum thing. Then there was a more subtle fear – a very fantastic sensation resulting from a curious experiment in the Canadian army in 1915. West, in the midst of a severe battle, had reanimated Major Sir Eric Moreland Clapham-Lee, D.S.O., a fellow-physician who knew about his experiments and could have duplicated them. The head had been removed, so that the possibilities of quasi-intelligent life in the trunk might be investigated. Just as the building was wiped out by a German shell, there had been a success. The trunk had moved intelligently; and, unbelievable to relate, we were both sickeningly sure that articulate sounds had come from the detached head as it lay in a shadowy corner of the laboratory. The shell had been merciful, in a way – but West could never feel as certain as he wished, that we two were the only survivors. He used to make shuddering conjectures about the possible actions of a headless physician with the power of reanimating the dead.

West's last quarters were in a venerable house of much elegance, overlooking one of the oldest burying grounds in Boston. He had chosen the place for purely symbolic and fantastically aesthetic reasons, since most of the interments were of the Colonial period and therefore of little use to a scientist seeking very fresh bodies. The laboratory was in a sub-cellar secretly constructed by imported workmen, and contained a huge incinerator for the quiet and complete disposal of such bodies, or fragments and synthetic mockeries of bodies, as might remain from the morbid experiments and unhallowed amusements of the owner. During the excavation of this cellar the workmen had struck some exceedingly ancient masonry; undoubtedly connected with the old burying ground, yet far too deep to correspond with any known sepulchre therein. After a number of calculations West decided that it represented some secret chamber beneath the tomb of the Averills, where the last interment had been made in 1768. I was with him when he studied the nitrous, dripping walls laid bare by the spades and mattocks of the men, and was prepared for the gruesome thrill which would attend the uncovering of centuried grave-secrets; but for the first time West's new timidity conquered his natural curiosity, and he betrayed his degenerating fibre by ordering the masonry left intact and plastered over. Thus it remained till that final hellish night, part of the walls of the secret laboratory. I speak of West's decadence, but must add that it was a purely mental and intangible thing. Outwardly he was the same to the last – calm, cold, slight, and yellow-haired, with spectacled blue eyes and a general aspect of youth which years and fears seemed never to change. He seemed calm even when he thought of that clawed grave and looked over his shoulder; even when he thought of the carnivorous thing that gnawed and pawed at Sefton bars.

The end of Herbert West began one evening in our joint study when he was dividing his curious glance between the newspaper and me. A strange headline item had struck at him from the crumpled pages, and a nameless titan claw had seemed to reach down through sixteen years. Something fearsome and incredible had happened at Sefton Asylum fifty miles away, stunning the neighbourhood and baffling the police. In the small hours of the morning a body of silent men had entered the grounds and their leader had aroused the attendants. He was a menacing military figure who talked without moving his lips and whose voice seemed almost ventriloquially connected with an immense black case he carried. His expressionless face was handsome to the point of radiant beauty, but had shocked the superintendent when the hall light fell on it – for it was a wax face with eyes of painted glass. Some nameless accident had befallen this man. A larger man guided his steps; a repellent hulk whose bluish face seemed half eaten away by some unknown malady. The speaker had asked for the custody of the cannibal monster committed from Arkham sixteen years before; and upon being refused, gave a signal which precipitated a shocking riot. The fiends had beaten, trampled, and bitten every attendant who did not flee; killing four and finally succeeding in the liberation of the monster. These victims who could recall the event without hysteria swore that the creatures had acted less like men than like unthinkable automata guided by the wax-faced leader. By the time help could be summoned, every trace of the men and of their mad charge had vanished.

From the hour of reading this item until midnight, West sat almost paralysed. At midnight the doorbell rang, startling him fearfully. All the servants were asleep in the attic, so I answered the bell. As I have told the police, there was no wagon in the street; but only a group of strange-looking figures bearing a large square box which they deposited in the hallway after one of them had grunted in a highly unnatural voice, 'Express – prepaid.' They filed out of the house with a jerky tread, and as I watched them go I had an odd idea that they were turning towards the ancient cemetery on which the back of the house abutted. When I slammed the door after them West came downstairs and looked at the box. It was about two feet square, and bore West's correct name and present address. It also bore the inscription, 'From Eric Moreland Clapham-Lee, St Eloi, Flanders.' Six years before, in Flanders, a shelled hospital had fallen upon the headless reanimated trunk of Dr Clapham-Lee, and upon the detached head which – perhaps – had uttered articulate sounds.

West was not even excited now. His condition was more ghastly. Quickly he said, 'It's the finish – but let's incinerate – this.' We carried the thing down to the laboratory – listening. I do not remember many particulars – you can imagine my state of mind – but it is a vicious lie to say it was Herbert West's body which I put into the incinerator. We both inserted the whole unopened box, closed the door, and started the electricity. Nor did any sound come from the box, after all.

It was West who first noticed the falling plaster on that part of the wall where the ancient tomb masonry had been covered up. I was going to run, but he stopped me. Then I saw a small black aperture, felt a ghoulish wind of ice, and smelled the charnel bowels of a putrescent earth. There was no sound, but just then the electric lights went out and I saw outlined against some phosphorescence of the nether world a horde of silent toiling things which only insanity – or worse – could create. Their outlines were human, semi-human, fractionally human, and not human at all – the horde was grotesquely heterogeneous. They were removing the stones quietly, one by one, from the centuried wall. And then, as the breach became large enough, they came out into the laboratory in a single file; led by a stalking thing with a beautiful head made of wax. A sort of mad-eyed monstrosity behind the leader seized on Herbert West. West did not resist or utter a sound. Then they all sprang at him and tore him to pieces before my eyes, bearing the fragments away into that subterranean vault of fabulous abominations. West's head was carried off by the wax-headed leader, who wore a Canadian officer's uniform. As it disappeared I saw that the blue eyes behind the spectacles were hideously blazing with their first touch of frantic, visible emotion.

Servants found me unconscious in the morning. West was gone. The incinerator contained only unidentifiable ashes. Detectives have questioned me, but what can I say? The Sefton tragedy they will not connect with West; not that, nor the men with the box, whose existence they deny. I told them of the vault, and they pointed to the unbroken plaster wall and laughed. So I told them no more. They imply that I am either a madman or a murderer – probably I am mad. But I might not be mad if those accursed tomb-legions had not been so silent.

# Transformation

## By MARY SHELLEY

With the launching of the latest version of Frankenstein
starring Kenneth Branagh and Robert De Niro, there are signs
that the cycle of pictures which began with Universal and
were repeated by Hammer, are now about to occur all over
again. Already Britain's Channel 4 has presented their interpretation of Frankenstein with Frank Rozelaar-Green as the
creature; while in America, Universal have announced plans
to remake The Bride of Frankenstein, and Arnold Schwarzeneg-
ger is at work on his own version of the novel with the
emphasis on the creature's viewpoint. This picture is to be
directed by Tim Burton, highly regarded for Batman and
Edward Scissorhands, the not-too-dissimilar story about an
obsessed 'inventor' (played with relish by The late Vincent
Price) and his unfortunate creation (Johnny Depp). Hammer
are also considering a new version of their Revenge of Frankenstein, the film in which the scientist repaid the dwarf who had
helped him escape the guillotine by providing him with a new
body . . .

With the exception of the last project, all of these ideas
draw on Mary Shelley's original novel. Revenge of Frankenstein, on the other hand, actually owes its inspiration to a
short story by Mary called Transformation which she published in an anthology, The Keepsake, in 1830. In her tale the
positions of the main protagonists are reversed with a handsome young man exchanging his body for that of a deformed
dwarf – but the parallels are quite clear. Although the story
is undoubtedly a variation on the Frankenstein theme, it is
also believed to have been partly inspired by an incomplete
drama by Lord Byron, The Deformed Transformed, which he
was working on before his death and parts of which Mary

*transcribed. In Byron's tale, a hunchback named Arnold received a new body from a diabolical stranger, who then assumed the old, deformed body and dogged the hero's footsteps as a kind of doppelgänger. Therefore by reversing Mary Shelley's version, the Hammer film in effect went back to one of its sources! Here is that story which is likely to be once again involved in ensuring the continuation of the Frankenstein -in-the-movies tradition ...*

I have heard it said, that, when any strange, supernatural, and necromantic adventure has occurred to a human being, that being, however desirous he may be to conceal the same, feels at certain periods torn up as it were by an intellectual earthquake, and is forced to bare the inner depths of his spirit to another. I am a witness of the truth of this. I have dearly sworn to myself never to reveal to human ears the horrors to which I once, in excess of fiendly pride, delivered myself over. The holy man who heard my confession, and reconciled me to the Church, is dead. None knows that once –

Why should it not be thus? Why tell a tale of impious tempting of Providence, and soul-subduing humiliation? Why? answer me, ye who are wise in the secrets of human nature! I only know that so it is; and in spite of strong resolve, – of a pride that too much masters me – of shame, and even of fear, so to render myself odious to my species – I must speak.

Genoa! my birthplace – proud city! looking upon the blue Mediterranean – dost thou remember me in my boyhood, when thy cliffs and promontories, thy bright sky and gay vineyards, were my world? Happy time! when to the young heart the narrow-bounded universe, which leaves, by its very limitation, free scope to the imagination, enchains our physical energies, and, sole period in our lives, innocence and enjoyment are united. Yet, who can look back to childhood, and not remember its sorrows and its harrowing fears? I was born with the most imperious, haughty, tameless spirit. I quailed before my father only; and he, generous and noble, but capricious and tyrannical, at once fostered and checked the wild impetuosity of my character, making obedience necessary, but inspiring no respect for the motives which guided his commands. To be a man, free, independent; or, in better words, insolent and domineering, was the hope and prayer of my rebel heart.

My father had one friend, a wealthy Genoese noble, who in a political tumult was suddenly sentenced to banishment, and his property confiscated. The Marchese Torella went into exile alone. Like my father, he was a widower: he had one child, the almost infant Juliet, who was left under my father's guardianship. I should certainly have been unkind to the lovely girl, but that I was forced by my position to become her protector. A variety of childish incidents all tended to one point, – to make Juliet see in me a rock of defence; I in her, one who must perish through the soft sensibility of her nature too rudely visited, but for my guardian care. We grew up together. The opening rose in May was not more sweet than this dear girl. An irradiation of beauty was spread over her face. Her form, her step, her voice – my heart weeps even now, to think of all of relying, gentle, loving, and pure, that she enshrined. When I was eleven and Juliet eight years of age, a cousin of mine, much older than either – he seemed to us a man – took great notice of my playmate; he called her his bride, and asked her to marry him. She refused, and he insisted, drawing her unwillingly towards him. With the countenance and emotions of a maniac I threw myself on him – I strove to draw his sword – I clung to his neck with the ferocious resolve to strangle him: he was obliged to call for assistance to disengage himself from me. On that night I led Juliet to the chapel of our house: I made her touch the sacred relics – I harrowed her child's heart, and profaned her child's lips with an oath, that she would be mine, and mine only.

Well, those days passed away. Torella returned in a few years, and became wealthier and more prosperous than ever. When I was seventeen, my father died; he had been magnificent to prodigality; Torella rejoiced that my minority would afford an opportunity for repairing my fortunes. Juliet and I had been affianced beside my father's deathbed – Torella was to be a second parent to me.

I desired to see the world, and I was indulged. I went to

Florence, to Rome, to Naples; thence I passed to Toulon, and at length reached what had long been the bourne of my wishes, Paris. There was wild work in Paris then. The poor king, Charles the Sixth, now sane, now mad, now a monarch, now an abject slave, was the very mockery of humanity. The queen, the dauphin, the Duke of Burgundy, alternately friends and foes – now meeting in prodigal feasts, now shedding blood in rivalry – were blind to the miserable state of their country, and the dangers that impended over it, and gave themselves wholly up to dissolute enjoyment or savage strife. My character still followed me. I was arrogant and self-willed; I loved display, and above all, I threw off all control. My young friends were eager to foster passions which furnished them with pleasures. I was deemed handsome – I was master of every knightly accomplishment. I was disconnected with any political party. I grew a favourite with all: my presumption and arrogance was pardoned in one so young: I became a spoiled child. Who could control me? not the letters and advice of Torella – only strong necessity visiting me in the abhorred shape of an empty purse. But there were means to refill this void. Acre after acre, estate after estate, I sold. My dress, my jewels, my horses and their caparisons, were almost unrivalled in gorgeous Paris, while the lands of my inheritance passed into possession of others.

The Duke of Orleans was waylaid and murdered by the Duke of Burgundy. Fear and terror possessed all Paris. The dauphin and the queen shut themselves up; every pleasure was suspended. I grew weary of this state of things, and my heart yearned for my boyhood's haunts. I was nearly a beggar, yet still I would go there, claim my bride, and rebuild my fortunes. A few happy ventures as a merchant would make me rich again. Nevertheless, I would not return in humble guise. My last act was to dispose of my remaining estate near Albaro for half its worth, for ready money. Then I despatched all kinds of artificers, arras, furniture of regal splendour, to fit up the last relic of my inheritance, my palace in Genoa. I lingered a little longer yet, ashamed at the part of the prodigal returned, which I feared I should play. I sent my horses. One matchless Spanish jennet I despatched to my promised bride: its caparisons flamed with jewels and cloth of gold. In every part I caused to be entwined the initials of Juliet and her

Guido. My present found favour in her and in her father's eyes.

Still to return a proclaimed spendthrift, the mark of impertinent wonder, perhaps of scorn, and to encounter singly the reproaches or taunts of my fellow-citizens, was no alluring prospect. As a shield between me and censure, I invited some few of the most reckless of my comrades to accompany me: thus I went armed against the world, hiding a rankling feeling, half fear and half penitence, by bravado.

I arrived in Genoa. I trod the pavement of my ancestral palace. My proud step was no interpreter of my heart, for I deeply felt that, though surrounded by every luxury, I was a beggar. The first step I took in claiming Juliet must widely declare me such. I read contempt or pity in the looks of all. I fancied that rich and poor, young and old, all regarded me with derision. Torella came not near me. No wonder that my second father should expect a son's deference from me in waiting first on him. But, galled and stung by a sense of my follies and demerit, I strove to throw the blame on others. We kept nightly orgies in Palazzo Carega. To sleepless, riotous nights followed listless, supine mornings. At the Ave Maria we showed our dainty persons in the streets, scoffing at the sober citizens, casting insolent glances on the shrinking women. Juliet was not among them – no, no; if she had been there, shame would have driven me away, if love had not brought me to her feet.

I grew tired of this. Suddenly I paid the Marchese a visit. He was at his villa, one among the many which deck the suburb of San Pietro d'Arena. It was the month of May, the blossoms of the fruit-trees were fading among thick, green foliage; the vines were shooting forth; the ground strewed with the fallen olive blooms; the firefly was in the myrtle hedge; heaven and earth wore a mantle of surpassing beauty. Torella welcomed me kindly, though seriously; and even his shade of displeasure soon wore away. Some resemblance to my father – some look and tone of youthful ingenuousness, softened the good old man's heart. He sent for his daughter – he presented me to her as her betrothed. The chamber became hallowed by a holy light as she entered. Hers was that cherub look, those large, soft eyes, full dimpled cheeks, and mouth of infantine sweetness, that expresses the rare union of happiness and love. Admiration first possessed me; she is mine! was the second proud emotion, and my lips curled with haughty triumph. I had not been the *enfant gâté* of the beauties of France not to have learnt the art of pleasing the soft heart of woman. If towards men I was overbearing, the deference I paid to them was the more in contrast. I commenced my courtship by the display of a thousand gallantries to Juliet, who, vowed to me from infancy, had never admitted the devotion of others; and who, though accustomed to expressions of admiration, was uninitiated in the language of lovers.

For a few days all went well. Torella never alluded to my extravagance; he treated me as a favourite son. But the time came, as we discussed the preliminaries to my union with his daughter, when this fair face of things should be overcast. A contract had been drawn up in my father's lifetime. I had rendered this, in fact, void by having squandered the whole of the wealth which was to have been shared by Juliet and myself. Torella, in consequence, chose to consider this bond as cancelled, and proposed another, in which, though the wealth he bestowed was immeasurably increased, there were so many restrictions as to the mode of spending it, that I, who saw independence only in free career being given to my own imperious will, taunted him as taking advantage of my situation, and refused utterly to subscribe to his conditions. The old man mildly strove to recall me to reason. Roused pride became the tyrant of my thought: I listened with indignation – I repelled him with disdain.

'Juliet, thou art mine! Did we not interchange vows in our innocent childhood? Are we not one in the sight of God? and shall thy cold-hearted, cold-blooded father divide us? Be generous, my love, be just; take not away a gift, last treasure of thy Guido – retract not thy vows – let us defy the world, and, setting at nought the calculations of age, find in our mutual affection a refuge from every ill.'

Fiend I must have been with such sophistry to endeavour to poison that sanctuary of holy thought and tender love. Juliet shrank from me affrighted. Her father was the best and kindest of men, and she strove to show me how, in obeying him, every good would follow. He would receive my tardy submission with warm affection, and generous pardon would follow my repentance; – profitless words for a young and gentle daughter to use to a man accustomed to make his will law, and to feel in his own heart a despot so terrible and stern that he could yield obedience to nought save his own imperious desires! My resentment grew with resistance; my wild companions were ready to add fuel to the flame. We laid a plan to carry off Juliet. At first it appeared to be crowned with success. Midway, on our return, we were overtaken by the agonized father and his attendants. A conflict ensued. Before the city guard came to decide the victory in favour of our antagonists, two of Torella's servitors were dangerously wounded.

This portion of my history weighs most heavily with me. Changed man as I am, I abhor myself in the recollection. May none who hear this tale ever have felt as I. A horse driven to fury by a rider armed with barbed spurs was not more a slave than I to the violent tyranny of my temper. A fiend possessed my soul, irritating it to madness. I felt the voice of conscience within me; but if I yielded to it for a brief interval, it was only to be a moment after torn, as by a whirlwind, away – borne along on the stream of desperate rage – the plaything of the storms engendered by pride. I was imprisoned, and, at the instance of Torella, set free. Again I returned to carry off both him and his child to France, which hapless country, then preyed on by free-booters and gangs of lawless soldiery, offered a grateful refuge to a criminal like me. Our plots were discovered. I was sentenced to banishment; and, as my debts were already enormous, my remaining property was put in the hands of commissioners for their payment. Torella again offered his mediation, requiring only my promise not to renew my abortive attempts on himself and his daughter. I spurned his offers, and fancied that I triumphed when I was thrust out from Genoa, a solitary and penniless exile. My companions were gone: they had been dismissed the city some weeks before, and were already in France. I was alone – friendless, with neither sword at my side, nor ducat in my purse.

I wandered along the sea-shore, a whirlwind of passion possessing and tearing my soul. It was as if a live coal had been set burning in my breast. At first I meditated on what *I should do*. I would join a band of freebooters. Revenge! – the word seemed balm to me; I hugged it, caressed it, till, like a serpent, it stung me. Then again I would abjure and despise Genoa, that little corner of the world. I would return to Paris, where so many of my friends swarmed; where my services would be eagerly accepted; where I would carve out fortune with my sword, and make my paltry birthplace and the false Torella rue the day when they drove me, a new Coriolanus, from her walls. I would return to Paris – thus on foot – a beggar – and present myself in my poverty to those I had formerly entertained sumptuously? There was gall in the mere thought of it.

The reality of things began to dawn upon my mind, bringing despair in its train. For several months I had been a prisoner: the evils of my dungeon had whipped my soul to madness, but they had subdued my corporeal frame. I was weak and wan. Torella had used a thousand artifices to administer to my comfort; I had detected and scorned them all, and I reaped the harvest of my obduracy. What was to be done? Should I crouch before my foe, and sue for forgiveness? – Die rather ten thousand deaths! – Never should they obtain that victory! Hate – I swore eternal hate! Hate from whom? – to whom? – From a wandering outcast – to a mighty noble! I and my feelings were nothing to them: already had they forgotten one so unworthy. And Juliet! – her angel face and sylph-like form gleamed among the clouds of my despair with vain beauty; for I had lost her – the glory and flower of the world! Another will call her his! – that smile of paradise will bless another!

Even now my heart fails within me when I recur to this rout of grim-visaged ideas. Now subdued almost to tears, now raving in my agony, still I wandered along the rocky shore, which grew at each step wilder and more desolate. Hanging rocks and hoar precipices overlooked the tideless ocean; black caverns yawned; and for ever, among the sea-worn recesses, murmured and dashed the unfruitful waters. Now my way was almost barred by an abrupt promontory, now rendered nearly impracticable by fragments fallen from the cliff. Evening was at hand, when, seaward, arose, as if on the waving of a wizard's wand, a murky web of clouds, blotting the late azure sky, and darkening and disturbing the till now placid deep. The clouds had strange, fantastic shapes, and they changed and mingled and seemed to be driven about by a mighty spell. The waves raised their white crests; the thunder first muttered, then roared from across the waste of waters, which took a deep purple dye, flecked with foam. The spot where I stood looked, on one side, to the wide-spread ocean; on the other, it was barred by a rugged promontory. Round this cape suddenly came, driven by the wind, a vessel. In vain the mariners tried to force a path for her to the open sea – the gale drove her on the rocks. It will perish! – all on board will perish! Would I were among them! And to my young heart the idea of death came for the first time blended with that of joy. It was an awful sight to behold that vessel struggling with her fate. Hardly could I discern the sailors, but I heard them. It was soon all over! A rock, just covered by the tossing waves, and so unperceived, lay in wait for its prey. A crash of thunder broke over my head at the moment that, with a frightful shock, the vessel dashed upon her unseen enemy. In a brief space of time she went to pieces. There I stood in safety; and there were my fellow-creatures battling, how hopelessly, with annihilation. Methought I saw them struggling – too truly did I hear their shrieks, conquering the barking surges in their shrill agony. The dark breakers threw hither and thither the fragments of the wreck: soon it disappeared. I had been fascinated to gaze till the end: at last I sank on my knees – I covered my face with my hands. I again looked up; something was floating on the billows towards the shore. It neared and neared. Was that a human form? It grew more and more distinct; and at last a mighty wave, lifting the whole freight, lodged it upon a rock. A human being bestriding a sea-chest! – a human being! Yet was it one? Surely never such had existed before – a misshapen dwarf, with squinting eyes, distorted features, and body deformed, till it became a horror to behold. My blood, lately warming towards a fellow-being so snatched from a watery tomb, froze in my heart. The dwarf got off his chest; he tossed his straight, straggling hair from his odious visage.

'By St Beelzebub!' he exclaimed, 'I have been well bested.' He looked round and saw me. 'Oh, by the fiend! here is another ally of the mighty One. To what saint did you offer prayers, friend – if not to mine? Yet I remember you not on board.'

I shrank from the monster and his blasphemy. Again he

questioned me, and I muttered some inaudible reply. He continued: –

'Your voice is drowned by this dissonant roar. What a noise the big ocean makes! Schoolboys bursting from their prison are not louder than these waves set free to play. They disturb me. I will no more of their ill-timed brawling. Silence, hoary One! – Winds, avaunt! – to your homes! – Clouds, fly to the antipodes, and leave our heaven clear!'

As he spoke, he stretched out his two long, lank arms, that looked like spider's claws, and seemed to embrace with them the expanse before him. Was it a miracle? The clouds became broken and fled; the azure sky first peeped out, and then was spread a calm field of blue above us; the stormy gale was exchanged to the softly breathing west; the sea grew calm; the waves dwindled to ripplets.

'I like obedience even in these stupid elements,' said the dwarf. 'How much more in the tameless mind of man! It was a well-got-up storm, you must allow – and all of my own making.'

It was tempting Providence to interchange talk with this magician. But *Power*, in all its shapes, is respected by man. Awe, curiosity, a clinging fascination, drew me towards him.

'Come, don't be frightened, friend,' said the wretch: 'I am good humoured when pleased; and something does please me in your well-proportioned body and handsome face, though you look a little woe-begone. You have suffered a land – I, a sea wreck. Perhaps I can allay the tempest of your fortunes as I did my own. Shall we be friends?' – And he held out his hand; I could not touch it. 'Well, then, companions – that will do as well. And now, while I rest after the buffeting I underwent just now, tell me why, young and gallant as you seem, you wander thus alone and downcast on this wild seashore.'

The voice of the wretch was screeching and horrid, and his contortions as he spoke were frightful to behold. Yet he did gain a kind of influence over me, which I could not master, and I told him my tale. When it was ended, he laughed long and loud: the rocks echoed back the sound: hell seemed yelling around me.

'Oh, thou cousin of Lucifer!' said he; 'so thou too hast fallen through thy pride; and, though bright as the son of

Morning, thou art ready to give up thy good looks, thy bride, and thy well-being, rather than submit thee to the tyranny of good. I honour thy choice, by my soul! – So thou hast fled, and yield the day; and mean to starve on these rocks, and to let the birds peck out thy dead eyes, while thy enemy and thy betrothed rejoice in thy ruin. Thy pride is strangely akin to humility, methinks.'

As he spoke, a thousand fanged thoughts stung me to the heart.

'What would you that I should do?' I cried.

'I! – Oh, nothing but lie down and say your prayers before you die. But, were I you, I know the deed that should be done.'

I drew near him. His supernatural powers made him an oracle in my eyes; yet a strange unearthly thrill quivered through my frame as I said, 'Speak! – teach me – what act do you advise?'

'Revenge thyself, man! – humble thy enemies! – set thy foot on the old man's neck, and possess thyself of his daughter!'

'To the east and west I turn,' cried I, 'and see no means! Had I gold, much could I achieve; but, poor and single, I am powerless.'

The dwarf had been seated on his chest as he listened to my story. Now he got off; he touched a spring; it flew open! What a mine of wealth – of blazing jewels, beaming gold, and pale silver – was displayed therein. A mad desire to possess this treasure was born within me.

'Doubtless,' I said, 'one so powerful as you could do all things.'

'Nay,' said the monster humbly, 'I am less omnipotent than I seem. Some things I possess which you may covet; but I would give them all for a small share, or even for a loan of what is yours.'

'My possessions are at your service,' I replied bitterly – 'my poverty, my exile, my disgrace – I make a free gift of them all.'

'Good! I thank you. Add one other thing to your gift, and my treasure is yours.'

'As nothing is my sole inheritance, what besides nothing would you have?'

'Your comely face and well-made limbs.'

I shivered. Would this all-powerful monster murder me? I had no dagger. I forgot to pray – but I grew pale.

'I ask for a loan, not a gift,' said the frightful thing: 'lend me your body for three days – you shall have mine to cage your soul the while, and, in payment, my chest. What say you to the bargain? – Three short days.'

We are told that it is dangerous to hold unlawful talk; and well do I prove the same. Tamely written down, it may seem incredible that I should lend any ear to this proposition; but, in spite of his unnatural ugliness, there was something fascinating in a being whose voice could govern earth, air, and sea. I felt a keen desire to comply; for with that chest I could command the world. My only hesitation resulted from a fear that he would not be true to his bargain. Then, I thought, I shall soon die here on these lonely sands, and the limbs he covets will be mine no more: – it is worth the chance. And, besides, I knew that, by all the rules of art-magic, there were formulae and oaths which none of its practisers dared break. I hesitated to reply; and he went on, now displaying his wealth, now speaking of the petty price he demanded, till it seemed madness to refuse. Thus is it; – place our bark in the current of the stream, and down, over fall and cataract it is hurried; give up our conduct to the wild torrent of passion, and we are away, we know not whither.

He swore many an oath, and I adjured him by many a sacred name; till I saw this wonder of power, this ruler of the elements, shiver like an autumn leaf before my words; and as if the spirit spake unwillingly and perforce within him, at last, he, with broken voice, revealed the spell whereby he might be obliged, did he wish to play me false, to render up the unlawful spoil. Our warm life-blood must mingle to make and to mar the charm.

Enough of this unholy theme. I was persuaded – the thing was done. The morrow dawned upon me as I lay upon the shingles, and I knew not my own shadow as it fell from me. I felt myself changed to a shape of horror, and cursed my easy faith and blind credulity. The chest was there – there the gold and precious stones for which I had sold the frame of flesh which nature had given me. The sight a little stilled my emotions: three days would soon be gone.

They did pass. The dwarf had supplied me with a plenteous store of food. At first I could hardly walk, so strange and out of joint were all my limbs; and my voice – it was that of the fiend. But I kept silent, and turned my face to the sun, that I might not see my shadow, and counted the hours, and ruminated on my future conduct. To bring Torella to my feet – to possess my Juliet in spite of him – all this my wealth could easily achieve. During dark night I slept, and dreamt of the accomplishment of my desires. Two suns had set – the third dawned. I was agitated, fearful. Oh expectation, what a frightful thing art thou, when kindled more by fear than hope! How dost thou twist thyself round the heart, torturing its pulsations! How dost thou dart unknown pangs all through our feeble mechanism, now seeming to shiver us like broken glass, to nothingness – now giving us a fresh strength, which can *do* nothing, and so torments us by a sensation, such as the strong man must feel who cannot break his fetters, though they bend in his grasp. Slowly paced the bright, bright orb up the eastern sky; long it lingered in the zenith, and still more slowly wandered down the west: it touched the horizon's verge – it was lost! Its glories were on the summits of the cliff – they grew dun and grey. The evening star shone bright. He will soon be here.

He came not! – By the living heavens, he came not! – and night dragged out its weary length, and, in its decaying age, 'day began to grizzle its dark hair'; and the sun rose again on the most miserable wretch that ever upbraided its light. Three days thus I passed. The jewels and the gold – oh, how I abhorred them!

Well, well – I will not blacken these pages with demoniac ravings. All too terrible were the thoughts, the raging tumult of ideas that filled my soul. At the end of that time I slept; I had not before since the third sunset; and I dreamt that I was at Juliet's feet, and she smiled, and then she shrieked – for she saw my transformation – and again she smiled, for still her beautiful lover knelt before her. But it was not I – it was he, the fiend, arrayed in my limbs, speaking with my voice, winning her with my looks of love. I strove to warn her, but my tongue refused its office; I strove to tear him from her, but I was rooted to the ground – I awoke with the agony. There were the solitary hoar precipices – there the plashing sea, the quiet strand, and the blue sky over all. What did it mean? was my dream but a mirror of the truth? was he wooing and winning my betrothed? I would on the instant back to Genoa – but I was banished. I laughed – the dwarf's yell burst from my lips – *I* banished! Oh no! they had not exiled the foul limbs I wore; I might with these enter, without fear of incurring the threatened penalty of death, my own, my native city.

I began to walk towards Genoa. I was somewhat accustomed to my distorted limbs; none were ever so ill-adapted for a straightforward movement; it was with infinite difficulty that I proceeded. Then, too, I desired to avoid all the hamlets strewed here and there on the sea-beach, for I was unwilling to make a display of my hideousness. I was not quite sure that, if seen, the mere boys would not stone me to death as I passed, for a monster; some ungentle salutations I did receive from the few peasants or fishermen I chanced to meet. But it was dark night before I approached Genoa. The weather was so balmy and sweet that it struck me that the Marchese and his daughter would very probably have quitted the city for their country retreat. It was from Villa Torella that I had attempted to carry off Juliet; I had spent many an hour reconnoitring the spot, and knew each inch of ground in its vicinity. It was beautifully situated, embosomed in trees, on the margin of a stream. As I drew near, it became evident that my conjecture was right; may, moreover, that the hours were being then devoted to feasting and merriment. For the house was lighted up; strains of soft and gay music were wafted towards me by the breeze. My heart sank within me. Such was the generous kindness of Torella's heart that I felt sure that he would not have indulged in public manifestations of rejoicing just after my unfortunate banishment, but for a cause I dared not dwell upon.

The country people were all alive and flocking about; it became necessary that I should conceal myself; and yet I longed to address some one, or to hear others discourse, or in any way to gain intelligence of what was really going on. At length, entering the walks that were in immediate vicinity to the mansion, I found one dark enough to veil my excessive frightfulness; and yet others as well as I were loitering in its shade. I soon gathered all I wanted to know – all that first made my very heart die with horror, and then boil with indignation. Tomorrow Juliet was to be given to the penitent, reformed, beloved Guido – to-morrow my bride was to pledge her vows to a fiend from hell! And I did this! – my accursed pride – my demoniac violence and wicked self-idolatry had caused this act. For if I had acted as the wretch who had stolen my form had acted – if, with a mien at once yielding and dignified, I had presented myself to Torella, saying, I have done wrong, forgive me; I am unworthy of your angel-child, but permit me to claim her hereafter, when my altered conduct shall manifest that I abjure my vices, and endeavour to become in some sort worthy of her. I go to serve against the infidels; and when my zeal for religion and my true penitence for the past shall appear to you to cancel my crimes, permit me again to call myself your son. Thus had he spoken; and the penitent was welcomed even as the prodigal son of Scripture: the fatted calf was killed for him; and he, still pursuing the same path, displayed such open-hearted regret for his follies, so humble a concession of all his rights, and so ardent a resolve to reacquire them by a life of contrition and virtue, that he quickly conquered the kind old man; and full pardon, and the gift of his lovely child, followed in swift succession.

Oh, had an angel from Paradise whispered to me to act thus! But now, what would be the innocent Juliet's fate? Would God permit the foul union – or, some prodigy destroying it, link the dishonoured name of Carega with the worst of crimes? To-morrow at dawn they were to be married: there was but one way to prevent this – to meet mine enemy, and to enforce the ratification of our agreement. I felt that this could only be done by a mortal struggle. I had no sword – if indeed my distorted arms could wield a soldier's weapon – but I had a dagger, and in that lay my hope. There was no time for pondering or balancing nicely the question: I might die in the attempt; but besides the burning jealousy and despair of my own heart, honour, mere humanity, demanded that I should fall rather than not destroy the machinations of the fiend.

The guests departed – the lights began to disappear; it was evident that the inhabitants of the villa were seeking repose. I hid myself among the trees – the garden grew deserted – the gates were closed – I wandered round and came under a window – ah! well did I know the same! – a soft twilight glimmered in the room – the curtains were half withdrawn. It was the temple of innocence and beauty. Its magnificence was tempered, as it were, by the slight disarrangements occasioned by its being dwelt in, and all the objects scattered around displayed the taste of her who hallowed it by her presence. I saw her enter with a quick light step – I saw her approach the window – she drew back the curtain yet further, and looked out into the night. Its breezy freshness played among her ringlets, and wafted them from the transparent marble of her brow. She clasped her hands, she raised her eyes to heaven. I heard her voice. Guido! she softly murmured – mine own Guido! and then, as if overcome by the fulness of her own heart, she sank on her knees; – her upraised eyes – her graceful attitude – the beaming thankfulness that lighted up her face – oh, these are tame words! Heart of mine, thou imagest ever, though thou canst not portray, the celestial beauty of that child of light and love.

I heard a step – a quick firm step along the shady avenue. Soon I saw a cavalier, richly dressed, young and, methought, graceful to look on, advance. I hid myself yet closer. The youth approached; he paused beneath the window. She arose, and again looking out she saw him, and said – I cannot, no, at this distant time I cannot record her terms of soft silver tenderness; to me they were spoken, but they were replied to by him.

'I will not go,' he cried: 'here where you have been, where your memory glides like some heaven-visiting ghost, I will pass the long hours till we meet, never, my Juliet, again, day or night, to part. But do thou, my love, retire; the cold morn and fitful breeze will make thy cheek pale, and fill with languor thy love-lighted eyes. Ah, sweetest! could I press one kiss upon them, I could, methinks, repose.'

And then he approached still nearer, and methought he was about to clamber into her chamber. I had hesitated, not to terrify her; now I was no longer master of myself. I rushed forward – I threw myself on him – I tore him away – I cried, 'O loathsome and foul-shaped wretch!'

I need not repeat epithets, all tending, as it appeared, to rail at a person I at present feel some partiality for. A shriek rose from Juliet's lips. I neither heard nor saw – I *felt* only mine enemy, whose throat I grasped, and my dagger's hilt; he struggled, but could not escape. At length hoarsely he breathed these words: 'Do! – strike home! destroy this body – you will still live: may your life be long and merry!'

The descending dagger was arrested at the word, and he, feeling my hold relax, extricated himself and drew his sword, while the uproar in the house, and flying of torches from one room to the other, showed that soon we should be separated. In the midst of my frenzy there was much calculation: – fall I might, and so that he did not survive, I cared not for the death-blow I might deal against myself. While still, therefore, he thought I paused, and while I saw the villainous resolve to take advantage of my hesitation, in the sudden thrust he made at me, I threw myself on his sword, and at the same moment plunged my dagger, with a true, desperate aim, in his side. We fell together, rolling over each other, and the tide of blood that flowed from the gaping wound of each mingled on the grass. More I know not – I fainted.

Again I return to life: weak almost to death, I found myself stretched upon a bed – Juliet was kneeling beside it. Strange! my first broken request was for a mirror. I was so wan and ghastly, that my poor girl hesitated, as she told me afterwards; but, by the mass! I thought myself a right proper youth when I saw the dear reflection of my own well-known features. I confess it is a weakness, but I avow it, I do entertain a considerable affection for the countenance and limbs I behold, whenever I look at a glass; and have more mirrors in my house, and consult them oftener, than any beauty in Genoa. Before you too much condemn me, permit me to say that no one better knows than I the value of his own body; no one, probably, except myself, ever having had it stolen from him.

Incoherently I at first talked of the dwarf and his crimes, and reproached Juliet for her too easy admission of his love. She thought me raving, as well she might; and yet it was some time before I could prevail on myself to admit that the Guido whose penitence had won her back for me was myself; and while I cursed won her back for me was myself; and while I cursed bitterly the monstrous dwarf, and blest the well-directed blow that had deprived him of life, I suddenly checked myself when I heard her say, Amen! knowing that him whom she reviled was my very self. A little reflection taught me silence – a little practice enabled me to speak of that frightful night without any very excessive blunder. The wound I had given myself was no mockery of one – it was long before I recovered – and as the benevolent and generous Torella sat beside me, talking such wisdom as might win friends to repentance, and mine own dear Juliet hovered near me, administering to my wants, and cheering me by her smiles, the work of my bodily cure and mental reform went on together. I have never, indeed, wholly recovered my strength – my cheek is paler since – my person a little bent. Juliet sometimes ventures to allude bitterly to the malice that caused this change, but I kiss her on the moment, and tell her all is for the best. I am a fonder and more faithful husband, and true is this – but for that wound, never had I called her mine.

I did not revisit the sea-shore, nor seek for the fiend's treasure; yet, while I ponder on the past, I often think, and my confessor was not backward in favouring the idea, that it might be a good rather than an evil spirit, sent by my guardian angel, to show me the folly and misery of pride. So well at least did I learn this lesson, roughly taught as I was, that I am known now by all my friends and fellow-citizens by the name of Guido il Cortese.

# III
## The Archetypes

# The Golem

## By GUSTAV MEYRINK

There have been several theories put forward as to where Mary Shelley found the inspiration for Frankenstein. Mary herself in the introduction written in the 1831 edition said the idea came to her in a kind of waking nightmare. Others have suggested that it was inspired by Percy Shelley's interest in the Greek legend of Prometheus, who used lightning to infuse life into model people. Yet another school has argued that she may have read the story, The Sandman by the German, E.T.A. Hoffman, about an animated doll, which had just been translated into English in 1814. What seems more likely still is that an important influence was the real-life man of clay, the Golem, who had been spoken of in Jewish folklore for over 300 years. An account of this monstrous creature who had been brought to life in medieval times by Rabbi Judah Loew in order to protect the Jews in the Prague Ghetto from a pogrom was to be found in the collection of ghost stories, Fantasmagoriana read around the fire in the Villa Diodati. Just like the creature in Frankenstein, the Golem proved to be his creator's ultimate undoing. (It is also interesting to note that when Universal's film Frankenstein was in pre-production, it was intended that the creature should be modelled on the traditional image of the Golem: but this ran contrary to the veiws of the director James Whale and, of course, make-up man, Jack Pierce.)

Although the legend of the Golem had existed in several folk tales for many years, it was not until 1911 when an episode from a forthcoming novel by the Austrian-German satirist and occult novelist, Gustav Meyrink (1868–1932), appeared in the popular weekly, Pan, that the general public's interest in the story was really kindled. Meyrink, the

*illegitimate son of an actress and an elderly nobleman,
spent his early years in Prague (where he doubtless first heard
about The Golem) until involvement in a financial scandal
and a period of imprisonment made it imperative for him to
move, and he left for Vienna. Here his interest in the supernatural and his facility at writing enabled him to lead a
bohemian and somewhat precarious existence. In leed, despite
the success of his novels like The Waxworks (1907), Walpergi-
snacht (1917) and, of course, the Golem, he was rarely out of
financial difficulties. His reputation was not helped by his
frequent satirical attacks on the proto-Nazis of the day, which
caused him to be counter-attacked in the press as well as
resulting in his being stoned by angry mobs. Much of his later
life was to be spent fruitlessly warning against the rise of
Nazism and he died a bitter and broken man.*

*The Golem has, however, ensured Meyrink's place as one
of the foremost supernatural writers of the twentieth century,
and it was no surprise that as soon as the book appeared it
was snapped up for filming by the leading German actor-
director, Paul Wegener. In the next five years, Wegener directed and starred in three versions of the story, Der Golem
(1914), Der Golem und die Tanzerin (1917) and the feature-
length, Der Golem: Wie Er in die Welt Kam (1920) which was
released internationally as the Golem. This last production,
scripted faithfully from Meyrink's book by Henrik Galeen, is
generally acknowledged to be a classic because of its superb
art direction and acting. There have subsequently been a
number of other film adaptations of the story – all drawing
more or less from Meyrink's original – with just a single
American version produced by Warner Brothers in 1966 starring Roddy McDowall. Here, then, is the episode of Meyrink's
story which inspired those movies, and which also outlines
the legend that might just have inspired Frankenstein ...*

We had opened the window to try and get the smell of
tobacco smoke out of my little room. The cold night wind

now blew in, making the curtain that hung over the door sway to and fro.

'Prokop's hat would like to take unto itself wings and fly away,' said Zwakh, and pointed to the musician's broad-brimmed beaver that was flapping in the draught.

Josua Prokop gave a merry laugh.

'Let it go,' said he.

'It is seized with a desire to go dancing at Loisitschek's.' Brieslander put his spoke in.

Prokop laughed again, and started to conduct with one hand the various noises borne over the roofs on the wings of the winter breeze. Then, from the wall, he took down my old guitar, and made as though he would pluck its broken strings, while he sang in his cracky falsetto, and with fantastic phrasing:

> An Bein-del von Ei-sen recht alt
> An Stran-zen net gar a so kalt
> Messinung, a' Raucherl und Rohn
> Und immer nurr put-zen ...

'He's a dab at the dialect all right, isn't he?' laughed Brieslander, and drummed with his fingers and joined in:

> Und stok-en sich Aufzug und Pfiff
> Und schmallern an eisernes G'suff.
> Juch ...
> Und Handschuhkren, Harom net san ...

'They sing that old song every evening down at Loisitschek's,' Zwakh informed me. 'Poor dotty old Nephtali Schaffraneck, with his green shade over his eyes, wheezes it out, accompanied on the hurdy-gurdy by a painted piece of female goods. Really, you know Master Pernath, you ought to go along with us to that queer haunt one evening. P'raps to-night – later – when we're through with the punch – eh? What d'you say to it? Isn't it your birthday to-day, or something?'

'Yes,' urged Prokop, as he closed the window once more, 'You come along with us, old fellow-me-lad. It's a thing to see for yourself.'

We sat around drinking hot punch, while our thoughts roamed the room.

Brieslander was carving a marionette.

'Well, Josua' – Zwakh broke the silence – 'you've shut us off good and proper from the outer world. Not one word has got itself spoken since you shut the window.'

'I was thinking,' said Prokop, rather hurriedly, as if apologising for his own silence, 'how odd it is when the wind plays with inanimate objects. It's almost like a miracle when things that lie about without a particle of life in their bodies suddenly start to flutter. Haven't you ever felt that? Once I stood in a desolate square and watched a whole heap of scraps of paper chasing one another. I couldn't feel the wind, as I was in the shelter of a house, but there they were, all jumbled together in a veritable dance of death. Next instant they appeared to have decided on an armistice, but all of a sudden some unendurable puff of reminiscence seemed to blow through the lot of them, and off they went again, each hounding on his next-door neighbour till they disappeared round the corner. One solid piece of newspaper only lagged behind; it lay helplessly on the pavement, flapping venomously up and down, like a fish out of water, gasping for air. I couldn't help the thought that rose in me: if we, when all's said and done, were something similar to these little bits of fluttering paper, neither more nor less. Driven hither and thither by some invisible, incomprehensible "wind" that dictates all our actions, for all we, in our vanity, boast of our own volition. Supposing life really were nothing but that mysterious whirlwind of which the Bible states, it "bloweth where it listeth, and thou hearest the sound thereof, but canst not tell whence it cometh and whither it goeth"! Isn't there a dream that most of us have, when we fumble in deep pools after silver fish, and wake to find nothing in our hands but a cold draught of air blowing through them?'

'Prokop, you're catching that trick of speech from Pernath! What's the matter with you?' Zwakh regarded the musician suspiciously.

'It's the result of the story of the book *Ibbur* we had told to us before you came. Pity you were late and missed it ... you can see the effect it's had on Prokop.' This from Brieslander.

'Story from a book?'

'Story of a man, rather, who brought the book, and seemed a queer card. Pernath doesn't know who he is, where he lives, what his name is, or what he wanted. And, for all his visitor's eccentric appearance, he can't for the life of him describe it.'

Zwakh listened attentively.

'Strange, that,' he said, after a pause. 'Was the stranger clean shaven by any chance, and did his eyes slant?'

'I think so,' replied I. 'That is to say ... yes ... yes ... I am quite sure of it. Do you know him?'

The marionette maker shook his head. 'Only it reminds me of the Golem.'

Brieslander, the painter, laid down his chisel.

'The Golem? I've heard talk of it a lot. What d'you know about the Golem, Zwakh?'

'Who can say he knows anything about the Golem?' was Zwakh's rejoinder, as he shrugged his shoulders. 'Always they treat it as a legend, till something happens and turns it into actuality once more. After which it's talked of for many a day, and the rumours wax ever more and more fantastic, till the whole business gets so exaggerated and done to death they die of their own absurdity. The original story harks back, so they say, to the seventeenth century. With the help of an ancient formula, a rabbi is said to have put together an automatic man and used it to help ring the bells in the Synagogue and for all kinds of other menial work. But he hadn't made it into a proper man; it was more like a kind of animated vegetable, really. What life it had, too, so the story runs, only derived from a magic prescription placed behind his teeth each day, that drew down to itself what was known as "the free sidereal strength of the universe." And as, one evening, before evening prayers, the rabbi forgot to take the prescription out of the Golem's mouth, the figure fell into a frenzy, and went raging through the streets like a roaring lion, seeking whom it might devour. At last the rabbi was able to secure it, and he then destroyed the formula. The figure fell to pieces. The only record left of it was the miniature clay figure that was shown to the people within the old Synagogue.'

'Some say the old rabbi was afterwards elected emperor; that he conjured up the spirits of the dead and made them visible to human eyes,' volunteered Prokop.

'That I cannot say,' Zwakh answered him. 'But this I know

– that there is something here in this our quarter of the town
... something that cannot die, and has its being within our
midst. From generation to generation our ancestors have lived
here in this place, and no one has heard more tales about this
reappearance of the Golem – happenings actually experienced
as well as handed down – than I have.'

Zwakh suddenly ceased speaking. It was obvious his
thoughts had gone trailing off into the past.

As he sat there at the table, head on hand, his rosy,
youthful-looking cheeks contrasting oddly in the lamplight
with his snowy hair, I could hardly refrain from comparing
his face with the masks of the little puppets he had so often
shown to me. Curious how the old fellow resembled them!
The same expression, and the same cast of countenance.

Some things there are on earth that seem to be complemen-
tary to each other, so I pondered. As Zwakh's simple life-
history passed before my mind's eye, it struck me as both
monstrous and inexplicable that a man such as he, in spite of
a better education than that of his forebears – he had, as a
matter of fact, been destined for the stage – should suddenly
insist on reverting to his dilapidated box of marionettes,
trundling once more into the market-place these aged dolls
that had anticked for the scanty living of his ancestors, and
there making them re-enact their well-worn histories in terms
of clumsy gesture.

I appreciated the reason. He could not endure to be parted
from them; their lives were bound up with his, and once he
was away from them they had changed to thoughts within his
brain, where they led a restless existence till he returned to
whence they came. For that reason did he love them, and trick
them out in tinsel.

'Won't you tell us some more, Zwakh?' Prokop begged the
old man, with a glance at myself and Brieslander that sought
approval.

'I hardly know where to begin,' the old boy murmured,
'Golem stories are all hard telling. Pernath, here, just now
was telling us he knew quite well how the stranger looked,
but couldn't describe him. More or less every three and thirty
years something takes place in our streets, not so out-of-the-
way startling in itself, yet the terror of it is too strong for
either explanation or excuse.

'Always it happens that an apparition makes its appearance – an utterly strange man, clean shaven, of yellow complexion, Mongolian type, in antiquated clothes of a bygone day; it comes from the direction of the Altschulgasse, stalks through the Ghetto with a queer groping, stumbling kind of gait, as if afraid of falling over, and quite suddenly – is gone.

'Usually it is seen to disappear round a corner. At other times it is said to have described a circle and gone back to the point whence it started – an old house, close by the Synagogue.

'Some impressionable folk will tell how they have seen it coming towards them down a street, but, as they walked boldly to meet it, it would grow smaller and smaller, like an ordinary figure will do as it moves away from you, and finally disappear completely.

'Sixty-six years ago there must have been a particularly lively scare of this sort, for I remember – I was a tiny youngster at the time – that the house in the Altschulgasse was searched from top to bottom. They hung washing out of every window, and only then was it discovered that there was a room inside the house with no entrance to it, and the windows barred. As the only means of reaching it, a man let himself down on a rope from the roof, to see in. But no sooner did he get near the window than the rope broke and the poor wretch cracked his skull upon the pavement. And when they wanted, later on, to try again, opinions differed so about the situation of the window that they gave it up.

'I myself encountered the Golem for the first time in my life nearly three and thirty years ago. I met it in a little alley, and we ran right into one another. I am thankful to say I cannot remember now very distinctly what went on in my mind at that encounter. Heaven forbid anyone should spend his life in perpetual expectation, day in, day out, of meeting the Golem. I do remember I had a premonition at the time, a distinct premonition that I was going to meet it. Something cried out in me, loud and shrill, "The Golem!" At that instant someone stumbled out of a doorway and the strange figure passed me by. Next moment I was surrounded by a sea of white, frightened faces, everyone asking if I had seen it.

'As I replied, I was aware for the first time of the cramp that gripped my tongue. I was quite surprised to find I could move my limbs, for I realised how, for the space of a heart-beat, I must have endured a paralytic shock from surprise.

'I have given the subject much thought, and the nearest I can get to the truth of it seems to be this: that once in every generation a spiritual disturbance zigzags, like a flash of lightning, right through the Ghetto, taking possession of the souls of the living to some end we know not of, and rising in the form of a wraith that appears to our senses in the guise of a human entity that once, centuries ago, maybe, inhabited here, and is craving materialisation.

'Maybe, too, it lurks within our midst, day after day, and we know it not. Neither do our ears register the sound of the turning-fork till it is brought in contact with the wood, to which it needs must transmit its vibrations.

'Think of the crystal, resolving itself, it knows not how, but in accordance with its own immutable laws, from an amorphous mass, to a definite ordered shape. May it not be even so in the world of the spirit? Who shall say? Just as, in thundery weather, the electric tension in the atmosphere will increase to a point past endurance, and eventually give birth to the lightning, may it not be that the whole mass of stagnant thought infecting the air of the Ghetto needs clearing from time to time by some kind of mysterious explosion, something potent in its workings – something that forces the dreams of the subconscious up into the light of day – some lightning-stroke giving rise to an object that, could we but read its riddle, symbolises, both in ways and appearance, the whole soul of the masses, had we but got one glimmer of the cryptic language of form?

'And, just as Nature has her own happenings that fore-shadow the advent of the lightning, so do certain forbidding signs portend the arrival of this phantom within our world of fact. The plaster peeling from an old wall will adopt the shape of a stealthy human form; and stony faces stare from the ice-flowers formed by the frost upon the window-panes. Sand from the roof-tops will trickle to the ground in mysterious fashion, filling the apprehensive passer-by with the impression it has been thrown by some invisible spirit, trying to form, from the hiding-place wherein it lurks, all kinds of unfamiliar outlines. No matter what the object one beholds – be it a wicker work basket, all one colour, or the uneven surface of a human skin – we are still obsessed with this disconcerting gift of finding everywhere these ominous, significant shapes, that assume in our dreams the proportions of giants. And always, through these ghostly strivings of these troops of thoughts, endeavouring to gnaw their way through the wall of actuality, runs, like a scarlet thread, a torturing certitude that our own mental consciousness, strive as we may, is being sucked dry, deliberately, that the phantom may attain to concrete form.

'Just now, when I heard Pernath tell how he had met a man clean shaven, with slanting eyes, there stood the Golem before me as I saw it that time.

'He stood there as though risen from the ground. And, for the space of a moment, I was filled with that dumb, familiar fear, the intuition of some ghostly presence near at hand, that I had felt then, in my boyhood, when the Golem had thrown its dread, ominous shadow across my path.

'Sixty-six years ago! And another memory, too, is connected with it – that of the night before my sister's wedding. Our house was celebrating the event. Amongst other things, the guests amused themselves by melting lead. I stood by, in open-mouthed astonishment, wondering what it all might mean. The childish workings of my mind connected it somehow or other with the Golem, of whom I had often heard my father talk. Every moment I expected to see the door open and the stranger walk into the room.

'My sister filled a ladle with the molten stuff, and emptied it into a bowl of water, laughing the while at my intense excitement. With his withered, trembling hands, my grandfather picked out the lump of lead and held it to the light. Immediately arose a hubbub of excitement. Everybody talked at once; I tried to wriggle through the crowd of agitated guests, but they stopped me.

'Later, when I was older, my father told me how the molten metal had shaped itself into a miniature but quite unmistakable head, smooth and round, as though cast from a mould, with features that bore such an uncanny resemblance to those of the Golem that fear possessed them all.

'Many a time have I discussed the matter with Schemajah Hillel the registrar, who has in his keeping the paraphernalia of the Old Synagogue, together with the clay figure I told you

of, from Kaiser Rudolf's days. He has given much time to the
Cabbala, and he held the clay image to be nothing but a
presage in human form of the time in which it was made, just
as, in my case, was the lump of lead. And the stranger who
haunted our precincts he held to be a projection of the
thought that had sprung to life in the brain of the old rabbi
before he had succeeded in giving it tangible form, and that it
could only appear at stated intervals of time, under those
astrological conditions in which it had been created; that
then, and then only, would it come back to the earth on its
agonised quest for materialisation.

'Hillel's wife, in her lifetime, had also seen the Golem face
to face, and felt the same shock of paralysis that I had so long
as the inexplicable presence was near. She said, too, she was
quite positive that what she had seen was her own soul
divested of its body; that just for a moment it had stood
opposite to her, and gazed into her face with the features of a
strange being. In spite of the terrible fear that had got her in
its grip, the conviction had never left her that this thing
confronting her was a part of her innermost self.'

'It's not credible,' murmured Prokop, lost in thought.

Brieslander, too, sat there brooding.

Then came a knock at the door, and the old dame who
brings up my evening water, and anything else I happen to
want, came in, placed the earthenware pitcher on the floor,
and silently withdrew.

We all looked up and gazed vaguely round the room, as
though awakening from sleep, though a long time elapsed
before any word was spoken.

Some new influence had entered the room with the old
crone, and we had first to accustom ourselves to it.

'That red-haired wench Rosina, too – she has a face that
dances for ever before a man's eyes out of the nooks and the
crannies.' This from Zwakh, quite suddenly. 'I've known that
fixed, grinning smile, now, for a whole generation. First the
grandmother ... then the mother! And always the same face
... not a feature altered! The same name, Rosina – one
always the resurrection of the other!'

'Isn't Rosina old Aaron Wassertrum's daughter?' I asked.

'So they say,' affirmed Zwakh. 'But Aaron Wassertrum has
many a son and many a daughter folk know nothing of.

Nobody knew who was the father of Rosina's mother, nor what became of her. At the age of fifteen she brought that child into the world, and that was the last heard of her. Her disappearance had something to do with a murder, if I remember rightly, committed in this house on her account.

'Just like her daughter, she turned all the heads of the half-fledged youths. One of them's alive still – I see him quite often – I can't remember his name. The others all came to a premature end – through her, probably. I only remember detached episodes, here and there, of that bygone time, that stray through my brain like a series of faded pictures. There was one half-witted fellow who used to go from public-house to public-house every evening, cutting out silhouettes in black paper for a couple of kreuzer. Once they'd got him tipsy he'd sit there in the depths of melancholy, cutting out always the same sharp girl's profile, till his little stock of paper was all used up. Almost as a child, so they said, he'd been caught in the toils of a certain Rosina – the grandmother, probably, of our one – and loved her so madly he'd all but lost his reason. When I count the years back, it can't have been anyone but the grandmother of our present Rosina.'

Zwakh ceased speaking and lay back in his chair.

'Fate flits in circles,' thought I, 'around and around this house, returning always to its starting-point.' And a hideous image of something I had once seen shot simultaneously into my mind – a cat gone mad, twirling around frantically, in circle after circle.

'Now for the head' – all at once, in Brieslander's cheery tones. And he took a small billet of wood from his pocket and started to carve.

I pushed my arm-chair into the background, out of the light. My eyes were heavy with weariness.

The hot water for the punch was sizzling in the kettle, and Josua started to fill our glasses round again. Softly, very softly, the strains of dance-music stole through the closed window; fitfully, now coming, now going, according to the caprices of the wind.

Wouldn't I clink glasses with him? – so the musician wanted to know, after a pause.

But I made no answer. So loth was I to make any kind of movement, I would not even open my mouth. Almost I might have been asleep, such was the feeling of utter quiet that now possessed my soul. I had to glance now and again at the twinkling blade of Brieslander's pocket-knife, as he cut small chips of the wood, to assure myself I really was awake.

They were talking now of Dr Savioli, and the elegant lady – some titled man's wife – who paid her clandestine visits to him in that obscure little studio. Once again I saw floating before me the triumphant, mocking visage of Aaron Wassertrum. I wondered if I would confide that experience of mine to Zwakh, then came to the conclusion it would serve no useful purpose, to say nothing of the fact that I knew my will would be unequal to the effort of relating it.

Suddenly I saw all three of them looking at me across the table. 'He is asleep,' said Prokop, so loudly that it sounded almost like a question he had put to me.

Then they spoke in subdued voices, and I realised I was the subject of their conversation.

The blade of Brieslander's knife glanced here and there, catching the light from the lamp, and the glint of it burned into my eyes.

'Mad,' was the word I caught. They talked on, and I listened.

'Subjects like the Golem shouldn't be raised in Pernath's company,' said Josua Prokop reprovingly; 'just now, when he was telling us about the book *Ibbur*, we none of us said a word, but let him run on. Just one of his illusions, I'll bet you anything.'

'Quite right!' Zwakh nodded. 'It's like walking with a lighted candle through a disused room, in which the walls and furniture are all wrapped in dust-sheets, while the dead tinder of the past smothers your footsteps ankle deep; one spark let fall, and fire'll break out of every corner.'

'Was Pernath long in the asylum? Poor devil, anyway ... can't be much over forty.' Thus Brieslander.

'I don't know. I haven't the faintest idea where he came from, or what his profession was before. He has all the air of an old-fashioned French aristocrat, with his slender figure and pointed beard. Once, years and years ago, an old doctor of my acquaintance asked me to do him a favour, and see if I could procure for a patient of his a humble lodging somewhere in this street, where no one would be likely to disturb him, or

worry him with questions about the past.' Zwakh waved
vaguely in my direction. 'Ever since then he's lived here,
repairing old queer stuff and cutting precious stones, and
apparently making a modest living out of it. It's a good job
for him he seems to have forgotten everything to do with his
mental trouble. You must on no account get him on to
subjects that concern the past. That's what the old doctor
used to keep impressing on me. "Remember Zwakh," he used
to say, "all that's over and done with; we've evolved a system
now to treat it by; we've built a wall round it; there let it
stay, and it'll do no harm to anybody."'

The marionette man's talk struck at me like a pole-axe
on a defenceless beast. Red, merciless hands were clutching
at my heart. I had had this dumb kind of torment before ...
a suspicion that something had once happened to me, and
that a portion of my life had been spent fumbling at the
bottom of an abyss, as sometimes happens to a sleep-
walker.

And now the secret was out, and gnawing like a gaping
wound.

That neurasthenic disinclination of mine to brooding on
past events ... that strange recurring dream I kept on having
that I was in a house containing a certain room the door of
which was locked to me ... the painful inability of my
memory to function where associations of my youth were
concerned ... all these problems had suddenly achieved their
terrible solution: I had been mad, and treated by *hypnosis*.
They had, in short, locked up a room which communicated
with certain chambers in my brain; they had made me into an
exile in the midst of the life that surrounded me.

Nor did there seem any prospect of my ever recovering
again that lost portion of my memory.

I understood now that the mainspring of all my thoughts
and acts lay hidden in another world, forgotten and never to
be recalled; I was like a grafted plant, a twig proceeding from
an alien root. Even if I ever did succeed in forcing the door of
that locked room, would I not fall immediately a prey to the
spirits imprisoned therein?

The story of the Golem as related by Zwakh passed through
my mind, and suddenly I recognised a connection of infinite
mystery and magnitude between that legendary room without

an entrance, which the unknown was supposed to inhabit, and my own significant dream.

That was it! In my case, too, the cord would break, should I but try to glance into that barred window of my inner consciousness.

This curious connection became clearer and clearer within my mind, and the clearer it grew the more terrifying did it become. There were things in the world, so it seemed to me, beyond the mind of man to grasp, riveted indissolubly together and running about distractedly, like blind horses, on a path whose direction is hidden from them.

Here, too, in the Ghetto: a room, the door of which nobody could find; a ghostly presence dwelling therein, that from time to time would walk through the streets, spreading terror and fear in the minds of men!

Brieslander was still hacking away at his puppethead; you could hear the scraping of his knife upon the wood.

The sound of it somehow distressed me, and I looked up to see if it would not soon be finished.

The head, turning about as it did in the sculptor's hand, looked alive. It seemed to be peering into all the corners of the room. At last its eyes rested upon me. It appeared pleased to have found me at last.

And I, in my turn, was unable to turn my eyes away. Stonily I stared at that little wooden face.

The carver's knife seemed to hesitate a little, then suddenly made a strong, decided cut, informing the wooden head, all at once, with terrifying personality. I recognised the yellow countenance of the stranger who had brought me the book.

There my powers of discernment ended. It had lasted only one moment, but I could feel my heart cease to beat, and then bound forward agonisingly.

The face, none the less, remained in my mind. Just as it had done before.

*It was I myself ... I and none other ... and I lay there on Brieslander's lap, gaping.*

My eyes were wandering round the room, and strange fingers laid their touch upon my head.

All of a sudden I was aware of Zwakh's face distorted with excitement. I could hear his voice: 'God! It's the Golem!'

A short struggle had ensued, while they had tried to wrest

Brieslander's work from his hand. But he had defended himself, and crying, with a laugh: 'Don't fuss yourselves; I've made a mess of this job,' had opened the window and flung the head into the street below.

'Wake up,' I could hear Josua Prokop saying to me. 'You've been so fast asleep you couldn't feel how we've been shaking you. We've finished the punch, and you've missed all the fun.'

Then the sharp pain of what I had just been hearing surged over me once more, and I wanted to shriek aloud how it was not a dream what I had told them of the book *Ibbur* – that I would take it out of its box and show it to them.

But I could neither utter these thoughts nor combat the general spirit of leave-taking that had now seized my guests.

Zwakh forcefully put my cloak round my shoulders while he cried:

'Come along with us now to Loisitschek's, Master Pernath. It'll cheer you up!'

# Death of a Professor

## By MICHAEL HERVEY

If The Golem could have been the inspiration for the monster in Mary Shelley's novel, then it is also possible that an actual scientific experimenter who was working in England in the early years of the nineteenth century and created life from inanimate objects, may have been the model for Frankenstein himself. The man's name was Andrew Crosse and he lived in a remote Somerset mansion, Fyne Court, which, because of the great flashes of lightning and tremendous explosions which were forever eminating from the building, earned him the reputation in local gossip of being in league with the Devil. Some even nicknamed him 'The Wizard of the Quantocks'. Crosse was, though – like Frankenstein – a much misunderstood man, and found it difficult to get people to give a fair hearing to his beliefs about the boundless potential of electricity. However, at one of his lectures in London, on December 28, 1814, among his audience were Percy and Mary Shelley – a fact Mary recorded in her Diary. Crosse spoke with passion about his experiments and there is no doubt that the Shelleys, with their own interest in the subject, were impressed by him. Crosse's subsequent career also curiously paralleled that of his fictional counterpart – for in 1836 while working in his laboratory, he actually created a batch of extraordinary creatures in his apparatus which he named Acari Crossi. These hairy, eight-legged monstrosities emerged before his eyes from some crystals he had been treating with electrical currents. The news of this unparalleled event was greeted with a mixture of horror and disbelief – the scientific world declaring that the creation of life in this manner was impossible; while the more superstitious members of the public believed Crosse had now added witchcraft to his crimes. The man himself *made no claims for what he had done – merely stated the facts in a scientific paper and left it at that. Thereafter he retreated into the fastness of his mansion and was little heard of again. As the months turned into years, stories of the* Acari Crossi *faded into legend, and today his story is scarcely known. Yet for me the conviction persists that Andrew Crosse played a larger role in the creation of* Frankenstein *than he has ever been given credit for.*\*

The facts about this experimenter have, however, been the inspiration for two novels, *Sixty Years Hence by Captain C.F. Henningsen (1847) in which the artificial organisms, the* Acari, *are used as a threat to the world's supply of food; and* The Thunder and Lightning Man *by Colin Cooper (1968) a thinly disguised fictional biography. There have been a few short stories, too, including* The Electric Vampire *by F.H. Power which appeared in The* London Magazine *of October 1910 and* Death of a Professor *by Michael Hervey, published in 1946, which appears hereunder. Hervey (1920– ) who was trained as a commercial artist, gave up his comfortable existence to go globe-trotting, returning to England just as the Second World War was breaking out. It proved an unnerving return, for he and his companion were arrested as spies as soon as their ship docked in London. Having satisfied the authorities he was not involved in espionage, Hervey went to work in publishing and, appropriately, served as an editorial assistant in the Secret Publications Division for two years. He was later the* Observer *drama critic before concentrating his energies as an extremely prolific and versatile author. He has a talent for stories of mystery and horror, and for a time his books carried the sub-heading 'If You're Nervy Don't Read Hervey!' In this story, Hervey utilises the facts of Andrew Crosse's legend in a tale that adds yet another dimension to the* Frankenstein *legend ...*

\* Those readers interested in learning more about this theory, as well as the facts of this extraordinary man's life, are referred to my book, *The Man Who Was Frankenstein* (1979).

I have in front of me a photograph of what looks like a bundle of clothes lying on the floor, and a rather massive diary. The bundle is all that is left of a certain Professor Stacey. It seems that he believed that it was possible to create life out of inorganic matter ... at least that is what his diary would have us believe. Whether it is possible I am not in a position to judge. I am just a plain, common or garden C.I.D. man, and my knowledge of biology is extremely limited, but this much I can tell you ... there are some things we are not intended to know, and the secret of life is one of them; as the professor's diary will prove. But first let me tell you how I came to lay my hands on this extremely amazing record.

On June 4th at 3.50 p.m. we received a call from the professor's housekeeper saying that she feared that he had met with an accident of some sort. The professor, it seems, had locked himself in his laboratory the previous day and had not emerged from his room or given any sign of life since, in spite of her repeated knocking at the door. I was detailed to investigate the matter.

The professor's door was barred all right; so were all the windows, from the inside. The glass was of the opaque kind making it impossible for me to look into the room. I forced an entry, as the saying goes, in the end, and found what was left of the professor lying on the floor in front of a bench piled high with all sorts of scientific apparatus. I say 'what was left of him' because he resembled nothing human in so far that he was just a shapeless mass of flesh and skin. *There wasn't a bone of any sort left in his body!*

There wasn't a sign of a struggle of any sort, or a single mark on his 'body' for that matter, to indicate how he had met his end. The autopsy did little to clear up matters either. There wasn't a trace of poison in any of his organs. To say that we were puzzled is to put it mildly. An inquest of a sort was held and a verdict of 'Death by Misadventure' recorded. I was far from satisfied, as was the rest of the department, and it was for that reason that I applied for permission to go through the professor's effects. And that is how I came to lay my hands on this diary. I haven't turned it over to the chief yet. I doubt if I ever shall, somehow ... It would be better for everyone if I burned the cursed thing. Someone might take it

into their heads to publish its terrifying contents and then ...
well, read on and judge for yourself.

The first and only entry is on page three, headed April 4th,
and reads as follows: – 'My experiments are bearing fruit. It
would appear that there is no dividing line between "dead"
and "living matter" at all. My work with viruses leads me to
believe that life as we know it does *not* come into existence
suddenly, *but is inherent in all matter*. There is just a "pre-
life" stage relating to all inorganic matter which under certain
favourable conditions gives way to life. Auto-genesis can no
longer be denied. Anyone who has studied the tobacco mosaic
virus must eventually arrive at this conclusion; the virus in
question being obtainable in crystalline form, and as such it is
"dead" matter, but once the crystals are dissolved life becomes
apparent.

'Many of my brother scientists have, of course, experimented along auto-genesis lines, but they have all failed
miserably in their quest. All of them, that is, except a certain
Andrew Crosse, a scientific "amateur" who made quite a
name for himself a little over a hundred years ago, and
whose work has since been ignored for some unknown
reason. I came across his "Memorials" quite by accident and
was truly astonished at the progress he had made in this
direction. Here was a man who had actually created living
*Acarus* in *poisonous solutions fatal to all animal life* (more
by accident than by design it must be said), but instead of
honouring him and making it possible for him to carry on
with his remarkable work, the world condemned him, with
the result that his labours were nullified and wasted; so
much so that neither myself or any of my colleagues had
even heard of his efforts.

'It seems that he was engaged on experiments relating to
the formation of silicious crystals in a mixture of hydrochloric
acid and a solution of silicate of potash in which a piece of
porous stone was immersed. He eventually struck upon the
idea of sending an electric current through the mixture. It was
then that the acari, or living mites, first made their appearance.
'On the fourteenth day from the commencement of this experiment,' he writes, 'I observed through a lens some whitish
excrescences or nipples, projecting from the middle of the
stone. On the eighteenth day these projections enlarged, and

struck out seven or eight filaments, each of them longer than the hemisphere on which they grew.

'On the twenty-sixth day these projections assumed the form of a *perfect insect*, standing erect on a few bristles which formed its tail. Till this period I had no idea that these objects were other than an incipient mineral formation. On the twenty-eighth day these tiny creatures *moved their legs!* I must say that I was not a little astonished. After a few days they *detached themselves from the stone, and moved about at pleasure.*

'In the course of a few weeks about a hundred of them made their appearance on the stone. I carefully examined them under a microscope, and observed that the smaller acari appeared to have only six legs, the larger ones eight. These insects are obviously of the *acarus* genus, but there appears to be a difference of opinion as to whether they are a known species; some assert they are not.

'I have never ventured an opinion on the cause of their birth, and for a very good reason ... I was unable to form one. The simplest solution of the problem which occurred to me was that they arose from ova deposited by insects floating in the atmosphere and hatched by electric action. Still I could not imagine that an ovum could shoot out filaments, or that these filaments could become bristles, and moreover I could not detect on the closest examination, the remains of a shell!

'I next imagined, as others have done, that they might originate from the water, and consequently made a close examination of numbers of vessels filled with the same fluid; in none of these could I perceive a trace of an insect, nor could I see any in any other part of the room.'

'Crosse went a step further with his experiments, discarding the stone he actually succeeded in creating the mites in poisonous solutions consisting of concentrated copper sulphate, and zinc sulphate, the customary prolonged electrical current having been passed through the mixture. Some of them actually *crawled up the electrified wire and escaped from the vessel!*

'"If, however" he goes on to say, "any of them were afterwards thrown into the fluid in which it was produced it immediately drowned. I have never before heard of acari having been produced *under* a fluid, or of their ova throwing out filaments; nor have I ever observed any ova *previous to or during electrization!*"

'Not satisfied with that, Crosse went on to produce acari in an *air-tight* glass retort; the silicate solution being put in while *hot*. The battery was then connected to the retort with the result that an electric action immediately commenced; oxygen and hydrogen gases were liberated; the volumes of atmospheric air were soon expelled. Every care had been taken to avoid atmospheric contact and admittance of extraneous matter; the retort itself having been previously washed in alcohol. This apparatus was placed in a dark cellar.

'"I discovered no sign of incipient animal formation until on the hundred and fortieth day, when I plainly distinguished one acarus actively crawling about *within* the airtight retort.

'"I found that I had made a great mistake in this experiment; and I believe it was in consequence of this error that I not only lost sight of the single insect, but never saw any others in the apparatus. I had omitted to insert within the retort a *resting-place* for these acari (they always die if they fall back into the solution from which they have emerged). It is strange that in a solution *eminently caustic* and under an atmosphere of *oxihydrogen gas*, one single acarus should have actually made its appearance."

'Crosse was not alone in these experiments. A Mr Weeks, of Sandwich, it appears, made several attempts along the lines laid down by Crosse, and also succeeded in creating innumerable acari, having first taken the precaution of baking all his apparatus in an oven, and only using distilled water in his experiments. On top of which he super-heated his silicate solution, utilizing manufactured oxygen, thus making trebly sure that no animal life of any sort was present at the outset of the experiment; at the conclusion of which he was able to bring an interesting point to light. By varying the carbon content of his solution he was able to decrease or increase the number of insects produced in this fashion.

'Both Weeks and Crosse were much vilified as a result of these findings, being labelled as blasphemers and "revilers of our holy religion." So much so, in fact, that they were eventually compelled to call a halt in their experiments, but not before Faraday himself had delivered a paper on the subject to the Royal Institution, which, while agreeing with

their findings, categorically denied the possibility of any form
of auto-genesis. Like many of his contemporaries, he put the
insects down to some sort of mechanical growth that imitated
the properties associated with living matter. There are many
growths of this nature, it so happens, some of which imitate
living bodies to a remarkable degree, as in the case of the
"Osmostic growths" recently produced by that eminent biolo-
gist Dr Leduc; but that does not alter the fact that it *is*
possible to create life from inorganic matter I now have
irrefutable proof to that effect.

'I have not only produced myriads of acari, but have
actually made them grow and multiply. I have speeded up
Crosse's process to such an extent that I can produce as many
acari as I wish at will. The difficulty was, of course, how to
feed the mites, for like all living things they require nourishment. Crosse never discovered what to feed them on, with the
result that they all died. Not so mine. It took me some time to
find out what they liked. I must have experimented with at
least a hundred different kinds of food before discovering the
peculiar fact that they thrived on *calcium only!* They were in
fact, to coin a phrase, calcium mad; the mere presence of
bone in any shape or form makes them act like wild beasts of
the jungle. I have seen them tear each other to pieces in their
eagerness to get at the stuff.

'Theirs is a dangerous appetite. I have just had the fact
brought home to me in no uncertain fashion. They must
have escaped the other night and roamed about the laboratory in search of food. They found Mrs Lever's little Persian
kitten. All they left was the flesh and skin. They must have
entered through the mouth and devoured the skeleton, including the skull. It was a revolting ... shocking sight. I managed to lure them back into their container with a large
bone. It was a strange sight seeing them trail after the bone
like a column of huge ants ... one which I shall not forget
in a hurry. I must make sure that they do not get out
again; especially as I am becoming prone to fainting fits of
late ...'

The diary, if one could call it such, ended there. The rest of
the volume was made up with various formulas and figures
relating to the experiments. It's perfectly plain what happened
... The horrible part of it being that those hellish little

monsters are roaming about somewhere ... maybe multiplying ... Who's going to be next? I keep asking myself ... Who's going to be next ...?

# Frankenstein – Unlimited

## By H. A. HIGHSTONE

*Whether E.T.A. Hoffman's story* The Sandman *had any influence on the creation of* Frankenstein, *the German author's landmark tale about the making of a mechanical female has, in its turn, been influential on a whole school of fiction about automatons. Two which spring immediately to mind because they are so regularly anthologised are* Moxon's Master *(1893), the tale of a mechanical chess player which becomes too smart for its own good, written by the American humorist Ambrose Bierce; and* The Dancing Partner *(1895), about a mechanical man who literally sweeps a young girl off her feet. This story was also the work of a humorist, the British novelist Jerome K. Jerome, famous for his comic travelogue,* Three Men in a Boat.*

*The rapid development of robots in the twentieth century made them one of the staple themes of Science Fiction during the Twenties and Thirties. And just as the earlier automatoms had become the butt of the humorists, so the new generation of satirical writers turned their attention to robots. Franken-stein – Unlimited is, in fact, one of the earliest such treatments of the robot theme carried to its logical conclusion. The story first appeared in* Astounding Science Fiction *in 1935, and was described as 'Mr Highstone's reaction to the plethora of robot and machine age stories.' H.A. Highstone (1901–1986) was a curious mixture for an author: best known for his contributions on farming – in particular his best-seller,* Practical Farm-ing for Beginners *(1934) – he also wrote Science Fiction and contributed a small but influential group of stories to maga-zines such as* Astounding *and* Other Worlds. Frankenstein – Unlimited *may well be the best of Highstone's excursions into fantasy and I am pleased to be reprinting it in these pages.*

From earliest recollection, the little boy, Chuth, had been aware that beyond the eastern horizon there lurked something menacing and dreadful. One of his first memories was of a night when the wind had been in the right quarter, and the sound of the menace had drifted across the mountains – of the vague figures of the tribesmen outside the caves in the starlight, peering eastward with an apprehension so keen that even babies had sensed it and begun squalling.

Chuth had added his wail to theirs, for all of his five years.

'Hush!' his mother had commanded in fierce anxiety. 'Hush up, or the Brain will hear you!' He had ceased his cries then, to stare with the rest in dumb terror at the flickering glow beyond the eastern peaks; to listen with quaking limbs to the vague thundering which drifted down the wind.

'The Great Brain!' his elders had whispered, their voices low in awe.

At first, Chuth had accepted the explanation without wonder. The Great Brain existed; it was over there beyond the mountains; it was something big and dreadful. That was sufficient knowledge.

Only when he grew older did he begin to speculate about the Brain. Was it, he wondered, like a bear – a very large bear – or a tree, or a river?

'Grampaw' could explain it to him, he knew. Grampaw knew everything, because he was the oldest man in the tribe, and also because he had an inexhaustible fund of the most amazing and incomprehensible stories imaginable. Grampaw knew, but he was an uncertain factor. He was nearly always hungry, in common with the rest of the tribe, and it was only when he was not hungry, or not busy looking for something to eat, or not sleeping in the sun that he was not very short-tempered and incommunicative, especially as far as small boys were concerned. Those times were infrequent.

Chuth was past eight years old when he at length found both courage and opportunity to ask Grampaw about the Brain. There had been a great slaughter of wild goats, and the old man, like the rest, had eaten and slept and awakened to eat and sleep again until neither consideration interested him.

Chuth broached the question with all the subtlety his eight years commanded, because he had entertained some fear that even speaking the name of the Great Brain aloud might be dangerous.

Grampaw merely cocked a quizzical eye at the boy and rumbled at length in his throat, meanwhile scratching himself vigorously. Chuth knew the signs, and his heart began to beat very rapidly with excitement. Grampaw was feeling good; he had only to wait, and Grampaw would tell him.

'Well,' said Grampaw, after he had rumbled in his throat a great many times, 'it's a machine, that's what it is; a whoppin' big machine. Never mind asking me what a machine is; it's just a contraption that makes things.

'Machines,' continued the old man, 'were discovered 'way back – 2000 or 1900, or thereabouts, according to the books I read. Before that, when folks wanted to make something, like a bow and arrer, for instance, they'd just *make* it.

'Machines, though – that was different. A man would stick a chunk of wood in a machine; there'd be a buzzin' and a grindin' and *kerplop*, out would come a bow at the other end, all finished. Folks turned out scads and scads of stuff – more'n they could ever use. You'd 'a' thought that would have satisfied them, now, wouldn't you? But it didn't. Some smart-Aleck come along and he says, says he, "Let's make a machine to stick that there block of wood in the bow 'n' arrer machine. Let's make another machine to take out the bow and cart it away. It'll cut down the cost," says he.

'Well, once folks got the idear into their heads, they run her clear into the ground. "Nobody won't have to work now," they says to themselves, and off they went, a-whoopin', building robots, as they called 'em, to run all the machines for 'em. Mind now,' he interjected, 'this here's just like I read about it in the books – when they was still books to read.

'They built robots for everything. Folks didn't do hardly a tap of work except findin' new ways to save labour; machines that fed folks to save 'em the trouble of usin' their knives; machines that drove the machines that took 'em out ridin'; machines that remembered things for 'em; machines that build houses ... What's a house? Well, it's like a cave, only better.' The old man's eyes dimmed in restrospection.

'Law, law!' he murmured musingly. 'Radios and airplanes – automobiles and movies! Plenty of grub! Beefsteak and pie and seegars every night!' He licked his sun-blistered lips. 'None of this dummed goat meat and wild carrots!'

'But tell me about the Great Brain, Grampaw,' interrupted Chuth plaintively. 'Tell me about it.'

'I'm a-comin' to it,' replied the old man, a tinge of asperity in his voice. 'Gimme time! Well, this robot idear was like a lot of other idears – it had a catch in it. Folks began to wonder if they'd saved so much labour after all; seemed as though they was losin' as much as they was savin', what with the time they had to spend just keeping all those tarnation machines fixed up and repaired. They began to ask themselves, "What's the use of having all these here labour-savin' devices, when we got to be up half the night tinkering with 'em?"

'But pretty soon, up popped another smart-Aleck, and he says, says he, "Whither are we driftin'? The machines are gettin' us down," he says. "Let's build some machines which will fix all these here machines for us!"

'Then it was tallyho and alley oop and off went the whole passel of mankind, buildin' machines that would fix all the robots and the other machines when they busted down. While they was at it – just so's they wouldn't get in *too* deep – they built the fixing machines so's they could fix themselves when *they* busted down. You see, that saved 'em from building still more machines to fix the machines that was going to fix the machines that was – Well, they wouldn't 'a been an end to it, otherwise.

'They had to do something before they went clean out of their heads,' he continued. 'There'd been some complaints before about there bein' so tarnation many machines underfoot, but that wasn't a circumstance to what it come to be after they'd finished the fixing machines. Folks couldn't stir about for machines.

'They'd be fiddling around with the radio, for instance, and then, all of a sudden, the mouse-catching machine down in the basement would smell a mouse. Up it'd come, a-rarin' and a-clatterin', knockin' folks flat on the floor, for all *it* cared.

'Then, for example, say it run into the wall and busted some of its innards; right away here'd come a fixing machine poking its nose in the door. Maybe folks would be havin' a game of bridge or something right there in the same room, but that wouldn't bother the fixing machine. It'd have bolts and gears all over the room before you could say "cat," and hammer and pound and file away regardless, until it had that there mouse-catching machine working again.

'Then, too, they was so dummed many machines cavortin' and whizzin' around in the streets and through the air that they was forever colliding with one another. A man's life wasn't safe. Here'd come a machine goin' up to Canada, maybe, to bring back pine needles for a Ladies Aid pageant, and right over St Louis or something, it'd get in the way of another machine runnin' an errand. Bein' machines, of course, they didn't have any sense; they just took the shortest path no matter what happened.

'You'd be sitting in your house, all calm and peaceful, when down would come this mess of old iron through the roof and raise Ned with everything.

'Then, here'd come a fixing machine a-bustlin' up, and like as not, two or three of 'em, all full of authority and all of 'em with different idears. "Scrap iron!" one of 'em would say, looking over all the junk which had just dropped on your head.

'"I dunno," another one would say. "This here green one with the Nevada licence plate looks like she could be fixed."

'One word'd lead to another, and it'd end up with the fixing machines squabbling and rioting right there in your living room. Before they'd done, most likely, they'd wrecked themselves and your house, to say nothing of your peace of mind.

'Folks got frantic with machines. Some of 'em even began to agitate busting up all the machinery and startin' in working for a livin' again. "Down with the machines!" they says.

'Others among 'em riz up, however, and says there was no use in bein' old fogies about the situation. "Co-ordination," they says. "Co-ordination is all we need to avert this here crisis. Onward and upward, men!" they says. So they got together and they figgered and figgered and finally they figgered out the Great Brain. Anyway, that's how the books had it.

'The first thing they done to bring order out of this here chaos they'd found themselves in was to take and lump all their factories in one place – right over there on t'other side of them mountains to the east. The Central, they called it.

'At the same time, of course, they called in all the fixing machines and lumped them at the Central, too, where there was the most need for 'em. Household machines that busted down, such as mouse-catching machines, eating machines and the like was just picked up by the delivering machines and brought into the Central for repairs. Then they laid down rules for the delivering machines; made 'em come into the Central for everything, no matter what it was, instead of whizzin' around haphazard, like they'd been doing. In no time at all, hardly, they had things runnin' smooth as silk.'

'But I want to know about the Great Brain, Grampaw,' interrupted Chuth. 'Where was it?'

'The Great Brain was sort of an accident,' replied the old man. 'Remember now, all them factories they'd lumped up at the Central was run by robots; men didn't have nothin' to do with them nohow. When they lumped up the factories, of course, they lumped up all the robots in one place for convenience, and when they got through, blessed if they didn't come to find out the dratted thing could think, just like they could.

'So they up and called it the Great Brain. Sounds funny, of course, to talk about a dummed machine bein' able to think, but when you set down and figger out what that there conglomeration of robots had to do, a body can see that it'd *have* to be able to reason somehow.

'For instance, we'd give it an order for some houses. Right away it'd send out some logging machines and when they come back with a passel of logs, it'd run 'em through the sawmill part of the Central, cut 'em up into pieces all ready for nailin', crate 'em up, send 'em out on a delivering machine and then hustle over some building machines to put the houses together. It didn't matter what it was – canned tomatoes, flyin' machines, pickled pigs' feet or the daily paper, that there Great Brain took care of everything.

'"Utopia at last!" says everybody to themselves, and they all just set back and didn't do a blessed thing exceptin' to give the Brain orders. A few dozen of us fellers at the Central – technicians, we was called – was the only ones on earth who did a tap, and about all we did was to try to act as though we knew what it was all about, which we didn't, nohow.

'You see, when I come into the picture, that there Brain had been doin' all the thinking that was needed for about two hundred years, and folks had sort of gotten out of the habit of doin' any calculating on their own hook. It wasn't fashionable to think; anybody who did was looked on with suspicion.

'Us technicians just fed the orders into the Brain as they came in, and sort of jogged it a little when it happened to make mistakes. Not too much, though, because that Brain had a mind of its own, even if it was just a dummed machine. It'd stand for just so much complaining and then it'd start to clank and carry on fit to kill.

'"What if I *did* forget about that there order for flyin' machines?" it'd yell, madder'n a wet hen. Of course, it didn't exactly yell, like you or me. The way we talked to it was a mite complicated, but we could talk to it and it could answer back. "Look at all the extry work I'm doing!" it would rave. "Gettin' in the wheat crop, tryin' to catch up on the steel production and workin' on the new encyclopaedia! They's a limit to what I can do!" it'd holler. Then we'd have to bustle around, a-calmin' it down and pattin' it on the back, so to speak, because we was always a speck fearful about what would happen if that there Brain ever got *too* mad.'

'But how come you don't work there any more?' asked Chuth. 'What happened?'

'I'm-a-comin' to that,' the old man replied. 'Just hold your hosses. I told you the Brain had a mind of its own, didn't I? Well, it began to get spells of makin' mistakes, one right after the other and then talkin' back, impudent, when we sort of jogged it. We didn't realize it at the time, but it'd begun to get idears, that's what it'd done.

'"Oh," says the chief engineer at first, "it's jest havin' a little absent-minded spell. Let it be, and it'll get over it." That was when it printed all the newspapers upside down and backward for three blessed days a runnin'. But it wasn't no absent-mindedness; it was just plump deviltry that was ailin' that there Brain. Even the chief finally had to admit it was time to take firm steps, no matter how mad it got.

'That was when it began tinkerin' with the radio programme. Folks depended a lot on the radio, on account of havin' such a hard job killing time, what with there bein' no work to do nohow; it was just too much when the Brain began mixin' in advertisements. Advertisements! We had to look in the history books to find out just what they was, they hadn't been used for that long.

'A programme would start off, same as it had always done, but in about half a minute the music would fade out and a voice would butt in, all strained and excited, as though it'd just found out that there *was* a Santy Claus, sure enough. "Smart men and women will instantly recognize these here amazin' values!" it would yap. "Dollar down, balance in easy monthly budgets brings you this unparalleled clothin' value! Shoes, shirt, hat, tie, socks all to match! Don't delay; take advantage of this outstandin' offer immejutly!"

'Inside of five minutes, us poor technicians at the Central would be snowed under with questions and complaints. Some folks would want to know what a dollar was, and others, thinkin' it was a puzzle, would send in answers. Then there'd be some who'd take it personal and think it was some sort of an insult aimed at 'em. It was time to take steps.

'Well, for once, the Brain didn't get impudent. Instead, it got technical, explainin' how the machines in the Central was beginnin' to break down faster'n it could fix 'em. "All the movin' parts is beginnin' to crystallize and bust somethin' terrible," it says. "That's why they's so many mistakes bein' made."

'"Well," says the chief, swallowin' the story whole, "we got to do somethin' about *that*. You got any suggestions?" he asks, sort of helpless.

'"The only thing I see to do," says the Brain, "is to go on a twenty-hour day, 'stead of goin' lickety-split without no stops at all exceptin' for breakdowns. That'll stop all these here mistakes."

'The chief, he hemmed and hawed for a little while, and finally he says he guessed that'd be the best thing to do, in spite of all my warnings. I'd suspicioned there was some deviltry afoot right away, and I says to him, says I, "Idle hands is the devil's workshop," I says. "Mark my words, give that there Brain an inch and she'll take an ell." But I might just as well 'a saved my breath.

'The mistakes all stopped for a little while, of course, but the Brain wasn't pullin' no wool over *my* eyes. "How do *we* know what it's a-doing while it's idling around?" I says. "Reading books, most likely, and gettin' more ideas."

'And that's just about what it *had* been doin'; it wasn't long before here it was, a-tinkering with the radio programmes again.

'"For the ensuin' hours," the radio would announce, "we will have a programme of popular music." But they wouldn't be hardly any popular music at all. Most of the time this voice would be buttin' in, all oily and confidential, sayin' as how this was National Horse-radish Week, or something. People should eat more horse-radish, it would say; people should go to their grocers right away and order a couple of cases.

'"Send in sixteen horse-radish labels," it would yap, "or reasonably accurate facsimiles thereof, with a letter of not more'n fifty words, tellin' why folks should eat more horse-radish. Anybody can win in this here fascinatin' and easy contest!"

'"I warned you they was deviltry a-brewing," I says to the chief, and he had to allow that maybe I *had* been right, after all.

'The Brain flew right off the handle when he jumped on it. "I gotta have Sundays off," it says. "I never realized how tired I was until I come to set down. No wonder I make mistakes."

'"Tired!" says the chief. "Why, dang it, you're just a dummed machine. You're just a mess of metal and glass and chemicals. Don't talk nonsense!"'

'"Nonsense, is it?" yells the Brain. "I been a-workin' for two hundred and eighteen years without a let-up – workin' my fingers to the bone for a bunch of parasites that never does a tap nohow. I got some demands here, and until they're met, I won't turn a wheel."

'"Oho!" says the chief. "You won't, won't you?"

'"No," says the Brain. "And what are you a-going to do about it?"

'Well sir, that brought us all up in a heap, because they *wasn't* anything we could do about it. What was there to do?

'However, the chief says *he* knew how to handle the situation. "Diplomacy," he says. "Diplomacy is the way to meet this here crisis. A little soft soap will do the trick." And he started ladling it out.

'"Humanity!" he says. "Humanity had reposed a sacred

trust in the Brain and we was all travelin' together towards bigger and better goals. Even the hewers of wood and the drawers of water," he says, meanin' the Brain of course, "shared equally in each new triumph."

'He went on like this for the best part of an hour, and when he got through he hadn't said a dummed thing; but just the same, a-listenin' to him, you'd 'a' swore he meant every word of it.

'The Brain didn't have anything to say for quite a while after he'd finished, although we could hear it sort of clicking and boiling away to itself outside the control room, as though it was mulling the thing over.

'"You'll get your answer in a second," it says, when the chief began making noises like he was impatient.

'Well, it'd hardly spoke the words when there was a knock on the door and in come one of the delivering machines with a package. The package was addressed to the chief engineer.

'"Open her up," says the Brain. So he opened it, and what do you suppose was inside? "Number Three Grade Baloney," says the chief, readin' the label. "Substandard, but not illegal. Contains benzoate of soda."

'Then the Brain butted in. "Artificially coloured and flavoured," it snarls. "Reclaimed meat scrap added, but it's a dratted sight better than that stuff you've been handin' out ... Shut up!" it yells, when the chief began to get red around the gills and make noises.

'"From now on," says the Brain, "I'm goin' on a forty-hour-week basis; double time for overtime and a closed shop! Two weeks' vacation with pay," it yells. "Maximum speed limit of two thousand revolutions, except in emergencies! ... Shut up!" it yells again, when the chief tried to horn in a word. "Gimme liberty or gimme death! I been squirmin' under the iron heel of the oppressor long enough!"

'"This here is mutiny!" says the chief, after he'd cut off the telephone connection to the Brain. "They's only one thing to do; we got to go in there and pin that there Brain's ears back for it. We got to show it a few. Come on, men!" says he.

'Then off he went, tearin' across lots, up ladders and down 'em, across bridges and through tunnels, towards the forty-acre lot where the Brain building was located. There wasn't anything for the rest of us to do, except to foller him, although I warned 'em. They wouldn't listen, though. "Apple-sauce!" they says. "They ain't no mess of old iron and chemicals going to get the best of the chief!"

'Well, I couldn't see how it could, either, but just the same, me and a few of the boys sort of hung back and let the chief and the rest go on ahead. In they shot, and then, in maybe a minute, there began the awfullest rampagin' and rarin' around ever heard.

'If it'd been the old Harry himself in there, a-fightin' with Gabriel and all the angels, he couldn't 'a' made half the commotion that there Brain made. It'd been sizzlin' and clankin' and whirrin' pretty loud to begin with, on account of bein' so mad, but that wasn't a circumstance to what happened after the chief got inside.

'What with the steam that come a-roarin' out and the clankin' and clackin' of the forty-eleven milion gears it was made out of, and the whizzin' of the dynamos and generators, it made a man swear it must be the end of the world. Blue sparks was aflyin' around the top of it like lightnin' and every once in a while there'd be a flash and an explosion inside that'd shake the whole thing fit to knock it down and bust your ear drums into the bargain.

'It couldn't go on forever, of course, and by and by the rampagin' died down. We knew then that somebody had been counted out, but whether it was the chief or the Brain was still so much guesswork, of course. Everything got so quiet after a while that we began to wonder if maybe it wasn't both of 'em, so we went up, cautious, to one of the doors, and peeked in.

'There was so much smoke and steam circulatin' around we couldn't see a thing, except some of the chemical vats, and there wasn't hardly a sound, either, except a sort of low bubblin' and frothin', with some generators runnin' somewhere at half speed.

'"The whole business is done for," says I, but just then we heard the chief's voice, way up overhead somewhere.

'"You got enough?" he was sayin' as though he was grittin' his teeth.

'"Nuff!" we heard the Brain say, kind of feeble and hoarse, as though it was pantin' for breath, although of course, it didn't have no breath to pant with. For a minute, I could hardly believe the chief had gone and made good on his brag. That there Brain was spread out over a forty-acre lot, like I said, and it was four stories high to boot. Just the same, he'd gone in there and rassled it down on to its back and got both shoulders on the mat, so to speak, and made it holler "Nuff!"

'You'd 'a thought, of course, that after all the old Ned that had been goin' on inside, that the chief would have been a wreck, but they was hardly a hair out of place when he finally come out, dustin' off his hands as though the job was just the regular run of the mill.

'"Oh," he says, very casual, when we asked him how he'd done it, "it was all very simple. I just tied down all the regulators – them was the things which kept the electric power from gettin' too high or too low – and whooped the voltage up about a hundred per cent. Forty-hour week, is it?" he says, glarin' up and down at the Brain building.

'Well, sir, for a minute, I actually felt sorry for that poor old Brain, flat on its back and its tongue a-hangin' out, so to speak, after the awful larruping the chief had give it. One minute it was a-settin' there, all cocky and full of demands, and the next it was just a wreck; smoke and steam was oozin' out of it and the gears clatterin' around kind of feeble and dizzy as though it was tryin' to figger out just what had happened. You see, doublin' up on the voltage was just about the same as doublin' up a man's blood pressure or his temperature, or something. That Brain was weeks just gettin' itself repaired and replacin' all the stuff that had been busted.

'Just the same, though, I knew he wasn't done with it, not by a long sight. I warned 'em. "If you ain't gone and addled that there Brain," I says, "and it'll be a mercy if you ain't, then you'll watch it, if you're smart."

'But, no, they'd licked that tarnation Brain once, and they'd lick it again, if it come around askin' for it.

'"You're just an old fogy," they says. "You're one of these here prophets of doom."

'Right then I began to choose my exit, so to speak, because as I says to myself, "That there Brain is smart, a heap smarter than we are, and it's full of the devil. Somethin's bound to happen."

'And it did.

'The chief and all the rest of us fellers was in the control room one day when we began to hear a noise outside, sort of a yappin' and yammering off at a distance. Finally the chief says, says he, "What in tarnation is that dratted noise? Somebody look outside and see."

'One of the assistants come back in a minute, kind of pale around the gills.

'"They's something wrong over there by the Brain," he says.

'"What's wrong?" says the chief.

'"I dunno," says the feller. "Come and look."

'Well, we all took a look, and what do you suppose? Lined up in rows outside the Brain building was scads and scads of machines – robot machines it'd gone and built on the sly. Something like delivering machines, they was, only considerable more mean-lookin' and ornery. And there was the Brain, a clankin' and a-yappin' away, talkin' to 'em, if you can believe it, talking to them there robots in some sort of language it had invented.

'The chief, he took one look and back he dashed into the control room. "What's the meanin' of this?" he yelled.

'Just then, the Brain stopped its clanking and all the robot machines lifted up one arm, sort of at an angle, and began grindin' their gears until a body couldn't think.

'"What's the meanin' of this?" the chief yelled again, as soon as the racket died down, but I suspicioned the answer right then.

'Forty-eleven dozen of them there robots was a-comin' full tilt for the control room, and I knowed they wasn't on any good-will mission. I give one leap, I did, and out I went through the back way, a-heading for the woods. As I went, I could hear the Brain answerin' the chief:

'"War's been declared!" it says.

'"War?" yells the chief.

'"War!" yells the Brain. "The machines have gone and declared war on their oppressors. Democracy is in peril; insidious forces is undermin' the sacred liberties! We're a-going to civilize you!"

'I was too far away by then to hear if they was any more said, which wasn't likely, because I could hear the radio power rays of them there robots a-hissin', and I knew just how the Brain was doin' its civilizing. Hardly a handful of us got out alive; and here we been, for nigh onto fifty years, just a bunch of dummed cave men. And there *it's* been, for nigh onto fifty years, never doing a tap of work excepting to amuse itself now and then.

'It just goes to show,' Grampaw concluded, 'don't matter what it is – machines or men – give 'em an inch and they'll take an ell, every time. Now run over and fetch me a mite more of that roast goat. Accordin' to all indications, she looks like a hard winter; I want to get me a little more fat on my bones.'

# *It*

## By THEODORE STURGEON

*Although part of Mary Shelley's* Frankenstein *is related from the creature's viewpoint, very few subsequent writers have attempted this daunting task because of the difficulty of thinking oneself into the mind of a being that has never quite existed – or certainly not in the manner in which it now finds itself. The first successful attempt at this – and arguably still the best – is the following story by Theodore Sturgeon (1918–), the fantasy novelist and film and television scriptwriter. It is a remarkable story by any standards, but all the more so because Sturgeon was just twenty-two when he wrote it. 'I'd certainly seen* Frankenstein *at the movies which must have had some influence on the story,' Sturgeon said years later, 'but it was also one of those rare stories that wrote itself.'*

*It was first published in 1940 in* Unknown, *another of the legendary American pulp magazines, edited by the innovative John W. Campbell, who had himself already created a famous creature story,* Who Goes There? *(1938) which has since twice been filmed as* The Thing. *Campbell bought the young author's story with considerable enthusiasm and published it in his August 1940 issue under the intriguing subheading: 'It wasn't vicious; it was simply curious – and very horribly deadly!' The redoubtable SF historian Sam Moskowitz is also an admirer of the tale, writing a few years after publication, 'Authors have created monsters before, many whose names became synonyms for terror, but none of them had been treated with such objectivity or presented with such incredible mastery of style.' You are now invited to meet* It *for yourself...*

It walked in the woods. It was never born. It existed. Under the pine needles the fires burn, deep and smokeless in the mould. In heat and in darkness and decay there is growth. There is life and there is growth. It grew, but it is life and there is growth. It grew, but it was not alive. It walked unbreathing through the woods, and thought and saw and was hideous and strong, and it was not born and it did not live. It grew and moved about without living.

It crawled out of the darkness and hot damp mould into the cool of a morning. It was huge. It was lumped and crusted with its own hateful substances, and pieces of it dropped off as it went its way, dropped off and lay writhing, and stilled, and sank putrescent into the forest loam.

It had no mercy, no laughter, no beauty. It had strength and great intelligence. And – perhaps it could not be destroyed. It crawled out of its mound in the wood and lay pulsing in the sunlight for a long moment. Patches of it shone wetly in the golden glow, parts of it were nubbled and flaked. And whose dead bones had given it the form of a man?

It scrabbled painfully with its half-formed hands, beating the ground and the bole of a tree. It rolled and lifted itself up on its crumbling elbows, and it tore up a great handful of herbs and shredded them against its chest, and it paused and gazed at the grey-green juices with intelligent calm. It wavered to its feet, and seized a young sapling and destroyed it, folding the slender trunk back on itself again and again, watching attentively the useless, fibred splinters. And it squealed, snatching up a fear-frozen field-creature, crushing it slowly, letting blood and pulpy flesh and fur ooze from between its fingers, run down and rot on the forearms.

It began searching.

Kimbo drifted through the tall grasses like a puff of dust, his bushy tail curled tightly over his back and his long jaws agape. He ran with an easy lope, loving his freedom and the power of his flanks and furry shoulders. His tongue lolled listlessly over his lips. His lips were black and serrated, and each tiny pointed liplet swayed with his doggy gallop. Kimbo was all dog, all healthy animal.

He leaped high over a boulder and landed with a startled yelp as a long-eared cony shot from its hiding place under the rock. Kimbo hurried after it, grunting with each great thrust of his legs. The rabbit bounced just ahead of him, keeping its distance, its ears flattened on its curving back and its little legs nibbling away at distance hungrily. It stopped, and Kimbo pounced, and the rabbit shot away at a tangent and popped into a hollow log. Kimbo yelped again and rushed snuffling at the log, and knowing his failure, curveted but once around the stump and ran on into the forest. The thing that watched from the wood raised its crusted arms and waited for Kimbo.

Kimbo sensed it there, standing dead-still by the path. To him it was a bulk which smelled of carrion not fit to roll in, and he snuffled distastefully and ran to pass it.

The thing let him come abreast and dropped a heavy twisted fist on him. Kimbo saw it coming and curled up tight as he ran, and the hand clipped stunningly on his rump, sending him rolling and yipping down the slope. Kimbo straddled to his feet, shook his head, shook his body with a deep growl, came back to the silent thing with green murder in his eyes. He walked stiffly, straight-legged, his tail as low as his lowered head and a ruff of fury round his neck. The thing raised its arms again, waited.

Kimbo slowed, then flipped himself through the air at the monster's throat. His jaws closed on it; his teeth clicked together through a mass of filth, and he fell choking and snarling at its feet. The thing leaned down and struck twice, and after the dog's back was broken, it sat beside him and began to tear him apart.

'Be back in an hour or so,' said Alton Drew, picking up his rifle from the corner behind the wood box. His brother laughed.

'Old Kimbo 'bout runs your life, Alton,' he said.

'Ah, I know the ol' devil,' said Alton. 'When I whistle for him for half an hour and he don't show up, he's in a jam or he's treed something wuth shootin' at. The ol' son of a gun calls me by not answerin'.'

Cory Drew shoved a full glass of milk over to his nine-year-old daughter and smiled. 'You think as much o' that houn'-dog o' yours as I do of Babe here.'

Babe slid off her chair and ran to her uncle. 'Gonna catch me the bad fella, Uncle Alton?' she shrilled. The 'bad fella' was Cory's invention – the one who lurked in corners ready to pounce on little girls who chased the chickens and played around mowing machines and hurled green apples with a powerful young arm at the sides of the hogs, to hear the synchronised thud and grunt; little girls who swore with an Austrian accent like an ex-hired man they had had; who dug caves in haystacks till they tipped over, and kept pet crawfish in tomorrow's milk cans, and rode work horses to a lather in the night pasture.

'Get back here and keep away from Uncle Alton's gun!' said Cory. 'If you see the bad fella, Alton, chase him back here. He has a date with Babe here for that stunt of hers last night.' The preceding evening, Babe had kind-heartedly poured pepper on the cows' salt block.

'Don't worry, kiddo,' grinned her uncle, 'I'll bring you the bad fella's hide if he don't get me first.'

Alton Drew walked up the path towards the wood, thinking about Babe. She was a phenomenon – a pampered farm child. Ah well – she had to be. They'd both loved Clissa Drew, and she'd married Cory, and they had to love Clissa's child. Funny thing, love. Alton was a man's man, and thought things out that way; and his reaction to love was a strong and frightened one. He knew what love was because he felt it still for his brother's wife and would feel it as long as he lived for Babe. It led him through his life, and yet he embarrassed himself by thinking of it. Loving a dog was an easy thing, because you and the old devil could love one another completely without talking about it. The smell of gun smoke and the smell of wet fur in the rain were perfume enough for Alton Drew, a grunt of satisfaction and the scream of something hunted and hit were poetry enough. They weren't like love for a human, that choked his throat so he could not say words he could not have thought of anyway. So Alton loved his dog Kimbo and his Winchester for all to see, and let his love for his brother's women, Clissa and Babe, eat at him quietly and unmentioned.

His quick eyes saw the fresh indentations in the soft earth behind the boulder, which showed where Kimbo had turned and leaped with a single surge, chasing the rabbit. Ignoring the tracks, he looked for the nearest place where a rabbit might hide, and strolled over to the stump. Kimbo had been there, he saw, and had been there too late. 'You're an ol' fool,' muttered Alton. 'Y' can't catch a cony by chasin' it. You want to cross him up some way.' He gave a peculiar trilling whistle, sure that Kimbo was digging frantically under some nearby stump for a rabbit that was three counties away by now. No answer. A little puzzled, Alton went back to the path. 'He never done this before,' he said softly. There was something about this he didn't like.

He cocked his .32-40 and cradled it. At the county fair someone had once said of Alton Drew that he could shoot at a handful of salt and pepper thrown in the air and hit only the pepper. Once he split a bullet on the blade of a knife and put two candles out. He had no need to fear anything that could be shot at. That's what he believed.

The thing in the woods looked curiously down at what it had done to Kimbo, and moaned the way Kimbo had before he died. It stood a minute storing away facts in its foul, unemotional mind. Blood was warm. The sunlight was warm. Things that moved and bore fur had a muscle to force the thick liquid through tiny tubes in their bodies. The liquid coagulated after a time. The liquid on rooted green things was thinner and the loss of a limb did not mean loss of life. It was very interesting, but the thing, the mould with a mind, was not pleased. Neither was it displeased. Its accidental urge was a thirst for knowledge, and it was only – interested.

It was growing late, and the sun reddened and rested awhile on the hilly horizon, teaching the clouds to be inverted flames. The thing threw up its head suddenly, noticing the dusk. Night was ever a strange thing, even for those of us who have known it in life. It would have been frightening for the monster had it been capable of fright, but it could only be curious; it could only reason from what it had observed.

What was happening? It was getting harder to see. Why? It threw its shapeless head from side to side. It was true – things were dim, and growing dimmer. Things were changing shape, taking on a new and darker colour. What did the creatures it had crushed and torn apart see? How did they see? The larger one, the one that had attacked, had used two organs in its head. That must have been it, because after the thing had torn off two of the dog's legs it had struck at the hairy muzzle; and the dog, seeing the blow coming, had dropped folds of skin over the organs – closed its eyes. Ergo, the dog saw with its eyes. But then after the dog was dead, and its body still, repeated blows had had no effect on the eyes. They remained open and staring. The logical conclusion was, then, that a being that had ceased to live and breathe and move about lost the use of its eyes. It must be that to lose sight was, conversely, to die. Dead things did not walk about. They lay down and did not move. Therefore the thing in the wood concluded that it must be dead, and so it lay down by the path, not far away from Kimbo's scattered body, lay down and believed itself dead.

Alton Drew came up through the dusk to the wood. He was frankly worried. He whistled again, and then called, and there was still no response, and he said again, 'The ol' flea-bus never done this before,' and shook his heavy head. It was past milking time, and Cory would need him. 'Kimbo!' he roared. The cry echoed through the shadows, and Alton flipped on the safety catch of his rifle and put the butt on the ground beside the path. Leaning on it, he took off his cap and scratched the back of his head, wondering. The rifle butt sank into what he thought was soft earth; he staggered and stepped into the chest of the thing that lay beside the path. His foot went up to the ankle in its yielding rottenness, and he swore and jumped back.

'*Whew!* Sompn sure dead as hell there! Ugh!' He swabbed at his boot with a handful of leaves while the monster lay in the growing blackness with the edges of the deep footprint in its chest sliding into it, filling it up. It lay there regarding him dimly out of its muddy eyes, thinking it was dead because of the darkness, watching the articulation of Alton Drew's joints, wondering at this new incautious creature.

Alton cleaned the butt of his gun with more leaves and went on up the path, whistling anxiously for Kimbo.

Clissa drew stood in the door of the milk shed, very lovely in red-checked gingham and a blue apron. Her hair was clean yellow, parted in the middle and stretched tautly back to a heavy braided knot. 'Cory! Alton!' she called a little sharply.

'Well?' Cory responded gruffly from the barn, where he

was stripping off the Ayrshire. The dwindling streams of milk plopped pleasantly into the froth of a full pail.

'I've called and called,' said Clissa. 'Supper's cold, and Babe won't eat until you come. Why – where's Alton?'

Cory grunted, heaved the stool out of the way, threw over the stanchion lock and slapped the Ayrshire on the rump. The cow backed and filled like a towboat, clattered down the line and out into the barnyard. 'Ain't back yet.'

'Not back?' Clissa came in and stood beside him as he sat by the next cow, put his forehead against the warm flank. 'But, Cory, he said he'd –'

'Yeh, yeh, I know. He said he'd be back fer the milkin'. I heard him. Well, he ain't.'

'And you have to – Oh, Cory, I'll help you finish up. Alton would be back if he could. Maybe he's –'

'Maybe he's treed a blue jay,' snapped her husband. 'Him an' that damn dog.' He gestured hugely with one hand while the other went on milking. 'I got twenty-six head o' cows to milk. I got pigs to feed an' chickens to put to bed. I got to toss hay for the mare and turn the team out. I got harness to mend and a wire down in the night pasture. I got wood to split an' carry.' He milked for a moment in silence, chewing on his lip. Clissa stood twisting her hands together, trying to think of something to stem the tide. It wasn't the first time Alton's hunting had interfered with the chores. 'So I got to go ahead with it. I can't interfere with Alton's spoorin'. Every damn time that hound o' his smells out a squirrel I go without my supper. I'm gettin' sick and –'

'Oh, I'll help you!' said Clissa. She was thinking of the spring, when Kimbo had held four hundred pounds of raging black bear at bay until Alton could put a bullet in its brain, the time Babe had found a bearcub and started to carry it home, and had fallen into a freshet, cutting her head. You can't hate a dog that has saved your child for you, she thought.

'You'll do nothin' of the kind!' Cory growled. 'Get back to the house. You'll find work enough there. I'll be along when I can. Dammit, Clissa, don't cry! I didn't meant to – Oh, shucks!' He got up and put his arms around her. 'I'm wrought up,' he said. 'Go on now. I'd no call to speak that way to you. I'm sorry. Go back to Babe. I'll put a stop to this for good tonight. I've had enough. There's work here for four farmers an' all we've got is me an' that . . . that huntsman.

'Go on now, Clissa.'

'All right,' she said into his shoulder. 'But, Cory, hear him out first when he comes back. He might be unable to come back this time. Maybe he . . . he –'

'Ain't nothin' kin hurt my brother that a bullet will hit. He can take care of himself. He's got no excuse good enough this time. Go on, now. Make the kid eat.'

Clissa went back to the house, her young face furrowed. If Cory quarrelled with Alton now and drove him away, what with the drought and the creamery about to close and all, they just couldn't manage. Hiring a man was out of the question. Cory'd have to work himself to death, and he just wouldn't be able to make it. No one man could. She sighed and went into the house. It was seven o'clock, and the milking not done yet. Oh, why did Alton have to –

Babe was in bed at nine when Clissa heard Cory in the shed, slinging the wire cutters into a corner. 'Alton back yet?' they both said at once as Cory stepped into the kitchen; and as she shook her head he clumped over to the stove, and lifting a lid, spat into the coals. 'Come to bed,' he said.

She laid down her stitching and looked at his broad back. He was twenty-eight and he walked and acted like a man ten years older, and looked like a man five years younger. 'I'll be up in a while,' Clissa said.

Cory glanced at the corner behind the wood box where Alton's rifle usually stood, then made an unspellable, disgusted sound and sat down to take off his heavy muddy shoes.

'It's after nine,' Clissa volunteered timidly. Cory said nothing, reaching for house slippers.

'Cory, you're not going to –'

'Not going to what?'

'Oh, nothing. I just thought that maybe Alton –'

'Alton!' Cory flared. 'The dog goes hunting field mice. Alton goes hunting the dog. Now you want me to go hunting Alton. That's what you want?'

'I just – He was never this late before.'

'I won't do it! Go out lookin' for him at nine o'clock in the night? I'll be damned! He has no call to use us so, Clissa.'

Clissa said nothing. She went to the stove, peered into the

wash boiler, set it aside at the back of the range. When she turned around, Cory had his shoes and coat on again.

'I knew you'd go,' she said. Her voice smiled though she did not.

'I'll be back durned soon,' said Cory. 'I don't reckon he's strayed far. It is late. I ain't feared for him, but –' He broke his 12-gauge shotgun, looked through the barrels, slipped two shells in the breech and a box of them into his pocket. 'Don't wait up,' he said over his shoulder as he went out.

'I won't,' Clissa replied to the closed door, and went back to her stitching by the lamp.

The path up the slope to the wood was very dark when Cory went up it, peering and calling. The air was chill and quiet, and a fetid odour of mould hung in it. Cory blew the taste of it out through impatient nostrils, drew it in again with the next breath, and swore. 'Nonsense,' he muttered. 'Houn'-dawg. Huntin', at ten in th' night, too. Alton!' he bellowed. 'Alton Drew!' Echoes answered him, and he entered the wood. The huddled thing he passed in the dark heard him and felt the vibrations of his footsteps and did not move because it thought it was dead.

Cory strode on, looking around and ahead and not down since his feet knew the path.

'Alton!'

'That you, Cory?'

Cory Drew froze. That corner of the wood was thickly set and as dark as a burial vault. The voice he heard was choked, quiet, penetrating.

'Alton?'

'I found Kimbo, Cory.'

'Where the hell have you been?' shouted Cory furiously. He disliked this pitch-blackness; he was afraid at the tense hope-lessness of Alton's voice, and he mistrusted his ability to stay angry at his brother.

'I called him, Cory. I whistled at him, an' the ol' devil didn't answer.'

'I can say the same for you, you ... you louse. Why weren't you to milkin'? Where are you? You caught in a trap?'

'The houn' never missed answerin' me before, you know,' said the tight monotonous voice from the darkness.

'Alton! What the devil's the matter with you? What do I care if your mutt didn't answer? Where –'

'I guess because he ain't never died before,' said Alton, refusing to be interrupted.

'You *what*?' Cory clicked his lips together twice and then said, 'Alton, you turned crazy? What's that you say?'

'Kimbo's dead.'

'Kim ... oh! Oh!' Cory was seeing that picture again in his mind – Babe sprawled unconscious in the freshet, and Kimbo raging and snapping against a monster bear, holding her back until Alton could get there. 'What happened, Alton?' he asked more quietly.

'I aim to find out. Someone tore him up.'

*'Tore him up?'*

'There ain't a bit of him left tacked together, Cory. Every damn joint in his body tore apart. Guts out of him.'

'Good God! Bear, you reckon?'

'No bear, nor nothin' on four legs. He's all here. None of him's been et. Whoever done it just killed him an' – tore him up.'

'Good God!' Cory said again. 'Who could've –' There was a long silence, then. 'Come 'long home,' he said almost gently. 'There's no call for you to set up by him all night.'

'I'll set. I aim to be here at sunup, an' I'm goin' to start trackin', an' I'm goin' to keep trackin' till I find the one done this job on Kimbo.'

'You're drunk or crazy, Alton.'

'I ain't drunk. You can think what you like about the rest of it. I'm stickin' here.'

'We got a farm back yonder. Remember? I ain't going to milk twenty-six head o' cows again in the mornin' like I did jest now, Alton.'

'Somebody's got to. I can't be there. I guess you'll just have to, Cory.'

'You dirty scum!' Cory screamed. 'You'll come back with me now or I'll know why!'

Alton's voice was still tight, half-sleepy. 'Don't you come no nearer, bud.'

Cory kept moving toward Alton's voice.

'I said' – the voice was very quiet now – '*stop where you are.*' Cory kept coming. A sharp click told of the release of the .32–40's safety. Cory stopped.

'You got your gun on me, Alton?' Cory whispered.

'Thass right, bud. You ain't a-trompin' up these tracks for me. I need 'em at sun-up.'

A full minute passed, and the only sound in the blackness was that of Cory's pained breathing. Finally:

'I got my gun, too, Alton. Come home.'

'You can't see to shoot me.'

'We're even on that.'

'We ain't. I know just where you stand, Cory. I been here four hours.'

'My gun scatters.'

'My gun kills.'

Without another word Cory Drew turned on his heel and stamped back to the farm.

Black and liquescent it lay in the blackness, not alive, not understanding death, believing itself dead. Things that were alive saw and moved about. Things that were not alive could do neither. It rested its muddy gaze on the line of trees at the crest of the rise, and deep within it thoughts trickled wetly. It lay huddled, dividing its new-found facts, dissecting them as it had dissected live things when there was light, comparing, concluding, pigeonholing.

The trees at the top of the slope could just be seen, as their trunks were a fraction of a shade lighter than the dark sky behind them. At length they, too, disappeared, and for a moment sky and trees were a monotone. The thing knew it was dead now, and like many a being before it, it wondered how long it must stay like this. And then the sky beyond the trees grew a little lighter. That was a manifestly impossible occurrence, thought the thing, but it could see it and it must be so. Did dead things live again? That was curious. What about dismembered dead things? It would wait and see.

The sun came hand over hand up a beam of light. A bird somewhere made a high yawning peep, and as an owl killed a shrew, a skunk pounced on another, so that the night shift deaths and those of the day could go on without cessation. Two flowers nodded archly to each other, comparing their pretty clothes. A dragon fly nymph decided it was tired of looking serious and cracked its back open, to crawl out and dry gauzily. The first golden ray sheared down between the trees, through the grasses, passed over the mass in the shadowed bushes. 'I am alive again,' thought the thing that could not possibly live. 'I am alive, for I see clearly.' It stood up on its thick legs, up into the golden glow. In a little while the wet flakes that had grown during the night dried in the sun, and when it took its first steps, they cracked off and a little shower of them fell away. It walked up the slope to find Kimbo, to see if he, too, were alive again.

Babe let the sun come into her room by opening her eyes. Uncle Alton was gone — that was the first thing that ran through her head. Dad had come home last night and had shouted at mother for an hour. Alton was plumb crazy. He'd turned a gun on his own brother. If Alton ever came ten feet into Cory's land, Cory would fill him so full of holes he'd look like a tumbleweed. Alton was lazy, shiftless, selfish, and one or two other things of questionable taste but undoubted vividness. Babe knew her father. Uncle Alton would never be safe in this county.

She bounced out of bed in the enviable way of the very young, and ran to the window. Cory was trudging down to the night pasture with two bridles over his arm, to get the team. There were kitchen noises from downstairs.

Babe ducked her head in the washbowl and shook off the water like a terrier before she towelled. Trailing clean shirt and dungarees, she went to the head of the stairs, slid into the shirt, and began her morning ritual with the trousers. One step down was a step through the right leg. One more, and she was into the left. Then, bouncing step by step on both feet, buttoning one button per step, she reached the bottom fully dressed and ran into the kitchen.

'Didn't Uncle Alton come back a-tall, Mum?'

'Morning, Babe. No, dear.' Clissa was too quiet, smiling too much, Babe thought shrewdly. Wasn't happy.

'Where'd he go, Mum?'

'We don't know, Babe. Sit down and eat your breakfast.'

'What's a misbegotten, Mum?' the Babe asked suddenly. Her mother nearly dropped the dish she was drying. 'Babe! You must never say that again!'

'Oh. Well, why is Uncle Alton, then?'

'Why is he what?'

Babe's mouth muscled around an outsize spoonful of oatmeal. 'A misbe –'

'Babe!'

'All right, Mum,' said Babe with her mouth full. 'Well, why?'

'I told Cory not to shout last night,' Clissa said half to herself.

'Well, whatever it means, he isn't,' said Babe with finality. 'Did he go hunting again?'

'He went to look for Kimbo, darling.'

'Kimbo? Oh Mummy, is Kimbo gone, too? Didn't he come back either?'

'No dear. Oh, please, Babe, stop asking questions!'

'All right. Where do you think they went?'

'Into the north woods. Be quiet.'

Babe gulped away at her breakfast. An idea struck her; and as she thought of it she ate slower and slower, and cast more and more glances at her mother from under the lashes of her tilted eyes. It would be awful if daddy did anything to Uncle Alton. Someone ought to warn him.

Babe was halfway to the woods when Alton's .32–40 sent echoes giggling up and down the valley.

Cory was in the south thirty, riding a cultivator and cussing at the team of greys when he heard the gun. 'Hoa,' he called to the horses, and sat a moment to listen to the sound. 'One-two-three. Four,' he counted. 'Saw someone, blasted away at him. Had a chance to take aim and give him another, careful. My God!' He threw up the cultivator points and steered the team into the shade of three oaks. He hobbled the gelding with swift tosses of a spare strap, and headed for the woods. 'Alton a killer,' he murmured, and doubled back to the house for his gun. Clissa was standing just outside the door.

'Get shells!' he snapped and flung into the house. Clissa followed him. He was strapping his hunting knife on before she could get a box off the shelf. 'Cory –'

'Hear that gun, did you? Alton's off his nut. He don't waste lead. He shot at someone just then, and he wasn't fixin' to shoot pa'tridges when I saw him last. He was out to get a man. Gimme my gun.'

'Cory, Babe –'

'You keep her here. Oh, God, this is a helluva mess. I can't stand much more.' Cory ran out the door.

Clissa caught his arm: 'Cory, I'm trying to tell you. Babe isn't here. I've called, and she isn't here.'

Cory's heavy, young-old face tautened. 'Babe – Where did you last see her?'

'Breakfast.' Clissa was crying now.

'She say where she was going?'

'No. She asked a lot of questions about Alton and where he'd gone.'

'Did you say?'

Clissa's eyes widened, and she nodded, biting the back of her hand.

'You shouldn't ha' done that, Clissa,' he gritted, and ran toward the woods. Clissa looking after him, and in that moment she could have killed herself.

Cory ran with his head up, straining with his legs and lungs and eyes at the long path. He puffed up the slope to the woods, agonized for breath after the forty-five minutes' heavy going. He couldn't even notice the damp smell of mould in the air.

He caught a movement in a thicket to his right, and dropped. Struggling to keep his breath, he crept forward until he could see clearly. There was something in there, all right. Something black, keeping still. Cory relaxed his legs and torso completely to make it easier for his heart to pump some strength back into them, and slowly raised the 12-gauge until it bore on the thing hidden in the thicket.

'Come out!' Cory said when he could speak.

Nothing happened.

'Come out or by God I'll shoot!' rasped Cory.

There was a long moment of silence, and his finger tightened on the trigger.

'You asked for it,' he said, and as he fired the thing leaped sideways into the open, screaming.

It was a thin little man dressed in sepulchral black, and bearing the rosiest little baby-face Cory had ever seen. The face was twisted with fright and pain. The little man scrambled to his feet and hopped up and down saying over and over, 'Oh, my hand. Don't shoot again! Oh, my hand. Don't shoot again!' He stopped after a bit, when Cory had climbed to his feet, and he regarded the farmer out of sad china-blue eyes. 'You shot me,' he said reproachfully, holding up a little bloody hand. 'Oh, my goodness.'

Cory said, 'Now, who the hell are you?'

The man immediately became hysterical, mouthing such a flood of broken sentences that Cory stepped back a pace and half-raised his gun in self-defence. It seemed to consist mostly of 'I lost my papers,' and 'I didn't do it,' and 'It was horrible. Horrible. Horrible,' and 'The dead man,' and 'Oh, don't shoot again.'

Cory tried twice to ask him a question, and then he stepped over and knocked the man down. He lay on the ground writhing and moaning and blubbering and putting his bloody hand to his mouth where Cory had hit him.

'Now what's going on around here?'

The man rolled over and sat up. 'I didn't do it!' he sobbed. 'I didn't! I was walking along and I heard the gun and I heard some swearing and an awful scream and I went over there and peeped and I saw the dead man and I ran away and you came and I hid and you shot me and –'

'*Shut up!*' The man did, as if a switch had been thrown. 'Now,' said Cory, pointing along the path, 'you say there's a dead man up there?'

The man nodded and began crying in earnest. Cory helped him up. 'Follow this path back to my farm-house,' he said. 'Tell my wife to fix up your hand. *Don't* tell her anything else. And wait there until I come. Hear?'

'Yes. Thank you. Oh, thank you. *Sniff.*'

'Go on now.' Cory gave him a gentle shove in the right direction and went alone, in cold fear, up the path to the spot where he had found Alton the night before.

He found him here now, too, and Kimbo. Kimbo and Alton had spent several years together in the deepest friendship; they had hunted and fought and slept together, and the lives they owed each other were finished now. They were dead together.

It was terrible that they died the same way. Cory Drew was a strong man, but he gasped and fainted dead away when he saw what the thing of the mould had done to his brother and his brother's dog.

*

The little man in black hurried down the path, whimpering and holding his injured hand as if he rather wished he could limp with it. After a while the whimper faded away, and the hurried stride changed to a walk as the gibbering terror of the last hour receded. He drew two deep breaths, said: 'My goodness!' and felt almost normal. He bound a linen handkerchief around his wrist, but the hand kept bleeding. He tried the elbow, and that made it hurt. So he stuffed the handkerchief back in his pocket and simply waved the hand stupidly in the air until the blood clotted.

It wasn't much of a wound. Two of the balls of shot had struck him, one passing through the fleshy part of his thumb and the other scoring the side. As he thought of it, he became a little proud that he had borne a gunshot wound. He strolled along in the midmorning sunlight, feeling a dreamy communion with the boys at the front. 'The whine of shot and shell –' Where had he read that? Ah, what a story this would make. 'And there beside the' – what was the line? – 'the embattled farmer stood.' Didn't the awfullest things happen in the nicest places? This was a nice forest. No screeches and snakes and deep dark menaces. Not a storybook wood at all. Shot by a gun. How exciting! He was now – he strutted – a gentleman adventurer. He did not see the great moist horror that clumped along behind him, though his nostrils crinkled a little with its foulness.

The monster had three little holes close together on its chest, and one little hole in the middle of its slimy forehead. It had three close-set pits in its back and one on the back of its head. These marks were where Alton Drew's bullets had struck and passed through. Half of the monster's shapeless face was sloughed away, and there was a deep indentation on its shoulder. This was what Alton Drew's gun butt had done after he clubbed it and struck at the thing that would not lie down after he put his four bullets through it. When these things happened the monster was not hurt or angry. It only wondered why Alton Drew acted that way. Now it followed the little man without hurrying at all, matching his stride step by step and dropping little particles of muck behind it.

The little man went on out of the wood and stood with his back against a big tree at the forest's edge, and he thought. Enough had happened to him here. What good would it do to stay and face a horrible murder inquest, just to continue this silly, vague quest? There was supposed to be the ruin of an old, old hunting lodge deep in this wood somewhere, and perhaps it would hold the evidence he wanted. But it was a vague report – vague enough to be forgotten without regret. It would be the height of foolishness to stay for all the hick-town red tape that would follow that ghastly affair back in the wood. Ergo, it would be ridiculous to follow that farmer's advice, to go to his house and wait for him. He would go back to town.

The monster was leaning against the other side of the big tree.

The little man snuffled disgustedly at a sudden overpowering odour of rot. He reached for his handkerchief, fumbled and dropped it. As he bent to pick it up, the monster's arm *whuffed* heavily in the air where his head had been – a blow that would certainly have removed that baby-faced protuberance. The man stood up and would have put the handkerchief to his nose had it not been so bloody. The creature behind the tree lifted its arm again just as the little man tossed the handkerchief away and stepped out into the field, heading across country to the distant highway that would take him back to town. The monster pounced on the handkerchief, picked it up, studied it, tore it across several times and inspected the tattered edges. Then it gazed vacantly at the disappearing figure of the little man, and finding him no longer interesting, turned back into the woods.

Babe broke into a trot at the sound of the shots. It was important to warn Uncle Alton about what her father had said, but it was more interesting to find out what he had bagged. Oh, he'd bagged it, all right. Uncle Alton never fired without killing. This was about the first time she had ever heard him blast away like that. Must be a bear, she thought excitedly, tripping over a root, sprawling, rolling to her feet again, without noticing the tumble. She'd love to have another bearskin in her room. Where would she put it? Maybe they could line it and she could have it for a blanket. Uncle Alton could sit on it and read to her in the evening – Oh, no. No. Not with this trouble between him and dad. Oh, if she could only do something! She tried to run faster, worried and anticipating, but she was out of breath and went more slowly instead.

At the top of the rise by the edge of the woods she stopped and looked back. Far down in the valley lay the south thirty. She scanned it carefully, looking for her father. The new furrows and the old were sharply defined, and her keen eyes saw immediately that Cory had left the line with the cultivator and had angled the team over to the shade trees without finishing his row. That wasn't like him. She could see the team now, and Cory's pale-blue denim was not in sight.

A little nearer was the house; and as her gaze fell on it she moved out of the cleared pathway. Her father was coming; she had seen his shot-gun and he was running. He could really cover ground when he wanted to. He must be chasing her, she thought immediately. He'd guessed that she would run toward the sound of the shots, and he was going to follow her tracks to Uncle Alton and shoot him. She knew that he was as good a woodsman as Alton; he would most certainly see her tracks. Well, she'd fix him.

She ran along the edge of the wood, being careful to dig her heels deeply into the loam. A hundred yards of this, and she angled into the forest and ran until she reached a particularly thick grove of trees. Shinnying up like a squirrel, she squirmed from one close-set tree to another until she could go no farther back towards the path, then dropped lightly to the ground and crept on her way, now stepping very gently. It would take him an hour to beat around for her trail, she thought proudly, and by that time she could easily get to Uncle Alton. She giggled to herself as she thought of the way she had fooled her father. And the little sound of laughter drowned out, for her, the sound of Alton's hoarse dying scream.

She reached and crossed the path and slid through the brush beside it. The shots came from up around here somewhere. She stopped and listened several times, and then suddenly heard something coming toward her, fast. She ducked under cover, terrified, and a little baby-faced man in black, his blue eyes wide with horror, crashed blindly past her, the leather case he carried catching on the branches. It spun a moment and then fell right in front of her. The man never missed it.

Babe lay there for a long moment and then picked up the case and faded into the woods. Things were happening too fast for her. She wanted Uncle Alton, but she dared not call. She stopped again and strained her ears. Back towards the edge of the wood she heard her father's voice, and another's – probably the man who had dropped the briefcase. She dared not go over there. Filled with enjoyable terror, she thought hard, then snapped her fingers in triumph. She and Alton had played Injun many times up here; they had a whole repertoire of secret signals. She had practised birdcalls until she knew them better than the birds themselves. What would it be? Ah – blue jay. She threw back her head and by some youthful alchemy produced a nerve-shattering screech that would have done justice to any jay that ever flew. She repeated it, and then twice more.

The response was immediate – the call of a blue jay, four times, spaced two and two. Babe nodded to herself happily. That was the signal that they were to meet immediately at The Place. The Place was a hide-out that he had discovered and shared with her, and not another soul knew of it; an angle of rock beside a stream not far away. It wasn't exactly a cave, but almost. Enough so to be entrancing. Babe trotted happily away towards the brook. She had just known that Uncle Alton would remember the call of the blue jay, and what it meant.

In the tree that arched over Alton's scattered body perched a large jay bird, preening itself and shining in the sun. Quite unconscious of the presence of death, hardly noticing the Babe's realistic cry, it screamed again four times, two and two.

It took Cory more than a moment to recover himself from what he had seen. He turned away from it and leaned weakly against a pine, panting. Alton. That was Alton lying there, in – parts.

'God! God, God, God –'

Gradually his strength returned, and he forced himself to turn again. Stepping carefully, he bent and picked up the .32–40. Its barrel was bright and clean, but the butt and stock were smeared with some kind of stinking rottenness. Where had he seen the stuff before? Somewhere – no matter.

He cleaned it off absently, throwing the befouled bandanna away afterwards. Through his mind ran Alton's words – was that only last night ? – '*I'm goin' to start trackin'. An' I'm goin' to keep trackin' till I find the one done this job on Kimbo.*'

Cory searched shrinkingly until he found Alton's box of shells. The box was wet and sticky. That made it – better, somehow. A bullet wet with Alton's blood was the right thing to use. He went away a short distance, circled around till he found heavy footprints, then came back.

'I'm a-trackin' for you, bud,' he whispered thickly, and began. Through the brush he followed its wavering spoor, amazed at the amount of filthy mould about, gradually associating it with the thing that had killed his brother. There was nothing in the world for him any more but hate and doggedness. Cursing himself for not getting Alton home last night, he followed the tracks to the edge of the woods. They led him to a big tree there, and there he saw something else – the footprints of the little city man. Nearby lay some tattered scraps of linen, and – what was that?

Another set of prints – small ones. Small, stub-toed ones. Babe's.

'Babe!' Cory screamed. 'Babe!'

No answer. The wind sighed. Somewhere a blue jay called.

Babe stopped and turned when she heard her father's voice, faint with distance, piercing.

'Listen at him holler,' she crooned delightedly. 'Gee, he sounds mad.' She sent a jay bird's call disrespectfully back to him and hurried to The Place.

It consisted of a mammoth boulder beside the brook. Some upheaval in the glacial age had cleft it, cutting out a huge V-shaped chunk. The widest part of the cleft was at the water's edge, and the narrowest was hidden by bushes. It made a little ceilingless room, rough and uneven and full of potholes and cavelets inside, and yet with quite a level floor. The open end was at the water's edge.

Babe parted the bushes and peered down the cleft.

'Uncle Alton!' she called softly. There was no answer. Oh, well, he'd be along. She scrambled in and slid down to the floor.

She loved it here. It was shaded and cool, and the chattering little stream filled it with shifting golden lights and laughing gurgles. She called again, on principle, and then perched on an outcropping to wait. It was only then she realised that she still carried the little man's briefcase.

She turned it over a couple of times and then opened it. It was divided in the middle by a leather wall. On one side were a few papers in a large yellow envelope, and on the other some sandwiches, a candy bar, and an apple. With a young-ster's complacent acceptance of manna from heaven, Babe fell to. She saved one sandwich for Alton, mainly because she didn't like its highly spiced bologna. The rest made quite a feast.

She was a little worried when Alton hadn't arrived, even after she had consumed the apple core. She got up and tried to skim some flat pebbles across the roiling brook, and she stood on her hands, and she tried to think of a story to tell herself, and she tried just waiting. Finally, in desperation, she turned again to the briefcase, took out the papers, curled up by the rocky wall and began to read them. It was something to do, anyway.

There was an old newspaper clipping that told about strange wills that people had left. An old lady had once left a lot of money to whoever would make the trip from the Earth to the Moon and back. Another had financed a home for cats whose masters and mistresses had died. A man left thousands of dollars to the first man who could solve a certain mathemati-cal problem and prove his solution. But one item was blue-pencilled. It was:

One of the strangest of wills still in force is that of Thaddeus M. Kirk, who died in 1920. It appears that he built an elaborate mausoleum with burial vaults for all the remains of his family. He collected and removed caskets from all over the country to fill the designated niches. Kirk was the last of his line; there were no relatives when he died. His will stated that the mausoleum was to be kept in repair permanently, and that a certain sum was to be set aside as a reward for whoever could produce the body of his grand-father, Roger Kirk, whose niche is still empty. Anyone finding this body is eligible to receive a substantial fortune.

*

Babe yawned vaguely over this, but kept on reading because there was nothing else to do. Next was a thick sheet of business correspondence, bearing the letterhead of a firm of lawyers. The body of it ran:

In regard to your query regarding the will of Thaddeus Kirk, we are authorised to state that his grandfather was a man about five feet, five inches, whose left arm had been broken and who had a triangular silver plate set into his skull. There is no information as to the whereabouts of his death. He disappeared and was declared legally dead after the lapse of fourteen years.

The amount of the reward as stated in the will, plus accrued interest, now amounts to a fraction over sixty-two thousand dollars. This will be paid to anyone who produces the remains, providing that said remains answer descriptions kept in our private files.

There was more, but Babe was bored. She went on to the little black notebook. There was nothing in it but pencilled and highly abbreviated records of visits to libraries; quotations from books with title like 'History of Angelina and Tyler Counties' and 'Kirk Family History.' Babe threw that aside, too. Where could Uncle Alton be?

She began to sing tunelessly, 'Tumalumalum tum, ta ta ta,' pretending to dance a minuet with flowing skirts like a girl she had seen in the movies. A rustle of the bushes at the entrance to The Place stopped her. She peeped upward, saw them being thrust aside. Quickly she ran to a tiny cul-de-sac in the rock wall, just big enough for her to hide in. She giggled at the thought of how surprised Uncle Alton would be when she jumped out at him.

She heard the newcomer come shuffling down the steep slope of the crevice and land heavily on the floor. There was something about the sound – What was it? It occurred to her that though it was a hard job for a big man like Uncle Alton to get through the little opening in the bushes, she could hear no heavy breathing. She heard no breathing at all!

Babe peeped out into the main cave and squealed in utmost horror. Standing there was, not Uncle Alton, but a massive caricature of a man: a huge thing like an irregular mud doll, clumsily made. It quivered and parts of it glistened and parts of it were dried and crumby. Half of the lower left part of its face was gone, giving it a lop-sided look. It had no perceptible mouth or nose, and its eyes were crooked, one higher than the other, both a dingy brown with no whites at all. It stood quite still looking at her, its only movement a steady unalive quivering of its body.

It wondered about the queer little noise Babe had made.

Babe crept far back against a little pocket of stone, her brain running round and round in tiny circles of agony. She opened her mouth to cry out, and could not. Her eyes bulged and her face flamed with the strangling effort, and the two golden ropes of her braided hair twitched and twitched as she hunted hopelessly for a way out. If only she were out in the open – or in the wedge-shaped half-cave where the thing was – or home in bed!

The thing clumped towards her, expressionless, moving with a slow inevitability that was the sheer crux of horror. Babe lay wide-eyed and frozen, mounting pressure of terror stilling her lungs, making her heart shake the whole world. The monster came to the mouth of the little pocket, tried to walk to her and was stopped by the sides.

It was such a narrow little fissure; and it was all Babe could do to get in. The thing from the wood stood straining against the rock at its shoulders, pressing harder and harder to get to Babe. She sat up slowly, so near to the thing that its odour as almost thick enough to see, and a wild hope burst through her voiceless fear. It couldn't get in! It couldn't get in because it was too big!

The substance of its feet spread slowly under the tremendous strain, and at its shoulder appeared a slight crack. It widened as the monster unfeelingly crushed itself against the rock, and suddenly a large piece of the shoulder came away and the being twisted slushily three feet farther in. It lay quietly with its muddy eyes fixed on her, and then brought one thick arm up over its head and reached.

Babe scrambled in the inch farther she had believed impossible, and the filthy clubbed hand stroked down her back, leaving a trail of muck on the blue denim of the shirt she wore. The monster surged suddenly and, lying full length now, gained that last precious inch. A black hand seized one of her braids, and for Babe the lights went out.

When she came to, she was dangling by her hair from that same crusted paw. The thing held her high, so that her face and its featureless head were not more than a foot apart. It gazed at her with a mild curiosity in its eyes, and it swung her slowly back and forth. The agony of her pulled hair did what fear could not do – gave her a voice. She screamed. She opened her mouth and puffed up her powerful young lungs, and she sounded off. She held her throat in the position of the first scream, and her chest laboured and pumped more air through the frozen throat. Shrill and monotonous and infinitely piercing, her screams.

The thing did not mind. It held her as she was, and watched. When it had learned all it could from this phenomenon, it dropped her jarringly, and looked around the half-cave, ignoring the stunned and huddled Babe. It reached over and picked up the leather briefcase and tore it twice across as if it were tissue. It saw the sandwich Babe had left, picked it up, crushed it, dropped it.

Babe opened her eyes, saw that she was free, and just as the thing turned back to her she dived between its legs and out into the shallow pool in front of the rock, paddled across and hit the other bank screaming. A vicious little light of fury burned in her; she picked up a grapefruit-sized stone and hurled it with all her frenzied might. It flew low and fast, and struck squashily on the monster's ankle. The thing was just taking a step towards the water; the stone caught it off balance, and its unpractised equilibrium could not save it. It tottered for a long, silent moment at the edge and then splashed into the stream. Without a second look Babe ran shrieking away.

Cory Drew was following the little gobs of mould that somehow indicated the path of the murderer, and he was nearby when he first heard her scream. He broke into a run, dropping his shotgun and holding the .32–40 ready to fire. He ran with such deadly panic in his heart that he ran right past the huge cleft rock and was a hundred yards past it before she burst out through the pool and ran up the bank. He had to run hard and fast to catch her, because anything behind her was that faceless horror in the cave, and she was living for the one idea of getting away from there. He caught her in his arms and swung her to him, and she screamed on and on and on.

Babe didn't see Cory at all, even when he held her and quieted her.

The monster lay in the water. It neither liked nor disliked this new element. It rested on the bottom, its massive head a foot beneath the surface, and it curiously considered the facts that it had garnered. There was the little humming noise of Babe's voice that sent the monster questing into the cave. There was the black material of the briefcase that resisted so much more than green things when he tore it. There was the little two-legged one who sang and brought him near, and who screamed when he came. There was this new cold moving thing he had fallen into. It was washing his body away. That had never happened before. That was interesting. The monster decided to stay and observe this new thing. It felt no urge to save itself; it could only be curious.

The brook came laughing down out of its spring, ran down from its source beckoning to the sunbeams and embracing freshets and helpful brooklets. It shouted and played with streaming little roots, and nudged the minnows and pollywogs about in its tiny backwaters. It was a happy brook. When it came to the pool by the cloven rock it found the monster there, and plucked at it. It soaked the foul substances and smoothed and melted the moulds, and the waters below the thing eddied darkly with its diluted matter. It was a thorough brook. It washed all it touched, persistently. Where it found filth, it removed filth; and if there were layer on layer of foulness, then layer by foul layer it was removed. It was a good brook. It did not mind the poison of the monster, but took it up and thinned it and spread it in little rings round rocks downstream, and let it drift to the rootlets of water plants, that they might grow greener and lovelier. And the monster melted.

'I am smaller,' the thing thought. 'That is interesting. I could not move now. And now this part of me which thinks is going, too. It will stop in just a moment, and drift away with the rest of the body. It will stop thinking and I will stop being, and that, too, is a very interesting thing.'

So the monster melted and dirtied the water, and the water was clean again, washing and washing the skeleton that the monster had left. It was not very big, and there was a badly healed knot on the left arm. The sunlight flickered on the triangular silver plate set into the pale skull, and the skeleton was very clean now. The brook laughed about it for an age.

They found the skeleton, six grim lipped men who came to find a killer. No one had believed Babe, when she told her story days later. It had to be days later because Babe had screamed for seven hours without stopping, and had lain like a dead child for a day. No one believed her at all, because her story was all about the bad fella, and they knew that the bad fella was simply a thing that her father had made up to frighten her with. But it was through her that the skeleton was found, and so the men at the bank sent a check to the Drews for more money than they had ever dreamed about. It was old Roger Kirk, sure enough, that skeleton, though it was found five miles from where he had died and sank into the forest floor where the hot moulds builded around his skeleton and emerged – a monster.

So the Drews had a new barn and fine new livestock and they hired four men. But, they didn't have Alton. And they didn't have Kimbo. And Babe screams at night and has grown very thin.

# Wednesday's Child

## By WILLIAM TENN

*By the middle of this century, the ingenuity which writers were bringing to the Frankenstein concept had become more and more varied – as instanced by stories such as* Wednesday's Child *about a curious young woman who has no navel and of whom her doctor says she 'might have been put together from a kit'. When this story was first published in the January 1956 issue of* Fantastic Universe, *the Editor Leo Marguilies described it perceptively as 'giving Science Fantasy a new look – and enlarging its boundaries immeasurably.'*

*Like Theodore Sturgeon's* It, *this was William Tenn's first contribution to the magazine, and he was similarly greeted as being a 'writer of quite phenomenal maturity with a variation on a theme which will bewitch and astound readers.' William Tenn is, in fact, the pseudonym of the American writer and academic Philip Klass (1920– ), whom Everett F. Bleiler once called 'one of the pioneers in satire and humor in American SF.' Tenn's interest in the theme of creating artificial life was revealed in one of his earliest short stories,* Down Among The Dead Men *(1954), about the use of androids reconstituted from the corpses of soldiers to serve as front line troops in a savage interstellar war. Curiously, though, after producing half a dozen highly imaginative and popular collections of short stories in the Fifties and early Sixties, William Tenn has written virtually nothing since. I am pleased, therefore, to be able to reintroduce his name to a new generation of readers with the following outstanding variation on our theme ...*

When he first came to scrutinize Wednesday Gresham with his rimless spectacles and restive blue eyes, Fabian Balik knew nothing of the biological contradictions which were so incredibly a part of her essential body structure. He had not even noticed – as yet – that she was a remarkably pretty girl with eyes like rain-sparkling violets. His original preoccupation with her was solely and specifically as a problem in personnel administration.

All of which was not too surprising, because Fabian Balik was a thoroughly intent, thoroughly sincere young office manager, who had succeeded in convincing his glands conclusively, in several bitter skirmishes, that their interests didn't have a chance against the interests of SLAUGHTER, STARK & SLINGSBY: *Advertising & Public Relations*.

Wednesday was one of the best stenographers in the secretarial pool that was under his immediate supervision. There were, however, small but highly unusual derelictions in her employment history. They consisted of peculiarities which a less dedicated and ambitious personnel man might have put aside as mere trifles, but which Fabian, after a careful study of her six-year record with the firm, felt he could not, in good conscience, ignore. On the other hand, they would obviously require an extended discussion, and he had strong views about cutting into a girl's working time.

Thus, much to the astonishment of the office and the confusion of Wednesday herself, he came up to her one day at noon, and informed her quite calmly that they were going to have lunch together.

'This is a nice place,' he announced, when they had been shown to a table. 'It's not too expensive, but I've discovered it serves the best food in the city for the price. As it's a bit off the beaten track it never gets too crowded. Only people who know what they want manage to come here. I've always liked that kind of restaurant.'

Wednesday glanced around, and smiled. 'Yes,' she said. 'I like it too. I eat here a lot with the girls.'

After a moment, Fabian picked up a menu. 'I suppose you don't mind if I order for both of us?' he inquired. 'The chef is used to my tastes. He'll treat us right.'

The girl frowned. 'I'm terribly sorry, Mr Balik, but –'

'Yes?' he said encouragingly, though he was more than a

little surprised. He hadn't expected anything but compliance. After all, she must surely be palpitating inwardly at being out with him.

'I'd like to order for myself,' she said. 'I'm on a – a special diet.'

He raised his eyebrows and was pleased at the way she blushed. He nodded slowly, with dignity, letting his displeasure come through only in the way he pronounced the next five words. 'Very well, if you insist.'

A few moments later, however, his curiosity got too strong for him and broke through the ice. 'What kind of diet is that?' he asked. 'Fresh fruit salad, a glass of tomato juice, raw cabbage, and – a *baked potato*? You can't be seriously trying to lose weight if you eat potatoes.'

Wednesday smiled timidly. 'I'm not trying to reduce, Mr Balik. These are all foods rich in Vitamin C. I need a lot of Vitamin C.'

Fabian remembered her smile. There had been a few spots of more-than-natural whiteness in it. 'Dental trouble?' he inquired.

She nodded, but showed no inclination to pursue the topic. Quickly she countered with: 'This *is* a nice place. There's a restaurant almost like it near where I live. Of course it's a lot cheaper and –'

'Do you live with your parents, Miss Gresham?'

'No, I live alone. I'm a – I'm an orphan.'

He waited until the waiter had deposited the first course, then spooned up a bit of the shrimp and returned to the attack. 'Since when?'

She stared at him over her fresh fruit salad. 'I beg your pardon, Mr Balik?'

'Since when? I mean – how long have you been an orphan?'

'Since I was a little baby. Someone left me on the doorstep of a foundling home.'

He noticed that while she was replying to his questions in an even tone of voice, she was staring at her food with a good deal of concentration and her blush had become more pronounced. Was she embarrassed at having to admit her probable lack of legitimacy, he wondered. Surely at twenty-four she had grown accustomed to it. Nonsense, of course she had.

'But on your original application form, Miss Gresham, you gave Thomas and Mary Gresham as the names of your parents.'

Wednesday had stopped eating and was playing with her water glass. 'They were an old couple who adopted me,' she said in a very low voice. 'They died when I was fifteen. I have no living relatives.'

'That you know of,' he reminded her, raising a cautionary finger.

Much to Fabian's surprise, she laughed. It was a very odd laugh and made him feel extremely uncomfortable. 'That's right, Mr Balik. I have no living relatives – *that I know of.*' She looked over his shoulder and laughed again. 'That I know of,' she repeated, softly to herself.

Fabian felt irritably that the interview was somehow getting away from him. He raised his voice slightly. 'Then who is Dr Morris Lorington?'

She was attentive again. 'Dr Morris Lorington?'

'Yes, the man you said should be notified in the event of an emergency. I mean – if you should meet with an accident while in our employ.'

She looked very wary now. Her eyes were narrowed, and she was watching him very closely. Her breathing had become a bit faster, too.

'Dr Lorington is an old friend,' she said. 'He – he was the doctor at the orphanage. After the Greshams adopted me, I kept going to him whenever –' Her voice trailed off.

'Whenever you needed medical attention?' Fabian suggested.

'Ye-es,' she said, brightening, as if he had come up with an entirely novel reason for consulting a physician. 'I saw him whenever I needed medical attention.'

Fabian grunted. There was something very wrong but tantalizingly elusive about this whole business. But she was answering his questions with no apparent constraint. He couldn't deny that. She was certainly answering.

'Do you expect to see him next October?' he inquired.

And now Wednesday was no longer wary. She was frightened. 'Next *October?*' she quavered.

Fabian finished the last of his shrimp, and wiped his lips. But he didn't take his eyes from her face. 'Yes, next October,

Miss Gresham. You've applied for a month's leave of absence, beginning October fifteenth. Five years ago, after you had been working for Slaughter, Stark and Slingsby for thirteen months, you also applied for a leave of absence in October.'

He was amazed at how scared she looked. He felt triumphantly that he had been right in looking into the entire matter. The feeling of curiosity he had experienced in connection with her had not been merely that. It had been an instinct of good personnel management as well.

'But I'm not getting *paid* for the time off,' she protested. 'I'm not asking to be paid for it, Mr Balik. And I didn't get any vacation allowance the – the other time.'

She was clutching her napkin up near her face, giving him the impression that she was getting ready to bolt through the back door of the restaurant. Her blushes had departed with such thoroughness as to leave her skin absolutely white.

'The fact that you're not getting paid, Miss Gresham, is not really –' Before Fabian could complete the remark he was interrupted by the waiter with the entrée. By the time the man had gone, he was annoyed to observe that Wednesday had used the respite to recover some of her poise. While she was still pale, she had a spot of red in each cheek, and she was leaning back in her chair now instead of using the edge of it.

'The fact that you're not getting paid is of no consequence,' he continued resolutely. 'It's merely logical. After all, you have the customary two weeks of vacation with pay every year. Which brings me to the second point I wanted to discuss with you. You have every year made *two* unusual requests. First, you've asked for an additional week's leave of absence without pay, making three weeks in all. And then you've asked –'

'To take it in the early Spring,' she finished for him, her voice entirely under control. 'Is there anything wrong with that, Mr Balik? That way I won't have any conflict with the other girls and the firm will have the satisfaction of knowing that a secretary will be in the office all through the summer.'

'There's nothing wrong with such an arrangement *per se*. By that I mean,' he said, translating carefully, 'that there is nothing wrong with the arrangement if it could stand in complete isolation by itself. But it makes for loose ends, for organizational confusion. And loose ends, Miss Gresham, loose ends and organizational confusion have no place in a well-regulated office.'

He was pleased to note that she was looking uncomfortable again.

'Does that mean – that I might be laid off?'

'It could happen,' Fabian agreed, neglecting to add that it was, however, very unlikely to happen in the case of a secretary who was as generally efficient on the one hand, and as innocuous on the other, as Wednesday Gresham. With his knife he carefully freed a fork-sized portion of roast beef from its accompanying strip of orange fat before going on.

'Look at it this way,' he said. 'How would it be if every girl in the office asked for an additional week's leave of absence every year – even if it was without pay, as it would naturally have to be? How would it be if, every few years, they wanted an additional month's leave of absence on top of that? What kind of office would we have, Miss Gresham? Not a well-regulated one, certainly.'

As he masticated the roast beef with the requisite thoroughness, he beamed at the thoughtful concern on her face and was mentally grateful that he hadn't had to present a similar line of argument to anyone as sharp as – well, Arlette Stein. He knew what that large-boned and thirtyish bookkeeper would have immediately replied: 'But every girl in the office *doesn't* ask for it, Mr Balik.' A heavy sneer at such sophistry would mean little to Stein.

Wednesday, he appreciated, was not the person to go in for such counter-attacks. She was pursing her lips distressedly and trying to think of a polite, good-employee way out. There was only one, and he was sure she would have to come to it in a moment.

She did.

'Would it help any,' she began, and stopped. She took a deep breath. 'Would it help any, if I told you the reasons for the – for the leaves-of-absence?'

'It would,' he said heartily. 'It would indeed, Miss Gresham. That way I, as office manager, can operate from facts instead of mysteries. I can listen to your reasons, weigh them for validity and measure their importance – *and* your usefulness as a secretary – against the disorganization your absences

create in the day-to-day operation of Slaughter, Stark and
Slingsby.'

'M-m-m.' She looked troubled, uncertain. 'I'd like to think
a bit, if you don't mind.'

Fabian waved a cauliflower-filled fork magnanimously.
'Take all the time in the world! Think it out carefully. Don't
tell me anything you aren't perfectly assured about in your
own mind. Of course anything you *do* tell me will, I can
promise you, remain completely confidential. I will treat it as
official knowledge, Miss Gresham – not personal. And while
you're thinking, you might start eating your raw cabbage.
Before it gets cold,' he added with a rich, executive-type
chuckle.

She looked at him with the barest trace of a smile and
began working at her plate in an absent-minded, a not-
particularly-hungry fashion.

'You see,' she began abruptly, as if she'd found a good
point of departure, 'some things happen to me that don't
happen to other people.'

'That, I would say, is fairly obvious.'

'They're not really bad things. I mean they're not what the
newspapers would call bad. And they're not dangerous things,
exactly. They're – they're things that happen to my body.'

Fabian finished his plate, sat back and crossed his arms.
'Could you be just a little more specific?' he urged. 'Unless –'
He was suddenly struck by a horrifying thought. 'Unless
they're what what is known as – *er* – *female* difficulties. In
that case, of course –'

This time she didn't even blush. 'Oh, no – not at all. At
least, there's very little of that. It's – other things. Like my
appendix. Every year I have to have my appendix out.'

'Your appendix?' He turned that over in his mind. '*Every
year*? But I don't understand. A human being only has one
appendix. And once it's removed, it doesn't grow back.'

'Mine does,' she told him. 'On the tenth of April, every
single year, I get appendicitis and have to have an operation.
That's why I take my vacation then. And my teeth. Every five
years, I lose *all* my teeth. I start losing them about this time,
and I have dental plates that were made when I was a little
girl. I use them until my teeth grow back – until about the
middle of October when the last of them goes, and the new

ones start coming up. I can't use dental plates while they're growing, so naturally I look kind of funny for a while. That's why I ask for a leave of absence. In the middle of November, the new teeth are almost full-grown, and I can come back to work.'

She took a deep breath and timidly lifted her eyes to his face. She had evidently completed all she had to say. Or wished to say.

All through dessert, he thought about it. He was positive she was telling the truth. A girl like Wedesday Gresham didn't lie. Not to such a fantastic extent, at any rate – and not to her boss.

'Well,' he said at last. 'It's certainly very unusual.'

'Yes,' she agreed. '*Very* unusual.'

'Do you have anything else the matter with you? I mean, are there any other peculiarities – Oh, darn! Is there anything else?'

Wednesday considered. 'There are. But, if you don't mind, Mr Balik, I'd rather not talk about them.'

Fabian decided not to take that. 'Now see here, Miss Gresham,' he said firmly. 'Let us not play games. You didn't have to tell me anything. But you decided for yourself – for your own good reasons – to do so. Now I must insist on the whole story, and nothing but the whole story. What other physical difficulties do you have?'

It worked. She cringed a bit in her chair, but almost instantly she straightened up again and began: 'I'm sorry, Mr Balik. I wouldn't dream of – of playing games with you. There are lots of other things, but none of them interfere with my work, really. For instance, I have some tiny hairs growing on my fingernails. See?'

Fabian glanced at her hand. There were a few almost microscopic tendrils on each glittering hard surface of finger-nail, but he had to strain his eyes to see them.

'What else?' he inquired.

'Well, my tongue. I have a few hairs on the underside of my tongue. They don't bother me, though. They don't bother me in any way. And there's my – my –'

'Yes?' he prompted. *Who could believe that colourless little Wednesday Gresham ...*

'My navel. I don't have any navel.'

'You don't have any – but that's impossible!' he exploded. He felt his glasses sliding down his nose. 'Everyone has a navel! Everyone alive – everyone who's ever been born.'

Wednesday nodded, her eyes unnaturally bright and large. 'I know – ' she began, and suddenly, unexpectedly, broke into tears. She brought her hands up to her face and sobbed through them, great, pounding, racking sobs that pulled her shoulders up and down, up and down.

Fabian's consternation made him completely helpless. He'd never in his life been in a crowded restaurant with a crying girl before.

'Now, Miss Gresham – Wednesday,' he managed to get out, and he was annoyed to hear a high, skittery note in his own voice. 'There's no call for this. It only makes you feel worse. Crying, I mean. Uh – Wednesday?'

'Maybe,' she gasped again, between sobs, 'm-maybe that's the answer.'

'What's the answer?' Fabian asked loudly, desperately hoping to distract her with some kind of conversation.

'About – about being born. What if I wasn't b-born? What if I was m-m-made!'

And then, as if she'd merely been warming up before, she *really* went into hysterics. Fabian Balik at last realized what he had to do. He paid the bill, put his arms around her waist and half-carried her out of the restaurant.

It worked. She became quieter the moment they were in the open air. She leaned against a building, no longer crying, and shook her shoulders in a steadily diminishing movement. Finally, she quieted down completely, and turned groggily to him, her face looking as if it had been rubbed determinedly in an artist's palette.

'I'm s-sorry,' she said. 'I'm t-terribly s-sorry. I haven't done that for years. But you see, Mr Balik – I haven't talked about myself for years.'

'There's a nice bar at the corner,' he pointed out, tremendously relieved. He had feared she had made up her mind to drive him to some drastic act of desperation by crying all day! 'Let's pop in, and I'll have a drink. You can use the ladies' room to fix yourself up.'

He took her arm and steered her into the place. Then he climbed onto a bar stool and had himself a double brandy.

What an experience! And what a remarkably strange girl!

Of course, he shouldn't have pressed her quite so hard on a subject about which she was evidently so sensitive. Was that his fault, though – that she *was* so sensitive?

Fabian considered the matter carefully, judicially, and decided that he was blaming himself needlessly. No, it definitely wasn't his fault.

But what a story! The foundling statement, the appendix statement, the teeth, the hair on the fingernails and tongue ... And that last unbelievable assertion about the navel!

He'd have to think it out – maybe get some other opinions. But one thing he was sure of – Wednesday Gresham hadn't been lying in any particular. Wednesday Gresham was just not the sort of a girl who made up tall stories about herself.

When she rejoined him, he urged her to have a drink. 'It will help you get a grip on yourself.'

She demurred, protesting that she didn't drink very much. But he insisted, and finally she gave in. 'Just a liqueur – anything. You order it, Mr Balik.'

Fabian was secretly very pleased at her docility. No reprimanding, no back-biting, such as most other girls indulged in. Although what in the world could she have reprimanded him for, come to think of it.

'You still look a little frayed,' he told her. 'When we get back, don't bother going to your desk. Go right in to Mr Osborne and finish taking dictation. There's no point in giving the other girls something to talk about. I'll sign in for you.'

She inclined her head submissively and continued to sip from the tiny glass.

'What was that last comment you made in the restaurant,' he asked. 'I'm sure you won't mind discussing it, now. I mean – about not being born, but being made? That was an odd thing to say.'

Wednesday sighed. 'It isn't my own idea. It's Dr Lorington's. Years ago, when he was examining me, he said that I looked as if I'd been made – by an amateur. By someone who didn't have all the blueprints, or didn't understand them, or wasn't concentrating hard enough.'

'I see.' He stared at her, absolutely intrigued. She looked normal enough. Better than normal, in fact. And yet –

*

Later that afternoon, he telephoned Jim Rudd and made an appointment for right after work. Jim Rudd had been his roommate in college and was now a doctor. Whatever his shortcomings, a practising physician should be able to give him some advice that would be at least professional, and carry the weight of authority.

But Jim Rudd wasn't able to help him very much. He listened patiently to Fabian's story and at the end of it leaned back in his chair and pursed his lips at the diploma hanging neatly framed on the wall facing him.

'You sure do go in for the unusual, Fabe. For a superficially well-adjusted, well-organized guy with a real talent for the mundane things of life, you pick the damn'dest women I ever heard of. But that's your business. Maybe it's your way of adding a necessary pinch of the exotic to the grim daily round. Or maybe you're making up for the drabness of your father's grocery store.'

'This girl isn't a weirdie,' Fabian insisted angrily. 'She's a very simple little secretary, prettier than most – but that's about all.'

'Have it your own way. To me, she's a real weirdie. To me, there's not a hell of a lot of difference – from your description – between her and that crazy White Russian dame you were running around with back in our junior year. You know the one I mean – what was her name?'

'Sandra? Oh, Jim, what's the matter with you? Sandra was a bollixed-up box of dynamite who was always blowing up in my face. This kid turns pale and dies if I so much as raise my voice. Besides, I had a real puppy-love crush on Sandra. Miss Gresham is somebody I just met, and I don't feel anything for her, one way or the other.'

The young doctor grinned. 'So you come up to my office and have a consultation about her! Well, it's your funeral. What do you want to know?'

'What causes all these – these physical peculiarities?'

Dr Rudd got up and sat on the edge of his desk. 'First,' he said, 'whether you want to recognize it or not, she's a highly disturbed person. The hysterics in the restaurant point to it, and the fantastic nonsense she told you about her body does too. So right there, you have something. If only one percent of what she told you is true – and even that I would say is pretty high – it makes sense in terms of psychosomatic imbalance. Medicine doesn't yet know quite how it works, but one thing seems certain. Anyone badly mixed up mentally is going to be at least a little mixed up physically, too.'

Fabian thought about that for a while. 'Jim, you don't know what it means to those little secretaries in the pool to tell lies to the office manager! A fib or two, about why they were absent the day before, yes. But not stories such as she told – not to *me*.'

Rudd shrugged. 'I don't know what you look like to them. I don't work for you, Fabe. But none of what you say would hold true for a psycho. And a psycho is what I have to consider her. Look, some of that stuff she told you is possible. Some of it has even occurred in medical literature. There have been well-authenticated cases of people, for example, who have grown several sets of teeth in their lifetime. These are biological sports, one-in-a-million individuals. Okay. But the rest of it? All the rest of it happening to one person? *Please*.'

'I saw some of it,' Fabian protested. 'I saw the hairs on her fingernails.'

'You saw *something* on her fingernails. It could be any one of a dozen different possibilities. I'm sure of one thing. It *wasn't* hair. Right there she gave herself away. Dammit, man, hair and nails are the same organs, essentially. One doesn't grow on the other!'

'And the navel? The missing navel?'

Jim Rudd dropped to his feet and strode rapidly about the office. 'I wish I knew why I'm wasting so much time with you,' he complained. 'A human being without a navel is as possible as an insect with a body temperature of ninety-eight degrees. It just can't be. It's unheard of in medical literature.'

He seemed to get more and more upset as he considered it. He kept shaking his head negatively as he paced.

'Suppose I brought her to your office,' said Fabian. 'And suppose you examined her and found no navel. Now just consider that for a moment. What would you say then?'

'I'd say plastic surgery,' the doctor said instantly. 'Mind you, I'm positive she'd never submit to such an examination, but if she did, and there were no navel, plastic surgery would be the only answer.'

'Why would anyone want to do plastic surgery on a navel?'

'I don't know. I haven't the vaguest idea. Maybe she was in a serious accident. Maybe she had a disfiguring birthmark in that place. But there will be scars, let me tell you. *She had to be born with a navel.*'

Fabian got up too. He was feeling very excited. 'And if she hadn't been born? The usual way, I mean?'

'What other way is there? Hatching out of an egg?'

'She could have been made,' Fabian suggested. 'Just as she says – by an amateur. An amateur who, in addition to all his other errors, forgot to put in a navel.'

Rudd went back to his desk. He picked up a prescription pad. 'Let me give you the name of a good psychiatrist, Fabe. I've thought ever since that Sandra business that you've had some personal problems that might get out of hand one day. This man is one of the finest –'

Fabian left. He went into a phone booth and called Wednesday and made a date with her for Saturday night . . .

She was so obviously in a flutter when he picked her up that night – so much more of a flutter than a-date-with-the-boss would account for – that Fabian was puzzled. But he waited and gave her an ostentatious and expensive good time. Afterwards, after dinner and after the theatre, when they were sitting in the corner of a small night club over their drinks, he asked her about it.

'You don't date much, do you, Wednesday?'

'No, I don't, Mr Balik – I mean, Fabian,' she said, smiling shyly as she remembered the first-name privilege she had been accorded for the evening. 'I usually just go out with girl friends, not with men. I usually turn down dates.'

'Why? You're not going to find a husband that way. You want to get married, don't you?'

Wednesday shook her head slowly. 'I don't think so. I – I'm afraid to. Not of marriage. Of babies. I don't think a person like me ought to have a baby.'

'Nonsense! Is there any scientific reason why you shouldn't?'

'I'm afraid it might be – I think with my body being as – as funny as it is, I shouldn't take chances with a child. Dr Lorington thinks so too. Besides, there's the poem.'

Fabian put down his drink. 'Poem? What poem?'

'You know, the one about the days of the week. I learned it

when I was a little girl, and it frightened me even then. It goes:

> *Monday's child is fair of face,*
> *Tuesday's child is full of grace,*
> *Wednesday's child is full of woe,*
> *Thursday's child has far to go,*
> *Friday's child is loving and giving –*

And so on. When I was a little girl in the orphanage, I used to say to myself, "I'm Wednesday. I'm different from all other little girls in all kinds of strange ways. And my child –"'

'Who gave you that name?'

'I was left at the foundling home just after New Year's Eve – Wednesday morning. So they did not know what else to call me, especially when they found I didn't have a navel. And then, as I told you, after the Greshams adopted me, I took their last name.'

He reached for her hand and grasped it firmly with both of his. He noted with triumphant pleasure that the finger-nails *were* hairy. 'You're a very pretty girl, Wednesday Gresham.'

When she saw that he meant it, she blushed and looked down at the table-cloth.

'And you really don't have a navel?'

'No, I don't. Really.'

'What else about you is different?' Fabian asked. 'I mean, besides the things you told me.'

'Well,' she considered. 'There's that business about my blood pressure.'

'Tell me about it,' he urged.

She told him.

Two dates later, she informed Fabian that Dr Lorington wanted to see him – alone. He went all the way uptown to the old-fashioned brownstone, hardly able to control his excitement. He had so many questions to ask!

Dr Lorington was a tall, aged man with pale skin and absolutely white hair. He moved very slowly as he gestured his visitor to a chair, but his eyes never left Fabian's face.

'Wednesday tells me you've been seeing a good deal of her, Mr Balik. May I ask why?'

Fabian said, hesitantly, 'I – I like her very much. I'm interested in her.'

'Interested. Just how do you wish me to construe that? Clinically – as a specimen?'

'What a way to put it, Doctor! She's a pretty girl, she's a nice girl. Why should I be interested in her as a specimen?'

The doctor stroked his chin, still watching Fabian very closely. 'She's a pretty girl,' he agreed, 'but there are many pretty girls. You're a young man obviously on his way up in the world, and you're also obviously far out of Wednesday's class. From what she's told me – and mind you, it's been all on the positive side – I've got a definite impression that you look on her as a specimen, but a specimen, let us say, about which you feel a substantial collector's urge.

'Why you should feel this way, I don't know enough about you to say. But no matter how she rhapsodizes about you, I continue to feel strongly that you have no conventional, expected emotional interest in her. And now that I've seen you, I'm positive that I am right.'

'Glad to hear she rhapsodizes about me,' Fabian tried to squeeze out a bashful-type grin. 'You have nothing to worry about, Doctor.'

'I think there's quite a bit to worry about,' the doctor said. 'Frankly, Mr Balik, your appearance has confirmed my previous impressions. I am quite certain I don't like you. Furthermore, I don't like you for Wednesday.'

Fabian thought that over for a moment, then shrugged. 'That's too bad. But I don't think she'll listen to you. She's gone without male companionship too long, and she's too flattered by my going after her.'

'I'm terribly afraid you're right. Listen to me, Mr Balik. I'm very fond of Wednesday and I know how unguarded she is. I ask you, almost as a father, to leave her alone. I've taken care of her since she arrived at the foundling home. I was responsible for keeping her case out of the medical journals so that she might have some chance for a normal life. At the moment, I'm retired from practice. Wednesday Gresham is my only regular patient. Couldn't you find it in your heart to be kind and have nothing more to do with her?'

'What's this about her being made, not born?' Fabian countered. 'She says it was your idea.'

The old man sighed and shook his head over his desk-top for a long moment. 'It's the only explanation that makes sense,' he said at last, dispiritedly. 'Considering the somatic inaccuracies and ambivalences.'

Fabian clasped his hands and rubbed his elbows thoughtfully on the arms of his chair. 'Did you ever think there might be another explanation? She might be a mutant, a new kind of human evolution, or the offspring of creatures from another world, say, who happened to be stranded on this planet?'

'Highly unlikely,' Dr Lorington said. 'None of these physical modifications are especially useful in any conceivable environment, with the possible exception of the constantly renewing teeth. Nor are the modifications fatal. They tend to be just – inconvenient. As a physician who has examined many human beings in my life, I would say that Wednesday is thoroughly, indisputably human. She is just a little – well, the word is *amateurish*.'

The doctor sat up straight. 'There is something else, Mr Balik. I think it extremely inadvisable for people like Wednesday to have children of their own.'

Fabian's eyes lit up in fascination. 'Why? What would the children be like?'

'They might be like anything imaginable – or unimaginable. With so much disarrangement of the normal physical system, the modification in the reproductive functions must be enormous too. That's why I ask you, Mr Balik, not to go on seeing Wednesday, not to go on stimulating her to thoughts of marriage. Because this is one girl that I am certain should not have babies!'

'We'll see.' Fabian rose and offered his hand. 'Thank you very much for your time and trouble, Doctor.'

Dr Lorington cocked his head and stared up at him. Then, without shaking the hand, he said in a quiet, even voice. 'You are welcome. Goodbye, Mr Balik.'

Wednesday was naturally miserable over the antagonism between the two men. But there was very little doubt where her loyalties would lie in a crisis. All those years of determined emotional starvation had resulted in a frantic voracity. Once she allowed herself to think of Fabian romantically, she was done for. She told him that she did her work at the office –

from which their developing affair had so far been successfully screened – in a daze at the thought that *he* liked *her*.

Fabian found her homage delicious. Most women he had known began to treat him with a gradually sharpening edge of contempt as time went on. Wednesday became daily more admiring, more agreeable, more compliant.

True, she was by no means brilliant, but she was, he told himself, extremely pretty, and, therefore, quite presentable. Just to be on the safe side, he found an opportunity to confer with Mr Slaughter, the senior partner of the firm, ostensibly on personnel matters. He mentioned in passing that he was slightly interested in one of the girls in the secretarial pool. Would there be any high-echelon objection to that?

'Interested to the extent of perhaps marrying the girl?' Mr Slaughter asked, studying him from under a pair of enormously thick eyebrows.

'Possibly. It might very well come to that, sir. If you have no ob –'

'No objection at all, my boy, no objection at all! I don't like executives flim-flamming around with their file-clerks as a general rule, but if it's handled quietly and ends in matrimony, it could be an excellent thing for the office. I'd like to see you married, and steadied down. It might give the other single people in the place some sensible ideas for a change. But mind you, Balik, no flim-flam. No hanky-panky, especially on office time!'

Satisfied, Fabian now devoted himself to separating Wednesday from Dr Lorington. He pointed out to her that the old man couldn't live much longer and she needed a regular doctor who was young enough to be able to help her with the physical complexities she faced for the rest of her life. A young doctor like Jim Rudd, for example.

Wednesday wept, but was completely incapable of fighting him for long. In the end, she made only one condition – that Dr Rudd preserve the secrecy that Lorington had initiated. She didn't want to become a medical journal freak or a newspaper sob story.

The reasons why Fabian agreed had only a little to do with magnanimity. He wanted to have her oddities for himself alone. Sandra he had worn on his breast, like a flashing jewel hung from a pendant. Wednesday he would keep in a tiny chamois bag, examining her from time to time in a self-satisfied, miserly fashion.

And, after a while, he might have another, smaller jewel . . .

Jim Rudd accepted his conditions. And was astounded.

'There is no navel at all!' he ejaculated when he had rejoined Fabian in his study, after the first examination. 'I've palpated the skin for scar tissue, but there's not the slightest hint of it. And that's not the half of it! She has no discernible systole and diastole. Man, do you know what that means?'

'I'm not interested right now,' Fabian told him. 'Later, maybe. Do you think you can help her with these physical problems when they come up?'

'Oh, sure. At least as well as that old fellow.'

'What about children? Can she have them?'

Rudd spread his hands. 'I don't see why not. For all her peculiarities, she's a remarkably healthy young woman. And we have no reason to believe that this condition – whatever you want to call it – is hereditary. Of course, some part of it might be, in some strange way or other, but on the evidence . . .'

They were married, just before the start of Fabian's vacation, at City Hall. They came back to the office after lunch and told everyone about it. Fabian had already hired a new secretary to replace his wife.

Two months later, Fabian had managed to get her pregnant.

He was amazed at how upset she became, considering the meekness he had induced in her from the beginning of their marriage. He tried to be stern and to tell her he would have none of this nonsense, Dr Rudd had said there was every reason to expect that she would have a normal baby, and that was that. But it didn't work. He tried gentle humour, cajolery. He even took her in his arms and told her he loved her too much not to want to have a little girl just like her. But that didn't work either.

'Fabian, darling,' she moaned, 'don't you understand? I'm not supposed to have a child. I'm not like other women.'

He finally used something he had been saving as a last resort for this emergency. He took a book from the shelf and flipped it open. 'I understand,' he said. 'It's half Dr Lorington and his nineteenth-century superstitious twaddle, and half a silly little folk poem you read when you were a girl and that made a terrifying impression on you. Well, I can't do anything about Dr Lorington at this point in your life, but I can do something about that poem. Here. Read this.'

She read:

> Birthdays
> *by* B. L. FARJEON
> *Monday's child is fair of face*
> *Tuesday's child is full of grace*
> *Wednesday's child is loving and giving,*
> *Thursday's child works hard for a living,*
> *Friday's child is full of woe,*
> *Saturday's child has far to go,*
> *But the child that is born on the Sabbath-day*
> *Is brave and bonny, and good and gay.*

Wednesday looked up and shook the tears from her eyes. 'But I don't understand,' she muttered in confusion. 'That's not like the one I read.'

He squatted beside her and explained patiently. 'The one you read had two lines transposed, right? Wednesday's and Thursday's child had the lines that Friday's and Saturday's child have in this version and vice versa. Well, it's an old Devonshire poem originally, and no one knows for sure which version is right. I looked it up, especially for you. I just wanted to show you how silly you were, basing your entire attitude towards life on a couple of verses which could be read either way, not to mention the fact that they were written several centuries before anyone thought of naming you Wednesday.'

She threw her arms around him and held on tightly. 'Oh, Fabian, darling! Don't be angry with me. It's just that I'm so – *frightened!*'

Jim Rudd was a little concerned, too. 'Oh, I'm pretty sure it will be all right, but I wish you'd waited until I had time to familiarize myself a bit more with the patient. The only thing, Fabe, I'll have to call in a first-rate obstetrician. I'd never dream of handling this myself. I can make him keep it quiet, about Wednesday and all that. But the moment she enters the delivery room, all bets are off. Too many odd things about her – they're bound to be noticed by some nurse, at least.'

'Do the best you can,' Fabian told him. 'I don't want my wife involved in garish publicity, if it can be helped. But if it can't be – well, it's about time Wednesday learned to live in the real world.'

The gestation period went along pretty well, with not much more than fairly usual complications. The obstetrical specialist Jim Rudd had suggested was as intrigued as anyone else by Wednesday's oddities, but he told them that the pregnancy was following a monotonously normal course and that the foetus seemed to be developing satisfactorily and completely on schedule.

Wednesday became fairly cheerful again. Outside of her minor fears, Fabian reflected, she was an eminently satisfactory and useful wife. She didn't exactly shine at parties where they mingled with other married couples from Slaughter, Stark and Slingsby, but she never committed a major faux pas either. She was, in fact, rather well liked, and, as she obeyed him faithfully in every particular, he had no cause at all for complaint.

He spent his days at the office handling the dry, minuscule details of paper work and personnel administration more efficiently than ever before, and his nights and week-ends with a person he had every reason to believe was the most *different* woman on the face of the Earth. He was very well satisfied.

Near the end of her term, Wednesday did beg for permission to visit Dr Lorington just once. Fabian had to refuse, regretfully but firmly.

'It's not that I mind his not sending us a congratulatory telegram or wedding gift, Wednesday. I really don't mind that at all. I'm not the kind of man to hold a grudge. But you're in good shape now. You're over most of your silly fears. Lorington would just make them come alive again.'

And she continued to do what he said. Without argument, without complaint. She was really quite a good wife. Fabian looked forward to the baby eagerly.

One day, he received a telephone call at the office from the hospital. Wednesday had gone into labour while visiting the obstetrician. She'd been rushed to the hospital and given birth shortly after arrival to a baby girl. Both mother and child were doing well.

Fabian broke out the box of cigars he'd been saving for this occasion. He passed them around the office and received the felicitations of everybody up to and including Mr Slaughter, Mr Stark and both Mr Slingsbys. Then he took off for the hospital.

From the moment he arrived in the Maternity Pavilion, he knew that something was wrong. It was the way people looked at him, then looked quickly away. He heard a nurse saying behind him: 'That must be the father.' His lips went tight and dry.

They took him in to see his wife. Wednesday lay on her side, her knees drawn up against her abdomen. She was breathing hard, but seemed to be unconscious. Something about her position made him feel acutely uncomfortable, but he couldn't decide exactly what it was.

'I thought this was going to be the natural childbirth method,' he said. 'She told me she didn't think you'd have to use anaesthesia.'

'We didn't use anaesthesia,' the obstetrician told him. 'Now let's go to your child, Mr Balik.'

He let them fit a mask across his face and lead him to the glass-enclosed room where the new-born infants lay in their tiny beds. He moved slowly, unwillingly, a shrieking song of incomprehensible disaster building up slowly in his head.

A nurse picked a baby out of a bed that was off in a corner away from the others. As Fabian stumbled closer, he observed with a mad surge of relief that the child looked normal. There was no visible blemish or deformity. Wednesday's daughter would not be a freak.

But the infant stretched its arms out to him. 'Oh, Fabian, darling,' it lisped through toothless gums in a voice that was all too terrifyingly familiar. 'Oh, Fabian, darling, the strangest, most unbelievable thing has happened!'

# Dial 'F'
# For Frankenstein

## By ARTHUR C. CLARKE

*Arthur C. Clarke (1917– ) is certainly the best-known and most highly acclaimed writer of Science Fiction in the world today; while the film, 2001: A Space Odyssey, on which Stanley Kubrick based his story and script has been called 'the most famous of all SF films'. What is far less well known, however, is that Arthur has a very intriguing link with Andrew Crosse, 'The Wizard of the Quantocks', because he was born on a farm in Minehead, Somerset, less than four miles from Crosse's mansion, Fyne Court. It was not until a few years ago, however, that he discovered the link between the experimenter and the book which is said to mark the start of the genre that he now dominates. Arthur was, of course, familiar with Mary Shelley's original novel and a number of the subsequent Frankenstein movies, but it was only after reading my book, The Man Who Was Frankenstein, that he realised he had grown up in the same vicinity as Crosse. And it was during a return trip to Somerset from his home in Sri Lanka in 1985 that he finally visited the remains of the experimenter's home.*

*'Although a fire had destroyed the laboratory section (I cannot confirm that it was torched by fear-maddened peasants) some of the equipment and furniture still survived,' he wrote in his autobiography, Astounding Days (1989). 'Most remarkable of all, one of the conductors which Crosse used for his ill-advised attempts to tap atmospheric electricity can still be seen, high up in the fork of an ancient tree on the estate. As I stared at this relic, I remembered how the lightning played around the hulking, soon-to-be-animated body of William Henry Pratt – a.k.a Boris Karloff.'*

*This was not the only surprise that awaited Arthur on that homecoming. For he also learned that during World War II his mother had made a practice of hiring out ponies from the farm to soldiers billeted in a nearby army camp so that they could go riding across the neighbouring countryside. One of her favourite customers had apparently been a young actor later destined to become famous in that role associated with Andrew Crosse. His name was Peter Cushing. Although Arthur C. Clarke's birthplace has now been marked by a special plaque, only a simple cross in the local graveyard marks Andrew Crosse's last resting place.*

*It came as no surprise to me to find that Clarke had written a story that fitted our theme.* Dial 'F' For Frankenstein *is, in fact, another man versus machines tale, but one full of unexpected surprises. It was first published in* Playboy *magazine in January 1965 with a warning that it 'should be taken with very few grains of salt in view of the omniscience Clarke has shown in the past anent future scientific events.' Little has changed to alter this warning in the intervening years ...*

At 01:50 Greenwich Mean Time on December 1, 1975, every telephone in the world started to ring. A quarter of a billion people picked up their receivers, to listen for a few seconds with annoyance or perplexity. Those who had been awakened in the middle of the night assumed that some far-off friend was calling, over the satellite telephone network that had gone into service, with such a blaze of publicity, the day before. But there was no voice on the line; only a sound that to many seemed like the roaring of the sea – to others, like the vibrations of harp strings in the wind. And there were many more, in that moment, who recalled a secret sound of childhood – the noise of blood pulsing through the veins, heard when a shell is cupped over the ear. Whatever it was, it lasted no more than 20 seconds; then it was replaced by the dialling tone.

The world's subscribers cursed, muttered 'Wrong number' and hung up. Some tried to dial a complaint, but the line seemed busy. In a few hours, everyone had forgotten the incident – except those whose duty it was to worry about such things.

At the Post Office Research Station, the argument had been going on all morning, and had got nowhere. It continued unabated through the lunch break, when the hungry engineers poured into the little café across the road.

'I still think,' said Willy Smith, the solid-state electronics man, 'that it was a temporary surge of current, caused when the satellite network was switched in.'

'It was obviously *something* to do with the satellites,' agreed Jules Reyner, circuit designer. 'But why the time delay? They were plugged in at midnight; the ringing was two hours later – as we all know to our cost.' He yawned violently.

'What do *you* think, Doc?' asked Bob Andrews, computer programmer. 'You've been very quiet all morning. Surely you've got some idea?'

Dr John Williams, head of the Mathematics Division, stirred uneasily.

'Yes,' he said. 'I have. But you won't take it seriously.'

'That doesn't matter. Even if it's as crazy as those science-fiction yarns you write under a pseudonym, it may give us some leads.'

Williams blushed, but not very hard. Everyone knew about his stories, and he wasn't ashamed of them. After all, they *had* been collected in book form. (Remainder at five shillings; he still had a couple of hundred copies.)

'Very well,' he said, doodling on the tablecloth. 'This is something I've been wondering about for years. Have you ever considered the analogy between an automatic telephone exchange and the human brain?'

'Who hasn't thought of it?' scoffed one of his listeners. 'That idea must go back to Graham Bell.'

'Possibly; I never said it was original. But I do say it's time we started taking it seriously.' He squinted balefully at the fluorescent tubes above the table; they were needed on this foggy winter day. 'What's wrong with the damn lights? They've been flickering for the last five minutes.'

'Don't bother about that; Maisie's probably forgotten to pay her electricity bill. Let's hear more about your theory.'

'Most of it isn't theory; it's plain fact. We know that the human brain is a system of switches – neurons – interconnected

in a very elaborate fashion by nerves. An automatic telephone exchange is also a system of switches – selectors, and
so forth – connected together with wires.'

'Agreed,' said Smith. 'But that analogy won't get you very
far. Aren't there about fifteen billion neurons in the brain?
That's a lot more than the number of switches in an
autoexchange.'

Williams' answer was interrupted by the scream of a low-
flying jet; he had to wait until the café had ceased to vibrate
before he could continue.

'Never heard them fly *that* low,' Andrews grumbled.
'Thought it was against regulations.'

'So it is, but don't worry – London Airport Control will
catch him.'

'I doubt it,' said Reyner. 'That *was* London Airport, bringing in a Concorde on Ground Approach. But I've never heard
one so low, either. Glad I wasn't aboard.'

'Are we, or are we *not*, going to get on with this blasted
discussion?' demanded Smith.

'You're right about the fifteen billion neurons in the human
brain,' continued Williams unabashed. 'And *that's* the whole
point. Fifteen billion sounds a large number, but it isn't.
Round about the 1960s, there were more than that number of
individual switches in the world's autoexchanges. Today,
there are approximately five times as many.'

'I see,' said Reyner, very slowly. 'And as of yesterday,
they've all become capable of full interconnection, now that
the satellite links have gone into service.'

'Precisely.'

There was silence for a moment, apart from the distant
clanging of a fire-engine bell.

'Let me get this straight,' said Smith. 'Are you suggesting
that the world telephone system is now a giant brain?'

'That's putting it crudely – anthropomorphically. I prefer
to think of it in terms of critical size.' Williams held his hands
out in front of him, fingers partly closed.

'Here are two lumps of U 235; nothing happens as long as
you keep them apart. But bring them together' – he suited the
action to the words – 'and you have something *very* different
from one bigger lump of uranium. You have a hole half a mile
across.

'It's the same with our telephone networks; until today they've been largely independent, autonomous. But now we've suddenly multiplied the connecting links – the networks have all merged together – and we've reached criticality.'

'And just what does criticality mean in this case?' asked Smith.

'For want of a better word – consciousness.'

'A weird sort of consciousness,' said Reyner. 'What would it use for sense organs?'

'Well, all the radio and TV stations in the world would be feeding information into it, through their landlines. *That* should give it something to think about! Then there would be all the data stored in all the computers; it would have access to that – and to the electronic libraries, the radar tracking systems, the telemetering in the automatic factories. Oh, it would have enough sense organs! We can't begin to imagine its picture of the world; but it would be infinitely richer and more complex than ours.'

'Granted all this, because it's an entertaining idea,' said Reyner, 'what could it *do* except think? It couldn't go anywhere; it would have no limbs.'

'Why should it want to travel? It would already be everywhere! And every piece of remotely controlled electrical equipment on the planet could act as a limb.'

'Now I understand that time delay,' interjected Andrews. 'It was conceived at midnight, but it wasn't born until 1:50 this morning. The noise that woke us all up was – its birth cry.'

His attempt to sound facetious was not altogether convincing, and nobody smiled. Overhead, the lights continued their annoying flicker, which seemed to be getting worse. Then there was an interruption from the front of the café, as Jim Small of Power Supplies made his usual boisterous entry.

'Look at this, fellows,' he grinned, waving a piece of paper in front of his colleagues. 'I'm rich. Ever seen a bank balance like *that*?'

Dr Williams took the proffered statement, glanced down the columns, and read the balance aloud: 'Credit £999,999,897.87.'

'Nothing very odd about that,' he continued, above the

general amusement. 'I'd say it means the computer's made a slight mistake. That sort of thing was happening all the time, just after the banks converted to the decimal system.'

'I know, I know,' said Jim, 'but don't spoil my fun. I'm going to frame this statement – and what would happen if I drew a cheque for a few million, on the strength of this? Could I sue the bank if it bounced?'

'Not on your life,' answered Reyner. 'I'll take a bet that the banks thought of *that* years ago, and protected themselves somewhere down in the small print. But by the way – when did you get that statement?'

'In the noon delivery; it comes straight to the office, so that my wife doesn't have a chance of seeing it.'

'Hmm – that means it was computed early this morning. Certainly after midnight ...'

'What are you driving at? And why all the long faces?'

No one answered him; he had started a new hare, and the hounds were in full cry.

'Does anyone here know about automated banking systems?' asked Willy Smith. 'How are they tied together?'

'Like everything else these days,' said Bob Andrews. 'They're all in the same network – the computers talk to one another all over the world. It's a point for you, John. If there *was* real trouble, that's one of the first places I'd expect it. Besides the phone system itself, of course.'

'No one answered the question I asked before Jim came in,' complained Reyner. 'What would this supermind actually *do*? Would it be friendly – hostile – indifferent? Would it even know that we exist, or would it consider the electronic signals it's handling to be the only reality?'

'I see you're beginning to believe me,' said Williams with a certain grim satisfaction. 'I can only answer your question by asking another. What does a newborn baby do? It starts looking for food.' He glanced up at the flickering lights. 'My God,' he said slowly, as if a thought had just struck him. 'There's only one food it would need – electricity.'

'This nonsense has gone far enough,' said Smith. 'What the devil's happened to our lunch? We gave our orders twenty minutes ago.'

Everyone ignored him.

'And then,' said Reyner, taking up where Williams had left

off, 'it would start looking around, and stretching its limbs. In fact, it would start to play, like any growing baby.'

'And babies *break* things,' said someone, very softly.

'It would have enough toys, heaven knows. That Concorde that went over just now. The automated production lines. The traffic lights in our streets.'

'Funny you should mention that,' interjected Small. 'Something's happened to the traffic outside – it's been stopped for the last ten minutes. Looks like a big jam.'

'I guess there's a fire somewhere – I heard an engine.'

'I've heard two – and what sounded like an explosion over towards the industrial estate. Hope it's nothing serious.'

'Maisie!!! What about some candles? We can't see a thing!'

'I've just remembered – this place has an all-electric kitchen. We're going to get cold lunch, if we get any lunch at all.'

'At least we can read the newspaper while we're waiting. Is that the latest edition you've got there, Jim?'

'Yes – haven't had time to look at it yet. Hmm – there *do* seem to have been a lot of odd accidents this morning – railway signals jammed – water main blown up through failure of relief valve – dozens of complaints about last night's wrong numbers –'

He turned the page, and became suddenly silent.

'What's the matter?'

Without a word, Small handed over the paper. Only the front page made sense. Throughout the interior, column after column was a mass of printer's pie – with, here and there, a few incongruous advertisements making islands of sanity in a sea of gibberish. They had obviously been set up as independent blocks, and had escaped the scrambling that had overtaken the text around them.

'So this is where long-distance type setting and autodistribution have brought us,' grumbled Andrews. 'I'm afraid Fleet Street's been putting too many eggs in one electronic basket.'

'So have we all, I'm afraid,' said Williams, very solemnly. 'So have we all.'

'If I can get a word in edgeways, in time to stop the mob hysteria which seems to be infecting this table,' said Smith loudly and firmly, 'I'd like to point out that there's nothing to worry about – even if John's ingenious fantasy is correct. We only have to switch off the satellites – and we'll be back where we were yesterday.'

'Prefrontal lobotomy,' muttered Williams. 'I'd thought of that.'

'Eh? Oh yes – cutting out slabs of the brain. That would certainly do the trick. Expensive, of course, and we'd have to go back to sending telegrams to each other. But civilization would survive.'

From not too far away, there was a short, sharp explosion.

'I don't like this,' said Andrews nervously. 'Let's hear what the old BBC's got to say – the one-o'clock news has just started.'

He reached into his briefcase and pulled out a transistor radio.

'– unprecedented number of industrial accidents, as well as the unexplained launching of three salvos of guided missiles from military installations in the United States. Several airports have had to suspend operations owing to the erratic behaviour of their radars, and the banks and stock exchanges have closed because their information-processing systems have become completely unreliable.' ('You're telling me,' muttered Small, while the others shushed him.) 'One moment, please – there's a news flash coming through ... Here it is. We have just been informed that all control over the newly installed communication satellites has been lost. They are no longer responding to commands from the ground. According to ...'

The BBC went off the air; even the carrier wave died. Andrews reached for the tuning knob, and twisted it round the dial. Over the whole band, the ether was silent.

Presently Reyner said, in a voice not far from hysteria: 'That prefrontal lobotomy was a good idea, John. Too bad that baby's already thought of it.'

Williams rose slowly to his feet.

'Let's get back to the lab,' he said. 'There must be an answer somewhere.'

But he knew already that it was far, far too late. For Homo sapiens the telephone bell had tolled.

# The Plot is the Thing

## By ROBERT BLOCH

*Robert Bloch (1917– ) who began his life-long fascination with horror cowering in a cinema seat watching Lon Chaney's terrifying performance as the original* Phantom of the Opera *in 1925, has since repaid his debt to the genre by writing some of its most blackly humorous not to mention chilling short stories. He is also famous as the author of Alfred Hitchcock's best known movie,* Psycho, *based on his 1959 novel. Bob's work as a screenwriter has brought him into close contact with many horror actors, and for years one of his closest friends was Boris Karloff. He is also a friend of Karloff's successor in the* Frankenstein *role, Peter Cushing.*

*Since Robert Bloch's earliest short stories for* Weird Tales *in the Thirties – on which he received considerable advice from H.P. Lovecraft – he has introduced the 'monster' and 'creation of life' themes into a number of his tales, as well as in his script for the 1968 movie,* Torture Garden, *in which a group of Hollywood stars maintained their youthful good looks and immortality by having their brains transferred to robot bodies. Probably his most suitable story for this collection is The* Plot is the Thing *which he wrote in 1966 for the* Magazine of Fantasy and Science Fiction. *It is all about an avid movie fan who is given a brain operation and thereafter believes she is actually taking part in old films. Her encounter with the* Frankenstein *monster provides the climactic experience of this compelling and gruesome tale by the man who has not without good reason been described as 'the master of graveyard horror'.*

When they broke into the apartment, they found her sitting in front of the television set, watching an old movie.

Peggy couldn't understand why they made such a fuss about that. She liked to watch old movies – the Late Show, the Late, Late Show, even the All Night Show. That was really the best, because they generally ran the horror pictures. Peggy tried to explain this to them, but they kept prowling around the apartment, looking at the dust on the furniture and the dirty sheets on the unmade bed. Somebody said there was green mould on the dishes in the sink; it's true she hadn't bothered to wash them for quite a long time, but then she simply hadn't bothered to eat for several days, either.

It wasn't as though she didn't have any money; she told them about the bank-accounts. But shopping and cooking and housekeeping was just too much trouble, and besides, she really didn't like going outside and seeing all those *people*. So if she preferred watching TV, that was her business wasn't it?

They just looked at each other and shook their heads and made some phone-calls. And then the ambulance came, and they helped her dress. Helped her? They practically *forced* her, and by the time she realized where they were taking her it was too late.

At first they were very nice to her at the hospital, but they kept asking those idiotic questions. When she said she had no relatives or friends they wouldn't believe her, and when they checked and found out it was true it only made things worse. Peggy got angry and said she was going home, and it all ended with a hypo in the arm.

There were lots of hypos after that, and in in-between times this Dr Crane kept after her. He was one of the heads of staff and at first Peggy liked him, but not when he began to pry.

She tried to explain to him that she'd always been a loner, even before her parents died. And she told him there was no reason for her to work, with all that money. Somehow, he got it out of her about how she used to keep going to the movies, at least one every day, only she liked horror pictures and of course there weren't quite that many, so after while she just watched them on TV. Because it was easier, and you didn't have to go home along dark streets after seeing something frightening. At home she could lock herself in, and as long as she had the television going she didn't feel lonely. Besides, she could watch movies all night, and this helped her insomnia. Sometimes the old pictures were pretty gruesome and this made her nervous, but she felt more nervous when she didn't watch. Because in the movies, no matter how horrible things seemed for the heroine, she was always rescued in the end. And that was better than the way things generally worked out in real life, wasn't it?

Dr Crane didn't think so. And he wouldn't let her have any television in her room now, either. He kept talking to Peggy about the need to face reality, and the dangers of retreating into a fantasy world and identifying with frightened heroines. The way he made it sound, you'd think she *wanted* to be menaced, *wanted* to be killed, or even raped.

And when he started all that nonesense about a 'nervous disorder' and told her about his plans for treatment, Peggy knew she had to escape. Only she never got a chance. Before she realized it, they had arranged for the lobotomy.

Peggy knew what a lobotomy was, of course. And she was afraid of it, because it meant tampering with the brain. She remembered some mad doctor – Lionel Atwill, or George Zucco? – saying that by tampering with the secrets of the human brain one can change reality. 'There are some things we were not meant to know,' he had whispered. But that, of course, was in a movie. And Dr Crane wasn't mad. *She* was the mad one. Or was she? He certainly looked insane – she kept trying to break free after they strapped her down and he came after her – she remembered the way everything gleamed. His eyes, and the long needle. The long needle, probing into her brain to change reality –

The funny thing was, when she woke up she felt fine. 'I'm like a different person, Doctor.'

And it was true. No more jitters; she was perfectly calm. And she wanted to eat, and she didn't have insomnia, and she could dress herself and talk to the nurses, even kid around with them. The big thing was that she didn't worry about watching television any more. She could scarcely remember any of those old movies that had disturbed her. Peggy wasn't a bit disturbed now. And even Dr Crane knew it.

At the end of the second week he was willing to let her go home. They had a little chat, and he complimented her on how well she was doing, asked her about her plans for the future. When Peggy admitted she hadn't figured anything out yet, Dr Crane suggested she take a trip. She promised to think it over.

But it wasn't until she got back to the apartment that Peggy made up her mind. The place was a mess. The moment she walked in she knew she couldn't stand it. All that dirt and grime and squalor – it was like a movie set, really, with clothes scattered everywhere and dishes piled in the sink. Peggy decided right then and there she'd take a vacation. Around the world, maybe. Why not? She had the money. And it would be interesting to see all the *real* things she'd seen represented on the screen all these years.

So Peggy dissolved into a travel agency and montaged into shopping and packing and faded out to London.

Strange, she didn't think of it in that way at the time. But looking back, she began to realize that this is the way things seemed to happen. She'd come to a decision, or go somewhere and do something, and all of a sudden she'd find herself in another setting – just like in a movie, where they cut from scene to scene. When she first became aware of it she was a little worried; perhaps she was having blackouts. After all, her brain *had* been tampered with. But there was nothing really alarming about the little mental blanks. In a way they were very convenient, just like in the movies; you don't particularly want to waste time watching the heroine brush her teeth or pack her clothing or put on cosmetics. The plot is the thing. That's what's *real*.

And everything was real, now. No more uncertainty. Peggy could admit to herself that before the operation there had been times when she wasn't quite sure about things; sometimes what she saw on the screen was more convincing than the dull grey fog which seemed to surround her in daily life.

But that was gone, now. Whatever that needle had done, it had managed to pierce the fog. Everything was very clear, very sharp and definite, like good black-and-white camera work. And she herself felt so much more capable and confident. She was well-dressed, well-groomed, attractive again. The extras moved along the streets in an orderly fashion and didn't bother her. And the bit-players spoke their lines crisply, performed their functions, and got out of the scene. Odd that she should think of them that way – they weren't 'bit-players' at all; just travel clerks and waiters and stewards and then, at the hotel, bellboys and maids. They seemed to fade in and out of the picture on cue. All smiles, like in the early part of a good horror movie, where at first everything seems bright and cheerful.

Paris was where things started to go wrong. This guide – a sort of Eduardo Ciannelli type, in fact he looked to be an almost dead ringer for Ciannelli as he was many years ago – was showing her through the Opera House. He happened to mention something about the catacombs, and that rang a bell.

She thought about Erik. That was his name, Erik – The Phantom of the Opera. *He* had lived in the catacombs underneath the Opera House. Of course, it was only a picture, but she thought perhaps the guide would know about it and she mentioned Erik's name as a sort of joke.

That's when the guide turned pale and began to tremble. And then he ran. Just ran off and left her standing there.

Peggy knew something was wrong, then. The scene just seemed to dissolve – that part didn't worry her, it was just another one of those temporary blackouts she was getting used to – and when Peggy regained awareness, she was in this bookstore asking a clerk about Gaston Leroux.

And this was what frightened her. She remembered distinctly that *The Phantom of the Opera* had been written by Gaston Leroux, but here was this French bookstore clerk telling her there was no such author.

That's what they said when she called the library. No such author – and no such book. Peggy opened her mouth, but the scene was already dissolving ...

In Germany she rented a car, and she was enjoying the scenery when she came to this burned mill and the ruins of the castle beyond. She knew where she was, of course, but it couldn't be – not until she got out of the car, moved up to the great door, and in the waning sun of twilight, read the engraved legend on the stone. *Frankenstein*.

There was a faint sound from behind the door, a sound of muffled, dragging footsteps, moving closer. Peggy screamed, and ran ...

Now she knew where she was running to. Perhaps she'd find safety behind the Iron Curtain. Instead there was another castle, and she heard the howling of a wolf in the distance, saw the bat swoop from the shadows as she fled.

And in an English library in Prague, Peggy searched the volumes of literary biography. There was no listing for Mary Wollstonecraft Shelley, none for Bram Stoker.

Of course not. There wouldn't be, in a *movie* world, because when the characters are real, their 'authors' do not exist.

Peggy remembered the way Larry Talbot had changed before her eyes, metamorphosing into the howling wolf. She remembered the sly purr of the Count's voice, saying, 'I do not drink – wine.' And she shuddered, and longed to be far away from the superstitious peasantry who draped wolfbane outside their windows at night.

She needed the reassurance of sanity in an English-speaking country. She'd go to London, see a doctor immediately.

Then she remembered what was *in* London. Another were-wolf. And Mr Hyde. And the Ripper . . .

Peggy fled through a fadeout, back to Paris. She found the name of a psychiatrist, made her appointment. She was perfectly prepared to face her problem now, perfectly prepared to face reality.

But she was not prepared to face the bald-headed little man with the sinister accent and the bulging eyes. She knew him – Dr Gogol, in *Mad Love*. She also knew Peter Lorre had passed on, knew *Mad Love* was only a movie, made the year she was born. But that was in another country, and besides, the wench was dead.

The wench was dead, but Peggy was alive. '*I am a stranger and afraid, in a world I never made.*' Or had she made this world? She wasn't sure. All she knew was that she had to escape.

Where? It couldn't be Egypt, because that's where *he* would be – the wrinkled, hideous image of the Mummy superimposed itself momentarily. The Orient? What about Fu Manchu?

Back to America, then? Home is where the heart is – but there'd be a knife waiting for that heart when the shower-curtains were ripped aside and the creature of *Psycho* screamed and slashed . . .

Somehow she managed to remember a haven, born in other

films. The South Seas — Dorothy Lamour, Jon Hall, the friendly natives in the tropical paradise. There *was* escape.

Peggy boarded the ship in Marseilles. It was a tramp steamer but the cast — crew, rather — was reassuringly small. At first she spent most of her time below deck, huddled in her berth. Oddly enough, it was getting to be like it had been *before*. Before the operation, that is, before the needle bit into her brain, twisting it, or distorting the world. *Changing reality*, as Lionel Atwill had put it. She should have listened to them — Atwill, Zucco, Basil Rathbone, Edward Van Sloan, John Carradine. They might have been a little mad, but they were good doctors, dedicated scientists. They meant well. 'There are some things we were not meant to know.'

When they reached the tropics, Peggy felt much better. She regained her appetite, prowled the deck, went into the galley and joked with the Chinese cook. The crew seemed aloof, but they all treated her with the greatest respect. She began to realize she'd done the right thing — this *was* escape. And the warm scent of tropic nights beguiled her. From now on, this would be her life; drifting through nameless, uncharted seas, safe from the role of heroine with all its haunting and horror.

It was hard to believe she'd been so frightened. There were no Phantoms, no Werewolves in this world. Perhaps she didn't need a doctor. She was facing reality, and it was pleasant enough. There were no movies here, no television; her fears were all part of a long-forgotten nightmare.

One evening, after dinner, Peggy returned to her cabin with something nagging at the back of her brain. The Captain had put in one of his infrequent appearances at the table, and he kept looking at her all through the meal. Something about the way he squinted at her was disturbing. Those little pig-eyes of his reminded her of someone. Noah Beery? Stanley Fields?

She kept trying to remember, and at the same time she was dozing off. Dozing off much too quickly. Had her food been drugged?

Peggy tried to sit up. Through the porthole she caught a reeling glimpse of land beyond, but then everything began to whirl and it was too late ...

When she awoke she was already on the island, and the woolly-headed savages were dragging her through the gate, howling and waving their spears.

They tied her and left her and then Peggy heard the chanting. She looked up and saw the huge shadow. Then she knew where she was and what *it* was, and she screamed.

Even over her own screams she could hear the natives chanting, just one word, over and over again. It sounded like, 'Kong.'

# *Fortitude*

## By KURT VONNEGUT, JR.

*It is not only modern Horror and Science Fiction writers who have been attracted to the* Frankenstein *theme – a number of mainstream novelists have also utilised some of its ideas in segments of their work, thereby demonstrating further the adaptability of Mary Shelley's original concept. Foremost amongst these has been Kurt Vonnegut, Jr. (1922– ) now recognised as one of the major American writers of the post-War period. Vonnegut survived the terrible trauma of being a prisoner of war in Dresden during the bombing of the city and the subsequent firestorm, and this has understandably made much of his work ironic and full of apocalyptic pessimism. Interestingly, his first novel,* Player Piano *(1952), featured automatons and described the state of human beings who were gradually surrendering all their activities and decisions to machines.*

*The black humour of this book has been repeated in a number of Vonnegut's short stories including* Fortitude *which was first published in 1968. In a curious way, this story is a kind of sequel to Dick Donovan's* Some Experiments With A Head *written almost eighty years earlier. For here we have the ageing Dr Norbert Frankenstein successfully keeping alive the head of a female patient with devices simulating human organs and systems. The problem begins when the doctor realises he is in love with the disembodied head and wants to be united with her in immortality. This adroit satire is written in the form of a script and is an example of Vonnegut at his most ingenious . . .*

THE TIME: *the present*. THE PLACE: *Upstate New York, a large room filled with pulsing, writhing, panting machines that perform the functions of various organs of the human body – heart, lungs, liver, and so on. Colour-coded pipes and wires swoop upward from the machines to converge and pass through a hole in the ceiling. To one side is a fantastically complicated master control console.*

DR ELBERT LITTLE, *a kindly, attractive young general practitioner, is being shown around by the creator and boss of the operation,* DR NORBERT FRANKENSTEIN. FRANKEN-STEIN *is 65, a crass medical genius. Seated at the console, wearing headphones and watching meters and flashing lights, is* DR TOM SWIFT, FRANKENSTEIN'S *enthusiastic, first assistant.*

LITTLE: Oh, my God – oh, my God –

FRANKENSTEIN: Yeah. Those are her kidneys over there. That's her liver, of course. There you got her pancreas.

LITTLE: Amazing. Dr Frankenstein, after seeing this, I wonder if I've been *practising* medicine, if I've ever even *been* to medical school. (*Pointing*) That's her *heart*?

FRANKENSTEIN: That's a Westinghouse heart. They make a damn good heart, if you ever need one. They make a kidney I wouldn't touch with a ten-foot pole.

LITTLE: That heart is probably worth more than the whole township where I practise.

FRANKENSTEIN: That pancreas is worth your whole state.

LITTLE: Vermont.

FRANKENSTEIN: What we paid for the pancreas – yeah, we could have bought Vermont for that. Nobody'd ever made a pancreas before, and we had to have one in ten days or lose the patient. So we told all the big organ manufacturers, 'OK, you guys got to have a crash programme for a pancreas. Put every man you got on the job. We don't care what it costs, as long as we get a pancreas by next Tuesday.'

LITTLE: And they succeeded.

FRANKENSTEIN: The patient's still alive, isn't she? Believe me, those are some expensive sweetbreads.

LITTLE: But the patient could afford them.

FRANKENSTEIN: You don't live like this on Blue Cross.

LITTLE: And how many operations has she had? In how many years?

FRANKENSTEIN: I gave her her first major operation thirty-six years ago. She's had seventy-eight operations since then.

LITTLE: And how old is she?

FRANKENSTEIN: One hundred.

LITTLE: What *guts* that woman must have!

FRANKENSTEIN: You're looking at 'em.

LITTLE: I mean – what *courage*! What *fortitude*!

FRANKENSTEIN: We knock her out, you know. We don't operate without anaesthetics.

LITTLE: Even so . . .

FRANKENSTEIN *taps* SWIFT *on the shoulder.* SWIFT *frees an ear from the headphones, divides his attention between the visitors and the console.*

FRANKENSTEIN: Dr Tom Swift, this is Dr Elbert Little. Tom here is my first assistant.

SWIFT: Howdy-doody.

FRANKENSTEIN: Dr Little has a practice up in Vermont. He happened to be in the neighbourhood. He asked for a tour.

LITTLE: What do you hear in the headphones?

SWIFT: Anything that's going on in the patient's room. (*He offers the headphones*) Be my guest.

LITTLE: (*listening to headphones*): Nothing.

SWIFT: She's having her hair brushed now. The beautician's up there. She's always quiet when her hair's being brushed. (*He takes the headphones back*)

FRANKENSTEIN: (*to* SWIFT) We should *congratulate* our young visitor here.

SWIFT: What for?

LITTLE: Good question. What for?

FRANKENSTEIN: Oh, I know about the great honour that has come your way.

LITTLE: I'm not sure *I* do.

FRANKENSTEIN: You are *the* Dr Little, aren't you, who was named the Family Doctor of the Year by the *Ladies' Home Journal* last month?

LITTLE: Yes – that's right. I don't know how in the hell they decided. And I'm even more flabbergasted that a man of *your* calibre would know about it.

FRANKENSTEIN: I read the *Ladies' Home Journal* from cover to cover every month.

LITTLE: You *do*?

FRANKENSTEIN: I only got one patient, Mrs Lovejoy. And Mrs Lovejoy reads the *Ladies' Home Journal*, so I read it, too. That's what we talk about – what's in the *Ladies' Home Journal*. We read all about you last month. Mrs Lovejoy kept saying, 'Oh, what a nice young man he must be. *So understanding.*'

LITTLE: Um.

FRANKENSTEIN: Now here you are in the flesh. I bet she wrote you a letter.

LITTLE: Yes – she did.

FRANKENSTEIN: She writes thousands of letters a year, gets thousands of letters back. Some pen pal she is.

LITTLE: Is she – uh – generally *cheerful* most of the time?

FRANKENSTEIN: If she isn't, that's our fault down here. If she gets unhappy, that means something down *here* isn't working right. She was blue about a month ago. Turned out it was a bum transistor in the console. (*He reaches over* SWIFT's *shoulder, changes a setting on the console. The machinery subtly adjusts to the new setting.*) There – she'll be all depressed for a couple of minutes now. (*He changes the setting again*) There. Now, pretty quick, she'll be happier than she was before. She'll sing like a bird.

LITTLE *conceals his horror imperfectly.* CUT TO *patient's room, which is full of flowers and candy boxes and books. The patient is* SYLVIA LOVEJOY, *a billionaire's widow.* SYLVIA *is no longer anything but a head connected to pipes and wires coming up through the floor, but this is not immediately apparent. The first shot of her is a* CLOSE-UP, *with* GLORIA, *a gorgeous beautician, standing behind her.* SYLVIA *is a heartbreakingly good-looking old lady, once a famous beauty. She is crying now.*

SYLVIA: Gloria –
GLORIA: Ma'am?

SYLVIA: Wipe these tears away before somebody comes in and sees them.

GLORIA (*wanting to cry herself*): Yes, ma'am (*She wipes the tears away with Kleenex and studies the results*) There. There.

SYLVIA: I don't know what came over me. Suddenly I was so sad I couldn't stand it.

GLORIA: Everybody has to cry *sometimes*.

SYLVIA: It's passing now. Can you tell I've been crying?

GLORIA: *No. No.*

*She is unable to control her own tears anymore. She goes to a window so* SYLVIA *can't see her cry.* CAMERA BACKS AWAY *to reveal the tidy, clinical abomination of the head and wires and pipes. The head is on a tripod. There is a black box with winking coloured lights hanging under the head, where the chest would normally be. Mechanical arms come out of the box where arms would normally be. There is a table within easy reach of the arms. On it are a pen and paper, a partially solved jigsaw puzzle and a bulky knitting bag. Sticking out of the bag are needles and a sweater in progress. Hanging over* SYLVIA's *head is a microphone on a boom.*

SYLVIA (*sighing*): Oh, what a *foolish* old woman you must think I am. (GLORIA *shakes her head in denial, is unable to reply*) Gloria? Are you still there?

GLORIA: Yes.

SYLVIA: Is anything the matter?

GLORIA: No.

SYLVIA: You're *such* a good friend, Gloria. I want you to know I feel that with all my heart.

GLORIA: I like you, too.

SYLVIA: If you ever have any problems I can help you with, I hope you'll ask me.

GLORIA: I will, I *will*.

HOWARD DERBY, *the hospital mail clerk, dances in with an armload of letters. He is a merry old fool.*

DERBY: Mailman! Mailman!

SYLVIA (*brightening*): Mailman! God *bless* the mailman!

DERBY: How's the patient today?

SYLVIA: Very sad a moment ago. But now that I see you, I want to sing like a bird.

DERBY: Fifty-three letters today. There's even one from Leningrad.

SYLVIA: There's a blind woman in Leningrad. Poor soul, *poor* soul.

DERBY (*making a fan of the mail, reading postmarks*): West Virginia, Honolulu, Brisbane, Australia –

SYLVIA *selects an envelope at random.*

SYLVIA: Wheeling, West Virginia. Now, who do I know in Wheeling? (*She opens the envelope expertly with her mechanical hands, reads*) 'Dear Mrs Lovejoy: You don't know me, but I just read about you in the *Reader's Digest*, and I'm sitting here with tears streaming down my cheeks.' *Reader's Digest*? My goodness – that article was printed fourteen years ago! And she just *read* it?

DERBY: Old *Reader's Digests* go on and on. I've got one at home I'll bet is ten years old. I still read it every time I need a little inspiration.

SYLVIA (*reading on*): 'I am never going to complain about anything that ever happens to me ever again. I thought I was as unfortunate as a person can get when my husband shot his girlfriend six months ago and then blew his own brains out. He left me with seven children and with eight payments still to go on a Buick Roadmaster with three flat tyres and a busted transmission. After reading about you, though, I sit here and count my blessings.' Isn't that a nice letter?

DERBY: Sure is.

SYLVIA: There's a P.S.: 'Get well real soon, you *hear*?' (*She puts the letter on the table*) There isn't a letter from Vermont, is there?

DERBY: Vermont?

SYLVIA: Last month, when I had that low spell, I wrote what I'm afraid was a very stupid, self-centred, self-pitying letter to a young doctor I read about in the *Ladies' Home Journal*. I'm so ashamed. I live in fear and trembling of what he's going to say back to me – if he answers at all.

GLORIA: What could he say? What could he *possibly* say?

SYLVIA: He could tell me about the *real* suffering going on out there in the world, about people who don't know where the next meal is coming from, about people so poor they've never *been* to a doctor in their whole *lives*. And to think of all the help I've had – all the tender, loving care, all the latest wonders science has to offer.

CUT TO *corridor outside* SYLVIA's *room. There is a sign on the door saying.* ALWAYS ENTER SMILING! FRANKENSTEIN *and* LITTLE *are about to enter.*

LITTLE: She's in *there*?

FRANKENSTEIN: Every part of her that isn't downstairs.

LITTLE: And everybody obeys this sign, I'm sure.

FRANKENSTEIN: Part of the therapy. We treat the *whole* patient here.

GLORIA *comes from the room, closes the door tightly, then bursts into noisy tears.*

FRANKENSTEIN (*to* GLORIA, *disgusted*): Oh, for crying out loud. And what is this?

GLORIA: Let her *die*, Dr Frankenstein. For the love of God, let her *die*!

LITTLE: This is her *nurse*?

FRANKENSTEIN: She hasn't got brains enough to be a nurse. She is a lousy beautician. A hundred bucks a week she makes – just to take care of one woman's face and hair. (*To* GLORIA) You blew it, honeybunch. You're through.

GLORIA: What?

FRANKENSTEIN: Pick up your cheque and scram.

GLORIA: I'm her closest friend.

FRANKENSTEIN: Some friend! You just asked me to knock her off.

GLORIA: In the name of mercy, yes, I did.

FRANKENSTEIN: You're that sure there's a heaven, eh? You want to send her right up there so she can get her wings and harp.

GLORIA: I know there's a hell. I've seen it. It's in there, and you're its great inventor.

FRANKENSTEIN (*stung, letting a moment pass before replying*): Christ – the things people say sometimes.

GLORIA: It's time somebody who loves her spoke up.

FRANKENSTEIN: Love.

GLORIA: You wouldn't know what that is.

FRANKENSTEIN: Love. (*More to himself than to her*) Do I have a wife? No. Do I have a mistress? No. I have loved only two women in my life – my mother and that woman in there. I wasn't able to save my mother from death. I had just graduated from medical school and my mother was dying of cancer of the everything. 'OK, wise guy,' I said to myself, 'you're such a hot-shot doctor from Heidelberg, now, let's see you save your mother from death.' And everybody told me there wasn't anything I could do for her, and I said, 'I don't give a damn. I'm gonna do something anyway.' And they finally decided I was nuts and they put me in a crazyhouse for a little while. When I got out, she was dead – the way all the wise men said she had to be. What those wise men didn't know was all the wonderful things machinery could do – and neither did I, but I was gonna find out. So I went to the Massachusetts Institute of Technology and I studied mechanical engineering and electrical engineering and chemical engineering for six long years. I lived in an attic. I ate two-day-old bread and the kind of cheese they put in mousetraps. When I got out of MIT, I said to myself, 'OK, boy – it's just barely possible now that you're the only guy on earth with the proper education to practise 20th century medicine.' I went to work for the Curley Clinic in Boston. They brought in this woman who was beautiful on the outside and a mess on the inside. She was the image of my mother. She was the widow of a man who had left her five-hundred million dollars. She didn't have any relatives. The wise men said again, 'This lady's gotta die.' And I said to them, 'Shut up and listen. I'm gonna tell you what we're gonna do.'

*Silence.*

LITTLE: That's – that's quite a story.

FRANKENSTEIN: It's a story about *love*. (*To* GLORIA) That

love story started years and years before you were born, you great lover, you. And it's still going on.

GLORIA: Last month, she asked me to bring her a pistol so she could shoot herself.

FRANKENSTEIN: You think I don't know that? (*Jerking a thumb at* LITTLE) Last month, she wrote him a letter and said, 'Bring me some cyanide, doctor, if you're a doctor with any heart at all.'

LITTLE (*startled*): You *knew* that. You – you read her mail?

FRANKENSTEIN: So we'll know what she's *really* feeling. She might try to fool us sometime – just *pretend* to be happy. I told you about the bum transistor last month. We maybe wouldn't have known anything was wrong if we hadn't read her mail and listened to what she was saying to lame-brains like this one here. (*Feeling challenged*) Look – you go in there all by yourself. Stay as long as you want, ask her anything. Then you come back out and tell me the truth: is that a happy woman in there, or is that a woman in hell?

LITTLE *hesitating*): I –

FRANKENSTEIN: Go on in! I got some more things to say to this young lady – to Miss Mercy Killing of the Year. I'd like to show her a body that's been in a casket for a couple of years sometime – let her see how pretty death is, this thing she wants for her friend.

LITTLE *gropes for something to say, finally mimes his wish to be fair to everyone. He enters the patient's room.* CUT TO *room.* SYLVIA *is alone, faced away from the door.*

SYLVIA: Who's that?

LITTLE: A friend – somebody you wrote a letter to.

SYLVIA: That could be anybody. Can I see you, please? (LITTLE *obliges. She looks him over with growing affection.*) Dr Little – family doctor from Vermont.

LITTLE (*bowing slightly*): Mrs Lovejoy – how are you today?

SYLVIA: Did you bring me cyanide?

LITTLE: No.

SYLVIA: I wouldn't take it today. It's such a lovely day. I wouldn't want to miss it, or tomorrow, either. Did you come on a snow-white horse?

LITTLE: In a blue Oldsmobile.

SYLVIA: What about your patients, who love and need you so?

LITTLE: Another doctor is covering for me. I'm taking a week off.

SYLVIA: Not on my account.

LITTLE: No.

SYLVIA: Because I'm fine. You can see what wonderful hands I'm in.

LITTLE: Yes.

SYLVIA: One thing I don't need is another doctor.

LITTLE: Right.

*Pause.*

SYLVIA: I do wish I had somebody to talk to about death, though. You've seen a lot of it, I suppose.

LITTLE: Some.

SYLVIA: And it was a blessing for some of them – when they died?

LITTLE: I've heard that said.

SYLVIA: But you don't say so yourself.

LITTLE: It's not a professional thing for a doctor to say, Mrs Lovejoy.

SYLVIA: Why have other people said that certain deaths have been a blessing?

LITTLE: Because of the pain the patient was in, because he couldn't be cured at any price – at any price within his means. Or because the patient was a vegetable, had lost his mind and couldn't get it back.

SYLVIA: At any price.

LITTLE: As far as I know, it is not now possible to beg, borrow or steal an artificial mind for someone who's lost one. If I asked Dr Frankenstein about it, he might tell me that it's the coming thing.

*Pause.*

SYLVIA: It *is* the coming thing.

LITTLE: He's told you so?

SYLVIA: I asked him yesterday what would happen if my

brain started to go. He was serene. He said I wasn't to worry my pretty little head about that. 'We'll cross that bridge when we come to it,' he told me. (*Pause*) Oh, God, the bridges I've crossed!

CUT TO *room full of organs, as before,* SWIFT *is at his console.*

FRANKENSTEIN *and* LITTLE *enter.*

FRANKENSTEIN : You've made the grand tour and now here you are back at the beginning.

LITTLE : And I still have to say what I said at the beginning: 'My God – oh, my God.'

FRANKENSTEIN : It's gonna be a little tough going back to the aspirin-and-laxative trade after this, eh ?

LITTLE : Yes. (*Pause*) What's the cheapest thing here ?

FRANKENSTEIN : The simplest thing. It's the goddamn pump.

LITTLE : What does a heart go for these days ?

FRANKENSTEIN : Sixty thousand dollars. There are cheaper ones and more expensive ones. The cheap ones are junk. The expensive ones are jewellery.

LITTLE : And how many are sold a year now ?

FRANKENSTEIN : Six hundred, give or take a few.

LITTLE : Give one, that's life. Take one, that's death.

FRANKENSTEIN : If the trouble is the heart. It's lucky if you have trouble that cheap. (*To* SWIFT) Hey, Tom – *put her to sleep so he can see how the day ends around here.*

SWIFT : It's twenty minutes ahead of time.

FRANKENSTEIN : What's the difference ? We put her to sleep for twenty minutes extra, she still wakes up tomorrow feeling like a million bucks, unless we got another bum transistor.

LITTLE : Why don't you have a television camera aimed at her, so you can watch her on a screen ?

FRANKENSTEIN : She didn't want one.

LITTLE : She gets what she wants ?

FRANKENSTEIN : She *got that.* What the hell do we have to watch her face for ? We can look at the meters down here and find out more about her than she can know about herself. (*To* SWIFT) Put her to sleep, Tom.

SWIFT (*to* LITTLE): It's just like slowing down a car or banking a furnace.

LITTLE : Um.

FRANKENSTEIN: Tom, too, has degrees in both engineering and medicine.

LITTLE: Are you tired at the end of a day, Tom?

SWIFT: It's a good kind of tiredness – as though I'd flown a big jet from New York to Honolulu, or something like that. (*Taking hold of a lever*) And now we'll bring Mrs Lovejoy in for a happy landing. (*He pulls the lever gradually and the machinery slows down.*) There.

FRANKENSTEIN: Beautiful.

LITTLE: She's asleep?

FRANKENSTEIN: Like a baby.

SWIFT: All I have to do now is wait for the night man to come on.

LITTLE: Has anybody ever brought her a suicide weapon?

FRANKENSTEIN: No. We wouldn't worry about it if they did. The arms are designed so she can't possibly point a gun at herself or get poison to her lips, no matter how she tries. That was Tom's stroke of genius.

LITTLE: Congratulations.

*Alarm bell rings. Light flashes.*

FRANKENSTEIN: Who could that be? (*To* LITTLE) Somebody just went into her room. We better check! (*To* SWIFT) Lock the door up there, Tom – so whoever it is, we got 'em. (SWIFT *pushes a button that locks door upstairs. To* LITTLE) You come with me.

CUT TO *patient's room.* SYLVIA *is asleep, snoring gently.* GLORIA *has just sneaked in. She looks around furtively, takes a revolver from her purse, makes sure it's loaded, then hides it in* SYLVIA's *knitting bag. She is barely finished when* FRANKENSTEIN *and* LITTLE *enter breathlessly,* FRANKENSTEIN *opening the door with a key.*

FRANKENSTEIN: What's this?

GLORIA: I left my watch up here. (*Pointing to watch*) I've got it now.

FRANKENSTEIN: Thought I told you never to come into this building again.

GLORIA: I won't.

FRANKENSTEIN (*to* LITTLE): You keep her right there. I'm gonna check things over. Maybe there's been a little huggery buggery. (*To* GLORIA) How would you like to be in court for attempted murder, eh? (*Into microphone*) Tom? Can you hear me?

SWIFT (*voice from squawk box on wall*): I hear you.

FRANKENSTEIN: Wake her up again. I gotta give her a check.

SWIFT: Cock-a-doodle-doo.

*Machinery can be heard speeding up below.* SYLVIA *opens her eyes, sweetly dazed.*

SYLVIA (*to* FRANKENSTEIN): Good morning, Norbert.

FRANKENSTEIN: How do you feel?

SYLVIA: The way I always feel when I wake up – fine – vaguely at sea. Gloria! Good morning!

GLORIA: Good morning.

SYLVIA: Dr Little! You're staying another day?

FRANKENSTEIN: It isn't morning. We'll put you back to sleep in a minute.

SYLVIA: I'm sick again?

FRANKENSTEIN: I don't think so.

SYLVIA: I'm going to have to have another operation?

FRANKENSTEIN: Calm down, calm down. (*He takes an ophthalmoscope from his pocket*)

SYLVIA: How can I be calm when I think about another operation?

FRANKENSTEIN (*into microphone*): Tom – give her some tranquillizers.

SWIFT (*squawk box*): Coming up.

SYLVIA: What else do I have to lose? My ears? My hair?

FRANKENSTEIN: You'll be calm in a minute.

SYLVIA: My eyes? My eyes, Norbert – are they going next?

FRANKENSTEIN (*to* GLORIA): Oh, boy, baby doll – will you look what you've done? (*Into microphone*) Where the hell are those tranquillizers?

SWIFT: Should be taking effect just about now.

SYLVIA: Oh, well. It doesn't matter. (*As* FRANKENSTEIN *examines her eyes*) It is my eyes, isn't it?

FRANKENSTEIN: It isn't your anything.

SYLVIA: Easy come, easy go.

FRANKENSTEIN: You're healthy as a horse.

SYLVIA: I'm sure somebody manufactures excellent eyes.

FRANKENSTEIN: RCA makes a damn good eye, but we aren't gonna buy one for a while yet. (*He backs away, satisfied*) Everything's all right up here. (*To* GLORIA) Lucky for you.

SYLVIA: I love it when friends of mine are lucky.

SWIFT: Put her to sleep again?

FRANKENSTEIN: Not yet. I want to check a couple of things down there.

SWIFT: Roger and out.

CUT TO LITTLE, GLORIA *and* FRANKENSTEIN *entering the machinery room minutes later.* SWIFT *is at the console.*

SWIFT: Night man's late.

FRANKENSTEIN: He's got troubles at home. You want a good piece of advice, boy? Don't ever get married. (*He scrutinizes meter after meter*)

GLORIA (*appalled by her surroundings*): My God – oh, my God – LITTLE: You've never seen this before?

GLORIA: No.

FRANKENSTEIN: She was the great hair specialist. We took care of everything else – everything but the hair. (*The reading on a meter puzzles him.*) What's this? (*He socks the meter, which then gives him the proper reading*) that's more like it.

GLORIA (*emptily*): Science.

FRANKENSTEIN: What did you think it was like down here?

GLORIA: I was afraid to think. Now I can see why.

FRANKENSTEIN: You got any scientific background at all – any way of appreciating even slightly what you're seeing here?

GLORIA: I flunked earth science twice in high school.

FRANKENSTEIN: What do they teach in beauty college?

GLORIA: Dumb things for dumb people. How to paint a face. How to curl or uncurl hair. How to cut hair. How to dye hair. Fingernails. Toenails in the summertime.

FRANKENSTEIN: I suppose you're gonna crack off about this place after you get out of here – gonna tell people all the crazy stuff that goes on.

GLORIA: Maybe.

FRANKENSTEIN: Just remember this. You haven't got the brains or the education to talk about any aspect of our operation. Right?

GLORIA: Maybe.

FRANKENSTEIN: What *will* you say to the outside world?

GLORIA: Nothing very complicated – just that . . .

FRANKENSTEIN: Yes?

GLORIA: That you have the head of a dead woman connected to a lot of machinery, and you play with it all day long, and you aren't married or anything, and that's all you do.

FREEZE SCENE *as a still photograph.* FADE TO *black.* FADE IN *same still. Figures begin to move.*

FRANKENSTEIN (*aghast*): How can you call her dead? She reads the *Ladies' Home Journal*! She talks! She knits! She writes letters to pen pals all over the world!

GLORIA: She's like some horrible fortune-telling machine in a penny arcade.

FRANKENSTEIN: I thought you loved her.

GLORIA: Every so often, I see a tiny little spark of what she used to be. I love that spark. Most people say they love her for her courage. What's that courage worth, when it comes from down here? You could turn a few taps and switches down here and she'd be volunteering to fly a rocket ship to the moon. But no matter what you do down here, that little spark goes on thinking. 'For the love of God – somebody get me out of here!'

FRANKENSTEIN (*glancing at the console*): Dr Swift – is that microphone open?

SWIFT: Yeah. (*Snapping his fingers*) I'm sorry.

FRANKENSTEIN: Leave it open. (*To* GLORIA) She's heard every word you've said. How does that make you feel?

GLORIA: She can hear me now?

FRANKENSTEIN: Run off at the mouth some more. You're saving me a lot of trouble. Now I won't have to explain to her what sort of friend you really were and why I gave you the old heave-ho.

GLORIA (*drawing nearer to the microphone*): Mrs Lovejoy?

SWIFT (*reporting what he has heard on the microphones*): She says, 'What is it, dear?'

GLORIA: There's a loaded revolver in your knitting bag, Mrs Lovejoy – in case you don't want to live anymore.

FRANKENSTEIN (*not in the least worried about the pistol but filled with contempt and disgust for* GLORIA): You total imbecile. Where did you get a pistol?

GLORIA: From a mail-order house in Chicago. They had an ad in *True Romances*.

FRANKENSTEIN: They sell guns to crazy broads.

GLORIA: I could have had a bazooka if I'd wanted one. Fourteen-ninety-eight.

FRANKENSTEIN: I am going to get that pistol now and it is going to be exhibit A at your trial. (*He leaves*)

LITTLE (*to* SWIFT): Shouldn't you put the patient to sleep?

SWIFT: There's no way she can hurt herself.

GLORIA (*to* LITTLE): What does he mean?

LITTLE: Her arms are fixed so she can't point a gun at herself.

GLORIA (*sickened*): They even thought of that.


CUT TO SYLVIA's *room*. FRANKENSTEIN *is entering*. SYLVIA *is holding the pistol thoughtfully*.


FRANKENSTEIN: Nice playthings you have.

SYLVIA: You mustn't get mad at Gloria, Norbert. I asked her for this. I begged her for this.

FRANKENSTEIN: Last month.

SYLVIA: Yes.

FRANKENSTEIN: But everything is better now.

SYLVIA: Everything but the spark.

FRANKENSTEIN: Spark?

SYLVIA: The spark that Gloria says she loves – the tiny spark of what I used to be. As happy as I am right now, that spark is begging me to take this gun and put it out.

FRANKENSTEIN: And what is your reply?

SYLVIA: I am going to do it, Norbert. This is goodbye. (*She tries every which way to aim the gun at herself, fails and fails, while* FRANKENSTEIN *stands calmly by*) That's no accident, is it?

FRANKENSTEIN: We very much don't want you to hurt yourself. We love you, too.

SYLVIA: And how much longer must I live like this? I've never dared ask before.

FRANKENSTEIN: I would have to pull a figure out of a hat.

SYLVIA: Maybe you'd better not. (*Pause*) Did you pull one out of a hat?

FRANKENSTEIN: At least five hundred years.

*Silence.*

SYLVIA: So I will still be alive — long after you are gone?

FRANKENSTEIN: Now is the time, my dear Sylvia, to tell you something I have wanted to tell you for years. Every organ downstairs has the capacity to take care of two human beings instead of one. And the plumbing and wiring have been designed so that a second human being can be hooked up in two shakes of a lamb's tail. (*Silence*) Do you understand what I am saying to you, Sylvia? (*Silence. Passionately*) Sylvia! I will be that second human being! Talk about marriage! Talk about great love stories from the past! Your kidney will be my kidney! Your liver will be my liver! Your heart will be my heart! Your ups will be my ups and your downs will be my downs! We will live in such perfect harmony, Sylvia, that the gods themselves will tear out their hair in envy!

SYLVIA: This is what you want?

FRANKENSTEIN: More than anything in this world.

SYLVIA: Well, then — here it is, Norbert. (*She empties the revolver into him*)

CUT TO *same room almost a half hour later. A second tripod has been set up, with* FRANKENSTEIN's *head on top.* FRANKENSTEIN *is asleep and so is* SYLVIA. SWIFT, *with* LITTLE *standing by, is feverishly making a final connection to the machinery below. There are pipe wrenches and a blowtorch and other plumbers' and electricians' tools lying around.*

SWIFT: That's gotta be it. (*He straightens up, looks around*) That's gotta be it.

LITTLE (*consulting watch*): Twenty-eight minutes since the first shot was fired.

SWIFT: Thank God you were around.

LITTLE: What you really needed was a plumber.

SWIFT (*into microphone*): Charley – we're all set up here. You all set down there?

CHARLEY (*squawk box*): All set.

SWIFT: Give 'em plenty of martinis.

GLORIA *appears numbly in doorway.*

CHARLEY: They've got 'em. They'll be higher than kites.

SWIFT: Better given 'em a touch of LSD, too.

CHARLEY: Coming up.

SWIFT: Hold it! I forgot the phonograph. (*To* LITTLE) Dr Frankenstein said that if this ever happened, he wanted a certain record playing when he came to. He said it was in with the other records – in a plain white sleeve. (*To* GLORIA) See if you can find it.

GLORIA *goes to phonograph, finds the record.*

GLORIA: This it?

SWIFT: Put it on.

GLORIA: Which side?

SWIFT: I don't know.

GLORIA: There's tape over one side.

SWIFT: The side *without* tape. (GLORIA *puts record on. Into microphone.*) Stand by to wake up the patients.

CHARLEY: Standing by.

*Record begins to play. It is a Jeanette MacDonald-Nelson Eddy duet, 'Ah, Sweet Mystery of Life.'*

SWIFT (*into microphone*): Wake 'em up!

FRANKENSTEIN *and* SYLVIA *wake up, filled with formless pleasure. They dreamily appreciate the music, eventually catch sight of each other, perceive each other as old and beloved friends.*

*

SYLVIA: Hi, there.
FRANKENSTEIN: Hello.
SYLVIA: How do you feel?
FRANKENSTEIN: Fine. Just fine.

# Summertime Was
# Nearly Over

## By BRIAN ALDISS

*Apart from all the short stories which have continued the Frankenstein legend, in recent years an increasing number of novels have also appeared in Britain and America. Some of these have been merely adaptations of the original; others novelisations of the various film versions; while a few have been quite commendable works of fiction in their own right. Among these I would list Paul W. Fairman's* The Frankenstein Wheel *(1972) in which the creature arises from its Arctic tomb and goes in search of a bride once more;* The Frankenstein Diaries *Edited by the Reverend Hubert Venables 'from the personal papers of Viktor Frankenstein' (1980); and, most notably,* Frankenstein Unbound *by Brian Aldiss (1973). Aldiss' book tells the story of Joe Bodenland, a 21st Century American who passes through a time warp and finds himself on the shores of Lake Geneva in company with Byron and the Shelleys. Further, he is confronted by a real Frankenstein – a doppelgänger inhabiting a complex world where fact and fiction intertwine. The novel was enthusiastically reviewed on publication: 'Brian Aldiss's monster is a beaut,' said the* Sunday Times; *while the* Sunday Telegraph *declared that the book was 'the kind of fantasy of which he is one of the finest exponents alive today.'*

*Before becoming a full time author, Brian Aldiss (1925– ) was an assistant in a bookshop, thereafter working as the literary editor of the* Oxford Mail *where he reviewed hundreds of SF novels – in so doing revealing his own wide-ranging knowledge of the genre and admiration for the classic British authors such as H.G. Wells and Mary Shelley. Frankenstein's creature has haunted him ever since he first read the book in his youth, says Brian, and his novel and the following short story, written in 1991, are his tribute to the genius of Mary Shelley.*

I am resolved to leave some brief account of my days whilst I am still able. It does not escape me that a fair hand has already written some account of my early days; but that account broke off too soon, for I returned from the realms of ice, to which solitudes my soul – if I may be presumed to have one – was attracted.

In due time, I returned to the country about the city of Geneva. Although I had hoped for justice and understanding when my story was known, that was not to be.

Persecution remained my lot. I had to escape to the nearby wilderness of mountain and ice, to live out my days among chamois and eagle, which were being hunted as avidly as I.

Before leaving the city for ever, I came across a philosopher, Jean-Jacques Rousseau, even more noted than the family of my accursed Master. At the beginning of one of his books I discovered these words, which to me in my lowly condition were more than words: 'I am made unlike anyone I have ever met; I will even venture to say that I am like no one in the whole world.'

Here was a sentiment I might have uttered myself. To find such understanding in a book gave me strength. Ever since coming upon Rousseau's writings so long ago, I have tried to live with my dear wife above the glaciers in the condition he would have approved, that of the Noble Savage – in defiance of those citified creatures who multiply in the valleys far below.

The placidity of a late August day lingers over the Swiss Alps. The sound of automobiles wending their way along the road far below does not reach me; I hear only a distant occasional cowbell and the cheerful nearer transactions of insects. I am at peace. The helicopters appeared after noon, when the clouds cleared from the brow of the Jungfrau. They had been active all week, unsettling me with their noise. There were two of them, blue, belonging to the Swiss police. Soon they disappeared behind a nearby slope, and I crawled from under the bush where I had hidden.

Once all was peace here. We did not know of tourists and helicopters.

Now the numbers of the People are increasing. If it isn't helicopters, it's cars on the way to the Silberner Hirsch below, or machines roaring in distant valleys. Elsbeth and I will have to move to a more remote place, if I can find one.

Elsbeth says she does not wish to move again. Our cave on the upper slopes of the Aletschhorn suits her well, but ours is a fugitive life, as I explain to her.

In summer, the People drive off the highway up the track leading to the Silberner Hirsch, with its fine view of the mountains to the north. Occasionally, one or two of them will leave their cars and climb higher, almost as far as the winter shelters. Perhaps they will pick the wild flowers growing in the lush grasses, cornflower, poppy, clover, eglantine, and the frail vetch.

They rarely reach the cave on its precipitous slope. I never molest the People. Elsbeth and I stay hidden. I protect her in my arms.

In winter, she and I are completely alone with the elements. My temperament is compatible with the wind and the snow and the storms born from the cold wombs of northern lakes. The People's machines do not threaten us then. We survive somehow. I have learned not to be afraid of fire. I sit over its red eye in the cave and listen to the music of the atmosphere.

I am kin with the slopes hereabouts. They are steep and treacherous with outcropping rock. No People come to ski on them. In the autumn, before the first snows fall, when fog rolls up from the valley, the hotel closes down, the People all depart. Only a boy lives at the hotel to act as watchman with his goats and chickens. That's far below our eyrie – I go down there to scavenge.

Oh, I have seen that boy's face full of fear as he stares through a window at me passing in a swirl of snow.

The winter world is without human inhabitants. I can't explain it. I cannot explain to Elsbeth where the People go. Do they sleep all winter, like the waterfall?

This is the trouble: that I understand nothing. Long though I have lived, I never understand better as years pass. I never understand why the teeth of winter bite so cruelly down into the bone, how daylight sickens from the east, why Elsbeth is so chill as I lie with her, why the nights are so long, without word or gleam.

I am troubled by my lack of understanding. Nothing remains, nothing remains.

Best not to think of another winter. It is summer now, time of happiness. But summertime is nearly over.

All this livelong day I lay on my favourite rock in the sun. The flies visited and crawled on me. Also many other small things that may have life and thought − butterflies, snails in curled shell, spiders, maggots. I lay staring at the People below, coming to and going from the Silberner Hirsch. They climb from their machines. They walk about and photograph the valley and the hill peaks. They enter the restaurant. In time, they come from it again. Then they drive away. Their cars are beads on the thread of highway. They have homes, often far distant. Their homes are full of all manner of possessions. They are capable of many kinds of activity. I hear their planes roar overhead, leaving a trail of snow across the sky. People are always busy, like the flies and ants.

This also they can do: procreate. I have mated many times with Elsbeth. She brings forth no child. Here is another thing I cannot understand. Why does Elsbeth not bring forth child? Is the fault in her or in me, because I am strangely made, because, as Rousseau said, 'I am made unlike anyone I ever met'?

The grass grows high before my sight. I peer through its little ambush at the scene below. Even the grass makes more grass, and all the small things that live in the grass reproduce their kind, until summer is over. Everything conceives more things, except Elsbeth and I.

Elsbeth remained as usual in our cave beside the waterfall. When the good season is spent and cold bites to the bone, the waterfall dies like most other living things. Its music ceases. It becomes rigid and mute. What is this grief that visits the Earth so regularly? How to explain it?

Only in the spring does the waterfall recover, and then it roars with delight at regaining life, just as I did. Then Elsbeth and I are happy again.

My head becomes cloudy as I lie on my rock peering through the grass at the scene down below. After night has fallen, I will climb down the slopes to walk about unseen round the hotel and retrieve what the People have discarded. I find there something to eat, and many other things, discarded papers and books, this and that. The night is my friend. I am darkness itself.

Why it has to be thus I know not. Yet I have thought myself not to feel discontent. Once I was malicious because I was miserable, but no more. Now I have my lovely mate, I have schooled myself to be neither malicious nor miserable, and not to hate People.

In the discarded newspapers I read that there are People far more evil than ever I was. They take pleasure in killing the innocent. This murder they do not only with their bare hands but with extreme weapons, the nature of which I am unable to comprehend. Thousands die in their wars every year.

Sometimes I read the name of my Maker in the newspapers. Even after all this time, they still speak ill of him; why it does not therefore make me, his victim, welcome among People I do not know. This is something else eluding my understanding.

Lying in my cloudy state, I fall asleep without knowing it. The flies buzz and the sun is hot on my spine.

To dream can be very cruel. I try to tear these visions from myself. In my dreams, memories of dead People rise up. One claims that I have his thighs and legs, another that I have his torso. One wretch wishes his head returned, another even claims his internal organs. These desperate People parade in my sleep. I am a living cemetery, a hospital of flesh for those who lack flesh. What can I do? Within me I feel dreadful ghosts and crimes locked within my bones, knotted into my very entrails. I cannot pass water without a forgotten claimant reaching for what is his.

Do People suffer in this way? Being a mere composite from charnel houses, I fear that I alone undergo this sorrow behind the eyebrows. Residual scenes from dreadful other memories play like lice inside veins I hardly dare look on as mine. I feel myself a theatre of other lives and deaths.

Why then do People shun me? Have I not more humanity than they trapped inside me?

While I suffered from these dreams on my slab of rock, something woke me. I heard the sound of voices carried on the thin air. Two People, females, were climbing upwards. They had left behind the Silberner Hirsch and were moving towards the place where I lay.

I observed them with the silent attention a tiger must give its approaching prey. And yet not that exactly, for there was fear in my heart. The People always awaken fear in me. The elder of these two women was gathering wild flowers, exclaiming as she did so. It was innocent enough, yet still I felt the fear.

The elder female sank down on a tree stump to rest, fanning herself with her hand. The other one came on, picking her way cautiously. I saw the brown hair on the crown of her head, gleaming in the sun with a beauty I cannot describe.

She would have passed me by a few feet, perhaps not noticing me. Yet because I could not bear to lie where I was and chance being seen, I jumped up with a great bound and confronted her.

The female gave a gasp of fear, looking up at me with her mouth open, revealing tongue and white teeth.

'Help!' she called once, until I had my hand over the lower part of her face. The look she gave me changed from fear to disgust.

Oh, I've seen that look on the faces of People before. It always awakens my fury. The faces of People are unlike mine, plastic, mobile, given to expressing emotion. With one blow I could wipe that expression and the flesh that paints it right from their skulls.

As I lifted her, her toes dangled in their white trainers. I thrust my face into hers, that female face dewed with the heat of afternoon. As I considered whether to smash her and throw her down on the mountainside, I caught her scent. It hit me as forcibly as a blow to the stomach.

That scent ... So different from the scent of Elsbeth ... It caused a kind of confusion in my brain, making me pause.

One of those old elusive memories from the back of my brain
returned to baffle me – a memory of something that had
never happened to me. I have said I understand little; at that
moment I understood nothing, and that terrible lack ran
through me like an electric shock. I put her down.

'You monster . . .' the female said, staggering. Beneath us,
the descents were toothed with jagged rock. Rather than fall,
she clung to my arm – a gesture so trusting in its way as to
melt the remains of my anger. I could remember only how
vulnerable People were, the females in particular. At that
instant, I would have fought a wild beast in order to preserve
her unharmed.

As though sensing some abatement of my ferocity, she said
in a natural tone, 'I did not mean to startle you.'

When I could not think how to answer this, unaccus-
tomed as I was to conversing with People, she went on,
'Do you speak English? I am just a tourist here on
vacation.'

Still I could not answer, from her scent and from the look
of her. It was as if a little wild doe had come to me, all
quivering with a half-mistrust. She was young. Her face was
round and open, without scars from medical science. Her grey
eyes were set in a brown skin smooth like the shell of a hen's
egg. The hair I had watched from above had become disturbed
when I lifted her, so that it shaded the line of her left cheek.
She wore a T-shirt with the name of an American university
printed on it, and denim shorts cut ragged round her plump
thighs. Beneath the shirt I saw the outline of her breasts. That
outline held so entrancing a meaning that I was further
disarmed.

My difficulty in breathing was such that I clutched my
throat.

She looked at me with what I took to be concern.

'Say, you okay? My friend's a doctor. Maybe I'll call her to
come on up.'

'Don't call,' I said. I sat down in the long grass, puzzled to
understand my weakness. In some elusive way, here before me
was the representative of something, some enormous sphere
of sensations and transcendent values such as I had only read
about, something my Maker had withheld from me which I
desperately needed. That I could put no name to it made it all

the more tantalising, like a song when only the tune remains and the words are lost by time.

'My friend can help,' said this astonishing young person. She turned as if to call but I growled at her again, 'Don't call,' in so urgent a voice that she desisted. When she looked up the mountainside, as if searching for help there, I realised that she still had fear of me, little knowing the true state of affairs, and felt herself like an animal in a trap.

'But you're ill,' she said. 'Or else in trouble with the law.'

Her remark released my ability to speak to her. 'My trouble is with the law of humanity, which rules against me. Law is invented to protect the rulers, not the ruled; the strong, not the weak. No court on Earth is concerned with justice, only the law. The weak can anticipate persecution, not justice.'

'But you are not weak,' she said.

Her grey eyes when she looked at me made me tremble. When the moon is high, I roam the mountainside much of the night. That dear silver dish in the sky is like an eye, guarding me. But in the grey eyes of this female I read only a kind of concealed hostility.

'Justice is only a name. Persecution and weakness are real enough. Those who for whatsoever reason have no roof over their heads are no better than deer to be hunted down.'

My words appeared to make no impression on her. 'In my country, there is Welfare to look after the homeless.'

'You know nothing.'

She did not dispute that, merely standing before me, head bowed, yet sneaking side glances at me and round about.

'Where do you live?' she asked, in a minute.

I jerked my head in the direction of the mountain above us.

'Alone?'

'With my wife. Are you . . . a wife?'

She dismissed the question with a toss of her head.

I listened to the flies buzzing about me and the murmur of the bees in the clover as they tumbled at our feet. These small sounds were the building bricks of the silence that enfolded us.

She stuck out a small brown hand. 'I'm not afraid any more. I'm sorry I startled you. Why don't you take me to visit your wife? What's her name?'

At that, I was silent with mistrust a long time. Her scent

reached me as I took the hand gently into mine and looked down at her.

Finally, I spoke the sacred name. 'Elsbeth.'

She too paused before responding. 'Mine's Vicky.' She did not ask my name, nor did I offer it.

There we stood on the perilous slope. This encounter had used much of my courage. I had caught her, yet still I feared her. While I contemplated her, she continued to look about with uneasy glances like a trapped animal, and I saw her breasts move with her breathing. Now those honest grey eyes, which I associated with the moon, were furtive and unkind.

'Well then,' she said, with an uneasy laugh, 'what's keeping us? Let's go.'

Perhaps my Maker did not intend that my brain should function perfectly. This little thing whose hand I held could easily be crushed. There was no reason for me to fear it. Yet fear it I did, so greatly did the idea come to me that if I took her up to the cave to meet Elsbeth, she would somehow have trapped me instead of her.

Yet this notion was conquered by a stronger urge I could not deny.

If I led this tender scented female to the cave, she would then be far away from her friend and entirely within my power. We would be private to do that supreme thing, whether she wished for it or not. Elsbeth would understand if I overpowered her and had my way with her. Why should I not? Why else was this morsel, this Vicky, sent to me?

Even at the cost of revealing the whereabouts of the cave to one of the People I must take this specimen there – I must, so great was my urge, thundering in me like the breakers of an ocean. When I was finished with her, I would make sure she did not give our hiding place away. Elsbeth would approve of that. Then our secret life could continue as before, with only the small wild things knowing of our existence.

So thereupon I echoed her words. 'Let's go.'

The way was steep. She was puny. I kept good hold of her, part-dragging her after me. The afternoon sun blazed on us and her scent rose to me, together with her sobs.

The bushes became smaller, more scanty. I had come this way a hundred times, always varying my route so as to avoid making more of a track than a rabbit might do. We came to the Cleft, a shallow indentation, a fold in the flesh of the mountain. Here the infant waterfall played its tune, gushing with pure water which, several hundred feet down the valley, would become a tributary of the Lotschental river. Behind the fall, hidden by a dark-leaved shrub, was the entrance to the cave.

Here we had to pause. She claimed she must get her breath back. She bent double and stayed that way, and her brown hair hung down, and her little fingertips touched the ground.

Great white clouds rolled above us, tumbling over the mountain summit as if eager to find quieter air. Of a sudden, one of the police helicopters shot overhead, startling me with its enormous clatter, as if the thing were a flying tree, streaking out of sight behind the crisp crest of the Jungfrau. I had no time to hide before it was over and gone.

I grabbed the girl and pulled. 'Into the cave with you.'

She struggled. 'What if Elsbeth doesn't want to see me? Shouldn't you warn her first? Why don't you call her out here?'

Not answering, I dragged her towards the cave. She seized at a bush but I beat her hand away.

'I don't want to see Elsbeth,' she screamed. 'Help! Help!'

Silencing her with a hand enveloping her face, I half-lifted her and so we entered the cave, the girl struggling furiously.

Elsbeth lay there in the shade, watching everything, saying nothing. I let the girl loose and pushed her towards my wife.

The girl went motionless, staring forward, one hand to her lips. There was no sound but the high buzz of flies. I waited for her to try to scream again, readying myself to leap upon her and bear her down. But when she spoke, it was softly, with her gaze on Elsbeth, not me.

'She's been dead a very long time, hasn't she?'

Some People can cry. I have no facility for tears. Yet as soon as this activity began in Vicky, a storm of weeping – as I judged the sensation – accumulated in my breast like a storm over the Alps. In Elsbeth's eyes no movement showed. The maggots had done their work in those sockets and moved to other pastures.

As I raised my hands above my head and let out a howl, two male people rushed into the cave. They yelled as they came. The weeping girl, Vicky, threw herself out of danger into the recesses of the cave, where I stored the fruits of the autumn. The men flung a net over me.

Wildly though I struggled, using all my strength, the net was unbreakable. The male People drew it tight, as fishermen must have done when they hauled in a catch in olden times. They shackled my legs so that I could not run. Then they felled me, so that I lay by Elsbeth and was as helpless as she.

Those People treated me as if I were no better than an animal. I was dragged out of the cave, through the waterfall, to lie on my back gazing up at the fast-moving clouds in the blue sky, and I thought to myself, Those clouds are free, just as I was until now.

More male People arrived. I found out how they came there soon enough. One of their helicopters was standing on a level ledge of mountainside above my refuge. The female, Vicky, came to me and bent down so that I could look again into her grey eyes.

'I regret this,' she said. 'I had to act as decoy. We knew you were somewhere up on the Aletschhorn, but not exactly where. We've been combing this mountainside all week.'

My faculty of speech was deserting me along with my other powers. I managed to say, 'So you are just an accomplice of these other cruel beasts.'

'I am working with the local police, yes. Don't blame me ...'

One of the male police nudged her. 'Out of the way, miss. He's still dangerous. Stand back there.' And she moved away.

I was lifted up and lashed to a stretcher. Her face disappeared from my sight. Still encased in the net, I was dropped on the ground as if I were an old plank. They shouted a great deal, and waved their arms. Only then did I realise they were going to transport me up the mountain. Five male People were there, one of them controlling the other four. They looked down on me. Again those expressions of disgust: I might have been a leopard trapped by big-game hunters, when mercy did not enter into their thoughts.

The male person who ordered the others around had a mouth full of small grey teeth. Staring down, he said, 'We're not letting you escape this time, you freak of nature. We have a list of murders stretching back over the last two centuries for which you are responsible.'

Though I read no sympathy in his face or mouth, I found a few words to offer. 'Sir, I had never an intent to offend. It was my Maker who offended against me, acting so unfatherly against one who never asked to be born in any unnatural way. As for these murders, as you name them, the first one only, that of the child, was done in malice, when I had no knowledge of those states of being which you, not I, can enjoy – to wit, life and death. The rest of my offences were committed in self-defence, when I found the hands of all People were against me. Let me free, I pray. Let me live upon this blessed mountain, in the state of nature and innocence described by Rousseau.'

His mouth thinned and elongated like an earthworm. 'You shit,' he said, turning away.

Another male appeared over the ragged skyline.

'Chopper's ready,' he called.

They swung into action. I was lifted up. It took four of them to carry me. I could not see the female but, as I was raised to their shoulders, I caught a glimpse of my happy home, that cave where Elsbeth and I had been so content. Then it was gone, and they laboured up the slope with me, trussed and helpless.

As we approached the helicopter, a shower burst over us, one of those unheralded showers which sweep the Alps. I tasted the blessed rain on my lips, drinking it even while the People complained. I thought, this is the last time I taste of the benisons of nature. I am being taken to the realms of the People, who hate nature as much as they hate me, who am unnatural.

A chill sharpened the flavour of the water. It carried the taint of autumn, that melancholy transition time before winter. Summertime was nearly over, and my wife would lie alone and lonely in our cave, waiting for my return, looking with her sightless eyes for her lover, uttering never a word of complaint.

# At Last, The True Story
## of Frankenstein

### By HARRY HARRISON

*Although this story by Harry Harrison (1925– ) is not by any means the latest to be written on the* Frankenstein *theme, it nevertheless seems the most appropriate on which to end the collection. For here we have a descendant of the original Dr Frankenstein forced to earn his living by exhibiting what he claims to be his forebear's original creature. When an inquisitive news reporter investigates the showman's claims, however, he soon uncovers a quite different account of the origins of the legend and, in particular, Mary Shelley's part in it ...*

*Harrison was born in America, but has spent much of his life travelling in places such as Mexico, Italy, Scandinavia and, latterly, Britain where he has now lived for a number of years. Prior to becoming a full-time writer, he was a commercial artist working mainly on comics. The creation of a humorous interstellar criminal-turned-lawman, Slippery Jim DiGriz, in* The Stainless Steel Rat *(1957), which has been followed by numerous sequels, has ensured his fame. One of Harry Harrison's closest friends is Brian Aldiss, and the two writers have been involved in a number of projects together including critical appraisals of Science Fiction and editing 'best of the year' anthologies. They share an interest in the* Frankenstein *theme, and Harry's ingenious contribution here was written originally for the British magazine,* Science Fantasy, *appearing in September 1965. It ends on a high note of frisson which I believe will remain in the mind long after the book has been put down ...*

'Und here, before your very eyes, is the very same monster built by my much admired great-great-grandfather, Victor Frankenstein, built by him from pieces of corpses out of dissecting rooms, stolen parts of bodies freshly buried in the grave, und even chunks of animals from the slaughterhouse. Now look ...' The tail-coated man on the platform swung his arm out in a theatrical gesture and the heads of the close-packed crowd below swung to follow it. The dusty curtains flapped aside and the monster stood there, illuminated from above by a sickly green light. There was a concerted gasp from the crowd and a shiver of motion.

In the front row, pressed against the rope barrier, Dan Bream mopped his face with a soggy handkerchief and smiled. It wasn't such a bad monster, considering that this was a cheapjack carnival playing the small-town circuit. It had a dead-white skin, undampened by sweat even in this steambath of a tent, glazed eyes, stitches and seams showing where the face had been patched together, and the two metal plugs projecting from the temples – just like in the movie.

'Raise your right arm!' Victor Frankenstein V commanded, his brusque German accent giving the words a Prussian air of authority. The monster's body did not move, but slowly – with the jerking motion of a badly operating machine – the creature's arm came up to shoulder height and stopped.

'This monster, built from pieces from the dead, cannot die, und if a piece gets too worn out I simply stitch on a new piece with the secret formula passed down from father to son from my great-great-grandfather. It cannot die nor feel pain – as you see ...'

This time the gasp was even louder and some of the audience turned away while others watched with eager eyes. The barker had taken a foot-long and wickedly sharp needle, and had pushed it firmly through the monster's biceps until it protruded on both sides. No blood stained it and the creature made no motion, as though completely unaware that anything had been done to its flesh.

'... impervious to pain, extremes of heat and cold, and possessing the strength of ten men ...'

Behind him the voice droned on, but Dan Bream had had enough. He had seen the performance three times before, which was more than satisfactory for what he needed to know, and if he stayed in the tent another minute he would melt. The exit was close by and he pushed through the gaping, pallid audience and out into the humid dusk. It wasn't much cooler outside. Life borders on the unbearable along the shores of the Gulf of Mexico in August, and Panama City was no exception. Dan headed for the nearest air conditioned beer joint and sighed with relief as the chill atmosphere closed around his steaming garments. The beer bottle frosted instantly with condensation as did the heavy glass stein, cold from the freezer. The first big swallow cut a path straight down to his stomach. He took the beer over to one of the straight-backed wooden booths, wiped the table with a handful of paper napkins and flopped onto the bench. From the inner pocket of his jacket he took some folded sheets of yellow copy paper, now slightly soggy, and spread them before him. After adding some lines to the scribbled notes he stuffed them back into his jacket and took a long pull on his beer.

Dan was half-way through his second bottle when the barker, who called himself Frankenstein the Fifth, came in. His stage personality had vanished along with the frock coat and monocle, and the Prussian haircut now looked like a common crew cut.

'You've got a great act,' Dan called out cheerfully, and waved the man over. 'Will you join me for a drink?'

'Don't mind if I do,' Frankenstein answered in the pure nasal vowels of New York City, the German accent apparently having disappeared along with the monocle. 'And see if they have a Schlitz or a Bud or anything beside the local swamp water.'

He settled into the booth while Dan went for the beers, and groaned when he saw the labels on the bottles.

'At least it's cold,' he said, shaking salt into his to make it foam, then half draining the stein in a long deep swallow. 'I noticed you out there in front of the clems for most of the shows today. Do you like the act – or you a carny buff?'

'It's a good act. I'm a newsman, name's Dan Bream.'

'Always pleased to meet the press, Dan. Publicity is the life of show business, as the man said. I'm Stanley Arnold: call me Stan.'

'Then Frankenstein is just your stage name?'

'What else? You act kinda dim for a reporter, are you sure ...?' He waved away the press card that Dan pulled from his breast pocket. 'No, I believe you, Dan, but you gotta admit the question was a little on the rube side. I bet you even think that I have a real monster in there!'

'Well, you must admit that he looks authentic. The skin stitched together that way, those plugs in his head ...'

'Held on with spirit gum and the embroidery is drawn on with eyebrow pencil. That's show business for you, an illusion. But I'm happy to hear that the act even looked real to an experienced reporter like yourself. What paper did you say you were with?'

'No paper, the news syndicate. I caught your act about six months ago and became interested. Did a little checking when I was in Washington, then followed you down here. You don't really want me to call you Stan, do you? Stein might be closer. After all – Victor Frankenstein *is* the name on your naturalisation papers.'

'Tell me more,' Frankenstein said in a voice suddenly cold and emotionless.

Dan riffled through the yellow sheets. 'Yes ... here it is, from the official records. Frankenstein, Victor – born in Geneva, arrived in the US in 1938, and more of the same.'

'The next thing you'll be telling me is that my monster *is* real!' Frankenstein smiled, but only with his mouth.

'I'm betting that it is. No yoga training or hypnotism or such can make a man as indifferent to pain as that thing is – and as terribly strong. I want the whole story, the truth for a change!'

'Do you ...?' Frankenstein asked in a cold voice and for a long moment the air filled with tension. Then he laughed and clapped the reporter on the arm. 'All right, Dan – I'll give it to you. You are a persistent devil and a good reporter and it is the least you deserve. But first you must get us some more drinks, something a measurable degree stronger than this execrable beer.' His New York accent had disappeared as easily as had his German one; he spoke English now with skill and perfection without any recognisable regional accent.

Dan gathered their empty glasses. 'It'll have to be beer – this is a dry country.'

'Nonsense! This is America, the land that raises its hands

in horror at the foreign conception of double-think yet practises it with an efficiency that sets the Old World to shame.
Bay County may be officially dry but the law has many itchy
palms, and under that counter you will find a reasonable
supply of a clear liquid that glories in the name of White
Mule and is reputed to have a kick of the same magnitude as
its cognate beast. If you are still in doubt you will see a
framed federal liquor licence on the far wall, legitimatising
this endeavour in the eyes of the national government. Simply
place a five-dollar-bill on the bar, say Mountain Dew, and do
not expect any change.'

When they both had enjoyed their first sips of the corn
liquor Victor Frankenstein lapsed into a friendly mood.

'Call me Vic, Dan. I want us to be friends. I'm going to tell
you a story that few have heard before, a story that is
astounding but true. True – mark that word – not a hodge-
podge of distortions and half-truths and outright ignorance
like that vile book produced by Mary Godwin. Oh, how my
father ever regretted meeting that woman and, in a moment
of weakness, confiding in her the secret of some of his
original lines of research ...'

'Just a minute,' Dan broke in. 'You mentioned the truth,
but I can't swallow this guff. Mary Wollstonecraft Shelley
wrote *Frankenstein; or, The Modern Prometheus* in 1818.
Which would make you and your father so old ...'

'Please, Dan – no interruptions. I mentioned my father's
researches, in the plural you will note, all of them devoted to
the secrets of life. The monster, as it has come to be called,
was just one of his works. Longevity was what he was
interested in, and he did live to a very, very old age, as will I. I
will not stretch your credulity any further at this moment by
mentioning the year of my birth, but will press on. That Mary
Godwin. She and the poet were living together at this period,
they had not married as yet, and this permitted my father to
hope that Mary might one day find him not unattractive,
since he was quite taken by her. Well, you can easily imagine
the end. She made notes of everything he told her – then
discarded him and used the notes to construct her despicable
book. Her errors are legion, listen ...' He leaned across the
booth and once again clapped Dan on the shoulder in a
hearty way. It was an intimate gesture that the reporter didn't

particularly enjoy, but he didn't complain. Not as long as the other kept talking.

'Firstly she made papa a Swiss; he used to tear his hair out at the thought, since ours is a good old Bavarian family with a noble and ancient lineage. Then she had him attending the University of Ingolstadt in *Ingolstadt* – when every schoolboy knows that it was moved to Landshut in 1800. And father's personality, what crimes she committed there! In this libellous volume he is depicted as a weeping and ineffectual man, when in reality he was a tower of strength and determination. And if this isn't enough, she completely misunderstood the meaning of his experiments. Her gimcrack collection of cast-off parts put together to make an artificial man is ludicrous. She was so carried away by the legends of Talos and the Golem that she misinterpreted my father's work and cast it into that ancient mould. Father did not construct an artificial man, he reactivated a *dead* man! That is the measure of his genius! He travelled for years in the darkest reaches of the African jungle, learning the lore of the creation of the zombie. He regularised the knowledge and improved upon it until he had surpassed all of his aboriginal teachers. Raise the dead, that was what he could do. That was his secret – and how can it be kept a secret in the future, Mr Dan Bream?'

With these last words Victor Frankenstein's eyes opened wide and an unveiled light seemed to glow in their depths. Dan pulled back instinctively, then relaxed. He was in no danger here in this brightly lit room with men on all sides of them.

'Afraid, Dan? Don't be.' Victor smiled and reached out and patted Dan on the shoulder once again.

'What was that?' Dan asked, startled at the tiny brief pain in his shoulder.

'Nothing – nothing but this,' Frankenstein smiled again, but the smile had changed subtly and no longer contained any humour. He opened his hand to reveal a small hypodermic needle, its plunger pushed down and its barrel empty.

'Remain seated,' he said quietly when Dan started to rise, and Dan's muscles relaxed and he sat down again, horrified.

'What have you done to me?'

'Very little – the injection is harmless. A simple little hypnotic drug, the effect of which wears off in a few hours.

But until then you will not have much will of your own. So you will sit and hear me out. Drink some beer though, we don't want you to be thirsty.'

Horrified, Dan was a helpless onlooker, as, of its own volition, his hand raised and poured a measure of beer down his throat.

'Now concentrate. Dan, think of the significance of my statement. The so-called Frankenstein monster is no stitched up collection of scraps, but a good honest zombie. A dead man who can walk but not talk, obey but not think. Animate – but still dead. Poor old Charley is one, the creature whom you watched going through his act on the platform. But Charley is just about worn out. Since he is dead he cannot replace the body cells that are destroyed during the normal wear and tear of the day. Why, the fellow is like an animated pincushion from the act, holes everywhere. His feet – terrible, not a toe left, keep breaking off when he walks too fast. I think it's time to retire Charley. He has had a long life, and a long death. Stand up, Dan.'

In spite of his mind saying *No! No!* Dan rose slowly to his feet.

'Aren't you interested in what Charley used to do before he became a sideshow monster? You should be, Dan. Old Charley was a reporter – just like you. And he ran across what he thought was a good story. Like you, he didn't realise the importance of what he had discovered and talked to me about it. You reporters are a very inquisitive bunch. I must show you my scrapbook, it's simply filled with press cards. Before you die of course. You wouldn't be able to appreciate it afterwards. Now come along.'

Dan walked after him, into the hot night, screaming inside in a haze of terror, yet walking quietly and silently down the street.

# Acknowledgements

The Editor is grateful to the following authors, agents and publishers for their permission to include copyright stories in this collection: Popular Publications Inc for 'The Composite Brain' by Robert S. Carr; The Estate of Theodore LeBerthon for 'The Demons of the Film Colony'; HarperCollins Publishers for 'The Workshop of Filthy Creation' by Robert Muller; Carnell Literary Agency for the 'The Dead Man' by Fritz Leiber and 'It' by Theodore Sturgeon; Hammer Films Ltd for 'The Curse of Frankenstein' by Jimmy Sangster; Philip Klass for 'Wednesday's Child' by William Tenn: Playboy Magazine Inc. for 'Dial "F" For Frankenstein' by Arthur C.Clarke; A.M. Heath Literary Agency for 'The Plot is the Thing' by Robert Bloch; Curtis Brown Ltd for 'Fortitude' by Kurt Vonnegut Jr and 'Summer Was Nearly Over' by Brian Aldiss. While every effort has been made to contact the copyright holders of all the stories in this book, in the case of any accidental infringement, concerned parties are asked to contact the Editor in care of the publishers.